SERIES WARNING

This series is only suitable for those 18+ and contains matters that can be triggering. This is a dark fantasy romance. The world is not kind, nor can be its people, or the main male character. He's an alpha-hole. This is an enemies to lovers story. This series is rough going, but they will have their HEA.... eventually.

For those that would like to go in blind, skip this.
If you have any triggers, scan the below or visit my website www.authorkellycove.com Under the books tab.

VROHI

- Wolvorn Castle
- The Drylands
- Vokheim Keep
- Aliseon
- Karion
- Entrance to Vahaliel
- Witches Rest

Legend
- .... Routes
- - - - - Pack lines
- Keep
- Village
- Ruins
- Castle

DEDICATION

To those that take comfort from the darkness.

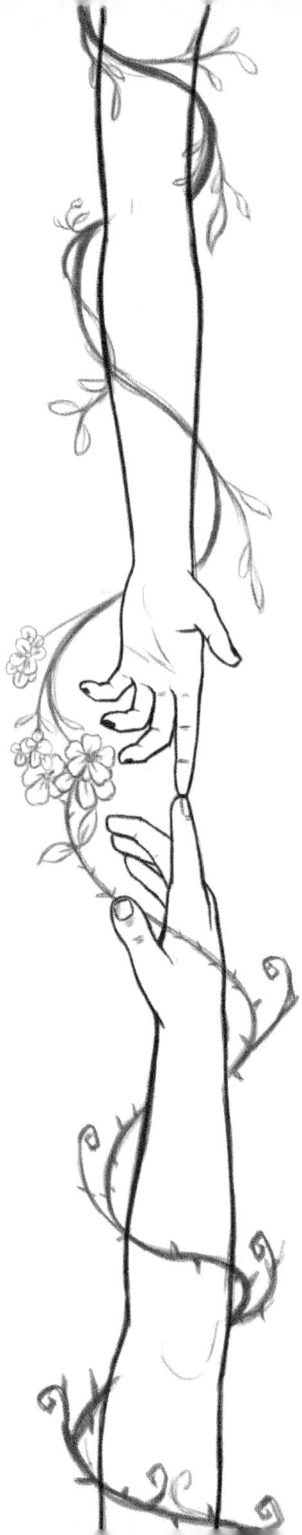

ONE

Darius

When I was a boy, I wanted to be strong like my father.

I wanted to make my mother proud, and protect my baby sister.

I wanted to be an Elite to the lands, doing anything I could to make sure it was safe for my sister to grow in—so she could thrive and live, and my mother could grow old in peace.

But when my mother and sister died, something inside of me went with them. I loved them deeply. They were my source of warmth and comfort, of softness and calm.

When they were no longer here, everything else turned cold.

Who could I make proud now? Who could I make sure the lands are safe for? Who would be the softness to my roughness to balance it out somewhat?

There was no one, until her.

Her, with ice-blue eyes that remind me of moonlight.

Her, who met my arrogance with snark.

Her, who was soft against my roughness.

And I *hurt* her.

It doesn't matter that I was given an ultimatum, that my men would be hurt if I didn't do it. I wasn't strong enough to be able to refuse Charles's order.

And that weakness makes me fucking *sick*.

At first, I raged upon the lands when I helped Rhea escape. I killed every creature that could be a threat, I hunted every rogure, anything to release this anger over what I had done.

But then I realized I wasted all that time when I could have been punishing myself for what I did to her.

Her justice.

I needed to bleed, I needed to hurt. I needed a reminder of what I fucking *did* to her.

It doesn't matter that I finally said aloud what I had done, that I told her I'm sorry, that it's my deepest regret.

I will bleed for the rest of my life for what I did to her.

What do words fucking matter anyway? It won't make it better, it won't go back in time and remove that whip from my hand.

Words are meaningless.

It means *nothing.*

And I knew they never would.

So when I wasn't looking for her or hunting for creatures, I would take the whip, one that is exactly the same as the one I used on her, and I would use it on myself.

At least, at first.

But it wasn't enough.

I couldn't hit right. I couldn't get an acceptable position for it to be truly like the way I did it to her. I couldn't get the angle.

So Leo had to do it.

He of course told me I was insane, and he refused to at first. It wasn't until he found me one night with more blood covering the floor than he had ever seen, that he finally agreed to do it, saying at least he could make sure I don't bleed out.

I wasn't going to bleed out, that wasn't part of my punishment.

From then on, Leo would come when asked, and he would whip me as I directed. In the same places I did to Rhea.

To give me my punishment.

To show my regret.

The scars, a stark reminder of my worst mistake.

They would be marked upon my skin for eternity, and I

would walk the lands in constant pain as a reminder.

And now she knows.

My little wolf was never meant to find out about this. Her heart is too soft, she would forgive me just to stop me from hurting myself because her heart is pure, and she hates others in pain.

I told her I don't want her forgiveness, that I don't, and never will, deserve it, but in the face of it, she would give it to me.

Her heart is her greatest weakness, but I will be her strength and refuse any forgiveness she offers me.

I will be that for her for the rest of our lives together, no matter how short that may be.

A lifetime isn't enough to be in her presence, isn't enough to sate my craving for her.

The Alpha of the Elites fell into her eyes, and he was captured at first glance.

And he will happily stay there.

He just has to make her leave this basement so her heart won't soften to the asshole who can't even turn around and face her.

He has to make her leave so he can continue what she interrupted.

He has to continue his punishment for the wrongs he committed against her.

He has to stop his soul from breaking underneath the weight of his crime every time he looks at her.

TWO

Rhea

Sometimes, when you feel pain, it can make you unable to catch your breath. Sometimes, it causes *you* pain, and you have to rub your chest to try and make it better. Other times… it can be enough to bring you to your knees.

Like now.

I hear Leo get up off the floor from where I sent him crashing into it, but I can't move my eyes to him, my single focus is on Darius. His back is torn to shreds, and there is blood everywhere.

And still, he sits there, his back to me, head bowed.

What has he done…

"Rhea." The hesitant voice hits me next.

I hold my hand up to stop Leo from talking further. "What is going on?" I ask.

My throat feels dry, my limbs shaky as I continue to stare at Darius's bloody back.

"He…" Leo sighs when Darius growls at him. "Darius will tell you. I did what I thought was best… I didn't want…" he trails off and sighs again, his voice tired. "I didn't want to hurt him." He clears his throat, and I can sense the sadness coming off of him, but I can't look at him.

I don't know if I will strangle him or collapse to my knees.

"If you need me, come and get me," he says. "I will keep the others out and give you both some time."

With that, he turns and leaves me all alone with Darius in

this cold dungeon.

This cold dungeon full of blood, pain, and misery.

There is a tense silence in the air as Darius breathes harshly, just as harshly as I am, I realize. My chest rising and falling deeply as I look down at the blood once more, feeling bile rise in the back of my throat at seeing him like this. He looks...weak.

Darius never looks weak.

I bring a hand up toward my mouth, only to realize that I'm still holding the whip. I drop it like it's burned me and stumble back as it lands on the floor with a *clack*, a whimper spilling from my lips.

"Leave," Darius repeats, and my eyes snap to the back of his head as his whole body tenses.

"I don't..." I squeeze my eyes shut, trying to get my thoughts straight. "Why was Leo whipping you?" I snap, letting my anger come through, my emotions swirling all over the place. "Why are you down here, bleeding, being hurt? Why!" I demand.

"Rhea," he growls in warning, and goosebumps pepper my skin. "Leave. This doesn't concern you."

I growl at his nonchalant attitude. "You cannot just dismiss me! For fuck's sake, Darius." I run a hand down my face. "Look at the mess of your back." I can barely stomach it. "Explain. Now!"

I scrub a hand down my face, wiping at a tear as it rolls down my cheek. I'm angry, scared, and hurt. After everything with the crystal, and now this, it feels like too much.

Sniffling, I make a move toward him, trying to breathe through my mouth as the metallic smell of his blood continues to make me feel sick.

He's hurt, wounded. I've never seen Darius so hurt before, I've never seen him on his *knees* before. I don't like it. It makes me uncomfortable. Like it's wrong.

"Darius Rikoth, answer me!"

I'm about three steps from him, my shaking hand reaching out, when a barrier is put up in front of me.

I gasp in surprise, looking at it with wide eyes, and then to Darius.

"No," I tell him, shaking my head. "You don't get to do this." I slap my hand on the barrier, calling my magic. It comes more easily as I guide it within me to the palm of my hand. I try to use it to disperse his barrier, but it doesn't work. "You don't get to ignore me, and expect me to shut up and walk away, that's not fair. Answer me, Darius!" I shout.

Silence.

Heartbreaking silence.

I stay where I am for a few minutes, watching his back, waiting for him to say anything at all.

He doesn't.

"Fine," I growl, but the sniffle I let out gives away my hurt. I sit down, my back to the barrier as I stare at the whip on the floor. "I'll stay right here then."

"Just fucking leave, Rhea" he shouts, and I squeeze my eyes shut, wrapping my arms around my knees. He's never sounded so... out of control.

"No," I croak out, putting my head on my knees. "Tell me why."

Nothing.

Runa releases a whine.

I stay.

THREE

Rhea

"Rhea?" I blink my eyes open, groaning at the ache in my limbs. Stretching out my back, I sit up from the cold floor.

"Yeah?" I say tiredly, rubbing my eyes.

"Come, eat." I look toward Leo, his eyes tired as he holds out a plate of food. I shake my head, looking at the bucket next to me that he put there for me to wash my face.

"Not hungry." He sighs, looking toward Darius.

"Are you really going to continue to do this? She's not fucking eating!" I watch as he tilts his head, scowling in Darius's direction. They must be speaking through the link. He shakes his head. "I'm not taking her out of here. You did this, now you can deal with it. I'll be back later, Rhea." He glares at Darius. "Hit him for me when you can." Then he leaves again.

"I don't know what's going on, but we are here, Rhea," Josh says down the link. He must have seen Leo leave the basement, waiting outside of it like he has since I came down here.

I know he's worried.

"I know, I'm okay."

"You are not eating again."

"I vow it, I'm okay."

Physically anyway. I'm not sure I can take any more emotional turmoil.

He sighs down the link and I shut it down.

I rest my head against the barrier separating me and Darius, looking through the light tinge of black to see that he still hasn't moved. It's been two days since I came down here and found him like this, two days since I saw my mother's throat being slit with a dagger.

I press my forehead further in, feeling Darius's magic greet me even though it's keeping me away from him right now.

Its coolness soothes my headache.

"You know, when I was younger, I used to think the lands were never-ending," I tell him, sighing as his magic seems to get colder. "I used to think it would go on forever, but it doesn't, does it?" I'm not even sure what I'm saying, but I'm tired, hurt and confused so the words just flow out of my mouth. "Land eventually turns to sea. That opened my eyes to something new that is ongoing." I bring a hand up, the tips of my fingers blue with my magic. "When I was in that basement," I say, and that gets me movement from him, the harsh, tensing of his shoulders. "I thought that would also be never-ending until the day that I died. I begged for it, wished, pleaded… but it never came."

I prayed for death, and when it didn't come, I wondered what I had done wrong to the Gods. Why wouldn't they bless me with death and end my suffering?

"I didn't die, no matter how many times I wanted it. I wanted to end my never-ending pain. But then my escape came."

I turn fully, crossing my legs in front of me and tracing the outline of Darius on his barrier, my magic leaving a shadowing mist behind. Runa sits up within me, her ears lowered as she waits patiently like I am.

"When I was roaming the lands, I thought that would also be my life, that it would also never end, and we would continue to move from place to place, never having a home or feeling safe," I sigh. "Then Eridian happened." I trace his back, swallowing over the lump in my throat as I look at his wounds. They have healed some, but they are still there, nonetheless. Dried blood cakes his skin, the floor, even splatters up the wall.

"What I'm trying to say is, that I thought all those types

of things were forever, when they weren't. But us, Darius, this connection *is* never-ending. Even when we take our last breaths, we are still connected. So regardless of how we got here, what we are now or will be, we are stuck with each other. So…" I place my palm flat, sending out tendrils of magic. "Answer me. Why was Leo whipping you?"

Silence.

"Do you like my suffering down here? Do you like me to remember when I was in a cell not so long ago?"

Darius stands suddenly, mist swirling from his feet as he moves to the table in front of him. He tries to quiet the grunt that comes from him, tries to quiet his pain, but I hear it all the same.

My heart beats roughly within.

Darius picks up a bucket with jerky movements, and I pick at my fingers as he lifts it and empties it over his head. The water washes away most of the blood, revealing more wounded and tattooed skin that once again turns my stomach.

I have to bite my tongue as I see old scars mixed into the new wounds.

He drops the bucket and it rolls towards me, hitting against the barrier. He then leans forward on the table at the back, his hands taking his weight as he hangs his head.

I wonder what's going through his mind as more blood seeps from the wounds as they split with the movement, but he doesn't make any move to help stop it.

"You don't need to be here, Rhea."

My eyes flick to the back of his head. "That's the first thing you say?" I whisper, my eyes automatically going to his back again as my brows furrow.

"Why are you still here?!" he demands, and I jolt at his anger. He's angry at me?

"You would leave during the night when I slept, sometimes you wouldn't even crawl into bed until the moon was high in the sky. But this time, you left going to get the crystal, so of course I came looking for you when you didn't come back," I tell him, rubbing my arms to stave off the chill down here. It's not like the coolness of Darius's power, that's like feeling it on a hot day and welcoming it. No, the chill down here is deadly. "I'm still here because you are!"

"You shouldn't have left the room, I would have been back soon."

"I had waited long enough."

I hear him growl beneath his breath. "Just leave, Rhea."

"No."

"I said leave!" He bangs his fists down on the table, and I hear it creak under the pressure.

"No." My voice breaks on the word, and he spins around, finally facing me.

"I'm warning you, Rhea." His hands fist at his side, and I shake my head.

He doesn't scare me.

"Why?" I croak out, and he looks away from me. I stand and take a step forward to the barrier, and he moves back, banging into the table. I pause at his reaction, looking over his face to try and figure out where his thoughts are. "Tell me, Darius, please."

"It's nothing for you to be concerned about."

"It's not nothing!" I shout, my body trembling. "Gods, it's not nothing," I tell him softly, blinking my tears away.

His jaw clenches as he stares at me, stares at my tears and his eyes harden before looking off to the side. I follow his gaze, and my stomach drops as I see another whip on the floor. Darius's eyes come back to mine, and I shake my head, pleading with my eyes.

The barrier turns a solid black.

"No," I whisper. My heart beats so wildly in my chest that I can hear it in my ears like a beating drum, like it's right next to me.

I hear movement.

"Darius, you can't mean to..." I press my palms to the barrier, my fingers digging into it. My fingertips glow blue as they sink in slightly, just as I hear the first strike.

I hiccup over a sob, placing my forehead against the barrier as I flinch.

"Stop it!"

Crack.

"Darius," I cry, pressing into the barrier and squeezing my eyes shut as my own memories threaten to surface. Runa whimpers within me, pacing restlessly.

Crack.

Stop it.

Crack.

Stop it.

I fall to my knees, hearing the whip slap against his skin again and again as I cry. Each strike goes through me, lances at my heart and cripples my soul.

Crack, crack, crack.

Stop it.

Stop it.

"Stop it!" I scream, forcing all the power I have into the barrier. It ripples, losing its solid color, but it doesn't break.

With blurry eyes, I see Darius on his knees again, facing away from me. He holds the whip in his right hand that hangs at his side, fresh blood coating it and his back.

"Please, Darius, stop this. It... it hurts me." I shake my head, pressing a fist to my chest to rub at it.

His shoulders rise and fall with harsh breaths as he stills.

"Why can't you just leave," he murmurs.

"I'm not leaving unless you do." And I'm not. "You cannot expect me to forget what I am seeing."

"It was something you were never meant to see. You wanted me to hurt like you did, I'm giving you what you want, and I'm just continuing what I deserve." His voice is rough, trying to hide the pain he no doubt feels.

I pause. I did say that, didn't I? I wanted to hurt him more than anything, I wanted my revenge on the way he had hurt me. I couldn't do it though, he knows that.

"Is this... is this my fault?" I ask, lead filling my stomach.

The shake of his head is instant. "No, never," he says vehemently.

Silence follows until I speak again.

"I did want you to hurt," I admit, swallowing over the lump in my throat. "You know I couldn't do it, but that doesn't mean I wanted this to happen. I thought after we had spoken that we were trying to move forward, to not stay in the past."

"The scars on your back are always going to be in the present!" He growls.

My heart cracks.

"And so shall yours now, won't they?" I say, my eyes roaming over his bleeding flesh. I rest my head against his barrier again. "Why are you doing this, Darius, tell me, help me understand. We saw the memory, and then you just didn't come back... to do *this*? Why?"

He laughs cruelly, and the hairs at the back of my neck rise. It reminds me of just before everything went to shit at Eridian. My heart beats faster.

"I whipped you because I thought it was you I saw who had caused the rogues, only now, who I saw wasn't you, was it? It was your mother." His knuckles turn white with how hard he grips the whip. I tense. "I've known it wasn't you for a while, but seeing it?" He hangs his head, his shoulders bunching. Anger rolls off of him as he growls, but it's not at me, it's at himself. "It was a reminder that I failed you."

So he came down here to hurt himself, but something doesn't make sense. "You have old scars, Darius. How long have you been doing this?" A pause. "Darius!" I shout when he doesn't answer me, banging my hand on his barrier.

A growl. "Since you escaped Wolvorn Castle."

I reel back, my breath catching. "But... But that was months ago."

"It was."

I look at the blood dripping down his back in horror. "How often have you done this?" I think back to the times he would disappear. I swallow. "Every few weeks?"

A shake of his head.

"Every few days?"

A pause, and then a grunt in confirmation.

My soul *hurts*.

How didn't I notice it? Thinking about it, I haven't even seen him fully naked since he had taken me here. Even in the shower he always faced me, when we fucked he's kept clothes on or made sure his back isn't to me. I think back to when I've been over his shoulder and hit his back, the grunts he let out, only now I realize it was from pain. In the bathroom when he was sweating through his t-shirt, that wasn't sweat at all... it was blood.

When he'd stretched his back out and rolled his shoulders like he was trying to shift some discomfort, had he been whipped during the night when he had left?

He's hidden it from me all this time...

He's punishing himself enough.

That's what Leo once said to me when he asked me to go easy on him. This is what he meant.

My eyes flick up to the back of his head. "You're punishing yourself."

"Of course I am," he says without hesitation, looking at me from over his shoulder. His eyes are tired, but hard. His scowl is angry but somewhat defeated. "Of course I'm punishing myself, it's the *least* I can fucking do, Rhea."

"But..."

"You think after our talk everything is forgotten after what I did to you?" He shakes his head, getting to his feet and stalking over to me, his steps heavy and harsh as he drops the whip to the floor.

I eye it, watching his blood drip from it before my eyes go back to him.

"Every time I close my eyes, I see the whip in my hand," he says harshly, a snarl on his face. "I see your flesh being torn by each leather strip, see it split and bleed, and I see your body tense and shake. I see what I did to you. Every. Fucking. Day." My eyes sting at his words, at his torment over what he did to me. His nostrils flare as he raises his hand to me, and I move my own trembling one to place it against his on the barrier, but he moves it just out of reach. "I see it all," he tells me quietly. "My punishment. My regret. My worst mistake that I couldn't even say aloud until that day with you in the willow gardens, like a fucking coward." He stares as his fingers hover before my palm on the barrier, watches as his hand moves back and forth like he wants to touch me, but refuses. "How could I not do to myself what I had done to you?"

He watches as my magic flows into the barrier, looking and searching for a way to break it. I need to be close to him, I need to... comfort him.

I never wanted this for him.

I hadn't thought much about how what he did to me may affect him. I didn't even know he was sorry until that day, but hearing him speak of how often he's tormented by it, how he sees what he did to me...

A tendril slips through, and I concentrate on it, moving it toward him. It reaches out, moving over his hand and resting there as I move it to his palm. Darius watches it, turning his hand over and a black strand intertwines with mine, holding there.

Keeping me there like he doesn't want me to disappear.

"What I did was unforgivable," Darius continues, never taking his eyes off of our magic. "I hurt you, so I hurt *me*. You bled so I will bleed. You were torn so I will tear, and you were scarred so I will fucking *scar*," he growls, his eyes coming back to mine as a tear falls from my eye. "There is no you, there is no me, there will forever be an us. Equal in every way." He watches as another tear falls, and his jaw clenches, shaking his head. "So don't cry for me, little wolf, I'm only doing what is deserved."

My heart is hit with a sharp pain, and I rub my chest again as more tears fall from my eyes. He's been harming himself for *months.* Even before the full truth was out in the open.

He's hurt himself more times than I ever was, and yet he didn't stop.

Hasn't stopped.

This isn't what I wanted. What I *ever* wanted. Especially after knowing he was threatened with his men if he refused Charles's order to whip me. I would do anything for my family, and that's what he did that day. He protected them.

I can see it from his side, I would have chosen my family in a heartbeat over him back then.

We were still enemies.

Now... I don't know what we are, but we are more than we were.

I think about the field of lesia flowers he made me, about the smile on his face as he watched over me as I played and spun for *hours.*

No. We are not enemies any longer.

"Stop it," I whisper, closing my eyes against the onslaught of emotions rattling through me. "You don't want me to cry?"

"Not like this."

"You don't want me in pain?"

"Of course not," he snarls, the ground trembling.

My eyes spring open, and I take a breath. "You don't want me to scar?"

"Never again!" He tilts his head, nostrils flaring as he growls. "I will not let another touch you to scar you, little wolf. Those that dare try will have a very painful death."

"No," I say, taking a step back, and my power along with it. His brows furrow as he watches me. "Not another...me." I nudge the whip on the ground that I took from Leo. Darius's eyes go to it, then slowly raises them to mine. They darken, those flecks appearing once again as he goes deathly still.

He won't stop? Then I will make him.

And he will never do this again.

"You don't want to do that," he murmurs, but it's deadly, a warning brimming inside of it. Tendrils of his power appear from behind his shoulders, swishing angrily as mist appears beneath his feet. "Don't even think about it."

"Try me." We stare at each other for a moment, and then I bend down, reaching for it. "You know how bad I am at doing as I'm told." My shaky fingers have just barely touched it when a hand is on the top of my arm and pulling me harshly away on a deep growl.

"You will never – *umph*."

My arms wrap around Darius's neck as I jump into his arms. His hands go under my ass, his power folding around me as I cling to him. I'm conscious of the wounds on his back as I bury my face in his neck, soaking his skin with my tears as I pull him closer to me. Just needing him closer.

"Little wolf?" His voice is wary, unsure.

Runa whines within me, and I feel her come as close to the surface as she can while Darius's wolf meets her.

"No more," I whisper into his neck. The smell of his blood like this makes me want to vomit, but I can't let go. "Vow it." He grunts, and I lean back, looking down at him.

He shakes his head slowly, his eyes telling me his choice.

I grip the side of his neck harshly. "I will never stop grabbing for it then." I look down at the whip and his whole body stiffens, more of his magic wrapping around me as he bares his teeth.

I show with my eyes how serious I am, that I won't ever stop. That if he continues to do this, then so will I.

"How do you expect me to give you justice for what I did if I cannot do this!" he says angrily, yet his touch on me is gentle as he doesn't let me fall. "I do not want your forgiveness in this."

I move my hands to his hair and yank his head back, baring my own teeth at him. "Vow it," I demand. "I do not need this from you, Darius, do you hear me? I do not want this, I don't condone it."

His jaw ticks. "Then what do you need? Tell me and I will do it. Tell me how to make it better, tell me how to take your pain away, tell me how I can go back and tear my own fucking heart out before I ever touched that fucking whip!" His eyes are a little wild, and I've never seen him like this.

He looks so lost on what to do, like him hurting himself was the only thing keeping him together.

I bring my forehead down to his. "Not this. I need you to stop it, okay?" His eyes harden, but I don't let up. I'm not backing down from this. "I don't want this from you, I never wanted this from you no matter how much I told myself I hated you. No matter how much I wanted to hurt you. This was never, not once, what I wanted to happen, so, vallier, stop," I breathe, imploring him with my eyes.

"These fucking eyes," he whispers, and he maneuvers me to bring a hand up to wipe my tears. "Then what do you want from me if not this?" he says gruffly, like there couldn't possibly be anything else.

His hands tighten on me, his eyes still a little wild like only I can give him the answers.

I take a deep breath before I reply.

"I want you to bring me my favorite flowers, to train with me, to feed me, fight with me, to hold me at night no matter how much I may grumble, to wash me in the bath, to let me read in your library, to kiss me under the moonlight, to not break this vow."

A pause. "Is that what you want?" he grunts, his magic tightening around my back for a moment, and I sigh in relief.

"I do." I stroke through his hair, soothing the sting I probably caused. "That's all I want. That makes me feel better."

His eyes bounce between mine, until he nods, his nose nudging mine. "Then I vow it."

FOUR

Rhea

"We need to clean you up," I tell him, wiggling in his arms. He's reluctant, but he eventually lets me down.

"You going to wash me, little wolf?" He raises a brow, and I scowl at him.

"Yes," I say haughtily, raising my chin and acting like it's not a big deal. "Now come on." His magic releases me and goes back into his body as he stares at me.

I already miss the cool sensation of it.

"No, go to bed, I will be up shortly," he says, looking around the room.

My heart drops.

"Darius," I whisper, and his eyes swing back to mine. "Let me clean them, I don't want to be down here any longer." We stare at each other until he eventually nods.

I hesitate for a moment, then I silently grab his hand in mine, and turn, leading him back to his bedroom. I don't ever want to come down here again.

The weight of his palm is heavy in mine, and even though his hand engulfs my smaller hand, he lets me lead him.

Runa comes closer to the surface where we are connected, and Darius grunts, no doubt feeling her. Then I feel his wolf there, so close that I hear Runa let out a purring noise.

Darius squeezes my hand, I squeeze back, pretending there isn't a lump in my throat.

"Where is everyone," I ask when we reach the hallway, the

door slamming shut behind us, hopefully forever.

A pause, then, "They are in the dining room going over more of the names we found."

I nod, not saying anything to that as my pack is the first to come to my mind.

One thing at a time, Rhea.

We hit the steps, and I duck my head when we reach the top, moving faster when we reach the room that I killed Maize in before we hit his bedroom.

I don't want to think about her, it makes me want to tear out her throat all over again.

Darius's scent immediately wraps around me when we go through the door, but it also has a hint of mine intertwined with it. It makes me pause for a moment until I continue.

I head to the bathroom, pulling Darius along with me. Grabbing a cloth, I turn on the tap to dampen it, letting it soak.

Darius watches me curiously as I gather the things I need, silent as ever as he crosses his arms. Both of us ignore the blood dripping on the floor.

When I have everything, I reach for him and guide him to the center of the bathroom, and he goes willingly. I'm not used to a compliant Darius, but I know he's doing it for my benefit, which I'm grateful for.

I'm sure he can sense the riot swirling inside of me. I need to do something. I feel responsible, even though it's not my fault. He did what he did because he wanted to punish himself, but it doesn't stop me feeling upset about it.

I quickly grab a stool. Then, pushing it behind him, I guide him to sit as I stand behind him, feeling his eyes on me from the mirror above the sink.

"This may sting a bit," I tell him, when I grab the damp cloth.

"It's fine, they will heal soon enough," he says.

I look down at the blood and open wounds on his back and swallow roughly. His markings will now have scarred flesh through them when they are healed.

I follow the harsh lines of his markings on either side of his back, following it down to the black pants he wears as they disappear beneath it.

Swallowing roughly, I bring the cloth to a particularly deep wound first, and I start to wipe around it with a shaky hand. I try to be gentle as I clean the wound, watching as more blood pumps out as I swipe around it.

When I stabbed Darius with a knife in his shoulder, I knew he would be okay, I knew I didn't hit anything vital... I knew it wouldn't damage, but instead cause some of the pain he caused me.

But this...

Focus Rhea.

Rinsing the cloth again, I think back to all the times I never saw his back when we were together, but then I do remember just one time.

"You gave me your t-shirt at Witches Rest," I begin, and his eyes flick to mine, nodding. My mind was in a haze at that point. It was far away after showing all my scars. "I saw your back, it was clear."

He tilts his head. "You are not the only one who can hide them. It had been a few days since I last...hurt myself."

"But you didn't hide them from me now?"

"You saw them. It would be foolish to attempt to trick you into thinking you didn't. I wouldn't do that to you."

We stare at each other for a moment before I continue again.

Darius doesn't make another sound as I work, as I go to the sink and rinse the cloth again and again before continuing in my task. His power comes out eventually, a tendril of it moving over my forearm as I clean, steading me.

Comforting me.

"You were never meant to know what went on down there," he says into the quietness of the room.

The only sound that has kept us company is that of the running water.

I hear the unspoken, *especially after finding out about your mother*. He doesn't say that, I can feel that he wants to but doesn't want to remind me.

"I assumed so," I mutter, cleaning around a particularly deep gash. I feel his eyes on me in the mirror, his gaze a comfort as they don't leave me as I get to work. "Your tattoos will not be the same now."

"They haven't been for months." I pause... right. "It does not matter, the most important one isn't affected." I flick my eyes to his neck briefly as his eyes do the same.

I continue on in silence, the only sound is the water every time I rinse the cloth to get it as clean as possible. As the blood is cleared away, and with me closer to his scars, I freeze when I notice something almost similar. My eyes flick up to Darius in the mirror before I take a small step back and look.

Really look.

"They are the same," he tells me before I can ask, and my eyes meet his in the mirror again. "I know where I put every mark on your body." His hands fist on his thighs. "I made sure to give myself the same treatment as close as I could."

This male...

He turns around on the stool as I stand there in shock. A large hand on my waist guides me between his spread legs, and then that hand is moving. It goes under my t-shirt and starts crawling up my back. I shiver at his touch, my eyes never leaving his as he traces one of my scars he can't even *feel*.

"We are the same in many ways, and completely different in others, but never forget this, little wolf. What is done to you shall be done to me." I shake my head, and his hands move to another scar, tracing it back down with a clenched jaw. I shiver. "The scars on your back are my reminder, the scars on my back are your reminder."

"My reminder of what?" I whisper.

"My regrets, my punishment, my vow and your justice," he says, pulling me onto his lap suddenly. My legs dangle on either side of his thighs as he brings us nose to nose. "We are one in ways no other can be. I'm a selfish bastard when it comes to you, so I won't accept anything less. So, the next time you threaten to hurt yourself, remember I will do the same. I will take advantage of that soft heart of yours and use it against you to keep you from harm."

The fucker isn't even sorry about that.

My eyes narrow. "It works both ways, Darius."

He rubs his nose with mine and nods. "I'm aware of that, little wolf." He nips at my chin. "And that is why I won't break my vow."

He lifts me, and then he's carrying me. "What are you doing, I'm not done yet," I protest.

"We are. I'm not going to let you stare at my back when it hurts you to look at them right now. Plus, you do know I can feel when your magic touches me."

"Yes." He turns and sits on the bed with me still in his lap.

"Then I know you used some of your magic to heal me."

"It still needs to be taken care of," I mutter. I did put some magic into his wounds, trying to speed up the healing process, and even though the wounds started to close, it's not fast enough for my liking.

"Other things need to be taken care of."

"Like what?" He grabs my hips and pushes down. I raise a brow. "Really? How can you be hard after that?"

"You only need to be in the room, Rhea, for me to get hard, no matter the circumstance."

"But your back..." I trail off as he rips my t-shirt off over my head.

"I don't care. I need to feel you." His voice is muffled as he places open kisses on my neck and shoulder, and my body instantly reacts to him.

"Darius..."

"Be a good girl and let me feel you." His voice is gruff, but with a hint of something I haven't heard before in his tone. "I just …" he inhales my scent. "Need to feel you."

I relent.

He wastes no time as he licks a path down to my breast and bites my nipple through my bra. That goes next, and then I'm on my back and he has me completely naked before him in seconds.

His eyes devour me as he stands at the end of the bed, the bulge noticeable in his pants. "Wait there." He turns and goes to the bathroom, and I hear the shower go on.

I wait impatiently as I squirm on the bed, my hands clenching in the furs as nerves rattle through me. My body feels hot, restless and in no time, Darius walks out the bathroom completely naked, dripping water. I raise up on my elbows, taking him in completely for the first time since my heat.

My eyes eat up the tattoos that travel from below his jaw all the way down over his shoulders, his sides, over his hips and then his thighs, and ending just above his knees.

During my heat, I vaguely looked over them, even knowing that the tattoos mirror those on his back, but now I can appreciate the art of his body even more.

I know writing in a language I don't know hides within harsh lines that sometimes have delicate curves flowing over them. If I look close enough, I can see wolf eyes, skulls and daggers, an assortment of things that only makes me think of battle, of bloodshed.

Darius pauses when he notices my perusal, letting me get my fill of him. This is the first time I have ever been able to.

I lick my dry lips, once again questioning if we should even be doing this. The last few days have been a lot.

"There is nothing wrong with wanting to find an escape when everything is too much," he says, like he can read my mind, tilting his head at me. My eyes lift to his in surprise. "It just depends on who you find that pleasure with, and make no mistake, it will only come from me, and I like to make you feel that. Something only I can do."

My eyes drift down to his extremely hard cock, and I squeeze my thighs together at the thought of him filling me, knowing this time will be different than all the rest.

Every time has been different.

But something has shifted even more.

Darius makes a rough sound, and I watch as he reaches a hand down to stroke himself. "Open your legs, little wolf, show me what I do to you. What only *I* do to you." His voice is like gravel, and I shiver, doing what he's asked even as my cheeks heat. Darius moves closer until he's at the edge of the bed. "Fucking soaking." His head lowers, getting a closer look. "That for me?" I nod. "Good girl."

I can't help but moan at his words as a drop of pre-cum appears. I lick my lips.

"Do you want some?" he asks me, and I nod again, not being able to speak, my eyes locking on the white bead.

Darius groans, then he's crawling over me. I'm too focused on his cock, that I haven't even noticed that his knees are on either side of my shoulders, or that he's guiding his cock toward my lips.

I freeze, my eyes lifting from his cock to his toned stomach. I don't move as he rubs the tip along my lips. Back and forth, back, and forth.

I part my lips automatically, knowing it's what I should do, and then he's pushing into my mouth slowly, just the tip. It rests on my tongue for a moment before he pulls out and pushes back in, a little further this time. All the while I count in my head, knowing it won't be too long—

Darius suddenly shifts his hips back, and then my mouth is empty. He brings a hand up and starts stroking my cheek, waiting patiently as I slowly raise my eyes to his, confused as to why he stopped.

He studies my features before staring deeply into my eyes. His own tighten in some sort of acknowledgement, his jaw ticking, but then he's crawling down my body and his lips are on my pussy.

"Darius," I gasp in surprise, the heavy feeling that was settling in my stomach now turning to something lighter. My hand goes to his head as I grip his hair in pleasure. This I feel, this I see instead of where my mind wanted to take me.

"You will give *me* something instead, little wolf." He devours me like he's starving, nipping, biting, and driving me crazy as he pushes me to the edge again and again so quickly. "You will give me something I am always fucking *aching* for, you will give it freely," he growls. He has two fingers inside me next, ramming into me at a fast pace as I squeeze his head between my thighs.

"Darius, please," I whine. His hands are a bruising grip on my hips as he nips and licks at the inside of my thigh, driving me crazy as I squirm on the bed.

Gods, just the sight of him between my legs could make me come.

"Begging already," he growls into my pussy, and then he's sucking on my clit and I'm soaring. "Fuck, what your noises do to me."

I haven't even come down from my orgasm when he fills me completely, but it's not the same.

It was slow, achingly slow, and my hands go to the sides of his neck as he hovers above me, staring into my eyes.

Those flecks appear, hovering just at the edge until they fill his eyes completely. He makes a rough sound in the back of his throat as I'm sure my eyes are doing the same.

It feels too much all at once, feels too deep.

I close my eyes.

"Look at me." His demanding voice with a particularly slow, deep thrust of his hips has my eyes peeling open. "Good girl," he says, starting a slow pace. "Let us bare it all. Let us finally show each other."

His eyes never leave mine, and mine never leave his.

I feel open, vulnerable.

Seen.

"I always see you," he groans, as he leans down, elbows resting next to my shoulders as he cages me in, sheltering me. My fingers dig more into his neck as I wrap my legs around his waist. "Now, see me."

A purr rumbles from his chest, the sound deep as he never takes his eyes off me, and I feel it wash over my entire body, heightening every touch.

The emotion in his eyes takes my breath away as he lets me in, lets me see everything. It's like for a moment we are fully connected.

I roll my hips experimentally and he growls, his hips stuttering for a moment. "Do that again, little wolf. Fuck." I do, enjoying the sight of his eyes rolling back at the pleasure *I'm* giving him.

His gaze roams over me, always coming back to my eyes at some point, but he looks everywhere he can, looks where we are joining.

He fucks me deep and slow, like he's savoring every single thrust as I match it, our bodies in sync because they know more then we ever did.

I whine as my clit rubs against his solid abs and I pull him down to me, kissing him softly, needing to taste him. His hands go into my hair, holding me as he starts to thrust a little faster, just enough to have another orgasm flowing over me.

I whine into his mouth, legs squeezing around him and then he moans, devouring the sound and then I feel him releasing inside of me as he fucks me slowly.

He doesn't stop when I come down, and when he's emptied himself, he just continues to fuck me slowly, like he can't get enough.

"Feeling you like this," he mumbles into my neck, careful not to put his weight on me as I catch my breath. "It's more than anything I have ever experienced. And I never want it to end. It also feels like the only way I can show you what you mean to me."

That's why he wants to feel me.

I blink unexpected tears from my eyes and I pull him closer, curling my arms around his neck and running my fingers through his hair.

"Me too," I whisper the truth of it. If he can say such things to me, then I can admit them back.

Maybe one day that will change, but letting Darius give me pleasure will never be a hardship.

I suspect he's never really felt for anything else apart from his family and brothers.

Tingles start on my forearm and I sigh into him.

"One day," he says after a long silence, still kissing my neck before he turns us, and I'm led on top of him, his cock still inside of me. "Your lips will be wrapped around my cock." I still, but he soothes me with his next words. "But make no mistake, little wolf, it will be on your terms only." He pulls me closer and places my face in his neck, his magic wrapping around me like he wants to protect me. "So don't open your mouth for me when you don't want it, do you understand? That is something I never want."

I pant into his skin, unsure what to say.

"Do you understand, Rhea?"

"I do," I croak out.

"Good," he rubs my back, and then he starts to slowly thrust up into me. "Now, again."

This damn male.

FIVE

Rhea

I watch Darius sleep.

It's not often I get to do this, but I woke before him, and now I'm watching his chest rise and fall as his hand circles my wrist, like he can't let go of me.

I squirm, deliciously sore from Darius's attention and I feel…content. I remember the way he never once looked away from me, never let his skin be far from mine, never let himself be removed from my body.

Darius more than fucked me last night, he stole a piece of my soul.

But did he really steal it when I let him have it?

Fingers flexing, I move my hands and trail them down the side of his ribs, following a line of a tattoo when I come to a stop.

I tilt my head and move closer to get a better look.

Is that…

"Enjoying yourself, little wolf?" Darius's voice is like gravel, and my head snaps up to his to see him watching me, a lazy smirk on his face.

I go to move my hand back, but he grabs it and places it back on his ribs.

"I got it as soon as I could, after I saw your eyes light up at one." I look down to the small lesia flower he has on the side of his ribs, and my chest warms.

"You could have gotten anything else," I mutter, unsure how

to respond.

"Why would I get something else when they are something you cherish?" A tendril of his magic slips around my waist. "They remind me of you."

My heart.

"Why there?" I wonder. I trace it as he still holds my hand.

"I put it on my side because that's where you will always be. Beside me."

"Will I?" I dare to question. We are at war, whether the lands know it or not. Not only do we have to survive it, what happens after, when we don't have a common goal to work toward? When we don't have to work together anymore?

In a sudden move, I'm hauled on top of him and he brings my face down to his. "Yes." He says it with absolute certainty, determination filling his eyes. "Do you not feel it?"

My eyes bounce between his and I nod, slowly. "I do."

The connection doesn't feel as frayed anymore, pulled as tight.

It feels stronger, pulling me to him more than I have ever felt.

Things feel different between us now. Not fixed, or even right, just…different.

He held me all night after he made me come again and again, and for once, I didn't argue or fight him on it. I wanted him there, no, I needed him there. To be close to him, to wrap his scent around me and he made me feel…safe.

Again, things are not right, and may never be. It's complicated what had happened to both of us and the reasons why. I haven't forgiven him, and he doesn't want to be forgiven. But maybe, we can finally begin to move forward now.

As long as he keeps his vow to not hurt himself anymore.

The thought makes me sick if he were to break it.

Darius rubs his nose against mine and breathes against my lips. "I will always be near you, no matter what that looks like, and you will always be with me." He lifts my arm and places a soft kiss in the middle of my forearm.

I suck in a sharp breath.

He smiles, nipping at it.

Asshole.

I allow myself to relax against him, and he brings his arms around me, hand running up my naked back and once again, he trails his fingers against the scars he cannot see.

It reminds me of his own.

Is it wrong of me to feel closer to him after that? That we both have something that's a reminder, but also something we will overcome?

"How is your back?" I ask, sinking more into his body and placing my head in the crook of his neck.

"Fine," he says, even as his body tenses. I go to sit up but he stops me on a sigh. "There is some pain, but nothing I cannot handle."

Are we being more honest with each other, more than ever now? Is this our something new?

"I'm glad," I tell him, and I am.

Never again.

He shifts beneath me and moves a hand to run it over my wrist, where red marks from the terbium cuffs once were. "You don't hide these ones?"

I shake my head. "I can't." He tenses at that. "I don't know why but I can't." I shrug. "I don't mind, they are a reminder to never be shackled again."

He growls beneath me and holds me closer. "Never." His magic comes around me next and I huff.

"So possessive."

"Protective," he corrects.

"Commanding."

"Assertive."

I bite at his neck in reprimand, and he groans beneath his breath. "Annoying."

"Adorable."

I hide my face more as my cheeks heat, but he chuckles like he knows anyway.

I sigh into him and eventually say, "We have to get up, don't we?"

He follows my sigh with one of his own. "There is much to do." I nod. "If I could keep you in this bed forever, I would." I'm suddenly hauled over his shoulder as he walks toward the bathroom. "But there is blood to be spilt, and we are first in line."

That we are.

"Ready?" Darius asks me, and I take in a shaky breath.

We are in his bedroom, sitting in the bed, crystal between us. I asked Darius to grab it, and he went without another word.

Did I worry the whole time he was gone that he would go back to the basement? Yes, but he came back to me quickly, and now we are sitting across from each other as I prepare myself.

I didn't want to do this in front of others again, and Darius didn't even question me, didn't even ask why.

I wanted privacy in case I react the same as before, and doing that in front of Darius doesn't seem to bother me.

He's seen me at my worst, seen me at my lowest, and yet he's still here, wanting me anyway.

The amount of weakness I have shown in front of others recently is nerve racking. Being wolves, we never show weakness in risk of being challenged. And though living in Eridian with my pack was peaceful, an Alpha does not show that weakness.

I can't seem to help it lately and I'm tired of feeling pathetic.

"I'm ready," I tell him and straighten my shoulders.

"I have you."

He does.

One thing about us starting as enemies, we have been through more than most in a small amount of time, and that means I know his intentions now.

His reasoning behind his actions.

How his words hold weight.

How he cares for me in his own way, even as he feels he doesn't know how.

We both reach out at the same time and touch the crystal, and then, we are instantly transported back into the memory.

I hold on to Darius's hand tightly as I look at the ground, gaining the courage to face what is before me once again.

Darius pulls me close, wrapping his arms around me as I take a few breaths to face the memory. We need to see if there is anything that may help us with the rogues, with Charles.

Placing my hand on his chest, I look up at him, taking in his strength as he strokes my cheek with the backs of his fingers, letting me know he's there.

Runa comes to just beneath my skin, and Darius's eyes flash black before I feel his wolf there.

They are also with us.

I nod and turn in his arms, taking in the scene once again.

Hooded figures chanting, Charles on the stone platform, another person off to the side. My mom is in the center, hanging by chains.

I swallow the bile that threatens to come up.

"You're okay," Darius tells me as he massages the back of my neck.

I inhale a few shaky breaths, trying to control the nausea I feel, the shake to my bones.

"I'm okay," I breathe.

"Do you know what they are saying?" Darius asks me quietly, rubbing my arms as if we can feel a chill.

I don't feel anything but heartbreaking dread.

"No," I say, my mouth dry. "But I think it is something to enhance power. At least, that's what it feels like." My brows furrow, trying to explain it but I can't.

"You feel a difference?" he asks.

"Yeah. The air feels charged almost, like a thickening blanket full of power, waiting to be placed."

"Hmm."

I take a step forward, Darius following at my back as we walk through the hooded figures. I look at the glowing platform, the runes placed there and fist my hands.

"A trap stone." I nod to the platform. "She couldn't escape even if she managed to get down."

He squeezes at the back of my neck again in comfort.

She was trapped, and I think she knew that, but she still fought until her last breath.

Oh, mom.

We walk to the platform, standing at the edge as I steel myself. Blinking rapidly, I raise my gaze and see her.

She is what I would imagine I would look like when I'm older. Full of grace and grit. A fierce protector and a gentle caretaker.

A warrior.

"She looks just like you." Darius says, his arms brushing mine as he stands next to me, his fingers tangling with my own. I nod. "I know where you get that wildness from." There is admiration in his tone, and a warmth fills me.

"She was too good for the lands," I choke out, watching as she fights, even knowing she will lose as she growls at Charles.

"It runs in the family." I flick my eyes up to Darius briefly, squeezing his hand, knowing what's coming next.

"Do not watch again, little wolf," he commands gently. He brings a hand up to cover my eyes so I can't see ahead or above. "You have enough nightmares, do not force yourself to have more."

I let him shield me, like he said he would, and I try to drown out the sounds, the chanting, the choking, the dripping of blood onto the stone that seems heightened.

My mom tells Charles of the beasts that will roam the lands, and Darius suddenly freezes.

"What is it?" I lift my hand to move his away.

"Don't," he says, the demand thick. His arm wraps around my waist, bringing me closer. I pause, then drop my hand. I still watch though, through the gap Darius has left me to see below.

I watch as that blood fills the groove of the stone, watch them glow to what seems to be a pulse of its own.

And then it blinks out.

My brows furrow as it looks like it seeped *down* into the stone.

Charles laughs, talking to someone about how they will see if it works, but I'm too focused now on the dark patch that has appeared off to the side on the short grass. It looks like it bubbles almost from a high heat, and then the edges dance as if it's a flame of darkness.

I take Darius's hand away from my eyes and point to it.

"Have you seen that before?" I ask him.

"No," he grunts, just as a shape starts to appear out of it. It seems almost like an apparition until it turns solid, and I swallow as two legs move forward on the grass.

Then I grip Darius's hand tighter as its eyes look directly at us and it lets out a piercing howl.

Rogure.

I look at Charles and the other hooded figure, ignoring the limp body hanging in front of them. "They haven't noticed," I tell Darius.

"How is that possible?" he asks. "It's right there."

But no one seems to see it, yet it's looking directly at us.

"This is just a memory, there is no way it can see us, so who is it looking at?"

Darius looks behind us and I do the same. "There is nothing but those that have stopped chanting, which I'm suspecting are the Highers's witches."

I turn back and startle as the rogue is now closer. "Darius…"

"What—" I push him to the side as the rogue lunges, its teeth bare and ready to tear.

I dive out of the way, shock rattling through me as the rogue spins to face me as it lands.

"Rhea!" Darius comes up behind the rogue, but it's already lunging for me again.

I roll, going through the hooded figures like they are not even there as I kick a foot out and connect with the rogues face. I have no time to wonder how the fuck it is a solid body as black saliva splatters on the ground, and a deadly growl comes from its throat as it comes at me again.

But it doesn't get the chance.

A black rope wraps around its neck, yanking it away from me. Darius appears behind it, his eyes furious as he gets on its back and wraps his hands around its neck.

We both know his magic could have done it for him, but because it came for me, he wants to personally do it.

The deafening crack seems to echo around us as Darius's angry breaths go along with it.

The rogue falls limp, and I look at it with wide eyes.

This is a memory, how the fuck is this possible?

Darius stands over the rogue like it will come back alive, his hands flexing, those two large masses behind his shoulders moving angrily.

"Dar," I say gently, and his eyes snap up to me.

At one time, that much fury in his eyes would have sent a shiver of fear down my spine, but I know it's not for me.

He seems to snap out of it when he takes me in on the floor, and he rushes towards me, landing heavily on his knees, hands on me in the next breath.

"Are you hurt? Did it bite you." His hands are frantic, looking for nonexistent injuries.

"I'm fine," I tell him, reaching out hesitantly, and then placing a hand on his cheek when he doesn't stop. "Darius," I say a little more forcefully, and his eyes snap to mine. "I'm okay."

His eyes bounce between mine for a moment, but then he breathes a sigh of relief, nodding. "Let's get the fuck out of here."

I couldn't agree more.

SIX

Rhea

"Took you long enough," Taylor says when I enter the dining room, his eyes looking for any sign of injury.

I huff at him. "I'm okay." He waits a moment, and then nods, coming to rub his cheek against mine.

"You need to stop leaving us for days at a time," Colten whines, next to rub my cheek when Taylor moves out of the way.

I pat his head and rub back. "Sorry," I say, and I mean it.

We have all been together for a long time, so being away from them is not something I like to do.

It makes me think of the others, of Kade, and my hands start to shake at the feeling of loss rattling through me.

Hudson squeezes my shoulder and moves to sit down with Colten, and then Josh is in front of me.

"I know," he says down the link and I nod, folding into his arms, a familiar growl at my back sounding. "Does he ever stop?" Josh mutters, nuzzling the side of my head.

I chuckle. "No."

He moves to take a seat next to Sarah, who waves and smiles at me. I nod my head at her, noticing how much healthier she looks. I'm glad.

Seb is here next. "Been up to no good without me?" he asks, wiggling his eyebrows and pointedly looking at my neck. At the bite Darius purposely left there in the shower this morning. "Invite me next time, I'm sure I can make it better than your babysitter."

I shake my head at him with a chuckle, accepting his hug. When he doesn't let go, just to piss Darius off, he's flying over the table in the next breath and slamming into the wall across from me.

I gasp and turn my wide eyes to Darius.

"Idiot," Leo mutters from his seat.

"I think he's got balls." That's from Damian.

"A death vow more like," Zaide mutters.

"Does he ever stop?" Jerrod asks Anna, who sits across from him.

"Nope," she says, taking a drink, looking over at Sebastian. "He's never one to control himself."

"And you are?" Zaide asks her, and they both stare at each other, not saying anything else.

Seb shakes his hands out as he stands, wiping invisible dirt off his clothes as angry breaths pant at the back of my neck.

"Was that necessary?" he asks Darius.

"Stop touching her!" He growls, and I ignore the pair of them as I move to sit down.

I won't be surprised if dicks are whipped out next.

Of course I don't get the chance to get to my own seat, because I'm hauled into a warm lap, limbs arranged just how Darius wants it and his power wrapping around my waist to keep me still.

I sigh in defeat, but also secretly liking it.

I don't want to be away from him either right now.

Darius grabs berries and bread, piling it onto my plate, along with some meat.

There is far too much, but I don't say anything.

I can feel the others watching us again, but my stomach rumbling makes me not care.

When Darius is happy with the amount, he holds a piece of bread up to my lips, and I turn, grabbing a berry and holding it up to his in return.

I take a bite of bread and he pauses, eyes trained on mine before he opens his mouth... then I launch the berry inside.

It must hit the back of his throat because he starts coughing and spluttering.

I smirk.

Damian and Seb howl in laughter, the others chuckling and I continue chewing my food. That's what he gets for shoving berries into my mouth in the bath.

Yeah, asshole, I say with my eyes as he glares down at me, *I remember that.*

He shakes his head, squeezing me with his power before he feeds me more food.

"The Alpha of Elites gagging on berries," Colten says, tearing into his bread. "I've seen it all now."

"Behave, pup," Hudson says, bringing Colten's plate closer so he can eat more.

Colten shrugs. "It's funny."

Hudson leans down and whispers something to him, and Colten's eyes glaze over for a moment, cheeks heating. I bite my lip to stop laughing, my eyes flicking to Josh and Anna who are hiding their smiles.

"Tell us what you found in the crystal," Taylor says and that sobers me up, the lightness I felt evaporating.

I take a breath and fill them in.

"So it was like it was real?" Josh asks. The fire crackles in the background as the tension rises, everyone focusing on the situation, plates now not being touched.

"It was like it was there. It was definitely solid, it wasn't part of the memory," I tell him.

"How is that possible?" Damian asks, leaning back in his seat.

"We don't know," Darius says at my back. "But it attacked us, and then I killed it." I snuggle into him, needing his body heat as ice fills my veins over seeing that rogue.

No one says anything to that, lost in their own thoughts. I'm surprised we are only discussing this. No one has said a word about where Darius and I have been the last few days.

I couldn't be more grateful about it.

I reach a hand down and rest it on Darius's thigh, feeling his power beneath my fingertips as he twitches. The arm banded around me tightens, pulling me even closer as he nuzzles the back of my neck, uncaring of the audience.

"Is there some type of magic that can reside in a memory stone to make this happen?" Zaide asks, not once looking up from his sharpening of his blade as Sebastian eyes him.

"I have never heard of it," Leo says.

"We never heard of a memory stone being able to change, so we can't rule it out," I tell them.

"We should look in the library, see if we can find anything?" Anna suggests.

My pack nods, Sarah more hesitant with her going to new places in the keep, but Josh laces his fingers with hers and kisses the back of her hand.

"You're so sweet with her," I tell him down the link.

Josh looks at me and raises a brow. *"And you willingly let him sit you on his lap like a little pet."*

My cheeks heat even as I scowl. *"I'm not some pet you—"* I sigh, and then turn slightly to look at Darius.

He tilts his head to the side, unapologetic in cutting out our conversation.

"Asshole," I mutter. He chuckles at my back, and then his lips are at my ear.

"This asshole had you dripping on my hand, my tongue, my cock—"

I shove my hand over his mouth as I feel everyone stare at my back. "Shall we go to the library then?" I say, my voice as steady as possible.

I hear chairs being pushed back and the shuffle of feet, along with some muffled laughs.

I glare at Darius, but he's unconcerned with the potential of losing his balls.

He grips the back of my hair and yanks my head back, invading all of my senses as soon as his tongue touches mine. He groans into the kiss, like a starved animal as he barely lets me come up for air, and I allow it.

Especially when he makes those satisfied noises along with a rumble coming from his chest.

Fine, maybe he can keep his balls.

A rustling starts, and then a deep groan. I sigh, exhausted from spending hours in the library and finding nothing.

There is another groan, but I realize that it's not from pleasure though, it's from pain.

I blink my sleepy eyes awake, trying to pinpoint in the room what woke me, when the warmth from my side leaves me completely.

I turn my head, watching as Darius sits on the edge of the bed, head low. He seems to shake it, running a hand through his hair.

He seems agitated.

He stands abruptly, but still quietly in that way he has always been able to move.

He moves toward the door, fist clenching and my stomach drops.

"Darius?" I sit up quickly, clutching the furs to my chest as moonlight peeks through the room, illuminating the scars on his back.

He stills at the sound of my voice, shoulders rising and falling roughly.

My feet hit the floor, and I pad over to him, not stopping until I'm in front of his body.

His eyes seem a little unfocused as he looks down at me, a

sheen of sweat covering his body.

My brows furrow. "Darius?"

He shakes his head, blinking a few times. "Go to bed, you should be resting." He moves to the side and passes me.

I turn and clutch his hand, squeezing it roughly as my heart beats wildly. "You vowed," I remind him, and I hear the breath release from his lungs.

He said he wouldn't go down to the basement again.

We stay like this for a long time in silence, me clutching his hand while he tries to calm himself from whatever woke him.

"Come back to bed," I whisper, pulling him gently.

I'm surprised when he lets me, but I continue until he's on the bed with me. I push him down gently, laying next to him.

He stares up at the ceiling, barely blinking and I bite my lip.

Decision made, I crawl on top of him, and his hands go to my waist instantly.

"What's wrong?" I ask quietly.

His eyes slowly come to mine, and the pain within them makes my breath stutter.

"It's nothing, rest, little wolf." He tries to pull me down, but I stop him. Once again, locked in each other's gazes, I ask with my eyes for him to tell me.

"It was just a nightmare." I tilt my head when he lets go of my waist and looks down at his hands.

I see the tremble in them and my worry mounts.

"What was it about?" I keep my voice low, quiet.

"My sins."

Me.

I run my hands over his bare chest as he still looks at his hands.

"I see blood, I see pain. I see betrayal." His words are low, like some secret.

I grab his hands and hold them in mine, running my fingers across them, over his knuckles and palms.

"Do you know what I see when I look at your hands?" I say,

and his eyes flick up to mine, his head moving back and forth slowly, like he's hanging on to my words. "I see the hands that fed me when I wouldn't eat, gave me water when I wouldn't drink." I turn his hands over so our palms are flat, together. "I see the hands that washed me when I didn't really have the strength to do it on my own. I see hands that planted seeds of my favorite flowers, made sure I had them again because he knew how much they meant to me." His breathing picks up, his eyes fixated on me. "I see hands that may have once caused me pain." He flinches, and a painful sound escapes him but I bring his hands to my chest, letting him feel my heartbeat. "But those hands have never hurt me again. They have cared for me, held me, and continue to do their best for me." I smile down at him, leaning forward and moving some of his hair off of his forehead, tenderly. "I think these hands may always be what's best for me."

I release his hands and they come up to my face, holding it. His thumbs rub back and forth under my eyes, just feeling me as I smile at him.

"Laeliah," he murmurs in a gruff voice. I huff out a laugh, but stop when he moves his hand over my heart. "Laeliah," he repeats, eyes bouncing between mine.

I understand what he's saying.

My heart is beautiful.

It's scary to fall, not knowing if you will be caught.

But the thing is, you have no say in it when it happens.

An invisible force pushes you off that cliff, and all you can do is hope there are hands waiting for you at the bottom.

And that's more terrifying than anything else.

SEVEN

Rhea

"Wow," Josh says, looking out through the field of lesia flowers. "He really did make you a flower field."

I smile, my fingers running over hanging branches of a willow tree. "He did." It's the most beautiful thing I have ever seen.

"I can hold this over him now." He nods to himself, a smile on his face.

I bump his shoulder with mine. "Leave him alone."

He raises a brow. "Did you just defend him?" I pause, horrified. "You just defended the enemy. It's over for us."

"Shut up." I hiss at him, wincing as the others up ahead turn around to look at me.

Fuck me.

I groan as they all laugh, my cheeks heating.

We walk more through the field, silence following.

Josh stares at me every now and then, and I know he's waiting for me to speak.

I sigh, pausing before I flop down on the ground.

"It was horrible," I tell him, looking up at the afternoon sun. "She was hanging there, being hurt, but still defiant of Charles." Tears spring to my eyes. "He killed her in cold blood. Slit her throat…" I gag over the words and squeeze my eyes shut.

Josh is there next, pulling me to a sitting position and hauling me into a hug.

"I'm so fucking sorry." He rocks me back and forth as I cling to him, feeling his comfort.

"She was so brave," I whisper. "She fought a losing battle right up until the end."

"Catherine was always like that when we were little. Remember that one kid that kept picking on us?" I release a wet laugh. "She went all mama wolf on him, and he never bothered us again."

They didn't.

"She thought of you as hers too, you know." I tell him, and he releases a stuttering breath.

"I know. I thought of her as my mother too."

I sigh into him. "I'm so tired of crying. I barely cried for years, and now I can't stop."

"You have been through a lot," he says, rubbing my back.

I go to dispute it, something I normally would do, but I *have* been through a lot. I can't keep shoving it aside.

"We all have." I relent a little, letting myself share these thoughts. I look over the flowers over his shoulder, then look toward the trees as a cold wind makes its branches flow. "So pretty."

Josh pulls back and turns to see what I'm looking at. "You and trees," he teases, and I huff out a laugh, shivering.

In a few short weeks, winter will be here and we can start to feel it.

Josh helps me to my feet and we follow where the others have walked ahead.

Colten and Hudson push each other, bickering as usual as Taylor looks over the field, probably thinking something is going to jump out at us. Anna crouches near a tree with Sebastian, probably trying to teach him about mushrooms, and failing.

He's probably over there to see if the tree is up to his standard for throwing knives into it.

"You know how I am," I finally answer Josh.

"I do," he agrees. "I just never feel what you do when you

touch them."

"Well, you aren't an Heir."

"Well you aren't an Heir," he mimics and I laugh, shoving him.

"Ass." I give him a small smile. "I can feel its life within, feel it all the way down to its roots, connecting to the earth below. It's like a whisper of innocence, bright and pure. There is nothing else like it." I look down at the flowers. "It's like breathing, something so natural but needed."

Seb walks over and makes a face. "It's a fucking tree, Rhea." I laugh at the look on his face. "They are good for holding someone up against it though. I could hold you up against it?" He looks me up and down like he's seriously thinking about it.

The memory of when Darius and I humped each other against a tree sends flutters through my mind, making my cheeks heat.

Seb smiles, all teeth, thinking he made me have that reaction.

"Gods," Josh mutters, side-eyeing me before he walks over to Hudson and Colten, shivering like the thought is the worst he could imagine.

Josh suddenly changes, shaking out his fur and Colten's eyes widen as suddenly, he's being pounced on.

Hudson folds his arms, smile on his face as he watches Colten change, and then two wolves are play-fighting in the flowers.

"There are some great flora around here," Anna says, holding a basket I didn't even notice.

"It seems you have collected a lot?" I nod to the basket.

She smiles. "Always good to keep extras around. Though there are some ingredients for some poison."

I blink at her. "Who in the Gods are you poisoning?"

She shakes her head, walking off and mumbling about silent knife wielders and my eyes go to Taylor in question.

"I have no idea," he says, moving to walk ahead and watching the two wolves yipping and nipping at each other.

I see Colten get the upper hand in the next moment, but

Hudson takes him by the scruff of the neck and pulls him off. Colten whips around and barks at him, but Hudson just raises a brow and Colten pauses, head lowering.

And then Josh is tackling them again.

I chuckle at their antics as I hear Anna up ahead talking about unruly beasts with Taylor and Hudson.

"Wanna tackle?" Seb says as he stands a few feet from me, those eyebrows wiggling again.

"Sebastian," I purr, and his eyes widen at my sultry tone. I crook a finger for him to come to me, and he swallows hard. He moves slowly, like he's about to walk into a trap, and I resist the urge to smile. "You know," I murmur low when he stops in front of me. I place my hand in the center of his chest, slowly moving it down as he makes a nervous sound. "If you weren't such a big flirt, you might actually find someone to tackle with." I shove him with my hand and he falls flat on his back, his eyes confused how he ended up there. I smile, my eyes moving to a solid line of my power that I put behind his knees that made him fall.

"Rude," he grumbles, but his eyes light in amusement when they move over my shoulder.

"Rude is correct," a deep, murderous voice says. I stiffen, a scowl on my face.

I didn't even hear him come up behind me.

"Darius," I say cheerfully, going to turn around, but I'm halted with a hand on my hip.

His chest touches my back and his breath hits my ear. "I do not share, little wolf." I shiver at his nearness, the possessiveness in his tone. He nips my ear. "Remember that or you will have one less pack member and then I will take you right here."

My cheeks heat.

Bastard.

His warmth leaves my back, and I turn and watch him stride over to Taylor, a blade in his hand as he talks about Gods knows what.

It's strange watching him converse with my pack, especially when Anna joins the conversation.

The head of the Elites and runaway pack members.

Who would have thought we would be here like this.

A chuckle brings my attention to the ground, back to Sebastian who has a huge grin on his face. "I love pissing him off." He sighs like it's the most majestic thing while I give him the stink eye.

"Idiot." I kick his shin, and he pretends to howl in pain before he shifts, his wolf leaping toward me.

I sidestep him, grabbing his tail and giving it a little pull, and laugh. He spins, snapping his teeth playfully at me and I chuckle, stroking my fingers through the light gray fur on his head. He nudges me, tongue out and I coo down at him.

"Who's such a good wolf?" His tail wags, his eyes lighting up and I do laugh, then. "Aww, you just want attention don't you?"

"Umm, Rhea, what the fuck are you doing?" Damian says, and I eye him.

"Telling this big baby what a good boy he is." Red colors his cheeks, and I smirk. "Go and get the other big baby," I tell Seb.

"Hey!" Damian says, stepping forward. "I'm not a baby—oof."

Seb knocks him down, and then another wolf is there. Damian's is brown in color, a few streaks of bronze. He's larger than Seb, but not by much.

They start nipping and pouncing on each other when I spot Jerrod and Zaide. They walk over to where Darius is, and I don't miss the way Anna throws them a glare.

I need to take those ingredients for poison away from her.

Leo chuckles as he slides up next to me. "They are like twins." He's looking at Seb and Damian, and I nod. They kind of are. Their personalities are similar.

I smile. "They get along well, considering."

"Considering what?" he asks.

"That we are enemies?" I question, like it's obvious.

"Is that what we still are?" I look at him, but he's looking over both my pack and Elites.

I look too.

There is no fighting, not a real fight anyway, and they are talking and listening, generally being in each other's company.

"No, I guess we aren't enemies anymore."

"Good," Leo says, and I raise an eyebrow at him. He hated me on sight, was someone who also didn't trust a word out of my mouth. He answers the question in my eyes as I feel Darius stare on me. "We have to be a unit in the coming war." My stomach drops thinking about the bloodshed to come. "But more than that. You are his." He nods his head over to Darius, but I don't look. "And we look after him, so we also look after you now."

Just like our pack. Who they care for is an extension of ourselves.

"In the basement..." he trails off when I hold a hand up to stop him.

"Darius explained, you don't need to." And I don't want to relive it.

He nods. "I know, but I wanted to say that he does truly regret what had happened, what he did. He was protecting us."

"I know," I whisper.

"He was put in an impossible situation..."

"Leo," I sigh, and turn toward him. "I appreciate what you're trying to do... to try and help me understand Darius's actions." He runs a hand down his face and I can tell this is bothering him. He doesn't want his brother to hurt. "You don't need to tell me. I know why he did it, I know the position he was put in. I was the enemy at the time, we barely knew each other and he had known you all for years." I shake my head at him. "I would have done the same if I was in his position. I would have protected my pack."

His shoulders slump in relief. "Good." He mutters awkwardly. "Good."

"You won't have to go in that basement again."

He nods. "Never again."

"Look at us, agreeing."

He laughs. "Are we friends now?"

"Oh, that's a bit too much," I say, forcing a look of horror on my face.

"He also thinks it too much."

I tilt my head. "Is he baring his teeth yet?"

"Oh yeah. You should hear how he's going to murder me in my head."

"Is it bloody?"

"Very."

"You better go then before you are decapitated."

He sighs as he begins to walk over to him. "Being close to the Alpha of the Elites is such a pain."

I grin and look over at the now four wolves all piling on each other, the sounds of their growls and playful yips filling the air.

It makes me mentally stroke Runa. She's missed out on so much. We both have.

Do you not want that? I say to her, running my hand down her head. *Do you not want to play?*

She whines, and my heart breaks for her.

We will figure it out.

Moving further into the trees and away from the others, I guide my hands over the bark as I pass. Their branches tickle me, gently caressing my face as I walk into the covered embrace of the weeping willow.

I feel protected inside the arms of the branches, hidden from everyone.

I know it's not true, but it's nice to pretend.

I kneel in the dirt as Runa settles, and then I place my palms on the ground, breathing deeply as I wiggle my fingers until I pour some of my magic into the soil. Flowers of blue pop up from the ground around me, painting the ground in a pretty color and I smile at its beauty.

I can't believe there are even lesia flowers here. It makes me wonder just how far Darius planted the seeds.

The ground trembles slightly beneath my hands and a quiet laugh spills from me as more flowers appear through the short blades of grass, this time an array of other colors.

Yellows, reds, some a deep shade of orange or purples.

I hear the sound of rustling leaves behind me, and this time I know Darius is there. He let me know he's there. I ignore his weighted stare on my back and continue to make my own little haven of a garden around me, inside the willow tree's branches.

Darius takes a seat beside me as I work, sitting in some of the flowers that I just sprouted, but he just shrugs as I scowl at him.

My poor flowers.

He leans back on his hands, face tipped upward toward the branches as some light peeks through in streaks. He closes his eyes and breathes deeply, and that breath sounds like the weight of the lands is on his shoulders.

I guess a lot of it is.

He has to get his men ready for war, and has to also make sure the people are safe. It's a reminder that he was betrayed by those in power. Everything was not as it seemed, and he and the Elites had been unknowingly doing the work of monsters.

While also painting himself as one.

The marks on his back show as much.

I pause at the thought, removing my hands from the ground and just watch him have this moment of quiet to himself.

He looks tired, but not any less attractive.

The slight stubble on his jaw makes me want to scratch my fingers through it, the hair falling on his forehead makes me want to run my fingers through it, and the tattoos along his neck make me want to lick it.

"Something you want, little wolf?" His rumbling voice makes my heart speed up a little.

Of course he knows I'm watching him.

I shake my head slowly, even though he can't see me, but his lips tip up into a small smile anyway. I smile too and lean back on my own hands, joining him in the moment of calm and just feel, sense. Breathe the life that surrounds us.

I'm used to Darius being close to me, the only constant since we came to Vokheim Keep.

It's a comfort now.

I pick a lesia flower between us and bring it to my nose, inhaling its sweet, familiar scent.

We are no longer enemies, or even friends or lovers, we are so much more. I guess we are both learning how to be with each other. But after we have both laid bare, bleeding each other, it's no wonder we feel comfortable.

When the other has seen you at your worst, you have nothing left to bare to them.

I squirm a little, feeling the gentle ache in my body and I welcome it, welcome how Darius makes me feel and how he seems insatiable with me.

I've never had someone who wants to touch me in the way he does. Though I suppose I haven't allowed it in the past.

I wonder if I had tried harder in all the years in Eridian, if I would have met someone. But looking at Darius now, the shine of light that peeks through the branches that caress his face, I know that even if my past didn't happen, I wouldn't feel toward another like I do with him.

I like how he always makes sure his Elites are well fed and cared for, I like how he always prioritizes those in a village that are in need of the most urgent support against the rogues. That he sends those that need a new home to Colhelm, at the temporary place they have set up to keep those of Vrohkaria safe. I like his loyalty to his men and his closest. I like how he is with me, protecting me, always watching me.

It's with that thought that I scoot closer to him, and without opening his eyes, his hand rests on my thigh, his thumb stroking back and forth without saying a word. Knowing I would feel embarrassed if he called out that I want his affection.

A relaxed sigh slips from me, and he makes a soft sound from his chest as my mind quiets down.

"Do you think we can stop the rogues?" I whisper, not wanting to ruin the quietness but needing to ask.

A pause. "We have no option but to stop them, little wolf, or all is lost." My heart cracks at that.

"I wonder what we did wrong to deserve this," I say aloud, thinking back to seeing that rogue appear out of that memory stone. "To right the wrong," I mutter, placing the flower I still hold down to the ground.

It will die, fade away into nothing over time, just like the lands if we cannot do anything.

A hand lands on the back of my neck, and I look at Darius, but he still has his eyes closed. He lets out a little of his power to stroke the pulse point at my neck.

"We will right the wrong, but the wrong wasn't done by you, it was done by others. Only we have the power to fix it."

"Because we are Heirs?"

"Because we were found worthy of the power bestowed upon us." I pause at that and look up at the branches above.

"I don't feel worthy," I tell him.

I whisper the words like a shameful secret, like I shouldn't have said it aloud.

"You are gaining more control with your power, and we will continue to work on getting your wolf out." At that, Runa scratches within me. "You will get there."

"We don't really have time." Frustration bleeds into my tone.

"No, we don't."

EIGHT

Rhea

Warmth surrounds me, wrapping me in its hold. I shift, letting out a small moan as I snuggle closer to it. A band around my waist tightens and pulls me closer, not wanting to let go.

My eyes peel open slowly, blinking in the dim light. The gentle smell of flowers surrounds me, but the scent of Darius suffocates me even more.

Looking down, I see a strong arm surrounding me, holding me close. I move my head, my nose grazing Darius's arm under my head that I'm using as a pillow, and I realize we must have fallen asleep.

I shuffle and try to sit up when I'm turned and planted on top of his hard body, that arm still wrapped around me while his other hand comes to the back of my head, holding me close to the curve of his neck.

He makes a sleepy sound and I grumble, blowing out a breath.

Those fingers caress the back of my head and I let out a content sound before immediately shutting it off.

"Don't hide your noises from me, little wolf," Darius murmurs, his breath tickling the top of my head. "You know how much I like them."

I do, he makes me sound all the noises, even when I try to refuse.

I chuckle before I move to sit up, my legs falling on either side of him. My gaze roams over his sleepy state, and something warm flutters in my chest, making my cheeks heat up.

He raises a brow at me, a smug grin curling his lips.

I smack his chest. "Shut up,"

"After having my tongue in your pussy and painting it with my cum, whilst also taking you many, *many* times, you're blushing at waking up in my arms, again?"

I groan. Do we really need to do this?

"Yeah well, it's different." I look away, watching as the branches of the willow tree blow in a gentle breeze.

"It's not the first time we have slept together."

"It's different now," I whisper, bringing my eyes back to him.

"It is," he agrees, staring at me intently. He picks up my hand, his fingers going to the blood oath on my wrist, watching the bite appear under his touch before moving his hand up, tracing the barely-there mark on my forearm.

"Do you regret it?" I blurt, and then curse myself internally for it. I'm not sure I want to know the answer to that question.

"Regret what?" he asks, still staring at the mark.

"Meeting me, because of what I did, who I am."

His brows furrow. "Killing some of my trainees?" I nod. "You did what you needed out of survival. You lied, killed, all to keep your pack safe." His eyes come to me, so bright, so green. "I won't ever blame you for that when it kept *you* alive."

The honesty in his eyes takes my breath away, and feelings bubble up within me.

He sits up, bringing us close and grips my chin in a firm hold, tilting my head back.

"I'll spend the rest of my days doing anything and everything just to have you keep your eyes on me. Do not doubt me in that. If they are not on me, Rhea, there is no hope for the lands. I would let it rot before you close your eyes and they never reopen. I would destroy anything that breathes life because you are life itself, and if you are not here, there is nothing. I will never regret meeting you."

"Darius," I breathe, my hands coming to rest on his arms. They twitch under my touch.

"I will spend the rest of my days looking after you and making sure you have a home again," he goes on, and my heart beats so wildly that I'm sure he can hear it. "I don't know where that will be, but I will give back what I helped get taken from you." He moves a piece of hair off my face.

"Is that even a possibility?" I ask, voicing aloud my fears.

"Yes. If that is what you want then I will give it to you." The determination in his eyes tells me he absolutely will. "We just have to hold out as long as we can so Charles doesn't suspect anything. So we can plan and *win*."

"I know," I whisper, my tone sullen. "But I want to go out and help others too when I can. I feel so helpless just sitting around. I don't know where my pack is, we cannot get to Kade yet unless we are willing to die."

"As much as it doesn't sound like it, he's safe there."

"But they are hurting him." It makes me feel sick to my stomach.

"I know," he says, stroking my head. "But with him there, we know where he is and the Highers think they have the upper hand. When we can find out where your pack is and get them, we will go for Kade after." I look down, but he doesn't let me, gripping my chin tighter. "If we went for Kade now, your other pack members will be in danger. I'm thinking as the Leader of the Elites, personal feelings are put aside. Getting to them first, along with the others that were stolen, we have a higher rate of success. We will have less deaths. You know if we went for Kade they would threaten and kill the others."

I know what Darius says makes sense, I just don't like it. I would do anything for Kade, and the need to get to him is so overwhelming sometimes.

"I know," I tell him. "It's just... he's mine, Darius."

"And you're mine. I will look after you." Darius pauses for a moment. "Come," he says suddenly, lifting me off his lap and standing.

"Where?" I ask as he helps me up and starts to walk out of the branches of our hidden bubble.

"You said you wanted to help more, so you can help me."

Nine

Rhea

Aliseon is a vibrant fishing town located on a huge lake that's central of Vrohkaria. People fill the market streets, the smell of the sea wafting through the cold air as I huddle down under my hood.

Both Darius and I are hidden beneath our cloaks, face masks firmly in place. With the weather getting colder, no one thinks it's unusual attire as we make our way through the market stalls.

"Get three fish for only two coins," someone shouts further up ahead.

Different varieties of fish fill almost all of the stalls, buyers haggling for a better price, coins being exchanged, and little kids running around. This town is… happy. I suppose as the only way to get here is by boat or port stone, like we did, the rogues can't touch them here.

It's like they are in their own little place, just for them.

We have heard of how the Highers are sending their guards to villages and demanding more food tax, whilst also charging those that resist, so seeing this town is… such a stark difference to the rest of the lands right now.

I watch a couple laugh, and then the male spins her, dipping her close to the cobbled ground before placing a kiss gently on her lips.

A hand at the small of my back makes me jolt, my head snapping up to Darius as he gently nudges me along. I didn't realize I had stopped to watch them.

"Did you enjoy watching them?" he asks in a low tone.

My cheeks heat slightly for some reason unknown to me. "Yes," I tell him, looking at a stall that looks as though it has glass figures.

I move over to it as Darius says, "Is that what you want? To be spun around and nearly having your head cracked open from the ground?"

A laugh huffs out of me as I shake my head. "No, they just looked so happy." He grunts, and I pick up a glass wolf, watching as a plethora of colors shine within, reflecting off its surroundings.

"Good," Darius tells me. "I'm not the type to do such things like that." Another small laugh comes from me.

Darius dancing in the middle of a cobbled road in the center of a town?

No, he wouldn't.

"I would think there was something wrong with you if you did that, Darius, but the thought of you doing this is funny. I can't wait to tell Damian."

"Don't you dare," he growls as I giggle.

Oh the amount of shit he is about to get. I can't wait.

"Three coins," an older woman says, nodding to the wolf.

"Oh, no thank you." I put it down and continue through the crowd. Darius's hand brushes against mine a moment later as he catches up to me, eyeing everyone who gets too close.

"I like it when you laugh. I don't hear it often," Darius says gruffly, like admitting it is the equivalent of walking over the glass we were just looking at.

I smile behind my mask, but it soon drops when I really think about it. It has been a while, and now I feel guilty because my pack is still out there, Kade is still trapped and I'm here... laughing.

I swallow, but a hand landing on the nape of my neck and hauling me into a solid chest instantly calms me.

I feel his magic seeping through the material of the cloak and cooling my neck, comforting me.

"Don't," Darius says softly, uncaring that others are bumping and knocking into him, making sure no one touches me. "You can laugh without sadness, little wolf, even for a moment."

How does this male always seem to know what's going through my mind?

I raise my eyes to meet his, my hand landing on his chest. "Are you a mind reader?"

Now he chuckles, and tingles spread through my body. "No, I just know you."

"How?" I wonder.

"Because I watch, I learn. It's impossible to keep my eyes off you, so naturally, I pick up on things." I blink, licking my lips behind the mask. His eyes drop, and even though he couldn't see it, his nostrils flare like he could. "Let's go before I make this town witness something indecent. Which I'm sure you would not appreciate."

I shiver, and look down as he grabs my hand and guides me along.

"My mom would have loved this," I say, smiling as a child darts past, what looks to be like her brother chasing her.

"You enjoy it, so I can believe that." I look over some brightly colored material I have never seen before. It looks as soft as a cloud. "It wasn't her fault," Darius says quietly.

"Hm?" I ask, not really listening.

"The rogues," Darius says. "It wasn't your mom's fault." I suck in a breath sharply and turn toward him. His eyes shine with honesty, and my shoulders slump in some sort of relief with hearing him say that.

Not knowing I needed it.

I know the circumstances were dire with what we saw in the memory, but I think my mom had no choice but to do what she did. I think the alternative we couldn't have known about would have been much worse.

"Thank you for saying that to me." He shrugs like it's nothing, but it's everything.

To know he doesn't blame my mother for what the rogures have done. For what they did to his family.

"Silk." He nods toward the material and I blink. Oh, it's called silk.

I run a hand down it. "It feels like... a cloud." My smile is wide when I turn to him. He looks into my eyes for a moment and turns away, arms folding over his chest as his nostrils flare. I huff out a laugh. "You're ridiculous." Another grunt.

We pass a long stall of fish being cooked over multiple small fires in circular pots. The kindling burns inside of it as two metal prongs hold up the fish in the center.

I've never seen anything cooked like this before.

"Do you want one?" Darius asks, and I wrinkle my nose.

"I prefer meat."

"Always a hunter."

"Always being hunted by you," I snark back, and he chuckles under his breath.

He doesn't deny it, and I don't say how much I like it.

We begin to walk through a large crowd that has seemed to have gathered. Darius stays close to me, pushing anyone in my way to move.

A group of giggling women come out of a tavern and I take a peek inside as the door swings shut. I haven't been in one of them before, but the melody coming from inside them makes me want to find out just what it's like.

"By the wolf of the high, take my prayer and save the night," a male voice shouts. "Clear the madness and take our thoughts, take the grace of Vrohkaria's hopes."

I scowl in the direction where the Highers's blessing was shouted from, then I move closer to it, peeking over other's shoulders to see a stall. It's full of the Highers symbol as an older male shouts.

"Kill the madness before it kills us all, capture the traitor once and for all."

Are they talking about me?

Darius growls beneath his breath, and then his voice is in my ear. "Do not move from this spot."

Huh?

I turn to look at him but he's already gone.

"The Highers save us so we shall save them, kill all who resist, and take their heads."

Gods.

The crowd shouts in agreement, and I have never seen the root of evil, but that male is spreading it like he was born to do so. "Find the traitor and bring her in, for she will be the highest sin. Take her against the— ahhh. Fire!"

What?

I'm jostled as the crowd begins to scatter, pushing others out of the way. A body slams into mine, and I tumble to the side. A large hand grabs me, pulling me close and I inhale the scent of Darius as he pushes through the crowd.

"Get water, quickly!" Someone screams as Darius leads us out of the fray.

"What's happening?" I ask when we lean up against another stall, further away from where we just were."

"Fire is cleansing," he says as he watches flames appear in the distance.

"Fire is destruction."

"No," he says as he turns to me. "I am."

We hold each other's gaze for a moment and I laugh.

Seems the Heir of Cazier showed some of his madness.

Runa purrs within me.

"I cannot believe you set the stall on fire."

He shrugs. "They deserve it for sprouting up bullshit."

It was bullshit.

"How did you even do it?"

"I took a cooking pot with a fish in it and slid it under the stall."

"What?" I splutter out a laugh, thinking of the fish stall.

"Then I knocked it over but the good news is, the fish will still cook."

I spot an older male rushing our way, a bucket of water in his hand to stop the fire. Suddenly, he goes flying through the air before landing with a thud.

"That had to have hurt," I say as I watch a few females go over to him to see if he is okay.

Darius smirks. "Well you did trip him, little wolf."

I did.

"This is the best outing ever."

Darius huffs out a laugh and then takes my hand in his, guiding us forward.

His hand is warm and heavy. I squeeze it. He squeezes back.

The central marketplace fades away, and then homes come into view. The light birch wood stands out against the blue backdrop of the lake as Darius walks along the path.

"What are we doing here anyway?" I ask. I forgot we even came here for a reason.

Burning stalls and tripping unsuspecting people will do that to me.

"I recognized a name on the list, or more so a last name," Darius replies. "The family lives on the edge of the lake. They run a small bakery, or they did when I last came here."

The list we stole from the Highers.

The lightness I was feeling instantly dries up.

"Are we going to talk to them?"

"Talk, or more…" he trails off and my stomach swoops with nerves.

"You want to know if they had a child and sold them? Like Sarah had said?"

He nods.

I hope they didn't.

The more we walk, the more the hustle and bustle of the center fades away, but so does the lightness of Aliseon.

We are close to the edge of the island, so close we are able to see the rocky terrain on the sand as water from the lake crashes against it.

We are also able to see a few poles scattered along it. They have loose ropes tied around them, the wood weathered like they have been there for a long while.

"What are they?" I ask.

Darius turns his head. "Punishments. They would tie them up on the edge of the water. Let them freeze in it as daily punishments were given. Sometimes it was a beating, sometimes it was having things thrown at them."

I'm instantly reminded of the fact that Anna came here and got tied up to a pole. Where stones were thrown at her.

I swallow and look away.

I guess this town isn't so happy after all.

We round a corner on the cobbled path and Darius halts. I come to his side and see a little bakery on the edge. A sign hangs off the side, looking worn and weathered, and I wonder why it's all the way out here.

"Shouldn't they be selling in the center?"

He shrugs. "It has always been here, some of my men would come here for their bread when we came to collect taxes."

"I thought the guards did that mostly."

"They do now, yes. We were too busy hunting."

Hunting us. Unknowingly.

Darius walks forward, dropping my hand and I want it back immediately. As we get closer, we see two shadows move around inside, the window having a display of a few loaves of bread and what looks like some kind of cake, maybe.

Darius's heavy footfalls vibrate the wood beneath the small steps leading up to it, and a chime rings as he enters, filling up the space with his presence entirely.

"Hello, welcome to—" an older woman stops mid-sentence, and I once again stand beside Darius.

Her wrinkled face shows her panic when Darius drops his hood back, pulling down his face mask and revealing himself.

She quickly shakes her head and then clears her throat.

"Welcome, welcome, Alpha Darius." She tilts her head to the side, showing him her neck.

An older male comes out from a back room, also baring his neck. "Is there something in particular you would like, Alpha Darius," he says, his bearded face wary as his eyes move to mine.

Darius grunts, then taking a step forward, he asks, "I have a few questions I would like you to answer truthfully." The pair share a glance before the woman speaks.

"Of course, would you like some tea? Maybe some of my sea cake?" Sea cake? I look at the one in the window and wonder if that's it.

"No. Do you have any children?" Darius is always straight to the point.

The air instantly tenses, and I wander to the side of the bakery to a set of shelves there. Preserves are in jars, a layer of dust covering them.

"N-no," the woman mumbles. "We unfortunately weren't blessed with any."

I turn and tilt my head at her, hearing her heartbeat increase.

"You're lying." Her eyes shoot to mine, and she sucks in a breath as I also pull my hood and face mask down.

"You're... you're the traitor," she gasps, hand on heart, eyes wide.

The male moves his hand below the counter and then lifts a blade the size of my forearm, pointing it at me.

A deadly growl has his eyes now moving to the very angry male in front of him.

"I wouldn't do that if I were you." It's a murmur, but no less deadly coming from Darius.

The blade shakes in the male's hand before he drops it on the counter.

"Talk. Now," Darius demands, letting his dominance flow out of him. While it makes the pair whimper, it caresses me like a blanket I want to wrap myself in.

It makes me want to climb him like a damn tree.

Darius's head snaps my way, his eyes heating for a moment as they trail over me before turning back to the pair.

The female is the first to speak. "We had a girl." My heart stops, and ice runs through my veins. "She was five months old when we last saw her."

I move to stand at Darius's side, my fingers twitching as a tendril of power comes to my back, slithering up to the base of my neck.

"Why was that the last time you saw her?" I ask.

"We do not answer to you, traitor," the male spits, but a black blur is suddenly over his mouth. His eyes widen in panic as he lifts his hands to pull it away, but he isn't strong enough to remove Darius's magic.

The woman's eyes start to water as her breathing picks up in fear.

"We... we had a visitor when she was born, he blessed her and said he would come back in a few moon cycles to see if she would be suitable."

"Suitable for what," I grind out as Darius eyes me.

"For... for him. Or more, for helping him. I don't know," she rushes out, looking at the male as he still struggles.

"Then what happened," Darius barks at her when she doesn't continue.

"He came back, and he said she would be a good fit." Bile rises in my throat. Darius moves a little of his magic down to the male's neck when she halts her words. She rushes over to him, trying to help. "Please, let him go."

Darius doesn't let up.

"Speak," he demands.

"He wanted her, and said he would give us a great reward for helping."

She didn't...

"What reward?" Darius asks.

"Three hundred gold coins and we would be exempt from

paying taxes."

The breath stalls in my throat.

Fury pours in my veins.

"You gave your daughter away for that?" My magic swirls dangerously inside of me, my voice shaking with anger. A cool glide against my hand helps me focus on it, and I know Darius is trying to help soothe me but it's not really working.

"You have to understand, we had nothing," she tries to defend her actions. "We barely had anything to eat when he came to us."

"So you do anything you can," I growl, stepping up against the counter to face her. "You bribe, you steal, you beg. You don't give away your fucking child!"

"What does it matter to you," she seethes, eyes blazing. "My daughter is mine, so I can do what I want with her. It has nothing to do with you."

"You sold your child for a measly three hundred coins," Darius murmurs, looking around the space. "You seem to be doing well for yourself." His sarcasm isn't missed. "Was it worth it?"

"Fuck you," she snaps. "We may be struggling now, but we ate well for *years*. And we didn't have a whiny baby in our ears all day and all night, wanting to be cuddled, wanting to be fed. Do you know how fucking annoying that is—" Her eyes widen as a gasp comes from her.

Her hands go to her throat, blood seeping through her fingers as her eyes widen in realization. I stare at her with cold eyes.

"You did not deserve a child," I tell her, thoughts of Kade running through my mind. He wasn't even my blood son, but I would *never* do what she did. I would die before then. "Your wrong doings have caught up with you, your punishment is death." My voice is calm, no hesitation as I watch the life bleed from her eyes as my arm drops, the blade that was on the counter dropping to the floor along with it when I let it go.

Her body falls, disappearing behind the counter and my breaths come out noisily.

No essence comes from her, she will join the below.

Darius sighs. "That will be messy to clean up, little wolf." My eyes go to his, but he doesn't reprimand me for what I just did, in fact, the asshole adjusts himself and then rounds the counter.

The male is openly sobbing behind his magic that is still on his mouth. And Darius lifts a hand, removing it.

"Oh Gods, you killed her."

My lips peel back in a snarl. "She deserved nothing less."

He backs up, but Darius's hand is around his throat in the next second, halting him. "Where is your child now?" he demands, but the male is still sobbing, his eyes going to the body on the floor. "Where?"

"I don't know," he cries.

"You don't know?" he asks incredulously.

"No!" he chokes out.

Darius shakes him a little. "Who did you sell your child to?"

The male's eyes come back to him, and he whispers the name we all suspected.

TEN

Rhea

Cleaning our hands off in the lake, I keep my eyes on the two bodies that are slowly sinking beneath the surface and will eventually be swept away by the waves.

I feel no remorse for their deaths. They will not be another stain on my soul.

They both deserved to die for what they had done. How could they sell their child? Why wouldn't they fight with everything they had to make sure she was safe.

They weren't forced to hand their babe over, Charles would have just stolen her and killed them. But we suspect Charles would rather offer them coins and titles rather than have people go missing in a high number.

There is already a harrowing amount of names on the lists we have, if you add at least one death of a parent to that, the number is doubled and more cause for concern among the villagers.

It's easy to say a child died of a fever then covering up multiple murders.

Darius shakes his wet hands off next to me, scowling into the lake.

"At least we confirmed that the list of names are accurate in what we suspected. They are missing people that Charles had taken."

I nod. "I thought I would feel some sort of relief after it was confirmed, that maybe we could now start to get somewhere, but I just feel... sad, useless."

Darius's hand comes to my nape. "We have to hope that those on this list, including your pack, are still breathing."

I close my eyes as he massages my neck, his thumb on my pulse. "There are so many names, Darius, so many," I whisper, swallowing roughly.

"There are," he says gruffly. "But it's a start. My father mentioned a place, Zaigar, in his notes. Maybe they are all in the same place."

I look out toward the lake, wondering how we are supposed to accomplish everything we want. The people need to know just who their Highers are, we need to protect them from the rogues, and we need to find those who are missing.

"How many more parents gave away their children, and how many died from trying to prevent it," I wonder.

A hand on my cheek has me turning toward Darius. "Questions like that will do no good wondering the answer." He puts a hand inside his cloak and pulls something out.

My eyes widen at it. "When did you..."

"When you weren't looking," he chuckles, holding up the glass wolf and twirling it between his fingers.

"It's beautiful." I say watching as the color shines on our cloaks.

"I know you liked it." He lifts my hand and drops the wolf into my palm.

"For me?" I ask, my fingers trailing over its tail. It reminds me of my carvings, and I realize I haven't done it in a while.

"I know you are struggling with not being able to get your wolf out, but maybe looking at this will help visualize it." He doesn't look at me as he says this, his eyes on the water and I smile.

This big, grumpy male.

"You don't have to look like you have eaten something vile when you say that," I laugh, nudging him lightly. He grunts. "Thank you, Darius," I say softly.

He turns toward me, his eyes dropping to my lips. "Little wolf—"

A squawk has our heads shifting as the dark bird comes flying between two homes and landing in front of us. My breathing picks up as I spot the rolled up letter tied around his neck, and I bend down quickly, petting his head in a calm manner even though my heart feels like it's about to explode from my chest.

"Hi, Illium."

He squawks, bouncing around my hand in excitement. I scratch under his beak, and then gently take off the leather strap around his neck. Darius assesses the area, like an enemy is about to jump out at us as I roll out the paper between my fingers.

Sucking in a breath, I read the contents and stand, handing it over to Darius with shaky fingers.

"What is it?" he asks, eyes reading.

"Hope," I whisper. "It's hope, Darius."

"Can we trust this?" He reads the contents again.

"Of course. He has helped me so much over the years. We just have to wait for him." I point to the place mentioned.

Darius's jaw ticks. "I will come with you."

"That's a given, that's why I said we."

I know he would never let me go on my own.

"Okay," Darius says, pulling out a port stone. "We will have some time to wait before I can look around the area while we do."

"It will be—"

I'm squished, the breath halting in my lungs and then we are on grassland.

I grip Darius's arm tighter then I should, glaring at him but he pays me no mind, immediately looking around.

I sigh, redoing my ponytail and sitting my ass on the ground.

Damn males and their Alpha bullshit.

I huff and fold my arms.

Yes I'm acting like a child. Nor do I care.

He should at least let me finish what I was saying.

"Do not pout, you know I find it adorable."

I scowl. The asshole doesn't even look at me when he says it.

He chuckles as he walks around the area, high alert as he scans through the trees. We are in the clearing near my old home, where I first saw Darius after escaping Wolvorn castle.

I smile as I remember Damian choking on grass.

Good times.

Darius comes back to me and sits down, his magic coming out to wrap around my thigh.

"Still pouting I see."

Hmph. Yes I am.

Darius's arm comes around me and then I'm falling backwards into the grass.

"What are you doing?" I grumble.

He gazes up at the sky. "Isn't this what people do?"

My brows furrow. "Do what?"

He clears his throat. "Look at the clouds together... or something like that."

I blink, then look up at the clouds too.

I guess kids do it. I did it when I was younger. My mom and dad also did it. I would look at them through the window when they said it was their time...

Wait.

"Do you mean this is what people do when they...mate?" I say hesitantly.

Darius doesn't say anything for a moment, and I kind of want the ground to swallow me up.

Just when I begin to pour my power into it, knowing I can try and get it to take me down, he speaks.

"Yes. I saw a mated pair do it once. I couldn't understand it, why the fuck are you looking up at the sky?" I huff out a laugh and Darius shifts uncomfortably. "I realize it's just about spending time together."

I lean into him further, looking as a cloud slowly passes by.

"I guess we can do this."

He grunts, but a rumbling purr comes from his chest and I can't help but snuggle deeper into him.

"My sister asked me once to do this," Darius suddenly says, and I tilt my head toward him a little, to let him know I'm listening. "I told her I was too busy, that father wanted me to train. She nearly cried that day."

Poor girl.

"She just wanted to spend time with her brother, she wouldn't have understood you had other things to do." I try to reassure him.

"Training wasn't important." His voice is low as he says it, and I can feel the regret he feels.

"But it was," I start. "Without the training you couldn't have protected those that needed it."

"I didn't protect her." My heart breaks for him. I sit and turn sideways so I'm looking down at him.

I realize at this moment that we both have no family left. We are all alone.

"What happened to them?" I dare to ask. Darius doesn't talk much about himself, or his family.

He looks at me, his throat moving on a rough swallow before looking back up at the sky.

"They were in a town. They wanted to look at the wares they had that day. My sister liked to collect little trinkets. It could be like the glass wolf you have, or it could be a holder for a candle. As long as it was pretty, she would want it. Of course my mother gave it to her, especially when she gave you pup eyes. How could anyone resist?"

I smile, moving to take his hand in mine. He tenses for a moment, but he relaxes when I turn it over and start moving a finger over his palm and around his wrist.

I just needed to …touch him.

"Rogures attacked the town. They didn't stand a chance. There were no defenses, there were little guards there and the townspeople couldn't face them. There were too many." He squeezes my hand, still not looking at me. "When I got there, it was too late. I killed and ripped and tore apart any rogure I came across, trying to find them, trying to keep them safe. But when I did find them, I was too late."

No. I swallow at the pain in his voice, the way his eyes are distant and I wished I would never have asked this.

"Mother held Isabell against her chest down the side of a home, facing the wall. They were both full of injuries all over their bodies, full of the black poison leaking out of them. The trail of blood before them made me think she dragged them both there, trying to get to safety. I can only hope their deaths came quickly."

Tears sting my eyes and I lean down on Darius, wrapping my arms around his neck and I hold him.

He doesn't move at first, but when his arms wrap around me and a deep sigh leaves him, I let a single tear fall.

Fall for him.

"I hope they are running free," I murmur.

He palms the back of my head. "I do too."

"Are you both okay?" a voice says, and I'm up on my feet and colliding with a body in the next moment.

"Edward!" He laughs as he folds his arms around me, pulling me close.

"It is so good to see you, Rhea." I choke on emotion as I snuggle into him before leaning back.

His midnight eyes look tired, and his blonde hair is ruffled. When did he start to look so much older?

"Are you—"

A thundering growl comes, and then I'm ripped away from Edward, pushed behind Darius as he grabs him by the neck.

"Darius!" I gasp, fighting his grip on me to no avail, especially when his magic wraps around my waist.

"You are Edward?" Darius snarls at him, and Edwards's face starts turning a shade of purple.

"Darius, stop. Yes this is Edward." Is he insane?

"This is Higher Warden," he growls, never taking his eyes off of Edward or loosening his grip on me.

"Darius," I growl, sinking my teeth into his arm. He just grunts.

"He is Higher Warden. He goes around the lands and deals with a lot of pack bullshit."

"I...help...the people..." Edward manages to rasp out, eyes on Darius but he doesn't even try to defend himself from him.

"Darius, let him down, let him speak." I say after I lift my teeth from him. He doesn't. "Vallier," I say a lot more gently, and Darius slowly lowers Edward to his feet.

When he lets him go, he steps back from him, taking me with him, still holding me protectively.

"I know he's a Higher, Darius," I tell him, and Darius swings his eyes to mine as I shuffle on my feet.

He stares at me for a moment, before he explodes.

"You didn't think it was important to mention that?" Oh, he's angry. "You didn't think that was important information for me to know?!" I swallow.

"I didn't find the right time to..."

"To let me know a Higher has been helping you all this time?" he thunders.

"No. How would I know you wouldn't endanger him, or, I don't know." I point between them. "Try and kill him!"

"He's a fucking Higher, what do you expect me to do!" Magic swirls around Darius's feet as his anger gets the better of him. "They hurt you, lied to me. Of fucking course I want to kill every single one of them!"

Okay so he has a point...

"It's." *Cough*. "Fine," Edward rasps. I look at him with an apology in my eyes, but he waves it off. "I am not the enemy, Alpha Darius."

"Every single Higher is an enemy, why the fuck aren't you?!" The ground begins to shake beneath Darius and the breath halts in my lungs.

"I am Rhea's guardian, I vow it, I am not a danger to her." His eyes are so sincere, and then he tilts his head to the side, baring his neck to Darius.

My eyes bounce between them, nerves rattling through me. Edward is important to me. He saved my life.

Darius breathes heavily, his body tense. "If you are her guardian, and you care for her. Why the fuck did you let her stay in that basement?"

Edward eyes lower, his face a show of sadness. "I didn't know."

"Darius, enough," I say quietly, standing between them. "He is important to me. He didn't know I was in the basement, just like you didn't. He didn't know I was alive and they were abusing me." Darius looks off to the side, knowing I'm right. "Shall we go somewhere less open and talk?" I look around the clearing, look through the trees. I don't like being so close to my old home.

Darius ignores my question.

"Are you going back to the Highers?" Darius asks. "What is your position?"

I move back a little so I can see them both.

"I am still present with the Highers. I am trying to gain as much knowledge as I can so I can pass it to Rhea. So we can make a plan. We have been trying for years." He shakes his head. "I think Charles knows I'm not fully loyal to him anymore. I cannot harm him with the Higher's bond we have because of the instinct to protect him, but I can tell you knowledge."

"And?" Darius says when Edward falls silent.

"And I have come with some news that is hopefully a good thing. Charles is sending me out more and more to the people, and looking for Higher Aiden who has yet to return." Darius and I say nothing at that. "The other Highers are frantic, and Charles is on the warpath looking for you, Rhea. He is more brutal, killing innocents who dare speak against him or do not have the information he seeks." Edward's face crumbles. "He is completely unhinged."

"And Kade?" I croak out, fear nearly rendering me speechless.

"I dare say he is safe there, for now," Edward says gently. "Everyone is far too busy looking for you and dealing with the people and the rogues. I have not managed to go to him without drawing suspicion. With me being your guardian, Charles has kept me far away."

A breath of relief comes from me. Darius is right. He is safer there than out here at the moment.

"Then how are you here if Charles suspects you are not loyal," Darius asks.

"I was given the command to go to the Aragnis pack and see how they are fairing on behalf of Alpha Paul. His son is also staying at the castle with him, but there have been murmurs of some movement that I am not sure of."

The thought of my family sets my teeth on edge.

"In the letter, you mentioned you may know where my pack is?" I ask him and he nods, but Darius speaks before he can respond.

"Come to Vokheim."

"The wards will know I am there," Edward replies instantly.

"I have changed them to mine."

Edward tilts his head at him. "And Lord Higher does not know?"

Darius shakes his head. "I don't think so. He would have questioned me on it."

Edward nods slowly. "Then let us go."

I watch as my pack crowds Edward in the dining room, smiles on their faces. They haven't seen him in such a long time. It's nice to witness.

Darius stands next to me, scowl on his face, arms crossed as he watches Edward's every move like he will attack at any moment.

He won't, but I understand why he's hesitant.

His men also stay standing, alert, and ready for anything and I have to roll my eyes.

Why won't they believe me?

I guess it didn't help that I didn't tell them about him being a Higher in the first place.

"Speak," Darius commands, those two misty shadows appearing at his back.

Edwards looks towards him and nods, my pack grumbling as they take a seat at the table.

I walk over to it, gesturing for Edward to take a seat. I take the one next to him, feeling Darius at my back.

I look at him over my shoulder, and he spares me a quick glance as he watches Edward with a scary amount of focus.

"You have news?" Josh asks, and Edward nods.

"I think—"

"Start at the beginning," Darius commands as his Elites go to the opposite side of the table, not one of them sitting.

"The tension is hot in here," Seb says, smiling as Damian scoffs.

"He is a Higher," Leo growls, fingers twitching at his side.

"He's my guardian."

"We all know titles and words don't mean shit," Damian says, and I say nothing to that.

"Why did you call yourself Edward when your name is Warden?" Darius demands.

"As I help others in the lands, I thought it better to go by Edward, which is my middle name, rather than the name Warden, which is well known as a Higher. I wanted to separate the two. The Male who wanted to help, and the Higher who unknowingly helped put a monster as the ruling authority."

He sounds so sad as he tells the Elites his reasons.

"Talk," Darius spits, and I growl at him.

"Would you stop it? He won't hurt me."

"It's okay, Rhea," Edward says. "I am glad you have others who are protective of you. Who can protect you like I have been unable to." He clears his throat. "Rhea's mother appointed me her guardian, along with Charles. We were friends for a very long time, all of us were." I can feel the sadness pouring off of him and I grab his hand on the table. He gives me a small smile, even as Darius releases a rumbling growl at my back.

We both ignore him.

"We all helped Charles become a Higher. I wanted to help the lands, to better lives. I also wanted to help put this ridiculous notion that Heirs were dangerous behind us. I thought Charles wanted the same. He did for a while, or he made it out to be that way. When he was appointed Lord Higher, I soon realized my mistake in helping him."

"You didn't know," I say.

"I should have known, I should have never let him become what he is. Others have paid dearly for my mistake." He shakes his head. "When I was told of Catherine's and Derrik's deaths, Rhea's mother, and father, I went straight to their home. Only to be told Rhea was also dead." His voice shakes with emotion and my throat clogs up. "Heavy with grief, and regret, I tried to help the lands in any other way I could. One day I found Rhea stealing some food, and then I took her to Eridian. Having known her story, what she had been through, *who* had put her through that... we have tried over the years to find a way to get rid of Charles with no luck without killing ourselves, and I won't risk Rhea. She will not die by their hand," he growls, and I sense his power rising within him, causing the Elites to tense.

I squeeze his hand and he takes a few deep breaths.

"With me being sent all over the lands, I get to talk with the people, see what others may not see. After some time, I started to send others who needed to escape with the help of others I had spoken to along the way. They took them to The Deadlands to then be taken to Eridian." He looks up at the rest of my pack who nod and smile at him.

"And we are grateful," Taylor says.

"We would be dead." Seb says next.

"I tried to put some good into the world, and then I found out that Charles was stealing children, using them for his sick experiments."

"What does he want exactly?" Darius says.

Edward sighs. "He has an obsession with Heirs, their power they gained from the Gods. I'm not fully sure, but he won't stop."

"We have the memory crystal that was shown when I was at Wolvorn Castle, it shows Charles as being the cause of the rogues, and my mom... maybe you can figure out something."

Edward sits up straighter. "Can I see?"

I nod, and Darius asks Leo to go and grab it. A moment later, Edward has his hand on the crystal, his eyes glazing over.

I wait until he is done, kicking myself for not mentioning the rogue in there.

Just as I'm about to pull him out of it, his eyes shimmer with tears as he looks at me.

"Forgive me," he says. "I failed in protecting you all."

I shake my head. "Sometimes the monsters are just too clever."

He grits his teeth but nods, placing the crystal down on the table.

"The ritual he did was to steal the power of an Heir and instill it into himself. But he didn't manage to get it all as your mother cursed the lands, or more so Zahariss did."

"She did?" I ask, feeling the weight of my mother being the

cause already lifting from me.

He nods. "I don't think Zahariss was very happy with what was happening to her chosen Heir, and she is punishing him for it. But in kind, it is punishing us all." We all sit with that knowledge for a moment. "When she did that," Edward continues. "Most of Catherine's power was drained, and therefore, Charles wasn't able to steal it all."

"And that's why he's still looking." Darius fills in the blanks, a growl building up in his chest.

"It must be," Josh says, a frown on his face.

"If Zahariss did curse the lands, how are we meant to undo it?" Leo asks, and silence fills the room.

I think about what Belldame said about the plane of the Gods and I catch Darius's eye. He's thinking the same thing, but also...

"Did you see the rogure?" I ask Edward, noting that he didn't mention it.

"Yes, I saw them coming out of the ground before the memory stopped."

I look at Darius. "No, the single one in there. It attacked us when we last went into the memory."

Edward shakes his head. "No… I didn't see that."

Then why did Darius and I get attacked?

"If Charles never received the full power of an Heir," Damian says. "It makes sense why he has never stopped stealing children."

"The children we have a list of names on," I tell Edward and his eyes light up.

"You do?" Taylor grabs the papers off the side and spreads them out along the table. "So many," Edward says, "and these names are familiar to me. I recognize some I have spoken to when I have been out in the lands."

"We were in Aliseon today to confront a family. They told us they sold their daughter to Charles."

The room fills with curses and growls at the news.

"You said you knew where my pack may be?" I ask him.

"And others," he nods. "I overheard Mathew and Frederick mention they are leaving for a while to a female servant. They ordered her to make sure their offices are kept clean, as well as their rooms that they stay in there. As they walked by the room I was in, they mentioned The Drylands, a place called Zaigar."

My heart rate kicks up. "We have heard of that name too, in Darius's father's notes."

"Then it must be important. You need to go there, but you have to be careful. If they find you there, there is no hope for us all." Edward turns to me, gripping my hands tightly. "I wish I could help you more, but my hands are tied with the Higher's bond. I can only do so much. I am sorry I am so useless to you."

I shake my head and draw him into a hug. "You saved me Edward. Saved us. You have never been useless."

And Darius must think so too as he doesn't growl at the contact between us.

"I cannot stay long. I have to report back," he says as he pulls back, his eyes sad. "Take care of her, Alpha Darius."

"With my life."

"I can take care of myself," I tell Edward, not wanting him to go so soon.

"I know you can," he replies. "But you shouldn't have to."

ELEVEN

Kade

"And who is this?"

The voice swirls around in my head as image after image flashes through my mind.

But the images are all warped, all wrong and ping pong around like an alternative reality.

What is real and what isn't?

What is true and what is false?

I grit my teeth and my back arches, a scream coming from me.

Axis growls within, wanting to rally to the surface but I'm quickly injected with something that makes him go quiet.

This always hurts.

Always, always, always.

Pain hits my cheek and I blink my bleary eyes open as my body relaxes for a moment, the pain dwindling.

"Who do you see?" the voice says again, dark eyes peering into mine.

"Her," I croak out.

"And where will she be?"

I shake my head, not wanting them to know where she could be. Some part of me wants to keep it a secret, to not let them know of our home.

It feels like a betrayal if I disclose where we live, where the people I love reside. I can't tell them, I can't.

"Again," the voice demands and that pain is back again,

digging into my brain and making itself a home there.

My arms and legs tense against the rope that binds me, and my head thrashes side to side as something scrapes down both of my arms.

A blonde-haired woman appears in my mind, covered in blood and a cruel smirk upon her face.

"She hurt you, killed who you loved."

Who?

"She made you suffer?"

How?

"She is your enemy."

Then why do *you* feel like the enemy?

"Why isn't this working?" the male growls and a blonde-haired male responds.

"He is fighting it."

"Then make him weak!"

"Yes, Lord Higher."

My body tries to catapult off the chair as pain so sharp makes me feel like my body is tearing in two. I chant for them to stop, shaking my head as whimpers come from me, but they ignore my pleas.

I don't know how long they do this. How long they tell me who my enemy is even though my mind tells me otherwise.

But it's all getting so blurry.

As I close my eyes, I see the silver butterfly, the only thing keeping me company in this dark place before I once again let the darkness swallow me.

TWELVE

Rhea

I wear another white dress, this one having some sort of ruffles at the neckline and ending just above my knees. White seems to be the only color around here, and when I asked Anna about it, she said the Elites didn't care for choice in color, just choice in clothing. Not that I mind, I don't really care either. It's not like I got to wear a dress every day, especially when I was out doing chores all the time so it's nice to feel something different against my skin.

Braiding my hair to the side, I look upon the lake from the balcony as I prepare to descend to the dining hall of the keep.

We have been back mere hours, and yet we leave again tomorrow.

This time to the Drylands.

Edward left a short while ago, and my heart is heavy not knowing when I will see him again.

I'm also scared of the danger he's in every time he sets foot inside that castle.

I can't lose him too.

A body presses at my back, and then hands are gently shoving mine aside as he takes my hair from me.

I don't flinch from him, my body so attuned to his in a way it has never been with another.

Runa practically rolls to her back, legs in the air and I would scoff, but Darius takes hold of my hair.

"You braid?" I ask, surprised as he tugs and twists my hair

with a movement that seems so familiar to him.

"My sister," he says gruffly, and I feel stupid for asking. "I haven't done this in a long time, so it may not be right."

We are silent as he finishes off my braid, placing it over my shoulder and my thoughts drift to Kade.

"Are you sure there is still no way to get to him?" I ask, unable to help myself.

"I'm sure, little wolf. Just like Warden... Edward said, he is safer there at the moment. As soon as we can, we will get him."

I know he's right, but my need to get him is only heightening. It's been so long without him.

Darius ties off the end of my hair with a leather strap, his fingers careful. I grip it when he's done, inspecting his work.

It's a little knotty, and he's missed a few bits of hair, but, "It's perfect." I tell him. And it is, because he did it.

That warm feeling flutters in my chest again.

He huffs out a laugh. "It's atrocious." I laugh too, shrugging.

"That's not what matters." And it's not.

He steps beside me, looking out toward the lands. Night is falling, and the last of the light glistens off of the lake's surface, the winter air feeling even cooler.

"Do you think it will snow soon?" I ask, glancing up like it will give me the answers.

"Any moment," Darius says. "We will have to travel in winter clothing." I nod.

Winter.

My birthday is in winter, along with my supposed only heat. I wonder if I will have a cycle this year, considering I have already had one early.

Remembering my last heat cycle isn't much of a pleasant memory, and I look to Darius, taking in the strong lines of his face, the large set of his shoulders.

Honestly, how this male didn't destroy me that night I will never know. Or any other night since.

Leaving Darius where he is, I step back into his bedroom and go over to the pack on the floor. Opening it up, I move over Belldame's bone and some of the carvings Darius saved for me, then I pick up the letter.

I read over my mother's words again, needing her comfort more than ever when I feel so damn helpless.

A shadow falls before me, and Darius peers down. "Your mother?" he asks.

Instinctively, I bring it to my chest, afraid it will be ripped from me, but then I settle, holding it back out in front of me.

Things are different now.

"Belldame gave this to me. Apparently my mother was a seer of sorts, and she knew her death was coming." I cough over the lump in my throat. "She wrote me this letter before I was taken, while I slept in my room."

He sits down beside me, a mass of magic curling around my back. His fingers trail down the side of the paper, looking deep in thought as I let him read it. "You are lucky the old witch gave you this."

I smirk at his name for her. "You like her, don't you?"

He frowns. "Of course not."

I chuckle. "Liar." He side-eyes me, but his magic moves along the top of my back, and my shoulders relax under the cool feel of it.

"What do you want to do with the book we found at my father's?" His voice is tight as he asks, like he didn't want to even do it.

My shoulders tense right up.

"You still have it?" I mutter, not wanting to think about it.

"In my office, I haven't read any more of it."

I sigh. "There isn't anything helpful in there, just what they did to me." Strangely enough, I don't feel like someone is choking me as I say the words. With Darius's magic caressing me, his scent filling my lungs, it's like he's opened my throat and let me breathe. "I didn't ever think I would come across a record of what they did to me. Stupid really, as your father always recorded what went on down there." A rumble builds in Darius's chest. "I want to burn it. I'm so sick of it having a hold over me." I turn to him. "I want it gone. I want to not relive that part of my life. I will have every single scar that was put on my body for the rest of my days." He flinches, and I reach up hesitantly to stroke his cheek. "But I will bear them like I have done. But maybe now…maybe now I can begin to see them as something I survived, instead of something I am ashamed of." I tell him, scratching at his stubble and his jaw ticks.

He reaches up and threads his fingers through mine. "Your scars are *nothing* to be ashamed of," he says vehemently. "Never. They mark you as a warrior."

My eyes bounce between his and I nod. "I want that book gone, and I want those who hurt me, dead."

His eyes flash black. "Their deaths are waiting for them, I will make sure of it. None will be left," he growls, and his power pours out from his feet. I nudge it with my foot, calling my own to caress his.

He shivers as they touch, and I move my foot back and forth through it, somewhat calming him. "Their death will be by my hand."

"And mine."

"Just mine," I say forcefully.

"There is no just you, only us."

This damn male.

"What are you doing to me?" I whisper, letting my hand drop to his chest as I release his fingers, feeling his strength.

His magic comes out in a tiny tendril and wraps around my fingers.

"Binding myself to you."

Our eyes lock, and once again, everything fades to just him and I. Our breathing is matched, the beat of his heart that I feel under my palm thumps with mine. And in this one little moment, I believe that maybe there could be an *us*.

A knock at the door has Darius turning with a growl. I

breathe out a breath, shaking my hand out as tingles spread through my arm.

The door swings open, and by the scowl on his face, I know who it is.

"I'm coming, Josh," I call out to him.

I place my mother's letter into the drawer beside the bed, hesitating for a moment before closing it.

"Hey," Josh says as I walk through the door.

Sarah's at his side, and she gives me a small smile.

I lean up and press my cheek to his, hearing the rumbling warning behind me. "Ready?" I ask him.

He nods as I lead the way with Darius at my back, knowing the rumbling coming from him will slow eventually.

It always does.

Josh and Sarah are not even bothered by it anymore.

I roll my eyes, staying close enough to Darius to satisfy him as we make our way to the dining hall.

"How are you doing?" I ask Sarah. We haven't spoken much since she came here. She is quiet anyway, but I need to make more of an effort when I can.

"I'm doing okay, adjusting." She shrugs, moving closer to Josh for comfort. He puts an arm around her, holding her close and I smile at the pair.

"That's good. Have you been out into the willows yet?" Some air would do her some good.

"Not yet, but I plan to."

"Good." I swing my arms as I walk. "You will see the lesia flowers I had spoken to you about one time in Eridian," I tell her. "You will see how the color turns a darker blue at the edges of the petals, how their scent is so sweet."

"Those are only for you," Darius grumbles.

"And I can do what I want with them," I reply, walking backwards to meet his eyes. "Beauty needs to be shared."

"I don't share you," he says quietly, for my ears only.

I nearly trip over his words, his hand grabbing my arm to

steady me. Our eyes lock once more, and the look in his makes my legs feel weak.

I can almost feel his want, his desire to keep me, feed me… fuck me.

Gods.

"Come on slow ass," Josh shouts from the end of the hallway with Sarah.

I blink, not realizing how long Darius and I were at a standstill before I follow them.

Things are definitely different between Darius and I.

Runa purrs within me so forcefully, I can feel it bubble up my throat. I clear it, my brows furrowing.

That's never happened before.

Darius stays behind me as we enter the hall. The Elites— as one, bow their heads for their Alpha at my back, but as I pass them, they also bow their heads to me.

A strange feeling fills me, almost glee that they show their respect to me, but also content that they accept me.

At least, I think they do.

Maverick stands at the end of the table closest to where Darius and his closest sit on the slightly raised stone. He nods his head to me, and then to Darius, a smile on his face.

I veer off to the side, seeing my pack seated at the table opposite Maverick's. They smile at me as I sit, grabbing food on the platters in the center.

Darius goes to sit with his closest on the platform, taking a seat with them but I feel his eyes on me.

"Gods, it's sooo good," Sebastian says around a mouthful, and I huff a laugh as meat juice dribbles down his chin.

"Disgusting," Taylor says, grimacing.

"Are you even an animal?" Seb replies, aghast.

"I could eat all the bread rolls here." That comes from Colten who's at the end with Hudson.

"Then you would give yourself a stomach ache," Hudson replies.

Colten sighs, patting his belly. "Worth it."

Hudson leans close to his ear. "That's only because I would rub it and make it better, pup."

Colten's cheeks actually turn slightly red, and I raise a brow at Josh who sits across from me. He smiles, cutting up some meat as Anna sips her drink to also hide her smile.

The chatter around the room continues at a low hum, everyone eating and drinking, acting like everything is okay.

I know better though. They know Charles could find out about Maize being dead, and could be knocking on the keep gates at any moment.

Maverick catches my eyes as he stares at me, and I raise a brow. I don't move my gaze from his, accepting the challenge.

He dips his head in respect in the next moment, and my eyes clash with another next to him.

This male doesn't avert his eyes, and I tilt my head at him. He's bulky, very short, dark hair with a scar running down the side of his cheek.

I don't think he's happy I am here.

I feel another set of eyes on me, and the rumbling, low tone in his voice makes my stomach flip.

"Rhea, with me." Everyone in the room seems to pause at his low command, and my head turns toward Darius, seated in the center of his table.

"And why would I do that?"

He tilts his head, and I think the whole of the Elites hold their breath at my attitude, probably wondering what their Alpha will do.

But I'm also an Alpha.

Darius though, he just smirks, leaning back in his chair like he finds it cute.

Rubbing his fingers across his lips, eyes heated, he says, "Shall I come down there and show you exactly how I can make you compliant?"

I'm up and out of my seat in the next moment, a scowl on

my face as I go to him even though my desire runs through me.

"Asshole," I mutter, rounding the tables and standing before him.

He grabs me on a chuckle, and then I'm planted on his lap. "Sit."

"Is this necessary?" I look at the Elites, and they try not to look up at what we are doing, but some are failing miserably.

"When my men are eye-fucking you?" He squeezes my hip. "Yes."

I still. "Are you jealous?" A thrill runs through me and I shift on his lap.

"Possessive." Hmmm.

I smile and face forward, grabbing his drink and taking a sip. The burn of the alcohol runs down my throat, but it's nice.

I drink and Darius feeds me bits of meat, relaxing into him as his hand grips my thigh, keeping me to him.

The scarred male from before is still watching us, and I can feel his hatred from here.

"Maverick, how many have come back to us since the attack on the keep?"

"Twenty, Alpha."

I feel Darius nod at my back.

"Sean," he calls, and the scarred male removes his eyes from me to focus on Darius.

"Yes, Alpha." His voice is scratchy, and I instantly recoil from it.

"Come." Darius gestures to in front of him, and the male hesitates before doing so.

He stops in the center of the room, in the aisle between the long tables there.

"Yes, Alpha," he says, bowing his head slightly.

Darius runs a hand up my arm, stroking the side of my neck and Sean watches his every move.

"Is there a reason why you are looking so closely at the Heir of Zahariss?"

Sean responds straight away. "No, Alpha. I apologize. I did not know I was."

"Hmm." Darius stays silent after that, stroking over my pulse as the male stands awkwardly, waiting for Darius to allow him back to his seat.

The other Elites and my pack watch on, whispering amongst themselves.

When the male starts to shuffle from one foot to the other, Darius taps my thigh and helps me off his lap.

When he stands, he guides me to take his seat, running the backs of his fingers down the side of my cheek.

I don't miss that he just openly claimed me in front of everyone, and I don't exactly hate it.

Something within me preens that I have what they cannot. Male, female, or anyone in between, it doesn't matter.

He chose me.

Darius rounds the table as his men smirk, leaning back like they are about to enjoy what is going to happen. I sit up, popping a grape in my mouth, and wondering what Darius will do.

Darius doesn't stop until he's in front of the table, just slightly to the right of me and leans back against it, crossing his legs at the ankles. Arms folded.

"You were at the attack against the rogures?" Darius asks.

Sean shakes his head, "No, Alpha. I was away on another scry location."

"I see." Darius tilts his head again, and I know his wolf is close to the surface with the animalistic way he did it. "So that means you were not included when others bared their necks to the other Heir of the Gods."

"No, Alpha." Darius stares at him, and we all wait with bated breath.

Slowly, the male lowers himself to the stone floor. He pauses for a moment, and he tilts his head, *just* enough that others would be satisfied with.

But not Darius.

He walks swiftly over to him, then, without hesitation, a booted foot lands on the side of Sean's face. He presses down until the male's head cracks off the floor.

"Now, this is how far you should go when baring your neck to her," Darius growls, his rage palpable in the air.

He looks back at me as the male scrambles with his hands to try and get up, but he must know he can't.

"Is this low enough, Vihnarn?"

The room breaks out in gasped shock, words and murmurs after Darius's revealing of what I am to him.

I look down at the male, watching his struggle, then my eyes lift back to Darius in answer.

His eyes flash black.

"So be it," he smirks, and without even looking, he pours some of his magic out to wrap around his neck, then the knowing *crack* follows.

Darius takes his foot away from the dead male's head and comes back to me.

He lifts me up and puts me back on his lap like nothing had happened.

"Anyone else have issues who have come back from a location search?" Silence. "Good. See that it stays that way, for you now know how it ends. I will not tolerate the disrespect. Clear?"

"Rah!" The thunderous reply comes instantly, and I see Maverick smiling. He clearly enjoyed that.

Eventually, Darius speaks up, gaining his Elite's attention.

"We leave for The Drylands," he tells them, looking at them all. "You know war will come knocking on our gates at any moment, especially after Maize's death." Guilt runs through me at that. I sped up the timeline. Darius squeezes my thigh, his magic forming under his fingertips. "While some of us are in The Drylands, I need you all to be vigilant, listen when you are out in the lands, protect our home. The people."

The Elites nod their heads, not once moving their gaze from their Alpha.

"We need to make sure papers are ready to distribute across the towns of the Highers deeds. It will cause much unrest, but hopefully, it will cause the people to fight back against the Higher guards in their towns. That they will fight with us when it's needed to gain back some control."

"What if they don't?" A male on the far right asks, and Darius's eyes swing to him.

"Then we protect them, like we have always tried to do." He nods at that, the others following suit.

Silence fills the room, and my head turns to look at Darius.

Underneath his rough exterior, at his core, Darius is full of protection. For his men, for his brothers...

He looks down and peers into my eyes, and I know that protection extends to me.

"Maverick," he says, not moving his gaze away. "Keep patrol alert for any more rogues, and you will devise a plan to get those that need sanctuary to Colhelm, we have a large farmstead there."

"Why can't we use the keep, there is plenty of room." You can hear the confusion in his tone. Darius finally moves his gaze away from me then.

"Because the keep will be one of the first things under attack when Charles finds out about killing those that were under him. When he finds out that we are no longer with him, but against him."

He's right, they will hit here first, and it could be at any moment.

"Be ready," he tells his men, "And say goodbye to your loved ones. We never know when the chance will arise again. If ever."

THIRTEEN

Darius

"That's it, feel it like it's an extension of yourself."

I watch my little wolf concentrate as she moves her head back and forth, holding a tendril of her power and controlling it.

Sweat dots her forehead, showing that she's working hard. And she is.

We have been doing this any spare chance we get, Rhea not wanting to let up because she feels so helpless.

I know she wants to go to the kid. I can't pretend like I understand because I don't. But he's important to her so therefore, I need to make sure we can get to him when we can.

"How do you hold yours so steady?" Rhea asks, hands on her knees as she pants.

I lift a hand and show her, moving my power this way and that, moving it towards her to wrap around her wrist.

She smiles down at it, hand stroking it.

"It is mine, I control it like I control every other part of myself."

"Not everything you can control," she mutters, pointedly looking at my crotch and I bark out a laugh.

"That is all you, little wolf. I cannot help what you do to me."

She turns, but I catch the smile on her face.

Little shit.

I send more power out around her and bind her legs. She falls face-first into the grass.

"It is rude to call out someone's erection." I stride past her as she grumbles, pulling at my magic until she gets it to release her.

"Asshole." A ball hits my back, and I whip around to her.

"Oh?" I ask, lifting a brow in challenge, a thrill going through me.

She huffs, calling her power to her hands that are glowing a soft blue.

I chuckle, and then I go for her.

She didn't expect the move, she thought we were going to throw magic at each other.

No.

I will hunt her.

She squeals in surprise, throwing her magic at me anyway before she takes off into a run.

The lightness in that sound makes my chest expand, a purr joining it at knowing the happiness she just felt.

I need to make more of it.

She runs through the fields, dipping in and out of the willow's branches.

We always come back to this place, always surrounded by her favorite flowers.

"You cannot hide from me, little wolf," I say, as she runs behind a tree, moving further out into the woods there.

"Are you tired?"

"To chase you?" I call. "Never."

I would chase her to the ends of the lands and back. I would chase her through dangerous waters and the darkness of the sea.

I will always chase the light she casts upon me.

We run for a while, her thinking she has the upper hand while I let her believe that as the thrill of the hunt rolls through me.

Better to tire her out, first. Better to catch my prey.

"Got you," I say when I round a tree and collide with her.

She screams, struggling in my grip as we tumble to the

ground, her magic wrestling with me as she laughs.

"You big fucker. Get off me," she pants, throwing magic in my face so I'm temporarily blinded.

"That wasn't very nice." I smile down at her, grabbing her wrists and pinning them to the floor. "That's better," I say, covering her hands with my power.

"It's not fair, you have the upper hand."

I shake my head, leaning over her. "You couldn't be more wrong."

"How so?" she asks, struggling in my grip. "I think this speaks for itself."

I shake my head. "When are you going to realize you have all the power here?"

She stills then, staring up at me.

I let her look, let her see the truth of it.

"And you freely give that power?"

The hold she has on me? No.

But power?

"Yes." I tell her, and she releases a stuttering breath.

She looks at me, imploring with her eyes what she won't say aloud. I wait a moment, watching as dark specks enter her eyes, sending a heat through my chest.

"You never need to ask for what you want from me, little wolf. Just take it, it's yours anyway."

I take her mouth with mine, demanding her to open for me, but I keep it gentle. I let her feel me, her little tongue exploring as she wiggles beneath me. I taste her too, something that is only ever hers and again, I want to capture it and keep it.

I slow the kiss before breaking it, rubbing my nose against hers.

"Do you think I will be able to control my power like you? Will I be enough?"

She looks at me like she's desperate for the answer, and I give her the truth, releasing her wrists and placing my hands on either side of her head.

"You are always enough Rhea, and when you fully control your power, you will be more."

She seems to relax under that, letting my words settle her. "And until then?"

"We keep practicing and keep trying to get your wolf out." Drax purrs at that.

Rhea nods and I stand, holding a hand out to help her up. I grab it, but I realize my mistake too late.

Her foot lands on my stomach and she pulls me down by my hand, and then I'm flying over her and landing into the dirt.

"You will pay for that!" I growl, getting to my feet.

Her laugh can be heard in the distance as she runs. "Catch me if you can!"

I race after her, and we play until the moon is high in the night sky.

When she suddenly stops, I pause behind her, listening as we both catch our breaths. When she raises her hand and spreads her fingers, I let out a chuckle.

"What are you doing?"

Her fingers part and she tilts her head up. "Looking at the moon."

"Through your fingers?" I grab hold of her wrist and bend a little, seeing what she's seeing. "Why?"

"It reminds me that we are small in a land so large. To remember that the little things matter too. Like these moments with you."

I stroke her fingers and then run them down her arm, watching as she shivers from my touch. "Then let's look together."

And we proceed to do just that.

Only she was looking at the moon, and I was looking at her.

FOURTEEN

Kade

"Maize is ignoring my calling to her. What did she say when you last saw her?" Aldus asks me, but I turn my face away, ignoring him.

Everything is confusing.

I keep having flashes of things that I'm not even sure existed.

Am I broken?

Am I going mad?

Where is the butterfly?

I sigh at that, and a slap rings through the air.

I turn my head, looking at Aldus who has rage in his eyes.

I never liked him. He's fake. Fake smile, fake words.

He hurts my head.

"What did you say to her? She is not answering my command to come back since she went to be mated to Alpha Darius." She tried to touch me and I nearly threw her out the window. "You were the last person to see her." He's shouting, and I look at his raised hand.

Oh. He must have hit me.

I blink.

I think someone would kill him for that.

I don't know for sure.

Just a feeling.

I laugh again at it.

He would have his throat ripped out.

Blue eyes and blonde hair, along with a kind smile flutters

though my mind.

Who is that female?

She feels warm and bright, not like the other one who laughs with a cruel smile.

I shake my head, starting to feel dizzy.

Darius…he hurts people too.

My cheek stings again, and the person in front of me doubles.

Why are there two of them?

"Stupid, useless boy!"

He moves away from me as Axis growls.

A silver butterfly follows him, and I stand on shaky legs, needing to catch it. Just like the other times.

It's back.

I follow, stumbling as the door comes into view,

Oh. I can't go there, it never opens. Always locked.

Always shut.

Always secure…

I pause, shaking my head again.

Light peeks through it and I tilt my head as the butterfly goes through the crack.

The door isn't shut this time.

It didn't close properly.

I shouldn't go though, I will be hurt.

Bad, bad, bad things will happen.

That's what happened last time…I think.

They will take me to that place again that makes me want to scream and rip my own head off.

It hurts down there.

It's dark down there.

I take a step back to retreat to my bed when that butterfly comes back to me.

It flutters in front of my face, always calling me. Fluttering its wings to entrance me.

I sway toward it, wondering if I catch it, if I can keep it to stop this darkness swallowing me whole.

Axis encourages me with a growl, pushing against my skin.

The butterfly still hovers, waiting for me.

I stumble forward and raise a hand, trying to grasp it, needing to keep it with me.

It dodges my hand, and I try again and again. It evades me every time.

It slips through the door again, but this time, I don't hesitate.

I follow it through.

I need to catch it.

But then blood is on the butterfly, his silver wings tinged with red.

What happened? Does it hurt?

It comes to a stop, hovers over a round object before it disappears.

I don't hesitate to follow it.

FIFTEEN

Rhea

Traveling though the rolling hills that will take us to The Drylands, I can't help but feel nervous about what awaits us there.

Dozens upon dozens of mountains litter the horizon, their snow-capped tips high up in the sky, nearly disappearing into the clouds. There has been no signs of anyone the closer we get to them, and a heaviness hangs in the air that I can't quite understand.

Since the rogures attacked the keep, and Maize's death, we are all on edge, waiting for the next strike from well, anything.

Darius has not been summoned to do the Highers's bidding and no new power spikes have been known, which Darius said it's normal to have lulls in them.

But with the rogure numbers increasing, I don't think it's normal at all, and I can't help the dread that Charles knows Darius is no longer loyal to him…

Add in that we have left the keep which has been a safe haven, not knowing when we will be back, it is hard to not let it get to us.

Darius stays close to my side like he has done for the past few days. We ported just outside a small farming village, remaining unseen by anyone that lives there. He said it was the closest he could get to The Drylands without being out in the open and not being seen by potential threats.

We all agreed, but it had cost us valuable time to get there.

I wrap myself up tighter in my cloak, fighting off the coming cold as I look at everything I can see. After living in Eridian for so long, it's still strange for me to see other parts of Vrohkaria. When we escaped my old pack, we never wandered this far west. We always stayed as close as possible to towns close by so we could steal food.

I take it all in and keep it close, not wanting to forget this moment at seeing this new landscape. I wonder if you can breathe at the top of the mountains with it being so high up. Would you freeze to death? Could anyone even climb it?

My nose begins to sting with the cold, and I sniffle a little, keeping pace with the others. Darius looks at me, concern in his eyes and I wave him off.

A little cold won't hurt me.

Leo and Josh are in front of us, talking casually and seeming to get along. Jerrod, Zaide, and Taylor are further in front, watching our surroundings closely while Hudson, Colten and Damian are at our backs.

We didn't organize this formation, it was an instinct to travel this way, and it's not lost on me that I'm central with Darius by my side. Two heirs from the land and below, protected at all sides.

We are the most powerful, most precious, and the most deadly beings in the lands—with a target the size of the mountains we are headed toward on our backs. Both of our lives have drastically changed since that day at Wolvorn Castle, taking a different direction to where we thought it was going.

But ultimately, the only thing solid in our knowledge is that we are tied to each other.

"Do you wish I didn't unblock your memories?" I ask Darius, peeking at him from the corner of my eye as his head constantly moves around, watching for danger.

"No, little wolf. It was something that I needed, something that only you could do."

"Me?" I wonder.

"Yes." He looks to his right, hand on the hilt of his blade. "My counterpart."

I look down, my chest warming. "Did you ever find out how it was blocked?" He never mentioned it, never even spoke of it really, like it wasn't important. But it was.

"It's not how it was blocked that is the main question. It was who tried to." I trip a little over my feet and his hand snaps out, steadying me.

"Do you know who?" I whisper, wondering if it was someone here with us. Can we not trust one of his men? Is he in danger? The thought has blue mist spurring from my palms and Darius's black covers it immediately, shaking his head at the unspoken question in my eyes.

I relax, letting my power flow back into me.

"Aldus," he tells me. He's the one who brought that crystal to Darius, who brought down the barrier around Eridian, who is with Kade. "I just don't know why. It's the least of our concern at the moment."

"But what if he does it again?" What if he forgets he's an Heir and conflict starts all over again between us?

What if he forgets... me?

"Then I will protect myself and you will unblock it again." My eyes widen at the finality in his tone.

"But what if I can't?" He knows my power is unpredictable, I can barely control it when it lets me. "I can't even turn into a wolf, how do you expect me to unblock your memories? I don't even know how I did it the first time."

"Instinct." Is all he says, as the ground begins to crack beneath our feet, letting us know we are now in The Drylands territory.

I see no water here, no plant life or animals. The ground is dusty as we walk toward the base of the mountains, and I wonder how anything could survive out here.

"How are you doing, pup?" I hear from behind me, followed by a scoff.

"Just fine," Colten replies, his tone hard.

I look behind me, my brows furrowed as I catch Hudson's concerned look toward him.

What's going on there?

I'm about to ask when Josh calls from ahead. "What the fuck is that?"

I walk faster toward him, Darius at my side and we both come to a stop.

"Darius," I whisper, my eyes unable to look away from the ground.

"Fuck." He runs a hand through his hair. "Weapons out."

The sound of weapons being drawn surrounds me as Darius creeps closer. I follow right behind him.

"How is this here?" I ask.

The black, circular patch on the ground is the exact same one from the memory crystal. The one where the rogue came out of.

"I don't know," Darius says, a frown on his face as he crouches beside it.

"Darius!" I snap in a panic, not liking him too close to it as I grip his arm. He looks to me, a smile on his face.

Asshole likes that I'm worried.

I look closely at the ground and just like in the memory, the edges of the patch have black flames, but these are smaller, barely moving.

Darius places his hand toward it, and I hold my breath, wary as he brings his magic out. A tendril flows from his palm and slowly glides down into the black earth, towards…nothing.

"It's dying," he says, eyes hard as his power moves deeper. "The land around it is dying."

"Dying?" I ask, as the Elites come near to investigate. "Like the trees in The Deadlands?" I crouch and place a hand on the cracked ground. I push my magic into it, and suck in a sharp breath. "There is no life inside of it." It's unnerving.

"It feels like it's spreading."

"Spreading?" He nods. "What could cause it to just...die though?"

"I don't know. The rogues are a plague to the people, but now, they are a plague to the lands itself." He calls his magic back and stands, holding out a hand for me. I grab it and he pulls me up, looking further ahead where we see more patches of black. "We need to be careful."

"I've never seen anything like this before," Leo mutters, looking curiously at the black earth near us.

"In the memory crystal, a rogue came out of something similar like this," Darius tells them and growls come next.

"Has a rogue already come out of it then?" Leo says.

"Maybe that's why it's dying," Zaide mutters, blades out.

Darius grunts. "Maybe,"

"There are so many of them," I say, looking further ahead. "It looks like it's coming from the mountains and spreading towards the other territories." I look behind me toward where life flourishes. "Does that mean the rogue dens could be in The Drylands?"

"Only one way to find out. Be careful not to step on any, you wouldn't want a rogue chomping on your leg," Darius tells everyone, and they nod.

I share a worried look with Josh as we continue on.

We eventually reach a stone path at the base of a small mountain, pausing to take in the knowledge that we are about to go there, but not knowing what is there.

"We go slow, I know some trails and caves we can rest in when needed. You find or see anything, let me know," Darius orders, and we all nod. "We don't know who or what could be lurking in these mountains. Trolls like the open ground, so if we see any, do not aggravate them, and they should leave us alone."

"Trolls?" I whisper, horrified. I've never seen a troll.

"Yeah," Damian says, coming to stand next to me. "Tall fuckers, and they have an aversion to clothing." He tilts his head in thought. "Though I'm not sure where they would get clothes from. Anyway, there are always more than one of them. They can be nasty fuckers when aggravated, and even though we are all skilled, many of them can cause us problems."

"That's not terrifying at all," I mutter to myself.

"Just don't stare at their dicks either," Leo chimes in, and I give him a blank stare. "They don't like it when you look at it without permission."

What?

"And you would know that how?" Who stares at a troll's dick?

"Ask Zaide over there," Leo chuckles, and my head whips around to Zaide, my wide eyes giving away my shock.

"You stared at a troll's dick?" I sputter a laugh.

"I did not expect that," Colten chuckles.

Zaide shrugs. "I hadn't seen one before, I needed all the intel I could get at the time."

I stare. "From a troll's cock?" He nods, and I pause, thinking for a second. "Was it normal?"

"Are we ready?" Darius growls, giving me a warning look, having had enough of our conversation, and I notice Josh taking a deep breath.

I walk toward him, slipping my hands in his and squeezing. He looks up from the ground, his light gray eyes full of apprehension.

"She's okay. Anna and Seb are with her. Though she may kill Seb by the time we are back." His flirting knows no bounds.

"We might not make it back," he says softly, his eyes going back to the path before us.

I dig my short nails into the top of his hand. "We need to get Kade and the pack back. You will not die on me now, and you will not die on me before you give me a niece or nephew."

He's always wanted a family, he just had to find the right one. No matter how the pack wanted him during their heat, and sometimes after, Josh wanted a connection with someone, and now he has.

A smile crosses his face and he pulls me close, leaning his forehead against mine.

We both ignore the menacing growl behind me.

"I don't think you're getting rid of your own babysitter anytime soon," he whispers, a small chuckle escaping him as I'm grabbed and hauled into a hard, muscular body.

"Not in this life or the next," Darius grunts, his voice low as his grip tightens on me.

I turn in his arms, looking up into my favorite green eyes that he doesn't know.

I go on my tippy toes and rub my nose against his as he freezes, his eyes wary, yet slightly dilated at my small show of affection I have given him.

Maybe he is right about me having all the power.

"If you want to keep your balls Dar, I would let up on babysitting duty." The male is always on me like green on grass, more so than ever lately.

He raises a brow and tilts his head. "You touching my balls? I fail to see how that is a bad thing?" His gaze drops to my lips. "You also know what will happen if you don't listen and go off on your own."

My body heats as I remember how Darius teased me until I was boneless after he carried me off into his room, after he caught me in the woods. He wouldn't stop until I gave him what he wanted, which was for me to follow his orders by staying close by his side.

I argued I was quite capable of looking after myself…to no avail.

I huff, and go to move back, but his lips are against mine in a quick, hard kiss. I'm a little dazed as he pulls back and he takes my hand, dragging me behind him as we take the narrow path between the mountains.

Dark, gray stone encases us on either side, and the dullness of it all starts creeping in. The light fades a little, and it feels like

I'm closed-in all of a sudden.

I grip Darius's armor at the back beneath his cloak, the leather creaking as I tighten my fingers against it. I do not do well in small spaces.

He squeezes my hand and draws me closer to his back, a tendril of power wrapping around my wrist.

Around my pulse I realize.

"You're good, Rhea, look up and see it's open," Josh says through the link, and I do, happy to see the blue, cloudy sky and also wondering why Darius didn't cut Josh off.

I breathe a little easier as I focus on the open space above me, trusting Darius to get us where we need to be. It's much colder in between the mountains, the base not getting much sun. I shiver a little, thankful for the thick, leather armor I'm wearing and the fur-hooded cloak for extra protection. I'm not sure if we will be able to make a fire when we stop, but I'll steal body heat if I have to. Even if it's from Zaide.

The thought makes me chuckle, and Darius looks at me from over his shoulder.

"Do you think Zaide's into cuddling?" I ask quietly, and he grunts, baring his teeth.

"There will be no cuddling," he growls.

"But—"

"No, now hush."

And hush, I do.

But not because he told me to. No. Because we have just exited the narrow pathway and are looking at an open canyon going far back until it hits the large mountains on the other side. Tall, spindly rocks are placed around erratically, and natural formations of stone are everywhere in an upside down semi-circle.

An eerie feeling washes over me at how deserted it all looks, yet so full of rock and stone. The gray color makes everything feel lifeless, even though the sky is blue. There is no sound here, no animals can be heard, no water trickling.

I move my gaze to the far right and spot smoke in the distance, curling up toward the sky. "That's not natural, is it?" I asked the group aloud, their gaze also on the white floating upward. I may not have ever been in here, but I know this isn't a regular thing.

"No, little wolf." Darius says, clutching my hand tighter and pulling me to him. "It isn't natural at all. Someone has a fire going."

Which means someone else is in The Drylands with us.

SIXTEEN

Rhea

We move through the bottom of the mountains after we trailed down to be truly encased inside of them. We can barely see the smoke in the distance now, but we know the direction we need to head. The breeze is cold, and it makes me shiver as we silently round a tall rock formation.

Darius stays at my back, keeping me close at all times, with Leo and Jerrod in front while the rest of the guys stay behind us.

We trek around a small mountain and down a narrow path between stones. Darius says it will lead us to another opening, and I'm hoping it won't take too long.

When we finally leave the tight passage, the barren earth in front of us opens out into a valley of sorts, with a body of water in the distance, the first I have seen. I feel like I can finally breathe again.

Damian heads straight on and we move down a small incline of rocky earth. Even with water nearby, no life can be seen or heard here either. Darius said there will be a cave to rest in for the night, and looking ahead, I can spot it a little ways in the distance. But none of that matters when a growl sounds to the left of us.

I still, but then spin with the others as a pair of eyes lock on to us.

"It's on its own," Darius says, twirling his blade in his hand. "Interesting."

"But they are never on their own," I say, looking around to find any more as my heart beats painfully.

"The one in the memory crystal was alone," he replies. "Leo, go ahead."

Leo huffs as the rogure perched on top of a large rock puts weight on his back legs. I go to call out to Leo to watch out, but before I know it, he's running head-on into the rogure just as it leaps and charges at him.

In the next breath, they collide. But it's not rogure and Leo, it's rogure and wolf.

Leo's dark brown wolf snarls into the rogure's shoulder, biting down with his teeth. The rogure whines, shakes, then spins roughly to shake Leo off. It works, and the wolf rolls to the side but quickly gets back on his feet.

The rogure lunges, teeth bared, dripping black foam, but Leo dodges to the left, spinning quickly, then his teeth are clamping down on the rogure's neck. Leo bites into it, gnashing his teeth until the rogure goes limp, bleeding all over the ground.

Silence ensues, and I breathe a sigh of relief when I spot no other rogures.

Leo gets up, shakes his fur out and then walks toward us. In the next second, he's a man, rolling his neck as he fixes his clothes. He has full control if he can keep his clothes on through the shift, Kade couldn't the last time he went wolf.

"Fucking rogure bastard," Leo says, continuing on. I look at Darius as he scans the surroundings, and I do the same.

Opening my senses more, I feel nothing but who we are with, and it makes me even more nervous that this lone rogure was out here.

"It was so skinny," I say to Darius as I walk beside him. He grunts in acknowledgement.

"Stay close."

We wander for a while. Around tall boulders, under stone archways, until eventually, Darius points to an opening in the side of a smaller mountain.

We head toward the cave with nightfall approaching. Wading through the small river to reach it, I make sure not to get anything wet higher than my boots.

Reaching a ledge that will get us into the cave, I'm about to lift my arms to climb it when hands at my waist lift me easily, letting my knees touch the top of the ledge before they let go. I look over my shoulder at Darius and he jumps, lifting himself up next to me, holding out his hand to help me up. I take it, rising to my feet as the others join us, raising a brow at him as he helps me.

We look into the darkness of the cave, and I swallow as nerves overcome me. I *hate* small spaces. It reminds me of the time I was stuck in the fucking cage Charles and my family kept me in.

Lips touch my forehead, and I let loose a sigh at Darius. Comforting male.

Dammit.

It's like he can feel my unease, feel my nerves and why I'm slow to move.

He's always noticed the little things.

Darius tugs on my hand to follow behind him as we enter, and though I can't see his back, I remember the scars he has there. Remember how they bled and tore.

I swallow back the bile.

"Call some of your power when we are a little further in," Darius says, and I give him a confused look. "The light will help, it's not much but it's something. Our wolves can only see so much in the dark, and my power won't give off light."

Runa perks up like Darius was talking to her, and I do as he says after walking another twenty steps, calling my power to my palms, concentrating to mold it into the shape of a small ball.

Well, as much of a ball as I can make it. It's more pointy in some places.

The blue glow caresses the walls gently, giving us a little light as we continue to move forward. We continue walking for another few minutes, silent and listening out for any movement, wondering if some unknown creature will come out and eat us for disturbing its home.

"Would you look at that," Leo says, and I turn, following his gaze to the ground.

I scowl. Bastards. "This is where they must have gotten it from them."

We move over to the dassil flower, and I remember how Sarah told me about what it does.

"I'll take some," Josh says at my back, looking at the flowers in anger.

"If my pack is here, in the name of that Zaigar place, it would make sense if they have a supply of this." The thought sickens me.

"It would be smart to set up a place, yes," Darius replies hesitantly, like he doesn't want to upset me but we all know I'm right.

"They will die," Colten snarls, walking ahead of us and Hudson goes after him.

"They will," Darius agrees and I watch as Josh carefully places some of the dassil in his pack.

"Anna could get some use out of this," he says and I nod. She could.

Eventually, we come to a more open space inside the cave, the almost circular room, clear, apart from the loose rocks on the floor. To the right, two more passages lead to Gods knows where, but it must be safe here as the Elites start setting their packs down and pulling out furs to sleep on.

I move to the back of the space, dropping my power and putting my pack down to get my own fur out, making sure I'm positioned so I can see all openings. Darius drops his pack beside me, looking around the room before his attention comes back to me.

"Come," he tells me as he starts to move away and heads to one of the other passages, collecting a small pack as he goes.

I drop my things and follow, curious to where he's taking me. Josh's chuckle sounds behind me, and I stick my tongue out at him. While Hudson and Colten are whispering to each other nearby.

Catching up to Darius, I keep close behind him as he takes us through the passage on the left. We walk without light for a little while until I hear the telltale sign of water.

"Where are we going?" I ask.

"You'll see," he says as we turn around a few corners before we come into another room inside the cave. I pause at the threshold, tiny streams of light shining down on the pool of water to the right and the small opening that a little waterfall seems to be flowing out of.

"Wow," I breathe. "It reminds me a little of my cave in Eridian."

Darius looks around. "It does a little."

I want to ask him about it. Does my cave look different? How did my home look? Is there anything even left of it?

But I'm too scared to know the answer.

Darius moves towards the water and drops the pack before taking off his weapons. Once he's disarmed himself, he takes off his leather chest armor, and drops it to the floor. Bare-chested, I watch as his defined muscles move as he stalks towards me, my eyes glued to his tattoos. I trace them going down to the side of his neck and over his ribs, making out small details as he comes closer.

A breath away now, I look toward the marking appearing on his neck, it's subtle, but seeing it fills me with a sudden warmth.

Darius takes the blades at my hips and throws them on top of his armor before unbuckling the straps on my own chest piece.

"Lift," he commands, and I raise my arms, letting him peel the material off my naked chest. He throws it onto the growing pile of clothes and licks his lips, his eyes roaming over my heaving chest.

He loosens the tie on my leather pants and kneels to take off my boots and socks, all before gripping the sides of the leather and pulling them down my legs. I hold onto his shoulders as he helps take them off my feet before he pauses, his face inches away from my panties.

"Needy little wolf," he murmurs. He leans forward, inhaling and placing a gentle kiss against me, causing me to tremble. He pulls his head back and smirks, pulling my panties down. Then, his hands grip my waist and he spins me suddenly. "Get in the water, little wolf." He bites my ass and I yelp, giving him a glare over my shoulder as I walk towards the water.

I feel his eyes on me the whole time, caressing all that's bare to him, and I don't feel shy about it.

I lift my foot and test the water's temperature. "It's warm," I say in awe, and move to enter fully.

"Hot water runs under the whole of The Drylands, warming any water above it. It comes from the pit."

"The pit?" I ask.

He nods. "It has caves filled with lava networking through it far from here, and that heats up the water running through the mountains."

"That's amazing," I groan as I lower myself into the water, feeling the heat loosen my muscles and warming my bones. A low growl has my head snapping Darius' way, and I suck in a breath at the heat in his dilated eyes.

He's removed his pants, standing in his naked glory of all muscles, markings—and dripping in power. I clench my thighs together, and he smirks.

He rummages through the pack while I turn around and take the tie out of my hair, letting it flow freely as I dip my head back to get it wet. Fingers are suddenly there, moving through the strands gently as I rise out of the water. I hear something being twisted open, and then the smell of wildflowers hits me.

Darius's hands lather the soap we use to wash my hair, his

fingers massaging my scalp in a way that makes me moan in approval.

This is something also unknown, this intimacy. We have fucked, he's had his tongue in and all over my body, but this is something that's so different, even from the last time he washed me in the bathtub.

"I can do it," I murmur to him, closing my eyes and enjoying the feeling of being cared for.

"I like my hands on you, little wolf, no matter how it happens." He presses closer to my back, running his soap-covered hands over my shoulders and dipping down the front, in between my breasts.

"Do you?"

He grunts. "Yes. It...calms me."

"Or excites." I huff out a laugh.

"Always with you, but that does not mean I have to act upon it."

He nips at my neck and I turn suddenly, splashing him right in the face. I laugh at the astonishment on his face as I swim away from him, kicking my feet as fast as I can.

"You think that's funny?"

I turn, hearing him coming for me again and splash some more. I laugh as he starts to splash me back, getting closer and closer and when he's near, I jump up and shove his head under the water.

Giggling, I turn and swim back to where we were originally, and a hand grabs my ankles, causing me to squeal out.

"Come back here, little wolf," Darius growls.

I turn, kicking out my leg to splash him again when Darius takes us both underwater. I push at him as he grabs my waist, letting me back up, only to dunk me again.

We play like this for a little while, splashing and seeing who can get who under the water. I know we are being too loud, but I don't care when splashing Daruis is this much fun.

He backs me up against the side of the pool a while later,

grabbing my hands as I laugh and try to splash him again. He turns me away from him on a chuckle, our breathing ragged as he inhales me at my neck.

I press into the hardness at my back, smiling at the soft groan he releases. He pinches my nipple in return, drawing a gasp from me as his lips touch my neck again, biting and licking my skin like he's starving.

"You make me feel as mad as the Gods are said to be," he tells me, biting down behind my ear. "I don't think even a lifetime will be enough for me to *get* everything I want from you."

He pushes me forward, staying at my back as he moves me to the edge of the water, pressing a hand between my shoulder blades.

"And what's that?" I pant.

"Everything, but I don't just want it once," he growls. "I want it again and again."

I lean over, bending so that my palms are on the cave floor, offering myself to him. I can't resist the pull to him. I always want him near me, inside me, and for once, I embrace it.

"This needs to be quick, little wolf."

"Better hurry up—" He thrusts into me in one hard stroke "Gods," I whimper as he stretches me.

He rumbles low in his throat in approval, and gives me another hard thrust. I moan loudly, gripping the flat surface as he withdraws and slams into me just as hard, again and again.

"Fuck," he grunts. "Your pussy always squeezes me so well, little wolf. Like it always wants me to stay inside of you, to never let go." I clench around him, my orgasm building quicker than I expected. "It's never enough, always not enough." Water splashes around us as he ups his pace, and all I can do is claw at the ground, me moaning and him groaning as the feel of us coming together like this. "Touch yourself," he orders, "I want you to drain the cum from my balls and coat your insides for all of the lands to know you are no one's but mine. Do it, now, Rhea."

Fuck. I move my hand at his harsh tone, the grip he has on my hips is bruising, fingers pressing into my skin with almost something like desperation.

I move my fingers over my clit, dipping them lower to feel him moving inside of me, loving the way he slides easily in and out of me with how wet I am for him. Only him.

"Harder," I pant. He grunts as my fingers squeeze around him before coming back to my clit and rubbing in circular motions.

"Gods, damn, this cunt." He removes my hand and replaces it with his own, moving even faster than before and angling his hips to hit the very spot inside of me that he knows drives me wild.

"Fuck! Darius," I whine.

"Shh, we don't want everyone to know that you're being fucked by the Alpha of the Elites, do you?" he taunts, and I gasp as pleasure runs through me. "Oh, you like them knowing? Even though none of them out there are a threat to you?"

I do. I can't help it when others know he's mine too.

"Possessive. Little. Wolf," he says with each thrust, and I moan, long and loud as his thrusts become erratic, almost animalistic as he ruts into me.

A finger is suddenly between my cheeks, and he eases his finger into my ass, moving in time with his strokes. Pleasure with a bite of pain spreads through my whole body, and I clench around him, my eyes rolling as my orgasm peaks.

He curses, burrowing his head in the crook of my neck before he stills, groaning my name into my skin as he releases inside of me.

We stay there, catching our breaths as he lazily continues to thrust in and out of me, making sure every drop stays within me. He pulls out when he's done, replacing his cock with his fingers when he shoves them inside of me, feeling our combined release.

He withdraws his fingers, placing them at my lips, coating

them before he shoves them in my mouth. I lick around them, swirling my tongue to get every taste of us as he hums his approval, while I hum mine.

Gods, I don't feel like myself when I get like this, but it's a need I can't explain. He's mine, and I want to taste us, scent us.

He kisses the nape of my neck before he moves back, picking up a bar of soap and starts to clean me. I'm still in a daze as he makes sure every inch of me has been cleaned by his hands and my eyes close over his attention on my body. He chuckles, running a finger down my cheek at the state of me.

I can't find it in me to care.

He rubs his nose against mine, and then bites down on my lower lip. I slowly peel my eyes open to find him staring at me with something I can't say.

Only that it is new, and I think I like it.

"Let's get you dressed, little wolf, so we can sleep."

"We?" I murmur, just wanting to curl up on the cave floor, but he's adamant about getting me dressed while I grumble and let him move me where he needs to, to get my clothes back on.

"Yes, *we*," he says, and throws the pack over his shoulder before picking me up behind my thighs and carrying me back the way we came. "The only way you're sleeping is in my arms. There is no other place for you to be."

SEVENTEEN

Darius

Holding the whip, my hand trembles subtly, blood dripping in splashes on the stone floor.

The people's faces blur around me as they shout and cheer, laughing at a particular curl of her body.

The way it shakes and strains.

The way it trembles.

My stomach revolts, Drax growling so violently within me, and my eyes move to the figure on the dais.

He smiles, his eyes on her, only her, as she tries to hold back her cries, as she doesn't make another sound after I raise the whip and mark her again.

I hold back my full strength, only doing it hard enough to appease him, but I'm still hurting her.

Her or my brothers, her or my brothers.

I repeat again and again.

I saw the crystal. It shows what she did. I'm doing what I need to for the lands, doing what I need to so I can protect my brothers.

They didn't betray anyone.

The rogues killed my family, took away any calm, any love.

Any softness in my life.

My stomach revolts as the whip comes down—

My eyes fly open wide, my heart beating so fast I can barely stifle the sound of my heavy breathing.

There is a shake to my limbs, a tightness in my chest as I clear away another nightmare.

Fuck.

A small sigh comes next to me, and my arm curls tighter around the body in my arms, sleeping soundly, feeling her warmth.

My nose comes to her hair, and I inhale, nuzzling the back of her head, knowing she's safe.

The urge to get up and find somewhere to stop the itch in my back nearly overwhelms me. It takes everything in me not to do it, just like the last time when Rhea woke to me leaving. It's hard to stop the habit I created to punish myself, especially after having a nightmare about it.

But I vowed to her, and I would not break a vow to her again.

"Another one?" a quiet voice asks, and I still, then sigh in defeat.

I loathe showing weakness to anyone, but he's seen it all.

I get my breathing under control before I gently, and reluctantly, remove myself from Rhea. She whines, her brow furrowing, and I quickly grab a spare fur next to me and roll it up, pressing it against her back so it feels like I'm still next to her.

Standing on silent feet, I stretch my neck out and walk over to where Leo rests against the wall. I slump down beside him and run a hand down my face.

"I thought maybe they would go after you two talked it out," he says on a whisper, not wanting to wake the others.

"I don't deserve them to go away."

Nightmares are the only thing I see when I sleep.

Leo only knows about them because most nights after I went to the basement, I would sleep in my office, and I would wake, sweating and panting, and he would be there, seeing it all.

Another punishment.

I'm close to all of my brothers, but Leo is my closest.

"No one deserves what *both* of you have been through," he says, his tone low and solemn.

I shake my head, feeling a slight tremble in my fingers like I'm still holding that fucking whip.

"What did she say after she found you in the basement?" he finally dares to ask, like he didn't want her to find me. Fucker.

I sigh, banging my head against the stone as I look up at the cave walls. We hadn't spoken about anything that had happened after that, and I get the feeling he didn't want to bring it up so soon in case I went back down there.

"She wanted me to stop, threatened to do it to herself if I didn't."

He huffs out a laugh. "I like her." My head snaps toward him, and he raises his hands. "Not like that."

He better not, it would be unfortunate if I had to send him away. I couldn't kill him, but I don't think it would be far off with the things I would do to keep Rhea.

He looks toward her sleeping form, and I follow his gaze. "I like her for you," he says. "She doesn't take your shit, calls you out on your bullshit and most of all," he says, serious all of a sudden. "She brings out things in you that I thought were lost forever." My brows crease at that. "Your heart, Darius."

I guess he is right in that. Years of bloodshed have hardened and hidden it away. But it beats for her now, and it makes me do things I would never have done.

Like planting hundreds of seeds of her favorite flowers, buying her a glass wolf, collecting her carvings, feeding her...

"It is not mine, brother," I tell him. "She has my heart now, and she can do with it what she wishes."

He hums. "She will take care of it," he says quietly.

She could destroy it if she wanted.

Rhea shuffles back against the rolled-up fur, her brows pinching like she knows it's not me. My chest puffs out at that, and Drax releases a purr.

She knows I'm not really there beside her, she knows she has peace in my arms even though they have shown so much violence.

She hasn't known true peace or been protected for so long, but I will give my dying breath to give her that.

She *deserves* that much.

"She's your match, everything you never knew you ever needed or wanted," Leo says, and I nod. I'm not going to deny it.

"She is…everything."

My moonlight.

She shines the brightest, even on the darkest of days.

Since my eyes locked with hers, the lands shifted, and so did I.

"We will make it right," Leo says, his voice strong.

"We will."

The Highers, the rogues… we will rid them from the lands, and Vrohkaria can have peace.

She will have peace.

Because she is who I will protect, and she is the one I will make sure the lands are safe for.

I press a hand to the side of my rib, where my sister's name has been so delicately intertwined with other markings.

Isn't that right, baby sister? I will do for her what I couldn't for you.

I vow it.

EIGHTEEN

Rhea

My shoulder jostles as a rough shake to my shoulder wakes me. My eyes spring open, seeing Darius looking at me intensely with a finger to his lips.

My brows furrow, and he moves his hand to his ear, indicating for me to listen while I calm my heart rate.

I tilt my head, opening my senses and hear nothing, until the sound of footsteps reach me. My eyes widen, and I sit up, my hand going to the blade at my hip to defend myself and the others.

Darius looks toward the opening of the cave as everyone rushes to pack up as quietly as they can. We join them, moving to our feet and gathering our things, putting them in our packs and making sure we have left nothing behind.

A sound reaches us, almost a groan with chuffing noises, and we all freeze in our movements. Leo slowly reaches behind him for his bow and notches an arrow, his aim on the entrance while Jerrod grips his axe in his hand, his stances ready. Darius moves me slowly behind them, nudging me along with Josh, Zaide, Taylor, and Damian.

Another sound, then a grunt, with what sounds like bark snapping. I tilt my head more, listening for any other sounds when another set of heavy footsteps reach us. *There is more than one.*

Holding our breath, our eyes pinned to the dark entrance, a shudder racks through the cave, bits of rock falling from the walls and then what sounds like a moan echoes toward us.

I raise my eyebrows, unable to believe what I'm hearing with the sound of skin slapping that comes next with groans and grunts following it.

I turn my head to Darius, my mouth parting while amusement glows in his light green eyes.

There is someone out there fucking.

Fucking…

Who in the ever loving Gods are they fucking in a cave?

Darius clicks his fingers softly, gaining the attention of the others and nods his head to the other passage.

He takes my hand, intertwining our fingers as he guides me over to the passage and we walk along the cave walls, the others trailing behind us. We're silent, slowly listening to the moans fading the deeper we walk.

I wonder why we aren't attacking them, why we are not gathering information but Darius seems intent on getting us out of here.

We round a corner into a narrow passage, and I squeeze Darius's hand, once again feeling trapped. My breaths come out faster and faster and I clench my eyes shut, trusting him to guide us as he picks up his pace.

My head starts to feel fuzzy, and a bout of dizziness hits me before I'm hauled up into strong arms.

I keep my eyes closed as Darius palms the back of my head, moving me to the curve of his neck as I breathe in his scent. A low, gentle sound comes from within his chest and I relax in his hold, knowing he's trying to calm me.

"Good girl," he whispers in my ear softly, nuzzling the side of my head before he picks up his speed once again.

I'm not sure how long he carries me for, but the sound of fucking is long gone, and my breathing turns steady by the time the soft light of morning hits me.

I peel my eyes open, noticing we are outside another entrance. The barren earth has a gentle river flowing through the middle now, and I watch as it seems to rise every second.

I lift my head to look around more, and see trees are dotting the area, grass sprouting through the once dead ground as I gape at it.

"How is this possible?" I whisper to no one in particular. There was nothing here before.

It's Damian who answers. "The Drylands are known for being barren of anything, but what most don't know is that it's always changing. You could look at an area, and the next day it's completely different." He waves a hand at the small valley now full of life. A surge of water sprouts out of the side of the mountain to the right, steam rising from it.

"This is amazing," I whisper, looking down at Darius as he still holds me.

"That's Vrohkaria, little wolf," he rumbles, his eyes tracing over my face, at the smile I have.

Then his eyes trail down to the side of my neck, and his nostrils flare, a deep rumbling sound coming from him. His eyes flash up to mine as I squirm under his gaze, dilating at my reaction as a smirk appears on those sinful lips.

"Behave you two, we have shit to do," Leo grumbles, and I flush, wriggling until Darius puts me on my feet.

My desire for him is getting stronger and stronger and I don't know why.

"Who was in the cave?" I ask, looking behind me as Josh does the same.

"Trolls," Damian answers, and my heartrate kicks up a notch. "Best not to pester them."

"I thought they were people," I whisper-hiss, looking back at the dark passageway.

"Definitely not people, and we definitely didn't want to cause a bloodbath. It would alert the rest of them," Leo says, and it makes me never want to come face-to-face with a troll in my life.

"Which way now?" I ask instead of voicing my fears.

"We follow the river and head toward where we saw the smoke," Jerrod says. "We have to be careful of the terrain changing."

I look over to the mountain of a man. His red central braid hangs over his shoulder, his eyes set in the direction with a fierce determination. I haven't talked to him much, but I remember the way he was at Eridian with little Oscar and Katy. I wonder if that's who he's thinking off when he stares into nothing. Then again, he didn't stop anyone from taking them.

I push the thought down. We are here now, not in the past where mistakes were made. We're going to get them back and that's all that matters.

"Usually it doesn't change until the next day," he continues, "but it has been known to be unpredictable the closer you get to the center."

What is in the center? I wonder but don't say aloud.

"Let's move," Darius says as he rummages through his pack and hands me some dried meat. "We can eat on the way." I chomp on the meat as we begin to walk.

I watch the river rise to the right of us, and I nearly choke at seeing fish jumping in and out of the water.

Where the hell did they come from?

I look around and take in the trees, noticing the fruit growing and wonder if we can eat them. None of the others seem to go near them so I take that as a *no* and continue forward. Taking everything in that I haven't seen before, I once again put it in that place to cherish for years to come.

We walk until the sun is high in the sky and the bitter cold that comes with being in here seeps into my bones. Everyone seems on alert, no doubt from the rogrue and the trolls in the cave.

Josh slides in next to me, and I don't miss the glare Darius throws his way.

I roll my eyes.

"I hope we can get to Kade after this," Josh says suddenly,

and pain spears through my heart.

Darius walks a little further ahead of us, reluctantly letting us talk, if the set of his stiff shoulders are anything to go by.

"Yeah," I whisper, glancing at him. "Gods I miss him." His absence has left a hole so deep, you can't see the bottom.

Runa whines within me, and I know she's struggling with him not being here. Just like Kade is mine, he's hers too.

"He's strong," Josh says. "He will be okay, he has had you to teach him most of his life."

"And you." I bump my shoulder with his. "I'm scared of what my family has done, and Charles. What if he doesn't want to come with me again?" The thought has me rubbing my chest.

"He will." Josh sounds so certain, but I'm not.

He didn't fully see the way Kade looked at me at Wolvorn, the way he would have done anything to get away from me.

"We will go to him after we are done here," Darius says, not looking back at me.

Of course he was listening.

It won't be that simple though. We all know it, we just don't voice it.

I lift my hand and call my power, watching as it floats on my palm. If only I could control it more, I could walk in there and have a better chance of walking out with Kade, alive.

It's hours later with my thoughts, and the sun dropping down when Darius speaks again.

"We will rest here tonight," Darius calls, and I look around, noticing we are nearing the end of the valley.

I walk over to the nearest tree, dropping my pack with a soft sigh and rolling my shoulders out. It's not exactly light.

"Come." I turn and see Darius walking a little ways away as the others look over at us.

I shrug my shoulders and follow behind him through the scattered trees.

Coming to a stop out of listening distance, he turns and a ball of his magic is already in his hands.

"Practice." He demands, and I scowl. "Let's see how you have improved."

"We have just been walking forever, why can't I rest a little while?" I can hear the whine in my voice but I don't care.

"That won't protect you. We have no idea what we are going into and you need to be safe."

I go to argue, but I see something in Darius's eyes that makes me stop short.

He's scared.

For me.

I give him a lingering look, but raise my hand. He must have sensed I called my magic, just like I can sense when he does the same, because he has balls formed in his hands the next second.

The air shifts around us and blue gently lights my palm. I focus on it, on the amount I let trickle into it, at the way I want to shape and mold it.

The circle grows slowly, and pulses bigger every few seconds as I lose hold on how fast magic pours into it.

I can create small balls to light the way, but anytime I do anything else with it, I just cannot grasp it enough.

Darius steps forward so he's right in front of me, his magic coming up and around my forearm.

"It's an extension of you, remember? So control the flow. Go too fast, and not only will it tire you more quickly, but it makes it volatile."

"I know all of this," I grit out, annoyed how his power just moves effortlessly along my arm, trying to soothe me.

"Knowing and doing are not the same." I huff out an annoyed breath. "Okay. Let's say hello to your wolf, shall we?"

"Wait," I manage to get out, but he's already putting a palm to my chest, and then blackness surrounds us again.

I blink my eyes open, looking around the dark space, the only light coming from my floating balls of magic.

"Is it even safe to do this now?" I ask Darius when he steps in beside me.

It's always strange being inside of myself, but even stranger when Darius is able to come too.

But to be honest, I wouldn't have even gotten this far without him.

"We are standing exactly where we are, frozen in place. The others will look out for us and this will be quick." He tucks a piece of my hair that's fallen behind my ear.

"Then what's the point if we are quick?"

He shrugs, taking a step forward. "I didn't want a certain wolf to feel left out in this training. No matter how small."

He didn't want Runa to feel lonely.

I blow out a breath at the emotions rising within me.

I stay back and watch as he moves forward into the darkness, but with him being made from it. It's almost like the darkness flows to him, crawling around his feet and up his body.

"Hello, wolf," he says, his tone controlled but somewhat soft. "Ready to come and see the lands?"

A snarl responds, and I walk toward where I see his back, anticipation running through me at seeing her.

I just need to see her, I need her to come to me.

"Runa?" I call, holding on to Darius's arm as a pair of blue eyes look toward me from the darkness.

I suck in a sharp breath, tears stinging the back of my eyes. I have felt her within me for so long, but I've never seen a part of her until now.

I stare, transfixed as Darius releases a rumbling purr. It's not one I hear from him a lot, so that must mean...

"Your wolf?" I manage to whisper, and he chuckles.

"He's waiting to meet her too."

"I am waiting to meet them both." I take a step forward, and the blue eyes blink, and then they're gone.

"Wait," I call, panic thrumming through me as I look around the space.

In the next moment, I'm looking at Darius's chest, my palm still out. I look around and notice we are back in the wooded area.

A dejected sound escapes me, and then a hand is on my nape, hauling me into a strong chest.

"Progress," he reminds me.

And though I don't agree, we don't have time.

He knows that.

I know that.

And everyone else will if I can't get my shit together.

Nineteen

Rhea

We carefully head down the steep incline to the bottom of the rocky hill we are on. Slowly and carefully I shuffle down, gripping boulders and trees as I go so I don't hurl myself down to the bottom.

"This isn't exactly safe," Colten says, losing his footing and slamming chest-first into a tree. "Fuck."

I laugh, grabbing onto a groove on the boulder as I look to where I'm heading next. "We used to climb the cliffsides, this is nothing."

"Sure," Colten groans. Hudson arrives at his side and peels him off the tree in the next moment. "I can do it," he snarls, and Josh and I share a look while Taylor huffs out an annoyed breath.

"Sure, pup, this way." With a hand on the top of his arm, Hudson guides Colten to another tree, his face set in a steely concentration.

I huff out another laugh.

"What's so funny?" Josh says, letting go of a branch and jogging down to another tree.

"Colten has been trained to be an Elite, but Hudson is always helping him. Colten acts like he hates it, but we all know better," I say quietly.

Josh snorts. "I'm not sure if they think we don't notice, or they don't care if we do."

I shrug, letting go of the groove and joining him against the tree with a laugh. "This is ridiculous," I blow out a piece of hair from my face.

Josh grins. "Nothing like going downhill first thing in the morning."

"It's so steep! I'm probably going to break an ankle." A hard stare hits the side of my face. "Or not, especially with my babysitter." I nod my head in Darius's direction.

"Really?" Darius says, stopping at the tree next to us. "I'm back to your babysitter?"

I eye him. "You have been on my ass since we left."

"And it's exactly where I will always be."

I scrunch my nose. "I can handle going down here without you being a constant shadow."

I don't know why I'm whining at him, it's not like I don't enjoy him always being at my back, watching me.

He eyes me back. "Are you being a brat?"

I blink. "Did you just call me a brat?" His face gives nothing away as Leo and Damion laugh. I call my magic and send it to the base of his tree.

It explodes on impact, and the tree Darius was using snaps at the base, then topples over.

Whoops.

I look at Josh and then head down the rest of the way together, laughing as Darius curses behind us.

"You are so dead," Josh whispers, looking behind him. "Oh he's mad."

I look too, and yep, he's mad.

"Way to show the Alpha, Rhea!" Damian calls and I smile.

Darius storms down the rest of the way, his eyes pinned to me as his face settles into a deep frown.

"Maybe you took it too far," Leo sighs.

I back away, hands held up. "Now just wait, you were being overbearing!" I say to Darius, defending myself. "I'm an Alpha too, or did you forget? You can't always—"

His hand is in my hair and my head is yanked back. "That

tree could have hit you on the way down," he says between gritted teeth while I blink up at him.

"But it didn't?" I try, making my face a picture of innocence.

An angry noise spills from him as his forehead lowers to mine. "Don't be so reckless! I'm already on edge with that rogue appearing and we have no idea what we are about to walk into," he hisses.

I soften at that, noticing the tension in his shoulders. "Okay, I won't do something like that again." I rub my nose with his, and he eyes me suspiciously. I raise my arm and tap my wrist, where the blood oath is. "I vow it."

He steps back, grunting in acknowledgement.

I didn't take into consideration that he may be feeling more on-edge than all of us. With having to leave Vokheim, the threat of Charles turning up at his keep at any time, and now walking into the unknown with his brothers and us... He has a lot to think about I guess.

A lot of worries to shoulder.

Maybe I shouldn't add to his load, but the tree was fucking funny.

Once we reach more level ground, I take in the massive boulders and small rock formations in the area. Some have formed bridges between levels and some look like they have steps at the side of them to reach the top.

It looks man made, rather than what the lands did.

"Does anything live down here?" I ask Darius, looking around.

"Many creatures live in The Drylands, the trolls are just one of those things," Darius answers, looking around for any signs of danger. "This is an area where they have been known to stay, but there are no signs they have been here for a long time."

I nearly trip over my feet. "What the fuck," I hiss. "Why in the Gods are we walking through here when there could be trolls?"

I do not want to meet a troll.

"Relax, little wolf. There is no one here—" he's cut off by a loud, growly chuffing sound, like the one back at the cave, and we all freeze in place.

"You were saying," I growl quietly at Darius, but in the next second, I choke on it as beings start appearing out of the rocks, seemingly coming out of nowhere.

I watch in horror as more and more are seen, and by the time I blink at the tall creatures, we find ourselves fully surrounded.

"Fucking trolls," Leo mutters as Josh looks over at me, worry written all over his face.

Darius steps up beside me, standing tall, like he's about to take them all on and get me out of here.

But even I don't think we can do anything, as there has to be at least forty of them, if not more.

Fuck.

They circle us, caging us within them and I can't help but look them over, even though I feel a slight shake to my legs.

They're tall, at least over seven feet, and their skin is a dusty beige, almost the same color as the rocks and boulders down here, making it easy for them to blend in. I look toward the one that's moving closer to us, my heart beating wildly in my chest the closer it gets.

The muscles in its biceps bulge, even as they hang by his side, and his chest is rock-solid. I move my gaze up to its mouth, and the tusks peeking out from the sides of it. They are white in color, but have dark patterns on them that must be in their own language. The troll has no hair on its head, its ears slightly pointed and my eyes move down when he reaches a few feet away from me.

Darius shifts at my side, stepping slightly in front of me as I look at its huge feet. Six toes and what looks like spurs circling his ankles which makes an impression in the ground. The troll makes another chuffing sound, this one deeper, and that's when my eyes move up to the fucking monster between its legs.

His legs.

It's soft against his thigh, but with my attention on it, it starts to slowly thicken and rise. I can't look away, the warning that the others uttered fleeting from my mind because I have never seen anything like this before, and I think that's the whole point.

My gaze moves over the bumps he now has on his fully, erect cock. The hair at the base is surprisingly groomed, with an array of small, colorful flowers nestled into them. His heavy set of balls are hairless, large, and smooth, just like the rest of him, and I watch as his tip leaks a scary amount of thick fluid.

"Don't look at his cock." Damian says quietly.

"I'm not looking at his cock," I reply.

"You're looking at his cock!" Josh whispers frantically down the link.

"I'm not!"

But I am. Oh Gods, I am.

The noise that leaves the troll next, like a quieter war cry, startles me from my staring and my head snaps up to his eyes, all white with just a black dot in the center. His gaze is pinned on me, and I swallow when his small nostrils flare.

Umm...

They told me not to look at a troll's cock, and I looked at a troll's cock and now we are all fucked because he looks at me like I'm something he wants. And I don't want him to look at me like I'm something he wants!

The troll takes a step forward, making a clicking sound, and I tense, feeling the others doing the same. We all reach for our blades slowly as the other trolls around us start stomping their feet, the dusty floor causing little flutters to circle where they stand. Nerves thrum through me as the troll in front of me bends his knees, and we prepare ourselves for an attack, to defend ourselves.

Just when I retrieve my blade from my hip, the troll starts to...dance?

I still, my mouth agape as he bounces up and down in his

slightly crouched position before rising and swaying his hips. He then begins thrusting forward violently, the fluid from his cock spraying forward in a splash. I jump back, my eyes wide, not wanting his thick, gray substance on me. I stare at the liquid in shock on the ground, following the trail back to his cock, my jaw still on the floor as I watch as he swings that monster from side to side, the flowers in his pubic hair seemingly vibrating with the movement.

All I can do is stare, flabbergasted as the stomping of the trolls surrounding us intensifies. We stay still, no one making a move as we are now all staring opened-mouthed, watching this troll do some sort of fucked up cock dance for us.

For me.

The troll suddenly slams his palms on the ground, and I flinch as rocks come to the surface out of nowhere. The troll grabs some small rocks in his hands, straightening to his full height and then begins to rub the smooth rocks over his body, his eyes closing as if he's in immense pleasure. He grunts, and more of that fluid spurts from his cock, that thing twitching. His hips start pumping, slow and sensual while making a chuffing noise, and his thick thighs bend, going lower as he pleases himself with the rubbing.

His eyes open suddenly, and pin me to the spot as the rocks crumble in his palms. Then he brings his hand down to his huge cock, gripping it tightly and starts to move his hips back and forth, thrusting into his hand.

I blink.

It doesn't take long before a deep, groan-like sound leaves him, and he uses his other hand to catch his own cum, making sure he collects it all. His body does a full shiver, and his hard cock softens, hanging between his thighs as he takes a step toward me, hand full of cum and all.

Darius tenses when he's a few steps away, a low growl peeling his lips back in a threat, and the troll's eyes snaps to his, a snarl on his tusk-filled mouth.

They eye each other in some sort of stand-off as the troll absent-mindedly passes his cum from hand to hand, and all I can do is stare at him in some sort of what-the-fuck trance.

The troll drops to his knees, the ground vibrating when his big body hits the floor, and then holds his hands out toward me, full of liquid. I look around at the other trolls, their faces stern but not harsh, and then look at the guys, who look like they ate something rotten. I lastly look towards Darius, his face full of anger as he still stares down at the troll, nostrils flaring and seemingly standing taller.

Another chuffing sound has my head swinging back to the huge troll on his knees, holding out hands full of cum to me like an offering.

"Oh, um... That's okay, you can keep it," I say gently, trying not to show the wince on my face. Another sound comes from him. "I'm okay, uh thank... you, though?" The sound is deeper, more demanding, and I raise a brow. "I don't want it, thank you. Maybe some of your... friends would like it?" The troll's eyes lower as I shake my head at him, a look of sadness crossing his face and I suddenly feel bad for him.

I go to take a step toward the troll when Darius hauls me in front of him, a murderous growl coming from deep within him as his hand goes to the front of my throat, his fingers tensing around it.

"She's mine," Darius says in a deadly tone as I feel his power accumulating. "Back, the fuck. Off."

TWENTY

Rhea

I stand still and hold my breath as the troll looks between Darius and I, his gaze moving down to the possessive hold Darius has around my throat, protecting my most vulnerable spot while also showing his claim.

I swallow against his hand, feeling him stroking the side of my neck with his thumb over my pulse as the trolls stare, watching everything. Darius lowers his head, like he can feel my nerves, and rubs his cheek against mine before letting loose his dominance.

It seeps into me, calling out my own, and some of the trolls knees hit the ground, unable to withstand the force of it.

They may not be wolves, but they can feel the power behind it.

I shiver at the display of it, goosebumps peppering my skin as an almost purr from Darius vibrates against my back, clearly happy with my reaction to him. But how can I not be when the male who won't leave my side, claiming me to be his, is showing just how strong he is to be able to keep me.

It settles that instinctive part deep within me that this male can fight for me to be his, that he has the power to back it up.

I lean further against him, rubbing my cheek back against his as he continues a low, deadly sound. Black wisps of power float out from him and come around to my sides, hovering there but not touching. With his hold on me, like I'm about to be ripped away, I know I'm not going anywhere unless he lets me.

The troll's eyes narrow at the black mist, then look over at the other trolls on their knees. He then does something unexpected. He smiles.

His surprisingly straight teeth show as he does so, and he rumbles a noise, his shoulders shaking.

It's then that I realize he's laughing.

Darius tenses at that, his low growl still going, and I move my hand up to his wrist, circling it with my fingers and calling some of my power to stroke over his skin.

"Dalie, Darius. Rey lo nok fel zah." *Calm, he will not hurt us.*

Darius's growl lessens at my words, his dominance slowly pulling back. I rein in my own, still clutching his wrist to keep him calm. I feel him tilt his head at the troll, the tension still thrumming through his body as we all stay silent.

"Dah lo nok," *I will not,* the troll replies, and I suck in a breath as my eyes widen. The troll smiles in return and raises a large hand, swiping it through the air and the other trolls stand at his silent command. "I understand, she is yours." He dips his head at Darius in acknowledgement.

"She is, do not try to mate her again," Darius snarls but the troll just smiles, nodding.

"Apologies."

Darius grunts.

"You speak the language of the old," I breathe out, my mind spinning with questions as Darius nearly whips his dick out in claiming me.

It is not bigger than the trolls, that's for sure.

"Kyt." *Yes,* the troll replies to me.

Oh my Gods.

Darius loosens his hold on my throat, his eyes still trained on the Troll. The rest of the trolls shuffle, and our small group tenses once again as they move toward the large troll before us, gathering behind him. The next second, they are dropping to their knees, heads bowed with two fingers resting over their hearts.

"Halis," *Heirs*, the troll's voice whispers, and the ground beneath us trembles.

I waver on my feet, Darius's hands coming to my waist to steady me as I look around in shock as smooth, polished stones appear around the trolls kneeling before us. The colors range from the darkest of black to the brightest of reds, to the deepest of blues, the brightest of oranges. The light reflects a prism of colors on the ground, shimmering in the sun so brightly I have to blink a few times.

"Well, shit," Leo chuckles, moving to stand next to us as the rest of our group follows.

"Where are they coming from?" Josh asks, stepping up beside me.

"What are they doing?" I wonder as I watch more and more stones appear.

Darius's breath tickles my ear. "They are an offering to us."

"An offering?"

He grunts. "Trolls keep these precious gemstones of the land buried deep within the earth. They are a rarity, spoken about in texts, the most prized possessions of the trolls. Not a single gemstone of the trolls has been seen in centuries."

I look upon the dozens of gemstones in awe, a kaleidoscope of colors littering the ground. "Wow," is all I say, not sure what it means, but in awe of its beauty. I've never seen anything like it.

"They are offering not only the gemstones, Rhea, but their loyalty." Shock courses through me, and I look over at the troll's lowered heads, seeing the smiles on their mouths.

"How do you know that?" I whisper.

Darius's breath tickles my ear. "My library has an abundance of knowledge."

"Remind me to read more." I want to know what other wonders are hidden between the pages at his keep.

The ground stops trembling and what I can only presume is the leader of this group lifts his head, a smile still on his face.

"We have been waiting for your return, Heir of Zahariss, Heir of Cazier," he says, reverence in his voice.

"Waiting for what?" Darius asks, the heat of his body still at my back, still protecting me.

"To right the wrong," he replies, and a harsh breath releases from me.

"Why do people keep saying that?" I turn my head to the side, looking up at Darius as he peers down at me. "Solvier said that... Belldame, and now..." I trail off, not even knowing the troll's name.

"Kruten," he says with pride, and stands, the other trolls still kneeling. "I am the leader of the Troxion Tribe," he waves a hand out. "Trolls."

"Nice to meet you, Kruten." If we ignore that he offered me his cum and made it spurt out of his cock like a waterfall. "Why do you say right the wrong?"

"Rogures," he spits, and I jolt, feeling Darius tense. "They are unnatural, caused by bad things. Bad blood."

"Bad blood?" I ask, my brows furrowing. My mind thinks back to what Sam once said about smelling bad iron.

"Do you know how to get rid of them?" Darius demands. "Where do they come from?"

The troll shakes his head. "I do not. Only that they are not meant for the lands. The bad is here too, similar, but more, maybe. Come. I will show you where you can rest safely and we can talk, Halis. It is not good to stand still for too long in The Drylands. It is much more unpredictable since more and more people come through here, as it is trying to defy the bad." He turns and starts walking between the kneeled trolls.

"What?" I say, peeling myself from Darius and ignoring his growl as I jog over to Kruten and stop him with a hand on his arm. Darius soon rips it off him a second later. A burst of my power coats my skin and I snarl at Darius, but he snarls back.

"Stop it," I growl at him, annoyed by his overprotectiveness at the moment. "What do you mean more people? Have you seen any wolf shifters?" I rush out to Kruten, my heart beating wildly within my chest.

"Kyt, many wolves. They seem to have set up further north." I turn my eyes to Darius as the others curse.

It's the same direction as the smoke.

Josh comes up to my side, linking his fingers with mine. Hesitance rests within his light-gray eyes as he squeezes my hand, knowing that this could mean our pack is there.

"It has to be them," Colten says, sliding up next to me with Hudson and Taylor.

"It must be," I tell Darius, who's scowling down at my hand in Josh's. But then his eyes move to mine, and soften, before looking at his men.

"Rhea," he says gently, moving a step closer. "They might not—"

"I know," I grind out. "Fuck I *know, okay?* But if they are there, they are strong, they have been through so much already." All members of my pack have been through their own torment. Torture. They will be okay. I just know they will.

I feel Josh's hand squeeze mine again as I babble that they will be fine, that they have to be there, and we can be together again. Bring them to Belldame where they will be safe behind her barrier. They can rest and heal.

They can go back to how things used to be.

All the while, the others look at me with concern, their eyes filled with pity that I loathe, but deep down, I know that my pack is there, and they are alive. Edward wouldn't have sent Illium to me otherwise. I know it.

They have to be alive.

They have to be.

We sit on the floor of a rock-made home around a small campfire. The warmth of it caresses our cold skin as the smoke flows out of an opening in the ceiling. The crackles and cracks are a balm to calm my racing heart over hearing the news about other wolves.

Elteru, one of Kruten's mates, places some very strange looking food down on a thin, stone slab in front of us all and fills our wooden cups with a sweet smelling liquid.

My cheeks heated when Kruten introduced us, knowing he had his cock out to pursue me to come into his home to join said mate, and others. Apparently with more females than males in this tribe, the females all agreed to share the males, if the males can seduce them with their dance.

The dance Kruten had given me.

I shiver and shuffle closer to Darius. Josh smirks at me, and I scowl, flipping him off knowing *he* knows I'm uncomfortable.

When Darius wraps an arm around my back, I stick my tongue out at him, knowing Darius is glaring at Josh over my head. I huff out a laugh when Josh rolls his eyes.

Ha, take that you shit, babysitter to the rescue!

Zaide clears his throat from across us, looking down and fiddling with his knife. Kruten looks at him, his frown clear to see as his nostrils flare.

"We meet again, wolf."

"We do." Zaide's voice is low, almost sounding bored, but his jaw ticks as Kruten makes sure the cloth he has wrapped around his waist is hiding the monster he pointed at me earlier.

I guess they do have clothes.

We thank Elteru when she finishes setting everything down and she moves over to Kruten, kissing one of his tusks and leaves the room.

I go to pick up a deep, pink strip of... something when Darius's fingers grab my wrist. My eyes connect with his, and he takes the meat from my hand, bringing it to his nose before taking a bite. I watch him chew slowly, eyes still on mine before he makes a small sound of approval and places the meat to my lips.

They part automatically for him, letting him feed me the meat and his eyes light in satisfaction of my easy acceptance.

I roll my eyes and he grins, feeding me more meat and paying no mind to the others that I feel are watching us closely.

His Elites and Josh have seen Darius do this on a few occasions since things have changed between us, but it still must be strange seeing us like this.

They don't know if we are enemies one moment or lovers the next.

"Good girl," he rumbles quietly. My cheeks heat at his words, knowing the others can hear him, but Darius doesn't seem to care about showing his affection, even in front of strangers.

"What do you know of the people coming into The Drylands," Leo asks as Darius continues to feed me after testing every piece, not trusting the troll in our presence.

I chew slowly, savoring the juices that flow on my tongue. Darius watches my mouth, his eyes darkening as I glare at him.

Now is not the damn time for him to devour me with his eyes, I nearly lost an eye to another cock just moments before!

"They have been coming to The Drylands for many years," Kruten says as he takes a sip from his cup. His words get my full attention, Darius's too. "We trolls have always had a comfortable, quiet life here, it is our home."

"That only the Elites and Highers are aware of," Zaide tells him, eating a strip of meat.

Kruten eyes him. "That seemed to be the case. Over the last thirty years or so, more and more have come to The Drylands. Many wolves. They didn't bother us trolls at first, and left us alone. We welcome all, but our home isn't for everyone." He picks up some meat on a bone and crunches it. "Then about two years ago, large numbers of wolf shifters started coming through here towards their encampment to the North. Whenever we are close to them, we don't see as many around than what we have seen pass through."

I push Darius's hand away as he tries to feed me more food, suddenly not hungry anymore at Kruten's words.

My eyes connect with my pack, and I know they are hit with the same thought.

Kruten has seen less than what has passed though. Will that be the same with my pack? And if so… that would mean…

Darius hauls me into his lap and holds me close to his chest. He makes a smooth, rumbling sound, knowing I need comfort without even asking. I breathe deep, looking at the other Elites whose eyes have turned hard at Kruten's words.

"They could be underground," Jerrod says, and I look at him. I forget the large male is here half the time. "That's why you might not have seen them around."

Fragile hope blooms in my chest at the thought. It's possible, more than possible if they are doing these… experiments on them.

My hope quickly turns to dread.

"This land changes though," Damian pipes in. "So they wouldn't be able to just stay there."

Kruten shakes his head. "It is more bad there. The land recoils from where they are, its presence not going near it. If it doesn't go near it, it does not change." He puts his hand to the floor and I watch as I see his fingers vibrate gently, like the ground is answering him. "We can stay here as we are with the land. They allow us and we accept it as they try to fight back the bad."

I lean forward and place my own hand on the ground, Darius's arm coming around my waist to hold me steady.

I bring my power gently to my palm, making sure the land knows I'm not a threat and ask for entrance. Once my power reaches the ground, a small, gentle glow of blue can be seen at the sides of my hand.

I feel something connecting with me, a soft *hello* that tickles, and I smile, closing my eyes. I feel the life inside, thrumming with power and gentleness. My magic pushes into the ground, twinning with something else, something almost playful, excited.

I haven't felt this response before, and I prod more at the ground, warmth filling me as a sense of peace hits my chest. It fills me, almost searching within me and I accept it, feeling like it's just another extension of myself.

"Little wolf," Darius says quietly by my ear. "Open your eyes."

I don't want to, I want to feel this way a little longer, but another strand reaches mine. Dark, quiet, but no less deadly if it wanted to be. But all I feel is comfort as Darius gently tugs my power from the land and guides my own back to me.

I slowly peel my eyes open and gasp.

I sit up straight, my eyes looking all around Kruten's home.

What was once just walls of rocks and slabs of stone acting as tables and units, is now covered in an array of flowers, stems, and vines. They crawl up the walls, a healthy green as they fill the room, with a bloom of color from the flowers.

A chuckle comes from my left and I see the look of awe on the Elites faces, and Josh looks at me with so much pride, my eyes water at the feeling. I clear my throat and smile sheepishly at Kruten.

"Uh, sorry." I shift in Darius's lap, unsure if I did something wrong when Darius holds me tight against him, forcing me to stop moving.

"Don't do that," he whispers roughly in my ear. That's when I feel the outline of his hard cock against me.

"Zahariss's Hali indeed," Kruten smiles, and I relax, knowing he's not upset with me.

"How do you know the language of the old?" Darius asks him as he leans down and picks up the wooden cup, bringing it up to my lips and making me take a sip of water.

"You call it the language of the old," Kruten replies. "But it is the language of Vrohkaria. The language of the—"

"Cannar," I interrupt, and he smiles at me and nods.

"Yes," he tells me. "The language of wolves."

"My mom told me all she knew about our line, about our Gods. The people have forgotten them even as they change into their wolves that they received from the Gods and run under the moon."

Kruten nods before he continues. "We may be trolls, but we have always been under the Gods's protection. They created the lands, ran around the earth, and played and danced. Creating rivers and caves and mountains and hills. Life. Without them, there is no us. No sun, no moon, no sky, land, or the below."

"Then why did they abandon us," Leo asks, and I look sharply at him. I know many feel that way, even I have at times when I have felt so low. But I just can't fully believe they would leave us. If I do, I lose all hope.

From what my mom told me, they loved the lands and its people. So why haven't they been around in so many years that they are now called the old Gods, and they are not prayed for anymore?

"They did not," Kruten says sadly, and my head flies back to him. "They were—"

"Leader," a troll rushes into the room, sweat beading his brow. "Something is happening to the land."

Kruten rushes to his feet. "What do you mean?" he demands, and we all stand at the nerves in his voice, Darius holding me close with a hand at the small of my back.

"It's splitting.

TWENTY ONE

Rhea

We rush outside, following Kruten and the other troll. A thunderous sound pierces through the air, and we look to the mountain side and see cracks forming in the rock. Stones fall down the mountain, tumbling and gaining speed until they crash onto the dry ground, smashing into pieces.

What the…

Another loud cracking sound draws my attention behind me to another mountain, seeing it split down the center so fast my eyes can't follow it. The ground rumbles beneath us, shaking like it's angry, and we waver on our feet, Dar's hand going to my arm to steady me. Another crack and shouts from around us spill into the air as trolls run out of their homes and come towards Kruten, their faces full of shock and fear.

Another crack, like roots splitting and my heart painfully beats in my chest.

"What is happening?" I shout over the crashing stones and splitting mountains. The ground starts to split in front of us, spider web cracks spreading and a gasp escapes me.

"We need to leave," Leo shouts, looking at the mountains in horror as one completely separates, and then starts to crumble.

"Move, now!" Darius orders us, and we do.

Kruten shouts for his tribe as we turn and run to the opposite end of this area, where it will be free of mountains and the threat of being crushed to death.

"Keep moving!" Darius pushes me in front of him, a hand

constantly on my back to urge me forward as I ask Runa for her strength.

She gives it, a whine coming from her as she can feel my panic.

Rubble crashes down on us at all sides, producing clouds of dusty smoke. I cough, rubbing my eyes as they water. A mountain to our right gives way next, and an almighty roar splits the air.

I almost trip over my feet, unable to believe what I'm seeing as I look to the skies. A large mouth, teeth bared, and then, a stream of fire follows it—spewing out like lava.

"Oh my Gods," I whisper to myself, my eyes wide as I take in another large ball of fire as it erupts out of its mouth and into the sky.

Its leathery wings the color of a coming storm in the sky spreading wide, gliding through the air with ease and I think... I think there is someone on its back.

"Is that a fucking dragon?!" I shriek, blinking the dust out of my eyes, wondering if I imagined it.

But there is no way I imagined that fire.

"Yes, now keep going," Darius growls, looking up at the fading dragon and ushering me forward. There was a dragon... a dragon! "Rhea," Darius snaps. "Focus!"

Right, yeah.

More stone gives way, tumbling around us, and I pick up the pace, Darius constantly at my back.

Josh pants at my side, his eyes glancing my way, then looking at Darius and nodding, picking up his speed with Colten, Hudson, and Taylor.

They know Darius won't let anything happen to me.

"Fuck," Leo curses, looking behind him as he runs next to Darius. "We need to move faster before they crash down on us."

"Don't let up," Damian says, running ahead of us before changing into his wolf.

Wait. *"Josh,"* I call down the link, and he tilts his head. *"Go wolf, tell the others.."*

"And the rest of you," Darius says to his men as he nods to Leo.

The next moment is a blur of fur and they take off. Thankfully, they are much faster on four paws.

"And you, Dar, go."

"You really think I would leave you, little wolf." I feel his magic at my back, like it's holding on.

No. I don't think he would.

I look around as more screams fill the air, and a troll gets crushed under a sheet of stone. I wince. What in the Gods caused the lands to do this.

I think back to the dragon. It looked like it came from within a mountain, but I don't think it caused this earthquake which is now turning into some rocky landslide at our back.

The rock-made houses of the trolls collapse in on themselves through the trembling of the ground, nothing but one with the earth as we keep moving around them, jumping over the rubble of their now destroyed homes. I cough, covering my mouth from the dust the devastation has created, blinking rapidly as it gets in my eyes again.

Trolls continue to be crushed under rock all around us, and I stumble as my heart clenches, slipping over stone, and that hand on my back urges me to keep going or we will be next.

Death surrounds us, cries, screams and rocks crunching and crashing are all that can be heard, along with the heartbeat in my ears. I take a peek behind me, to the rocks tumbling our way and I think we have enough time to get to the end of the valley, we can make it.

A devastating scream comes from up ahead, and my ears hone in on it. My eyes lock onto a female troll picking up rocks with desperate cries, moving them away from what looks like what was once her home.

The noises she's making are one of pain and heartbreak, and

I can hear them so clearly over the screams and shouts of others. I nudge Runa in her direction, demanding she give me more of her strength. I feel my power swelling within, filling me with a need to help her.

I will it to my feet, and then I'm moving, gliding, the fastest I have ever moved. I rush past trolls, avoiding their path as they run toward the cries.

"Rhea!" Darius shouts behind me. "Where are you going, it's not safe!"

I reach the troll within moments, ignoring the shouts at my back. I can feel Darius's furious growl in my soul, but I can't ignore the painful sounds coming from this troll.

"What's wrong," I ask her, stepping up to her side. She points towards the rubble with a trembling hand, panic in her wide eyes. I look down, heart hammering within my chest when I can just make out a small hand peeking out. "Fuck."

I lean down and grab the boulder that's on top of the body, digging my hands into the stone as best as I can and push. The female troll's palms land next to mine, trying to help with tears streaming down her dust covered face, but the boulder isn't moving.

Come on, Come on.

"We need to go, now Rhea!" Darius demands at my back when he reaches me, and I shake my head and grit my teeth, trying to push harder. Trying to get this fucking stone to move. To get to the small body beneath it.

The female troll is openly sobbing now, words and pleas coming from her mouth as she puts everything she has into it. She pulls back and throws her shoulder into the stone. It cuts her, red leaking out of her skin but she doesn't seem to notice.

"Help me Darius, vallier," I plead, not looking at him as I grunt and will my power to my hands. It doesn't listen, does not move from where it's settled at my feet.

"Rhea, fucking move!" he growls, grabbing hold of my shoulder.

I shrug him off aggressively. "No, help me."

"I will not risk your life over others!" He grabs my arms next, but I push him on a cry.

"Then help me so we can all get out of here!" I growl, trying to yank on my power, to move it, grab it, fucking shouting at it in my mind to move, but it doesn't.

I let out a frustrated sound.

"Gods dammit, little wolf."

Strong hands land beside mine, his body pressing into my back, and I watch inky blackness surround both of our hands and spreads over the boulder. I continue pushing, noticing the Elites and Josh have joined us, no longer in wolf, to try and move this small fucking mountain.

Darius grunts behind me, and I try to call for my power one more time, and this time, it answers.

Light blue mixes with Darius's black, the glow of my hands radiating on our faces as I put my all into pushing this boulder away. Black surrounds my blue, encasing it within as more of Darius's power is called from his hands.

The boulder groans, moving a little and hope surges within my chest.

"Together," Darius tells me against my ear as more of the mountains around us fall, the ground vibrating at our feet. "Now."

I push with everything I have, letting power rush out of me in a huge surge, not even trying to control it. Spider webs of cracks forms underneath my fingertip, the light of my blue and the dark of black peering out from within, almost having a purple tint to it.

Then the boulder shatters in a blast.

Stones fly out suddenly in an explosion, and I clench my eyes shut, waiting for the pain of it to hit me. Only it doesn't. I peel my eyes open, seeing a barrier of black surrounding me. But not only me, the others with us as well.

I reach behind me and squeeze Darius's hip in thanks before

he drops the barrier and we rush forward, the female troll the first to reach the limp form as she picks the child up and cradles him within her chest, crying loudly.

I swallow the lump in my throat and rush towards her, knowing we don't have a lot of time and need to move. I look at the child in her arms and without conscious thought, my shaky hands are moving and land on the boy. One on his forehead, the other over his heart.

My markings form upon my face, my fingertips once again glowing blue without my command. I can't stop it, can't change it, can't force it away as all I feel within me is the desire to see this child live as his labored breathing makes my stomach drop.

I feel it then, my power sinking into his skin and beneath his flesh. Muscle, ligaments, tendons, organs, cells. I feel it all, feel everything.

And I feel the damage.

Urgent voices echo around me, but I can't hear them, not really, it's just noise. The small child is bleeding within, near his chest and lower stomach, bones shattered and broken. I close my eyes as a familiar hand lands on my shoulder, but I don't move, I can't, it won't allow me.

I aim for the bleeding first, my strands flowing through his body to get to its destination. I reach for it, feeling where the torn tissue is, and my strands of power split off, using itself to stitch the wounds and begin to repair the damage. They crisscross with the flesh, pulling and tightening the tears closed.

I suck in a breath when I sense the blood slowing, my strands acting like it's a part of his body. I feel all this happening in all the places his body is damaged, in every single strand of my power and in every single piece it heals.

Once the last stitch is done, my power flows around the boy's entire body, leaving strands of my power within to hold further healing, going to the broken bones, and attaching itself to them to help the healing. Then it retreats back to me, less power than what I gave, and I slump back into a hard chest and open my eyes, seeing us once again caged within the dark.

"Breathe, Rhea, fuck!" Darius demands. "Not again." And suddenly, Josh is in my face, eyes full of worry.

Droplets of sweat flow down my temples and there's a burning sensation in my lungs, my heart slowing. My brows furrow, and my vision wavers, but then suddenly a large hand appears from behind me, forms a fist, and thumps my chest.

I gasp in a breath, cough and splutter at the force of it, taking in lungfuls of air when I can.

"Gods, Rhea," Darius says from behind me before I'm spun and picked up in his arms. "Don't fucking do that ever again," he growls as he drops his barrier and runs. His power comes around me, holding me steady.

Thicker dust clouds have formed around the area, the sounds of crashing stones hitting me so fast my head spins. Darius moves, still carrying me as we all run to the clearing that should be just up ahead. A small cry has my head snapping to the side, and I see the boy crying in his mother's arms as she weeps, kissing his head and holding him tightly as she keeps up with us.

Our eyes connect as I'm still coughing and spluttering, and they're full of gratitude and tears. I give her a small smile and wave her off, still trying to catch my breath.

"Jump it, now. There is no time to go around," I hear Zaide call, and I look in front of us, Darius holding me closer as he picks up speed.

"No, no fucking way are we making that," I screech, my fingers digging into Darius's shoulders.

The land has split completely ahead of us, like someone took a giant axe and cleaved it in two. The side we're on is slightly raised compared to the other side that's lower. I couldn't tell you how big of a gap has formed between them, but I know we are not going to make it to the other side.

"We're going to die, this is not how I die, Darius," I snarl at him. "I will not die by falling down a fucking hole!"

"You're not going to die," he scoffs at me like I'm ridiculous when he suddenly thinks I've sprouted fucking wings and can fly. "Hold on," he tells me, and I whimper, shoving my face into Darius's neck and closing my eyes. "I won't let you fall, Rhea."

I feel the moment his powerful legs bend, putting strength into them as he launches himself up and off the ground. I feel air brushing past me, feeling weightlessness as I scream into his neck, my stomach in my throat.

Oh shit, oh shit, oh shit.

Then, we descend.

My hair whips around us and my thighs squeeze his waist as I scream.

We are so going to fucking die.

But then I feel solid fucking ground and my teeth rattle on impact

Ow, that hurts.

An *oomph* leaves me as we roll, Darius's power leaping out of him and around me as we continue to tumble over the hard, rocky ground. His hand comes to the back of my head, holding me close, trying to protect me from any damage as he grunts in pain.

We roll one more time, and then come to a slow stop, Darius below me and me on top. Groans sound around us and I pant into his neck, trying to calm my racing heart.

Darius rubs my back, and I lift my head tentatively, moving the hair away from my face.

"I got you, it's okay," Darius murmurs to me as I try to calm my racing heart, sucking in deep breaths.

I sit up, my hands planting on Darius's chest as he moves his hands to my hips. I quickly look around.

The Elites, Josh and trolls are all sprawled out on the dirt ground we're on, breathing heavily as they catch their breath. Crumbling sounds pierce the air behind us, and I look back to the bit of land we just jumped from as parts of it break off and fall into the large ravine that separates us.

The ravine we could have fallen to our death in.

"Gods," I mutter, waiting as the last of the mountain on the other side falls, dust climbing in the air from it, forming a cloud and obscuring my vision of the other side.

"Well," Damian mutters, and my eyes go to him star-fishing on the floor next to Taylor. "I don't want to do that again."

Leo rolls his eyes and Jerrod kicks his legs. A laugh tumbles out of me on its own accord as everyone agrees.

Definitely do not want to do that again.

A squeeze on my hips has my eyes going back to Darius, a smirk upon his lips. I narrow my eyes at him.

"Don't say a word," I warn, my eyes glaring as my cheeks heat.

His smile stretches, knowing I'm embarrassed about thinking we would fall to our death.

In my defense, there is a giant fucking hole in the ground.

I ignore Darius's smile and look over him, searching for any injury as he does the same to me. Apart from the dirt that clings to us, we came out unscathed other than a few scratches. More on Darius than me as he protected me.

"I told you that you weren't going to die," he says smugly. "I never took you as a dramatic one." The amusement on his face is plain to see, and I scowl down at him.

"We are wolves, not fucking dragons. We like the ground."

A laugh rumbles from his chest and the sound goes straight to my heart. "Imagine where I could fuck you if we had wings," he muses, and I raise a brow.

"That is the first thought in your mind after we took a leap of death?" Is he insane?

"Oh, little wolf," he purrs, and I dig my fingers into his chest. "I'm always thinking about fucking you."

"What is wrong with you," I groan, leaning forward and putting my face back against his neck to hide my heating cheeks again.

"When you are one with your wolf, you will feel the same and want to fuck me all the time too," he chuckles again, bringing a hand to the back of my head and running his fingers through my hair, a hum leaving him.

"What now," I mumble against his chin as the fingers on his other hand move up and down my spine.

He sighs. "We continue forward. I don't think it's best to stay in one place for a long period of time if the land is just splitting."

"Why did it do that?"

"I don't know, little wolf, I don't know."

I get up, groaning at the stiffness in my limbs as the others all get to their feet. Darius places a kiss to my lips, his nose rubbing mine before moving past me to speak to his men.

I look around and spot Josh still on the ground, holding his leg with his face twisted in pain. Rushing toward him, I crouch down and put my hand over his own on his leg.

"What's wrong?" I ask, moving his hand out of the way frantically and seeing a gash in his leg.

"Just a scratch," he says gruffly as I wince and press my hand down on the bleeding.

"Just a scratch my ass," I mutter and close my eyes, wondering if I can heal him somehow like I did to the boy.

I concentrate as the palm of my hand warms, moving some of my power slowly toward it, and it does. I ignore Josh's protests, and I block him out and let my strands seep into his leg.

The damage isn't much, but it's far from just a scratch.

The wound is deep, but thankfully nothing serious. He would heal in no time thanks to his wolf. But we haven't got time and I don't want to see him in any pain either.

I feel my strands hooking themselves into the skin on either side of the cut while others are inside of it, adding power to his own cells to heal it faster. I also feel my power grabbing little bits of grain like stone and pushing them to the surface, removing them from his body. My strands circle each one, finding anything foreign that shouldn't be there and clearing it out.

I never knew I could ever do this, and I have to wonder why I can now.

Once the bleeding has stopped and I feel the last of the wound being stitched together, I open my eyes and suck in a sharp breath. The gentle glow of my power shines against his skin, showing how it weaved itself into his flesh and closed the wound.

"Wow," Josh says and I look up at him to see his wide eyes staring at his now closed wound. "How did you do that?"

"I have no idea," I sigh, feeling tired. After healing the little boy, and now this, exhaustion runs through me but I can't stop and rest now. "Anna would be proud though, she loves her stitches."

He chuckles and nods. "She would."

I search inside of me and feel Runa, mentally stroking my hand over her head in thanks for lending me her strength. She's tired too.

My power also feels calmer, less chaotic, but I can tell it still has that wildness that's ready to move at any moment. I can't imagine what it would feel like if it is fully settled, if it was always balanced, calm, like an extension of myself like Darius said his was.

I stand on shaky legs and Josh stands beside me, gripping my arm when I falter to the side. "Rhea," he says, the worry clearly heard in his tone. He looks down at his leg. "You shouldn't have done that," he chastises.

I give him a small smile. "I'm fine, promise." I wave him off and we walk over to the others. I feel his eyes on me, knowing I'm lying, but we don't have time to fuck around.

I'm a little tired, I'm not dead.

"Where will you go," I hear Leo ask Kruten as we reach the

group.

"We will go to the west lands," Kruten says as he looks behind him at his tribe. "The further away from the bad, the better. We will search until we find a new home to settle. I cannot risk any more of my tribe, we have lost many whom we need to honor." His face falls when he thinks about those that got crushed under the falling mountains, and my own heart aches.

Losing someone is never easy, but always inevitable eventually. Only you want it to be from old age, not to be taken far too soon.

A tap on my arm has me looking to the side, and I see the female troll we helped. The braids of her dark hair fall loosely over her chest, and the boy that must be her son, plays with one. He looks at me warily, and I give him a smile, raising my hand slowly to touch the short hair on his head. The male trolls must shave it when he's of age as the other older males are all bald.

"I thank you, Hali," the female says, her voice soft. "I am in your debt." She bows her head and holds her son tighter.

I shake my head. "You owe me nothing," I tell her softly. Looking down at the boy, my heart clenching at the sudden memory of me doing the same with Kade when he was younger, holding him close when his nightmares got too much or he hurt himself. Gods I miss him. "Just hold him close and keep him safe." I swallow roughly, giving her one last smile before I move to stand beside Darius.

He runs a finger down the side of my cheek as I peer up at him, noting the softness in his gaze as he follows his finger along my skin. I'm sure my heartache is clear to see on my face, and what the cause of that ache is.

I look around the area, noticing all who came with us to The Drylands are safe. They look a little worse for wear, especially Jerrod who has a large wound running down his cheek. He doesn't seem to care for the droplets of blood that drips from him and is collecting in a small pool at his feet.

His eyes meet mine briefly, and he answers the unvoiced question in my eyes of healing him by the small shake of his head.

"We will continue toward where we saw smoke, and then leave The Drylands," Darius tells Kruten.

He nods. "It will be wise if this is how the land is acting."

"Why did it do that?" I ask.

"I do not know, Halis. It seems as though we are not the only ones it disturbed." He frowns as he looks to the west, and then back at his tribe. "I just hope it does not happen again. We cannot lose anymore."

I look behind him at his tribe huddled together. Some weep, and some stare into the distance.

"I hope they run free," I tell him, referring to the dead.

Sorry won't make it okay, it won't bring back the dead.

He dips his head to me. "We thank you for your help. We stand with Halis, with the Gods." His eyes come to meet mine. "The Gods didn't abandon us, Hali, do not think they did. They were stolen from us." Stolen? "Call through the lands if you need us, we will come." My brow furrows as the guys look at me. "You will know what to do." I go to open my mouth to speak, but he bows his head again and turns towards his tribe that's preparing to leave.

I shift uncomfortably as the guys stare at me.

"What?" I grumble, not liking the too-intense eyes on me, not liking that I just realized I'm the only female here.

If Anna was here, she would back me up and tell them to stop staring.

"You seem to be collecting beings wherever you go," Leo says, eyeing me.

"Do you think it's witchcraft?" Damian says, tilting his head. "She does have that blood witch in her pack."

Zaide grunts. "The witch wouldn't put something so pathetic on anyone."

We all look at Zaide in surprise, but he takes a knife out and sharpens it.

"I'm not spelled," I say. "They just want what's best for the lands, like we do."

Though call them through the lands?

How am I supposed to know how to do that?

"Let's move. I don't think we want to stay here and risk the chance of having the land cracking beneath our feet again," Darius says.

That, I agree with.

We head further into The Drylands, my eyes looking at Josh's injury and seeing that he's walking fine on it.

I look down at my hands in wonder, wiggling each finger.

"We will speak on it later," Darius says to me and I nod.

The smoke can be seen more clearly the deeper we go, just a day or two away.

A day or two from hopefully seeing my pack again. Alive.

Gods, please be alive.

A chill settles in my bones, and I pull my hood up over my head, hating that we didn't manage to grab some of our packs so we don't have any extra clothing.

I stroke over my pocket, feeling the port stone and the glass wolf Darius gave me there, safe and sound.

It will be okay, it has to be.

TWENTY TWO

Darius

Grabbing another small log, I heft it up into my arms as Leo and Damian do the same beside me. We are exposed, staying out in the open for the night instead of a cave, but with the land acting strangely, we don't want to risk being crushed under stone.

"Do you think her pack is there?" Leo whispers quietly, and Damian looks over at him.

I sigh. "For her sake, I hope so, and alive."

"We have no idea what we are walking into," Damian mutters, picking up a stick. "We are completely blind apart from information from a Higher."

Just like me, he doesn't trust the male either.

"We are Elites," I remind him, "We are always walking into situations with limited knowledge." Turning to walk back. "As for the Higher. Rhea trusts him, that has to mean something."

"Doesn't mean we trust him though," Damian mutters.

"Correct," I agree.

Leo huffs. "I can't wait to kill some pricks anyway, it's been too long, I'm getting itchy."

Damian smiles. "Bloodthirsty fucker, we just sparred the other day. You nearly broke my nose."

Leo shrugs. "Yeah, but I don't want to actually kill you. Zaide and Jerrod are agitated too."

I suspect both are for different reasons.

One being away from a certain witch, and the other to get

to a mother and her child.

"Just don't mention anything to Rhea, I don't want her to be more upset than she already is." I check ahead to see that she is far away from being able to hear us.

She's sat next to Josh, both of them building a campfire we will have no choice but to use. Taylor stands with his back turned, looking out into the distance for threats.

Zaide and Jerrod are opposite, doing the same while Hudson and Colten sit on the ground.

When Rhea suddenly smiles at Josh for whatever he says, a growl builds in my throat, but for once, I swallow it down, knowing that she needs his comfort.

Just until I get back, I tell myself, still wanting to remove his head from his shoulders.

"It is strange seeing you like this," Leo muses, amusement filling his tone. My eyes flick to him. "I never said it wasn't a good thing, drop your glare," he chuckles.

"I agree, very strange," Damian reaches up and snaps a branch. "But I like her, we all do. We also like her giving you shit. She has you wrapped around her little paw."

"Fuck off," I grumble.

"Ha!" he says. "Don't pretend you don't love it." I smirk but say nothing. Then his tone becomes serious as he stops and turns fully toward me. "We will take care of her like our own. You know that, right?"

I straighten to my full height at his seriousness, and walk over to him. "I know that." I place a hand on his shoulder and squeeze. "I know, brother. I appreciate it."

Leo comes to my side and nudges my arm. "Always."

"Come on, let's head back," I say, having gathered enough wood.

Reaching Rhea, her head lifts instantly, and the satisfaction that her attention comes to me right away makes a rumbling purr begin in my chest.

We put the wood in the center, and Hudson moves forward,

scraping stones together to cause a spark. Once flames start to appear, I call my power and put a barrier up around us.

It's completely solid, no one being able to see us but I leave an opening at the top for smoke to escape through.

The fire will keep us warm tonight. I would rather we didn't risk drawing any attention to ourselves, but our body heat won't suffice.

I feel a tingle and look to my right, watching as Rhea strokes her fingers down my barrier.

Unable to resist any longer, not that I would want to, I move toward her, watching as her eyes stay on mine.

Josh moves to the other members of his pack, and I grab Rhea by the waist and lay her down next to me, encasing her body as much as I can with mine.

The others settle down for the long night, keeping close to the fire as Rhea and I just watch each other.

The things I would do to keep her eyes on mine...

"Healing?" I ask, keeping my voice low so it feels like it's only us here.

If this is something she can do, she can heal herself if she were ever to be injured.

She nods, raising a hand and placing it on my chest. The contact has that purr softly releasing from me.

"It seems so," she says, and I notice how tired she looks. "It was a surprise, but it just felt like I needed to do it with that child. It was a calling I could have never refused."

I nod. "Then don't refuse it, but if it puts you in danger, I will remove you from it."

She huffs out a laugh, but then yawns. "Ever the protector."

She will one day understand my need to keep her safe.

When she is one with her wolf, she will feel the connection fully between us, feel the way I crave her all the time.

I can't wait for that day where she will be fully mine.

As soon as we are done in The Drylands, I'm getting her wolf out and we will stand under the moonlight.

Like we were always meant to be.

"Sleep, little wolf, rest up."

She hums, snuggling closer to my chest, into the safety of my arms and my purr gets a little louder in satisfaction as both of our wolves greet each other.

I inhale her, wanting to bathe in her scent as she slowly drifts off to sleep.

Trusting me.

I know then that there is nothing I wouldn't do. No one I wouldn't kill, and nothing I wouldn't remove if she was ever taken from me.

I pull her even closer, closing my eyes as I hold the most important thing in my arms.

TWENTY THREE

Rhea

Walking and barely sleeping for three days really strains the body, especially when it's been over a week since we entered The Drylands.

The mood is tense between us, like a thick cloud among our small group, even though we have been as normal as ever with each other.

But we are full of aches, pains, and frustration. We are all exhausted, barely resting as the land continues to change, making it hard to rest for a long period.

Making it harder for my magic to recover.

We can smell the fire from where the smoke is coming from up ahead, as we navigate through thick woods. The trees are full of life for the time of year, and I never would have expected to see such vibrant green of the leaves on the trees considering the ground is so dry.

So dead.

We navigate around the trees, all of us eating meat from a deer Zaide caught the night before. Jerrod, Damian, and Taylor made us water skins, which we used to collect water from a small river we came across.

Darius wouldn't let me take a sip unless he tasted it, even after arguing with him long enough that I could do it myself. I just gave up, accepting that he wanted to be the one to provide for me.

Insufferable male.

I should count myself lucky I was even allowed to eat the strip of meat without him holding it to my mouth, watching me so intently as I took small bites.

I've never been fed so much in my life, but I think his wolf side is driving him to provide for me in any way he can. It's unusually more intimate than anything we have ever done, but now it's not uncomfortable anymore. It's natural, almost.

I know he will take the best pieces of meat and hold it to my mouth to eat, and then I know he will always look around while I eat or drink, making sure no danger is near.

It's foreign having someone focused so intently on me and protecting us. I don't hate it, I almost wait for it now.

To watch him as he watches me, before scanning the area with sharp eyes until they return to me. It makes something inside of me warm, and my chest feel tight.

I look at Darius out of the corner of my eye now, seeing him do just exactly what I'm thinking about.

His gaze travels all around us, but then his eyes dart in front of me to the ground, making sure nothing is in my way as I walk. Once satisfied, he turns to me briefly, making sure I'm eating and then repeating the process all over again.

I smile to myself, my cheeks heating as I spot Josh next to me, wiggling his eyebrows, and I lightly shove his shoulder. I worry about him being away from Sarah.

He's anxious, and twitchy to be back to her. He wanted to come with us though, needed to. It's been him and I since we left the Aragnis pack, and I know he wants our pack back just as much as I do. And Kade.

Your child always comes before anything and everyone. And that is what Kade is to me, to Josh. We treat him as such, love him as such, and we will do whatever we need to do for him.

Consequences be damned.

If I need to go up to Wolvorn Castle and exchange myself for him to get him back, I would, but I know Charles would never do that. He would say he would, but then he would keep us both and use Kade against me.

I can't put him through any more than he already has been, so I need to find a way to get to him.

As soon as we get my pack back, the next focus is Kade, just like Darius said. If I can find a way to sneak into Wolvorn and kill them all, I will. But I need to be sure I can do it.

Runa growls inside of me, liking the bloodshed that will happen. If only she would come out and help us, help us with my Heir power so I can be what I need to be.

And I need to be able to kill all Highers.

We round another set of thick trees, the smell of smoke hitting us stronger than ever and we come to a halt. My gaze fixates on the camp in front of me, my breathing picking up. Darius motions for us to crouch low, and we do, looking around at the males standing guard around a dark, stone, one-story building.

There's a campfire in front of it, and I count five males surrounding the structure. Their armor black with their wrist and shin guards green, letting us know they are the Highers's guard.

This must be where Edward mentioned? Or else why would the Highers's guards be here?

I grind my teeth and look at Darius. His nostrils flare and the anger in his eyes sends a shiver down my spine. He is furious.

"What now?" Leo whispers, looking at Darius for the command.

I can hear Darius grinding his teeth. "We kill them and infiltrate the building. They are clearly guarding something and we need to find out what."

"Our pack," Josh whispers and my heart rate picks up.

"Be prepared for what we may find in there," Darius says quietly to me, nodding to the building. "It is small."

I know what he means. Too small to hide many pack members, or none at all.

I give him a nod, letting him know I hear him as I try to stop my heart from crumbling.

Darius unsheathes his blades and we all follow his lead. "Let's go."

We head back into the cover of the trees and walk silently to the left so we can get around the back of the building. Keeping our eyes on the guards, we trail after Darius.

Leo has an arrow already nocked in his bow, Zaide has his twin blades ready, and Jerrod has his axe in his hand with Taylor at his side. Josh, Hudson, Colten, and Damian are at the back with me, faces set into hard lines and I pull my mask up to cover the bottom half of my face.

Killing never comes easily, but it does with the enemy. We could just render them unconscious, but there is no guarantee we can do it quick enough that the others won't port out and call for backup and inform the Highers's witches. Then the Higher's themselves could come, knowing we are here and Darius's plans to keep them in the unknown for as long as possible will be forfeit.

We know that the Higher's guards aren't out in the Drylands for a fucking picnic or a change of scenery.

They are guarding something important.

Darius motions for me to move forward toward the tree line. "Wait here with Josh," he whispers to me, begrudgingly. I open my mouth to protest, but he puts a palm over my mouth. "We know how each other works," he says, nodding to his men. "I'm sending Hudson, Colten, and Taylor to watch the other side. We can handle this easily, I don't need to be worrying where you are. I know you can fight," he tells me quickly, and it soothes me a little. "But when we need to take them down as fast as possible, just know we can do it without a hitch. Tell me you understand and you will do as you're told." He implores me with his eyes.

I look deeply into them, and I see the worry there he's trying to hide from me.

"Kyt," I whisper to him. "I understand."

And I do. They have fought together for years. Their moves and placement will be natural, throwing my pack and I into the mix and risk being known, it's not worth it.

Darius's shoulders relax instantly, and he leans forward and pulls my mask down, rubbing his nose against mine before putting my mask back in place. Everyone follows suit, hiding their faces as Darius nods to his Elites. With one last look at me, he moves, his men following and my pack to do his bidding, leaving me with Josh.

Two guards appear at the back of the building, not even scanning the area, far too comfortable to not know the threat that lurks within the trees.

Josh and I watch as the Elites silently pick up speed and walk toward the back of the building where the two guards begin to talk quietly.

Too relaxed for their own good.

I see Leo adjust his bow, and not a second later, the arrow flies through the air, hitting its target in the side of the neck. The other guard barely has enough time to blink before a small knife from Zaide lodges in his throat.

Both their hands lift to their necks, blood seeping out of their mouths before they collapse to the floor, just as the Elites reach them. Darius places his blade on one of the guards chest and pushes deep while Jerrod brings his axe down on the other. Leo pulls his arrow out of the now-dead guard's throat and they all split up.

All of that happened in mere moments.

Darius, Leo, and Damian move to one side of the back of the building, as Jerrod and Zaide move to the other. I look across and see my pack in position to watch them as we do, our gaze moving to the remaining guards up front around the campfire.

They heard nothing of the Elite's silent attack behind the building.

Then without warning, they attack the remaining guards.

They don't bother to hide themselves this time as they emerge around the building and the guards turn, shouts of surprise coming from them.

That's when I hear it, a twig snapping.

I move to stand, the sound of footsteps reaching me.

"Josh."

"I know." He replies instantly.

We didn't even hear them until they were practically on top of us, too focused on the others. That is a mistake that shouldn't happen.

Nerves running through me, and I turn as Josh gets to his feet. I take the blade from my hip, tightening my grip on it as two guards emerge from behind a tree and come straight for us.

With no other choice but to act, I go for the one on the left, Josh on the right.

I raise my blade and swing, aiming to take off his head as Runa growls within me. The guard's ragged face twists into a snarl, leaning back to avoid the strike, then raises his foot to kick me in the stomach.

Fuck.

I let out a small growl when it connects, pain flaring inside of me.

"We have a rabbit in the woods," the guard says, coming for me again. "What are you doing out here, hmm?"

I push my blade hand outward, the clink of metal on metal sounding around us as I block his sword away from the side of my head.

"Who the fuck are you? Reveal yourself!" the guard demands, his dark eyes assessing me as he briefly looks over at Josh and the other guard.

I ignore him as he pushes forward on his blade and I push back, knocking him a few steps. He growls and comes at me, and I block him the best I can as I go on the defense.

Damn, he's strong.

He swings his sword back and turns with it, swinging it down on me. I bring my blade up above my head to stop it, the strength behind it causing me to stumble back, shocked that the blade in my hand didn't break.

He moves again, his sword stabbing straight towards my chest and I turn quickly. Hissing as it connects with my arm but managing to avoid it going through my chest. I move forward and grab his wrist when I dodge his lunge and I pull toward me.

Using the momentum, I bend forward, using my shoulder to propel him over my back. He lands on the floor with a thud, and I turn quickly, but his sword lashes out and gets me on the top of my thigh.

I waver a little, but then I'm stepping on his sword hand and pressing down with my good leg. Bringing my blade up quickly as I pant, I don't waste any more time shoving it straight through his chest unaimed, just needing to subdue him as his other hand comes toward me.

He groans, moving to grab the blade but I take it out and then it's in his heart. He goes limp beneath me, unseeing eyes wide as they stare at me, no essence leaving him.

I gasp heavily, taking my blade out of his body and look to see Josh coming toward me, a body laying still on the floor behind him.

"You good?" he asks, looking at my injuries. I nod. "Let's move, I don't know if there are others but I can't sense them."

"I can't either, I think it was just these two. We need to get inside the building in case there are more." I move forward, trying not to limp with the gash in my thigh and ignore the pain in my arm.

Josh follows close behind me, checking our backs.

I look across from me and see the rest of my pack making their way to the Elites as we emerge from the trees and head around the side of the building, aiming for the front. When we reach it, I spot Damian striking the last guard in the stomach, his face thunderous before he does it again and again, until the guard drops to the floor.

The others stand over four more dead guards, wiping their weapons on the bodies to clean the blood off.

I move to the double doors and turn the circle handle, twisting it to open, not bothering to wait for Darius as desperation runs through me with a heavy dose of dread.

Please be here, please be alive.

The blood rushes in my ears as complete silence reaches me as we step into the dark building illuminated by a single torch on the wall.

Josh stays at my back as the door slams behind us.

The room is practically bare, only a single table and a few chairs to be seen.

"No," I whisper, devastation washing over me. I limp further into the room, going into an open doorway further to the left, but only finding bed rolls on the floor and nothing else. "Fuck."

"Rhea," Josh starts.

"They should have been here!" I run my hands through my hair, messing up my ponytail as I pull my mask down.

A harsh *creak*, and then heavy footsteps reach my ears before I'm spun around and facing a furious Darius. "Don't ever fucking walk into a building blind like—"

A muffled scream rents the air, stilling us, and my heart.

We leave the room of bedrolls and look toward the back of the stone building—like the others are, seeing nothing, but we all heard it.

I swallow. "Where did that come from," I whisper, shivering as cold seeps into my bones.

Another scream, and all of our heads turn to the stone floor at the very back. I take a tentative step forward, but I'm halted by a hard grip on my arm.

Darius looks at the blood seeping from my arm and leg, his nostrils flaring at my injuries. "I'm fine," I tell him.

"Heal yourself!" He demands, his eyes murderous but another scream reaches us.

"Later," I say quietly, even knowing that I can't.

Darius growls quietly and moves in front of me, his steps light until he reaches the back wall.

His brows furrow as he reaches out, moving his hands over the dark stone, checking the grooves. I see the black color of his power at his fingertips seeping into the cracks, grazing them along the stone when his head suddenly snaps to the floor.

"Rhea," he murmurs, "come."

"What is it?" Leo asks, but Darius doesn't reply.

I didn't even know everyone was in here with us.

I move and stand beside Darius, ignoring how my blood subtly leaves droplets as I go. He grabs my hand and pulls me down to a crouch with him gently, but I hiss at the burning in my thigh.

He growls low. "Who the fuck did that to you?"

"Dead."

"Good, now speed up your healing," he demands.

"I don't know how," I admit. I need to save my energy anyway in case we need it.

Darius's stare is hard on the side of my face and I don't want to see the look on his face.

Growling, he stands suddenly, lifting his armor to the t-shirt beneath. He rips off a piece easily, and then he's crouching back down beside me again.

"Rise." I hold his shoulder as I stand, and he carefully wraps my thigh, his eyes hardening as blood pulses out as he tightens it.

He rubs over the t-shirt gently, and then guides me to crouch again.

"Okay?"

I nod. "I'm okay."

He grabs my hand and places it onto the stone floor. My power answers the call of the runes placed there instantly.

My eyes widen as my palm heats, and our magic seeps into

the runes as they glow, breaking them up and un-writing them, just like they did in his father's basement.

"Dar," I say, hating the tremble in my voice, but hating what we could find even more if it's anything like what we found in his father's basement.

He squeezes my hand in comfort and we watch as the runes glow one last time before they disappear. We stand as one and move back as the stone trembles at our feet. The ground unravels, moving aside to reveal stone steps leading down into the dark.

"What the fuck," Damian says, and Zaide comes closer, looking down.

"Can we all fit in there?" Jerrod asks.

"It will be a tight squeeze, but we will," Leo says, coming up to stand next to Zaide, eyes hard.

"We need to be careful," Taylor says, and Hudson and Colten nod.

Darius looks at me and another muffled scream comes from below. I flinch.

"Stick close, be on guard. Attack first, no questions," he orders. "Questions could get you killed."

Darius holds my eyes a moment longer, and I answer with my own.

I'm ready.

He starts his descent, gripping my hand to pull me behind him before he lets go when I'm close to his back. My palm hits the damp stone as stale water hits my senses, and I try to get my breathing under control in the tight space.

It's like it's getting worse. Like I can feel the dread we are about to enter.

I hear cursing from the others behind me, knowing the larger Elites will feel cramped.

"Rhea, light," Darius says in front of me, and I raise my other hand, letting a small ball of power form so we have a subtle glow.

Earth and stone surround us as we go further down in the dark, down to Gods knows where. I grip the back of Darius's armor once more. The feeling of being suffocated creeping in, but it's not as bad now, letting my will to see if my pack is down here keep the worst at bay.

"We're here," Josh whispers behind me.

"I know," I reply through the link, unable to speak aloud right now.

The scream comes again, and my stomach rolls when I realize it's female.

Light appears at what seems to be the end of the steps, and I have no idea how deep we have gone down. When we reach the bottom, Darius pauses in the narrow stairway, tilts his head to listen for a moment, and then he opens the door.

I grip my blade, ready for anything as I leave the ball of magic on my hand in case I need it, hoping I can at least do something accurate with it.

But the room is empty as we all shuffle in.

There is evidence that many are here, though. There are tables, food and more bedrolls than the other room. Weapons are in stacks in one corner while another large table holds papers and scrolls recklessly stacked all over it.

Darius and I go over to it, quickly scanning them to see notes and numbers, vials and orders for more ingredients.

Ingredients that are familiar.

Darius and I share a look.

A single door at the back of the room calls all of our attention, and we move slowly as one. No one says a word as we make for the wooden door, briefly glancing at the items in the room again while remaining silent.

Darius grips the handle, looking back at us one more time, making sure we're ready, before he pulls it open slowly.

My heart beats wildly within my chest as the scent of blood follows with sweat and mildew, and something else I can't place. I breathe out through my nose and in through my mouth as I put my mask back in place, not wanting to take the scent in.

Darius moves forward and we follow, then pause. We've entered a long, narrow room, balls of light hanging from the dark ceiling, casting their glow on the stone rows on either side of the room. Rows that have bars.

I move forward cautiously, Darius at my back as I lift my hand to cast some light inside one of the cells. I clear my throat quietly when I spot the unmoving body within.

Gods.

This is worse than Darius's father's basement.

Taking a breath, I look at the female's belly that's swollen and bulging, like it was about to burst. Her sides have claw-like marks on them, deep and oozing with blood that is still very much fresh. She doesn't twitch, her chest still and her head is turned away from us. Her hair matted and cast over her face.

What in the Gods did this to her.

Darius's chest rumbles angrily as my stomach drops, thinking about the last cage we saw, thinking of what may have happened in my own.

I move to the next one, my hands shaking as I see another female. This time, she is on her back, legs wide open. All that is left between her thighs is a gruesome hole. She also has claw marks on the inside of her thighs, her breasts, and shoulders. Her dead eyes look up to the ceiling, her face blank.

Tears prick my eyes at the sickening scene, my brain taking it all in but then not at all.

"Fuck," I hear Josh whisper, and see him looking in another cell across from me, his eyes full of pain.

Colten gags while Hudson rubs his back, drawing the younger male into his chest as Taylor's fists clench at his sides.

"What the fuck is this," Leo croaks out as the other Elites shake their heads.

Darius moves from my back, looking into the next one, and his jaw ticks, his hand tightening around his blade. We all move forward, looking in cell after cell at the horrors that lay within.

With each one I hope not a single one is my pack member. Some we can't even tell though, their faces ripped open as well as their bodies.

One thing is common though, they are all female.

The second-to-last cell on our side, Darius stares within it longer than the others, his face a mask of cold, hard fury. I come up next to him, bracing myself for what I'm about to see when I let out a startled noise.

I grip his arm as I look over the gray, clumpy skin of hind legs, recognizing it instantly. But then I move my stare up to the pale legs on either side of the rogures's hips on the floor, my heart hammering within my chest as I move my eyes up and up and up.

Claw-like hands are piercing the shoulders of the female, its wolf-like face next to a head of dirty, blonde hair,

"W-what?" I stutter, my hands clammy as a scream wants to escape from my throat.

A rogure, but not.

It's more humanoid. Its hind legs are like a rogure, but its torso is like us. Arms with clawed hands, it has human-like unseeing eyes but still with a small muzzle. Dark hair covering everything but its bottom half and its head. Its ears are smaller, just slightly pointed at the ends and from the looks of it, its cock is inside the woman. And they're dead.

Both dead.

I choke on the vomit that wants to come up, quickly moving my mask out of the way as I rest a hand against a pillar that separates the cells, releasing the contents of my stomach.

I hear the other guys come over to the cell, my back to them as I hear murmuring words, but I can't make it out as my vision blinks in and out.

What the fuck is that kind of rogure, and why the fuck was it inside that woman?

Gods, it was fucking her. Fucking her and they are both

dead, and he's still inside her.

I gag again, bile burning my throat and my vision blacks out longer. I slump against the wall, sweat peppering my skin, the room spinning. I hear a harsh curse and then I'm hauled into a hard body, and my face is moved into a warm, familiar neck.

I breathe in Darius, knowing it will help calm me as he murmurs quiet words. His hand moves in a circular motion on my back, and he rubs his cheek against the top of my head. I breathe him in deeper, needing to be closer, to make him stop what I just saw from replaying in my head.

Once I'm calm enough, his words register, and I pull away from his neck and shake my head. "No," I choke out, "We're not leaving. We need to find them, even if...even if they are no longer of this land."

Another scream has me flinching, this one much louder, and all of our eyes go toward the double doors at the end of the row.

Darius looks at me intently, seeing the determination on my face before he nods. He places me on my feet, moves my mask back in place and covers my hair with my hood.

"We have no idea what's in that room," he tells me, and I swallow roughly, nodding. "Can you handle that?" he asks.

"I can," I say firmly, straightening my shoulders. My voice is strong and sure. I can handle it, I think. I just didn't expect whatever the fuck that was in that cell.

"You might see more of whatever the fuck that is," Darius says, nodding towards the cell in question. I nod again. His eyes tighten, concern creeping into his gaze, those silver flecks appearing before they wilt away. "It's taking everything in me not to remove you from here, to make sure you are somewhere far away from this place." I let out a shuddering breath as he comes closer. "Do as I ask, when I ask." A pause. "Vallier. My instincts are riding me hard."

I can see the struggle in his tense body, the way his eyes are flickering with specks and flashing black. The least I can do is make it easier for him.

I lift up on my toes and bump my nose with his. "I will."

He releases a breath that is so unlike him, and then looks toward his men that are still looking into that cell, their faces more pale than I have ever seen.

Josh stares at the ground, face ashen and hands loose. He's just as disturbed as me at what is in these cells…and what could be of our pack members. Of Sarah.

I've never seen whatever the fuck that thing is in that cell, and I don't ever want to again.

My mind goes back to the notes in Darius's father's basement, and I feel sick all over again.

It couldn't be… could it?

"The sketches…" I begin, and Darius's eyes sharpen. "We have seen sketches of them from your father."

He looks away for a moment in thought. "We need to port back here and take any information we can," Darius tells his men, and they nod, their faces a mixture of disgust and anger. To me, Darius says, "stay close," as we move toward the double doors.

I steel myself for what we may find on the other side, at finding out what this woman is screaming for, and to hope it's not one of my pack members.

TWENTY FOUR

Rhea

The large, wooden doors loom over us as we halt in front of them.

It feels like an omen, an entrance to death and all that is wrong in the lands.

Nerves rattle through me, causing my hands to shake. We can still hear the screams of the woman, but now that we are closer, I can hear murmured voices beyond the closed doors.

That, followed by unknown growls that makes the hairs on the back of my neck stand to attention, makes me want to rush inside or hide.

It's unnerving, this fear I have.

I don't know if it is those growls itself, or what we will find, but seeing what was left of those females in those cells…

I swallow roughly again, saliva filling my mouth as Darius brings a finger up to his lips, letting us know to keep quiet as he slowly turns the handle. He begins to pull the door open on another scream, and a subtle light shines through the crack. I move out of its way before it hits me, standing next to Josh.

Blades ready, we pause, waiting to see if anything happened. We cast worried glances at each other as we wait, but when it doesn't, we nod to ourselves.

A *creak* from the door opening more has my eyes snapping to it, but another scream, followed by a growl, covers the sound. The scent of more blood reaches us.

Please, Zahariss, not them. Vallier, I chant to myself.

Knowing we haven't been noticed, Darius quickly slips through the opening of the door on silent feet, and we follow.

A large, tall stack of wooden shelving is directly in front of us and we move to hide behind it, crouching low. It's full of different herbs, materials and vials of liquid, the color of burnt orange inside of them.

I scrunch up my nose at the odd smell.

Peeking through the shelf at my level, I search the vast room between the items.

It's large and oval, with torches placed throughout the space to cast a dull light upon everything, which makes it feel eerie. Some light shines down through cracks in the ceiling between the rock, creating bright spots on the uneven stone floor, making me wonder how close the surface is up there.

Cells line either side of the room, mirroring each other but they stand freely off the underground walls, not attached to a wall in any way. Stone pillars separate the cells, but that is the only solid thing holding them up as you can see directly through the other side of the bars. I don't see a door of any kind attached to it to open them, and a sick feeling settles in my stomach.

My eyes move to the center next, a raised platform sits where a crude, large rectangular stone rests, and one of those beasts we saw in the other room is chained down upon it.

My hand tightly grips the shelf as its odd, beastly form violently shakes, rattling the chains around its wrists and ankles.

I give a wide-eyed glance at Darius, seeing his jaw tick.

My eyes go back to the beast, and it tilts its head back suddenly, letting loose a terrifying growl from its muzzle that sounds like it's screeching.

It is almost the same sound a rogure releases…but much deeper.

Rogures sound unhinged, this beast sounds…angry.

I scan its body, which is exactly like the rogure-human-thing we found in the other room. I trace my gaze lower, looking over the clumps of gray skin from the waist below until I reach in between his thighs. Vomit threatens to rise within me once more.

I resist stepping back, fear running through me at what I'm seeing, at what one of those things did to that woman.

I avert my eyes back to the cells on the left, seeing shadows moving in one of them three down from the one closest to us. There is someone in there...

A painful scream has my head whipping to the right at the other cells. A naked female body is suddenly slammed up against the front bars, causing me to startle. I go to get up, but in the next moment, one of those human-rogure beasts comes up behind her.

My hand goes to my mouth as it pins her still, then she screams again, her hands gripping the bars as her body shakes with sobs as she's pushed into the bars again and again in a rhythm. The beast's claw-like hands grip her naked hips, causing blood to start dripping down as it moves forward and backwards against her, his grunting growls causing me to shiver.

Oh Gods.

It's...it's fucking her.

I thought maybe what happened in the other room was just an anomaly, that it was a mistake to put a beast in a room with a female. That the notes we found were just a coincidence...

But what I'm witnessing now, it's the same. It's purposefully done.

The notes we found confirmed exactly how a new rogure was claiming a female, how she was in heat, how she fell pregnant and was moved somewhere else.

Is this what he was doing in his basement? Are these beast-like humans the new rogures that were mentioned?

My wide, teary eyes turn to the others, and they have similar faces of shock and disgust, mixed with pain at seeing the woman being brutally raped by that beast.

Darius's eyes meet mine, and I see the rage bleeding into them, slowly seeing the wolf within taking over.

Seeing his rage for this woman makes me suck in a shuddering breath and I wipe at my tears angrily, getting my shit together. I grind my teeth but I don't look away from him, letting him see a mirrored version of himself.

The fury of an Heir.

I nod my head to the woman, wanting to go to her quickly, to get that fucking thing away from her. I check my mask and adjust my blade, ready to do so on his command, but his hand halts any movement.

My eyes widen when he shakes his head.

He can't be serious, he can't leave her like that!

The woman's sobs become weaker, and he squeezes his eyes shut for a moment but shakes his head harder.

No, no, no. We can't leave her like that.

"Give him another dose of ultrian," a voice says, and I swear that my heart stops.

I don't breathe, don't move apart from my head turning slowly to the newcomer's voice.

That's why Darius was shaking his head at me, he knew someone else was there…

The male comes in with another at his side, both of them wearing cloaks but with their hoods down. Two Highers, Frederick, and Mathew, make their way to the center of the room.

To that beast.

Another shadow catches my eye.

Another beast presses its body to the bars, watching the one across from it rape that woman. He snarls, saliva dripping down its muzzle as its slightly-pointed ears twitch.

Just how many are there?

A little body comes up to the bars of another cell further down from it. His little hands appearing first, and then a teary-eyed face and dark hair.

My heart beats wildly within my chest.

Oh, Gods, Oscar. He's here.

I grab Darius more tightly, my nails digging into him as I place another hand to my mouth, swallowing the cry I want to release.

"Josh, look." I see him following my gaze, but I don't move my eyes from the cell.

Another shadowed body appears, quick hands grabbing onto the little body with urgency, but I saw her swollen face before she moved back into the cell. Katy, his mom.

Runa growls low inside of me, seeing what I'm seeing, wanting to go to them as I try and control my relief and terror at them being here.

"They are here," Josh replies, his relief evident that we have found them, though we don't know if all of them are there with this angle and the low lighting.

My hand moves to Darius's hand, and he squeezes it, and nods. He saw them.

A shuffle to my left has my gaze settle upon Jerrod. His eyes are harsher than I have ever seen on the giant of the man as he stares at the cell they are in, the harsh grip on his axe causing his knuckles to whiten.

We're coming, just hold on.

"It shouldn't be long now," Mathew says, his dark eyes looking at the beast raping the woman. "Hopefully this bitch will survive." Survive? I think back to the dead woman. Gods, how many have there been like her?

"We have had three successful deliveries this month," Frederick says. "All boys, unfortunately, but they will be useful."

"Of course." Mathew nods, looking down at the beast laying before him. It snarls up at him, those chains clanging harder as it looks like he's trying to rip his throat out.

Frederick lifts up a vial that looks similar to the ones on the shelving in front of me, and takes the cap off. Moving it toward the beast's head, he brings his hand up to grab its lower jaw.

The beast growls and tries to twist out of Frederick's grip, but ultimately, it's chained down and has nowhere to go.

Frederick tips the liquid contents into the snapping mouth, uncaring that some spills down the sides as the beast starts to shake wildly, growling and grunting.

"There," Mathew says. "Unchain him and put him in the cell with the new female. Let's hope they can produce what we need. I don't want to disappoint Lord Higher again."

"I think we will get a female this time," Frederick says, beginning to unchain the shaking beast who doesn't even look coherent anymore, its eyes are glazed. "We always go through phases of boys, it's time for females now."

"The beast has been examined and determined to be a successful breeder, at least to get a pregnancy." He looks to the other beast raping the woman. "We have been doing this for a very long time now. He will get her full of his seed and she will birth a new generation like the others, no matter what that looks like. I have no doubt."

A long time? New generation?

Darius lets out a small growl, and all of our heads whip toward him, terrified of being detected, and also terrified of what Darius will do. His powers float out around him in tendrils, two thicker and longer mass-like tails moving up and slightly away from his back, the tips showing above either of his shoulders.

Shit.

"Dar," I whisper as quietly as I can as more growls pierce the air, and his eyes hit mine so fast that if I had blinked I would have missed his head turning to me.

I see it then, why he's so angry.

This is what was meant to happen to me, to breed the new generation like Charles had told him.

"We need to get Katy and Oscar, we need to see if there are any more of my pack here." His head tilts, the whites of his eyes bleeding black.

We can't be found yet, I need to get my pack somewhere

safe, I need to get to them.

"Darius," I say in a low, warning tone as quietly as I can, and his nostrils flare. "My pack first, destroy later." I reach forward and let a little power come to my fingertips and press into his arm.

The blue wraps into his black, welcoming and calming, a gentle prodding until finally, Darius's eyes return to normal, the black strands coming from him, slowly retreating back into his body.

I let out a quiet breath as his nostrils flare, getting himself under control. We don't lose eye contact the whole time, and I wait him out, knowing he can come back.

When he nods and tilts his head toward the cells where Katy and Oscar are, I breathe a sigh of relief.

"You, your pack, and Jerrod will go to them," he murmurs quietly, jaw ticking. "Port out when you have them. We will go to the other side and cause a distraction once we have cleared the cells and found no other members. Or anyone else."

"How will you distract them without them knowing?" I ask as I watch Frederick drag the still-shaking, and not fully conscious beast over to a cell on the right using a chain around its neck.

He opens the bars with a wave of his hand and shoves the beast inside, releasing the chain. So magic is how they open it.

Another scream, another ferocious growl, I know that beast is raping someone else inside the cell he was put in.

"Oh, he's really going for it," Frederick laughs, and my eyes squeeze shut, my grip tightening on Darius's arm as her cries and pain fill the air.

How can they do this? How can they openly throw that thing in there whilst they rape a woman. Is this what would have happened to me? Has this happened to my pack? Has this happened to those that were stolen?

"They are beasts, whatever fucking kind," Darius whispers, and I open my eyes, looking around the space. "They are in a rut, I can sense it, all males can." I look at the others, seeing their tense faces, knowing what Darius said is true. "It was brought on by whatever they gave it. It will be protective against any intruder trying to go near what is his at the moment, we can use that."

"Won't it harm the female more?" I ask him, my eyes coming back to him.

Darius's eyes tighten. "We don't have a choice. It's a risk we need to take. I think death would be welcomed by any female having to take that beast unwillingly."

He's right. I saw what they did to them in the other room, but can I let them die?

Darius reaches a hand out to me, his eyes briefly going toward the Highers as they laugh, making sure we are still unnoticed. His fingertips run along my forehead before he places a kiss there.

I feel his wolf brushing along my skin, Runa responding.

"There is nothing else we can do unless we want to alert them to our presence and risk them porting your pack members out of here," he whispers against my skin. "I want to gut them, Rhea. I want to torture, maim, and behead them for all they have done." His body shakes with every word. "The only thing stopping me from going around these shelves and shoving my blade in their bodies is I know how important your pack is to you, so therefore, it is important to me." I let out a shuddering breath. Forgive me, Zahariss, more souls will be coming to you. "Once your pack is safe," he grits out, just slightly over a quiet murmur but no less deadly, "I will go for them, if I can. We are not prepared for them, and I can sense others in a back room."

What others?

"It may just be better to get in and out unnoticed," I reluctantly say. "I want them dead more than anyone, but you are right, we are not prepared for this."

We didn't think any Highers would be here... but if there are also more somewhere. More Highers? Their witches maybe?

"Get your pack ported out of here," Darius commands. "Once they are gone I can try and take one for questioning if we can keep our identity a secret."

I give him a resigned nod. "Okay."

His eyes bounce between mine. "I need you safe Rhea. Having you this close to them…" He looks away before his eyes come back to mine. "Port out of here as soon as you can, Vihnarn."

I breathe in his scent and nod.

Then with one last lingering look, we split up.

I creep toward the end of the shelves with Josh, Taylor, Colten, Hudson, and Jerrod. I look back toward the Highers, who have now moved to the back of the room, looking down at a table. With their backs to us, we have the advantage.

But another cloaked figure suddenly joins them from somewhere in the back, just like Darius sensed.

I wait as the newcomer, a guard it looks like, joins them at the table until I proceed.

Sweat beads my brow as I wait until they are completely immersed in looking down at the table before I dart out from behind the tall stacks and run to the end of the cells, heartbeat in my throat.

When I reach it, I slide down the long wall at the end on a crouch, waiting to see if they have spotted me.

They hadn't.

I wait as the others do the same, one at a time and then Jerrod takes the lead and peeks around the cell wall.

We hear the Highers talking louder now, Mathew angrier and we make our way to the back of the cells, quiet and cautious as we can see straight through the bars…just like they can.

As we pass, I look inside the cells.

More dead bodies, all females, all failures.

This could have been me, this could be my pack.

I'm going to make them all suffer for what they have done.

I won't rest until I do. Whether that's now, or later.

Magic coats my hand without warning, and I place it on my chest, willing it to go away as anger flashes to the surface so quickly, I have to grab on to a bar to steady myself.

"What's wrong?" Josh asks. He looks at my hand. *"Fuck, not now Rhea, control it."*

"I'm trying." Runa growls within me, pacing and restless, and I mentally stroke her head, trying to calm her to help calm me.

I look through the bars and see Darius's eyes on me from the other side, his men already there too.

The two rows of cells may be between us, but just his eyes on mine begins to calm me.

Runa whines, and I settle, pulling my magic back before Darius comes over here.

I nod my head at him, letting him know I'm okay and with a lingering look, he carries on.

"You good?" Josh's tone is full of worry.

"I'm good." My eyes go to the others and I nod, letting him know to continue.

Taking a fortifying breath, we aim for the cell that Oscar and Katy are in, not making a sound as the beasts on this side and Darius's side are still fucking the females *to death*.

The sounds of their cries shred my heart. It feels like something is dying inside of me as I'm choosing my pack over saving them.

But it's not just them.

If the Highers see us, it's over. They will know Darius is against them, and then the rest of Vrohkaria will continue to be in their clutches.

We can't let that happen.

Raised voices reach my ears as the beast on the other side of the room roars in anger, and we quicken our pace, knowing Darius did something.

I take a peek through the bars of the next cell to the other side of the room and see the beast grabbing the female hard, and shoving her down to the floor, his entire body covering her as he ruts into her while looking around, snarling, and roaring.

Forgive me.

Fingers, along with a small cry grip the bars of the next cell, and that's what has my head snapping to it and away from the horrid scene.

Jerrod kneels next to it, holding tiny hands. "Shhh, mighty axe," he says quietly. He's talking to Oscar whose little body is shaking.

Hudson, Colten, and Taylor are further down, reaching their hands through the bars, whispering words frantically.

I crouch down next, my knees giving way to relief as I look into the cell, my own tears flowing as I see nearly all of my pack members inside.

"He's with us," I say straight away for Jerrod. They don't know what has happened since they were taken, and the look of horror on their faces says as much, as they look at him in fear, neck bent in submission.

Finn, Axel, Eliza, Katy, Oscar. Elijah, Leah, her mom, Nathen, Lacy, and Sam, who's leaning against the cell wall, squished between two members as she stares ahead blankly, Sybil holding her hand as some more members huddle together.

I spot a body on the other side and notice it's Ben…

"Alpha," Katy's trembling voice hits me as she looks at her son and the Elite who took her away from Eridian in the first place. "You're alive," she says, and I nod, placing a hand to my lips for silence, then reach forward and squeeze her hand.

"Others?" I croak out, and more tears spill down her cheeks, looking at Ben.

I nod, grief curling around me.

"We're getting you out of here," I tell her quietly, looking at what is left of my pack that is huddled in this cell. Seventeen of them. "Come, gather round, all of you," I tell them, and my pack rushes towards me, the pups crying and the others barely keeping it together. "Jerrod, take them back," I tell him, and he looks toward me, conflicted. "Hudson, Colten, Taylor. Go with him."

"This is not a good idea," Taylor tells me as Hudson and Colten share a look.

"They will need you," I say, looking at my pack. "They won't go if you don't."

They nod at that, knowing they are scared of Jerrod.

Jerrod looks across the room to his brothers. "Dari—" he starts.

"I trust you to keep them safe, Jerrod." I give him a pointed look, moving my eyes to Katy and Oscar who are now huddled together. "I need to stay here with Darius and kill every motherfucker in this room that deserves it." I am trying to keep my rage in check, my powers—and I don't know how much longer I can keep hold of it.

Jerrod still looks unsure, knowing it will be going against Darius's wishes. So I do something I have never done before.

"I am the Heir to Zahariss, you will do as I order." His eyes widen slightly, feeling the command in my tone before he gives me a small smirk.

"It's your head, Rhea. Darius will send you to an early grave." I shrug, I can handle it.

"Go with him, you will be brought to safety, I promise," I tell my pack who look panicked. "Go." I rush Jerrod, and he takes out a port stone from his pocket. Only a few of us carried one as the others were lost with our rucksacks.

My pack moves toward us at the bars, Eliza and Sybill dragging Sam, and I make sure they are all touching each other. Jerrod holds the stone in one hand while he slowly moves his hand through the bars. I put his hand on the back of little Oscar's head, Jerrod's eyes on Katy, and then they are gone.

In the blink of an eye, they are safe.

I sag forward against the bars, tears of relief trailing down my face. I feel Josh coming up next to me, his forehead resting on my temple and I lean into it.

I knew he wouldn't leave me, so there was no need for me to even ask.

"We couldn't get here in time for them all," I breathe down the link to Josh.

"No, but we managed to get some of them. The rest can now run free in peace," he replies, nuzzling my hair through the hood of my cloak. I can feel his grief mixed in with relief, and we both need the comfort for just a moment.

The Higher's voices are suddenly closer than expected, and my heart throbs with nerves. But another roar pierces the air, and my eyes glide across the room to Darius through the bars.

The darkness is visible to see from here.

He looks at the now-empty cell in front of me, his lips peeling back into a silent snarl at knowing I'm still here. But there is nothing he can do.

"Did we give him too much?" Frederick asks.

"I don't think it would cause him to behave like this." That comes from Higher Mathew.

"Then fix it!" Frederick shouts. "If he kills her before she's pregnant it will be on your heads, do you understand!"

"And yours!" Mathew says, floundering. "We both are assigned to this."

"I will not be put under Lord Higher's wrath for you."

I rise, unsheathing my blade from its holder and tell Darius exactly what I'm thinking with my eyes.

We can maybe save those females.

He paces back and forth, the tension visible from the other side of the room before he stops and tilts his head again. I follow suit, wondering what he's hearing.

"If we lose this one, we will have to move some to go through the compatibility tests," Frederick growls. "We won't have time to do that. Lord Higher expects results."

"What about Kaden?" Mathew asks, and my heart rate picks up, Runa standing to attention within me.

Josh tenses at my side, tilting his head.

"Charles wants to bring Kaden down here anyway and give him the ultrian serum, we can just speed up the timeframe. Kaden won't be able to deny the need to fuck, and then we will throw him in a cell with a few females. I'm sure he will be able to take the serum, so we don't need to test him," Frederick chuckles. "He has the original line running through his veins, though weaker, he will be able to produce an Heir for Lord Higher while we test the others."

Frederick hums. "That's not a bad idea. We will have to beat him a little before restraining him…"

My vision whitens at their words, blood rushing through my body and a pounding begins to thrum in my ears. My power rushes through me, I can't stop it, can't even attempt to.

I don't even know I'm moving, I don't even know that I'm now standing out from behind the cells and moving towards the center of the room near the stone slab.

All I feel through my body is two thoughts—

Kill. Protect.

And then, both Highers and the guard turn around from the table, sensing someone else in the room. Their eyes widen briefly in the presence of someone unknown, but I snarl at them, feeling Runa so close to the surface it feels like she will burst out.

"Who the fuck are you!" Frederick demands as his guard unsheathes his blade.

Guess there is no hiding now.

TWENTY FIVE

Rhea

I move my mask down and remove the hood from my head. I growl low, my lips peeling back as I bare my teeth at them.

I sense the air change around me instantly. Malice and a wrongness trying to suffocate me. It's like a blanket of invisible thickness that coats my skin. Coats the area as the Highers turn to fully face me.

"Well if it isn't Lasandrhea," Higher Mathew says, a grin splitting his lips.

I can still hear the beasts raping the females, still hear them cry as they have no choice but to be taken by those monstrosities.

I need to help them, but they need to tell me fully what they plan to do with Kade. Why are they doing this to begin with?

I won't make the same mistake I made with Maize.

"Now, isn't this a surprise," Frederick hums and moves away from the table that had him so occupied. Another snarling grunt sounds, and his lips tilt into an arrogant smirk. "Do you like the new and improved rogures, Lasandrhea?" he asks, and my body jolts.

New and improved?

"Rhea, what are you doing!" Josh shouts down the link, and I know he's readying to come out of hiding.

"Stay there," I commanded back. *"They do not know anyone else is here."*

I say nothing to Frederick, sensing the Elites still hiding

behind the cells that he and the others haven't noticed. What I have noticed, however, is more of the Highers guards entering the room from another door at the back. Their armor on and blades ready as they form a half-circle behind Frederick, Mathew, and what must be the head guard of their squad.

"Not that I am in any way complaining about you being here, in fact, this is perfect," Frederick says as he waves a hand to his side. Mathew's smile is sinister as he moves over to the right and crouches before a large grate. "Not only will Lord Higher reward us for your delivery, but you can be introduced to your new life."

"Which is what," I say between clenched teeth.

"A breeding body. A hole for another to fuck. Don't worry though," he says, his eyes changing to reassurance. "We can heal any rips or cuts. We will look after you."

"Why are you doing this, what is it that you want?"

Mathew moves his hand over the grate, a rune appearing before it disappears and the sounds of growls reach the room. Many. So fucking many.

Frederick smirks. "The next generation will be powerful. Those that don't make the cut will go to Lord Higher, he likes to get them around eight weeks before he does their check."

Eight weeks for what...

"Why must the next generation be stronger?"

Mathew lifts the grate and reaches a hand inside while I watch intently, my heart pounding with the movement. He lifts his hand out and moves further back, revealing a chain. Lifting his other arm, dark purple strands pour out of him, and I suck in a sharp breath as the room fills with that power.

It feels like mine and Darius's magic that was given from the Gods.

How did they get that power?

My eyes snap to Fredericks for a moment as he laughs. "They need to be stronger for what we want."

I resist moving my eyes to Darius and his men, to not give

them away as I continue to watch the purple strand that feel wrong attached to him.

Another chuckle brings my attention back to Frederick, but making sure I watch that magic out of the corner of my eye.

"Ahh, yes," he says. "You didn't know the Highers have Heir power, did you?"

"How do you have it?" I grind out between clenched teeth, my hand tightening around the hilt of my blade.

"We Highers have had Heir power in some way, shape or form for over twenty years now," he hums, smiling as more snarling comes from the hole where the grate was lifted. "Now, some have more than others, but what a gift it is that we have received. You can thank your mother for that, Lasandrhea."

My heart lodges in my throat at the mention of my mother. "What?" I barely get the words out, the word no more than a whisper, but the malicious glint in his eyes lets me know he heard me.

"She was a beautiful woman," he says wistfully while I try not to throw up for Gods knows how many times now. "But alas, she was off limits to us."

Mathew pulls the chain harder, moving towards the center of the room and I step further away, wanting to make sure I have all of them in view as I see more guards join the others.

Gods, we are outnumbered.

But that's the least of my problems with what I see next.

A clawed hand appears from the hole in the floor, the sharpness of them able to dig into the hard stone and grips it tightly. The dark violet of Mathew's power thickens slightly as the male grunts, and another clawed hand emerges before a snarling beast appears.

I finally move my panicked eyes to Darius, and he begins to move through the shadows.

"Rhea…" Josh says worriedly.

The beast lifts himself out of the hole, the huge mass of his body revealing itself as he gets a hind leg up, and a clawed foot is placed on the floor. Mathew's powers is wrapped around its waist, and I realize it was used to help the rogure out of whatever the fuck is below.

I move further back, looking toward Darius again, but don't see him there.

My hands start to sweat, and my legs shake slightly as the new rogure stands to its full height of over seven feet. The lower half of his bottom rots off in chunks like a rogure, as hair covers the rest of him. Just like the others.

It lifts its head and inhales deeply through its still wolf-like snout, and lets out a terrifying, screeching growl.

"Do you see? It's magnificent," Frederick says, but I keep my eyes locked on the beast. "It has been many years in the making, and finally, we have succeeded," he laughs, holding his arms out to the beast.

"Succeeded in what?" I ask him through trembling lips, dreading to know.

"In making these new rogures of course. We can breed them, we can control them, we have an army of them," he boasts. I lock my knees, willing them not to fail me with the words he is telling me. "My, Lasandrhea, this is perfect timing that you have arrived. This beast hasn't been tested yet for breed ability, but it would be good to work you in." Work me in… "And you have been wanted since Lord Higher found out you were alive to be fucked and bred. It's perfect timing." I gag. "Your mother saw to foiling his plans, but alas, Lord Higher has been working toward this new goal for some time."

Mathew clicks his fingers, and the snarling beast stops, every sound stops. "Ricurium," Mathew murmurs as he runs a hand down its hairy side.

The rogure, beast, whatever the fuck monstrosity it is, snaps its head toward him, and Mathew drops the chain while recalling his magic.

Fuck.

My eyes bounce between them and the new rogure, sweat

beading my brow as a roll of familiar power fills the room. My head snaps to where Darius was, and I see him now walking out from behind the row of cells.

"Higher Frederick, Higher Mathew of Vrohkaria, you are guilty of treason and are sentenced to death under the laws of the land," he announces, and comes up to my side, power flowing from him that calls to my own without hesitance. My marking appears as he continues. "You are going to die today," he tells them. "Have no doubt about that." The other Elites and Josh come behind us and stand at our back, ready.

Nerves rattle through me as Frederick lets out a booming laugh, his manic eyes alight.

"My, my, Alpha Darius," he says. "Who knew a wet cunt would make you commit treason against the Highers. I can smell your scent on her, boy." Darius snarls, inky tendrils of his power coating his body like a second skin. "I cannot wait until we let Lord Higher know that your loyalty has changed. He will have his fun with you. Your father would be disappointed." He frowns like he's upset about that.

"I do not claim a man or a wolf who kidnapped people and experimented on them against their will, or abused others as my father did."

"Ah, but he was your father," Frederick smiles cruelly as Mathew laughs, their eyes on me. "And he very much liked watching females getting their throat fucked and playing with their body while they were unconscious, as did we. We very much enjoyed visiting you in your home, Lasandrhea."

My vision blurs, and I grip onto Darius's arm, trying to keep the memories at bay, trying not to let myself sink into them so they can suffocate me.

Darius stills at my side, not moving, not twitching. He's a solid form under my grip as I breathe heavily through my nose. The ground trembles slightly beneath his feet, his power coming from the ground like a swirling wind up to his ankles.

His palm comes up slowly from his side and I watch, my

eyes following it until it reaches my cheek. It's like he did it without thought, the movement automatic, and I let his warmth comfort me as he moves his hand until his fingers come under my chin.

Lifting my face gently, my eyes move up his chest and rest on his neck where his dark Heir markings pulse, feeling mine repeat in kind. When I finally reach his face, his eyes are completely black apart from his glowing, light green pupils, and those silver flecks.

I sense his wolf within, so close to the surface now that I can sense destruction, but I don't falter my gaze even as I know he can see the shame in my own, sense the pain from Frederick's words no matter how hard I try to banish the feeling.

"Do not listen, Vihnarn," he rumbles, his voice deep and I clench my eyes shut at him calling me that. "I will bring his heart to you," he continues. "I will rip it from his still-breathing body. I will show it to him while he takes his last breath. The last thing he will see is the Heir of Cazier carrying out vengeance for all that was done to what is his." I shiver at his words, my eyes springing open to see the tails of his power floating behind both shoulders.

Frederick and Mathew laugh.

But I don't think they should.

"You think you can go against a Higher?" Mathew says, eyeing the beast still standing next to him.

I harden my gaze before looking back at them, feeling myself sink deeper into cold rage for the little girl who ran though flowers and danced underneath the stars, before she had it ripped away by those in power for their sick deeds.

"Dar," I whisper. He doesn't answer, but I know he's listening by the tilt of his head. "If you think I'm going to stand back and let you take his heart without my involvement, you don't know me very well at all."

He lets out a breathy laugh. "Little wolf," he rumbles from deep in his chest, that lights me up from the inside. "If I don't find at least one wound on their bodies from your blade, I will be very disappointed." I turn my eyes to him and they become determined. "But get yourself hurt and I won't be responsible for what I do to you." I blink, then blink again before nodding.

Darkness surrounds us suddenly, and I call my power to my palms to light the area we are enclosed in.

I don't think about how to control my magic, I don't gently try and will it do as I ask.

No.

I can't think much at all as we split up, and I open my senses to focus on the heartbeats I can hear.

I know Darius's magic surrounds everywhere here, but it's only us in the barrier. We move around in a wide circle, listening to their shouts of alarm, along with their guards.

Josh breathes quietly beside me, his eyes furious and his grip strangling his blade. He glances at me, nodding that he's ready. The Elites don't even so much as look at each other, they don't communicate in any way, already knowing what's about to happen as they have probably done this a hundred times together.

The Highers shout for back up, and I can hear the head guard moving around. A sudden purple glow can be seen, and the beast roars, making the other beasts in the cages roar with them.

My heart pounds as Darius looks at me as we settle behind them all, roaming his eyes over the cut on my thigh and arm, then the next second, the darkness evaporates.

I lunge forward and my blade is in the guard's neck, dead before he can even do anything.

I see the Elites go directly for the Highers as Josh turns around, growling as more guards pour into the room.

Trusting the others to go to the Highers, we go for the guards as that beast roars again. I lash out with my blade, catching the shoulder of one guard and I call my power to my hand. Feeling it concentrate at my palm, I lift it and push. A wave of magic follows, slamming into some of the guards and their front line topples over.

Josh is on them, slicing and stabbing until a puddle of red can be seen as I join him.

More guards come from the back, and I have a sickening feeling that maybe they ported in. And if they did, that means someone went back and asked for back up.

That means the other Highers could know.

Fuck, fuck, fuck.

"Darius!" I shout, leaning back as the curve of a blade comes for my head.

"Yes, little wolf," he grits out, and then a ball of purple flies past me, hitting a guard in the chest.

We all seem to watch as he coughs, blood spewing out of his mouth, the ball of power sinking into his chest, eradicating through his body, growing smaller and smaller the deeper it goes until it evaporates.

I see a thin layer of skin in the center of his chest, which must be his back, and then the body drops.

"Rhea, move!" The panicked tone from Josh has me instantly diving out the way to the floor. Another ball.

I look back and see Frederick smiling, not even caring that he just killed one of their guards.

Darius growls and goes for him.

I get up off the floor and lift my blade as another sword comes for me, brown eyes full of hatred.

"They don't care about you," I try to reason with him. "They will kill you all just to get to me. Leave."

He sneers. "Traitorous whore." Gods dammit.

I let loose my dominance, and he whimpers, his body folding in on himself a little and I stab him in the heart.

I'm suddenly knocked to the side, a heavy weight on me, sending my blade flying. I groan, getting my hands up to push the fucker off me as Josh shouts my name.

I push power out of my hands and it sends the guard soaring across the room, landing against some other guards and they topple to the floor.

More shouts, and more fucking guards come in as Damian can be seen slicing through them. An inhumane whimper has me turning my head to watch Zaide fighting with the beast, its huge claws gliding through the air at him.

Darius and Leo are dodging the Highers balls of power, keeping them busy but I see Darius sending out his own magic, his face furious. A black mass turns to short spikes and propels them out of his hand, but the Highers put up their barrier, protecting them.

A hand on my ankle has me sucking in a breath, and I don't even look as I kick out with my other foot, aiming for their face. I hear bone crunch over it, and then my hand is to his chest, sending power into him.

He stumbles back, and my eyes go to the grates below me that I landed on. To the snarls and growls.

The glow of eyes look back at me.

Hundreds and hundreds of eyes, and my body trembles.

Gods.

I get to my feet, hissing at the pain in my thigh as the guard just sort of stands still, then collapses. Seeing how many of our enemies are still here, I drop back down and place my hand on my thigh, letting the blood soak into it. Once I have enough, I place my palm on the stone floor. "*Va ka reidu, lec fa dienn,*" I chant. "Zahariss, grant me protection."

A wave of magic coats the floor, and some of the guards drop to their knees as Josh, Damian and I back up and reassess.

Darius and Leo are where the shelves are, fighting with the Highers as Zaide is fighting the beast near the center, rolling over the stone in the middle as a clawed-hand crashes against it, instantly crumbling the side.

"I'll go in the back," Damian says, as he nods his head to a doorway where the guards were coming out of. Josh and I nod.

As he goes, Josh and I back up to one side of the cells, eyeing at least twenty guards who are coming closer and closer. Once they hit my wave of magic, I pick up a discarded blade and we pounce again.

We get lost in the fray of battle, dodging and slicing, stabbing, and hitting.

I pant, swinging my leg around and kicking a guard across the face as I turn and stab another in the shoulder. Blood coats me and the stone floor, the sound of the others fighting reaching us.

I need to take these out before I can take a Higher's head.

Runa growls within, liking that thought.

A guard manages to catch Josh in his stomach, and I send out a ball of my own magic, knocking him to the side when it connects. He cries out, holding his ribs. When his hands come away, they're full of blood.

"You okay?" I ask Josh, leaning back before a sword takes my head.

"Fine," he growls.

I slice my blade through the air, clashing with another guard as I kick my leg out, hitting him in the ribs while I turn and send out another ball, hitting the guard in the face. He's knocked back, tripping over a body on the floor, I bring my blade down through his chest, the vibration of hitting through both bodies and the stone floor, traveling up my blade and shaking my hand.

"Roll!" I don't know who the command is for, but both Josh and I do so, then an arrow is lodged in a guard's face.

Ducking one blade and side-stepping another, I bring my own up to clash with a new one.

We spin in a circle, his back to the Elites. I kick out, catching him above the knee and then ram my blade through his stomach. He gurgles and slumps forward, his hand coming to my face as he starts hitting me.

I grab his hand with my own and bend it back, listening for the snap of his bones. He screams as he bleeds out on my blade, then slumps further into me. Fuck, he's heavy. I stumble back from his weight, trying not to trip over my feet. I grunt as I try to dislodge him, but with my blade running through him, it's not easy.

A glint to the side has my eyes widening. I can't move, I can't defend myself from the sword that's coming for me.

The guard looks me dead in the eye as he starts to bring his sword down, but then a blade is suddenly in the side of his skull.

I blink, then look to where it came from to see Darius's arm dropping. He threw his blade to protect me…

And then he's suddenly off of his feet, getting hit with magic.

"Darius!" I shout, as he gets thrown back, panic thrumming through me.

He rolls on the floor as he lands, over and over, but then his magic comes out and stops him from crashing against the cell walls, rising to his feet in one swift movement with cold fury on his face.

I breathe out a sigh of relief and finally dislodge the guard on my own blade. All I see is red and guards, the clanging of metal and grunts the only sound I hear as the beast's claws can be heard scraping against stone. I don't know if we can—

"Ahhh." A blow to the side of my head has me stumbling, and then falling to the floor. A thunderous growl from Darius sounds as a weight crashes on top of me, hands instantly wrapping around my throat.

I bring my blade up and stab into whoever is on top of me, blindly as I try to clear my blurry vision. He cries out in pain, but after releasing one hand from my throat, he grabs my wrist and slams it to the ground again and again.

I drop my blade as pain vibrates down my arm, and I growl up at the guard. His face twists as he still digs his other hand into my throat, and I groan as it feels like he's crushing my windpipe.

I wriggle and buck, eventually getting the other hand and throwing him off of me. I punch him in the face as I cough and splutter, taking in ragged breaths. Then I pick up my blade and stab, anywhere and everywhere until I'm sure he won't survive, but I realize too late when his blade comes my way and scores my side.

Fuck.

I bring the blade down to his neck, and when blood spurts out of it, I know he's dead.

Blood covers me, dripping down my body as I collapse back, staring up at the stone ceiling as I catch my breath for a single moment. Knowing I don't have much time to be vulnerable, I get my hands under me, lifting to a sitting position before using my blade to help me stand.

A pained growl has me lifting my head and see Zaide fighting with the beast still. Claw marks track down his arm as he circles it and blocks his clawing attacks while slicing at its flesh. Darius's black tendrils snap the necks of two guards trying to sneak up on him before they travel my way, not once looking.

His magic reaches me, traveling up my legs until it rests on the side of my neck. Its coolness seeps into me, caressing my sore neck and I swallow over the lump in my throat over his carefulness with me.

I raise my hand and place it over the top, feeling his magic wrap around my fingers before I check on Josh.

His hands are around a guard's neck as his face twists in pain before turning a shade of blue. The guard's hands come up but it's no use, he drops to the floor. Dead.

There are still a few guards left, and Damian slides up to Josh, having come out of the back room at some point, panting but nowhere near done if the look on his face is anything to go by.

He hands Josh his blade, and he takes it without thought. Then, Damian's wolf is there, teeth and claws as he lunges on the next guard as their numbers dwindle.

His screams fill the air.

Wobbling over to the cells, I make my way down the front, mindful of Zaide and the beast as I try to come to the side of Mathew and Frederick. Leo and Darius are keeping them busy, and if I can get the right angle, when they drop their barrier to attack, I may be able to hit him.

But I forgot about the beast that is still in the cell.

Clawed hands rake down my shoulder and I cry out, stumbling forward as my opposite hand goes to the wound. The beast snarls and grunts, black foam dripping from its muzzle as I stare at it with wide eyes.

A roar comes from behind me, so fierce that I sense its vibrations on the floor, and then a slimy voice hits my ear the next moment.

"Are you wanting to come to us, traitor of Vrohkaria," Frederick says, closer than expected. I spin around, seeing he has separated from Mathew who throws magic at Darius and Leo, holding them back as he puts the beast and Zaide between them.

"Fuck you. If anyone is a traitor it's you!" I snarl, lifting my hand. He's a good distance away, but he's slowly creeping closer.

He laughs. "But only we know that, don't we?"

I move to the side, further down from the cell with the beast, Frederick mirroring me. "Where is Kade?"

"Why, at the castle of course."

"What have you done to him?"

He smiles.

I go for him.

Frederick's laughter still surrounds us as I leap over the bodies between us, blade in a death grip as all my focus is on one of the people that turned my childhood into a monster, swallowing it whole.

Darius calls my name, his voice urgent as Frederick aims a blow at me. I dodge it as he walks backwards, and as it crashes into the wall, rock tumbles down from above, nearly hitting me.

I pause, looking at it and then the ceiling.

I don't think it can take a lot of hits.

"Kade is a good boy, when he listens." My head snaps Frederick's way as a cry comes from the other side of the room.

Mathew is on the floor with his arms raised as Darius goes for him, Leo now helping Zaide with the beast.

I let my power out, aiming for Frederick but his barrier appears. My magic hits it, causing ripples, but it doesn't disperse it.

"Come and fight me you coward!"

"Like you haven't been a coward, hiding away for years,"

That stops me short.

"Think about it. All of this," he twirls a finger around the room. "Was done because you got up and left. If you were where you were supposed to be, well, no one else would have suffered."

"You're lying," I spit. They would have been greedy and done this anyway.

"Am I?"

"What is the purpose of this, what do you want!" I scream at him, letting another ball fly.

"Power."

"You have it. You rule over Vrohkaria. This is pointless!"

"Vrohkaria is just a start."

What.

He looks at my face and laughs. "Vrohkaria is nothing to the rest of the lands. And we will all get a slice of it."

"The other lands?" He smiles, and his barrier drops.

I duck as another ball comes for me, and I barely manage to miss it. The ground shakes when it lands into the wall, more rock crumbling down.

They are doing all of this for *power*? To rule the other lands outside of Vrohkaria?

They are insane.

"You're all fucking crazy," I pant, and then I'm sprinting, crashing into his barrier with gritted teeth.

He laughs like he's crazy too. "I can't wait to have you. Not to breed, no, that's for Lord Higher and the beasts, but I want to feel your cunt wrapped around me at least once."

"You're sick." I try to sound strong, but my voice wavers.

"I am a Higher. Now, let's see how strong you are." Then he drops his barrier.

I lunge, but he's faster, sending out a wave of magic that sends me flying back. I gasp for breath as I land against the cell bars, Darius roaring on the other side of the room when I collapse to the floor, smacking my head off the stone.

I can see Frederick coming closer through my blurry vision, and I groan as I try to get up, wetness spilling down the side of my temple and cheek. I try to move, do anything.

I will not be taken by him.

Come on, come on. I will my power as Runa whimpers inside of me, my body feeling sluggish.

But I feel it then, a little spark of it, and then another surge.

I raise my hand and aim.

Frederick, caught off guard, manages to dodge most of the attack, but some catch his side.

He cries out, going to one knee as his face turns into something painful.

I grip the bar of the cell hauling myself to my wobbly feet and raise my hand again.

Now's my chance. I can get him, knock him out and get him to tell us everything, how we can catch Charles off guard.

I stumble forward, about to aim at his temple when his hand comes up faster than I was expecting, and then it's around my throat, bloodied teeth smirking.

"Do you ever wonder how that memory crystal ended up in Eridian, how Aldus found it? There was already one there… waiting for the perfect time to strike after Lord Higher found out there was a hidden pack. You are not the only traitor we know of," he says, and I freeze, his words rattling around in my mind. He lifts a knife in his other hand and sinks it into my shoulder. I cry out, wrapping my own hand around his wrist, trying to call my power but there is nothing there. He laughs, head tipped back at the look on my face. No... "Oh, this is going to be fun you stupid bitch—" He gurgles suddenly, eyes widening and then his hand goes slack.

I blink, watching as he crumbles to the floor, blood blooming from his chest and then there is Darius— Pure Alpha, rage pouring off of him, bloodied blade in hand as he snarls down at Frederick.

"You do not. Fucking. Touch her!" he roars down at him, and then he's on him.

His fists pummels all over. His face, his chest, his ribs. Bones break, screams erupt, blood splatters. He doesn't stop. Just growls and snarls, his magic flowing wild around him.

I slump down, watching as blood goes everywhere.

I don't even try to stop Darius, don't even open my mouth to tell him to keep him alive so we can get information.

I can't.

My mind is stuck on what he said, about the crystal.

A hand on my shoulder has me flinching, and my head turns to Josh, eyes full of concern. He sees my exhaustion, the wounds still bleeding all over my body.

But it's emotionally where I am wrecked the most.

It cannot be.

"What is it?" he asks, brows furrowed. He knows something isn't right.

"Come with me," I tell him down the link.

He's confused, I know he is, but he nods when he sees the look on my face, trusting me. We have been together long enough for him to know I need to do something.

"Where to?"

Darius's head lifts suddenly, his eyes on me.

I can feel his confusion at why we are talking down the link.

I don't look at him, I can't, I just keep my eyes on Josh.

I pull the port stone out of my pocket and hold it in my bloodied hand, and then grip Josh's arm with the other.

"Rhea..." Darius questions, breathing heavily. "What are you doing?"

I do look at him, then. His face is hard, bloody. I can still see the fury residing in his eyes as his hand is still in a fist, aimed for the now barely-breathing Frederick.

"I'll be back," I croak out to him.

I need to see, I need to do this now and not have him wonder if the area is safe or even try to stop me.

Darius's eyes flash, hand reaching for me, but I'm already gone.

TWENTY SIX

Rhea

We land softly, the feeling of being squeezed, leaving me as I blink my eyes open in the afternoon light. Another wave of dizziness hits me and Josh is there, steadying me.

"Shit, Rhea. You good?" No, I'm not. I think I tore open my thigh wound even more, my throat feels like it's closing up and a rib may be broken. I nod at him anyway, my eyes squeezing shut as I breathe through my nose. "We shouldn't have come here, we should have stayed and then gone back to Vokheim Keep and had Anna look you over." I peel my eyes open, seeing the blood and bruises on his face, and it instantly makes me feel guilty.

I reach up and place my hand over his own on my arm. "I'm sorry, Josh. I shouldn't have brought you here. You need to get back to Sarah."

He shakes his head, squeezing my hand. "Of course I would go with you." I go to open my mouth but he cuts me off. "No, I'm not going to leave you to do this alone, whatever we are here for."

I sigh, releasing his hand and rubbing my eyes. "We are about to find out." He eyes me, but says nothing.

We move through the trees that surround Eridian, the eerie quietness around us unsettling as we listen carefully for anyone.

"It's strange," Josh says as we walk through the forest.

"It is. It doesn't feel like just months ago the pack were running through the woods, howling to the moon, and playing with each other."

"We had no idea what was coming for us," he sighs.

"We didn't, and we didn't have a chance to stop it."

I pause when we come to the lilk trees that were once full of vibrant color, but are now lifeless and dead.

"Gods." Tears prick my eyes as I move forward, feeling the fallen branches snap beneath my feet. I place my hand on the dull, birch bark, closing my eyes as a tear finally falls.

I sense nothing within, not a beat of life, not a source of company. Nothing.

My hands dig into the tree and I grit my teeth at the unfairness of it all, of the wrongness.

It is more proof that Solvier is no more. The guardian who protected this place, who was also my friend.

A pull on my hand has me opening my eyes again, and Josh nods his head toward our home. Or what *was* our home.

With one last sorrowful look at the lilk tree, I follow him, our steps slow and steady to avoid anyone who may be here.

But not a single heartbeat to be heard, or any sign of life. It reminds me of The Deadlands, and I shiver at the thought.

It doesn't take us long to come across the first cabin of our home on the outskirts, the windows broken and pieces of furniture lay carelessly outside, trashed on the ground and in shambles.

"There is no one here," Josh whispers as he looks around.

He's right, there are no guards, not even any creatures.

"They must have thought it pointless to send anyone here when there is no one to guard," I murmur as we continue to walk.

We pass more cabins and then the gathering. What was once a place where meals were shared and stories told, is now a pile of wood everywhere, like they were making a large campfire.

The memory of the man who appeared there, him handing Darius the memory stone and destroying everything, flashes in my mind. I swallow over the lump in my throat and tighten my hand on Josh's as we move forward again.

If I stay in one spot I won't be able to stand. The grief will send me to my knees.

And it nearly does as we pass Josie and Danny's cabin next, and I can't help the pained noise that escapes.

"I know, Milal. I know," Josh whispers roughly and pulls me to him. His arm curls around my shoulders as we walk.

"They didn't deserve it Josh. None of them did." They didn't deserve their throats being slit.

"You didn't deserve what they did to you either, Rhea." We move past the healer's cabin next, and Josh grits his teeth at seeing the window to Sarah's old room open, seeing the destruction within. "All we ever tried to do was survive. We knew it was a risk coming here and staying. There was nothing we could have done to stop the Elites from coming here and what happened after."

"If I accepted my Heir powers—"

"It wouldn't have mattered, Rhea." His tone is full of conviction as he looks at me. "Whether you accepted your Heir power sooner or not, there were too many. Too skilled and we were massively outnumbered. Unprepared. We didn't stand a chance."

We didn't, but that doesn't make me feel like I couldn't have done something. Bought them time, handed myself over to Charles sooner. But then I suppose Darius was always going to be ordered to come to The Deadlands to search for Sarah.

It still doesn't change the fact that this is another failure that will make my soul ache until the end of time.

So many could-haves. So many what-ifs. I suppose none of it matters now, and looking around at a deserted Eridian, I know it doesn't.

We start to slowly walk up the dirt path towards my home. The Cabin looms over us in the late afternoon sky, looking more like a destination of doom than my one place filled with love and some semblance of peace.

We reach the bottom of my porch steps full of broken planks and I look at the slightly open door. I halt in place, gripping the railing to try and gather myself.

"Is this where you needed to go?" he asks, waiting patiently at my side. "Is this why you needed to come back here?"

I nod, breathing deep before we move up the steps and to the door. Every step sends pain through my thigh, and I resist the urge to pause, knowing there is blood dripping on the floor from it.

Reaching the door, the creak of the wood unsettles the silence around us as I push it open.

I walk through on shaky legs, my heart pounding in my ears. Looking around my now trashed home, where Kade and I once lived, where we sat and ate dinner, where he gave me his drawings, where I held him when he woke from nightmares, where he laughed and smiled and told me all of his secrets...

Devastation rocks through me like an avalanche.

My knees buckle and I hit the floor.

Hard.

Chest heaving, my sobs wrack through me, noises of pain that I didn't even think possible, leaving me. My hands tremble as they land on the floor at the feeling of loss, love and life.

At the loss that Kade isn't here, in his home where he should be.

Safe. Safe. Safe.

It was a fucking lie, it wasn't fucking real.

We were never safe.

Who in the Gods was I kidding in thinking I could protect him? Making sure no harm came to him when he's been suffering since the day he was born. Being birthed into our family, being starved, and used as a pawn, being tormented with memories before I had them hidden. Finding a mate for her to die, for getting his wolf to have no control over and now...

Now to be in the hands of our family to be forced to fuck to try and create an Heir?

You cannot create an Heir.

You're *chosen.*

"Shh, Rhea," Josh says by my ear, and I didn't even realize he is on the floor with me, his arms around me, rocking me. "We will get him back. As soon as we're done here, we will go to Wolvorn, we will get him."

Runa whines within me, a sorrowful sound coming out of her and it makes more tears track down my face.

"The other Highers, our family," I hiccup. "What if he's not even there anymore? What if they have started to make him... do things?"

Josh pulls my face out of his neck and waits until my eyes hit his. "We will find him, Rhea." His gray eyes are full of determination, full of emotion. "We will bring him back."

"Frederick said something to me," I tell him, trying to calm myself. I don't want to think about it, don't even want to know if it is true... but if it is. "He said, where do you think Aldus got the crystal from in Eridian." Josh's brows furrow. "There was only one crystal I received before the Elites came."

Josh's eyes narrow, and then surprise washes over his face. "I...Let's look." I nod and he stands, reaching down to help me up. I hiss at the pain running through my leg, and he looks at me with concern.

"Rhea..."

"I'll be fine." He doesn't believe me...and shit, I don't either, but we need to hurry, I need to get back to Darius before he really loses it.

I look over my shoulder at the dining room table, at the grandfather clock that lay in pieces on the floor. I dread to think what we might find once we go inside my office.

We dodge bits of wood and broken pictures that have been thrown down the hallway, before coming to the open doorway at the end. I steady my breathing and follow Josh's lead as we enter my office.

It's destroyed. The books and shelves are scattered all over, the furniture in pieces, and the objects I had on my shelves are all in bits.

Bastards.

We both look toward the desk though, the only thing that seems untouched. I let go of Josh's hand and move around it, apprehension slithering down my spine. Coming to stand next to my office chair, I look down at its drawers, and a *woosh* of breath leaves me.

Josh comes to stand on the other side of the desk, his hands leaning on the wood as he waits.

I crouch, running my hands down the grooves of the drawers before I come upon the last one. Bringing a hand to my thigh, I collect some blood before I place it on the drawer. The rune appears, changes color and then I place my hand on the drawer handle.

I flick my eyes up to Josh for a moment, before bringing them back down as I pull it open.

My eyes look over the letters I have gotten over the years, and I rummage through the belongings in there.

But one thing is noticeably missing.

I shake my head at Josh, letting him know that what I'm looking for isn't here.

"There are only three people who know how to open that drawer," he says, his fist clenching on top of the desk as my heart beats wildly, rapidly. "You are one of them, me the other."

I nod and stand, breathing heavily through my nose as I lean on the desk, my head hanging. "It doesn't make sense." I shake my head in denial, hoping that someone else knew, hoping someone else got in. But I know it can't be the case. "He taught me how to place the runes," I choke out, feeling confused and hurt. "Frederick said I wasn't the only traitor they know of… and here is the proof."

Josh drops his head back on his shoulders, eyes full of anger. "All this time, he could have—"

His words are suddenly cut off by a howl that's full of pain and confusion, and we both freeze, our eyes widening.

"Rhea... is that?" Josh begins, but I am already leaping over the desk and rushing out the room, ignoring the ache in my bones, ignoring wherever I'm bleeding from.

Josh is right on my heels and we jump over the mess in the cabin and fly out of the front door.

I pause on my porch, my stomach swirling, breath halting in my lungs as the howl comes again.

That's...

We take off, running down the path and toward the howl, which came from the direction of the gathering. Josh falls behind as I push Runa to give me strength, her ears perking, and I move through the scattered trees, my breaths coming fast.

I skid to a stop when I reach the first pile of wood, but that doesn't have my attention. That doesn't have my eyes fixed on it.

The gray wolf in front of me, on the other side of the gathering, does.

"K-Kade?" I call, noting the darker blue eyes and silver bleeding around them. No, not Kade. I stop, my hand reaching out toward him in the air. "Axis," I whisper, "It's okay." I move over the broken benches slowly, wood scraping into me, but I don't care.

I watch as the wolf's eyes turn wary, and then flicker to pain. His coat is covered in a little blood, and he's filthy. He lifts a paw and takes a step back and I hold the sob in my throat that wants to burst out of me. I don't know why he's here, how he's here, but it doesn't matter, he came home.

"Kade," I whimper, climbing over another pile of broken benches.

The wolf steps forward, his paws hesitant, but then more sure of himself, and I hear Josh suck in a breath behind me, finally catching up and seeing Kade.

"Carzan," Josh mutters, shock in his voice.

"Kade," I try to say down the link, and instantly have the shocking reminder that it's no longer there.

I continue to move carelessly toward him, but slowly slipping and being stabbed by wooded pieces. The pain is nothing when bits scrape against my hands, as I move pieces out of the way to get to him. Nor do I care when a particularly sharp one pierces through my skin at my shin.

Kade's movements seem just as rushed, looking around for the best way to get to me, a whine in his throat that brings tears streaming down my face.

"I'm coming, I'm coming," I cry, and Runa whines inside of me, agreeing with my need to reach him. Of needing to be near him.

We're so close, just a few feet away when a voice shouts through the open air, stopping us in our tracks.

"Rhea!" Darius calls, and my breath halts, my whole body locking up as Kade's head turns toward the sound, his ears flicking up, on high alert.

No...no!

Kade starts moving backwards, moving away from me.

"No, no Kade. It's fine," I tell him in a rush. "It's fine. You are safe. A lot has changed... everything has changed. He's not your enemy," I babble, but he's not listening, he keeps moving further away. "Shit, Kade. Don't. Please."

But he does. He turns and sprints out of the gathering while I climb over the wood faster, hauling pieces away from me and not caring where they land. I shove what's left of the benches away, growling at them like it will make them move until finally, I'm on the other side.

"Rhea, wait," Josh shouts behind me, trying to follow me.

"He can't run away, Josh. I need to get to him. Stop Darius from following me. He's scared of him."

"Little wolf, don't you move," Darius growls out from somewhere behind me, but I'm already moving.

Already running again.

TWENTY SEVEN

Rhea

Runa gives me a boost the best that she can to chase after Kade, sprinting along the dirt path. I call my power to my feet, trying to get it to give me anything that is left, but there is nothing.

Just my determination and desperation.

Kade is here, he is home.

It doesn't matter why, or how. I just need to get to him, make sure he's okay, to keep him safe.

I don't take in the other ruined cabins. I don't take in more destroyed furniture that's thrown onto the ground as I pass home after home. I faintly hear the others chasing after me and I pick up speed.

I just need to get to Kade.

It's been so long since I last set eyes on him, so long since I held him. And with that is the reminder of the last time I saw him. Of the hurtful words he spewed at me, then cutting the link and refusing to come with me.

But I don't let that stop me now. He wasn't himself then, I know it. They had to have done something to him.

I don't know how but I will fucking fix it, whatever they have done.

"Kade!" I call again, breathing heavily. I can just see the end of his tail up ahead. I rush past the dead lilk trees, paying no mind to them as I continue to pick up speed.

"Rhea," Josh calls down the link. *"Just wait and we will get him together. Darius is coming, I tried to stop him but he wouldn't listen."*

I ignore him, needing my focus to be on Kade.

"Carzan," I shout when I lose sight of him, panic driving me faster. Pain rattles through my body with every step, my throat is on fire and my leg feels like it will snap, but I keep going.

Spilling blood as I go.

I follow his tracks through the trees, then across the river, the cold of it seeping into my bones, then I follow until I realize the direction in which he must be going.

Lovers Falls.

I feel like my heart will give way at any moment.

I come to a stop at the river where it splits into two different directions, and catch my breath. I can't hear the others behind me, but I know it won't be long until they come and I have to get to Kade before he's spooked again.

Bending forward and resting my hands on my knees, I waver slightly, stumbling toward the river's edge before righting myself.

Fuck. I haven't got much left in me.

My body is going to give out before I reach him, but I can't let it. I can't stop now.

"Zahariss, be with me," I breathe to myself.

Taking a deep breath and wiping the sweat from my forehead, I lock my damn knees before I take a chance and go right. I don't see any prints on either side, but I think he would go this way.

Jogging alongside the river, memories flash through me of the last time I did this. Where me and Darius were on opposite sides looking for Sam.

Is this why Kade has run this way? Does he think he will find Sam? Or is he just running blindly?

I realize at this moment that I don't know what Kade thinks at all anymore.

It's been months since I last saw him, the longest we have been separated, and it's felt like I lost a part of me. A part of me only he can fill again.

Runa whimpers in agreement.

I try not to hold onto the words he said to me in the hall at Wolvorn Castle to upset me, try not to let myself believe that's what he actually thinks of me, that I mean nothing to him.

But even though I know something is wrong with him, that sliver of doubt creeps into my mind the further I go.

What if he does believe I am a traitor?

No matter. I just need him away from our blood family and the Highers, even if it means I'm not in his life anymore.

I cough over the lump in my throat and hastily wipe tears that I hadn't realized had fallen as I continue on.

Finally reaching where the river joins again, I watch as the rapids flow hastily, angrily spilling over the edge into the Unforgivable Sea. Slowing my pace, I look around and toward the statues on either side. The female on my side first, and then over to the male on the left.

No sign of Kade.

Did he not come here and veer off in another direction? Did I get it wrong?

Panic still strikes me.

"Kade," I say through trembling lips, pressing a hand to my chest as pain rockets through me. It feels like with every beat of my heart, a sharp pain flares up in some part of my body, traveling through it like lightning.

No, not yet. Not yet.

"Kade?" I cough out, gasping for air as Runa whines within me. I walk forward on shaky legs, scanning the area for him as I wheeze.

I tilt my head and hear nothing out of the ordinary, only the silent breeze as it brushes past me. A rock tumbles down the cliffside in front of me, the sound barely heard over the rushing water, but my head snaps to it, regardless.

I follow its journey down, watching as it bounces on the floor, bits of stone splintering off of it before I lift my gaze to the top of the cliff.

I blow out a breath, my body locking up as I gaze upon the one I have called my own for eleven years.

"Carzan," I whisper as we lock eyes with each other.

His blue to my blue, just slightly different.

He stands on top of the cliff, his body tense, head tilted down.

His hair is longer, grazing his eyes and he's dressed in a t-shirt and cargo pants. I have to wonder if he has gotten more control over Axis since we have been apart if he's wearing clothes, but that doesn't matter much right now.

He's skinnier, his face more drawn with a little stubble, and though he is eighteen, I want nothing more than to hold him to me and tell him everything will be alright.

To remove that look in his eyes.

When he says nothing, I gulp over my nervousness and take a step forward, craning my neck further back to keep my eyes on him. He still doesn't say a word, just continues to look down at me.

Why won't he say anything?

I go to open my mouth when he suddenly steps back, leaving me unable to see him and I move in a rush of panic.

At the rocky cliffside next to the female statue, I place my foot in an indent in the stone, then moving my hands up and gripping onto the jagged rock. With a deep breath, I start to move myself up on shaky arms.

Rocks dig into my skin and slice my arms as I push forward, creating a path of red behind me as I continue my ascent. My whole body trembles, and exhaustion threatens to take me under— but my sole focus is on reaching the top, which makes me too careless to rest.

A particularly sharp rock scrapes down the side of my already wounded arm, as I lift it to find the next grip. Then a burning sensation pulses through my leg, and my foot slips on the next groove. I cry out in alarm through gritted teeth as the rock slices into my hands as I hold on. Kicking my leg up to have my foot catch on something, I manage to find a place where my foot grips and I breathe heavily, leaning my forehead to the cliffside and squeezing my eyes shut just to rest for a moment.

It's a long fucking way down.

Steeling myself, I lift my head and open my eyes, blinking the sweat away as I scan for my next move. Come on Rhea, look, look! You have done this hundreds of times.

There!

I lift my hand and grip the rock sticking out, double checking my foothold as a crumbling stone falls below me. I swallow roughly, my mouth dry. My arms shake as I pull myself up to the next one, and my thighs scream at me to stop, to rest and take a breather, but I can't.

I won't.

My fingers eventually find flat, dirt ground as I reach the top, my blood dripping from all sorts of scratches and wounds from my body, as I grunt and pull myself up. Crying out as I heave myself over, I collapse on my front, coughing as I can't take in enough air.

My fingers digging into the earth as I calm my racing heart and wait until the dizziness subsides, forcing myself to take slow, deep breaths.

A scuffle of feet has my heavy head lifting, and I spot Kade at the pointed edge of the cliff, looking down onto the waterfall that leads into the Unforgivable Sea. The sound of the crashing water hits me, and some birds chirp in the distance, but all I see is him.

Whimpering, I get my knees under me, and then I push myself off the floor, rising to my feet. I stagger forward toward him, always toward him as I wipe my cheek, cleaning off some of the grainy dirt there.

"Kade," I pant softly as I watch his back. His body tenses at the sound of my voice, but he doesn't reply.

Noises come from below as I move closer toward him, and where the cliff becomes thinner into the point where he's at.

My eyes move down as I spot Josh coming into view on my

side of the river, his eyes wide as he sees us.

"You found him," he whispers down the link.

"He's scared. Stay down there," I reply, my gaze moving down and to the other side of the river.

Darius bursts through the tree line with Leo and Damian, his body practically vibrating with rage. I can't see his eyes clearly from up here, but I know they are hard and cold as he looks up and sees me. I sense his eyes scanning me from head to toe, and I can almost feel his displeasure and concern as he takes me in.

He is definitely not happy with what he sees, and Darius knows no bounds when it comes to me, apparently.

He needs to stay there, he needs to stay away.

Just as I think it, he moves, Leo and Damian hot on his heels as he gets closer to the male statue on his side. When he reaches it, he looks from me to the cliff wall on his side, and to the top of it.

He's not. He wouldn't.

But he does.

I shake my head wildly down at him as Darius puts his foot on the stone, and then starts to climb.

Shit.

I shuffle forward, moving closer to Kade who tenses at the arrival of the Elites. The gap between our side of the cliff and the one Darius is climbing is too far to jump across, but Darius doesn't need to be close to intimidate.

Ignoring how clumps of dirt fall off the edge as I get closer to Kade, I reach out a tentative hand to him.

Kade turns sharply, and I nearly tumble back from him, not expecting him to face me so suddenly.

I really take him in, my eyes watery as I look upon a face I know so well, yet seems so different.

He's changed. I feel it in my soul.

"Carzan," I whisper, biting my lip as he looks over my face.

"Butterflies, they aren't here," he mumbles to himself, frowning.

My brows furrow. "Butterflies?" I ask gently, not daring to move any closer just yet. "Let's just get down from here, okay?"

"They were supposed to be here, waiting for me...." He shakes his head, looking around. "What are you doing here?" he asks me, voice gruff, and just the sound of his voice makes me want to launch myself at him. To hold him tight and never let go.

Runa makes a sound of agreement within me.

"I came to look for something and then I saw you," I tell him, making a move to take a tiny step closer, but halt when he takes a small step back.

I let out a shaky breath as I see how close he is to the edge, how close he is to falling down into the water, never to be seen again. You don't come out of the sea, it's unforgivable to those that enter it, swallowing them down in its depths.

"Be careful—"

"You shouldn't have come here," he cuts me off, and my eyes move back to him at the dead tone in his voice now. Oh no. "Or maybe you should have." He tilts his head and his features turn...cold. So cold that it sends a shiver down my spine.

I let out a shaky breath as his eyes have this faraway look in them, just blank.

This is not the boy who would cry out for me when he had a nightmare and cling to me as I soothed him. This is not the boy that would have the brightest smile on his face as he showed me his drawings he did for me. This is not the boy who would come to me and tell me everything he was thinking and feeling.

No.

This is the male he has turned into over the last few months. The male they *made* him.

What happened? I want to ask him. What did they do to you?

I'm sorry I couldn't protect you, I love you. Forgive me for letting them have you.

I want to say all the things to him, but the look in his eyes stops me.

"Are you okay?" I ask hesitantly, not really sure what to say from his demeanor as I look over his body for any sign of injury. He has what looks like healed wounds on his arms, and I dread to think what put them there. Then I look at the scar that runs down from his elbow, through the link it cut.

It sticks out clearly, the thick, white of the scar carving a path through the black markings, through the blood link.

I want to grab it, rub it and make it go away.

Kade scoffs, and I internally wince. "Am I okay?" he scowls at me and I swallow, ignoring Darius's progress with the others on the other side. "Do I look okay to you?"

"I'm sorry I didn't come sooner. I'm sorry I wasn't strong enough to protect you. Let's just...let's just go home, okay? And we can talk about it," I plead. "I've been so worried. Whatever is wrong we can fix it, just come away from there," I hedge carefully.

"I have no home," he shouts, and I flinch back at his sudden outburst. A growl sounds in the wind and I know it came from Darius, a warning to him, but Kade pays no mind to it.

"Your home is with me," I manage to get out, trying not to cry, to scream and fall to my fucking knees at the unfairness of all of this.

"You were never my home." And just like that, my heart shatters.

It bleeds and burns, withers within me at those words.

I struggle to take in air, struggle to see past my eyes through the overflow of tears I couldn't have held back, even if I tried.

"Rhea!" Someone calls, or shouts. I'm not sure which, but it has no effect on me. Has no power to turn my face away from the boy that I call my own.

"You can hate me all you want, just let me help you." I stagger forward, unable to hold back. I'm so close now we nearly touch, and I look up into blue eyes I know so well, ignoring the cold look in them.

For a moment, for one *small* moment, I swear his eyes fill with pain and longing. I swear he looks just like my Kade.

"Get back away from the fucking edge, Rhea!" Darius shouts, his voice full of worry.

Snow begins to fall, dotting everything white as flakes land on us.

Winter is coming, and I will bleed upon its snow to make it right.

I'll make it better, I can make this better.

"Kade," I whisper, lifting my shaky hands to his face, my thumbs stroking the apple of his cheeks. "You don't mean that," I tell him as he just stares at me. He's not seeing me. "You are my home, and your home is with me," I cry, unable to keep it in as I dig my fingers into his cheek gently. "My life was not worth living until I took you out of that kitchen and held you tight. It wasn't worth the pain of living with what they had done to me, to us. None of it was, until I looked into your blue eyes and I vowed to myself...I fucking vowed to myself, Carzan, that I would do everything to protect you. Even live in this deep-seated, vile, crushing curse of pain within me that never leaves, if I can just make your life what it was always meant to be."

He stares at me, eyes clearing a little as he shakes his head.

"Arbiel canna. Always," I choke out. "You are my azari." *My son.* "Come back to me, come home, vallier."

He lets out a stuttering breath, and his head leans forward, touching his forehead to mine. A sob spills from my lips as Runa pushes up against my skin where Kade touches.

I soak it in as his scent surrounds me and for that moment, the land is right. My soul is at peace.

Gods I've missed him.

My hand moves from his cheek to the back of his head, running my fingers through the longer hair there.

Just like I had always done.

I can bring him home to us, he will just need time.

After a deep breath, I sluggishly move my hands up his face until I land on either side of his temples. The move was not my own, but I didn't resist anyway. I call whatever power I have left to spring to my fingertips, and just like I knew it would, it comes effortlessly—like an instinct.

Then I push it into his mind.

Kade's eyes widen, filling with tears as he gasps for air, but I never take my eyes off of him. I ignore my own chest caving in, and blood dripping from me. I ignore my body's call to lay down and rest, I just push everything I have left into him and what greets me is a ball of black, like thick mud.

My power aims for it, making it the target to eradicate and get rid of it. To evaporate the wrongness.

It collides, and I feel it breaking in, feeling it cover it whole, slowly disintegrating whatever it is holding Kade hostage in his own mind.

I hear Axis within him, then I hear Kade cry out.

I release him, dizziness washing over me with being completely depleted, but Kade stumbles back, his face full of anguish before his eyes roll in the back of his head as he loses consciousness, and I cry out in alarm as he starts to drift backwards.

I don't think as I grab onto his arm, hauling him back as much as my strength will allow and turning my body so the momentum will carry him safely behind me.

But that means I've switched places with him, and the move makes my foot slip on the edge.

"Rhea!" The sudden shout, the alarm in Darius's voice has my eyes flying open.

I tumble over, and I reach a hand out, managing to grab the edge with a cry, as pain rockets through me. I lift my other hand to hold on, trying to get a grip but it keeps slipping.

"Fuck, Rhea hold on!" My feet try to find purchase in the rock, but all it does is break it off.

I whimper, squeezing my eyes shut for a moment as Runa whines within me.

"Rhea, I'm coming now. Fuck, fuck," Josh says down the link, his voice a rush of panic.

"Just make sure Kade is okay?"

"Rhea—"

"Vow it," I plead.

"Of course I will, but I need to get you up first, I'm half way up!"

I say nothing as the arm I'm dangling from begins to tremble. I try again to grip something with my other hand, but I just keep slipping.

A breeze hits me and I look down at the rushing water below, waiting for me to drop in its hungry waves. Turning my head, I see Darius crest the top of the opposite cliff, his eyes full of fear as he rushes toward the edge and reaches out a hand to me, like he could somehow grab me.

But we are too far apart.

"Hold on," he says after shouting at Leo and Damian to try and find something to help me. I look down again. "No, little wolf. Eyes on me. Good girl. Keep them on me okay?"

I nod, whimpering again as I feel my fingers slipping further.

"Josh, hurry up!" Darius shouts and he reaches out again, his magic coming for me but the fight must have also depleted him, it doesn't come anywhere near.

I see the desperation on his face as his mouth moves, talking to me but I can't make it out. A buzzing fills my ears and sweat beads my brow, and we both know I don't have time to wait.

Darius shakes his head, shouting behind him and still trying to get as close to the edge as possible to reach me. Rock crumbles at his feet and I shake my head frantically at him.

"Don't!" I cry, scared he's about to fall.

"Then do not let go, understand?" I look into the eyes I love so much. A reminder of fresh grass poking through snow at the first sign of spring. My favorite. "Just hold…little wolf, you…make…" He's saying words, but they aren't quite registering again. "Rhea!" he shouts when I continue to look at him. "That's it, keep those pretty eyes on me," he demands, but his own eyes are full of fear he cannot hide.

I can see it.

He never really lets me see him.

A sharp pain spreads through my body and I cry out, squeezing my eyes shut as I try to keep both of my hands on the rock.

I look at Darius again. We have been through a lot since we met. We have caused harm to each other, making our lives more difficult, but right now, I'm scared and I need him to make it all go away.

I need him to make it better.

And I'm slipping.

Bleeding.

Fading.

And Darius can see it in my eyes.

"Don't you fucking dare, little wolf. You don't get to leave me when I just got you. Climb up, now." When I don't move, he continues. "Just move up a little for me, okay?" he pleads. Darius never pleads. "I'll be across soon." He looks back as Leo and Damian continue to cut down a tree to get to me. "Just hold on, just fuck, please!"

His hand is still reaching out toward me, and I lift mine, wiggling my bloody fingers, wanting to feel his skin against mine. Tears drop from my eyes as I stretch my hand out as far as they will go, as I reach for him.

It's strange that at this moment we are mirroring the statues below us who once reached out to each other from across the river. To try and get the other person to hold them tight and never let go.

But they failed.

And so have we.

My fingers slip, and I'm falling, the water below ready to take another victim into its depths.

At one point in the early days of Eridian, I stood atop the cliff, so close to letting the Unforgivable Sea have me, and now it's going to take me when I want to stay.

A roar sounds above me, the sound thundering and my body turns on its own accord so my back faces the water below. My hair whips around my face as I look up to the top of the cliffs where Darius is, when the other half of me gets smaller the further I fall.

Take care of him, Cazier. He will need you.

My vision wavers, and a wheezing breath leaves me as I continue looking up toward Darius, but then, he jumps.

He's coming for me, hand outstretched, body coated in darkness and all I can do is watch as I get further away from him.

Just as I hear the water about to engulf me, just as the cold, icy depths take me, a blur has me blinking, and then I'm looking into the eyes of a wolf before I'm swallowed whole.

TWENTY EIGHT

Darius

I hit the water, my hand reaching out to grab Rhea as I land exactly where she went under.

I dive down when I feel nothing, my eyes open, scanning the darkness frantically. My hands spread out, clawing, reaching, trying to grab any part of her body, but I only touch water.

Still, I swim deeper and deeper, the ice of the water threatening to freeze the blood in my veins. But what the Unforgettable Sea doesn't realize is that if not for her, the heart in my body wouldn't pump blood around it to keep me alive.

There!

My hand grabs hold of something solid, and I grip it as tightly as I can, trying to see in the dark to no avail. I feel fingers, my lungs burning for air as bubbles release from my mouth as I try and pull on a growl.

Then it's gone, slipped through my hand and I'm left scrambling, searching, spinning this way and that to try and grab that hand again.

Something reaches my shoulders, grabbing my arms and pulling me.

No. No!

I have to get to her.

I fight with the other body, trying to kick out but I suck in water, my lungs stalling as they fill.

I'm pulled up, light cresting the surface that I see with bleary eyes and then we are at the surface.

I cough up water, gasping for air as Damian shouts in my ear, slamming his hand down on the top of my back.

"Are you fucking stupid! How can you get her if you're dead!" He's holding me up, making sure I don't sink back down, keeping us afloat.

"Do you see her?" I say instead of replying, watching as Leo is now on the cliffside, scanning the waters for her.

"No, brother," Leo shouts, his blonde hair wet from the spray of water every time it splashes against the rocks.

"Josh?" I call out as I see him descending, and his gray eyes meet mine. He shakes his head, looking down frantically as he moves to another foothold before lowering himself.

"Keep fucking looking!" I roar at them, pushing Damian away from me to dive back down.

He comes with me, never leaving my side as I once again go as far as I can go until the need for air overtakes me.

Damian is right, I can't get her if I'm dead, but I cannot get far enough down.

"Again," I say to Damian, and I see Josh hitting the water, also diving.

Down we go, my hands reaching out, my senses open and alert to catch a glimpse of her.

But I don't.

Not now, not in the next dive, and not hours later.

Snow begins to fall more heavily, making it even more difficult to see as I take a breath, waves crashing over me.

"Darius," Damian says, floating next to me, teeth chattering. "We need to get out for a bit, It's freezing." I shake my head, preparing to go back down again. "You're not thinking clearly, brother."

I grit my teeth and keep looking into the water, my heart beating wildly when I still see no sign of her.

This can't be it; I couldn't have lost her.

We have barely begun.

Barely started something neither of us wanted but cannot

deny.

Something neither of us can be without now.

She was right fucking there, within my grasp, but I wasn't able to hold on to her to bring her to me.

I wasn't enough.

Why did she even come here? Why did she port out on her own to where I couldn't protect her? Did she think I wouldn't allow her to come to Eridian? I would have come with her after I checked to make certain it was safe.

And why was the kid here, the kid that was fucking stupid enough to stand on the edge of a fucking cliff.

My limbs stiffen at the memory of it happening, and of me unable to do anything other than watch as Rhea tried to hold on, her fingers slipping slowly.

"Rhea!" Josh shouts across from me with so much anguish, and my jaw ticks when his voice cracks. I don't even care how his love for her right now comes across in his voice, I don't feel a shred of jealousy or possessiveness, not when I can't find her.

Not when I can't even feel her.

I won't accept that she's gone. I won't accept that I won't see those glass-like eyes on me so intently that she's carved out a space within me, made it her home and never left from the moment our eyes locked in The Deadlands.

She is made for me, and me alone.

She is mine in everything I am, and I can't.

Fucking.

See.

Her.

Rage and panic build up inside of me, a ball of everything I am made of, and I roar, the sound loud enough to be heard over the crashing waves as I dive back down into the Unforgivable Sea.

I will not accept this. I refuse.

I sink down, the ice cold instantly filling my veins and injecting into my bones. I keep my eyes open, looking around for her, but I see nothing.

Rising to the surface again, I take in gulps of breath just as a strong wave sends me under. It causes me to turn and spin, not knowing which way is up or down.

But I don't close my eyes, not once.

When I tumble once more and then to a stop, I look up and find the moonlight reflecting off the water's surface. Needing air again, I swim up once more.

Turning around, looking, searching, I still see no sign of her, I hear my men yell and shout for me, telling me to come back and rest for a while.

I won't.

"You cannot have her!" I roar into the waves as they splash up against me. "Do you hear me? You. Cannot. Have. Her."

I feel my eyes turn black and the last of my power swells inside of me before it coats me like a second skin. It moves downwards until it touches the water, and then it flows along the surface.

Looking.

Searching.

Reaching for the other half of me.

My magic is as frantic to find her, to gather her in its embrace and bring her home.

To me.

"Brother," Leo's voice says through the link. I keep my eyes on the water. No one will take my focus away from searching for her. *"There is no sign of her. Come back and we can search in the daylight."*

"No," I say, moving my head left and right in my search.

"We have been searching for hours in darkness. We can barely see."

"I don't care, we will find her," I shout back.

"Darius—"

I dive again.

TWENTY NINE

Rhea

Down.
Down.
Down.
Darkness surrounds me.
Cold suffocates me.
I feel nothing else.
I see nothing else.
Just sinking down, down, down.

The Unforgivable Sea has a new soul, only this time, it didn't willingly go in its deadly embrace.

THIRTY

Darius

I heave myself up the cliffside and then lay on my back, my body exhausted. Still, I roll over on my side, my eyes going back to the water's surface, still looking, still searching.

Always searching.

It's been days of nothing.

Gripping my chest, I feel the emptiness within it as I dig my fingers into the dirt with my other hand, begging once again for Cazier to go to her, to keep her safe, to keep her breathing and bring her back to me.

And yet I still don't see her, or feel her.

I never thought I would beg for anything, but for her, I would get down on my knees, bare my neck, and plead to the Gods.

Gripping the sides of the cliff, I move to sit up and dangle my feet over the edge. Everything stopped when she fell, the look on her face of defeat and resignation. I haven't done anything apart from look for Rhea ever since.

My men are scouring the shores in case she ends up there, and the rest have been told to guard Vokheim in case of an attack. With Mathew and Frederick disappearing, and the many guards that were at that place in The Deadlands, it's likely someone ported out and Charles has been told of my betrayal.

But as long as I can keep looking for her, everything else will have to wait. Including Charles and the people of Vrohkaria.

They can burn for all I care, nothing matters but her.

A figure appears further down the cliff's edge, and I see Josh looking into the waters below with her other pack members.

I snarl.

He must have come back from seeing the Kid. The Kid that hurt Rhea, the Kid that should be dead.

I haven't seen him yet. I'll kill him if I do. I would tear him limb from fucking limb and throw what's left of him into the Unforgivable Sea bit by bit.

The only thing stopping me is *her*.

If he wasn't there, she would be fucking here.

She's alive, she's alive, she's alive, I chant to myself, trying to keep the rage from overflowing.

If I let it out, I won't think clearly, and if I don't think clearly, how could I ever find her?

Yet my chest feels like it's caving in, my heart dying within as it beats a slow, cold rhythm. There is no warmth. No softness that it feels like when she's around.

Nothing but coldness, which is what I felt before I found her.

No.

This is worse than what I felt before.

Before I set eyes on her, after my mother and sister died, I was a walking vengeance in a body of flesh.

Now without her...

I'm a walking corpse who won't feel if you cut me, a dried, withered husk left to rot— but only left with rage.

No life flows within my veins.

Without her, there is nothing.

No moonlight to show how she shines when she stands under it.

No stars to glisten in her eyes as she looks up at them.

Only darkness in an empty space remains.

A space only she can illuminate.

I look through the waves below me, wanting to see anything that could resemble her as I lean forward on my knees and clasp my hands in front of me. But once again, I don't see her.

I sigh and scrub my hand through my hair, my tired eyes blurring for a moment until I shake my head to refocus.

"She's not dead," Josh says. I ignore him. "She is not. Dead," he says louder, a growl slipping through his words, and that causes me to look toward him.

He's still looking down into the water as Hudson holds Colten, murmuring words into his ear. Sebastian and Taylor are wet, having just come back from another search and Anna kneels at the edge, throwing things into the water while chanting under her breath.

"Of course she's not fucking dead," I spit, my nostrils flaring. "She is strong, a fighter, a warrior. You should have gotten to her sooner!"

He was on her side, he could have made it to her.

"She asked me to wait, Darius. She told me Kade was scared. If I had known…" Seb puts a comforting hand on his shoulder and squeezes.

I can see the guilt on Josh's face.

Good.

Let him rot with it.

"She's not answering the blood link," he says after I don't answer him. "Where is she?" His hands clench at his sides as he stands at the edge.

"I don't know," I mutter. "You can go back; I'll go down soon to continue looking."

"I just got here," Josh says, hands now on his hips.

"I'll go back in with you," Taylor says, wiping a hand down his face and Seb nods as Colten also strips off.

"You also need rest, Darius," Josh mutters. "She will need you when she's back."

"Don't tell me what she will fucking need!" I'm her Vihnarn, I know her better than anyone. I shake my head and get to my feet as he sighs.

"I'll bring you some food then." Josh says as he turns and

starts to head back down.
 I almost laugh at the thought that he thinks I will eat.
 I can't.
 Not without her.

THIRTY ONE

Rhea

Floating.
Down.
Down.
Down.
I feel weightless as my hair tickles my face, my arms reaching out uselessly above me as I sink deeper.
Falling.
Falling.
Falling with no ground beneath me.
I feel nothing else, sense nothing else as I keep my eyes closed and hold the blood in my mouth that wants to escape.
My chest burns, pain filling me with every shallow breath I take. My eyes sting behind my closed lids, my body just…done.
The beating of my heart slows and tries to pump more blood around my body, but it's flowing out of my wounds at a steady pace. I can't heal, I have nothing left in me.
Runa is silent, curled up in a ball, her back facing me. I wish I could reach out and comfort her. She knows I'm struggling as I have no magic left in me, not a sprinkle as a cloud-like feeling spreads beneath me and then, I stop.
Suspended wherever I am.
Am I still in the Unforgivable Sea? Is this what it feels like when it takes you into its depths and captures you?
This isn't so bad. The pain in my heart is more than the pain

throughout my body. Is that what others felt like when they went to Lovers falls to jump off the top of the cliffs when their minds became too much?

Did they feel free? Relieved? Or were they scared? Lonely? Desperate?

A whine escapes my lips and I startle, scaring myself with the sound as it echoes around me.

Where am I?

I breathe deep and take in the smell of cedarwood. It's a comforting smell, and I drag it into my lungs.

But...how is his scent here? It's cruel, taunting, and I want nothing more than to feel warm, strong arms around me.

I want Darius.

I want him more than I have ever wanted anything before.

He would make it better, he would hold me and look after me.

I can't do this on my own.

A gurgled cough comes from me then, and the blood I was keeping in my mouth finally escapes onto my chin and chest.

Still, I keep my eyes closed.

I don't want to open them just yet. I don't know what I'll find.

I'm still breathing, no water entering my mouth and flooding my lungs, so where am I?

I hit the water, and yet I feel none around me. I feel no clothes around me. I am just bare to it all. Whatever this is.

A deep whimper comes from my right, and I turn my head, my hair hanging beneath me. I feel a puff of air across my face next, and then a wet, cold touch against my cheek.

I jolt at the unexpected feel of it and slowly open my bleary eyes.

A black nose enters my vision first as I blink, and I follow it up the hairy muzzle until I'm looking into two piercing green eyes surrounded by black fur. The subtle marking of a crescent moon on its forehead glows gently, the color silver so stark against the black.

My eyes widen, and the large wolf tilts its black head, ears down as he hovers over me.

He's huge, taller than me if I were standing.

His eyes stay locked with mine, and I can't help but feel safe with him as I cough up more blood. My hands tingle and pinpricks of pain travel from my fingertips to the tops of my arms. I take in a wet breath, and the wolf whimpers again before his massive head turns and looks behind him.

I slowly look around too, the space looking empty. I look up and see a soft light far above, but enough that for some reason, it's able to shine down here.

There is nothing else in here but me, and the wolf.

Where am I?

The wolf turns his head again and sits on…nothing?

Am I still floating?

I wiggle my fingers, and then my hands, the feeling of numbness fading into more pain as I wiggle my toes next. Carefully. Tentatively.

The wolf shuffles closer, that nose of his nearing my chest where the pain is the strongest, and a soft cry leaves my lips.

Please don't touch there, it hurts! I scream in my head and Runa releases a startled cry. The wolf's eyes snap to mine and I freeze.

Did he hear me?

He moves his head back and stands, his large paws walking on nothing as he pads alongside my body and walks around my feet. That's when I see it. His tails hanging low, two of them.

Two tails.

My body flinches, more blood spluttering from my mouth and white, hot pain cascades through me at the movement.

Gods it hurts.

The wolf comes around to my other side and licks at my face softly as I try to move my head away from him. For some reason, I know he won't hurt me, but I'm unsure what is going on, and how I'm going to get out of here.

Darius must be losing his mind, and Kade and Josh? Are they okay?

"Josh?" I try down the link, but I'm met with emptiness, a block.

Panic threatens to overcome me but the wolf's wet nose comes to the side of my neck next, and takes in a deep breath, nuzzling into the crook of my shoulder and I relax, my body limp.

I move my hands, stretching out my fingers, clenching and unclenching before I gingerly move my arm toward the wolf. He sits and lowers his head again, moving until my palm meets the center of his forehead.

Tears slip from my eyes and a whimper escapes me as my fingers glide gently through his soft, black fur. I trace the crescent moon next, feeling a slight tingle from it.

A low growl comes from my right suddenly, and I grip the black wolf's fur tightly on its neck, the sound scaring me which causes my body to lock up. Pain thrums through my chest, piercing and sharp, and the dark wolf next to me growls.

It's not at me though, it's for the pain I'm in. I don't know how I know; I just do.

I swallow more blood, the metallic taste rolling my stomach and I run my tongue over my teeth.

"You saved me, didn't you?" I croak to the wolf in barely a whisper. He makes a gentle purr-like sound as his eyes once again hold mine. "When I was little," I start, trying to catch my breath through the pain. "I was running away from the Highers. I saw you in the woods behind my house. You walked past me and stopped them from getting to me, didn't you?"

He just stares at me before nudging his head into my palm, but I know it to be true.

How is this possible?

Another growl from the darkened space has my muscles tensing once again and I cry out, my eyes squeezing shut.

The wolf barks at the darkness, and a deep growl replies. It is so much deeper than this one's, so much more aggressive.

I open my eyes and look where it came from. I sense something there, moving, watching, and I feel so fucking helpless.

I wish I had some magic left, but I gave it all to Kade, to the smog that covered his mind.

I felt it.

It was dark. It was evil.

I just hope I did enough to clear it, enough to save him, even if it cost me my own life.

I don't regret it, but as green eyes with silver flecks flash through my mind, I regret not spending more time with Darius.

We could have worked things out, talked more, I could have told him that forgiveness is hard, but I would let him earn it and I'm okay with that. That I am willing to give him that time if it meant that maybe... maybe I could have someone for my own in this life.

And I can't see anyone but him.

I never expected Darius, and I want more time with him, and right now, it feels like another thing that was stolen from me.

How we started to what we could become is something that I would never have thought would happen. How he cares for me, how he looks at me, how he makes me feel.

He can be my peace, I realize.

When I'm in his arms, that's my peace.

And now I won't have that.

It seems my life wasn't meant to get its happy ending, and with that realization comes a feeling of defeat that I have never experienced before.

To have the potential to have everything, only to then realize you never even stood a chance, is more soul-crushing than to have never had it at all.

The wolf nudges me gently, and two large, bright, violet eyes shine within the darkness. I make a surprised sound, and the wolf stands at my side, his stance protective as he faces whatever it is.

The eyes move closer, and a shape finally appears. His head first, large and surprisingly darker than the wolf beside me. He stalks forward, his paws silent on the ground and my heart beats so wildly within my chest that I feel like it's going to give out from overuse.

I try to move my body, trying to get up and move away, but it doesn't listen.

I can't move.

I look at the wolf beside me, more tears slipping out of my eyes as the massive wolf comes closer, wanting him to leave, get out of here before he's hurt.

He can't fight that, he's at least over eight feet.

He's a giant.

But he doesn't move from his spot besides me.

I move my head to face the violet-eyed wolf as dread slithers down my spine.

This is it, isn't it? This is the last thing I'm going to see before I die.

As he comes fully into view, I suck in a sharp breath at the chains wrapped around his body, pulsing with untold magic. Not only that, what looks like spears are sticking out of him in all sorts of places and I swallow roughly.

The massive wolf stops just beyond my feet and tilts his head to the side, his eyes roaming over me before he looks at the two-tailed wolf. He makes a low sound, not friendly but not exactly threatening I don't think, and the two-tailed wolf looks down at me.

I watch them both, my eyes going back and forth, wondering what is going on.

Then, the violet-eyed wolf lowers his head and I hold my breath, wanting to close my eyes and not see his teeth come for me, but I can't look away.

His eyes now this close, they look to have the night inside

of them, with tiny dots that look like glittering stars.

My fingers twitch at my side as his mouth gets closer and closer, and my breaths come faster and faster.

I cough up more blood, choking on it, and the massive wolf pauses, looking down at my chest, then back up to my face.

There is something in his eyes, something I'm not sure what it means.

But then he opens his mouth slightly, positioning himself so I can see all of his many, many teeth.

I can't move, I can't tell him to stop.

I'm frozen as I silently cry.

It's only when a purple glow comes from his mouth, only when he growls and releases it, do I then make a noise.

It's only then that I scream.

THIRTY TWO

Darius

"Where's the kid," I dare to ask Leo as I enter Rhea's cabin, making my way to the kitchen.

My men and some other Elites have set up here, restoring it as best as we can to what it was before we destroyed it.

I want something Rhea can come back to, some comfort.

I don't think she will get that at Vokheim so I'm making sure things are ready for her. Most of the cabins have been repaired and the gathering will have new benches soon. We replaced all pots, cutlery, and mugs, made new furniture and even brought in protection crystals which have been placed next to the dead lilk trees.

It's been nearly fourteen days since I last saw Rhea. Fourteen days of this dead thing within my chest beating cold blood around my body to keep me moving.

"He's been put in a cabin on the outskirts," Leo replies, and I grunt, crouching to put the last of the table together. "Brother, you need rest."

I shake my head even as my shoulders slump. I haven't stopped in two weeks, searching day and night for any sign of her. Fuck, the only reason I'm here now is to finish off the table, and to make sure my Elites are doing what they were ordered to, even though my brothers are seeing that they do.

I just needed to see it for myself. Needed to see that when she's back, she sees comfort and not destruction.

"The lands?" I pick up the large piece of wood, placing it on the four legs and adjusting it.

"Chaos," Leo replies on a sigh. "From last we spoke, there have been more hangings, more trials, but the Highers have been silent apart from that."

"They must know by now that something is wrong." First Aiden, now Frederick and Mathew are missing? Charles must know something is wrong. "What else?" I demand.

Leo huffs, knowing *I* know he's stalling. "You received a letter to attend Wolvorn and take your place as Higher."

My body locks up, and I hammer a nail in with a bit too much force that I have to physically restrain myself. "That won't happen."

"I know, brother, but you need to reply."

"No."

"Darius."

"No. I won't reply, and I won't give them what they want."

"We don't know if someone ported out in The Deadlands and told the Highers what they witnessed, but if you don't at least respond with a letter, they will be suspicious."

"Let them," I grunt. "Let them fucking come. And while we wait, have those posters released into the lands."

I can feel his tension instantly. "Do you think now is the right time?"

"Are you questioning me?" I ask, body tense.

"No, brother, of course not." I pick up a knife and start carefully carving into the wood. "But you need rest."

"I'll rest when this organ in my chest stops beating all together," I tell Leo then turn, facing him.

His blue eyes tired, his blonde hair all over the place as he scrubs a hand down his face. "Darius, I know how you feel."

"You have no idea how I fucking feel!" I growl at him, my temper short. Patience short. "Do you feel like half of your heart is gone? Like it's missing a beat and cannot work properly without its other half?" His eyes look between mine as he shakes his head slowly as I walk toward him, aggression spilling from my pores. "Does it feel like the air is tainted in poison with every breath you take? Like you are constantly running out of air? Does it feel like every step you take, your legs are about to break, like you can't move without a fracture, like your bones rebel at every simple step?"

Another shake of his head as his shoulders tense, pain in his eyes for me. "Brother…"

"Does it feel like your soul is torn in two, like it has split, ruptured, and ripped in half and it's searching in an endless circle for it to be whole again?"

"No," he whispers, his shoulders slumping.

"Then you have no fucking idea how I feel," I tell him, moving around him and out the front door before I unleash everything that is inside me and flatten Eridian.

I can't do that.

Rhea would hate that.

And then hate me.

And we are far past hate. Far past anger, disgust and despise for each other. We would never feel that way toward each other again.

No, I am so far from hate that she ended up being my everything.

She may be my weakness, my pain, my anger.

But more than that, she's my softness, my comfort. My home.

And I will not rest until she is back in my arms.

I walk into the cave, running my hand over the glowing ore here as I follow it to the space that Rhea claimed as hers. Where I claimed her for the first time.

She didn't know it then, but I knew what I was doing when

I followed her here.

No, followed isn't the right word. *Hunted.*

When I smelled her coming into her heat, that's when I began my hunt.

I stalked her from a distance, never too far from her unless I was pulled away to speak to my men. I watched her with her pack, and then watched her handle her business and get her hands dirty with chores that needed doing around Eridian. Sometimes she would laugh and smile, other times she was quiet.

That's when she would go off on her own, walking amongst the trees, deep within her own thoughts. I would have given just about anything to know what she was thinking in those moments.

Then she was in their gardens and her heat had begun. She raised her pretty, ice-blue eyes to me, half-lidded, her chest rising and falling with her heavy breaths. I don't think she knew how she reacted to me then. Her back slightly arched, her thighs rubbing together and her eyes silently begging me to take her.

And I did.

I hunted after her through the forest and to her cave.

I waited outside for a time, a small part of me knowing if I went in, it would be a mistake. But I couldn't resist because the thought that someone else may come and claim her drove my first steps into her space to make her mine.

I'll never forget the first time I was inside of her, the way her body wrapped around me like it was always meant to be. And it was.

In the end, it wasn't a mistake, I didn't regret it.

But I regret what I said to her afterwards.

Sighing, I run my hand through the cascading water when I reach the center. It's cold—as cold as my body feels as I look toward the middle of the pool, remembering her standing there, body wet, curves on display, hair dripping.

She was a vision of wildness and beauty.

I move to the side and walk to her carvings in the crevasses of the rock wall. When the barrier fell around Eridian and my Elites and the Higher's guards came, I didn't tell anyone about this place. I couldn't.

Some part of me felt it would be a betrayal to her. Even if at the time I thought her a traitor and the cause of the rogues, this is just one thing I couldn't do. Everything within me rebelled at someone else in this space.

Our space.

Because when I made her mine here, it became ours.

Looking over the carvings I left behind, I pick one up that she made of her and Kade. She's carved it so he's young, maybe eight, and she's holding him protectively against her chest as her hand holds him at the back of his head.

I squeeze the wood, hearing it creak and groan before putting it down.

I growl, and it vibrates off the walls as I turn away, wanting to rip his existence from those carvings like he never took his first breaths.

Rhea told me that something is wrong with him, that the Highers or his family fucked with his head, but logic is not at the forefront of my mind right now.

She only fell because he was there, because he stumbled back.

I move past her furs, remembering the last time we stayed here together. I sit on the dirt ground, bringing my arms up to rest on my bent knees. Looking around the space, I notice the lilk trees are still in bloom here, their pink and dark-orange petals swaying with no breeze that I can feel.

The ones that surround Eridian died when the barrier fell, so how are these still alive?

I look up to the moon shining down through the center of the cave, hoping it's showing the way for my own moonlight to get back to me.

To get back to where she belongs.

In my arms.

A flash of a glow has my head turning toward it, and I see a small ball of light peeking out from behind a lilk tree. It hovers there, like it's watching before it disappears behind the bark, only to slip out the other side.

I watch it, watch me, wondering how it's possible when the wisps around Rhea all dimmed, evaporating through the rainfall of the barrier when it broke.

I thought there were no wisps left.

It slowly comes out from beneath the branches and floats toward me, moving around the water that flows down around the pool until it hovers in front of me.

I can sense it studying me, sizing me up.

"I didn't expect to see you," I murmur to it, and its misty, green-blue body wiggles from side to side.

It zips forward suddenly, shooting around me again and again in a circle until it rests in front of me once more. More wisps appear behind the trees, looking like fireflies as dozens of them emerge. They float closer, swishing around each other until a wall of them are before me.

"I guess you didn't die." Rhea will be happy about that.

They move as one, swirling around, spinning, and spinning in a cyclone until the shape of a body starts to appear. A female. They move within the shape, creating feet, legs, torso, arms, and fingers. The last to take shape is the face and flowing hair.

I watch, my heart beating painfully in my chest as familiar features start to take shape, and I hold my breath, jaw clenching as wisps of Rhea appear before me.

My hand raises on its own accord, the tremble in it visible as the wisps move her own hand out toward me, reminding me of how close I was to grabbing her on the cliffs before she fell.

The wisps touch the tips of my fingers, and their subtle warmth tingles my skin, spreading up my arms before they disperse, tiny balls of her body coming apart as they once again float in front of me.

I drop my hand down, my head following as I grit my teeth through the pain, staring at the dirt below me. My hands land on the ground, my fingers digging in as black mist appears, spreading out around me.

I growl low, and even I can hear the pain in it. Anger. The fear.

A small wisp comes forward and floats down, the first that came to me. It hovers over my power as a tendril reaches for it. It moves curiously up to the wisp, and the wisp stays there, letting it explore.

My power gently wraps around it, and the wisp jiggles, its glow seen from within the black and I suck in a breath at the familiar feel of its power. My eyes lock on the wisp, then to the others and I shoot my power out toward them. Wanting more of that feeling, needing more.

I wrap them up one by one, not covering them completely but holding them, and they let me. They can feel my need when these little balls of power feel like Rhea. So exactly like her, but on a smaller scale.

I close my eyes, feeling everything from its warmth to its wildness.

"Where are you, Rhea," I say aloud, my voice hoarse. If this is her power, then she's alive. This is a confirmation I desperately needed, and something loosens within me at the knowledge.

I feel warmth on my face and peel my eyes open. A wisp covered in my power hovers, and I hold out my hand letting it rest in my palm.

"How do you have Rhea's power in you?" I ask it, knowing it will have no answer. "Are you made from her?"

I tilt my head in thought. They were always around her in the quiet moments, and they seem to stay here in her cave. How did she do this?

I call my power to my palm, unwrapping it from around the other wisps and close my eyes again, imagining a ball of darkness, imaging the wisps and I feel a stronger heat in my hand.

Opening my eyes, a ball takes shape in my palm and slowly wiggles, like it's shaking itself out before it floats on its own. I watch in fascination as the other wisps come closer to it, curious of their new friend as my black wisp floats higher, wobbling from side-to-side just as a new fawn would be standing for the first time.

The wisps that first came to me go toward it, bumping it gently before circling it in what seems like excitement. It curves around it before stopping and bouncing up and down, the black wisp copies, then hovers closer to the others as they surround it, all of them touching it briefly as if in greeting. Welcoming it.

I call on more of my power and make more, enough that in front of me, all I can see is a glow of blue-green and black, all dancing around each other.

Powers of the opposites hovering in perfect harmony.

I lift my hand, releasing the last wisp that now has a life of its own and watch them play, imagining the way Rhea's eyes would light up if she was here to see this now. The colors would reflect in them, and her smile would mesmerize me. Then the happiness that would radiate off of her would make my chest loosen, make it feel like it can take a full breath for the first time.

She would smile again, and then laugh as she would run into the wisps and play with them, giggling when they tickled her and I would watch on.

Protecting her as always.

I frown, rubbing my chest as pain shoots through it before my hand goes to my neck, to the marking that has been slowly filling since the day I met Rhea.

Running my thumb over it, the need for it to be filled consumes me. A want so deep and instinctual that I nearly growl in sorrow that it is not completed. It feels wrong for it not to be whole.

Soon, I tell myself. As soon as she's back in my arms, we will complete it under the moonlight.

A yip comes from behind the wisps and my head snaps up, seeing a young, dark gray wolf approach. Its eyes meet mine, hesitant, scared even, and then it bounds over at full speed, crashing into me.

I can't help the small, sad smile that appears on my face. "Rhea would be happy to see you, Leif." He yips, tongue coming for my face, and I playfully grab his nose, shaking him. "Where is your Mother? Brothers and sister?" He nuzzles into me, fur in my mouth as a whine comes from him in response. My brows furrow. "Let's go and see if we can find them, hmm?"

THIRTY THREE

Rhea

"She will survive it…. Yes, I'm sure, I gave her enough to get to… you chose well…It's not… Of course…soon."

I hear the deep voice as my eyes slip open. My eyes are blurry once again, just shadowy masses as I turn my head to look for who spoke. I'm sluggish, stiff, like I haven't moved in a while. I take a deep breath, the slight rasp of it echoing and the pain in my chest making me pause for a moment, as everything comes crashing back into me.

I gasp, or at least I think I do, and my hands scramble for my chest before I pause.

I shake my head, trying to get my vision to clear but it's no use. It's like I'm looking through water that's murky, and dark. I tentatively bring my hands the rest of the way to my chest, slowly, carefully, as I place them on my skin. My bare skin.

Where are my clothes?

My fingers move gently, and I feel burned flesh, to mottled skin, feeling a slight ache. I will my body to move as I gingerly sit up, groaning as my muscles protest. How long was I out for?

Blinking until my vision clears, I look around the dark space. Where is the wolf?

I see nothing, *feel* nothing.

There's no air but I'm able to breathe, no surface beneath me but I'm floating, no water but a ripple moves outward beneath me every time I move. Like water yet there is none below me.

A shape moves in the darkness, and my eyes lock on to it as

it moves closer, wrapping my arms around myself. I hold my breath, my hands clenching into my skin, but I sense no malice from the shape. No anger or violence.

I tilt my head as it comes toward me slowly, my long hair tickling my lower back. I can barely make out the shape of the head, but the small, glowing crescent moon on its forehead has me relaxing.

The wolf comes into full focus, and a cold nose touches my forehead. I breathe out a breath as it breathes me in and I press into its touch, needing to feel anything right now. He nudges me, licking my skin and purring softly. I raise a hand, stroking its muzzle and up to its ears before clasping it around its neck.

Runa stirs quietly within me, but she's still so sleepy.

I pull him closer, needing to feel his warmth and some familiarity, and the wolf obliges. Stepping forward, he rests his head on my shoulder, and I place my nose into his fur.

I don't know what's happening, or where I am, but having him here makes me feel safer.

I tentatively look around the dark space from my hiding spot in the wolf's fur, looking for the larger wolf, but I don't see him at all.

I don't remember much after that wolf sent the ball of flaming purple into my chest. I just remember my eyes locking onto his violet ones, and I felt like that moment was important.

That this needed to happen to move forward.

But forward to what? I don't know, I'm sure I blacked-out from the pain, from a power filling me.

I woke a few times I think, the memories of it unclear, but I remember the wolf. He would rest his head on my chest and occasionally lick my neck. He would purr softly, nudging my face before protecting me again.

I also remember tiny, violet balls, like a million lights swirling around me like fireflies, like the stars in the night sky. They reminded me of wisps. They got less and less until I saw no more, and I see none now.

A warmth starts to bloom in the center of my chest and spreads throughout my body. I take a hand off the wolf and touch it, feeling the slight tingle there. It suddenly flows up to my neck, the side of my face until it reaches my temples.

I gasp, gripping the wolf tighter as scenes flash through my mind at a speed I can't keep up with.

Lands, castles, people, wolves. Waterfalls, moonlight, blossoms, silver eyes and long nights.

I can't determine what is what or what it means. I feel it all though. The sadness, rage, hurt, disbelief, love, happiness, distress, and most of all, heartbreak.

Soul-destroying heartbreak.

Wetness coats my cheeks and a sob escapes me as I squeeze my eyes shut, my body jolting with my cries with what I see next. Fire, screams, blood, teeth, claws, and death, I see darkness and thousands of eyes looking, I see a wolf looking down from above and feel longing.

I feel love and loss.

The wolf whines, snuggling into me further and I cry into his neck, the emotions I'm feeling are so strong that they feel like my own but I know they aren't.

The wolf lays down next to me, and I clutch him closer as the memories fade out of my mind, like fog dissipating and I'm left with Runa, curled up in a tight ball, shivering.

She whimpers, her ears flat, eyes closed, paws twitching. I mentally reach out to her, stroking her face as she continues to make these sad noises that break my heart.

"It's okay, Runa. I'm here, we're here." The wolf starts to do a soft purr into my neck, the sound coming from deep within him making Runa's ears twitch, her body tensing before it eventually relaxes, the whimpers becoming softer until they eventually stop.

A growl comes from our left and I raise my head, my eyes locking on violet ones in the dark. The large wolf tilts his head, but makes no move to come closer as I grip the wolf's fur tighter within my fingers. He moves back out of my grip, and I suck in a breath, my hands dropping to my side as he nuzzles my cheek as if to reassure me. He walks over to the larger wolf, and my fingers twitch the closer he gets to him, worried the larger one will attack, but all he does is bend his head down to see the smaller wolf better.

They stay locked in their stare, and I watch them, wondering what they are doing. The larger one releases a smaller growl suddenly and looks up above him. I follow his gaze and see where light pierces into this darkness further up. It's like light glistening on a water's surface, and I slowly move to stand up, my legs trembling, my eyes flicking to the wolves to keep an eye on them.

I wobble on my feet, ripples circling around me, and I start to fall to the side. A black blur is suddenly there, his back coming up to my shoulders and I use him to steady myself, hanging on to him.

A huffing sound comes from the violet-eyed wolf, and my head turns to him. I think if he were human, he would have just scoffed at me.

His eyes move down to my chest before looking back at me, head tilted, but then he walks closer, his steps making no sound as small ripples come from each paw beneath him. Fear once again makes itself known within me, but I just clutch the wolf closer. He doesn't seem bothered by him, so I should be okay.

Once the large wolf is close enough, I crane my head up, keeping my gaze on him. He brings his head down, and I tense again, but the look in his eyes has me slowly relaxing.

It's not friendly, but it's not cold either.

His large nose nudges my arm, and I stumble more into the smaller wolf. My eyes widen as he does it, again and again, and I have no idea what he wants, until the smaller wolf lowers himself.

I look back and forth between the two wolves, my brows pinched together until a particularly harder shove from the violet eyed wolf has me falling on the smaller one's back. I scramble, and the wolf shuffles as my legs end up on either side as I scowl at him.

"You could have just asked, you know. I already have someone who man handles me," I grumble, my voice quiet, but then I instantly freeze. I slowly lift my eyes to his, hoping he doesn't eat me for talking, or complaining, but then I hear another huffing sound. This one like he just laughed at me. "Um…"

He shakes his large head, his violet eyes seeming to brighten further until he looks up again. The smaller wolf moves under me, and I grip his fur at his neck in a panic, not wanting to fall. He stands at his full height and moves from side to side like he's adjusting me, then settles again.

The larger wolf growls, looking down at me before once again looking up. The smaller one moves now, only it moves closer to the other one. I may have let loose a noise in fear as he moves along the larger one's front leg, pressing himself—and my leg, against him. I look at the chains around his body, so tightly against his skin that he's bleeding, something I hadn't noticed before.

The wolf comes back through the middle of his front legs and turns to face him once more. Gods he's huge.

We stare at each other, violet to ice-blue, and I slowly reach out my hand to him. I'm petrified of him, having no idea who he is, but he saved me with whatever he did.

He looks at my hand and then to my eyes, until he lowers slowly, and my shaking fingers touch the tip of his nose. He closes his eyes, turning slightly until I gently stroke up his snout.

"Thank you," I whisper, and he opens his eyes again, only this time, it's brutal. I can see the torment in them, the hurt. It's so unexpected that my eyes begin to water, and I sniffle, sucking them back. I don't want to cry again.

But it feels just like what I saw in my mind, that heartbreaking feeling again.

Did it come from him?

"I can help you, maybe?" I say, gesturing to the chains and the spears, but he moves and licks my hand, giving it a small nudge before he steps back.

More ripples spread out from under him, moving towards me but I don't see the cause. Fear penetrates me again at the thought of something else down here, an unseen creature.

Just as I nearly call out to the large wolf, the one beneath me gives a small, low purr, and then he starts to run.

But not straightforward.

No.

He goes up.

My fingers clench in his fur, my thighs locking around him to keep myself from falling as he runs up violet, mist-like steps. They appear the higher we go, coming from the bottom.

I look down, seeing the larger wolf watching us, his eyes glowing before he seems to melt into the shadows.

"Wait!" I call out, but he's gone.

I look back up and see the light shining above. I see waves turning back into themselves, bubbles appearing before we suddenly crash into it. I try to scream, but water invades my lungs as I'm knocked off the wolf's back in an instant. I close my mouth, scrambling as ice cold water surrounds me. I start to swim, to rise to the surface that seems so far away, but I can't seem to rise, my limbs feeling heavy.

A shadow appears next to me, and I hold on to the wolf's wet fur as he swims to the top, taking me along with him as my lungs burn with the need for air.

He moves as fast as he can, his eyes focused as I squint for the light, holding on to him tightly.

Just as I feel myself start to slip, we break through the surface.

THIRTY FOUR

Darius

Following Leif through the forest surrounding Eridian, I pull the hood over my head as more snow falls. Leif yips ahead of me, his nose going to the air before he starts to cross the river. I follow, the ice-cold feeling of the water instantly seeping into my pants and boots. But I press on, wondering why he was away from his family and in Rhea's cave.

I haven't seen him since the last time Rhea was playing with the pups. Which seems like a lifetime ago now when I watched her from within the trees, seeing how happy she was playing with them. She would love to see them all again, I know she would.

But her home isn't the same anymore.

The Higher's guards have destroyed anything they could inside the cabins, splintered wood and belongings litter outside homes as if it wasn't everything Rhea's pack had.

I admit, my Elites helped them, but only to round up the members of Rhea's pack when the barrier fell, we didn't set out to destroy anything. The Higher's guards saw to that, and then monitored Eridian for a time before they left it abandoned.

But that's when they must have searched their homes. What for? I have no idea. But seeing the shell of what was once Eridian pains me. Not for me, but for Rhea.

This was her home for so many years, a safe haven for her and others. They built it from the ground up, and now it's in shambles.

Because of my ignorance.

Because of my anger.

But I will fix it.

Another yip, and I know we are getting close to where Leif's den is. He comes running back to me, a little clumsily on his paws in his excitement and I reach down and pet his head. He runs alongside me as we continue on, not wanting to rush off for some reason to see his pack.

He suddenly stills before we break through the trees, a whine in his throat and I sharpen my senses, my blade in hand in the next moment.

I pause when the smell of blood hits me.

I move on and rush around the last tree, stopping in my tracks. Blood. So much blood covers the ground. And when I raise my eyes to the entrance of their den, I see one of the reasons why.

A low howl comes from Leif, before he takes off and tries to run past me, but I think fast and I grab him by the scruff of his neck, unsure what has happened here. And even though I can't hear anything close by, you never know where danger lurks.

He growls at me and I growl back, letting loose my dominance and he relents, going slack in my grip. His eyes dull with pain as they tentatively reach mine and I swallow roughly. I lift him higher and pull him to my chest, stroking the back of his head.

"It's okay, you're okay." He whines and buries his face in my neck as I walk closer to the scene before me.

I slowly let Leif go, my eyes telling him to stay put as I move closer. Bloody, torn paws are what I see first, a torn chest and a head with lifeless eyes.

I let out a ragged sigh at seeing his mother. I step closer, making sure I stay alert and look into the den. Leif's brothers and sisters are at the back, their bodies close together but none of them are alive.

They must have starved to death.

Leif whines behind me, and I grit my teeth, reaching down to stroke his head. I look toward the ground, examining the blood and see some veer off to the right.

I grab Leif and take him away from his family and put him next to a bush. "Stay." I tell Leif, instantly following the trail.

It goes deeper into the forest, with broken branches along the floor and two sets of paw prints, one different from the other and unease rises within me. I pick up the pace, seeing more and more blood as I go, until I find the culprit.

Rogures.

Two of them, and Leif's father.

I rush toward them, knowing I don't sense any more but I keep my blade ready. The rogures are both dead, their graying skin torn and chunks of flesh missing.

Fuck.

I hear raspy breaths, and that's when I see Leif's father's chest rise and fall slowly. I go to him and crouch down, ignoring his growl at my presence.

His head whips around the best he can in this state, but it tapers off when he realizes who it is.

Dark eyes meet mine, apprehension swirling in them when I raise a hand and place it over the wound on his side. He growls again, and I shush him.

"None of that," I tell him. "Rhea will already be upset when she learns of what happened here, so you need to let me help you so you can get back to your son." He looks at me for another moment, and then lays back down, accepting it. *"Leo, call for Anna, I need her help."* I call down the link.

"What's wrong? Where are you?" He demands, his voice agitated.

"Rhea was close to a pack of wild wolves that live in Eridian, the only members of that pack left are its Alpha and his son. The Alpha is in bad shape, Anna should be able to fix him." I say, pressing down harder on the wound as blood seeps through my fingers.

"I'll have her port in now."

I check around me, not sensing any more rogues and wonder how the fuck I'm going to move him.

"Come find me East of the river, if you head straight, you will find us. Rogues killed them, but the Alpha took them down and there aren't any signs of more."

"Got it," Leo says. *"I'll be there soon and I'll have some men check the perimeter."*

I reach a hand out and touch the Alpha's head, checking for any other injuries as his breathing becomes even more labored. "You drew them away to try and protect your family, didn't you?" He growls low when my hands move down his spine. "Your son is still alive, so you need to hold still and let us help you," I tell him, feeling no other injuries. "You fought well, rest now."

As if understanding me, he closes his eyes, and his tense body relaxes.

"He's lucky their bite didn't poison him," Anna murmurs, putting her healing salve onto the wound on the wolf's side. "This is the worst of his injuries," she says before moving her hand to the puncture marks on his chest. "These will heal on their own, but the salve will help. He should be fine in a week or so if infection doesn't grab hold of him."

I nod, running my hand between his ears. It's to help him stay calm, but also to be able to grab him if he decides he doesn't want Anna helping him anymore and tries to bite her.

Leif lays at my side, his front paws touching his fathers as they watch each other. Not long after Anna and Leo arrived, he came bouldering over and hasn't left since, whimpering for his father.

I should have known he wouldn't stay put, and it makes all

the more sense why he likes Rhea. Neither do as they are told.

"Elites are doing their checks. There are signs of them having been here, but none have lingered," Leo tells me, running a hand through his blonde hair and looking at the dead rogues we are burning a little ways from us.

The smell makes my nose twitch, but I don't want any trace of them left here.

Eridian has already been tainted enough.

"It seems they were killed yesterday according to the wolf's injuries. Maybe they were moving on and caught the pack's scent," I say, watching Anna apply the rest of the salve. She puts the bowl down and reties her red hair before blowing out a breath.

She looks tired, the darkness under her eyes visible. She has been working tirelessly on spells to try and find Rhea. She spends her time at the cliffside, throwing all manner of things in there while chanting.

I know she feels like a failure, and I know this because I feel the same.

Zaide leans against a tree, blade in hand, watching her work. I've noticed him watching her a lot, but I don't say anything.

I couldn't really care.

"That's all I can do, it's in the Gods hands now. If he gets worse, I can call my Grandmother but she is busy looking through our archives to find a spell." Anna pats the wolf's side and stands. "Where will you keep him as he recovers?"

I tilt my head, wondering if it's the right place to port him, but I can't think of anywhere else. "I have a place; I'll port him with Leif."

"You will need help taking them both, I'll come." Leo makes a move towards me, but I shake my head. His brows furrow.

"No, I'll take them on my own." I ignore his inquisitive look and hold out my hand for the port stone.

Anna picks up her bowl. "Any news?" she asks gently, like anything sudden will send me over the edge. I would say there is no need to be cautious, but that would be a lie.

"None," I grunt.

Her shoulders slump, and she walks away without another word, her head down.

Zaide follows.

I grab Leif by the scruff of the neck and move him to my lap, keeping my hand on the Alpha's head, and then port out without another word.

The lands spin, and my body compresses but it's over quickly. Then I'm sitting just before where the water falls from the opening in the top of Rhea's cave.

The Alpha tries to stand, a growl on his snarling lips but my own growls shut him up. Leif turns in my lap, raising his paws to my chest and licks my cheek before running off to the lilk trees, finding a wisp to play with.

"You all good?" Leo asks down the link.

"I'll be back at Lovers Falls soon," I reply.

His sigh follows. *"You need to rest, Darius."*

"No, I don't."

"Darius," he starts, and a deep growl is already building in my chest. *"You need to think of the possibility that she may not come back."* I snarl, power exploding out of me so harshly that even the wisps hide within the trees. *"Darius, brother,"* he says more gently. *"Its been a long time. You haven't stopped, you're barely talking to us unless you ask us for updates. We're worried."* I know they are but what do they want me to say?

That my heart isn't inside of me anymore, that it belongs to the only person it ever could and she's not here? That my skin feels like it's eating me alive, and nothing will make it stop until she's back in my arms?

Or that I will unleash destruction upon the lands if she's not with me soon because I'm barely holding on.

"I'm dealing," is all I can say to him. If he knew my thoughts, they would all be here in an instant, locking me down before I go to a place where I can't return from. A place I didn't

nearly return from after I whipped Rhea and she left to where I couldn't find her.

"Just," he begins, tone concerned. *"We are here, brother. We can't know what you're feeling, but we all have come to like Rhea. She's one of us, and with what's between you two, she's family."* I clench my hands into fist and watch Leif take a drink of water in the middle. *"We want her back too. Just call if you need us, I'll keep you updated as soon as I hear news from the coasts."*

The link closes and I tilt my head back and close my eyes. I rub my chest, feeling the ache there, something only she can fill.

I'll make sure the Alpha wolf is settled before I head back out to Lovers Falls, hoping I can catch a glimpse of her before I do what the stories told us about the Gods.

Go mad.

THIRTY FIVE

Rhea

I gasp for air, my lungs on fire as I sputter out water. I move my arms, trying to float whilst kicking my legs, but I sink under again as a wave crashes into me.

I swallow the sea, my feet like stone as I raise my arms and move my legs. My head breaks the surface once again, but it's no use, I'm under before I know it. I claw at the water, desperate to get air into my lungs as panic runs through me.

I can't breathe, I can't breathe.

A body moves next to me, four legs kicking toward me and I grasp his fur, holding on as he begins to rise. I scramble at his side when we break through, leaning over his back as I throw up the water I inhaled. Waves flow over us as I take in gasping breaths.

The wolf moves beneath me as I cough up anything and everything, but I hold on tight, knowing if I let go, I'm more than likely going to drown.

Once he stills again, I move my wet hair from out of my face and look around us.

Where are we? All I see is water, so far around us that it seems never ending. But I know too well about never-endings. I don't see the cliffs of Eridian, or the waterfall. I move my head and look behind me, and just there in the distance, I see land.

"Over there," I tell the wolf, my voice croaking as I point in the direction we need to go. He doesn't waste any time and turns, heading that way.

I hold on and kick my heavy legs next to him, trying to help us get ashore as my thighs scream for rest. The large wolf may have given me a boost of some kind, I mean, I am alive, but my whole body is aching with a desperate need to rest.

I pull myself up further onto the wolf's back, my naked body draping over him and he sinks a little. A panicked noise escapes me and I back off, but still grip his fur tightly in my hands to keep afloat.

His head turns my way, and his green eyes flick to his back. Without complaint or hesitation, I climb on and swing a leg over, holding onto his neck as I straddle him. We sink deeper into the water a little, goosebumps peppering my skin, but we are still afloat as he powers his legs.

I shiver from head to toe with how cold the water is, my hair plastered to my back and each drip that falls from it feels like ice stabbing me. My teeth chatter as he swims forward, and I hunch down a little, trying to curl in on myself from the wind that slices against us, but I'm just hit by the freezing waters more.

I don't know how long I was out for; I don't know how much time has passed, only that nightfall soon approaches as I turn to watch as the sun begins to dip in the horizon.

A tear escapes me as exhaustion washes over me. I just want a bed and to have Darius curl up around me, holding me possessively like I would leave him in his sleep.

Even though it annoyed me to begin with, I never did leave, and I would give anything to feel it right now. Those strong arms holding me, his breath on the top of my head as I would sleep in the crook of his neck, the warmth from his body seeping into mine.

I want to go in the protection his arms will give me.

But another thought seeps in.

"Josh?" I say down the link. *"Josh, I'm here."* Nothing. Worry begins to take root within me.

Is he okay? Is Kade okay? I hope that Josh has protected him from Darius. I have no doubt he will blame him for me falling in. But it was my choice to switch places.

Rather I fall than him.

But there is one thing I have learned about Darius when it comes to me; he doesn't like seeing me upset, and I have to hope he hasn't touched Kade in risk of him doing just that.

After everything that happened at Wolvorn Castle, he's done nothing but try and make it all better in the way he is with me, always feeding me, touching me, holding me, giving pleasure to my body I have never known before.

And he has also hurt himself for what he did to me.

Constantly.

A sob builds up in my throat before I blow out slow, even breaths, trying to get myself under control.

I accept his effort to make it better for me.

I accept that I am his and he is mine.

Always his.

It's what I want, and he's shown me it's what he wants in the way only Darius knows how.

Being an asshole about it.

And I want him, now.

It feels like years by the time we reach the shore, the wolf's panting breaths hitting me over the sound of the smaller waves. As soon as the wolf hits solid ground, his legs fold underneath him, and a *umph* releases from me as I'm knocked off and land face-down on the sand.

I pant, groaning whilst my muscles ache like never before, and I feel like I could sleep until the next moon cycle.

I keep my eyes closed as I catch my breath, uncaring that I have sand all over my naked body as the wolf pants next to me.

The waves crash against my ankles, and the cold wind causes my whole body to shake. Eventually peeling my eyes open, I get a good look at the wolf to make sure he's okay. His breathing is fast, but he doesn't seem to be dying or anything.

I gingerly rise on my arms and look around us. It's night

time now, the moon is our only light source and I gaze at it, wondering where everyone is.

Is he looking at the moon too?

Is he feeling this ache in his chest that will only go away once we are together?

I groan as I sit back on my heels, crossing my arms over my chest to stave off the wind but with no luck. I can see no one on the shore, it's just me and the wolf. But I spot some lights peeking through the trees in the distance.

It must be a village of some kind, a place to get dry and warm.

My teeth continue to chatter as I rise on wobbly legs. The wolf whines next to me before he also gets up and walks toward me, nuzzling my neck. When he pulls back, I look into his eyes and reach out, stroking his head.

"Thank you," I whisper to him, smiling softly as he tilts his head and I scratch deeper behind his ear. "Let's get you back to where you belong too, yeah?" He moves forward and puts his wet nose against my neck. I huff out a laugh when Runa perks her tired ears up. "Come on." I turn, moving toward the lights with him right next to me, slow and steady as his wet fur brushes my sides.

I really take him in now. His head stops above mine, his fur black with no other color apart from the light blue of the crescent moon and his eyes. He has an almost mist-like coating on top of his fur. Like tiny flames coming off him yet I don't burn when I touch them. Looking back at his tails, I watch as they swish behind him, mesmerized that this is the wolf that saved me all those years ago.

His ears twitch as he looks down at me for a moment before he looks around us, alert. I watch as his paws move on the sand, leaving large prints behind and I wonder for a second if we should cover them up.

I realize though that we don't have time. Not with my shivering body and his exhausted one.

The trees give us a reprieve from the wind as we stroll

through them, though being naked isn't helping the coldness in my bones. I stop when we reach the tree line and I see a small village. It's quiet, no one is around at this time of night, but it's so quiet you would think it was abandoned if it wasn't for the glow of lights coming from the windows. I turn to the wolf.

"Stay here," I tell him quietly, "I need to get something to cover myself up with, and then we can figure out how to get home." Though I don't know where to go. Vokheim Keep to the Elites? Witches Rest with Belldame and my pack? Or do I go back to Eridian in hopes Darius is still there?

No, I know he will still be there, waiting for me. And hopefully not destroying anything while he waits.

I shake my head and move forward, no time to think of these things. I'm freezing and I can't stay out here with a target on my back.

I swallow over the lump in my throat and jog over to the side of a house. I crouch below the windows and skirt along the wooden wall, keeping my senses open. Peeking around the back, I breathe out a sigh of relief as I see clothes hanging on a line.

This isn't the first time I have stolen clothes, and seemingly, it won't be the last. I feel bad for what I'm about to do, but I need to get warmed up.

I need to survive.

After everything, the damn winter cold won't take me out.

I just need to get to him.

Always him.

I glance at the back door of the home, and look to the window there, noticing they have the shutters closed. I dash forward as much as my frozen legs can take me and rip off some pants and a tunic from the line, then I dive back to the side of the house, my breaths coming fast but softly as I listen for any movement.

When nothing reaches my ears, I grab the pants and pull them up my legs. The material sticks to my barely-dry skin, but I finally get them on and tie the laces there. I quickly pull the tunic over my head next and put my arms through. It's a little big but I'm not complaining. I look down at my now dirty bare feet and wonder if I should look and see if anyone left any boots outside of their doors, but I quickly think against it.

This will do for now.

I take one last look at the back of the home before rounding the side again, wanting to get back to the wolf quickly when I crash into a solid form.

I hiss as leather smacks against my body and look up into a scowling face with stern eyes.

The male looks me over as my heart rate kicks up. His confusion doesn't last long though and his eyes light up in knowledge.

"Well, if it isn't the traitor of Vrohkaria." He grabs me, fingers digging into my arms.

Fuck.

I shake my head, panic setting in. "No," I croak, "you've got it all wrong." I try to dislodge the grip he has on my arms, but he holds firm as I wriggle.

"No girl, I don't have it wrong. Your face is drawn on posters all over the lands. You will bring in a pretty coin."

"Let me go," I smack him, pushing at his chest but it does nothing. "I am not a traitor, and the Alpha of the Elites wouldn't like you touching me like this." I try to call my magic, but nothing happens.

I am an Alpha, he can get fucked.

I kick him right between his legs instead and he grunts, his hold on me loosening.

I turn, ready to run to the wolf but a hand is in my wet hair the next moment, his other over my mouth as I'm dragged back with no care. I try to bite and kick, but my body doesn't have the strength behind it.

He starts dragging me around the home and through the center of the village. I trip over my feet a few times as I claw at his hand, trying to get him to release me and screaming into the hand that covers me.

"As soon as I get a port stone, we are going to Wolvorn Castle, and I'll be rewarded for my capture of the traitor." He comes to a stop and looks over me and licks his lips. "I'm sure I could warm you up first, I am a good wolf, after all." I gag a little behind his hand and try to bite him, but his fingers dig into my cheeks.

He pulls me by my hair harder as he continues to drag me along, my eyes stinging from the pain. I claw at his hands, my nails digging in when a deep growl comes from behind us and the male pauses, his grip tightening further as he turns around, dragging me with his movement.

The wolf stands there, teeth bared and ears low, his stare on the male.

"What the—" is all the man gets out before the wolf lunges.

THIRTY SIX

Rhea

"Good boy," I say to the wolf as I look down at the mess he left of the male.

My heart beats uncontrollably in my chest as I slide up closer to him, putting my hand on his back as he continues to growl down at the remains.

My head stings where he pulled my hair, and I reach up with my free hand to rub at it. "Come on," I whisper to him. "We need to leave."

A gasp comes from behind me and I freeze. The wolf whips around at the sound, teeth bared and ears perked. I turn with him, my fingers gripping his fur tightly.

A woman stands still at the corner of the house, her eyes wide with a hand over her mouth. She looks toward the remains on the floor, then to me and the large wolf in fear.

I hold up a hand, taking a step back. "We're leaving," I tell her, pulling on the wolf to get him to move, but he's locked in on the woman. "Hey," I hiss at him. "Come on."

"Elrick?" The woman mutters, her eyes on the mutilated body before once again looking at the wolf. Her brown eyes taking in the blood on his muzzle that's barely visible on his dark fur, before again coming to me.

Her eyes suddenly light up in recognition and I go still with shock as she drops to her knees, head bowed, neck exposed.

"Heir of Zahariss." I blink, then blink again before looking around, wondering if this is some kind of trick and she's stalling me so the others in this village can capture me.

I move even closer to the wolf, wishing I had a blade of some kind so I can protect myself.

"You are safe here," she says, and I raise a brow at her when she looks up and then move my eyes to the body at our feet. She shakes her head. "He was a tyrant, the self-proclaimed leader of our village and treated us worse than livestock." She spits toward his body, her face twisted in anger. "You have done us a great service by getting rid of him, or the...wolf." She swallows roughly before she lowers her eyes to the ground again when he growls.

"You're not wanting coin for my capture," I ask, suspicion lacing my voice. She shakes her head adamantly.

"We want peace that was stolen from us by him, you have now restored it." I look around once again, but I see no signs of anyone else coming for me. "We do not pray to the Highers, Heir of Zahariss." My eyes sharpen at her words. "We have seen the posters that branded you as a traitor, but we have seen the posters about the Highers too."

"Posters?" I trail off.

She nods her head. "Of their deeds, of them stealing children." The breath halts in my lungs...They released the posters. What has happened since I fell? "Some may have lost belief in the Gods of old, but we have not."

"We?" I question, watching her for any sudden movements.

"Our village," she answers. "We may be small, but for generations past, our village has only prayed to the wolf Gods, even when we were forced not to utter their prayers." The wolf shifts next to me and she eyes him warily. "The Highers, they do not care for the common folk, for those who till the land and grow the crops that provide them with bountiful feasts to fill their bellies. They do not care that the rogues are killing us all, and they refuse to let us seek sanctuary in their castle. My mother took my little sister and baby brother to seek safety there, but they were turned away and a riot ensued. It was too dangerous for them to continue to try, and they came home. But rogures caught them." I grip the wolf's fur tighter. "Thankfully, the Elites came and killed them before they were hurt, and they managed to flee and come home. But it was close, a few more moments and they would have been dead." Her eyes fill with tears. "The Alpha of the Elites is also the Heir to Cazier, is he not?" Her fingers shake when she places them in her lap, d gripping the material of her dirty dress. I nod my head in affirmation. "If...I beg of you." She bows her head and places it on the ground before her, and a lump forms in my throat at the sight, at the sound of desperation in her voice. "Please, ask the Alpha of the Elites for sanctuary on behalf of our village, of my family."

Slowly letting go of the wolf's fur, I move a step forward, my feet wet from the dew on the grass here and I sink a little into the mud. The wolf moves with me, but I halt him with a palm to his chest. Green eyes lock with mine, and I tell him with my eyes to stay put. He makes a low sound, but he doesn't follow when I continue forward.

When I reach the woman, my knees hit the ground, partly because I want to be on her level, to show her that we are equal, but also my legs just can't hold me up any longer.

I reach out tentatively when she sniffles, gently peeling her fingers from where they clench her hole-ridden dress. She flinches, but then squeezes my hand— almost painfully, but I ignore it. Lifting my other hand to place it under her chin, I raise her head until her eyes are on me.

"What is your name?" I ask her gently.

"Mivera," she hiccups.

"Do not beg, Mivera," I say sternly.

She releases a sob. "Please, my sister is only young, my brother younger still, maybe just take them? I don't have much, but take anything," she cries. "I'll do whatever you—"

"No," I tell her, and she cries even harder, tears dripping onto my hand that she holds on to so tightly. "Do not beg me for this, you shouldn't need to beg anyone for safety." Safety is all most ask for in the lands, it is all I have ever asked for, and I won't make another do the same, let alone beg for it. Her watery eyes meet mine. "I am going to Eridian, you must have heard of it, I assume?"

"Inside the Deadlands?" she says through trembling lips. I nod. "The Highers released an announcement when you were captured, and posters were pinned to every board in every town and village. It told all of who you are, what you did, and where you came from. It also told us we were not allowed to enter The Deadlands or Eridian, and if you were to do so, punishment would be brought upon those who do."

Bastards.

"I'm going to Eridian. I was…taken somewhere and I need to get back. Darius should be there."

"Alpha Darius?" she sniffles.

"Yes, you can come with me."

"But what about my family?" she says, looking around her.

"You can all come with me, however we get there." Her eyes go wide in alarm and she looks above me. A warmth hits the back of my neck and I look up into a chest of fur as the wolf stands behind me, his legs on either side of me as his head swivels left and right. "Don't be afraid, he's a softy," I tell the woman and he huffs, nudging my head with his before continuing to look around.

"I… I have never seen a wolf so large before," she says quietly, almost like she doesn't want to spook him as her other hand grips mine.

"He is no normal wolf, but he also needs to go back to where he belongs." She gives me a questioning look, but I press on. "Do you want to come with me to Eridian? If the Elites are still there, you will be safe, and they could also take you to a place in Colhelm where they have been taking others to safety."

"Colhelm?" she asks, and I nod. "But we are in Colhelm."

We are in Colhelm? "I don't know where the place is, I don't think anyone does except Darius and his inner circle. Have you seen anything in Colhelm? A place where maybe too many Elites are?"

"No," she whispers, "I haven't seen anything like that at all."

Dammit. I thought maybe if she knew, we could go there, and they will take me to Darius. "If you come with me to Eridian, they will take you there. Your family and the whole village."

"And what of the Highers? They said no one should leave their homes and to just continue with their jobs. We have guards coming to the village weekly to make sure we are doing what we are told."

Their sins are getting worse and worse. "The Highers won't know, or at least, it will be too late when they do."

She looks around and bites her lip, her face unsure of her decision. Then what could possibly be the worst sound we could ever hear hits our ears, and we both lock eyes. Fear sinks into me as more and more join in on the howls.

"You need to decide now!" I say in a panic as I rise to my feet and drag her up with me as best as I can. The wolf growls low, a snarl on his lips. "Hurry!" I tell her, trying to keep my voice low.

"We will go, I need to get my family." She turns and starts running around the house with me following behind her.

"Please tell me you know where that bastard's port stone is?" Port stones are not cheap to come by for a village like this, so I don't imagine she has one.

"Elrick always kept it in his home, but I don't know where." She points to a house, by far the largest one and I grab her hand to halt her.

"Did everyone in the village see the posters of the Highers deeds? Do they pray to the Gods?" I ask her, my head turning to the sound of doors opening. Panicked voices soon follow as the people of the village come out of their homes at the sounds of screeching howls.

"None pray to the Highers, even when Elrick beat us to do so, this is one thing we have refused."

I nod and look at twenty or so onlookers who have stopped in their tracks when they see me, all panicked from the sound of those howls.

The wolf stays close to me, ears twitching.

"Gather everyone to come inside Elrick's home, I'll find the port stone and then we will get out of here." Another howl, this one louder. They are getting closer. "But we have to fucking hurry before they get here."

"What if you can't find it?" she asks, her body shaking in fear.

"I will, we have to."

Otherwise, we will all be rogure food.

"Now, go." She runs off toward the other villagers, and I rush to the house Mivera pointed out.

I slip in the soggy mud, ignoring the protest in my body at just wanting to lay down and rest. Runa whines inside of me, knowing I'm pushing myself too much, but this isn't a rare occurrence for me or my body. I just need to hold out until we are all safe. I won't leave these people to be torn apart by rogures.

"Don't let any rogures near here," I tell the wolf as I rush up the steps and pull open the door. I hear a small growl in answer, but I look around the spacious living area and start with the drawers of a nearby desk, looking for the port stone.

The sound of the rogure's howls is a haunting song in the background as I rummage through every drawer and piles of trinkets around the room. With no luck here, I rush to the room next to it. It looks like some sort of storage space, but I look through the crates and inside of a moldy box of apples anyway.

Nothing.

The kitchen is next, while I'm rummaging through cupboards I hear the front door opening, followed by plenty of footsteps.

I don't ask them to help me, they could panic and could just port themselves out of here leaving us to fend for ourselves. I wouldn't blame them; they are protecting themselves and their family. But I can't risk it.

I need to get back.

With no luck in the kitchen, I head into the hallway and up the stairs, ignoring the astonished looks I get when the people of the village see me. Cries of children add to the haunting song, along with hushed whispers of calming voices from mothers and fathers.

I pant as I reach the last step and head to another room, falling into the door with a *bang*. Giving myself a moment to catch my breath, I brace myself on the wood before I head inside.

It's a bedroom.

I rummage through drawers to the left as menacing growls come from the wolf protecting the doorway to the cabin. I turn to the window and rush over, gasping when I see a pack of rogues entering the village to the far right. I grip the windowsill, my body going taut as dread washes over me.

I see more people running toward the home I'm in, their screams of fright only ramping up the rogues as their bone-colored eyes track them. Their gray bodies begin stalking forward, black dripping from their mouths, and I can feel my heart in my throat.

A couple stands frozen in the middle of the street, their fear making them unable to move. I bang on the window as hard as I can, hoping they can hear me over the rogue's snarls.

The wolf looks up at me from below and follows my eyes to the frozen couple. Without hesitation, he rushes forward and stands in front of them, growling at the rogues, facing off against them.

The couple finally move, rushing to the home and I breathe a sigh of relief as I hear them downstairs, but my terror now takes over as the rogues move their eyes to the wolf standing tall and ready in the center.

"No," I whisper, my fingers digging into the glass.

As if he heard me, the wolf's eyes lock with mine. It's so intense that it feels like he's pushed himself inside of me. Runa stands up suddenly, howling as she charges and I jolt forward as Runa presses up against my skin so forcefully that I bang my head on the glass.

I cry out, my skin splitting on impact and she charges again and again. The wolf gives me one last look before it takes a step forward and growls at the pack of rogues, as blood trickles down the corner of my eyebrow.

I move, turning to look around the room for the port stone. I have to find it, now!

I head to the drawers beside the bed, opening them so roughly that it comes out and ends up on the floor. Papers and odd items scatter everywhere, some rolling under the bed. And that's when I see it. The gray stone that I need.

I get to my knees, lowering to the floor and crawling on my stomach as the stone rests beneath the bed. Growls and snarls can be heard from outside and tears prick my eyes at not knowing what's going on, thinking the worst.

I crawl right under the bed, my arms rubbing along the rough wooden floor, but I reach it. Grabbing the port stone next to a suspicious stain, a breath of relief escapes my lips as I feel its magic within.

Rushing out from under the bed, I leave the room and go down the stairs two at a time as Runa still continues to slam against me. I don't know what she's doing and I don't know how to help her.

The small crowd of people look at me as I enter the room, but I search for Mivera, spotting her against the wall with an older woman and a young girl and boy. It must be her family.

I run toward her. "Is this everyone?" I ask her quickly and she nods her head.

"Yes, everyone is here." A long, deep howl comes from outside and everyone shouts, moving as far back in the room as possible and away from the window.

"Everyone grab onto the person next to you," I raise the port stone and they all hone in on it like predators. "We are all getting out of here." They rush to do as I ask, and I grab Mivera and place her before me in front of the door. "When I open this door, I want you to hold your arm out." She starts shaking her head instantly at my request. "Be brave, you are wolf," I tell her. "And I'm not leaving without the wolf outside. I'm the only one who can take us to Eridian, a few seconds of courage, that's all you need. Can you do that for me?"

She looks around the room at everyone waiting, and then to her family who are holding on to her as tightly as possible. "Yes," she croaks out before clearing her throat. "Yes," she tells me with more determination this time.

"Okay." I turn and open the door.

Mivera keeps the door held open as I sneak forward and down the steps. Crouching down by the railing as I watch the wolf attack two rogues in front of me. My hands shake as I watch a blur of teeth, claws, and blood as the sound of their growls fill the air. Clumps of gray flesh spew from the wolf's mouth and the snarls coming from the rogues will probably haunt my dreams in the near future.

I look around and see nothing I can use as a weapon, nothing I can use to distract them so I can get the wolf close enough to port.

My gaze moves to the other rogues further behind them. They are at a home, scratching and clawing at the door, their teeth biting into the wood as if they could tear it down. It makes me wonder if some are still in there, but Mivera said everyone is present.

I shuffle closer, trying to discreetly get the wolf's attention and not the rogues, but neither pay any mind. I swallow roughly when a yelp comes from the wolf, and blood spills to the floor as a rogue swipes at its side.

Suddenly, the wolf lets out a low snarl, whipping around and baring its teeth at it. The wolf lunges, jaw wide and it clamps its teeth down on the rogure's neck, knocking it over and onto its back. The wolf shakes his head back and forth, snarling around its kill. The rogure doesn't even cry out in pain as the wolf continues to bite down on its neck.

The other rogure leaps onto the wolf's hind, its jaws snapping open and biting down at the top of its leg.

Fuck.

The mist-like fire on the wolf seems to become larger, and the rogure yelps, shaking its head back and forth like it's in pain as the black fire seems to be spreading along its body.

My feet move me toward them without thought, without preservation as the other rogures begin to gather again and make their way toward the wolf. Us. Me.

Because now I'm in their sights, now their bone-colored eyes track every one of my moves before they raise their heads and release a hunting howl.

Then they come for me, not hesitating to get their kill. I can feel their bloodlust dripping off of them like water flowing over rocks. No. They are playing with their food, spreading out in a formation I didn't know they were capable of even considering.

They are more intelligent than we thought.

My mind goes back to The Drylands and what we found there. The experiments, the liquid they gave those rogure-like beasts, and what was in Darius's father's basement.

Have they done experiments on normal rogures too?

When I looked down into the grates on the floor in that place, there were so many of those creatures, too many to count. It was an army of them, an army to take over more lands than Vrohkaria like Frederick said.

The wolf turns its head back and forth as it moves its body to try and get the rogure off its back. It's biting into its shoulder now, even as the flames cascade over his body and rotting flesh drips from it.

The wolf yelps again, and it shoots straight to my heart. I feel inside for my magic, hoping for a tiny spark, anything to help him. Runa cries within, looking through my eyes as we watch on in dread.

I look toward the ground, seeing if I can spot anything, and I see it, a rock amongst a small tuft of grass. I go for it, looking behind me at the door where Mivera still holds her hand out, her eyes looking at the rogues nervously. I bend down and pick up the rock, sliding my eyes over to the now semi-circle that the other rogues have made as they close in on us.

The breath wooshes from me as I stand tall, knowing I only have one shot to try and make this work. My eyes stay glued to the rogue on the back of the wolf as he moves his body around, trying to dislodge him. He suddenly whines at a particular bite, and I wind my hand back, waiting.

Just as the rogue rears its head to land another bite, I let the rock loose, pushing all of my strength into it as it soars through the air. It smashes into the side of the rogues head, and it loses its balance at the unexpected blow. It falls to the side, and the wolf spins, knocking the rogue off completely.

"Come!" I call to him. The wolf turns his dark head to me, and I move to make my way back to the door. "Hurry!" He moves toward me at a fast pace, though he's limping on one of his back legs.

The other rogues howl, that screeching sound echoing around us and they charge toward us just as the one that attacked the wolf gets to its feet and joins them.

I rush the steps to the door, to Mivera's hand and I clap it on my own. I reach into the pocket of the pants I stole, and take out the port stone, setting the location in my mind and my eyes stick to the wolf coming to me as fast as he can.

The rogues are closing in on him, that black foam dripping from their mouths as they rush at us.

"Please," Mivera whimpers, "Get us out of here."

"We are going to die."

"Gods, save us."

The villagers all start shouting, begging me to go.

But I won't leave him.

"Come on, come on," I chant to the wolf, "Nearly there." I watch on in fear as the wolf stumbles a little, the rogures nipping at his hind legs and I grip Mivera's hand, dragging her out of the door a little to get closer.

She's openly crying now, trying to get me to let go of her as the others scream in terror.

The wolf's eyes lock with mine, so green, so familiar and I don't look away from him.

"Come home with me," I whisper, and with a powerful push, the wolf moves faster, then his nose touches my hand and we port out to the sounds of howls and snarls.

THIRTY SEVEN

Darius

My power pours out of me, a swirly, raging thing as I let it roam the land, curling around any bora that decided to take me on today.

I know Leo is looking for me, I know it won't be long so I have to do this quickly and move on. I already shut down the link so he couldn't hound me, but Leo being Leo will find me anyway.

I know they are worried, but I just need time to expel this…rage bubbling within me before I can go back to the cliffs and search again.

I growl, slashing and stabbing my blade again and again as we take on this family of them.

They howl, their spiked tails high as they come for me again and again.

I welcome it.

I welcome the burn of battle, the exhaustion that will hopefully soon take me to slumber before I completely lose it.

I get hit in the side, a spike entering me and I swing back in anger, blade forgotten as I punch the side of its head.

Once.

Twice.

When it's knocked on its side, I stab it through the head.

Lifting my hands, I push power to it and shape it into spikes as I dodge another attack. Rolling and then coming to a stand, I let those spikes loose, releasing them to the three bora that are charging for me.

A buzzing suddenly fills my ear, and I shake my head, disorientated for a moment, but then I pause, arms hanging loosely as I turn. I look through the dead trees aimlessly, blinking the sweat from my eyes at this feeling...

I take a step, then two, but then a bora knocks me over from the side as Leo speaks to me.

THIRTY EIGHT

Rhea

We land with an *oomph*, my legs giving out instantly and I hit the ground hard. The now useless stone rolls from my hand and I crawl over to the wolf as he drops down. I wrap my arms around his neck, my face hiding in his fur and I grip him tightly, my heart crashing against him.

Gods, that was close.

I can sense the others behind me, murmuring and whispering, comforting the young ones as I collect myself for a moment.

I eventually lift my head and pull back, placing my hands on either side of the wolf's muzzle. They look so small against his large head as we just look at each other, trying to calm our breathing before I lay my forehead against his nose in relief.

Getting to my feet gingerly, I look over the wolf's injuries. He's bleeding in all sorts of places, his back leg is especially bad and I move to it, placing my hand upon it. He makes a sharp huffing sounds, and I shush him, trying to comfort him as I try to find my power and come up empty again.

Someone moves in our direction and I turn my head, baring my teeth. The villager steps back, hands raised in defense.

They won't come near him when he's hurt.

I try again to heal him, to send anything to him but nothing happens. I pant through my breaths, wiping the sweat beading on my brow as I rise to my feet again.

"Where are we?" I hear Mivera ask somewhere behind me,

and I answer without looking.

"The edge of The Deadlands." They all gasp and make noises of fright. "It won't be long now until we reach the top of the cliffs that surround Eridian. Come, we have to move, the glow of the tree sap will help guide us."

The wolf gets to his feet when I encourage him to do so as we start walking, making sure my pace isn't too fast to help the wolf take his time. I stick to his side, my legs barely holding me up. My chest heaves as pain shoots through the center of me, spreading to my arms and up my neck. I grit my teeth, my hand gripping the wolf's fur as sweat beads on my forehead. I'm panting after walking for a short while, damn near collapsing as I lean into the wolf. His head turns and nudges me, and I make a noise, not able to talk.

His teeth come to the back of my tunic and pulls me to him. I look up at him in question and he nods to his back.

I shake mine. No way is he carrying me in his current state.

He lowers himself down to the ground, refusing to move and I try and catch my breath, all the adrenaline leaving me. I relent and try to lift my leg, but it's like stone.

A hand comes to my arm, and I growl at it, not wanting to be touched.

Mivera looks at me in surprise for a moment before her brows furrow and her eyes fill with concern. "You okay?" she asks, and I nod my head. She looks at me like I'm full of wolf shit. And I am. I'm not okay. "Let me help you." I give her a curious look and then she's at my back, reaching around and lifting my leg.

I grunt and lean forward, gripping the wolf's fur so hard it pulls a few tuffs out, but the wolf doesn't seem bothered. I squeeze my eyes shut and will my leg to move as I try and help her get my leg over. She eventually gets it over the other side and pushes me so I'm completely on the wolf's back. I lean my head forward into the back of his neck, my breaths heavy.

Mivera rubs my back, and I bristle, hating the vulnerability I just showed, the *weakness*, but I'm honestly too tired to tell her to back off.

"Thanks," I whisper to her, and she squeezes my shoulder before moving away. I raise my head, the dead trees before me mixing together and multiplying, the pain in my chest radiates through me again. I press my palm to it, not wanting to let out the pained sound that fights to be free from my lips.

I'm mindful of the wolf's injuries as he walks, my hands buried in his fur at the back of his neck. The flame-like mist on him is small now, I notice, subtle as it flows over me.

It feels just like him, and I run my fingers through it, taking in some comfort.

Mivera walks at my side with her mother, younger sister, and brother. The boy on her back has his small arms wrapped around her neck to hold on while her sister holds her mother's hand. Their faces are all showing their nerves, and with them having never entered The Deadlands before, I understand their unease.

I'm uneasy too but not from being inside here. I can feel my body giving up, feel that whatever that larger wolf did to me is dwindling.

I just need to reach him.

I sigh and slump forward a little on the wolf's back, the warmth of his fur sliding through my fingers, and I just want to rest for a little while.

I can see the edge of The Deadlands in my peripheral, and I lift my head and pull on the wolf's fur gently, stopping him from going any further.

I walk him tentatively forward, watching as the snowflakes fall on the treetops of Eridian when we come out of the dead trees. Winter is harsh, deadly, it's no wonder I was born in it. I had barely ever known peace in my life, but just for a moment as I watch the snow-covered tree tops upon the wolf's back, and the few birds that can withstand the weather flying above, I can breathe a little life into my lungs.

I lift my head and close my eyes, feeling the caress as a breeze finally rushes past me, smelling the lands, opening my senses to the scuttles of small creatures burrowing deeply into the ground. I look to the twin lakes next. The one on the left always freezes completely, while the one on the right doesn't. I remember the pack going on that frozen lake one day, slipping and sliding until it felt like we were gliding across the surface.

It became a thing we did every winter, and became part of our simple life.

My gaze goes to the end of the valley next, as memories of falling at Lovers Falls rushes through my mind. At Darius reaching out his hand to try and reach me, save me. But he couldn't and I fell.

I frown, then shiver. The peace disperses and a sadness creeps in. The wolf shifts beneath me and we walk back into the dead trees and onto the path we need to take, watching as the villagers wait for me.

"This way," I tell them, and they follow without question.

The thought of Darius, at how close I may be to him makes me realize that I don't want to go back to that simple life any more.

That simple life didn't have Darius in it.

Is that selfish of me?.

I look down at my forearm and run my fingers over the marking that's nearly filled there.

Darius is that part of me that has always needed to be filled, that part of me that I thought would be empty until my days end.

I want him, I crave him.

I *need* him.

I have always been someone who made sure to never need anyone, instead looking after everyone, it's all I have ever done for a long time.

But for once…for once I want someone to help me.

I want Darius to take some of this pain away that I feel in my heart and body, and just… save me.

I turn around and look at all who watch me, their gazes nervous and apprehensive.

"There is a path down to the forest a little further ahead, we will have to go very slow, but we need to be as quiet as we can. I'm hoping the Elites are still here, and if they are, you will be safe." They look around at each other, but they eventually nod. I begin walking again.

I clench my jaw, my hand gripping the wolf's fur to hold me steady as sweat beads on my forehead. My breaths come out more slowly, and I vow as my heartbeat fills my ears that it's weakening. My chest heaves and more pain shoots out through the center of me, spreading to my arms and up my neck.

Zahariss, let him be here.

"Rhea?" a voice of disbelief hits me and my head swivels at the sound. "Gods, fuck." Leo rushes toward me, dropping his bow he must have aimed at us.

"Leo?" My vision turns hazy as I take him in. "What are you doing in here?"

The villagers all scream in fright, huddling closer as Mivera tries to calm them. Leo suddenly stops when the wolf growls softly at him, his eyes turning wide. I look past him as Damian comes through the trees.

"Is that—" Damian begins, but Leo cuts him off.

"It is." Leo's eyes snap to mine. His head tilts, eyes glazing for a moment. "Get food and water, along with blankets." He looks behind me at the villagers. "Looks like the Heir of Zahariss brought new guests." He smiles at me, and I try to smile back but it's more of a grimace.

"Darius?" The ground suddenly starts to shake, the trees rattling, and it seems like all the air is sucked from around us. The villagers start to cry in panic.

"He's on his way," Leo says, looking over me with concern before looking at the others.

"Kade? My pack?" I dare to ask.

Damian eyes me for a moment, but his eyes soften. "They are safe, Rhea. Are you okay?"

I ignore his question as my shoulders slump in relief. "Which way is he," I whisper, my voice cracking as I look around.

"I think North somewhere, but I don't know where, he's never told us," Leo says, shaking his head and coming closer. "Rhea, where the fuck have you been...Rhea!"

I don't hear the rest, I'm already moving.

"Go," I urge the wolf, and he picks up speed as we rush past them. Shouts follow, but I don't care. "Quickly," I say, and he growls low as I hang on, my eyes looking around to spot him.

The trees continue trembling, the ground shaking but we don't stop. We run through dead tree after dead tree.

"Faster, faster," I urge the wolf more. My need to see him outweighs the danger of falling off.

I don't care that I can barely breathe.

I don't care that I'm in so much pain.

I just care about being in his arms.

A tree snaps up ahead, breaking from the force of the ground trembling, then I see a figure I know so well, glowing within the luicium sap.

A whimper spills from my lips.

His power coats him, the black creating a second skin around him and those damn tails are at his back, forming on either side of his shoulders. His eyes meet mine briefly as he comes for me, but I see the emotion in them so vividly.

They are full of fear, concern. Full of relief.

The wolf stops suddenly, jolting me forward so forcefully that I nearly go over his head. He purrs as in an apology, but I'm too focused on what's in front of me.

I pant as I watch his approach, his hurried steps aiming straight for me, and me alone. A cry slips past my lips, my hands shaking as a single tear falls down my face.

Home.

"Darius," I croak, and his beautiful green eyes meet mine

after looking over my body frantically.

The green of fresh grass sprouting after winter, the green of my dreams that watch over me as I sleep. The green that is my favorite as I reach out a hand and tilt to the side, my grip loosening in the wolf's fur as I'm unable to hold on any longer.

I can finally, *finally,* rest now.

"You found me, little wolf." Large arms wrap around me. The scent of cedarwood. Power. A warm body. The cool touch of his magic. The nuzzle of a wolf. A tingle in my arm. A touch to my forehead.

Comfort.

Strong.

Safe.

Home.

My body is jostled, a rumble of panicked words, movement. I'm rocked in the cage of arms that I have been waiting to be held in at last, as it feels like he's running. No, the wolf is running beneath us.

"Rhea."

Darius.

"Open your eyes."

I can't.

"Fuck, stay with me."

I am. I'm finally here.

"Just, hold on."

You're holding me.

"Wake up."

I'm so tired.

"We are nearly there."

Where?

"Little wolf."

Just let me rest.

"Show me those pretty eyes of yours."

Soon.

"I've got you."

I know you do, but panic grips me and I must make a sound of distress, because in the next moment, I'm being shushed and caressed and told that everything will be okay.

Then I hear more voices, another growl, the grip on me tightening and then coldness is all that's left.

And then everything goes dark.

THIRTY NINE

DARIUS

Sixteen Years Old

"So stupid," I grumble as I walk out of the Alpha's home at the Aragnis pack. I slam the door behind me, letting my father know just how I feel about being left out, once again, with their meeting.

Alpha Derrik wanted me to stay, but my father said I was too young to understand what they were talking about. I scoff to myself and head toward the trees at the back of the home.

I've been training to be an Elite for years already, my father starting when I was just six years old. I will be heading into The Deadlands to do my rite of passage to become an Elite in a few short years, and I will eventually take over from my father when he accepts the position as a Higher, so why can't I sit in on their meetings? To learn everything I need to know about this pack, as I will need to do the same for others when I become the Alpha of the Elites.

Instead, he sent me out like a scolded child.

I should have just stayed home with mom and Isabell.

I head into the trees, pissed and frustrated when a heat suddenly spreads up my neck. I pause, moving a hand to it and feeling pinpricks along my fingers.

I've been feeling this sensation for over a week now. There is no pattern to it, no explanations for it, yet every time it happens

I don't feel threatened.

I haven't told anyone about it, especially father, he will look at me like I am unfit to lead one day and I can't bear for him to look at me like that.

I will be the greatest Alpha of the Elites there has ever been. I will protect the lands so my mother and sister will always be safe.

I will keep the peace, and kill all that are a danger.

So no, telling my father will just let him know I have a weakness in my body because of this…thing. I thought about telling Leo once, but thought better of it. He's training for the rite of passage too, he doesn't need a distraction.

Angry voices reach my ears the further I walk, and my eyes move to the direction it's coming from, tilting my head to try and hear better. Are pack members arguing?

I move further into the woods, toward the voices. If I handle the situation, if there is one, I can go back to my father and prove to him I'm ready to be an Elite, that I'm ready to be the Alpha when I come of age and can sit in on pack meetings and aid them. He won't be able to deny that I'm capable.

The heat spreads up my neck more forcefully the deeper into the trees I go. The raised voices become more distant, and I pick up the pace, trying to keep up when I round a cluster of trees and a scent hits me. It halts me in my tracks, the burn in my neck on either side intensifying and I hunch over, gritting my teeth.

I bring a hand up to my neck as my vision wavers in and out.

What is going on?

A scream pierces the air next and I freeze, my body locking up yet my muscles strain under my skin. A flash of a violet color appears before me, until it's blinding me and then it's gone.

But I'm on my knees.

My hands hit the ground as something inside of me expands…shifts and moves. My skin feels like it's crawling, bristling, and rearranging. My fingers dig into the earth as I grunt, my insides turning. I growl low, with a snarl on my mouth and I dip my head and close my eyes as *something* reaches the last layer of my skin, and then it's out.

I breathe heavily, sweat dripping down my back, my heart beating wildly within my chest.

I'm confused, disoriented and feeling strange.

Then, two black paws come into view.

I tense up, slowly raising my head and my gaze connects to piercing green eyes.

The connection locks, the heat on my neck cooling slightly and the wolf before me moves forward, putting his nose against my forehead. I close my eyes, the feeling of completeness washing over me and I know.

I know this wolf is mine.

A cry comes from within the trees. It's scared, pleading, and desperate and I'm instantly on my feet, but not before the wolf before me whips around and charges forward, a deep, low growl coming from it.

I follow this irrational need to go to that cry more than anything I have ever felt. To go and…do what… I don't know.

I run, barely seeing the dark wolf up ahead of me as he wastes no time in darting over bushes and tree roots. I try to keep up with him on foot, but a wolf is much faster than I am.

The sound of angry voices gets closer, twigs snapping in hurried, panicked steps and my protective instincts rise within me. I don't know what for, all I know is I need to get there.

A sob reaches my ears and a sound starts within my chest, reaching my throat and releasing into the air in a *purr*. Everything stops for a second at that sound, as if the lands are holding its breath before it exhales again.

I come through the trees, onto what looks like a made path, like someone takes this route often. I see my wolf ahead, his stance defensive, and my eyes move to the area in front of him.

Light hair whips past a young face, tears pouring down her cheeks as she runs past. Her eyes were wide, her body trembling as she looks at my wolf in panic, before looking toward me as she passes by. A cry passes from her lips as I move closer, and then she's gone. Her little legs taking her away.

My wolf races off to the direction she came from but I can't move. My limbs refuse to cooperate as I watch where she disappeared.

My heart pounds within me, my neck once again heating and I don't even touch it this time, my hands stay loosely by my sides as I take in the fact that everything just changed.

Later, when I asked my father about a girl with light hair, he told me he didn't know of anyone like that, that I imagined it.

After looking and not finding her... I stupidly believed him.

FORTY

Darius

Now

"What is wrong with her!" I snarl, pacing back and forth as Belldame and Anna look over Rhea.

I'm close to her, watching their every move as they start to remove her clothes.

I turn and snarl at my brothers standing at the entrance to the cave, and they get the message and slowly back away. Their concern for me making them hesitate for just a moment.

"We will be here," Leo tells me.

They all came when I ordered them to get Belldame down the link. I had to tell them exactly where I was, how could I not.

They need to help her, knowing where Rhea's cave is, be damned.

"Grab the salve, Anna, start at her thigh." I look on closely as I see her injured thigh, a furious growl releasing from me as I mentally catalog all of the other bruises and cuts.

"Fuck!" I run my hands through my hair, gripping it tightly as my power moves at my feet with every step I take.

"Alpha Darius, control yourself," Belldame chastises.

But how can I when they have my moon in their hands? And she's not. Waking. Up.

It's been too long since I laid eyes on my little wolf. Of

feeling like I'm torn in half and there is no light to guide me from the dark.

It's been a slow torture, a slow decay of my soul. And now she's finally here, within my sight. And she's like *this*.

I look at her now.

At the sweat dotting her naked skin, my eyes go to her chest to make sure it moves.

One beat.

Two.

It rises, and my breath rushes out of me in relief. I move closer, sitting on the furs next to her head, uncaring that Belldame and Anna can see my weakness as I place my hand on her head and stroke it through her hair.

I will gladly let the lands know she is my weakness and revel in it if they can make her better.

"She's hurt here too," Anna says gently, placing salve on her arm. My jaw clenches, and Belldame raise her eyes to me in warning.

I squeeze my eyes shut to control the anger that's threatening to bubble over. My power swirls where I sit, moving closer to her and touching her bare shoulder.

Goosebumps pepper her skin at the touch as I try to cool her. She's burning up.

A huff comes to my left, and then a nose is nudging my arm. I run my hand over his head as he looks down at Rhea.

"You did good taking care of them, Drax," I tell him, and he growls softly, nipping me.

When he came from me, as he can with being an Heir, I felt his loss, felt our separation but I knew he would look for her, and my only hope would be that he finds her and keeps her safe. I couldn't know if he succeeded, but then I felt her enter The Deadlands.

I had that same feeling that I had many moon cycles ago, that pull that drew me to her.

When Leo told me he saw her through the link, he just

confirmed it.

I killed all the bora to cross my path and rushed to her.

Always to her.

Seeing her on the back of Drax, knowing he kept her safe and he helped bring her home to me nearly brought me to my knees.

It was like I could finally breathe again, like my soul could rest and be at ease. I was close to losing myself, lost to the madness that was creeping up within me at her not being near.

But now she's here and like this, it is threatening to take me under.

Belldame mumbles to Anna quietly as they work on her, their eyes full of concern that sets me even more on edge. I have no idea what they are doing, but she's not waking up.

Why isn't she waking up?

Cazier, do not let her be taken.

I place a kiss on her forehead and get up, pacing again. Draxton lays next to her, his nose touching her arm as he watches over her.

"She's full of cuts and bruises," Anna says before sniffling.

My jaw clenches.

"She may have hit some rocks when she fell," Belldame replies.

I growl again, my fists clenching at my sides before I swallow roughly as I look over her. She's so pale, her skin has a bluish tinge to it and her lips are cracked, bleeding slightly. By the looks of her body, she must have been in so much pain.

My chest tightens in a way that's almost painful to take a breath. Where has she been? And who the fuck are the others?

"Who are the people that came with her?" I ask my brothers.

"Villagers from Colhelm," Zaide says.

"They say she saved them." Damian mentions.

Always the savior.

"They said rogues attacked and she managed to port them out of there with the wolf," Leo murmurs.

I tense at that.

"Was she well when she came to them?" I question.

"We will ask," Leo says before the link shuts down.

"Is she okay?" Josh asks then, and my head snaps toward him as he rushes into the cave.

I growl, covering Rhea's nakedness with a barrier and then stand in front of her, protecting her.

Josh comes to a stop as my power flows out of me, a snarl on my lips as I watch his every move. Drax growls in warning.

"Fuck, Darius, I'm not going to hurt her," he barks at me.

"Stay away," I say between clenched teeth, and I hear Drax rising and coming to stand next to me. His head is just above mine, ears back as he bares his teeth.

Josh growls, lowering his head, preparing to try and get past us.

"Enough." My body heats suddenly, feeling like I'm being burned from the inside and I turn, snarling at Belldame and the hand that is raised toward us. "I said enough, she wouldn't want this."

That stops me. Fuck.

I call my power back and Drax goes back to her side as I run a hand down my face.

I hear Josh moving, and then he's at the end of the furs that one of them must have covered her with, eyeing Drax carefully before he sits.

"Tell me," he says gently, looking at Rhea's face in concern.

"She's very weak," Belldame says, and my eyes go to her. "Brave girl. Whatever happened, she fought like the Gods to get here. I don't even know how she made it." She picks up her hand and strokes over her bruised knuckles. I want to go over there and rip her hand away. "She is beyond exhausted; she must be if she hasn't even healed."

"No other problems," I ask, coming to a stop next to her. We can work with her needing rest. She can rest for as long as she needs.

She looks down at Rhea in concern. "I think she has used up her magic." I freeze at her words, breath stalled, heart not beating. "I can barely sense it; you must know this." She turns to me and I look away.

I wanted to believe that my fear of her not waking up was overriding my senses, but she just confirmed it.

I sense no magic within her.

None of that wildness and light.

"She needs time, and rest to wake up." Beldame pauses. "If she wakes." Anna bows her head and Josh's eyes squeeze shut as he places his hand on her leg over the furs.

I still. I don't move as I look over Rhea's face.

"It was like this when she first came to Witches Rest," Anna says, and my gaze reluctantly moves to her. "After everything that went on at Wolvorn Castle, she made it to my grandmother and collapsed. She was out for a while." Guilt threatens to send me into a fit of rage, to go and find a whip to take it out on my back, but I meet her gaze head on. No matter the shame I feel for what I did, the regret that is always there. I will look Anna in the eyes as she tells me what had happened. "She had nothing left in her then, but she did wake up, Darius. She did." A tear drips down her cheek as she says the last words.

"Get out," I say hoarsely, my voice even unrecognizable to myself. "Get out!" I roar when no one moves, the cave walls shaking with the force of it.

Belldame sighs, but she gets up from the furs as Anna collects her things. I hear them mumble to Josh, trying to get him to follow them, but I can't make out much of what they're saying.

They eventually move to leave when Belldame stops and puts a hand on my arm.

"Stay close to her, Heir of Cazier." Like I would leave her. "Just be next to her, your bond will help her." With those last words, she exits the cave and I'm left with silence apart from the water flowing down the opening and Rhea's soft breathing.

I look at her. Taking in her pouty lips that are slightly parted, her little nose that I can't help myself touching when I can, and then finally, to her closed eyes.

"Let me see those pretty blue eyes, little wolf," I whisper into the air. I only saw them briefly when I was going to her, and it was far too short for me. I need them on me, and I need mine on hers. I go and kneel down beside her, tracing a finger on her forehead and running it down the slope of her nose. "Please Vihnarn. I need my moonlight."

Nothing.

I close my eyes, breathing in her scent to try and calm my racing heart before I move the furs and get beneath them. Lifting an arm, I reach over and gently pull her closer, moving her how I want her until she's laid on top of me, where she always loved to be, even if she didn't admit it to herself.

I bring a hand up to the back of her head and guide her to my neck, keeping my other arm wrapped around her waist as I let her inhale my scent. She's so small compared to me. Small but mighty. My little warrior, my little wolf.

I stare up at the cave ceiling, and I reach a hand out and call Drax to me. His nose touches my hand, and then he's within me, resting as he should be.

Vrohkaria is in chaos outside of these walls. Rogure numbers have increased tenfold, my Elites aren't able to slaughter the ones that are plaguing towns and villages, but instead, evacuating them to Colhelm to try and keep them safe.

Posters are all over the lands, accounting the Highers deeds which no doubt is leaving them scrambling and the people in an uproar...but none of that matters if the being in my arms doesn't wake up.

She will hate that I'm not out there helping, but how can I move without my heart?

I clutch her tighter to me, breathing in her scent as I call my magic to my palms and gently stroke it over her skin, letting it absorb into her.

When she wakes, I vow that before I take my last breath in

the lands, there will not be a single Higher or member of Rhea's family alive.

I will make sure the lands are safe if it's the last thing I do for her.

Always for her.

FORTY ONE

Darius

I run my hands down my face, a heavy sigh leaving me as I stare into the water. My back is to Rhea, her soft breathing the only thing left that's making me not snap.

It's been five days since she came back to me, and five days since I saw her pretty blue eyes, which feels like a lifetime. I thought not seeing her after her escape from Wolvorn was bad....I was wrong.

I look over my shoulder at her, my heart clenching in that unfamiliar way that only happens with her. I fist my hands on my knees and look back to the water.

How this female has a hold on me...

No one has had the ability to make me feel as much as she does. Not even my brothers, or my family. Why did the Gods choose me for her? What is the purpose when I am no good?

When have I ever done anything right by her? Us meeting just made her life worse, so why?

She's laying there now because I was unable to protect her, again.

How many times have I failed her? Hurt her?

I loathe myself for it, but I can't keep away from her when I feel like I can only breathe when she is near. So I'm the selfish bastard that kept her with me, and now look what has happened.

I shake my head at myself. It would be easier if we didn't have this connection, if we had never even laid eyes on each other. I wouldn't have this constant worry for her, the need to protect and possess, and the need to just *be* in her presence. I would just go about my days as normal without her constantly on my mind.

And she would have been safe.

I never wanted her, now, I can't bear the thought of life without her.

It makes my skin crawl and an uncontrollable rage bubbles up within me, thinking about the possibility that she won't ever wake. That I will never see her glare, or smile, or the fight in her, or hear her soft moans that she makes when I make her come alive beneath me.

It's unbearable.

I growl to myself, and Leif and his father lift their heads to look at me from across the pool of water. They are laying between the trees, keeping their distance while the Alpha recovers fully.

I call some of my Heir power from my palm, watching the black form into a small ball. I push a little more to it, making it the size of my hand before I guide it to her. I turn and watch as it moves above her chest, the furs covering her to keep her warm. It takes a moment before it lowers into her, disappearing from sight.

I've been doing this daily when I'm not wrapped around her, making sure she can always feel me in some way. Belldame said my power will help, but it's done nothing.

A sound at the cave entrance has my head snapping in its direction, and I rise to my feet, instantly on alert. With a growl on my lips, I march over, my steps quick and heavy.

No one is entering this cave with her vulnerable.

She cannot defend herself, she cannot let me know her feelings on others seeing her this way.

I come to a stop and block the way as Josh rounds the corner with Leo. I scowl at them, noticing the pack Josh has in his hand before I bring my eyes back to theirs.

"Food," Leo says gruffly, looking over my face as he throws me the pack. I catch it, holding back my need to throw it. I don't need fucking food, I need her. "You look like shit," he says, and I clench my jaw and look away.

"You need to eat," Josh says and I shake my head.

"Not hungry."

Josh sighs and Leo grunts, folding his arms. "Brother," Leo starts, and my gaze moves back to his, my eyes giving a warning that he refuses to heed. "You need your strength, you're dead on your feet." I may as well be dead without her.

"I'll eat when Rhea does."

They look at each other, and my fingers grip the strap of the pack tighter. "She would kick your ass for this," Josh says, a frown on his face. "This isn't helping anyone, especially her. She will hate this."

Will Rhea forgive me if I rearrange his face? Wake to him being buried?

I tilt my head at him in thought, it may be worth it.

"Leave if there is nothing else." I go to turn when a hand lands on my shoulder. I pause, my body rigid, trying to control the urge to lash out. To kill, maim and hurt.

Josh walks past me to go and see Rhea, and I have to control my breathing as Leo's grip on me tightens.

"Darius, things are getting worse. I know you need to be with her, but we also need you out there," Leo says quietly, as if he didn't want to say the words but had no choice to.

"You don't know the need I have." I shrug his hand off my shoulder and turn to him. "You couldn't possibly know the need." I laugh, but it's hard, cold. "Don't tell me what I need, and fuck everyone out there in the lands. What have they ever done apart from lick the asses of the Highers?"

Leo shakes his head. "We also did the Highers bidding, you are not thinking straight, brother." He doesn't need to remind me of what we have done. "They have started calling in the alliances of packs, they are traveling to Wolvorn Castle as we speak."

"What for?" I grind out.

"I don't know, no one does," Leo pauses. "They have rogures with them."

"Rogures," I repeat. He nods. "What do you mean by that?"

He swallows roughly, stealing a glance at Josh before continuing. "They are traveling with them instead of porting. I don't know why, but the rogures are protecting those they are with."

My brows crease. Rogures are traveling *with* them and not killing them all, and they aren't killing the rogures? What the fuck.

I remember my traitorous men in the Bayson forest that had rogures with them, they didn't attack them, they stared and watched. No, they waited for a command.

And then I think to that place in the Deadlands that I have some of my men guarding, the way that beast was controlled to attack us...

"They are controlling them," I say, and he nods.

"But how?" Josh asks, eyes wide as he comes back to us.

"It must be the concoction they used, or maybe something similar to it." I scrub my hands down my face. "Have a few of the others follow them, stalk them and gain information." I tell Leo, and he nods. "I can't leave here right now."

"But—" Leo begins.

"No, do not ask me, brother," I tell him firmly. "I physically *can't*."

"What do you mean," Josh asks, a curious look on his face. "I can stay with her."

"My need to be near her won't let me. My instinct to watch over her won't let me. My wolf won't let me." I place a hand on my neck, feeling the warmth that's pulsing gently beneath my skin. "I can't leave, I won't. She is where I will be for now."

Leo sighs and runs his hand through his hair. "Then I'll devise a plan with the others." I nod. "I will speak to Maverick for an update on The Deadlands, and we will continue dealing with things and keep you updated." I reach out and place a hand on his shoulder, grateful he just accepts it.

"The people?" I ask him.

Leo shakes his head, a frown on his face. "Daily hangings and beatings. After the posters, most are rebelling, and the guards have been ordered to keep the peace at any cost."

"To keep them loyal, you mean."

"Exactly," Leo grits out, anger pouring off of him.

"Take those who need it to Colhelm."

"I will," he says, "the barrier is holding up." I nod and with one last squeeze of my shoulder, he turns and leaves.

"She will wake up, Darius," Josh tells me quietly. I say nothing as I watch them leave the cave, only moving away from the entrance once I'm sure they are gone. I move back over to Rhea, dropping the pack on the floor before crouching down.

Running my fingers over her forehead and temples, I stare at her delicate face. "Wake up, little wolf." When nothing happens, I lay down next to her, turning so I'm on my side as I stroke her hair. "You may not have been wanted in my life. I never wished for you, prayed for you, yearned for you." I run the back of my fingers down her cheek. "But Gods, Rhea, I can't be without you now. There was only ever you. My lumniva, my Vihnarn." I reach back and grab a damp cloth, wiping her forehead before I rub my nose against hers. "I need you to wake up. I....you cannot leave me."

I watch her when the night turns to day, and the days turn to night. And all this time, she doesn't wake.

FORTY TWO

Darius

Numb.

There is no other way to describe it.

The pain radiating through me feels like an avalanche crashing down on my soul.

She's not waking up.

Won't wake up.

I can barely feel her warmth anymore.

Just cold. So, so cold.

It's been sixteen days.

Sixteen days of concoctions and spells, magics and recipes, and the result has been... nothing.

"What am I supposed to do, Rhea?" I ask her, looking down at her pale face. "Tell me what to do," I beg her.

I press my own forehead to hers, feeling just how cold she is and a shiver runs down my spine. Draxton whines within me, his ears down, sitting solemnly in the center and watching through my eyes. He's been quiet apart from the distressed noises he makes. Just as quiet as I have been.

I only talk to her now.

I lift my head and peel back the furs. I put her in a white, cotton dress this morning. I didn't want anything too heavy on her that she may feel suffocated by, but I didn't want her naked beneath the furs either.

She didn't say it, but she liked wearing the dresses I picked out for her, and I would see a shy side of her that peeked out which I found adorable.

How I wish for that now.

I pick up her hand, stroking my fingers in circular motions on the back of it. I move them to her wrist, tracing her veins before I rub up and down, trying to warm up her skin. My hand pauses in the center of her forearm and my thumb traces the marking there. Our marking. One that may never be filled completely.

My own tingles in response on my neck and I swallow roughly, closing my eyes against the onslaught of despair that instantly fills me. This can't be it.

It just can't.

I keep rubbing her arm to warm her as I look around her cave. "You need to wake up to see your lesia flowers, little wolf," I say quietly as I look at the cave filled with blue. "I had them brought here because I knew you would like to see them when you woke up." My throat tightens as I look at the candles lit around the cave.

They rest on small wooden circles, surrounded by wildflowers and a prayer of good health. To be blessed by the Gods.

A last resort to heal the nearly departed.

I hear footsteps behind me, but this time I don't move, I don't stop them from entering. I turn my head when they are close, watch their distraught faces as they pale and place their newest blessing down in the cave.

They walk over to me, to the other side of the fur bed that Rhea lay in. Josh kneels down next to her and grabs her hand, squeezing tightly as tears gather in his eyes. "Rhea," he chokes out. I look away briefly, watching the flames of the candles flicker, unable to take the look of devastation in his eyes.

It means there is no hope.

It means she is going.

Colten kneels down next to him, Hudson at his back with a hand on his shoulder. "I can't believe this." He shakes his head, his voice raspy. "I just can't."

Hudson grips his shoulder tighter as he looks down at Rhea. "I know, pup. Life does not grant you mercy. Even to those most deserving."

Anna, Taylor, and Sebastian move to the bottom next. Anna's eyes are puffy from crying, and Taylor's scowl is deep while Sebastian remains quiet.

"There must be something else we can do," Anna sniffles.

"We will try the library again," Taylor grunts as Sebastion nods.

"She doesn't deserve this," Josh says eventually. "Not her. She saved us all and this is how she's repaid?"

I say nothing. What can I say?

I should have saved some of my magic so I could have used it to catch her before she fell? I should have crossed the river and gone to the other side so I could have caught her? I should have never set foot in The Deadlands in the first place, and she would have still been living her life.

Everything was set in motion as soon as Charles gave me an ultimatum for me to go there, and I should have refused.

I should have fucking refused and just became a Higher.

I may see you sooner than intended, baby sister.

I sit next to her for a long time, holding her hand as the others speak around me. To Rhea, with each other, it doesn't matter. I can't hear them anyway. I sit there long enough that they all leave, and I'm left in a cave with the woman who is my everything, who won't wake up.

Hope is no more.

It's been too long for a body to come back from this. She exhausted herself too much to get back to me and it caused her the most damage. She was warned of the dangers, we both were…and now this is how it ends.

I've known this for days, deep down I knew this. I just didn't accept it.

Another set of footsteps penetrate the fog of my mind. These ones are more soft, hesitant, and I growl.

"You really want to die if you have dared to come here." My hand tightens around Rhea's, and I quickly lighten my touch, not wanting to hurt her.

There is a stagnant pause, and then, "I needed to see her," he says quietly, and it takes everything within me not to get up and tear his head from his shoulders. I haven't seen him since that day he was atop the cliffs with Rhea.

The reason she was there in the first place.

I breathe deep to try and calm myself as magic curls at my feet, trying to remember what Rhea would want.

The rage that fills me nearly makes me lose my grip on remembering that.

Only she can have power over me and sway me.

So I sit there, rigid and tense as he gets closer.

I open my eyes when I hear him stop, take in a shuddering breath, followed by a rough swallow.

He looks a mess. Dark circles under his eyes, his blonde hair choppy and he's lost weight. I feel no sympathy though as his stare never leaves her face.

His knees give way the next second, and he drops to the hard floor, his shaking hands reaching out for her.

"Mom." That's all he gets out before he begins to break.

Just like he broke her heart.

He leans forward and places his head on the side of her shoulder, his hand gripping hers as he sobs. His whole body shakes as his guttural cries fill the cave, and I have to get up and move away as he babbles words to her.

Apologies, forgiveness, pleading, begging. Telling anyone and everyone he will do anything to make her wake up.

How the kid can now just come to his senses makes me want to snap his neck.

She loves him so deeply, fuck, she fell off a cliff because of him!

Yet all I have seen him do since I met Rhea was cause her pain.

All I have seen in her eyes when it comes to him, is pain.

The need to rid that which hurt her is getting harder to ignore. And then my back itches.

I stretch it out and breathe deeply, trying to remember my vow to her.

Kade moves his hand and runs it over her hair, tears falling down his face as he barely breathes. "I'm so sorry. I'm so, so, so sorry."

He stays like that for a long time. Holding her, always touching her. Continuing with his words.

He eventually leaves when Belldame retrieves him, promising her he will be back, and then I'm once again left alone.

The day turns to night, the only light in here from the hundreds of candles of the blessings, and the moonlight coming through the opening.

Despair and grief grips itself tighter around me, covering me in hopelessness as it tightens in my chest.

Rhea's breathing has slowed, labored, and I swallow over the lump in my throat.

I go to her, pressing my finger to her pulse point and my eyes close in pain.

Breathing deep, taking in her scent like it can become one with me, I stand and remove my clothes so I'm left in nothing, so I can feel every inch of her. Bending down, I get an arm under the back of Rhea's knees and the other underneath her shoulder blades.

Lifting her, feeling how light she has gotten, I cradle her against my chest, putting my nose to her hair to breathe her in.

Hopelessness makes my legs feel heavy as I walk toward the pool, making sure I don't stand on any of the gifts of blessing or lesia flowers as I pass them. I walk through an opening in the water and enter the water slowly.

It's cool against my skin, I recognize this, but I don't feel it.

Wading further to the center, Rhea still cradled tightly against my chest, I watch as the ends of her hair dampen. It has gotten so long now.

I stay there for a while, watching how the light cascades on her skin before I tip my head back.

"Why does it have to be this way," I whisper. "You helped in her creation, Zahariss, you are Cazier's mate. And yet you take her from me?" I look down at Rhea, the light of the moon making her skin look like it shimmers with every breath I take. "You are taking away my moonlight, the one you gifted to me." My head hangs forward and I shut my eyes tightly. "She is mine ." My voice cracks on the last word and I growl. "She is not who you take. She has spilled enough of her blood, and her soul into these lands. So *please*, Cazier, Zahariss." I clutch her tighter and her arm falls limply at her sides, the tips of her fingers touching the water below. "Do not take my moonlight away."

I watch Rhea's face. So pale, so weak as I move her head closer to my neck on my shoulder.

Then, I feel her heartbeat falter, and I think mine just stopped.

Not like this. No.

"My Vihnarn." I rub my chin on the top of her head, clutching her tighter to me before I lower her down into the water.

I support her weight under her head and her legs as she gently floats in the center. Her hair fans out around her, the light strands darkening a little with the water. Her pale skin glows in the moonlight as I lean over, rubbing my nose to hers as I'd always done, unable to help myself.

"Where you go, I go."

Then placing a soft kiss onto her cold lips, teardrops fall onto her cheek, rolling down as I kiss her gently. Showing her what she means to me, begging her to stay, wishing I could feel her warmth against me once again.

When I get myself under control, I pull back a little, breathing against her as I open my eyes and beg the Gods to see those pretty blue eyes.

But her lids stay shut, her eyes hidden from me and my chest caves in as her heart beat stops.

Silence.
Nothing.
Despair.

FORTY THREE

Darius

I hold her to me, the cotton dress clinging to her wet skin as I bury my nose in her wet hair. Magic pours out of me and along the water's surface as her coldness sinks into me.

Her body is limp in my arms. I can't feel her magic within her, her essence, her soul.

I failed her. I failed her in every fucking way since we met. I harmed her, and was cruel to her.

I didn't protect her.

I don't deserve her.

This is my punishment, it must be.

All these thoughts swirl in my head as my chest tightens, pain flowing through me.

I'll never get the chance to make her happy. To show her that I can be her everything. I wanted to give her a stable home, lands to be safe in, a reason to smile, and laugh and play in her field of flowers that she loves so much.

Now she doesn't get to see the future that is planned out. To have the wrongs righted as she has been told many times.

She gets to see none of it because I didn't fucking protect her.

"I'm sorry, Vihnarn." I squeeze her tighter, my lips press to her forehead.

Wetness coats my cheeks, but I ignore it as it passes to her. It's the visible bleeding of my soul coming out, and nothing will make them stop.

I squeeze my eyes shut and grit my teeth to stop another pained sound from escaping me. The cool water coming up to my waist feels like blades stabbing against my skin every time it sloshes against me, and the ringing in my ears feels like they are about to explode.

I deserve it. This pain.

I deserve this pain until I go to the below.

A glow penetrates my closed lids, and I slowly blink my eyes open. A small wisp hovers in front of us, the one that first came to me in here that day.

It bounces a little as I watch it, then it moves closer, resting just in front of Rhea's face. The small glow from it lights up her features, making her look ethereal.

Laeliah.

Too beautiful for these lands that have hurt her.

The wisp moves closer, almost touching her nose until it seems to shiver, quickly moving back and zipping to the lilk trees that are scattered around the cave. I watch it go behind one, and then my eyes go to the blessing that fills the stone floor.

I didn't even make her one, I realize. I just wanted her surrounded by her favorite flowers.

Would she be disappointed in me? Rhea has always been proud of following the Gods. Her belief in them, though sometimes it wavered, it has always been strong. To not have blessed her as the old Gods once did, would she be hurt by that?

I kiss her forehead again, ready to get out of the water with her when light catches my attention again. I turn my head and see the little wisp moving closer to me, but this time, it's not alone.

Slowly, wisp after wisp comes from behind the trees, too many to even count. I look up to see others coming in from the opening above me, almost looking like stars falling with the night sky at their back, and the moon watching over them.

A heavy breath leaves me as they gather around us, hovering

just inside the water's flowing edges of the pool. I turn slowly, making sure Rhea is safe in my arms as they line up next to each other.

I watch them all, their green-blue glow bright, and then I feel their subtle warmth, even though they are not too close to us.

But then they start moving closer, almost as if they are one.

I stop, watching as their own circle becomes tighter around us and I wonder if they know she is gone too. Their warmth becomes greater, but not hot, like a soft caress from Rhea when she touches me. The wisps become a circular wall around us, and I'm only able to see the water below me and the night sky above.

I start to wonder what they are doing, if I should just walk through them, but Rhea loved the wisps. Her face would light up, she would always have time for them when they were near.

Maybe they are saying goodbye in their own way.

The small one breaks off from the wall, coming closer to Rhea. It floats down until it touches her hand that rests against her chest. It sits there, gently rocking back and forth when another one comes to sit on her arm, then another on her leg, chest, head, feet.

More and more break off and touch her where they can, making sure no part of her is uncovered apart from her face.

I watch with fascination and sadness. They loved her just as much as she loved them.

I swallow roughly, rubbing my chin on her head softly.

There are still wisps that are surrounding us, unable to touch her, but now they move, all connecting with the other wisp, resting next to them. Their warmth sinks into my body, and I shiver from the difference between hot and cold, but then the water begins to heat up.

I look down, and it's like a sea of wisps. I can't even see the water I'm standing in anymore. Suddenly, they begin to glow beneath the surface, ripples rushing out from them as they all seem to rush for Rhea.

Her body jolting has my head snapping to her, wondering what caused it. My grip tightens on her, making sure she's safe as I ready my own power to get rid of the wisps in case they hurt her.

But one of them floats down and touches her forehead.

It was barely a touch, but it did something.

The green-blue glow of all the wisps dims a little, all of them in sync and then, from the center of Rhea's chest, ice-blue, the color of her power, starts to come through.

My heart beats painfully as one single, flowy strand comes first, then another, and another, and another, like a flower blooming. Hope fills my chest, and my eyes go from Rhea's face then back to her power.

If she has power...she's still in there, right?

It's so thin that I can see through it, I can see the wisps beneath it as her power becomes a gentle sea of its own. It flows over her chest and down her middle, I slowly relax my hold on her and lower her into the water once more. I support her again, making sure she floats there, and the wisps retreat from her suddenly.

They fly up and hover above us as I watch Rhea's power bleed into the water.

The pool slowly turns blue, glittering like stars as my eyes constantly move back and forth from her face, to her chest, to the water surrounding us.

Draxton is silent within me, watching carefully. My markings appear on my neck and shoulders, I feel them appearing down my back as I move my magic to my palms. Slowly, as gently as I can, I release my power into Rhea, mixing it with hers. I tilt my head, praying for any sound from her.

A breath, a heartbeat, a twitch from her fingers.

I watch as the last strand of her power leaves her body, the color almost blinding as we are surrounded by it. My heart rate kicks up, wondering what the fuck just happened. Does she not have any left within her now?

I look up to the wisps as they hover above us like fireflies, for any sign of something wrong, but they hover there content, their glow slowly getting stronger.

Ba-bump.

I still.

Ba-bump

I don't breathe.

Ba-bump.

I slowly begin to move my head down. Scared, hopeful.

Ba-bump.

My eyes land on Rhea.

Ba-bump.

The glow of the water brightens.

Ba-bump.

Her power that bled into the water is suddenly sucked right back into her.

Ba-bump.

Her body arches.

Ba-bump.

A gasp.

Ba-bump

Her eyes flutter.

Ba-bump.

They open.

Ba- bump, ba-bump, ba-bump.

And then, my knees buckle.

FORTY FOUR

Rhea

Green eyes lock with mine as we crash into water below us. I suck in a breath at its coldness, my eyes fluttering as I'm hauled into a warm body.

"Rhea," Darius breathes, and his arms tremble around me. "Fuck…Fuck!"

"Darius?" I whisper, bringing my arms up to come around his neck as I cough.

Why is my throat so dry?

Darius's face goes into my neck as he hauls me closer, my legs on either side of his waist. His breaths are choppy on my neck, his body trembling as his fingers dig into me.

I blink, looking over his shoulder and recognize my cave. Flowers are scattered everywhere, and is that…are they blessings?

"Vihnarn." His trembling intensifies, and a sound comes from him that I have never heard before. "Vihnarn."

It makes my heart beat faster, and he moves a hand to it, fingers digging in.

I try to speak, but all I can do is release a choked sound, my throat thick.

What has happened?

He pulls his head back, hands on my face as he looks at me so intensely, touching me everywhere.

It feels like he's looking within me. At all the jagged pieces and torn strands that reside there.

But I'm looking at him, too.

I see pain, fear, rage…relief.

My body is hot, my lungs feeling like they have air for the first time since the last time I saw him. How long has it been?

"Rhea," he breaths again, and then I'm hauled upright. "Fuck." His voice is a guttural whisper, low and haunting.

My legs tighten around his waist, water lapping at my body as I run my hands around the back of his head. I close my eyes, placing my head in the crook of his neck as I breathe him in. He exhales heavily against me.

A shudder wracks through him, and I run my fingers through his hair, gripping the strands as tears prick my eyes. I lock my ankles, not wanting to move an inch away from him.

I remember.

I remember falling, hurting. Going to the shore, the male in the village dragged me, rogues, porting out and then going to him.

I remember my breathing turning shallow, the pain radiating through me, the feeling of falling.

But he caught me.

We hold each other, the need for us to be wrapped together is a need that is more profound than anything else at this moment.

I kiss his neck gently, and his shaky breath hits the top of my head. He runs a hand up my back, twining his fingers in my hair as he gently pulls my head back.

The tears fall then, looking up at his beautiful face that looks so exhausted, so haunted.

His lashes are wet, and I feel a sob bubble up at the back of my throat. "Darius." I manage to get out. His eyes close, almost relishing his name on my lips so I say it again.

I bring a hand up, running my fingers over his forehead, down the side of his eye and moving to his stubble. His eyes open then, the softness in them taking my breath away as he leans closer and touches his nose with mine.

I crumble.

His hand leaves my head, and the one still clutching over my heart moves to my face as he wipes the tears away while I sob, as if he wants to take away my sadness.

But these tears are more relief than anything.

"I told you, little wolf," he whispers, his voice thick with emotion. My skin peppers with goosebumps at his nickname for me. "You don't cry tears like this."

"I...I thought..." I swallow and lean into his touch. "I thought I would never see you again."

His nostrils flare, eyes flashing black. "Fuck, Rhea, I thought I lost you." His voice is raw, full of pain and I place my hands on his face. "I can't...I can't." He squeezes his eyes shut and shakes his head, but then he quickly opens his eyes like he wants to keep looking at me. "Fuck."

Seeing him like this, so distraught. I watch his face shape into something I had never seen before. Grief of what could have been.

The Heir of Cazier is showing me this side of him, suspecting I'm the only one he has fully let in, and an emotion so strong fills me that I place my lips against his. Lost for words.

Lost on him.

He makes a guttural sound in the back of his throat before he groans and lets *me* in. Our tongues tangle, greeting one another like it has been forever since the last time. This kiss isn't from lust, but the desire to feel closer. To almost become one.

I need him in me, around me, I need that peace only his arms can give me.

His hand moves to the back of my neck, holding me still as he kisses me softly, demanding I give him more, give my submission to let him devour me.

"Vihnarn," he whispers reverently against my lips, and pleasure coils through me at that word. "Vihnarn."

A moan rises in my throat and he groans at it, his arm squeezing me around my back. My own hands move to his hair, his neck, his shoulders, and I realize for the first time that he is completely naked.

I want to touch him everywhere.

He gentles the kiss after a while, slowing down as he saviors me before he pulls back. Our breaths mingle with each other, eyes locked like he doesn't want to look away from me. Like I could vanish at any second.

Gods, I've missed him. "I've missed you," I whisper against his lips, unable to stop myself from saying it.

He releases a heavy breath, stroking my hair, and running his fingers through the strands. I didn't even notice it was wet.

"You have no idea how mad I've been without you," he grunts, his body tensing and I stroke the pulse over his neck, trying to comfort him. "I don't." His body shakes and he leans his forehead against mine. "Rhea…you wouldn't fucking wake up. No matter what I did. You wouldn't wake…up." He shakes more forcefully, a growl beginning in his chest. "Fuck."

Suddenly, his power explodes out of him, spreading out in every direction.

I feel my body tingle in its presence, watching as it flows out of him in thick strands. I'm not scared, not one bit.

Not when the walls shake, not when stone crumbles down, and not when small cracks appear in the ground.

Two black mass-like tails appear from behind his shoulders, and I smile softly, reaching for them with a hand. I gently touch his power, and he shivers at my touch, as the end of a tail wraps around my hand.

"It's okay," I tell him quietly, even though I'm not sure I understand, but he shakes his head with a groan and pulls me close again, using his hand on the back of my head to guide me back to his neck.

His power comes around me, cocooning us from the shoulders down and I feel like I'm finally home.

"It's okay, Darius, I'm here." He shakes his head.

He says the next words like they tear from his throat. "I

couldn't find you, little wolf. I tried, but I couldn't find you."

The devastation in his tone fills me with heartbreak. "I know you tried. I felt you." And I did. I remember a hand trying to grab mine, and I knew it could have only ever been him.

"I wasn't enough."

I pull back and put my hands on either side of his face. "Darius...you...you are enough," I tell him, emotion clogging my throat as I try and find the words. "I wanted to come back to you. I fought with everything I had to get back to *you*." He stills, eyes intently on mine. "Let that be enough to show you what I think of you."

He pulls my head back into his neck, but I don't miss the flash of emotion in his eyes that he's trying to hide from me. "I don't deserve you. I never will." The words are so quiet, I can barely hear them.

I sniffle, about to refute his words when I look up as soft light flutters down.

"Wisps," I say on a gasp as I watch them all come closer, my eyes wide. "I thought they were all gone."

Darius looks up before his eyes come back to my face. "So did I. After the barrier..." he trails off, and my eyes come back to him as he swallows. "They have been here, waiting.

"Waiting for what?" I wonder.

"You. Us." My brows furrow and he continues. "You love them."

I nod. "I do." I reach up and stroke a small one when it's close, and it wiggles.

"That's because they are a part of you," he tells me, and lifts his own hand. I watch in awe as a small, black ball forms in his palm. It glows gently, the shape almost stretching before it rises and hovers.

"What?"

"Watch," he says, and then all of a sudden, black wisps come through the openings between the water pouring down. So many of them, more than the blue-green wisps I'm so used to.

They swirl around us, before mingling in with the others, creating a circle of blue and black lights around us.

"Wow," I breathe, leaning my head on Darius's shoulder as I watch them. He purrs, running a hand up my back.

Then the wisps suddenly part, and my mouth drops open as they merge and change shape. Legs, torso, arms and...

I gasp, sitting up straighter in his arms. "That's us." Darius nods, but he's not looking at them, his eyes are solely on me as I smile.

I watch the wisp figures of me and Darius stand there, just looking back at us. They look so real, so life-like.

The figures turn towards one another, and wisp Darius raises its hand to wisp Rhea's face. She leans into the touch, bringing her own arm up to clutch at his wrist almost desperately.

I swallow roughly, my eyes stinging as I look back to Darius. "How?"

"They are me, and you." He looks away for a moment. "When I came here, wondering where the fuck you were. Angry with myself, at how I failed you."

"Darius, it wasn't your fault." How could he think that?

He shakes his head. "I was hanging on by a thread. All I wanted to do was destroy everything around me. But when I'm in here, I remembered how much you love it, and I was able to control myself. *Barely*." He strokes my cheek, just like the wisp version of him had done. "They came to me." He nods toward my version. "They created the body of you and when I touched them, I *felt* you. That was the hope I grabbed onto." His finger runs up to my temple. "How could they feel like you if you were dead?" He clenches his jaw, the pain in his eyes so visible that it takes my breath away. My heart aches for the sorrow in his voice. "That's when I made my own and I realized that they are us. Our essence."

I turn to the wisp couple, who are now embracing each other. "They are us," I whisper.

"We are Heirs, the Gods gave us their power. Eridian...they

blessed it when they created the barrier around it all those years ago, like you said. When it fell…"

"They needed more power," I finish for him.

He nods. "I think they have been hiding away here to recuperate."

"Does this mean we can replace the barrier?" I ask him, my eyes still roaming his face. I can't help it, I don't want to look away, and it seems he can't either.

"I think so, but there is something more important to do first." His voice turns into a growl at the end.

"What?"

"You're going to eat and drink, and then you are going to tell me where the fuck you have been!"

FORTY FIVE

Rhea

Darius carries me out of the water, his power still wrapped around me, refusing to let go. The wisps spread apart as he steps onto the stone ground, and I cling to his neck, my eyes refusing to leave his face.

I look into his eyes, at his nose and the small scar there. His strong jaw and stubble, then finally to his neck. I shiver, suddenly feeling cold having been in the pool and Darius tenses before walking faster.

He squeezes me gently before lowering me, my feet touching the soft furs beneath. His hands trail down my waist to the top of my thighs before he grabs the hem of my dress, pulling it over me in one swoop. The wet *slap* of fabric hits the floor and his eyes darken as he takes in my naked body.

Yes, desire is there, but it's more than that. It's me being here. Alive.

I didn't think I was going to make it, and the thought makes me feel as though there is a noose around my neck.

My arms hang loosely by my sides, letting him get his fill before his gaze is drawn to the wounds still healing on my body. Especially the one on my thigh. I suck in a breath when he raises his hand and trails his fingers over the scar there, his eyes filling with rage.

I grab his fingers in my hand, squeezing them before I move them up and bring them to my lips. Wanting to calm the rage I see building again, I place a kiss on his palm before moving it to my cheek. He cups my face, and I once again lean into it, closing my eyes and just…breathe.

His heavy sigh reaches my ears and the warmth of his hand disappears, causing me to open my eyes as I look at him rummaging through a pack. I look at his strong shoulders, his defined arms and torso, and of course the tattoos he has there. My eyes instinctively go to his neck again, seeing the marking there that is now nearly complete.

My heart skips a beat and warmth fills me, suddenly not cold anymore as he hands me a water skin and urges me to drink. He suddenly grunts, and my eyes go to him, noticing where his gaze is before bringing them to my own forearm.

I look down, my chest fluttering.

"Under the moonlight," he says, and I nod.

He hands me some dried meat next, but I bypass it and put my hand on his chest, my fingers trail down over his abs, stroking the hair there.

"Rhea, you need to eat and rest," he grits out between clenched teeth, and I shake my head.

He's hard, but he makes no move to do anything about it.

"Talk first," he grunts, his eyes wandering to my heaving breasts. "Then I will fill you." Gods. I clench my thighs together, and he smirks at me, noticing. He always notices. His nostrils flare before blowing out a breath. "In." He nods toward the furs and I do as he says, laying down under them as he slides up next to me.

Then I'm on top of him, my legs on either side, my chest to his and my face in his neck.

I relax, my body melting into his as he grabs the fur to make sure we are covered. He moves my hair out of the way, stroking the back of my neck until his fingers rests on my pulse point. He seems to breathe me in.

"Why did you leave?" he asks, after a while of just being in each other's arms. Heartbeat to heartbeat.

I take a breath. "Frederick said something about a crystal I had in Eridian."

"What crystal?"

"I received it from Edward along with a letter telling me you were in The Deadlands."

Darius is silent as he takes that in. "And the crystal could be the memory one?" He puts it together without me having to say it aloud.

He tenses as he waits for my answer, "I came to check it and the one he gave me isn't there."

"So he's betrayed you?" he growls and I sigh.

"I don't know, it hurts to think about it but only him, Josh and I knew how to get into my drawer. Edward taught us how to lock it with a rune."

"I could have gone with you, to check."

"I wasn't thinking straight. I just needed to go and see straight away, and you would have waited until you knew it was safe for me to go."

"Of course I would have." I snort, my point proven.

"Where were you," he asks. "After you fell."

"I'm not sure," I begin, remembering everything that has happened since I fell. "I really don't know where I was, only that I was safe."

His chin rubs against the top of my head. "Explain."

I sigh, snuggling closer. "It was...blackness," I tell him, and he tenses. "When I fell off the cliff, I thought that was it." I swallow roughly, feeling my body hitting the surface all over again. "I was filled with relief that it was me and not Kade. He lost consciousness." He growls but says nothing. "And then I thought selfishly that we didn't have enough time, that it was unfair that I had finally found..."

"What," he whispers.

I sigh, bracing myself for my next words. "That I had finally found someone who's just mine, for me alone. That I wouldn't get to have time with you." Tears sting my eyes, and his hand comes to my chin, raising my head. My watery eyes meet his and they look so pained. "I've never had that with anyone, until you, and everything else that had happened, it just...didn't matter anymore."

And it didn't.

"You are right to think that. I am yours, only yours. No matter where I am, or where you are." His jaw ticks. "You will always be mine, and I yours. It's infinite, Effiniar. Always," he reassures me, and then places a gentle kiss on my lips before guiding me back to the crook of his neck. He must really want me to scent him. "What happened after?"

"I sunk." His body turns stiff and I bring my hand between us and place it over his heart, rubbing circles there. "I sunk and it felt never-ending, but we both know how most never-endings work." He holds me closer at that and I continue. "I didn't drown, and I don't know how long I was sinking for, but it was more like floating then. I was weightless and nothing surrounded me but black. And your wolf." My lips quirk into a soft smile as he grunts.

"Draxton," he tells me, and I memorize his full name. It suits him. "I couldn't stop him from coming out, not that I would have. I had hope he would reach you, but I had no way of knowing that. I just had to hope he would find you and keep you safe."

"He did," I tell him. If it wasn't for him, I wouldn't have made it back here.

"Why didn't you show him to me before?"

"I didn't want to make you think I tricked you. I didn't want to make you more upset than you already were after everything that had happened."

"Because I would know it was you and him who saved me in the woods that day behind my house when I was little." He nods. "Did you always know?"

"No, it wasn't until I was in your cave and saw a carving of him."

"The one with two tails." Another nod.

"I was surprised but it also just made so much sense after Wolvorn. The way I was drawn to you. I didn't know what to say after I saw that... I needed to get back to stop the Rogues, it didn't want distractions... which was pointless. You are always my distraction, little wolf."

I smile softly at the affection in his tone.

"And he can come out separately?" I had never herd of that before, though really, I shouldn't be surprised.

He nods. "Heirs have different powers, you know that. Seers, strength, healing..." I smile. "I can have Drax separate from me."

"Like that day?"

"Yes, thought I didn't understand it then."

"What happened after I ran?" I ask.

"I was only sixteen."

"Sixteen!" I think for a moment. "You are thirty seven?" he nods. So young to be an Alpha of the Elites. So young to carry so much weight on his shoulders for the long life we have.

"Thirty eight this winter," he tells me.

"You were born in winter too?" He nods. Both born in harsh climates but survived nonetheless.

"I followed Drax that day," he continues. "That was the first time my Heir powers came to me. I think it was because you were near, I'm not sure. But I followed him and when I saw you, I knew everything had changed from that moment, even though I didn't understand it." He plays with my hair. "I caught up to Drax, but he was growling at nothing. They must have ported out."

He doesn't even question my story, believing me instantly about what happened all those years ago, even though he himself saw no one there.

"After that," he continues. "My father came, and we had to head home. I wanted to stay and find you, talk to you and make sure you were okay, but he refused to listen and said he saw no one like you, and then we left. I came back about a moon cycle later but you were gone."

"Not gone," I whisper, "just in the basement." A rumbling growl sounds in his chest and I continue rubbing circles over his heart. "That was a long time ago."

"A time you will never get back."

"I'm here now, that's all that matters, isn't it?" I raise my head and he scowls. "Anyway, Draxton was with me in this blackness, and I couldn't move at that moment, but we weren't alone. Another wolf was there," I hedge, and his eyes flash black. "He...spoke to me, in here." I raise my hand to my head and his own comes over the top of it. "I was scared. I couldn't move, I was so weak. He came closer and I thought, this is really it this time, but all he did was come over to me and put magic into me, and then I blacked-out from the pain."

Darius looks thoughtful for a moment. "He saved you." I nod. "Do you know who it was?"

I shake my head. "No, but he was huge, way bigger than Draxton and had violet eyes."

"What happened next?"

"When I awoke, the wolf was there and then I was on Draxton's back. Steps appeared and we made a break for the surface. We made it to Colhelm, I stole some clothes and then I ported out of there with the villagers when rogures attacked." I don't want to tell him about the male that tried to take me. "The people of the village there said they do not want to live under the Highers rule. I wonder how many others would help us get rid of them, now that posters of their evil deeds are out in the open."

"We can only go to them and see."

I nod.

"Why didn't you go to Vokheim?" he asks quietly. "It would have been the safer choice."

"I...I just wanted to get to you."

"To me?"

I lean my forehead to his. "To you." I can't explain the need,

I can't find the words.

"No more talking."

"But what about the people that came—"

He growls and his mouth descends on mine.

It feels different this time.

There is a hunger in his kiss, desire, but more prominently, there is affection, relief, need and a craving I also feel as I sink into his kiss.

It's slow and sensual, like he's savoring all of me, like he can't believe I'm here and most of all...it's so gentle.

"Darius," I breathe against his lips, my heart beating wildly with emotion, and he groans, but it's like he's in pain.

His hand is on my pulse point for a beat or two, and then it's at the back of my head next, his fingers tangle in my hair as his tongue presses against my lips. I open instantly, hearing the satisfied purr coming from him as his other hand trails down to my hip.

It squeezes there, rubbing and moving over my skin like he wants to crawl inside of it.

I rock above him, his cock leaking between us and my wetness coats it.

The moan that tumbles from his lips, and the almost-silent *fuck* that follows makes me feel lightheaded over the hold I have on him.

I want him.

I need him.

I want to taste him.

"No," he says suddenly, halting my hips. "Rest, Rhea, fuck."

"By the sounds of it, I have done more than enough of that." He goes to open his mouth again but I just kiss him more.

When he starts to move his hands up my sides, tracing my ribs and the underside of my breasts, I break the kiss.

I rise onto my knees and slowly move down his body. The furs come away, revealing more of his skin as I bend down, licking his side where his tattoos are, and his breathing turns ragged.

"Rhea," he breathes, never breaking eye contact with me, never once letting go of my hair.

I feel nerves trying to halt me in my tracks, but I keep moving lower. When I get to that trail of hair, I inhale him, taking his scent into my lungs and my own moan tumbles out.

Gods.

Mouth watering, I shove my nerves aside and when I lower, I feel the tip of his cock at my chin. Without breaking eye contact, I tilt my head down and lick the head.

Just one, small lick.

What that does to the male before me is instant.

His other hand is buried in the furs, knuckles white. He hisses through his teeth, eyes, dark pools of desire as that grip in my hair tightens.

"You don't have to do that, little wolf," he grits out, his cock so painfully hard.

"I'm not scared, Darius," I tell him, knowing what happened the last time his cock was near my mouth. I go in for another lick. He tastes so good. "You won't hurt me."

His eyes squeeze shut then, and something astonishing happens.

Darius sinks into the furs and gives me *his* submission as he lets go of my hair and brings his arm to his side.

This male just gave me more than he could ever know. Even though I told him I wasn't scared, he still made it so I knew this was all me. That he will let me do what I want.

With one last lick, I'm suddenly overcome with the need to taste him fully, I take the head in my mouth. Darius groans, hips punching forward a little before he retreats, holding himself back and taking his taste away.

That kind of pisses me off.

I suck the head, tasting his pre-come instantly on my tongue and I moan, shuffling my hips with the need to be touched.

"Fuck, little wolf," he groans, looking down at me. "I'm not going to last if you do that again. You should see how you look with my cock in your mouth, how your lips stretch around me." His eyes look wild, already on edge and it makes me preen inside.

I smile the best I can around his dick, and his eyes narrow.

Then I suck him as deep as I can, being careful not to gag and his hand flies to my hair. "Fuck. *Fuuuck.*"

I bring my other hand up and stroke him with my movement, bobbing my head up and down in a smooth rhythm.

"Rhea, I don't want to come in your mouth." I double my efforts, wanting it, needing it. "No," he growls.

I'm suddenly underneath him, and his cock is right there, filling me up. My hands go to his arms, my nails digging in as I whimper at the slow stretch.

"I want you wrapped around me," he says, thrusting slowly. "I want my essence inside of you, I want yours on me. I want us leaving here scented of each other so deeply after I fuck you again and again, that even bathing won't wash it off," he groans on a deep thrust. "This is where I belong."

Pleasure coils through me, building and building. "Faster, Darius," I gasp, my nails digging into him.

He comes down on his elbows on either side of me so we are face to face. "No, little wolf," he murmurs, going slower. "This isn't a fast fuck. I'm going to savor you, cherish you." He rubs his nose against mine. "I'm going to show you what you mean to me."

And then he kisses me, his tongue entering my mouth like he's fucking me and my arms go around his neck, his words forming a lump in my throat.

His hands move over my body, squeezing my sides softly, roaming over my breasts, hands on my ass as he pulls me impossibly closer.

He kisses my neck, nipping at the skin there as my head tilts back in pleasure.

He grinds into me, and with each thrust he rubs against my

clit and I know I'm about to come.

"I feel you squeezing me," he says against my skin, licking and nipping as our gentle pants echo in the air. "Give me you, so I can give you me." And then he bites down, hard, and I come.

The moan that comes from me is long and loud as he clutches me tighter, and his thrusts turn jagged until he stills.

Warmth fills me, and a satisfied sigh comes from my lips as my hand goes to the back of his head as he groans into his bite.

Marking me as his.

Darius lazily rubs a hand down my back as I begin to wake up after being satisfied again and again. We slept for a while in between, but he couldn't keep his hands off me, and if I'm honest neither could I.

Admittedly, some of the times that I woke him was just for him to hold me in a different way. I always ended up on top of him though, secured in his arms like I am now.

Light shines through the opening of the cave as I peel my eyes open, and I let the sound of water flowing down invade me as I snuggle closer to him.

"I found this cave by accident," I tell him. "As soon as I entered here, I knew it was mine."

"Just yours?" he rumbles beneath me.

"Maybe ours," I whisper, sighing into his warmth.

"Our scent is all over it." I can hear the satisfaction in his tone and I huff out a laugh.

A *yip* comes from the side and I lift my head, a gasp spilling from me as Leif comes bounding over.

"Leif!" I squeal when he jumps, licking all over my face as he wriggles himself between Darius and I. "Oh look how big you've gotten. Who's a big wolf cub now?"

Darius sighs in exasperation, but he holds me by my sides as I sit up and cuddle him. "Don't pay him too much attention, he will get used to it," he grumbles, and I stifle a laugh at him.

He's Alpha pouting.

"Why is he here?" I ask in a giggle as Leif turns and starts to lick Darius's cheek. What's even more shocking is that he lets him get on with it. Like this is a normal morning.

"I found him hiding in here," he begins, lifting a hand to stroke down the back of Leif's nape. "When I got to his den…" He trails off and my stomach drops.

I pick Leif up and hold him to me, burrowing my face in his fur. "What happened?"

His face pinches. "Rogures."

I close my eyes, a sob building as Darius sits up and holds me to him as Leif snuggles closer.

I loved that pack, I watched the mama swell with her babies, watched as her mate brought her food when she was too tired to leave her den. I watched when the pups were born.

"It's not fair." I sniffle into Leif's fur as he gives me one last lick before running off. I watch with bleary eyes as Darius pulls me back down onto him and I spot Daddy wolf over by the lilk trees, that I am just now realizing are still blooming.

"He killed the rogures," Darius tells me. "He took them away from the den to try and save his family but…" He was too late.

Leif goes to his dad, and he nuzzles him before the Alpha nudges him further into the trees, a slight limp to him as he goes.

"Thank you," I say to Darius, and I feel him shake his head.

"You loved them, of course I would look after them. I couldn't save them all, but I saved him and buried the others."

He secretly likes them, I know he does.

We are quiet for a long while, both of us with our thoughts until Darius breaks the silence.

"Ask," he murmurs against me.

"Did you break your vow?" He freezes for a moment and my heart drops.

Like he can feel it, he nuzzles the top of my head. "I didn't expect that to be the first thing you ask," he admits. "No, little wolf, I didn't."

I sigh in relief, and then, "Kade?" I begin, hedging the question.

I would have asked Josh down the link, but I soon realized he had blocked it.

Darius grunts, sitting up and taking me with him. The furs fall to my waist, and his hands run down my sides to clasp my hips. My own hands go to his neck, stroking his skin, keeping my eyes there.

"Look at me." I do, raising my eyes to his gaze. "You should always be looking at me."

"Like you do with me?"

"Always."

I blush, and his lips tip up. "Adorable."

"Ass."

His smile fades, and I wait for him to tell me.

"Josh has been taking care of the kid." The breath that releases from me is so full of so much relief that I sag against his chest. "He came here once, when you wouldn't wake up," he grits out. "It took everything within me not to take his head."

"It wasn't his fault," I say, placing a kiss on his neck as tears sting my eyes.

"He has caused you nothing but pain since I met you," he says quietly, but I hear the rage underneath.

"He's just a kid," I defend.

"He's eighteen," he counters. "He is old enough to get his wolf."

"I know," I tell him, my arms running over his chest. "I know I need to realize that he's a man now, not the little kid I held in my arms that would wake up screaming from his nightmares." Deep down I know he's not a kid anymore, though Darius calls him that. He is grown now, has a wolf like Darius says, and maybe I do need to stop defending him so much. But me falling isn't his fault. "He's mine, Darius. Through his faults, his mistakes." I lift my head and stare at him. "He's mine, just like you are."

His eyes flash black at that. "Are you going to say that a lot?"

"I am brave enough now." Nearly dying will do that to you.

"You have always been brave." My eyes shine with tears at that and I duck my head. Gods, I'm sick of crying.

He places a hand on the back of my head and gently takes my hair in his fist, pulling my head back. His eyes bounce between mine as he frowns.

"I hate your tears," he murmurs, watching one fall as his eyes darken. "But there is no shame in it, even if I wish you wouldn't let them fall. I'm sure you have wanted to cry many times and stopped yourself, you do not have to do that with me, little wolf. Never with me." He places a gentle kiss on my lips and I let his words wash over me.

I look into his green eyes, and I'm still in disbelief that we are here, him holding me and me touching him.

I didn't think I would ever be in this position.

He's the only one who ever could. There is no other but him.

"My pack?" They were all so scared when I left them, so... lost within their horrors.

"Resting in their homes in Eridian." I nod, thinking how that must be a comfort, if not for the fact that all cabins were raided. "What else has happened since I've been gone?"

"That didn't take long, did it?" I shake my head, smiling softly. I need to see my pack...Kade. "The Highers are rallying at Wolvorn Castle as more of the people try to get past their gates. Rogures are more rampant than ever and then we got some news."

"What news?"

"Patrick was seen with other Alphas that have pledged their loyalty to the Highers moving toward Wolvorn."

My brows furrow. "Why didn't they just port there?"

"They are being protected by rogues; it seems."

"Rogues?"

"They are controlling them somehow. They are not attacking them or going off path. I've sent others to watch them."

"I know what we saw in The Deadlands showed that those beasts were able to be controlled, but if rogues can be too, then the attack on Vokheim Keep…"

"Was coordinated," he finishes for me. "I had some thoughts on that for a while. The rogues don't attack keeps or castles, so why my keep? It didn't make sense, but if they can be controlled, then it does."

"But who is controlling them?"

"After seeing the Highers experiments, I think we have a good guess."

"But why attack the keep? For what purpose?"

"To kill me." I rear back. "I have not been doing as I am told and it seems they want a replacement."

"Who?"

"Your cousin."

"Patrick?" I shiver at his name on my lips and he rubs my arms, frowning.

"It doesn't matter what they want to happen, what they think will happen, they are *all* dying."

"Are we ready for that? Strong enough?" I think back to the fight, to Frederick and Mathew. "What happened in The Deadlands?"

"Mathew is dead, the beast is dead, and my men are watching over the many beasts and rogues that were below it through the rubble, killing them a few at a time."

"Frederick?" I ask, lifting a hand to my throat as his phantom hands grab it.

"Being questioned." He moves my hand from my neck and inhales me there. "He is restrained and waiting for you."

I lean back and see the fury in his eyes, the fury he restrained for me to be able to decide what to do with him.

I nod. "Are we ready to attack? To go after the Highers?"

"I don't know," he says honestly. "But we are quickly running out of time, little wolf. In the end, we will have no choice but to be ready."

"And the people?"

"Some will rally, some are barely surviving, having no crops left from either rogures or the tax Charles demands."

"We need to get them to safety, or at least get them food."

He nods. "We will."

I swallow roughly, my body tensing. "Where is he?"

Darius looks off for a moment. "He's in a cabin, being guarded."

"I don't think that is necessary."

"It is. He was with the Highers for a long time, we don't know if we can trust him."

"He's Kade, of course we can trust him."

He gives me a look. "Look what happened at Wolvorn, when you tried to get him to leave with you." The reminder has pain shooting through me. "He is not well, Rhea, he is not safe for you to be around."

"What do you mean?" I ask, my brows furrowed.

"He has these outbursts, and when that happens he thinks everyone is the enemy."

My stomach drops and a harsh breath comes from me. Did it not work when I tried to clear his mind? Was it not enough?

Was I not enough?

"I will help him," I say vehemently. Darius eyes me, but he doesn't say another word.

I feel Draxton beneath Darius's skin rubbing up against mine, and Runa comes forward then, greeting him.

She has been quiet until now.

"He wants to meet her," Darius says.

"So do I."

He lifts a strand of my hair and twirls it around his fingers.

"We need her to come out, little wolf. The lands are in chaos, and I'm not sure we will see the other side if we don't have all of us at full strength."

"I know," I say, picking at my fingers between us. "How do we get rid of the rogues?"

"They need to be gone from the lands, but we still need to figure out how." He pulls me closer. "For now we rest, and then we will begin."

"I need to see my pack, and Kade," I say, but he rolls me beneath him in the next moment.

"Not yet,"

"Darius—"

"No," he growls down at me, his face harsh but I see the pain residing in his eyes. "Not yet, little wolf. I can't…I thought you were gone forever. So no, the others can wait a little longer. Don't make me force you to stay, don't make me make *you* angry at me right now."

I look at him watching me. His breathing is choppy, his shoulders bunching up and I see what he doesn't say aloud.

His fear is that I'll disappear.

"I can't Rhea, not yet."

I let my hands rest beside my head and spread my thighs so he easily slides in between them.

"Then show me I'm alive," I tell him, sighing as he enters me on a rough groan. "Show me what it means to be yours."

FORTY SIX

Rhea

"Rhea," Josh calls out as he runs toward me.

I fall into his arms as he scoops me and spins us, clutching each other tightly.

Darius growls from behind us, but for once, he makes no move to get him away from me.

"I was so fucking scared." Josh puts me on my feet while checking me over. "Are you okay?"

"I'm okay," I tell him, looking into his tired, gray eyes.

I'm scooped up again and Seb is there, clinging to me as Colten comes to my back, shoulders shaking as he holds me.

"Stop scaring us," Seb says gruffly.

"It's not fair to keep doing this," Colten tells me, and I hold them, closing my eyes to their warmth. Then Taylor and Hudson are there, then Anna.

She cries, tears dripping down her cheeks as we hug each other tightly. "I will boil you alive if you ever do that again!"

I laugh against her, her red curls sticking to my face as my own tears drop. "I don't want to make it a habit," I chuckle.

"Ah, she wakes."

"Belldame!" I say on a gasp, and I go to the older woman as she embraces me, those bones on her neck clanking together.

"I knew you would wake, child, all you needed was more than your own within you."

"What do you mean?" I ask, and pull back while grasping her hand.

"You needed him," she nods her head and I look over my shoulder to Darius, watching me, his brothers next to him grinning at me.

I huff out a laugh. "I think he would have gotten me from the below, himself."

"Oh child, you don't belong in the below."

Before I can ask her what she means, Leo comes over to me.

"I don't appreciate you running off when I am talking to you." I raise a brow at him. "You scared the shit out of me."

Then he wraps his arms around me.

I'm too stunned for a moment, but then I awkwardly pat his back. Damian hugs both of us next, laughing as he rocks us from side to side.

"Aww, we are one big, happy pack," Damain shouts.

"Shut up," I laugh, punching his arm playfully. He runs back over to Darius, saying something about abuse.

I spot Zaide and he nods his head at me in respect, I nod back. I don't see Jerrod though, or Sarah.

"She is helping the villagers that you brought with you," Josh says.

"Are they okay?"

"They are now with food in their bellies and a safe place to rest." Warmth pulses through me at that. "Just…don't leave us like that again."

Darius's warmth touches my back as I'm hauled back into him. His hands wrap around my waist, nuzzling into my hair. I lean back, feeling my magic swirl within me. "She won't." Darius tells him.

Josh rolls his eyes. "This is going to be worse now, isn't it"? he asks, pointing at Darius and then to me.

I shrug. "Honestly, I think it goes both ways," I tell him somewhat shyly, bringing my hand up to land on Darius's arm, scratching slightly there.

"I'm so fucking happy you're awake." Josh looks at the ground, running a hand down his face to cover his emotions.

"Me too," I tell him, swallowing over the lump in my throat and leaning further back into Darius.

I look at my pack, standing strong, eyes on me and I couldn't have wished for a better family. And as the Elites move at their back facing Darius and I, I can see now that it has grown some.

We are united in our goal to end the Highers and see the rogues purged from these lands, but in the meantime, we have become one in our little inner circle, one I think that will only get closer over time.

"You are ready, child," Belldame says, and I look into her light, violet eyes.

"Am I?" I wonder. "Because I feel pretty useless."

She shakes her head. "You are on the path you are supposed to be."

"What will I find at the end?"

She holds my gaze for a moment, sparing a glance at Darius. "Everything you have ever wanted."

"That is very vague, Grandmother," Anna says.

I turn to look up at Darius and see him already looking down at me. I see in his eyes what could be, what I want.

I look to my pack next, who nod their heads, telling me they are with me.

"Where is he?" I eventually ask Josh, a notable member of the family missing.

Josh's eyes turn sad for a moment. "He's in a cabin close to the west side of Eridian. He...he wanted to stay there, and Darius has an Elite guarding him." He glares at Darius at the mention of it, who doesn't seem affected in the slightest. "He's not doing so well, Rhea."

I take in a stuttering breath. "Tell me." Darius strokes my waist, the touch comforting while I wait.

"He barely talks to anyone, and when he does talk, it's mostly to himself. He just sits there, other times he's staring at the walls— day and night. He hardly eats, either. He calls out in his sleep, shouting and sometimes...screaming."

Rage and heartache bubble up within me. "Take me to him," I tell Josh, moving out of Darius's grip. He hauls me right back.

"Stay beside me," he growls, and I growl back, spinning to face him fully.

"Not now, Darius. I am not dealing with your—oh for Gods's sake."

He jostles me over his shoulder. "You can calm down up there as we go to the cabin."

"You can't be serious." What in the lands is he doing right now? "Darius!"

I'm aware of the others laughing at our antics, even Belldame laughs at us.

Where is the loyalty?!

"No, you decided to give me attitude, you go over my shoulder." He turns and heads west. "Are you just going to stand there?" he asks Josh, and I see his legs move in my upside-down view.

"Aren't you going to say anything?" I ask Josh, gripping Darius's waist to try and see him better.

"Nope," Josh replies, but I can hear the smirk in his voice. "What you two get up to is none of my business."

"Really?" He has to be joking. "Who's the traitor now," I mutter.

"Yup, who am I to get between you two Vihnarns. I like my life, thanks." I scowl and he chuckles, bending down so we are face-to-face as I lean up. "Despite everything, I'm happy you have him, Rhea," he says quietly before patting my head.

"I think I am too," I tell him down the link, which gets me a swat on my ass.

"Behave," Darius warns, and I twitch on his shoulder from the sting. "I can help you with that." He kneads my ass cheek.

"Later," I whisper, my cheeks heating instantly at the word. Darius rumbles a pleased sound and I roll my eyes.

Damn Alphas.

We arrive at the cabin a short while later, the laughter

quickly leaving us behind.

Darius sets me down in front of a cabin that we used to use for members who were prone to violence, the ones that we had to separate when the females were in heat.

It isn't lost on me that Kade is now in here for his outbursts.

An Elite stands up straighter as he notices Darius, raising a fist to his chest in respect and bowing his head.

"Alpha," he says in a nod, and then his eyes flick to me. "Alpha."

I'm stunned for a moment, and then I wave him off. "Just Rhea."

He gets a panicked look on his light brown face as he looks to Darius for a moment "Sorry, Alpha, um— Rhea. Alpha."

Josh laughs behind his hand as Darius speaks. "Don't worry, Kieth, Rhea doesn't like the pack structure."

He's kinda right. We should all be treated as equals, but there is a time and a place for pack structure to be needed. To calm and reassure your pack members. To keep them safe.

Otherwise, I'm just Rhea.

I kick Josh in the shin when he mimics me being called Alpha. He pinches me in return and the glare on Darius's face stops us both from continuing.

"Any changes?" Darius asks.

Kieth's eyes glance to mine. "He was throwing things around in the room a while earlier, Alpha. But that has since stopped for some time."

Darius nods. "Go stretch your legs, I will have someone else posted here for the remainder of the day.

Kieth fists his chest, and then there's a flash of dark fur before he's off, running into the trees.

The cabin is silent when I look at it, no sign of any movement within.

"He's in there?" I ask Josh, making sure. He comes to stand next to me.

"He is." He takes my hand in his, squeezing gently. "He's

struggling, Rhea. Just, prepare yourself."

I peek at Josh as he looks at the cabin, eyes a little sad. My eyes follow it to the door, knowing Kade is in there and scared to enter.

What if it's like last time?

What if he can't look at me? What if he does and it's full of disgust?

What if he's frightened of me?

"Breathe, little wolf." Darius's calm tone hits my ear as he whispers into it. "I'm here."

I know he is, but maybe he shouldn't be.

"I'll go in first."

"No."

"Darius."

"Rhea." He moves until he's in front of me. "I won't leave you alone with him until I know it is safe to do so."

I look at Josh. "It's just Kade, I will be okay, won't it?" Josh's eyes move away from mine, and I swallow. "Before I fell, I… I put my magic into him, like I did with you, Darius."

He tilts his head, his eyes darkening. "And that's why you had none left." He realizes.

"I cleared the wrong in his mind, I felt it. I thought it had worked but…" But what if I wasn't enough?

"He is confused, Rhea," Josh says. "Sometimes he's okay, sometimes he's not. We don't know the mood he will be in."

"Okay," I whisper.

My palms sweat as I take a step forward. Darius is at my side in an instant, moving with me as we climb the short, wooden steps.

He opens the door for me and I take a breath before I enter the room. I expect to see Kade straight away, my eyes going to every corner to find him, but all I see is furniture.

I look over my shoulders at Josh and he tips his head toward a door at the back. I clench my hands and wipe them on the pants that Darius gave me. I step toward the door, apprehension swirling inside of me.

Don't hate me, don't hate me.

Reaching the door handle, my hand shakes as I grab onto it. I don't push it down yet though, something inside of me is too scared to.

I don't know what I will do if he reacts the same as he has done? What if he doesn't even *want* to see me.

Runa whines within and I feel her sorrow so deeply that I have to take a few ragged breaths.

A hand comes on top of mine, and Darius wraps himself around my back, breathing into my nape.

I can feel his want to take me away from here, from something that could hurt me, yet here he is, trying to comfort and reassure me because he knows it is what I need to do.

He places a kiss to the side of my neck, a nip of encouragement, and that gives me the strength to push down on the handle and open the door.

It creaks, the sound deafening in the silence, and I move forward and take in the room as Darius's magic swirls around my waist. Smashed furniture litters the floor, holes in the wooden walls as though fists have crashed through them, windows half-broken with glass on the floor...

And then a lone figure, sat in the corner of the room at the back.

My heart clenches with the sob building in my throat as I look to my cousin who has always been a son to me.

His head is in his hands, elbows to his knees that are pulled to his chest as he huddles against the wall. He doesn't even look up as I enter, doesn't even tense or twitch.

I shuffle forward slowly, not wanting to startle him with Darius at my back. Reaching a hand back, it lands on his hard stomach as I halt him. I stroke there in a silent question.

Will you stay back?

I sense his body tensing, locking up in a way that screams he isn't going to allow it, but after a moment, he runs his hand over mine, withdrawing his power.

I breathe a sigh of relief and continue forward.

The closer I get to Kade, the urge to suddenly flee grows stronger when he doesn't move. I don't know if I can do this. I don't know if I can take any more hurt from him, if I can have him look at me the same way he did that day in the castle. It will break me this time, I'm sure of it.

But then, he lifts his head.

Blue, unseeing eyes pierce me so sharply that I freeze mid-step. He just stares at me for a moment, seeing through me as we seem to pause in time.

But then he blinks, a furrow to his brow as he slowly sits up straighter. When I continue to do nothing, Kade's eyes widen and he scrambles to his feet.

Pain so acute fills his eyes, a cry lodged in his throat as he says a word I have never heard from him before. A word that nearly brings me to my knees.

"Mom?"

A sob bursts free from my throat and I don't hesitate any more. I rush toward him.

I crash into him, and he falls into my chest, clinging to my sides as that cry finally escapes him. My hand goes to the back of his head on instinct, comforting him like I have always done, and his legs give way, taking us to the floor on our knees. I grab onto him tightly, tears streaming as I rock him slowly back and forth.

He says something into my skin, I can't make it out as it's so quiet, but it's so full of torment and regret. As he continues on, I eventually make out the words.

"I'm sorry, I'm sorry, I'm sorry."

"Oh Carzan," I whisper into his hair. "Shhh," I tell him, still rocking back and forth, gently. "I'm here, I'm here." He cries even harder, his whole body shaking from the force of it.

"I— I'm sorry." He starts gagging over his sobs and his words. I pull him out of my neck and grab both sides of his face, wiping away the tears that never seem to stop falling. "I'm so, so sorry."

"Hush now," I tell him, sniffling and trying to get my own emotions under control. I feel his pain like it's my own and I just want to reach inside of him and take it away.

No one wants to see their child in so much pain.

Kade shakes his head, his face distraught. "What I said at the castle, what I believed, what I did...the cliff—"

"I know, I know, it's okay," I tell him again, but he doesn't seem to be listening as he mumbles his sorry's, barely breathing over his rushed words.

"I didn't mean to..."

"I got you."

"I never would have..."

"I'm here now."

"I'm sorry..."

He falls into my chest again and I just hold him, sitting back against the wall and taking him with me.

It isn't until he starts screaming into my neck and clawing at himself that I think I feel the worst pain I ever have. Worse than anything I have ever been through.

Hearing the anguish in his screams, the raw devastation...

That is a pain that has no rival.

Kade sits beside me against the wall, leaning into my side as I hold one of his hands in both of mine. My eyes feel scratchy, heavy, and I know they are red and puffy from crying with him.

We cried for so long.

Kade finally calmed down a little while ago, preferring just to sit in silence and be next to me rather than talk. But that's okay, Runa and I are basking in his presence, like he is ours.

I look over at Darius across the room. He leans against the wall, arms crossed, but he is no doubt alert. His eyes haven't left mine since he stood there, always making sure I'm okay.

He tried to come to me a little while ago when I tried to get my own sobs under control, and I can see he still wants to now with the tension running through his body, but I need to be with Kade right now.

"I'm sorry," Kade eventually croaks for what seems like the thousandth time.

"I know you are, Carzan," I whisper, lifting a hand and moving some of his blonde hair out of his face. He needs it cut.

He sighs heavily, and I feel the weight of that sigh down to my bones. "Do you feel okay?" I ask him, needing him to know that if something is still wrong, I can find a way to help him.

"I'm not sure." My eyes flick to Darius as he now watches him. His jaw ticking. "I didn't know what was happening to me," he begins quietly, and I squeeze my eyes shut at the sound of his voice. It's so lost, lonely...bleak. "I didn't understand, my thoughts and every memory were... twisted. I would remember one thing, but then the next it would change, and I didn't know which one was real or not." His voice cracks on the last words and he clears his throat. "I didn't understand how I had two memories of the same thing. The things I said, did, believed...And then what they did when I chose the wrong memory." He swallows roughly and his hand begins to shake in mine.

I look down at the scratch-like scars on his arms, only visible because of the t-shirt he's wearing. My nostrils flare as I wonder what they did to him, at the pain he must have gone through. I want to ask him what he means by the wrong memory, I want to ask what they did, but I don't want to trigger him. I have to bite my tongue to keep the growl in my throat over the rage I feel.

"How can you ever forgive me," he asks, and I realize I never said anything to what he just told me, to focus on not lashing out, myself.

"I know it wasn't you," I reassure him. He truly didn't mean the things he said, he was confused and manipulated. "It's not your fault what they did to you. You never deserved that, Carzan."

"I hate myself," he says quietly. Bluntly. "I should have been stronger. I should have been who you have taught me to be."

This boy. No, not boy, not anymore.

"You are always who you were supposed to be. I failed you if you think that way, Carzan," I tell him. "And I'm so fucking sorry for that."

He sits up straighter, turning toward me with pain flaring in his eyes. I see Darius unfold his arms.

"All you have ever done is protect me. You raised me, taught me, nursed me. You. No one else." He's getting angrier now as he stands up and starts to pace. I rise to my feet slowly. "How could you have ever failed me? I failed you in every way! I disobeyed orders, I ran away from my issues, I caused others to invade our home that caused its downfall, but you are blaming yourself!? I wouldn't fucking be alive if it wasn't for you. Not those who spawned me. You!" He's shouting now, and I can't help but flinch at his aggression, even though it isn't for me.

"Don't shout," Darius orders from his spot on the wall, noting my reaction. He doesn't raise his voice, but the command is there.

"Why not shout?" Kade throws his hands in the air as he turns toward him. "How can you stand there and let her say this shit to me? She failed me?" he scoffs, running his hand through his hair, and I note the change in the color of his eyes, his wolf peeking through. "I shouldn't expect anything different from you though," he says to Darius. "I don't even know why you are here. To ruin our home again?"

"Kade" I reach for him, trying to get him to calm down, but he moves away from me.

"You fucking whipped her," he says to Darius, and my eyes

squeeze shut for a moment. "I may have been the cause that brought you to our home, but you didn't protect her when she needed it most!"

"Watch it," Darius warns, a deep rumble coming from his chest. He steps away from the wall and my panic rises, heartbeat in my throat.

"How does she know how special she is when we all treat her like shit, especially you," he snaps at him.

"Do not do this in front of her," Darius replies on a growl.

"Why? You don't want her to remember what a piece of shit you are?"

"Kid. Last warning."

He steps up to Darius. "Or what? Going to whip me too?"

Darius's fist flies out and connects with the side of his face.

"Darius," I gasp, rushing toward them, but Darius's power comes out and wraps around me, rooting me to the spot. "Darius, let me go!" But he's not listening, his focus solely on Kade.

Kade laughs, wiping blood from the corner of his mouth. "That's all you got?" Darius hits him again, then again, and I start screaming at him to stop, shouting for Josh who is nowhere to be seen for help.

My power, just a small spark within me, flickers to life for a moment and I try and grab onto it, holding it and begging it to rise. "Darius, stop it!" I scream at him again, and finally, he does stop.

I sag against his power, my heavy breathing echoing around the room as I look at Kade on the floor.

Darius crouches down next to him, arms on his bent knees and my whole body tenses. "Feel better now?" he asks Kade, and my brows furrow, confusion spreading through me.

"A little," Kade replies, grunting as he sits up and wipes more blood from his face. Darius hums and then moves over to me.

I glare, my arms struggling at my sides where his magic has pinned them. "Don't look at me like that, little wolf. Now isn't the time." I snarl at him, and he raises a brow. "We can make time though," he chuckles, and I growl, turning my head away from him. "We don't do that." His thumb and finger grip my chin, bringing my face back to his. "I thought I would never see your eyes again," he says quietly, just for me. "Don't hide them from me now." My body relaxes at his words, and he nudges his nose with me, calling his power back.

My eyes move to Kade as Darius comes at my back, an arm wrapping around my waist. "What was that about?" I ask him tentatively.

"He wanted me to hit him, little wolf," Darius says into my hair. "But you should know, kid, if you want me to hit you, just ask, I have no problem doing so, but watch your mouth." His voice is cold as he scolds Kade, and an unwanted shiver runs through me.

"No." My own voice is hard.

"That is not up to you," Darius tells me.

"Darius, no." I try to spin in his arms, the grip he has across my waist doesn't let me. "You will not hurt him."

"He isn't a little pup, Rhea, stop treating him like one. I'd rather it be me than something else. Be it wolf, creature or rogure," he says, and the thought stops me dead. Looking at Kade, I wish for him to tell me he wouldn't, but he just stares at me, eyes so full of pain that I know he would.

A furious rumble starts in Darius's chest. "You don't have to lash out to get your ass beat, kid, and don't shout in front of Rhea," he warns him, and Kade nods his head before it lowers, chin to chest. Darius lets me go and walks to him, as a panicked noise gets lodged in my throat. "I'm not going to hurt him again, little wolf." I move to the side, keeping an eye on them as Darius stops in front of him. "I did whip her," he admits, and Kade's head snaps up to him. "It is my worst regret, my greatest shame, and something so unforgivable that I shouldn't be breathing." He takes a deep breath. "But Rhea has not killed me, and until she does, I will spend all my time with the impossible task of making it up to her. To give her happiness she has always deserved, to make sure she is safe and content."

I look down at his words, rubbing my chest.

I feel the conviction in his tone, the vow and determination that he would absolutely spend the rest of his days doing just that, for me.

"The reason you are still breathing and not dead for the hurt you've caused her, is because she would hate me for it." He slams a heavy hand on his shoulder and brings himself down to eye-level. "So, you will make up for the hurt you've caused, whether your fault or not, the hurt happened, and you will spar with me to take out your own self-loathing, otherwise you will cause Rhea to worry. I will not have her worry about that, understood?" Kade nods his head, his eyes flicking to mine. "You are a man now. Act like the son she sees you as."

Darius stands and turns, walking right over to me.

"I will be right outside the door if you need me." He bends to rub his nose with mine and then the door is shutting.

His steps aren't heard walking away, so I know he is literally right outside of the door, and I sigh, scrubbing my hands down my face.

"Gods."

A chuckle brings my attention back to Kade, the sound so unexpected that my mouth drops open. "I guess a lot has happened since I have been gone."

"Yeah." I go toward him, wiping the blood he missed from his face. "Don't get yourself hurt," I whisper to him, but he says nothing. I run my hand down his arm and lift it. My fingers trail the scar from his severed bloodlink, and it makes me feel that emptiness inside my mind.

"I want a new one."

My head lifts. "We can do that." I want nothing more than to repair what was broken.

"Will you stay for a while?" he asks.

"We are going home, Kade."

"Do we even have a home anymore?"

I nod. "It is a little broken and needs some care. Some time to be repaired the best it can be, so at least the walls still stand."

"What if they don't stand?" he says quietly, and I know he isn't talking about the homes anymore.

"Then you can have others help hold them up, all you need to do is ask." I hold him to me. "Arbiel canna. Always."

He hugs me back. "Arbiel canna."

FORTY SEVEN

Rhea

As soon as we port in, we make our way up the path to my home, Darius at my side, while Josh and Kade walk behind us.

"I'm not sure how to make it feel like a home anymore," I tell Darius, looking at the windows that have now been replaced. "Did you do this?" I ask him as Kade and Josh move around us to go inside.

The last time I was here, everything was trashed, and broken.

Darius moves to my back and wraps his arms around my waist, his chin on my head. "I wanted you to come back to some normality. To your home."

My heart flutters. Even though I don't think things will ever be simple again, he did this for me.

"What else have you done?" I wonder, turning in his arms and looking up at him. Darius isn't the type to just do one thing, and he proves it with his next words.

He strokes his hand through my loose hair, playing with then ends. "We cleared out all the broken furniture in all of the cabins. Fixed doors and windows, even started making benches for the gathering." He pauses, his eyes bouncing between mine. "Made sure all the furniture has been replaced. Beds, tables, things like that."

My hands slide up his chest and his nostrils flare. "Are we safe here?"

"I have men all around Eridian, protection crystals in place. We are as safe as we can be."

"Does anyone know we are here?"

He shakes his head. "Only those that need to be informed."

I nod, feeling the warmth of his skin at his neck. I stroke over the mark there, and I watch as he tries to contain a shiver, but fails. I smile.

"Something funny, little wolf," he rumbles, pulling me so I'm flush against him.

"Nothing at all." I step back and head home. For as long as it will be again.

When I enter this time, it nearly looks just like it always did before it was destroyed. Sofas have been put in the sitting room, bookshelves at the back. When I enter the dining room, I halt in my tracks and take in the table.

My eyes fixate on it as Josh and Kade sit around it.

"It was the best I could do," Darius says at my back as I move toward it, my fingers trailing over the top.

I see Kade look down at his spot, his hand rubbing the markings there from him and Cassie, proving this is the exact table we made.

And when I get to my spot, I stop.

My finger follows the grooves of the wood, over the letters there as my whole body fills with the warmth of a thousand suns.

R and D.

My eyes flick to Darius who looks extremely uncomfortable. His arms are folded, and he's looking down at the table, his throat bobbing with a rough swallow.

"How are you doing now, Carzan?" I ask as I take a seat."

He shrugs. "I think I'm okay. Whatever you did that day on the…on the cliff, helped."

I sit up straighter. "It did?"

"Yeah. It calmed Axis down and it made everything less fuzzy, but sometimes old memories creep up. Not real ones." His brows furrow as he rubs his head. "At least I don't think they are real…No. They can't be. You wouldn't hurt someone unless you had to."

I glance at Josh with worry. "Of course Milal wouldn't hurt someone unless she needed to."

"I know," Kade says, slumping back in his seat. "Everything gets so muddled sometimes and I get confused. I don't know what's true or not and I just get so…so angry." He lowers his head like he's ashamed and I grip his hand.

"We will get through this, okay?"

"We will," Josh reiterates. "If you are ever confused, come and talk to us. We are here. We can make sure whether your memories are true or not."

"Okay," he says quietly, but he doesn't look convinced. "I'm going to rest for a while." He rises to his feet, and then I hear him going up the stairs.

"He will be okay, Rhea. He just needs time," Josh says as he stands. "I'll be at the gathering preparing for dinner."

I look down at the table, my fingers going back to the initials carved there.

"You defiled my table?" I say, glancing up at Darius to find his eyes already on me.

"I made it permanent."

I tilt my head. "Made what permanent?"

"Us."

We gaze at each other until I stand and come around the table. He tracks my movement, his body going impossibly still. Nerves rattle through me, but I won't let it deter me.

Everything has been a lot today, but seeing those initials carved in the table make me feel like I'm floating, and it makes me want to repay him.

Through it all, he is always standing when I feel like a soft breeze could push me over.

Once I'm in front of him, he gives me a questioning look before I slowly lower to my knees.

His eyes flash black, his chest heaving. "What are you doing, little wolf."

I don't say a word, I can't as his scent wraps around me as I look at the bulge in his pants.

With shaky but firm fingers, my hands are in the ties and then pulling down. He isn't wearing anything underneath, so his hard cock springs out and he hisses through his teeth, his arms now at his sides.

I look up at him, his eyes alight with desire, a hand in my hair, steading me—or himself as I lean forward and lick.

Just a little one.

A tiny one.

His reaction however, is not.

He groans, his eyes fused to my mouth as his hips thrust forward on a growl.

I want to say thank you. I want to ask him what made him mark the table with our initials.

I want to ask why he made an effort to do all of this.

But I already know.

His home is with me, where I go, he goes.

I don't look away from him and part my lips, wrapping them around the head of his cock as he leaks onto my tongue. His groan is low, full of desire and I'm instantly wet.

I may be on my knees, but I'm the one with all the power. The power he hands over to me.

I wrap my hand around the base of him and his hand strokes my hair. "Good, little wolf," he praises. "Just like that. Are you happy with your table?" I moan, taking more of him into my mouth as I move my hand with the motion.

He groans when I take him deeper, and the muttered *fuck* that comes from him has me squirming.

"Are you wet from sucking my cock?" he asks, punching his hips forward gently. But I can feel the tension brimming in him to let loose, to use my mouth as he fucks into me. But he won't, and I don't think he ever would in fear of hurting me.

It just makes me fall deeper.

The flowers.

My home.

His wolf.

His commitment to me and only me.

I'm petrified for when I land, but I think— no, I *know* he will catch me at the bottom. Because this is what he has been waiting for, patiently.

He has always told me he has no patience when it comes to me, but he does with this.

I run my other hand up his thigh, feeling the muscle tense there as I nod my head in answer. I'm soaked for him.

Needy for him.

I reach his balls, rolling them in my palm and he hisses, his fingers tightening in my hair as he drags me off his cock.

I whine when he picks me up and bends me over the table, wanting to taste him more, but then my pants are down around my ankles and he's there, filling me, owning me, scenting me.

"As much as I want to come down your throat, little wolf, as much as I want to stretch those lips around me, feel you gag and dribble on my cock." His hands are at my hips, digging into them as I whimper, feeling the pleasure building inside of me. "I want you to look at that carving as I fuck you, as I make you come on my cock."

My eyes roll. "Darius," I whimper.

"I can feel your pussy fluttering, come with my name on your lips."

As I look down at our initials, I do just that.

I hold Darius's hand as we walk to the gathering. I look down at the size difference and squeeze, watching as snowflakes land on them. It is far too cold to do this now, but I can't think of a better time.

I can see a pot bubbling on the fire as we near, and I see those I brought from Colhelm bustling about.

"Heir of Zahariss," Mivera calls and she rushes over to me. "You are back?"

I nod, smiling lightly at the flush of her cheeks. "I am, is everyone okay?"

"We are great, thanks to the Elites. Alpha Darius has helped us so much." She looks down, her booted foot playing in the dirt on the ground as she peeks up at Darius.

I raise a brow.

"I'm glad," I say slowly. "Are you staying here or going back to Colhelm?"

"I think most will go to Colhelm, I'm staying here, with my family and I think a few others are too for now. We are so grateful for your help and sanctuary." Another peek, more redness in her cheeks and I take a deep breath.

"You are more than welcome to stay, but Mivera…"

"Yes?" she says softly, hands clasped in front of her.

"If you keep looking at Darius like that, I will tear your throat out."

She blinks at me and then laughs, but it soon tapers off when I don't return it. "You…you're not joking."

"Absolutely not."

She looks at Darius, a question in her eyes. "My little wolf wouldn't joke about such a thing," he tells her, pride in his voice that has me preening.

She swallows roughly and then nods. "I see. I didn't mean to be disrespectful." She goes to drop to her knees but I grip her arm.

"No need for that, and I know you weren't, but I am just letting you know. Okay?"

"Of course," she says. "I best see if the stew is ready." She runs off back to the cooking pot as Darius chuckles, moving to my back. "I think you scared her."

"I didn't want to…"

His arms wrap around me. "Do you not like others looking at me, little wolf?"

"You're mine," I growl, and then take a deep breath.

"I am," he reassures me. "And you have me so fucking hard right now."

I move my hand behind me and squeeze his erection, causing him to groan in my hair. "This is only mine too."

"Yours," he says, shifting his hips into my hand more.

"Let's get some food." I wiggle out of his arms and enter the gathering while he curses about me not sating his hard dick.

"You will pay for that, little wolf" he grumbles, taking a seat next to me as the others do the same.

The Elites are here, along with my pack and the villagers. Kade sits beside me on one bench, while Josh, Seb, Taylor, Hudson, and Colten take another bench. Anna sits next to Zaide on the bench with more of the Elites resting on it.

When Darius hands me a bowl of stew, I wait for everyone to start eating before I start my own.

I wish the rest of my pack was here.

I look at Darius when he nudges me. "We will go after you have eaten."

I nod my thanks, leaning against him further.

It is also time to bring them home.

FORTY EIGHT

Rhea

I look upon the mist of Witches Rest, side-eyeing Darius. "Still going to tear it down?"

He grunts. "I would have done it to get to you."

"Of course you would have."

"You don't believe me?" he asks skeptically.

"Oh, I do. I just think your balls would have been boiled before then."

"You would have been right, child," Belldame says, emerging from the mist and I run to her. "I saw you not too long ago," she laughs.

I squeeze her harder. "I know." She pats my back and then holds her hand out to Anna.

"Come, Granddaughter." Anna goes to her with a smile, her red hair down today.

We walk with Belldame through the mist as she welcomes us and tells me about my pack.

"They are doing as well as can be expected," she tells me. "We have healed those who were injured, now all they need is a good rest, and time."

"Injured?" I question, worry at the forefront of my mind.

Belldame nods. "Yes, child. Though we can only heal so much with our hands, we cannot heal the mind."

I nod my agreement and continue on, nerves slithering down my spine. I feel Darius at my back like a beacon of strength.

It's funny because I never wanted him at my back, knowing what a threat he is, now he's my ever protector, watching over me.

We emerge to a familiar bridge and my breath stalls in my throat.

My pack stands on the other side, watching, waiting.

We don't waste any time and run to them.

I gather Katy in a hug with little Oscar, rubbing my cheek to theirs as Josh and the others do the same.

"Alpha," Leah cries and I bend down and gather her in a hug.

"I missed you," I whisper in her hair, looking up to her mother whose tears gather in her eyes.

We spend time hugging and relishing in the fact that we are back together again. That we survived our ordeal. I notice the Elites stand back, not wanting to encroach on this moment.

Darius had already told me that they know things have changed between us, and they have been informed about what has happened since they've been away.

When I get to Sybill last, I grab her and haul her to me. "It is so good to see you."

"It is, Alpha," she says, her cheek against mine. "I thought we were all dead." The terror in her voice makes me hold her tighter.

I remember a time when brief hugs were all that I wanted, but now, I hold on to them all for as long and as tight as possible.

I pull back, holding her hands between us. "Are you alright?"

She shrugs. "As much as we can be," she replies, and the others nod. "We are just so thankful you came that day…they…they were planning to give us over to those beasts."

I shiver at the thought. "You are safe now, thank the Gods." I look around the group. "Where is Sam?" Sybill's eyes turn sad at that.

"I asked if she was coming to wait for you with us after Belldame told us you were coming, but she just shook her head." My brows furrow. "She hasn't spoken since we have returned."

My heart squeezes at that, and I automatically look for Kade, knowing how close they are.

When I don't see him with us, I turn and see Darius, nodding his head to the right. I look and see Kade's retreating back and go to follow him, but the shake of Darius's head makes me halt.

"Let him go, child," Belldame says, coming to stand next to us. "He is also where he is supposed to be. Now come everyone, let's go back to the house where you can all catch up."

My pack turns and they start to follow Belldame, all talking amongst themselves. Seb starts flirting straight away while Taylor watches over them. Hudson and Colten take up the rear, their shoulders brushing as Colten holds Leah's little hand.

I stand back with the Elites and watch my pack for a moment, noting Jerrod walking alongside Katy and Oscar, whose little hands are reaching for him. I'm not too surprised when Katy hands Oscar over to him, smiling gently as Oscar plays with his long, red braid.

"Little wolf?" Darius asks as he comes to my side.

"I'm okay," I whisper as Anna comes over to me.

"Come on," she says, "Grandmother will have our hide if we make her wait too long."

I laugh as she pulls me along by the hand before dropping it, glancing in the direction Kade went one last time.

He's not a kid anymore Rhea.

We walk through the made paths, looking at the icy rivers that flow all around and in between the homes on stilts. Children still play out in the cold weather, and they eye the Elites with fear and curiosity as we pass by.

"Have you been here before?" I ask Darius.

"I haven't," he says as he moves to walk next to me. "I wasn't exactly welcomed here."

"Not surprising." I tell him, and he raises a brow. "You don't exactly have a great record of doing good by the people, and only being the Highers hounds."

"That is not what the Elites stand for, not what we set out to be anyway."

"You can change the people's feelings toward you, it will just take time," I reassure him.

"Time I'm not sure we have," he sighs.

"You will show them the good you can do; I have no doubt."

I know he feels guilty for his role in the Highers bidding for so many years. He was blindsided, just like many others. But they will see who he really is, and I have no doubt that in time, the people of Vrohkaria will look to him for guidance.

When we pass a particular home, Janette comes out of her door, a male following close behind her. I eye them as she sneers, grabbing the male's hand quickly. The show of partnership is not lost on me.

"Where have you been?" Anna makes a noise at her sister's question as she walks past her, shaking her head. "Ahh, with the delinquents I see. I am surprised you haven't been around them *all* yet."

Did she just call Anna a whore?

"Insecurity does not look good on you, Janette. Do better," Anna replies.

Janette follows after her, releasing the man and grabbing Anna's arm. "You think you are something special, when all you are is a whoring bitch!" Janette spits, shoving her.

"I don't want your husband, I never have," Anna says, fire in her eyes. "He had a crush on me years ago and I rejected him, you know this. If your husband has wandering eyes, maybe you should take that up with him."

A slap rings out as Janette hits her.

I grab the back of her hair and yank her to me. "I wouldn't do that again if I were you," I growl down at Janette who raises a red hand filled of her magic.

"And I also wouldn't do that," Darius says, his power wrapping around hers instantly.

The male who must be her husband, steps forward. "Let's just...calm down. Okay?"

"Let her go, Rhea, she isn't worth the energy," Anna says, I do so reluctantly as Janette stands straight, flattening her hair down while she glares at me.

"You are all just rabid. Why grandmother lets dogs in, I will never know."

"Just stop, Janette," the male says, coaxing her away but she is having none of it.

"Are you sticking up for her, Jake?" She asks him, anger crossing her face. "Do you want to be with her?!"

"Of course not."

"Let's go," Anna says and continues down the path as her sister and Jake argue.

Or more, she argues while he tries to placate her.

Zaide and Leo walk ahead, and when Jake tries to pull Janette back toward the home, she pushes him and stumbles into Zaide. Without any warning, Zaide takes her legs from under her and carries on walking like nothing happened.

I stare, stunned for a moment until I cover my mouth with a laugh as Janette screeches on the floor.

Anna turns and looks from her sister to Zaide for a moment, before continuing on.

"Brutal," Damian says as he walks over her. "Maybe be nicer, yeah?"

"Shut up, *dog*," Zaide jests.

"Pft, maybe you are a lost cause," Damian sneers.

Darius grabs my hand as we follow the others, leaving a screeching Janette behind.

"I don't like her," I tell him as his magic wraps around our hands. I call my own to join his.

"She thinks your witch wants her husband."

"She definitely has a grudge, but I saw the hatred in her eyes. She could really hurt Anna."

Darius grunts. "She wouldn't get close enough, not with

who is watching over her."

"Who is?"

Darius chuckles, but he halts in his tracks and tilts his head. His eyes turn unfocused, and I know he is speaking to his brothers. His jaw ticks, a rumbling coming from him. He blinks suddenly, and then he's looking down at me. "What is it?" I ask.

"A public Hanging." My stomach drops.

"Where?"

"Wolvorn." I feel sick.

"What is the hanging for?"

"I don't know, but we need to find out."

FORTY NINE

KADE

I watch on as my pack hugs each other, tears and sniffles following. I know I should go to them, let them know I'm happy they are safe, even though we lost a few, but I can't.

I don't feel like I'm a part of it, like I don't belong there which I know Josh and Rhea would think it's ridiculous, but I can't explain it.

Loneliness wraps around me like a rope and my shoulders tense as Axis moves within me, wondering if I can control his urges to be free.

At the castle, I did learn somewhat to control it, I had no choice, the end result would end in pain otherwise. Some part of me thinks there still may be pain that follows after a shift, but my logical side wins out. Knowing we are not in that place anymore.

As my pack continues to express their relief, I realize I'm just standing here with the Elites, once our enemy.

I know things have changed, a lot has actually, but it makes me feel a little on-edge to be standing with males that are the best warriors in the lands.

I feel inadequate.

A flutter catches my eye, and my head turns, blinking in disbelief as I think…no…I *know* I saw a silver wing just now.

Veering off from the group, I walk off path and follow that glimpse of silver. No one stops me, I don't think anyone even noticed I'm not with them anymore, and sadness wraps around me, but still, I focus ahead as I round a tree and see the silver butterfly.

So I wasn't imagining it.

I watch it hover for a moment, and I feel like it's watching me as I watch it.

What's it doing here?

I followed it in Eridian and then it just...disappeared.

It flies up and down and moves again, this time a little faster. I pick up the pace as I follow, trailing over roots, careful of the boggy water in some areas around here, the further I go from the main village I guess you can call it.

The butterfly flies a little higher though the trees that have purple flowers wrapped around them, and I panic a little when I can't see it.

I move into a full-on sprint, my heart kicking up as my feet slam against the ground, some sort of desperation flowing through me.

I end up on another path next to a rushing river when the butterfly comes into view again. It's at chest-height now, and I'm so focused on it that I don't notice we are coming up to a bridge.

Or the figure on it.

I stop before I hit it, catching my breath as the butterfly slows down.

I stare at it as it goes toward the figure, who's looking down over the bridge, only focused on the water. I take the first step onto the wooden plank, heart beating almost painfully in my chest as the figure's head snaps my way.

I freeze as amber eyes connect with mine, so sad and distant that a sharp pang goes through my heart.

The butterfly hovers above her head, and she doesn't react at all to it. Does she even see it?

We stare at each other, noting the difference in both of us since we last saw each other.

Since I left her in bed after she fell asleep.

Memory after memory crashes through my mind, of her first shy smile at me, the way she would clutch onto Axis, her laugh, the way she would always run to me when she saw me. Pain radiates through my head but I try to focus on them, trying to determine whether they are true or not but I know they are. I can feel it.

Only she isn't running toward me now, and the butterfly disappears.

I take a step toward her, and after a moment of hesitation, she does the same.

A breath escapes from her, like she was about to say something but can't.

I take a breath, then two.

If she can't do it, I'll do it for her. I think I'm the only one who can.

"Hi, Winglet."

FIFTY

Darius

Rhea and I port in with Leo, leaving the others behind to not draw attention to ourselves with a large number. I turn and make sure Rhea's hood is all the way up, her mask in place as she waits patiently until I'm satisfied she is hidden.

Once I am, I make sure my own face is covered and grab her hand, the act now so familiar, always wanting her palm against mine.

We wade through the large crowd that has gathered just outside Wolvorn Castle to the center. It will be easier to blend in that way.

Rhea makes a distressed noise, and I hold her in front of me and discreetly let some of my power comfort her. She leans back heavily against my chest, her body shaking as none other than Higher Charles, Higher Warden, or should I say, Edward, and Alpha Christopher walk the battlements.

Rhea tenses, and I rub her shoulder, trying to comfort her as rage settles in my gut.

"Where do you want me," Leo asks down the link.

"In the back, get a vantage point of the whole area."

Seeing Charles here makes me want to storm up there and tear his head off of his shoulders, but I know I can't. Guards line the walls, archers at the ready for any disturbances.

Edward shuffles his feet and I look to the male Rhea adores. He may have betrayed her, and I want his heart for it because the way she speaks about him is close to how a daughter would a parent.

I don't care for him, but she does and that's what matters.

"People of Vrohkaria, after a thorough investigation, we have deemed the culprits of those heinous posters that were distributed across the Lands," Charles's voice rings out, and Rhea curls into me more.

I look around at the crowd when they start shouting. Some don't believe him; some agree with him, and some are just pleading to be saved from the rogues.

He ignores them all as guards at the front keep them back from the gates.

Fucking coward.

"Can we just kill him now?" Rhea says to me under her breath.

"I don't think we would even get close to him. Plus, Edward would be inclined to protect him as he is a Higher. The bond they have will deem it so. Do you want to fight him?"

Her shoulders slump in answer.

Truthfully, I don't think we are prepared to fight Charles just yet, and there are other Highers to take out one-by one first. It will weaken Charles as we do, and we need the best chance of winning as we can get.

So as much as I want to rush him to his death, we have to be as patient as our anonymity allows it.

Alpha Christopher raises a hand to settle the crowd. "We are doing this hanging here to show that no matter where those who commit a crime are, they will be punished, they will not get away with it."

"More like they don't want to open the castle gates and be at risk of others getting inside and staying," I mutter in Rhea's ear. She nods, her hand coming back to grip my side.

"These males were found to have multiple piles of posters in crates beneath their home," Charles continues. "And after being questioned, they finally admit to their crimes in wanting to rebel against myself, and against the Highers. Those that protect you!" Three males are brought forward on the battlements. Hands tied behind their backs and mouths stuffed with cloth.

Typical that they haven't allowed them to talk.

"Darius," Rhea mumbles and I lean down to hear her better. "Why are there only three males when there are four nooses?"

I look up at that and see she's right.

Four dangle down from the stone, ready and waiting. Why make four when there are only three males.

"We need to help them," she mumbles, her body stiff. "We both know they didn't do it."

I do, but it's only us, we have no chance of doing anything to help them.

"It is too dangerous, little wolf. It is a risk, and we may do more harm than good," I say quietly. Maybe it wasn't a good idea to bring her here. She will feel guilty just standing here and watching, I know she will.

"We can't do *nothing*," she hisses at me.

Fuck.

"Because of the heinous slander spread across the lands, these males instilled anger and panic across the people, which resulted in multiple brawls and many left dead. They have their deaths on their hands with their actions," Charles booms.

"And that is before taking into consideration their treason against the Highers," Alpha Christopher tacks on.

Edward says nothing, his eyes sad as he watches the three males get put in their nooses by the Highers's guards. They struggle, of course they do, they are about to die, and a woman screams in the front row.

Begging.

Crying that her mate has a young pup.

I grind my teeth and Rhea's shoulders shake.

"Not only will these traitors lose their life, but they will also lose the home where they carried out these traitorous acts." He points in a direction, and we all turn, watching as smoke appears in the distance. "It will burn as a reminder that these crimes will not be tolerated!"

Rhea makes a devastated noise, I turn her in my arms and pull her close. "Don't watch, little wolf." My hand goes to the back of her head as she grips me tightly.

I definitely shouldn't have brought her here; I should have refused her. But I was afraid she would run off on her own again.

I go to fetch the port stone out of my pocket, but Charles's next words hit us like he's speaking directly to us.

"We also have one more traitor." Rhea turns, a gasp spilling from her as Edward is pushed forward.

A noose is placed around his neck like the others, and he looks over the crowd below. He doesn't even fight it. I know the moment he sees Rhea though. His eyes widen, a hard set in his jaw before he lowers his eyes.

A bird squeaks, and we both look up and see Illium circling above, squawking as he looks down at him.

"No," Rhea says. It's quiet, but full of devastation.

She moves so fast that she slips through my fingers and with a muttered curse, I follow her through the crowd.

"Little wolf, fuck!" I shove people out the way, and that causes Charles to look into the crowd with furrowed brows.

"Quiet down," he demands as someone punches me as I pass them. I turn quickly and hit him back, sending him crashing into others and that starts a full on fist fight.

People start shoving and pushing, blood spilling as I hear the guards ahead trying to calm them.

"You will not disrespect me in my home!" Charles fumes, and then what feels like a shockwave of lightning passes through us.

I grit my teeth, managing to grab the back of Rhea's cloak and drag her to me.

"Stop," I tell her as I feel the painful current spreading through me. "You are going to be seen—"

Her watery, blue eyes look up at me as I turn her toward me, her panting breaths being seen in the cold air. My shoulders sag at the grief in her eyes.

"Always these fucking eyes," I tell her, as Higher Charles calls out to the people to behave. "Okay, little wolf."

"If I do not have silence in the next moment you will be joining the traitors in being hanged!" Charles roars. The crowd becomes silent, though I notice their eyes. Some fearsome, some full of anger.

Guards step up behind the males and Edward, moving them to a slot in the low walls.

Charles tells the crowd how Edward has been working against the Highers for his personal gain for many moon cycles. How he has orchestrated the whole thing with the posters and caused many deaths, and has collected deceivers and rebels along his way.

"It is so very disappointing to know one of our own has betrayed us. This is just more proof that you may not know who you work with at all," Charles says with fake sadness. One I have come to know over the years to try and get sympathy.

Rhea's shoulders shake harder, desperation in her eyes but they soon widen as all of a sudden, the males are pushed over the edges.

And bodies are being dropped.

"Let this be a lesson to you all!" Charles declares as the males all choke, their faces turning purple.

"Leo, arrow!"

Rhea turns, hands out and her magic pulses from them. People scream and jump out of the way when they see the magic, and the crowd gasps when that ball of power hits the guards directly in front of the gate, the hanging men above them.

The wood splinters and breaks, and then the whole thing comes crashing down as the people scream.

And Chaos ensues.

Two guards fall from the battlements, and most topple over from the surprise impact, including Christopher and Charles.

Leo's aim is true, and within moments, arrows cut through all four ropes and the hanged men fall. I call my power, letting it out to roam around the crowd and toward the guards at the edges.

I rush forward with Rhea as Charles bellows in anger. Leo fires arrows off toward them and the guards on the battlements as the people fight the guards.

I shove people out of the way until we are eventually in front of what is left of the gate, people stampeding on the hanged males to rush inside. Rhea hits a guard in the face and I grab another and throw him into the crowd. I mold my magic into a spike in the next moment and I stab another guard in the neck as Rhea rushes for Edward, cutting the rope around his neck and then doing the same with the males.

I make sure to cast a barrier around them, holding people back from trampling her.

"We need to go, Brother," Leo says, *"They are ready to do an attack."*

I look up at the battlement above and see Christopher looking over the wall, directly down at us. An arrow lands in the center of his head next, and then he's falling down. I watch as his body becomes broken on impact.

"Who dares attack your Lord Higher!" Charles roars, and I grab Rhea's shoulder as magic crackles in the air.

She grabs Edward's arm and I touch the port stone.

But my eyes lock onto Charles's as he looks down directly at us.

And I know he saw me.

And now he knows I'm a traitor too.

Landing in Eridian, I drag Rhea away from Edward and the other males as he coughs and splutters on the forest ground.

"Stay next to me," I tell her and for once, she doesn't fight me on it. *"Warn Vokheim, Charles knows I am no longer under his paw,"* I say down the link to my brothers.

We are not ready for the consequences of that, not ready to fight, but we have no choice.

He definitely saw me.

I saw his eyes widening and then quickly turning to fury. And I have no idea what he will do with that.

I look down at Rhea, lifting her hands and inspecting the blood on them. It isn't hers, so she must have caused some damage to the guard she punched.

She says nothing, just stares at Edward with a mixture of hurt and hope. Leo ports in next, brow sweaty and bow hanging loosely in his hand.

"That was interesting." He says, eyeing me for a moment before he looks down at the three males. He sighs, putting his bow over his shoulders and going to them with a knife. They panic, trying to roll away. "I'm not going to hurt you, I'm going to undo your hands."

They are still tense as he does just that, looking over to me and Edward with fear in their eyes.

"Come," Leo says, "We will get you patched up and then we can figure out where you go from there."

As the males follow him to Eridian, we stare down at Edward as he wrestles with himself to a sitting position.

He stares at Rhea as she stares back, a familiar *squawk* coming to us as Illium lands on the ground next to him, chirping.

"Are you okay?" Edward asks Rhea, and she firmly shakes her head. "I didn't mean for you to ever come to the Nightshade Pack. It was dangerous. I don't know how you knew I was there, but I didn't know anything until a moment before Charles stepped up on the platform, that he knew I was a traitor. He told me he caught me handing out those posters and…"

"Did you plant the crystal?" Rhea says, cutting him off.

Edward's head rears back. "What?"

"The memory crystal, did you send Illium to give it to me to then have it be used against me."

I tense as I wait for his answer, and I see the moment it all clicks into place what she is talking about.

"No, Rhea, Gods no. Why would you think that!? I didn't even know that was the same one I looked at." He frowns, his eyes pleading. "The crystal I gave you was a memory saved of you and Kade in the river one day, when he learned how to swim." When Rhea says nothing, he continues. "Did you not see it?"

She shakes her head. "The crystal is gone. I put it safely in my drawer with runes you only taught Josh and I. If you didn't plant it there, if you didn't give it to the others, how is it gone?"

"I don't know." His eyes plead with her to believe him. "I...Rhea, you are like a daughter to me...I would never..." He takes in a shaky breath, head hanging low and I hear Rhea's rough swallow.

I know she wants to go to him, give him comfort, while he will give her some in return.

But she doesn't need comfort from anyone but me.

I bring her to me, putting her in the instinctual position of her back to my chest as I rest my chin on her head. My arms wrap around her waist, protecting her back as I can protect her from any danger at the front.

"Aldus gave me the stone in Eridian," I tell him, and his brows furrow before he curses.

"What!?" Rhea asks, bringing her hands up to clutch my forearm.

"He was the one who taught me the runes," he said, face crumbling.

"So he could have gotten the stone," Rhea says slowly, her shoulders relaxing a moment.

"I don't know, he must have, but I didn't plant anything

Rhea, I wouldn't…"

Rhea stares at him for a moment, and then squeezing my arms, she moves forward and I release her.

She believes him.

I, however, will be keeping a close eye on him.

What he said makes sense, and his past actions were only ever to help Rhea and others. That is the only reason he still has his heart.

Rhea drops down in front of him and reaches behind to cut the rope, Edward hauls her to him, closing his eyes in relief as he murmurs words I can't hear to her.

Then he says, "I'm sorry if I have done anything to make you doubt me."

Rhea shakes her head. "I'm sorry I ever did. It's just, everything is just so much."

"It's okay," he says before reaching down to stroke Illium's head. The Croneian squeaks happily, bouncing around. "Charles knows of my deeds against him. How far back that goes? I don't know, but…he knows. I cannot be of help to you that way anymore."

"You are safe, that's all that matters," Rhea says as she hugs him again.

Edward looks over her shoulder at me. We both know he isn't safe.

"We need to prepare," I tell Rhea as they both stand.

"Prepare what?" Rhea's face is a picture of confusion, letting me know she had no idea.

"Charles saw me."

Her eyes widen. "Are you sure?" Her hands come around herself, and I hate the way that male makes her feel.

"I'm sure, little wolf."

"What do we do now?"

"Get ready for what is to come."

"And what's that?" she asks in a small voice.

"Anything."

FIFTY ONE

Rhea

I drag the deer as my pack runs around me, playing, excited for dinner. In wolf form, they nip and play in a way I am envious of.

Runa huffs her agreement.

I wonder what it would be like to run with them, fully. Sure I do anyway, but two legs over four has to make a difference.

Drax however, stays beside me, watching over me while Darius is with the Elites. He did go for a little run, but he soon came back.

"I don't need another babysitter, you know," I tell him, changing my grip on the deer's legs to pull better. "Your keeper does a good job of that already."

He nudges me, but that's the only response I get as Runa sits up straighter at his attention.

A rustle ahead in the bushes has me tilting my head as a familiar wolf walks through. I pause, eyeing Drax and the little black flames on his back with trepidation.

Axis walks forward a few steps, but halts when Drax moves toward him. I drop the deer, ignoring the blood dripping off of my hands as I watch on. I don't know how much control Kade has, we didn't manage to have that conversation, and since we got back here, he has been spending all of his time with Sam.

Axis bares his teeth when Drax draws near, but he pays him no mind and huffs at him like he's a little pup. Axis doesn't like this, he growls, head lowering.

Shit.

But then, Drax just walks up to him and nips his nose. I pause, and Axis seems to do the same, unsure what just happened.

I see the moment Kade comes through, and my shoulders relax that he has control. He sits, tilting his head up at Drax before the change comes over him.

Being fully clothed, it's a relief to know the progress Kade has made, but he is also more vulnerable with a large wolf towering over him.

I go to them, running a hand along Drax's side and then I face Kade, a hesitant smile on my face. "Hey, Carzan," I say, rubbing my cheek to his.

"Hey," he murmurs, looking up at Drax still. "He's big."

"Yeah," I chuckle, turning to look up at him too. "Biggest one you have seen, right?"

He nods, and Drax seems to stand taller as we become silent while he just lets us stare at him.

"Wanna help me?" I ask Kade, tilting my head to the deer and he nods.

We both know I don't need help.

Kade grabs the deer and we walk with Drax at our back, heading through the forest and to the gathering.

"Is Edward okay?"

"Better," I say. It will take some time but he will be okay.

"And he's the one who helped with my…memories?"

I'm quiet for a moment when we come up to a river. Gesturing for him to leave the deer, we go to the water and sit. Drax takes a drink as I watch the water ripple. It's cold out, but not unbearable.

"When you were younger, you would have these nightmares that felt like no other. Or I guess, I knew what they felt like because I had them too." I don't look at him as I talk, but I know he's watching me. "They hurt you, Carzan, and they hurt me." I turn to look at him then. "They are family but there is no love there...no warmth and comfort. All they gave us was pain."

His brows furrow. "I don't...really remember."

I nod. "I made it that way. I would say I am sorry, but I'm not. I asked Edward to block those younger years from you, and Kade...that night I have never seen you sleep so peacefully." I reach for his hand and squeeze his fingers. "You smiled for the first time three days later, a day after, you laughed." I smile softly at the memory. "You would play with Josh and I, you would ask questions and learn things about the lands. You were a totally different kid after those memories were blocked...how could I ever regret that?"

He looks to the water, deep in thought.

I swallow roughly.

"I...I never did the things they said about me, Carzan... I could never." I shake my head. "I just wanted to protect you, give you the life you deserved. And then that expanded to others. I didn't want that at first, but now they are my chosen family. It is hard to trust when for so long all you did was hurt."

"Did they hurt you badly?" I nod.

When he says nothing, my heart drops and I pull my hand away, but he grabs onto it, still not looking at me, but he squeezes my hand.

"I don't think you did what they said, not when I'm thinking clearly," he says the last words quietly. "I'm thankful I had a mom like you." I have to hold back the sob that wants to escape with those words. "I'm glad I had Josh. You were both the best parents I could have ever wanted. I don't see *them* as my family. I know I can get confused and...and it may seem like it but..." He turns to me then. His eyes are full of untold words. "You will always be my family, and I'm sorry. Thank you for always taking care of me. I'll do better."

I lift a hand and stroke the back of his head. "All you need to do is be you."

"What if I don't know who that is anymore," he whispers it

like some secret.

"Then you find it."

"And if I don't like it?"

"Maybe you don't like it because it is different from what you used to be, and that's okay. You can learn to love it."

"Are you different from what you used to be?"

My answer is quick.

"Yes." He frowns at that. "But moments peek through," I tell him, thinking about running through the lesia field. "Sometimes you find someone who brings out the things that you thought were lost forever."

"And if they can't?"

"You do it yourself, but then, you also don't have to. Do not put too much pressure on yourself to be like you once were. Life molds you, situations change you, but you have the power with what you do. You can decide the path you take, and you can decide how to take the path that was thrown at you."

His sigh is heavy, like he has so much inside of him and he doesn't know how to release it. "Can we do the blood link again?" he asks, and I have to breathe deeply a few times to choke my words out.

"Of course, Carzan. We can do it after dinner?" He nods, and I feel his relief like my own. "How's Samantha?" He shakes his head. I nod, understanding. "Let's get back for dinner."

We stand and drag the deer the rest of the way, Drax at our backs again. It doesn't take long before we are at the gathering and the meat is cut up and put in the bubbling pot.

"That should do it," Josh says, sitting next to Kade and ruffling his hair.

"It almost feels normal," Colten says, relaxing back on the bench and tilting his head back, closing his eyes.

"You mean with just us?" Hudson asks, sitting next to him, shoulders brushing. Colten grunts in reply.

"We can always get naked." We all look at Seb as he wiggles his eyebrows. "What? It would be fun."

"Shut up." We laugh as Taylor smacks him on the back of his head.

"You guys are no fun." Seb comes and sits down on the ground in front of us anyway, and we all just take a moment to just... be.

It does remind me of the time we spent together before we went into the Deadlands, how we laughed and looked up to the sky.

We all have weights on us now, though.

We listen to the stew bubble, and I notice Drax has wandered off. Probably going back to Darius.

"Is Sarah doing okay?" Colten asks.

"I feel like a weight has lifted off of her now that her father is dead. He deserved more than an arrow, but she is glad he is rid of these lands," Josh says. "She's spending a lot of time with Anna and learning how to help treat wounds. She said if she can save someone else's life like hers was saved, she feels like she is giving back."

"That is a good skill to have," Taylor says.

Josh nods, pride in his eyes. "She's really good at it, too."

Seb smiles at that, but I notice the residing pain in his eyes and I wonder if he is thinking about his mate he lost.

"She's going to be great," Colten chimes in, his eyes moving to Kade. "Wanna spar later?"

Kade takes a moment to think. "Wolves?"

Colten grins. "Fuck yes."

Hudson sighs. "I'll keep watch."

"I'll count points," Taylor tells them.

"I'll throw knives in for an extra flare." We all look at Seb who shrugs. "You are never fighting just one opponent."

We pause, and then we all nod.

He has a point.

Katy comes over and puts some herbs in the pot. Her and a few others have been tending to the gardens and salvaging as much as they can. It is working so far, and the younger kids love learning as they help.

Sam and Sybill come here next, and Kade gets up, walking over to Sam and nodding to the bench. When she takes a seat, he sits next to her and Sybill gives Kade a grateful smile.

The rest of my pack file in with the pups, and when some Elites come along, I notice Darius isn't with them. I give Leo a questioning look.

"He went to the cabin a while back," he says, nodding his head in the direction of it.

My brows furrow and I stand, making my way to my home. It isn't like him to be away from me this long. Since I woke in his arms, he's barely left my side, always kept me within his sights so why isn't he here now?

When I get to my door, I push it open and hear him in the dining room. Going in, I see him frowning down at a bit of wood as he has a knife to it. His gaze is intent on it, so much so that he doesn't even blink.

I tilt my head curiously. "Are you okay?" I ask, and his head snaps up to me.

Did he not even realize I was here?

Worried, I walk toward the table and notice him grabbing the wood in his hand, like he's hiding it.

"Darius?"

His jaw ticks and he looks away from me, but he must have seen the concern in my eyes because he slowly opens his hand.

Getting closer, I round the table and step up beside him, looking down into his palm.

"I can't do it like you," he mutters. "I just keep taking off more chunks."

Pulling a chair out, I sit next to him, and then I think better of it. Lifting his arm, I move it while I lift a leg. Knowing what I'm doing, he scoots back a little and helps me into his lap, an arm going around my waist.

I grab the wood and turn it over so the back of my hand is in his palm as he breathes into my neck. "I don't think it's bad at all," I tell him, picking up the knife. "Can I show you?"

He nods against my neck, his hand curling around the one holding the wood and then I show him how I move the knife over it.

"You have to follow the grain, making sure there is no stuttering in the movement and getting it at just the right angle." He listens intently as I show him a few times, and then I hand over the knife. "Try it."

Placing the wood on his hand, I put my own hand on the back of his and go through his movements, giving advice here and there.

"It looked easy when I would see you do it," he says, getting used to the glide of the knife.

"I've done it for years." I lean back against him, making my power come to my fingertips as I still hold the back of his hand. "I'm still not great."

He chuckles. "At least I can make out what you are carving,"

"And what are *you* trying to carve?" I feel his smirk against my neck.

"You will have to see."

FIFTY TWO

Darius

She sleeps in her own bed for the first time in a long time. I made sure the room was prepared as I painstakingly placed every piece of furniture in here. The bed, the table, the dresser.

I didn't let anyone else help me with this, and they wouldn't dare go in her room in fear I would retaliate.

They know not to touch anything of hers, especially from me.

I also made my scent strong here, and she liked it instantly.

No. She loves it.

As soon as I brought her here after dinner, I don't think she even realized how deep of a breath she took. How her eyes glazed or the small smile on her lips.

What this female does to me…fuck.

I stroke her hair, my chest expanding at the small, happy purr that leaves her parted lips.

I would give everything up for this creature that is mine.

A strong female.

An Heir.

My moonlight.

I've barely let her out of my sight since she woke up, but the thing is, when I do leave for a few moments, her eyes look for me, searching.

She's just as needy for me as I am for her, and I'm not even ashamed of it.

I never thought I would ever see her eyes again, so I'm going to make sure they are on me for as long as I can.

She whimpers in her sleep, her hands clutching the pillow by her head and I lay down again for a moment, bringing her hand to my lips as I gently run them over her knuckles.

I feel her wolf there, and I let Drax come to greet her.

He's desperate to meet her. Not only is Rhea the other half of me, but her wolf is also the other half of Drax.

A balance that's needed to be kept, yet he's missing his counterpart.

Rhea may hate me for the lengths I may have to go to get her wolf out, but now it is more urgent than ever knowing Charles saw me.

We are in more danger than we ever have been, I don't think we are ready.

The burden lies heavy on my shoulders as I stroke Rhea's cheek, moving down to the pulse in her neck to make sure it is beating.

The memory of it halting will forever haunt me.

I have to make sure she is safe, and then the ones she loves, along with my own men and the people.

The people are a burden the Highers are supposed to have, but it has been left on my shoulders to get us through with whatever is to come. To end the suffering and to make sure the right decisions are made, to make sure we train and are ready to face off against an enemy we never have before.

We don't know all of the Higher's powers, but what was showcased in The Deadlands may only be a snippet.

I fear what had happened to the rest of the crowd when we left, was no less than brutal.

Charles can be evil, but in anger? There are no words. But I had to get Rhea out of there, I couldn't stay and protect them and I don't regret that.

"We have news." Leo says down the link, and I bend down, inhaling Rhea's scent before I reluctantly move from the bed.

I guess the start of what's coming has arrived.

Rhea's brows crease, her hand reaching out for me as I move and I grab a pillow, running my cheek across it before gently laying it next to her. As soon as her hand touches it, she pulls it to her chest, burrowing her face in it so she has my scent.

I swallow roughly at her reaction, my heart beating almost painfully at how adorable she is, at the way she wants me.

With one last lingering look, I leave the room and pause outside the kid's door. I hear nothing inside but gentle snores. Rhea said he's a deep sleeper, but he doesn't sleep much anymore according to the guards I have watching over him.

I quietly yank down the handle and open the door. He's asleep in the bed, the furs tangled around him and sweat beads on his head.

I know he went through some shit at the Wolvorn, I know they hurt him and messed with his head, but I have no sympathy for those that hurt my little wolf.

Hurt people will hurt people, but that doesn't mean we have to accept it.

He is a different case though, with his twisted memories and all, so for Rhea's sake, I'm trying to be…cordial toward him. I'll happily beat his ass when needed, but I can see the strain on Rhea's face when tension thrums between us.

My jaw ticks and I leave the room, heading down the stairs. As soon as I'm out on the porch, I look to the moon and wait for my brothers.

I won't go further than this to leave her right now, everything rebels at me even trying.

I lift my hand and Draxton comes out. He shakes his fur, leaning down to stretch himself out. I shake my head at him as he turns and puts his nose to my neck, greeting me.

I run my hand over his head, playing with the flames only he possesses. "You will meet her soon." He huffs into my neck. "Go run, and then check the perimeter."

He growls playfully and I scratch his ears before he turns to do just that.

I look down at my hand and play with my power, rolling strands between my fingers.

I never let him out in front of Rhea before he barged out of me. I didn't want our already complicated relationship any more messy, with adding in the fact he was the wolf she saw when she was younger. That we both saw each other.

If I could kick my sixteen year old self back then to grab her. To go after her and take her away someplace safe, I would.

Footsteps approach and I turn to my brothers.

"What news?" I ask Leo as Damian yawns, stretching his arms over his head.

Zaide and Jerrod are on night duty tonight, but I know they probably filled them in.

"Maverick says he caught a few stragglers around Vokheim last night. And now we haven't been able to get in contact with him."

I stand up straighter. "Rogues?"

"And witches," Damian says, a concerned look on his face.

"They definitely know," I tell them.

Leo nods. "We think so."

"Casualties?"

"None, the rogues were taken care of and when one of the Elites on patrol confronted a witch, she said she was powering up the wards." Leo runs a hand down his face, stress lining his eyes. "What do you want us to do?"

"So they knew I had been slowly changing the wards to my own." They nod. "Send some more Elites to the keep, have some from Colhelm follow." He nods as Damian takes his blade out. "Damian, you go on ahead with them." He nods, face turning into a coldness I am familiar with as he readies himself. I look back at the cabin. "Leo, stay with her, let her know I won't be long when she wakes.

"I'm more useful to you."

"I can't...I can't trust anyone else with this. I need to know she is safe and you are that direct link."

He stares at me hard for a moment before his shoulders slump. "She's going to kick your ass," he mutters.

"Probably, but I'm not sure how long I can stay away from her to be honest."

They both give me a sympathetic look.

"And after we are done there?" Damian says, coming closer as I mentally call Drax back to me.

He comes through the tree line, aiming directly for my outstretched hand.

"We prepare."

As soon as Drax is with me, I gather the extra men near the gathering, and with one last look at the cabin, we port.

Only, we port into a bloodbath.

My men battle with others in the courtyard, archers on the battlements getting blasted by witches' magic. Wolves and rogues tearing each other apart as balls of fire hit the side of the keep.

What the fuck.

"How did they get in?!" I shout, grabbing a guard by the scruff of his neck and sending him flying back as he nears one of my men.

Fucking Highers guard.

"They breached the west wall, Alpha." I send out my magic and it splits off into five sharp points, hitting a few more enemies. "They came with witches and a trebuchet. The witches got through the wards and then the trebuchet hit, smashing through the wall." He spins, slicing a guard in his neck. "Then rogues followed."

"Damian, find Maverick and get an update. Sean," I say to the Elite as he finishes off another guard. "Grab the injured–" A whooshing sound reaches my ears, but I'm too late, the arrow imbeds in the center of his forehead and then he goes down. "Fuck," I growl.

I spin, looking for the culprit and see a smirking guard that's infiltrated the battlement, notching another arrow. I snarl, my markings appearing on my neck and down my back. More power instantly comes to the surface and my tails are at my back.

My eyes lock on him when I raise my hand out, and then Drax is there. My power coats him, the black flames licking at his fur but never burning him.

But he will burn them all.

"Go hunt," I tell him, never straying my eyes from the guards as he falters.

He releases the arrow aimed for me anyway, but my hand comes up, catching it in midair before it hits me right between the eyes. I turn and lodge that same arrow in the eye of a guard attempting to wound me. I tilt my head and smirk back at him, cold overtaking me as screams follow Drax in his wake.

Black flames hit the floor where he walks, and if you were to touch them? You'd catch fire, and then slowly be engulfed by them until there is nothing left of you.

Grabbing another arrow he sends my way, I clench my hand around it, then I'm coating it with my magic. Pulling my arm back, I send it flying.

Rhea would be proud of that throw. Especially when it hits him right in the chest and my magic rushes up to his neck, squeezing, crushing.

It isn't long until he falls off the wall and—would you look at that, into the waiting jaws of Drax.

I gather my blade and fight in the courtyard, defending our home. Chaos is everywhere, with bloodshed and pained cries.

"Have you found him yet?"

"No, Zaide and Jerrod are here." Damian replies. *"They are helping to look."*

"Keep me updated."

I slice through the stomach of a guard and dodge a magic attack from a witch. Picking a sword up off the ground, I throw it at her, I watch as it impales her shoulder and she stumbles to the ground. Not a moment later, she disappears. She must have ported out.

I see my men at the entrance into the main rooms of the keep, not letting the guards enter as more rogures snarl in their hunt.

I catch one on its hind legs, slicing through the flesh and it turns, whipping around to bite me. I punch it in its nose, then stab it through the chest when it's momentarily stunned. I see Drax ahead, a few people in flames trying to attack him as he chomps and bites his way through.

I end up near one of the side entrances, taking the fight there. More bodies of my people litter the ground. Kitchen staff, cloth makers…and then I notice a familiar, bloodied face on the ground.

Ellian, the omega.

Fuck.

I go to him, shoving a guard out of the way and slicing through another. My hand is on his neck in the next moment and a growl builds up in my chest.

No heartbeat.

Rhea will be devastated.

Magic spurs out of me, winding and sprawling out through enemies's legs as I slow them down. They grunt, trying to move but to no avail, and I don't think as I cut them down one by one.

Blood covers me, my clothing soaked, my hands slippery by the time it feels like I blink again. Still, I don't stop because it feels like we are getting nowhere.

I end up inside the keep, ascending the stairs that will take me to my room. Guards have gotten inside, and I grab one by the back of the neck, slamming his head against the wall. Once. Twice.

When he crumbles, I carry on and enter my room. I don't waste time as I go directly to the picture of my mother and sister, then grab Rhea's things and her pack.

With it secured over my shoulder, I make my way back

down to the hall where we eat. Fighting ensues inside, and I help my Elites to eradicate them and push them back.

A ceiling collapses from the inside and I look up to the walls of the home I have known for so long. The walls shake and stone falls.

It isn't safe here anymore.

"Everyone, outside!" I roar the command to any Elites within hearing distance. I grab one of my injured, helping them stand as we make our way to the courtyard.

"Thank you, Alpha," He croaks as I place him against the wall. "I have failed you, I'm sorry."

"You have not failed me, you fought well to protect our home." I squeeze his shoulder in reassurance.

"Where is Maize?" I hear a guard shout, holding one of my men by the throat. "Where is the witch!" When my warrior says nothing, a blade is stabbed in his stomach before I can get to him.

Fuck, they must have realized Maize is not here.

Magic attacks continue on the keep, trying to get into the building itself and I growl, looking in the direction it's coming from.

"Wolf!" Someone screams as I spot them running away from Drax. Only, he crashes into a witch who's just about to aim her magic.

It flies out of her hand and hits the top of one of our towers with a mighty crash.

A few seconds, then one more, and the brick begins to tumble down.

"Move!" I order my men below as I start rushing toward them. It's then that I notice Maverick is also there.

But he's locked in a battle with a guard while another wolf is with a rogure. There are two injured on the ground behind them that they are protecting.

I see the roof collapse and it follows the bricks down.

They are going to be crushed.

"Darius!" I hear Damian shout, but I'm nearly there.

Just as I'm a step away from being able to drag the guard to safety, the rogue spins unexpectedly, clamping his jaws down on my arm, and then we are under the rubble.

FIFTY THREE

Rhea

I flip through the pages of the old book, careful not to damage the pages as I read about the history of the lands.

Darius isn't back yet after leaving for the keep, and half a day has gone by with no word. Leo assures me everything is fine, but a little while ago when we were talking, he stopped suddenly and said he would be right back.

He hasn't been back since.

I sigh and lean back, looking out the window.

"He will be back soon," Sarah says, a small smile on her face as she sorts out the cupboard of supplies.

We are in the healers cabin, and it looks pretty much like it used to, with a few added touches.

"I know what it's like to miss someone, to need them near." Her eyes go to Josh at the other end of the room as he looks through his own book. Their eyes meet, a softness in them as they look at each other.

I shift uncomfortably in my seat. "I know he will be okay, he always is."

Damn Alpha seems invincible.

"Any more luck?" she asks, nodding to the book in my lap.

"Just that the Gods seem to favor the last place they created, though I don't know where that is. It's said that it was the last place they made after running around the lands. They would go there, raise their heads to the moon and howl a song that would bring life to everything around them."

"That's beautiful," Sarah says with a faraway look in her eyes.

"The Gods are what made us, what gave us the lands, and along with that, its beauty."

"I haven't seen much beauty," she says sadly, and Josh makes a sound in the back of his throat.

Apart from Eridian, I hadn't either, But then my mind goes to the field of flowers Darius made me and I think...it doesn't matter.

"Beauty can be found," I tell her, a gentle smile on my face. "It can also be made. Given." I tilt my head in thought. "Created."

She looks at me for a moment and grins. "You're right. I just need a certain male to make something for me."

"I made you a drawing the other day!" Josh protests, coming to stand behind her, hands on her waist.

"Oh, was that what it was?" His mouth drops open. "I couldn't tell!"

"You little—"

"I am trying to rest up here," Edward croaks from the bed he's in.

I raise a brow. "You were pretending to sleep to hear gossip."

His eyes open, and though they are full of pain, they are filled with mirth. "Maybe."

I smile and place the book down, dragging my chair to his side. "You okay?" I ask as Sarah hands him some water.

"I'm okay." He pats my hand that's covered in healing bruises and I frown.

We wolves always had better healing, but Edward is much older, and with that, our healing slows.

"Reading anything good?" He nods to the book.

"Just how the lands were formed. Belldame told me that we needed to go to the plane of the Gods, and I figured I had nothing else to do at the moment so why not see if I can find anything more."

"Ah, the Gods." He sits up more, coughing as he does. I

watch on with worry. "The Gods always loved creating things. It's why Heirs exist." I smile at that. "They enjoyed Zakith, it was the last place they were."

It isn't lost on me that it happens to be my home.

"I don't remember anything there that could possibly be the plane of the Gods."

Edwards smiles, his eyes crinkling. "They wouldn't have made it easy, however much has been lost over the years." I nod. "What else did Belldame say? She is the Blood witch?"

"Don't be saying anything bad about my Grandmother or I won't heal you," Anna says as she comes into the room with a bowl in her hands.

"I would never. I respect her too much for that," Edward says, his eyes conveying more than he wants to say.

Hmm. We have a few who do that around here.

A commotion sounds from outside the room, then footsteps running, words and then shouting.

"Get them down on the ground and make sure they don't move."

Leo?

"What is going on?!" I get to my feet, rushing for the door. I swing it open, uncaring as it bounces off the wall while I watch as man after man is ported into Eridian. "What…"

"Oh my Gods," Sarah says behind me.

A scream comes from a male further ahead, his leg resting at an odd angle and I seem to come out of my frozen state and move.

"Josh, grab hot towels and cloths." I look over some wounds as more arrive. "Then start a fire, we need to cauterize some wounds. Sarah," I start, and she blinks at me. "Bowls…no. Buckets of clean water, ask for help to gather it at the river. We need as many as you can get!" She blinks at me. "Can you do that?"

"Yes," she says quietly, but then she straightens her spine. "Yes!"

Anna is already rushing off, barking orders as I go for the male with a broken leg. "Hey, lay back and stay still."

"Fuck, it hurts." He looks to be in his late twenties, but his eyes speak of battles far more than they should be able to.

"Yeah it will," I tell him and then grab my knife from my boot and start to cut his leather pants around the bone.

Blood seeps out of it in spurts, and the metallic taste hits my mouth. I pull and tear until I have his leg clear, trying not to throw up. Then placing a hand on his leg near the open wound, my face warms as I push some power into my palm, willing it to go to the wound.

It reacts, strands probing into his legs and the subtle glow lights my face. I close my eyes and concentrate. The last time I did it with Josh, it was going on a whim, but I can't do that here.

I feel the tears, the ligaments and muscle torn from the bone snapping through his skin.

I open my eyes and look at the male who's panting, sweat dripping from his neck. "You there," I say to an Elite as he passes. "Get me a small piece of wood." His brows furrow and I release a little dominance and try with a more forceful tone. "Now."

We can't be fucking around here.

I rest my hand on the guard's arm. "Now, this will hurt," I tell him, and I see him swallow. "But it will only be for a moment, okay?"

He nods, and then the Elite is back, handing me some wood.

"Thank you," I say to him. Lifting the wood to the man's lips, I tell him, "Bite down."

I don't wait until he's even fully doing so as I grab his leg, the bone, and push them together. He screams around the wood in his mouth, his back arching and then he's moving, trying to get away from the pain.

"Stay still," I grunt, trying to keep a hold of his leg as he lifts his arm and accidentally hits the side of my face.

"I wouldn't do that," a growling Leo says, his hand stopping me from getting hurt again. "You will be in worse pain than you are now."

I continue to take the strips of leather that I cut and wrap them around his leg, all the while continuing to work on stopping the bleeding.

"Keep it still," I tell the male, "Don't move until a healer has seen you."

"Rhea," Leo says as I check him over before rising. "You need to come with me."

"What is it?" I ask, looking at all the other injured men. "What happened Leo?"

I see Sarah and Josh helping, along with more Elites and those that came to us from Colhelm. Anna is with a bleeding Zaide, and I'm so shocked at the fact he's hurt that I don't move for a moment, until Leo's words hit me.

"Darius got hurt."

My heart lodges in my throat. "Where is he?"

"He was trying to save others. We pulled him out but..."

"But what," I whisper, my hands trembling.

"Just come."

I follow him as I weave through injured men... and dead ones. He leads me to the bottom of the cliffs, and I see Jerrod and Damian there, looking down at the ground.

I rush forward, my heart beating hard against my chest.

They both turn at my approach, faces full of concern, but I go between them, pushing them out the way and there he is.

Darius lays on the ground, sweat beading his brow and blood... everywhere.

I get to my knees, putting a hand to his chest and feeling his heart beating. Then my eyes go to the wound on his arm.

"No," I whisper, sucking in a sharp breath.

"What are you doing here, little wolf?" His brows furrow, and then he tries to get up. He hisses in pain, his glare going to his arm before he lays back down. "Fucking rogure."

"We can fix it," I say, starting to mumble. "We can have Belldame come here, maybe she knows what to do."

"Rhea."

"And who knows, maybe my power can heal it, right?"

"Little wolf, stop."

"And then the poison won't take hold and everything will be fine." I start peeling back the leather of his arm. Panic has my hands shaking, my eyes watering but I still tear and grab at the material.

"Rhea, I'm fine," he says, halting me with his hand.

"You are not fine!" I shout, chest heaving.

He's been bit by a rogure, and its poison is making its way into his body, slowly stopping his organs, and killing him.

Oh Gods…

A strand of magic comes to my face, stroking my cheek. "I'm immune," he says, and I stare at him.

"What?"

"It hurts, but I'm immune," he says slowly, and my mouth drops open, "I am Heir of Cazier, of the below. They can't hurt me, not like that."

I sag against him, my forehead on his chest, uncaring about all the blood that must be getting on me. The others around him all murmur at Darius's words, their own shock evident.

"Leo said you were hurt, and I thought…"

"Leo," he says on a growl, and I hear him shuffling back. "Is going to get his ass kicked for worrying you like that."

"Hey!" Leo says, "I didn't know you were fucking immune! How did you even know?"

"I knew the moment the poison didn't take hold, but like I said, it hurts." Darius shrugs. "And I don't care about your reasoning, you don't ever worry her like that!" His hand comes to the back of my head. "Though I'm not complaining about you caring, little wolf."

"Asshole," I grumble into him and he chuckles. That's when I notice the pack he's gripping in his other hand. "What's that?"

He hands it to me. "Important things."

I open the bag and see its contents. "Darius."

"I made sure to get them." He went inside the keep whilst under attack to make sure he brought me my things. "I couldn't find Belldame's bone, though."

Inside the bag is a picture of his family, but also my mother's letter and carvings.

"Thank you," I whisper to him.

He nods, sitting up on a grunt. "I will be fine soon, and then I need to help my men." His fingers go down my cheek. "Why do you have a red mark here?" Magic comes from his fingertips, cooling the sting.

"I was helping and I got hit by accident."

His eyes darken. "Who."

"It's fine." His eyes go over my shoulder, and his eyes glaze. "Darius," I say, my hand gripping his own, squeezing. I know he's asking Leo down his link if he knows. "I'm fine, now tell me what happened?"

His jaw ticks. "The Highers, they know."

I swallow roughly. "Are you sure? Are we out of time?"

He nods. "I don't think they know we are in Eridian, but it won't be long until they do."

And my home is at risk again. "What do we do?"

"We recover and heal, then we get a wolf out and go eat our enemies."

I huff out a laugh. "It is not that easy."

"I know," he says, running a finger across my lips. "But anything worth having was never easy."

FIFTY FOUR

Rhea

After putting more protection crystals around Eridian, we helped tend to the wounded. Darius told me about the attack on the keep and about those we lost.

My heart is heavy with that, especially Ellian. Edward and I blessed him when I told him. The omega didn't deserve that fate.

Darius thinks he was trying to escape with his kitchen staff...and that breaks my heart even more.

We don't know the number of the dead with most under the rubble of what used to be Vokheim now, and I can tell Darius is not only furious about his home being destroyed, but I think he's also grieving a place that had been his for so long. Along with his men.

He told me he had been there since he became Alpha of the Elites at eighteen. That's a long time to become attached to a place, though he hasn't outright said it.

The attack has put things into perspective. We don't have time, and this is why we are here.

"Will it work this time?" I ask Darius as he stands before me. Snowflakes drop around him, and in his hair, giving him a softer look rather than the harsh male of the Alpha of the Elites.

Just like he said, he was immune to the rogures poison after being bitten, and it must be because of Drax, because Darius tells me he's fine too, just tired.

We are all tired.

We are a little ways into the forest, just past the lilk trees. Darius wanted us to come out this way to where it is silent, where no one can disturb us.

"It has to work, little wolf, we are running out of time," he reminds me. "We don't know when we will be attacked, and we have to start fighting back."

And if I don't fully connect with Runa, I will be a liability, I'll be of no help to anyone.

I have to save my family from the Highers's wrath, I have to keep them safe, along with all the innocents dragged into this.

"Okay," I nod, and straighten my spine. "Do it." Darius smiles and places a hand on my chest.

Pride fills his eyes. "Good girl."

I close my eyes, breathing in the cold winter air around us as Darius pours his magic into me. I welcome it now, I let him in instantly.

So different from the first time we did this.

I realize I trust him now.

My chest heats, and then I peel my eyes open and look around the dark space. Small, glowing balls float around us, some scattering further back.

When I look into the pure darkness, I swallow roughly. Darius doesn't miss my unease, aware of my reactions more than ever.

"What is it?" he asks. He stands in front of me, just like he was before we came here. With his hand still on my chest, he rubs there gently, as if he can make it all better.

"It just reminds me of what happened after I fell," I tell him honestly. I remember the darkness, the thought of not being able to breathe, invisible hands dragging me down.

His eyes darken, a tick in his jaw. "You are not there now, you're with me." He runs his hands up and down my arms. "Safe."

I look up at him and nod. He will keep me safe, I know that. He wouldn't let anything happen to me even if he can't help it.

He rubs his nose with mine and pulls back, his eyes going over my shoulder.

"Hello again, wolf." My eyes widen at Darius's words. I try to spin around, needing to see Runa, but he stops me. "Are you going to come to me?" A growl comes from behind me, and Darius smirks. "Your human counterpart needs you, so you either come out willingly, or I drag you out."

"Darius!" I hiss. I know deep down that it will be that way, but he doesn't have to be so harsh about it. I'm hoping it won't come to that.

"No, Rhea." He looks down at me. "For every time she refuses, it puts you in danger, you nearly fucking died because you used up too much power from not being able to control it properly!"

Oh. I thought he was thinking about how we need my power to help in the coming battles…but I didn't think of this. It should have been obvious because his eyes are full of fear as he says it, and it's fear for me.

"Dar," I say gently, but he shakes his head and storms past me.

"Wolf, let her lead you out," he says, and I turn and see glowing, blue eyes watching him, a ferocious growl spilling from her lips the closer he gets. "You have to come out or it will kill her. Is that what you want? Is that my punishment for what I did? You want her to die—"

I blink, but Darius isn't there anymore. I look around, trying to find him but he's just…gone.

My eyes go back to Runa, and she's already watching me as my chest heaves with nerves.

She doesn't growl at me, she just…stares.

I take a breath and try to relax my posture, wiping sweaty hands on my pants.

"Hi," I whisper to her. She's not kicking me out this time, she's not doing anything.

As we watch each other, I think of all the things we have

been through over the years, all the things that they did to us in the basement. It kind of feels like I'm facing my past all wrapped into her stare.

"When I was fourteen and they…" I squeeze my eyes shut from the onslaught of memories, but then I shake my head. No. They won't drag me down "When I was fourteen and you came to me after they were putting me through so much pain, I couldn't have been more thankful for you," I start, not moving from my spot. "You saved me from agony, and then you tried to rip them apart, we both did. But they were much stronger, weren't they?" I say softly.

I watch as those balls of light float around, hovering to her a little, showing just a smidge more of her.

"When they started on you, Runa…" My eyes sting and I clear my throat. "I wasn't thankful anymore. They were hurting you, and you wouldn't let me come back because you were trying to protect me, weren't you? You took that pain in my stead."

She makes a sad sound, and a tear finally drops. I quickly wipe it away.

I need to be strong here.

"I hated and loved you then. Hated you because I had to bear witness to your pain, and loved you because you did that for me. I had you come to me at fourteen, but then they quickly took you away from me because you have never come out again.

Her eyes blink at me.

"I know you are scared, I have been scared too, and I have let you live within me, and be your grumpy self when I should have encouraged you to come out more, worked with you sooner. I'm sorry for that." I pick at my fingers. "But Runa," I say, shaking my head. "We need you to come out. I need you."

She doesn't move, doesn't make a single step toward me as my heart crashes against my ribs.

"I can't do this without you." I point to the glowing balls of power around the space. "I cannot control it fully, you know that, you have felt that. We need to protect those we love."

She makes a chuffing sound.

"We need to protect Josh and our pack... we need to protect Kade." A whine. "Let me see you, come to me Runa, Vallier."

I don't think she will move at all, and my heart begins to sink that this isn't working, but then, she takes a step forward. Just one, slow, hesitant step.

"We were hurt when we were young, far too young," I continue to keep talking, hoping it will help. "We didn't deserve any of that. We were innocents in the hands of monsters. I don't want the monsters to keep a hold of us any longer. We are stronger than that."

Another small step, and I nearly go to my knees. "That's it, you are safe with me."

Another step.

"You are safe with him."

Another.

"He wouldn't let them touch us again. He would rampage across the lands."

Another.

"You know that, don't you?"

Two more.

"You have *felt* that."

Three more.

"So come to me and let's show the lands just how amazing you are." I hold out my hand to her, and she stops. "We cannot be scared, and you need to see that you can come out without harm."

I hear the thumping of my pulse in my ears as the glow of the light shows the color of her fur.

I release a breath.

"Gods, you are beautiful, Runa," I say gently, softly. Another tear falls from my eyes as I smile at her. "You are more than I had ever hoped for."

Her head lowers a little at that.

"You are coming with me now," I tell her, determined, and she tilts her head. "Okay? We are going to show the lands just how beautiful you are, and how deadly your teeth can be."

I drop my hand and take a deep breath, hoping I don't scare her, but I can't hold myself back, not with all the emotions coursing through me.

"I'm tired of running, Runa, aren't you?" I start walking toward her. "Instead, let's run to each other." After a hesitant moment, she takes a step. "Let's overcome our fear."

I nod encouragingly as I take one too, and then we are both taking steps. Runa follows me, and I follow her, eyes locked on each other.

And then, I'm running.

Running to my wolf that I haven't properly felt since I was fourteen, running to a future we can only have together.

And she's running too.

A wet laugh comes from me, full of elation and happiness as we close the distance.

"Let us take care of you," I tell her, so close now. "We will, I promise."

And then we are there, colliding with each other as I crash into her chest.

In the next moment, we are out of there, and she is taking us to her freedom.

FIFTY FIVE

Darius

I watch as every possible emotion takes over Rhea's face as she stands before me, eyes closed.

After Runa kicked me out—something the wolf is getting far too comfortable doing, I've been watching over Rhea, ready to be here for when she comes back.

I could force my way back in, but I hope the time they have together, helps.

Drax growls restlessly within me, impatient in his anticipation that he may get to meet her, and I have to hold him back tightly, making sure nothing can distract me while I watch over her.

Snowflakes fall lightly around us, coating the trees and plant life. The winter wind blows and I pull the hood of Rhea's cloak over her head, wanting to keep her warm as her eyes flicker beneath her closed eyelids.

Maybe I should start a fire to keep her warm, I don't know how long we will be here.

Just when I begin to move to go gather firewood nearby, I sense it.

The change.

I freeze, my body thrumming with anticipation as my eyes roam over her. Then I feel it gradually getting stronger, the air around us filling with it and I straighten to my full height.

"Rhea?" I ask, but she doesn't acknowledge me.

Drax moves within, ears perked as he comes to my eyes. Is

this it? Is she finally coming out?

When I feel another strong surge, I step back to give her space, my eyes locked on Rhea when suddenly, she twitches.

Just the slightest bit in her finger first, then another, then her entire hand.

My breathing picks up, my own hands flexing to grab her, hold her and make sure everything is alright.

"I got you Rhea, let her come," I say gently. I don't even know if she can hear me. "I'm here." Calling my power, I move a tendril forward and wrap it around her middle finger, loosely, solidifying my words to her.

A whimper comes from her lips, and I take a step forward before halting myself.

I cannot interfere with this.

"You can do it, little wolf, relax as much as possible, it will hurt less."

The change hurts when you first receive your wolf, and it's only after a few times of doing so that your muscles become used to the way they stretch, the way your body molds and moves.

She hasn't done it since she was fourteen.

A small cry comes from her next, and I grit my teeth. If I go to her, I could disrupt this, I could make Runa retreat and then she will have to go through this all over again.

Her face crumples, and I want to take it away. All the discomfort, all the pain.

"I'll take care of you," I tell them both, because now her eyes are open and on me, and it's Runa looking from within. Those black flecks float in her eyes as she stares. "I won't hurt you." I shake my head. "Never again," I growl to her, to myself. "I vow it so just…come out and ease Rhea's pain."

I take another step back and squeeze Rhea's finger with my magic. She looks down, lifting her hand and following the strand back to me. Where we are connected.

My eyes show my truth, my honesty to them both.

My vow.

I raise my arm and pull the sleeve up, showing the bite mark. "We made a blood vow, if my words aren't enough, this should be." It glows a subtle violet as I reveal the mark to her, hating that it is even needed.

She closes her eyes, and then a sudden shimmer overcomes her, a scream following on parted lips as she hunches over.

One moment, she's there.

The next, she's wolf.

A breath escapes me as I watch the wolf shake out her fur, standing on wobbly legs as she sneezes. My chest warms at finally seeing her, and then pride fills in my chest for them both, for actually shifting.

"Laeliah," I tell her softly. "Just like your keeper." Her head snaps to me at the sound of my voice, and her whole body freezes.

She's large, not as big as Drax, but still larger than any other wolf. Her coat shines silver, the snowflakes disappearing as soon as they land on her. Her eyes are a striking blue, so full of life and innocence that emotions rise within me, overwhelming as it reminds me of Rhea when she sees something for the first time.

I swallow roughly at how strong my reaction is.

I take in the crescent moon on her forehead that mirrors Draxton's, only hers is black where his is silver.

Fitting isn't it, how clever the Gods are with their balance.

They knew what they were doing when they created our wolves separately, and then gave them to Rhea and I.

I call my magic back and Runa tenses, her ears lowering, tail tucking between her legs.

I don't remove my own stare from her as I let her see the pride in my gaze, the wonder that she is finally here.

"Runa," I say, dipping my head as Drax tries to force himself out of me.

Not yet. You have to wait, or you will scare her.

Runa whines, the fear evident in her eyes and I loathe it. So much like her keeper's at one time, and I won't allow it.

I spread my hands out in front of me slowly and then crouch down so I'm below her.

"I won't hurt you." And I won't. I hate that I need to tell her this, to reassure her, but after everything that has happened to her, and then what I did to Rhea...I don't blame her.

Runa backs up on unsteady legs, tripping over herself and I rise, an instinct to go and help her, but she yelps at my advance, snapping her jaws at me and I pause once again.

"It's okay, just take your time." I don't think I have ever sounded so gentle in my life, maybe when my baby sister was born, but I need to try before she does something like bolt.

The forest doesn't pose a lot of danger, but she may hurt herself, or get caught up in the river.

Her eyes dart around, tail tucked tighter and I take in a measured breath.

"I will let Drax out soon, but he's eager, too eager, and he will just barrel you over in excitement." Her ears perk a little. "We need you steady, okay? You need to at least be able to stand so you can bite the fucker when he gets to be too much." Drax huffs within me, turning his head away as he sits down.

He can't deny my words, he knows that's exactly what he will do.

Runa eyes me for a moment, then she moves a little, just side to side, then back a step to get her legs where she wants them to be.

"That's it, good girl," I praise, letting her know how well she's doing.

She shakes her fur out again before sniffing the ground, taking in all the scents while still keeping her eyes on me.

The snow falls a little heavier now, our every breath can be seen, but she doesn't seem to care as she gets a light dusting of snow up her nose.

I smile at her, holding in a chuckle as she goes to a nearby bush , taking a bite from a leaf. She immediately tries to spit it out, her tongue wiggling as the leaf gets stuck on it.

She snaps her head my way suddenly, seemingly forgetting I was there in her curiosity.

I must have let loose that chuckle as she pauses again, tongue out with that leaf stuck there, and her eyes locked with mine.

I watch with a smile still on my face, one that I can't seem to hide, and I realize, I don't want to. So I grin wider as she eventually gets the leaf off of her tongue.

She lowers her head, sniffing the ground again and letting her nose lead her. I follow her around trees and past boulders as she takes it all in, letting her sate her curiosity.

She hasn't been out in so long, I want her to take everything in, get used to her legs. Explore and chase after the little squirrel that was climbing a tree.

I have to hold in a laugh as she barks and growls up at it.

As the hours pass, I eventually take a small step toward her when she stops by what she has deemed to be a suspicious twig. She bares her teeth at me when she notices, all the while I never lose my grin.

All this time I have kept a distance, making sure she's okay while she makes sure I'm far enough away, but now I need to push a little.

"You will need those for our enemies, wolf, but not for me," I say to her sharp teeth. I ignore her warning growls as she backs up, her legs working far better than the first time, but I keep moving toward her slowly.

I don't think she will come to me willingly, but I need to go to her.

"My Vihnarn sleeps within you, I imagine?" I say, taking another step. "And while she sleeps, we can sort out our differences." Another step. "Rhea's life has been at stake while you have refused to come out, I'm angry at you for putting her at risk, at your stubbornness, though I know it comes from a place of pain." Another. "And you loathe me for what I did to your keeper. I understand that, and I accept it." I keep going, guiding her back into a tree. She yelps in surprise, emotion filling her eyes as they lock with mine, still growling.

Two more steps and I'm so close I can almost touch her. She comes up to my head in height whereas Drax comes above. That means she can have the advantage with him and go for his neck when he gets to be too much.

Drax growls like I betrayed him, but he can't pretend he wouldn't want her to.

Runa continues her growls and snarls as I watch on, showing her I won't retaliate. That I won't harm her.

She snarls violently and lunges when I take the last step, biting the top of my arm and still, I don't move. I feel her teeth tear into me, feel the blood now dripping down my arm and onto the ground as I grunt in pain.

I have to smirk though.

"Just like your keeper, she likes to bite too." I tilt my head. "She would be proud of you for that," I tell her, feeling the blood dripping from my fingertips as it runs down my arm.

She pauses in her biting before she takes a few steps back, realizing I'm not going to do anything to her for hurting me.

I take a breath before I crouch again as I ready myself for what I am about to do. She watches me curiously, looking down at the snow-covered ground that's slowly turning red.

"You know, I have never done this to anyone, not even your keeper." I eye her. "Though I willingly let my Vihnarn put her teeth in me, encourage it, even." I chuckle at the reminder. "I would do this for your keeper in a heartbeat if she asked it of me, but first, I will do it for you, because I don't think there is any other way to show you that I won't harm you."

After a moment's pause, I tilt my head further to the side, baring my neck to her. The most vulnerable part. But also the part where there is a mark that claims me as Rhea's.

"I will look after you, I vow it. She trusts me, and you can too." She looks from me to my neck, her eyes turning curious.

"I will make sure you are safe. I will be her shield, as Drax will be yours."

Tension stretches between us, until finally she takes a step toward me. I hold my breath and wait for her, patient as I can be. Two more hesitant strides come next, and they land in front of me, her breath hitting my face.

I don't move, don't take my eyes off her as she eventually lowers her head to my neck.

Her cold nose touches my skin as she inhales a breath, not once, but twice. And then I hear it, the small whine in her next breath, a tremble running through her. Slowly, I bring a hand up to the side where she can see it, and I see her body shake.

"I won't hurt you." I move my hand toward her face when she pulls back, always where she can see it and then I'm there, touching the side of her head near the start of her jaw.

The shaking worsens as I move to behind her ear, stroking down the center of her head, and then I'm bringing the other hand up on the opposite side, slowly guiding her head down until we are forehead to forehead.

I close my eyes and feel all of her, but I also feel my little wolf deep inside, and I rub my head on hers. Runa relaxes, letting more of her weight rest on me and we just get used to each other, taking in our scents.

She accepts it. Accepts me.

"Now then, let's go for a run, shall we?" I pull back and she licks my face, and then I let the change follow and I'm no longer male, but wolf.

She steps back in surprise, but her tail comes up, wagging a little. I shake my fur out and stretch my front legs, relishing the movement.

It's been a long time since I have been wolf.

I won't let Drax take over this time, this is between me and her, but when I look back at Runa, a certain glint in her eyes has me pausing.

Hmm. I tilt my head. I don't think Rhea is asleep anymore.

THE LANDS DEFYING

She trots toward me, still a little unsteady but sure, and I let her walk around me, letting her nose sniff my fur. She comes back around to the front and looks up at me before inhaling at my neck. I let her, not caring that she could actually tear my throat out.

But like I said to Runa, I would willingly let her do it.

I draw the line at biting my tails, however. So when she goes back around me and she tries, I whip around and pounce.

She snarls as I get her on her back, playfully nipping at her as her back legs try to shove me off from my stomach. I can tell she gets frustrated when she growls low, but I just carry on nipping and hovering over her, nuzzling anywhere I can.

When her eyes meet mine, I lick the side of her face a few times, then I turn and run.

She barks after me, and she sounds like a damn boulder coming through the forest, but she will learn in time to be silent when she's wolf.

I don't run too far from her, letting her chase me until she jumps at me from the side. We go rolling, and I nip at her front leg as we both stand again. Walking further into the forest, she rubs up against me, never leaving my side until a rabbit catches her attention.

Her head lowers and she gives chase, making all the noise for the rabbit to easily go back to its burrow. She looks down into it, waiting for one to come out, but they won't.

I grab her by the scruff of her neck, pulling her to me to follow. When we come across another rabbit, I stand in front of her, and lower myself a little. With a pointed look, she copies me.

I take slow steps forward, making sure it is only one paw at a time, and being as quiet as possible. Runa comes up beside me, following everything I do and when the rabbit turns, she pounces.

I watch as she misses its tail by a hair and she shakes her head back and forth, growling.

I huff and nudge into her before nipping at her tail. She spins, legs down, hind in the air as her tail wags as she barks at me.

We run and play in the forest until the sun begins to set, until the ground is fully covered in snow and we are panting wildly. We go to the river last, taking a drink and I think playtime is over…until she jumps on me.

We waver to the side, landing on the ground hard, and I'm about to bark at her, to tell her it's enough and that she could hurt herself, but all she does is nuzzles my neck and licks my face.

I'll allow it, I suppose.

When she's done, she moves between where I have laid down and curls up between my front and back legs, soaking in my heat. I nuzzle behind her ear, curling myself around her and resting my head on hers, watching over her as she rests.

Because whether male or wolf, I'll always watch over her.

FIFTY SIX

Rhea

I wake to a body pressed against mine. Warm, tight, safe.

I peel my eyes open to the morning light and stretch my limbs out. A fire burns next to us, keeping us warm through the winter night and I have no idea when Darius had done that.

I groan at the ache spreading through my muscles, but then I suddenly sit up, gasping.

Daruis wakes, magic out and widely looks around.

"What is it, what's wrong?!" he demands and I laugh, jumping on him so he's laying down again.

An *oomph* comes from him as I straddle his waist and smile. "She came out!"

"What?" Darius's eyes turn concerned, but then realization hits and he pulls his magic back. "She did." His hands go to my waist as he lets loose that smile of his and I laugh again.

"I can't believe it!" I tell him. "She's amazing. Isn't she?" I stroke Runa within me, feeling her puff up her chest at my words.

"She is," he chuckles, now playing with a strand of my hair.

"She can jump so high too! When you jumped over that huge stone, I thought there was no way I can do that, but with Runa being so tall, we did it with ease. And Gods," I say, laughing. "We can run *so* fast, did you see us? And we didn't even get tired for ages…" I taper off as Darius chuckles beneath me. "What?" I grin, even as my cheeks heat.

Darius sits up, his grip steadying me and it's then that I realize how very naked I am. I look down at the cloak wrapped around me.

"Yours?" He nods, and then chuckles. "What's so funny?"

He shakes his head. "Your excitement, little wolf. It feels like you are breathing life into me."

My cheeks redden further at his words, and I bring my hands up to his shoulders. "Thank you," I breathe, and then I lean in to kiss him.

I'm hesitant at first, but when he groans and pulls me closer, I'm the one that deepens it, my hands going to his hair, trying to get as close as possible.

Feeling Darius relax from my touch, feeling him grab and pull me close, gripping tightly so as not to let me go, is a feeling I think I will always cherish.

It shows how badly he wants me; it shows me what *I* do to him.

We break the kiss, panting for breath as we just look at each other, those damn eyes once again drawing me in.

"It's time for our wolves to have their playtime," he says. I pull back and watch as he lifts his hand, and then Drax is there.

I smile at him as he stretches out, and I don't miss the almost side-eye he gives Darius, curling his lip at him.

"Shut up, they both needed time," Darius says to him and I laugh at the huff that Draxton gives back. "Little shit," Darius mutters. And that's when I let out a full belly laugh.

They are arguing like an old, mated couple.

Fingers are at my sides, tickling me. "Are you laughing at us, little wolf?"

"No!" I say through my giggles, trying to stop his hands. "Stop it."

"Adorable," He tickles me further. "Don't lie to me."

"But you both act like an old couple." I scream as he gets me on my back and tickles me harder.

He uses his magic to wrap around my waist, keeping me still and then I'm gasping at the cold seeping in through his cloak.

"Cold." I mutter, and he's instantly hauling me into his lap and dragging me near the fire.

"Silly little wolf."

"It was funny though." I bring a hand to my lips to stifle another chuckle.

He wraps me up in his arms as Drax sits a little to the left, patiently waiting, or I guess not as he stamps his front paws one by one.

Runa's head tilts and her eyes are much brighter than ever before as she wags her tail. My magic caresses her, not just hovering nearby and I feel it deep within me.

It's…calm.

The calmest it has ever been.

I lift my hand and open my palm. Calling my magic there, it happens in an instant. I blink in surprise. I push some more out of my hand and form a perfectly shaped ball.

"I…I did it!"

Darius squeezes his arms around. "You did."

I let the ball go, and we all watch as it floats high into the sky.

I feel whole within me, feeling nothing volatile or out of control, I just feel both Runa and my power…waiting for my call.

I lift my other hand and aim it toward Drax who suddenly stands, ears perked.

"Feel her within, and call her to your hand. Like you are pulling her.

"Like my magic?"

"Yes, but Runa has her own mind, if she doesn't want to, give her a small tug if needed."

"You like shoving."

He nips at my neck. "It works"

I close my eyes. "Come on Runa, come out and meet Draxton, officially. He will be able to teach you things that even Darius and I cannot."

I thought she would hesitate, I thought I would need to talk her into it, but my eyes fly open as she's right in front of me, but then lunging at Drax.

I gasp, and Darius chuckles as snarls and barks come from them. I go to stand, worried, but Darius halts me.

"Let them work it out. Drax won't hurt her in the slightest, but he will pin her down when he's had enough."

We watch them break apart and then she goes for him again.

"Did she do this with you?"

"You didn't see?"

I shake my head. "I woke up to seeing you as a wolf, but I saw nothing before that, only sensed that something had happened."

He kisses the side of my neck and then plays with a strand of my hair. "I just showed her that she can trust me." I watch as he pulls his hand back and realize it is covered in blood. "It's nothing, we just needed to work it out."

I grab that hand and push my magic into it, feeling it run up his arm and to the bite on his shoulder. Closing my eyes to concentrate, I push the ruined muscle back together, feeling it stitch itself. When I open my eyes, Darius's eyes are nearly black, the heat in them burning me alive.

I look at Runa as she goes for Draxton's front legs as a distraction.

"She does trust you, just like I told her to."

"You did?" He sounds so surprised at that and I turn my head to him.

"Of course I did. I trust you, so why shouldn't she?"

His eyes flare and he groans into the side of my neck. "You would find it inappropriate to fuck you with our wolves right there, wouldn't you?"

I squirm. "Yes," I clear my throat. "Absolutely inappropriate."

"Later" he growls into my neck, pulling me closer to make sure I feel all of him.

I guess he approves of my trust in him.

Suddenly Runa yelps, and we look at Drax who has her pinned down on her back, just like Darius said.

"Well that's familiar," I mutter. "That's what you did to me."

He chuckles. "We are like our wolves in many ways."

We watch on as Drax moves backward off of Runa, and I can't help the awe I feel at seeing them both.

Runa stands and looks to Drax, head lowered. Draxton walks over and nuzzles the side of her face, a purr coming from him as he licks her there before going to inhale her neck. Runa's tail wags, and when Drax nudges her again they run off into the forest.

"They will be okay, won't they?"

"He will look after her," He assures me.

I look back to the fire. "What do we do now?"

Darius starts to peel the cloak off of me. "Well, there are no wolves near anymore, so let me warm you up."

FIFTY SEVEN

Rhea

I'm running.

Me, with my pack, running as a wolf and not on two legs.

I huff out a laugh the best I can being wolf, nipping at Josh excitedly by my side who nips back. My tongue hangs out, my tail low to help me gain speed as I rush on ahead, elated to finally feel…free.

Sarah runs at his side, staying close and Colten and Hudson come barreling past, racing each other. Seb is leaping in the air around Taylor as the serious male looks like he's about to bite into him.

And it couldn't be any better. Well it could be if Kade were here, but he went for a run before us. I tried to contact him down the link but I think Axis is running free.

Darius runs to the side of me, away from us to give me time with them— but doesn't he know yet that I want him near?

I *yip* at him and his head swivels toward me.

I bounce—sort of, or at least I think I do, but then I'm tumbling to the floor.

I roll, letting out a wheezing breath until I'm stopped as I land in a nearby bush, all four legs spread out at my sides as I let out a huff.

A chuffing sound comes, and then a black muzzle is peeking through, green eyes full of laughter.

I roll mine and stand, shaking out my fur.

Darius comes into the bush, nudging my head this way and

that as he inhales my neck. He walks around the back of me, checking me over, or at least I assume he is. But when I feel his breath near my tail, I spin, baring my teeth.

He gets me on my back in an instant, pinning me.

Why do I always end up like this, damn him and his huge ass for not moving.

I'm about to bite him in warning when all of a sudden, Darius is there and Drax is out, his tails swishing as he looks down at me with humor in his eyes.

"It isn't funny," I tell him. Even the fucking wolf is laughing at me.

Darius looks down at me, smiling wide, and I close my eyes, willing me and Runa to part.

It comes easier now after days of practice.

Within a few moments, Runa is out and I'm below Darius, clothes fully intact.

I'm proud to say it didn't take me long to manage the clothing situation, much to Darius's dismay. Darius thinks that although Runa and I have never been connected like this, the time we have spent with one another has made the transition easy.

"What are you doing," I pant, gripping Darius's shoulders.

He bends and nuzzles my nose. "Let's run."

Huh? "But we were?"

He stands and brings me with him, chuckling as he picks twigs out of my hair.

"No, we haven't run with our wolves."

I eye him for a moment and turn to see Drax and Runa. I can hear my pack in the distance, their howls calling to me and I smile.

"Want to race?"

Darius's lips tip up. "You want to play, little wolf?"

Without warning, I take off, laughing as Darius growls about cheating.

"Come on, Runa, let's show them how to move."

I guide my powers to the soles of my feet, and as soon as I hear Darius and Drax gaining on us, I really *move*.

I feel like I'm gliding as I sprint ahead. No tree slows me, nor do roots or large rocks. Runa and I run side by side, and I notice the slight blue glow to her paw prints every time a paw lands on the ground, I gasp, my eyes wide.

Runa side-eyes me as I look at her, and she huffs happily, picking up speed.

Is she always using power at her paws?

I grin.

"You brilliant wolf, you," I say to her, and she holds her head a little higher at that. I lose my smile though when I hear Darius and Drax gaining on us. "We are so fucked when they reach us, you know that?" She huffs. "What do we do, split up?"

She shakes her head and when a particular growl of excitement sounds behind us, I grip her fur to keep next to her.

They love the hunt.

Looking ahead, we are coming up to another river, and I know it will slow us both down. Well, more me as Runa can probably jump it.

I blink.

Runa can probably *jump* it.

"Hey," I say to her breathlessly, "Wanna give me a ride?" I ask. She eyes me and then ahead. I rode Drax, and Runa isn't that much smaller than him. I feel her amusement before she gives me the slightest head nod. "Really?" I didn't expect her to say yes.

I look at the distance between us and the river and hope I can pull this off.

"Here goes nothing." Gripping Runa's fur with the opposite hand to her, then using the hand closest to me to grip between her shoulders, I wait one moment, then two, then...

I push off from the ground, using the strength in my legs and arms to haul me up onto her back.

Yes! Thank you, wood chopping and forever running on

these damn two legs.

Next, I adjust myself just right before we are leaping over the river.

I scream, throwing my head back with a wide smile on my face as Darius's amusement-filled laugh reaches me.

We land with an *oomph* on the other side, and I nearly fly forward off of her back but manage to hold steady.

"Fuck yes!" I tell Runa, stroking her head. "You are the best, you know that?" She does this little tappy-dance thing, but then we are *both* tumbling to the ground.

I'm still laughing as I fall off her back, a shield of darkness encasing me before I land. I pant up into the sky as a heavy weight is back on top of me, his darkness like a familiar caress of when I sunk into the Unforgivable Seas tickling the back of my mind.

"You are bold, little wolf," he says down to me, "You cheated."

"I did no such thing," I pant, lifting a hand to stroke his jaw. His eyes instantly darken at my touch. "I just raced, like we said."

"Clever."

"Always," I whisper.

"You were made for each other."

"And made for other things," I didn't mean to say that out loud, but he instantly gets my meaning.

I can tell by the way his body locks up, those intense eyes of his burning with some kind of new emotion, and then, last but not least, the way his mouth lands on mine.

It's deep and possessive, his hands clutching me closer to him and he groans at my taste. I may have let out a moan, a sound or something, because his touch turns almost desperate.

I know the moment he shields us to hide as the light begins to fade away from behind my closed eyelids, then he possesses my mouth in a way only he ever could.

Darius's hands land on the back of my head, his fingers

tangling in my wild hair as he moves me to thrust his tongue deeper. He seems to want to reach everywhere inside of me, and I can barely breathe as he devours me.

But it doesn't matter when he has become the very air I breathe.

He softens the kiss after a long while, gently nipping and swiping his tongue across my lips like he can't get enough. He nuzzles his head into my neck, a tortured 'Rhea' spilling from his lips as he kisses me there.

I don't know why he said my name like that, why he's chanting it into my neck with his kisses, but goosebumps cover my body at it.

I bring my hands around his neck, pulling him closer as I peel my eyes open and see complete darkness. I call my magic, and small balls of lights glow next, making me able to see his face as I pull him from my neck.

We stare at each other, chest heaving and full of tension, but the good kind as I stare at him.

And I see everything in this moment.

Past, present, future.

His brows furrow, his eyes changing from confusion to adoration, switching from one to the next until it lands on something even deeper.

"Rhea..."

He trails off when we hear, "you fuckers, how long are you going to keep us waiting?"

Darius's eyes turn angry and he growls at the voice.

Moment gone.

"We were coming Josh, we just wanted to... play?"

I realize how that sounds and Darius smirks down at me as my cheeks redden.

"Ew, Milal, really?"

The barrier is gone in an instant and I'm up on my feet the next. I dust myself off. "Yes, problem?"

Josh shuffles where he stands. "Well, I don't want to see my sister doing…that?" he waves a hand at us, and I laugh.

"You idiot, we were actually playing. We raced, I won," I say proudly.

Darius huffs next to me. "You cheated, you mean,"

I face him. "No, I took initiative."

"By running off before we even began." His voice is deadpanned.

"You were slow."

"And you are a bold little wolf." He steps toward me.

"Um…I don't want to be a part of your guys' fucked up foreplay, I'm just— *Oomph*."

We both turn and see Drax standing there, glaring down at Josh.

"Gods, you are too big." Josh shakes his head up at him. "Don't tell me you hate me talking to her too? Come on," he says, exasperated.

Runa comes beside Drax, rubbing up against him before she bends down and licks Josh's cheek.

"Thanks…" Josh says, wiping her saliva off as I laugh into the side of Darius's arm.

Drax growls at Runa for that, and I shake my head.

Possessive, just like his keeper.

A dark, gray wolf emerges next, slower, hesitant, and I straighten as I move toward Axis.

"Hey," I say, smiling at him. "Come here."

They have all met Runa and Drax, but Axis hasn't been this close to them.

Axis eyes me for a moment, but then walks toward me. I feel Darius tense as he comes to my back, and I would roll my eyes at him but the truth is…I don't know what will happen.

Kade is still having…issues with what is real and what isn't. He has outbursts, random bouts of anger and I've seen him a few times with cuts on his lips and bruising, but Darius told me to keep out of it. That it's better for him to go to him for a fight than picking one with the wrong person.

I'm thankful in a sense that Darius is willing to do that after everything. It's not lost on me that Kade isn't Darius's favorite person, but he won't kill him.

He promised me.

When Axis is within distance, I place a palm on his head and stoke behind his ears. "Did you have a good run?" I ask, he huffs.

I smile at him and watch as Runa slowly comes to us. Axis tenses, turning his head toward her but then he slowly relaxes. Runa dips her head and nuzzles his neck, and when Axis leans into the touch, I want to cry.

Darius wraps an arm around my waist, sensing my emotions and I place a hand over his, squeezing it in gratitude.

Drax comes over next, never leaving Runa alone for long, and when Axis looks up at him I see it then, the change.

Not from wolf to male, from Axis to Kade.

I swallow my surprise at how easily that came for him after fighting for control for so long, but the longer Drax stares at Kade, the more he comes through and straightens.

He shakes out his fur, stretching a little and then he walks toward Drax.

I hold my breath nervously, but Drax nudging the top of his head with his nose is all that occurs, and they are all off, running through the trees.

I sag back into Darius with relief.

"I never thought he would ever get control," Josh says, looking to where they ran off also. "I'm glad he's getting better."

"I am too." We can only hope it lasts.

FIFTY EIGHT

Rhea

We are going to torture a man today.

No, not man, a monster.

Frederick has been kept in a makeshift shack on the outskirts of Eridian, in The Deadlands. I had pushed his being alive out of my mind for a little while, not ready to face him. But I am now.

Darius says he's held securely, that he is guarded all times of the day, but having a Higher that close to us— to my family, has me wanting to tear my skin off.

It feels…wrong.

We port in at the top of the cliffs, and I look to Darius as he glances toward the Unforgivable Sea. I step toward him and look more closely at him, no, he's looking at Lovers Falls from up here.

"Hey," I say gently, reaching out for his arm, ignoring my own shiver running down my spine.

He blinks, seemingly coming out of whatever moment he was in, and looks to me. "Yeah?"

"Are you okay?" I feel awkward asking, and I regret it instantly when he smirks.

"Are you caring for me again, little wolf?" His arms wrap around me and I try to push him off.

"Forget it," I mumble, not in the mood for his teasing.

"Don't do that," he says, pulling me in tighter. His jaw ticks, seemingly uncomfortable. "I just don't like seeing it. All I see is you going over the edge, landing in the water and I can't get to you."

He looks off to the side and a pang shoots through me. I don't want him to think about things like that if they affect him so much, but it warms me to know he has to care for it to bother him.

Darius has staked his claim on me many times, he's told me as much. But I'm not sure what he *feels* for me. Not really. Is it just possession? Our connection? Or is it something deeper?

I'm sure I see it residing in his eyes sometimes…but having never experienced this, I don't want to make a fool of myself by asking him.

I don't even know why I'm thinking about this now, of all times. I guess I'm feeling unsure of what's next for me, for us…my family.

"I'm here," I tell him instead. He looks down at me, eyes bouncing between mine and he nods.

We walk to where Darius placed Frederick in silence, the glow of the luicium sap our only light, I begin to feel invisible hands squeeze my throat. Just like Frederick's.

"You don't need to be nervous," Darius says. "I won't let him hurt you."

I shake my head. "I just want all of this to end, to be over and done with."

"We need answers first, and we need to find the other stolen people."

"I know."

We move through another set of dead trees, their branches looking even more depleted of life and my brows furrow. Looking around, I sense nothing else close by, but there is an eerie feeling in the air.

I rub my arms.

Bora can be heard in the distance, calling to their family members and luckily, we are far away from them. "Are there any families close to here?" I ask Darius and he shakes his head.

"No, and any that came near were redirected."

We reach the shack just a little further on, and it's just that, a shack.

The wood is rotten, barely holding itself together. As we near, I can see through spaces between the walls and see a chained hand on the ground.

I swallow.

Darius nods to one of the three Elites keeping guard here, but my eyes stay fixated on that hand.

It twitches and I flinch.

Get it together, Rhea. You are an Alpha. I chide myself.

Runa growls her agreement and my spine straightens. Fuck him. Fuck them all.

Darius gives me one last look before opening the door. It creaks and whines, bits of wood breaking off as we enter.

It's small in here. If I reach my hands out at my sides, I can nearly touch both of the walls, but space isn't what Frederick deserves.

The male in question kneels before us, his chained hands resting on the floor and I'm transported to a vision of me.

I was in a similar position not long ago.

No. Rhea. Stop it.

I have the power here now, not him.

Frederick looks up after a moment, a deranged smile on his face. He doesn't look like he's all there. I can see it in his eyes, the way his tongue peeks out and licks his lips, the way his hands clench.

"Hellooo traitors of the lands," he laughs, his head tilting to the side. I eye Darius as he watches him closely.

"We have a few things to ask," he says. "Answer and it will be less painful."

Well, he doesn't waste any time getting to the point.

Frederick chuckles. "Like I would answer—" Darius fist flies through the air and lands on his cheek.

I blink.

That was fast.

"I don't have the patience, so let's begin." Darius shrugs out of his cloak and throws it on the dirty floor, uncaring.

I watch as he shakes out his hands, how the muscles in his arms move, and I have to force myself to look away from him.

His strength attracts me, it always has.

"Where did you take the other missing pack members?" I start. Frederick just stares at me. He gets another punch. "We know you have taken them somewhere. We have lists to prove it."

"Some were sold," he shrugs.

"And?" I demand. He says nothing. Darius takes a finger and snaps it. Frederick grunts in pain but otherwise, his eyes never leave mine.

"Why couldn't you have just been the bitch we taught you to be, and stayed to spread your legs?" he wonders, his eyes closing as he takes a deep breath. "Ahh yes, you will be up to breeding soon."

"Shut the fuck up," Darius barks, taking his other hand and starting on those fingers.

I look at Darius in confusion, but he focuses on Frederick.

"We are not here to talk about me, where are those people?" Nothing. "Did you steal most of them? Because those that sold their children will soon die." A laugh.

I can feel my heart rate kick up at him refusing to answer.

How can he be so cruel?

"They were just children!" I move toward him, getting in his face. "Tell me where you took them, you sick fuck."

He spits in my face.

I freeze, Darius freezes.

But then I move.

My hand flies out and I hit him again and again, focusing on his cheekbone, his jaw, his eye.

Blood splatters my face, but I don't fucking care, this piece of shit thinks he can stay silent.

No.

He will scream.

My power comes to my hand and then it's around his throat, squeezing, tensing, wanting to crush it. My face heats, and the glow of my markings reflect in his, now one good eye.

"Tell me where they are, now," I growl.

I feel a tendril of Darius magic wrapping around my waist. It's not only for comfort, no, it's to also pull me back if Frederick tries anything.

"If you let me breed you, I'll tell you," he laughs, and I have to swallow the bile rising in my throat.

"You will *never* touch me," I spit, feeling my insides twist.

"But I did, I suppose you don't remember, but I do." He smiles, all bloodied teeth on display and a tremble starts in my body. "It was a good time. I told them we should fuck you then, even Lord Higher nearly agreed. But your cousin, Patrick got greedy and wanted you first. Always the teacher's pet." He snipes as jealousy flares in his eyes.

I have never been more thankful for Patrick wanting me so badly, that he got them to wait before they raped me when I was of breeding age, but I can work with Frederick's jealousy. If Darius doesn't snap his neck first.

I feel him behind me, a mass of fury at Frederick's words, and now *I'm* the one who wraps a rope of magic around his arm to calm him. I can feel his anger like it's my own, his angry breaths are all I hear from behind me.

"He did want me all to himself," I say, the words tasting like ash as I speak them. "But Charles said to wait until I was eighteen."

"Yes," Frederick says. "And that's because he didn't want to waste a good, virgin, breedable pussy in the meantime. He knew what would happen."

I move a strand of magic on Darius soothingly, letting him know I'm doing okay.

"What would happen?"

He tips his head back, his eyes rolling like he's in pleasure. "We would rip your pussy apart, tear it in two." He cackles. "Gods, we would have fucked it together at any time. That was what we all planned. Just the thought of breeding the daughter of an Heir…" he groans out the last word and shifts his hips.

Looking down, I can see he's hard.

I feel sick.

"And those you stole; did you breed them too?" I have to ask. I have to know what fate they suffered while I hid myself.

"Oh yes," he moans, his hips now thrusting, his eyes on mine, pupils blown. "Many times, fuck, so much virgin eighteen year old pussy.

I have my blade through his dick in the next second.

No one moves.

Darius doesn't,

Frederick doesn't.

But I twist, grip the handle tighter, and then I slice down.

Oh, that finally prompts Frederick's agonizing screams to unleash. I smile, baring my teeth at him as he thrashes in my grip.

"You think it's funny that you were raping women?" I tut. "Even the Gods below won't want you when I'm done with you."

I step back and watch as he continues to flail about in pain, his cries and screams fulfilling something inside of me.

"Good girl," Darius purrs in my ear. "Now, more."

This male.

He doesn't shy away from what I just did, he encourages it.

He really is the Heir of Cazier, the darkness of the lands…but people seem to forget.

Zahariss was just as ruthless, and I'm hers, after all.

"The people you all stole, where are they?" Darius snarls, digging his blade into Frederick's shoulder.

"Argh," Frederick grunts. "They are in...are in the back rooms of Zaigar. The place you were in, in The Drylands."

That was Zaigar? The place Darius's father mentioned in his notes. It seems everything in there is true.

I think for a moment and remember where the guards came from in the back of that room. But Darius said it's buried under rubble.

I cast Darius a worried glance. We need to go back there.

"The beasts in The Deadlands, what are they?" I ask, wiping my hands on the cloth that Darius gave me. Not like it would do either of us any good.

"Oh them," Frederick says tiredly. His head twitches, making his beaten face scrunch up. "They will help take all the lands. All, all, all, the lands," he giggles, his head falling back on his shoulders as he sighs. "They make great breeders, many breeders we have."

I eye Darius as his brows furrow. He takes a step closer and crouches down in front of him.

"What was the liquid that was given," he asks.

"Hmmm?"

I look down at the blood dripping from his body. Shit, maybe we went too far.

"The vial you gave the Beast in The Drylands."

"Oh, Ultrian," he mumbles. "It makes the beasts want to breed."

That's what they gave that beast? I think back to the notes we found about it and swallow roughly.

Sick. Bastards.

"And you want these beasts so you can take over more lands, to be able to breed powerful pups for your army?"

"Yes, yes, how brilliant is that?!" He grins. "So clever, our Lord Higher. All he did was take rogures and mix them up, add some females in the mix and poof, bred a beast deadly enough to take the lands."

"What are the beasts made of? Rogure and people?" Darius snaps, agitated.

"Rogures. Those little bastards were an annoyance when they came. Only for a short while though, Lord Higher made a plan and now they are his." He slumps forward, and Darius slaps his cheek to wake him up.

"Hey, answer me."

"They are very…loyal…" He trails off, blood dripping from his open mouth.

He doesn't move again.

"Fuck." Darius stands, running a hand down his face.

"All the people the rogues have killed…Darius," I begin.

His body is tense, full of fury and I know he's thinking the same thing. Charles killed his family if he sent those rogues into that town that day.

"He needs to die," I croak out, reaching a hand out to grip Darius's arm. "No wonder you could never find how to stop the rogues, Darius. He's been controlling them all this time, which means he has had you running around, getting rid of these creatures and for what? Why did he bother doing that?"

"He kept me busy, like a fucking guard dog so I wouldn't find out what he was doing." His tone is so low, full of threat and danger as he lets me guide him out the shack. "He will pay for what he has done."

I can't imagine what he must be feeling right now. The look on his face tells me he's experiencing his mother and sister's deaths all over again.

The Elites's faces are pale as we emerge. They won't look us in the eyes, and I think one of them may have actually been sick, no doubt hearing the torture we just put Frederick through.

"Are you okay?" I ask him. He nods shakily, wiping his mouth with the back of his hand. Poor male.

"New recruits," Darius grunts, shrugging.

I shove at him. "Don't be mean."

"War isn't clean, he needs a stronger stomach."

He has a point.

"What do we do now—"

A sound reaches my ears and I tilt my head.

It can't be.

No.

I know that sound.

That howl.

Darius and I both turn and see the bone-colored eyes glowing in the distance. There are so many of them, like drops of pearls hanging from the dead branches, and I gasp.

"But how?" I say to Darius as he hauls me back to him. "How did they get here and no one noticed?" Elites were guarding further into The Deadlands, we would have been notified unless. "They're dead."

"Fuck, we need to get to Eridian, now." He pulls the port stone out. "To me."

As soon as the Elites are near, two things happen.

One, the Elites trip over themselves to get to us, and two…

The rogues run, and they run right for us.

We land at the edge of Eridian, rushing forward as their haunting howls follow us.

"There are still injured people here Darius, we need to get them moved," I say as we run through the protection crystals at the lilk trees.

"I know, I'll gather my men to attack and defend, can you move them?"

"On it." I say, and then I'm grabbed into strong arms.

"Be fucking careful. I need you to be safe, so just focus on getting the injured out of here."

"I can help!" I protest.

"I know you can, little wolf," he says more softly. "But I don't think I can help anyone if you are near. I would walk past anything to get to you. My men dying, the rogues destroying, it won't matter if you need me. We both know Charles sent them, he knows we are here."

I know this.

My heart stutters, and I reach up and rub my nose with his. "For me, you can try, vallier. I cannot just stay back while they come into my home, Dar."

He looks off to the side and then gives me a hard kiss. "Hit hard and fast, and stay with someone if you need to, okay? Vow it Rhea," he growls, body tense.

"I vow it." With one last, lingering look, we split up.

"Josh, rogures are upon us, gather everyone to fight, and then we need to start moving the injured to my cabin to port them somewhere safe."

"Fuck .Where are they coming from?" he replies.

"The Deadlands."

FIFTY NINE

Rhea

"Come on," I say to the Elite, who has half a leg missing from the attack on the keep. "Hold on to me and we can get you there."

I wipe the sweat from my brow and hold the male up as best as I can. It's times like this that I wish we had enough port stones for everyone, but we just don't have that many in our supplies, and we can't risk going back to the keep right now with it being mostly destroyed.

"Shit," the male grunts, and then he falls forward, taking me down with him.

"Gods," I say, rubbing my elbow but rushing to my feet. "Get up," I demand, "Do you want to die?"

"Of course not," the male growls, gripping my arm and then managing to get his leg under him.

"Then we need to move! I need to help the others protect this place."

More howls, and my heart beats in time with our steps as we move toward my cabin.

They cannot get in here, but all we have are protection crystals.

"Josh, update?"

"I have most of them," he replies down the link. *"Anna and Seb are rounding up some to the west, while Taylor guards those already inside. Hudson and Colten said they are going through each cabin to grab anyone left."*

I grunt as I hold more of the male's weight. *"Kade?"*

"Looking for Sam," he says in a rush. I pause at that.

"Where would she be?!" She needs to be home.

"Probably at the river. Kade told me she has been going there a lot lately," he says.

But she barely went to the river before she was taken…

"Okay. Just let me know if he's not back soon. His link is closed right now." I shuffle down the dirt path to my home, the male bleeding from somewhere, but I haven't got time to inspect it.

Runa is alert inside of me, her teeth already bared to the danger she knows is coming. We are one this time, and we will not let those creatures hurt our family.

She growls low in agreement.

I push the door open to the cabin and Taylor is there, relieving me of the male.

"You okay?" he asks, and I nod my head, touching his arm in thanks.

My home is overrun by the injured and my pack. Katy and Oscar sit near the wall, huddling together tightly as Sybill looks after some of the pups, while their mom's help the injured.

"I'm going to go back out and help," I tell Taylor. "Eliza, grab the furs in our rooms if you have to," I tell her, and she nods.

"I can come," Taylor says, propping the male up against the wall.

I shake my head. "I need you to defend here in case any rogues get through. Kade and Sam should be here soon and then I need you to port out with them to Colhelm. I think Damian is coming here so he can take you to the location. I trust you to keep them safe."

He looks around, eyes conflicted. "An order?"

"No," I say, "But it can be."

He knows I never want to pull rank, but I will.

He chuckles. "I got them." He tilts his head to the door. "Be safe."

"Arbiel canna."

"Arbiel canna," he repeats.

I head back down the dirt path, looking for anyone else who may not know what's going on. The howls can definitely be heard here now, but they may not know where to go.

I spot Hudson and Colten coming around a cabin, five people in tow. "Do you see anyone else?"

"We didn't see anyone," Colten says.

"We will do one last pass after we get these ones to the cabin."

"Be safe," I call, as I make my way through the gathering, looking through the trees but I don't see anyone else. I can hear the Elites's war cry further into the forest, and I know what that means.

The rogues have come down from the cliffside and are now in the forest.

Shivers run up my spine.

"Kade?" I say down the link. *"Have you got Sam?"*

"I have her, just —"

"Kade?" I say, turning in a circle. *"Kade?"* I repeat, heart thrashing in my chest when the link remains quiet.

A branch snaps behind me and I freeze. A huffing sound follows, heavy steps, another snap.

What the...

I turn slowly, blade already in hand when my eyes zero-in on the treeline to the forest.

The bushes move violently. Whoever is there is not trying to be quiet.

Another noise, and I call my magic, the glow of blue in my hand a comfort. Another rattle of leaves, and then Kade comes barreling through, Sam on his back as he runs past me, heading toward the cabin.

"Kade? What's wrong..."

I would celebrate that he has her, that Axis is now taking care of her, but I now know why he was running so hard.

I suck in a horrified breath as a hairy body comes into view.
Tall.
Gray flesh.
Human-like face.
A snarl and teeth that could, and would, rip me in two.

"*You have to port, now,*" I shout down the link.

"*We can't, no one's here to take us to Colhelm,*" Josh replies. "*What's wrong... Kade is here now with Sam.*"

"*You need to leave, now!*"

The beast's eyes land on me, and he sniffs the air, once, twice. And then he's coming for me.

I raise a hand and put a barrier around us as far as I can, my hand trembling with how wide I managed to get it, but he can't get to the others. He just can't.

I know what these beasts are capable of. Gods, are there more?

"*There are beasts here, Josh. You need to keep them safe. Try my office for a protection crystal, there should be one somewhere in there.*"

"*Rhea—*"

I shut down the link, concentrating with the enemy right in front of me.

The beast comes, clawed hand raised and ready to swipe at me.

I dodge the first one, but I didn't realize he could move so fast when the other catches me in the side.

Fuck, that *hurts*.

Blood splatters the ground, and the beast seems to inhale. Disgust runs through me as his erect cock shows through the fur on his body, and the contents of my stomach want to come up.

I get in a defensive position, holding my weight on my back foot to move faster.

The beast roars, and it rattles the trees, the birds that were once resting in there for protection against the cold, now flying high above.

A clawed hand comes for me, and I dodge the attack, turning my knife and slicing down his arm. The beast doesn't even seem to notice, its black blood dripping everywhere as it comes for me again.

I roll, swiping at the back of his leg, and then coming to a stand, I gather a ball of power and fling it at him.

"You will not get to my family!" I growl at it. My power hits him in the shoulder and he's pushed back, hitting the wall of my barrier.

I throw my magic out, tightening the magic strands like ropes just as Darius showed me one time, around his legs and arms, fusing it to the barrier.

He screeches, jaws snapping, eyes dilated as his angry growls continue in his struggle to be free. I get close, raising my blade and bringing it down into his chest. I lean back away from its teeth, trying to dodge it as I stab the blade in as deep as possible without getting hurt.

But with an almighty roar, the beast frees himself from my hold, and then he's on top of me.

Clawed hands scratch and tear at me, my clothing splitting in places and I scream, stabbing the knife in again and again, calling my magic and pushing it into him.

But no matter the wounds, no matter how much I make it bleed, it's not stopping. Focused on one thing and one thing only as I feel that disgusting appendage trying to rut into me.

Cold air hits my stomach.

No, no, no.

The tops of my legs.

It's not yours.

Claws slicing into my hips.

It's. Not. Yours!

Runa is out of me immediately without hesitation, and in the next moment, her teeth are in the beast.

She goes straight for its neck, ripping her head back and forth until finally, the beast's attention is off of me as he's toppled to the side.

Those hands go for Runa, and I panic for a moment but she is not a normal wolf, she is *mine.*

Glowing paws press on his chest as her teeth sink deeper into the beast. I get to my feet on shaky legs as I pant, agony thrumming through me, but I pick up the blade not even realizing I had dropped it. I come around the back of it, but then the beast gets its claws into Runa's side and she yelps.

"You do not touch my wolf!" I leap onto its back. He's momentarily surprised by that, and that's enough time to raise the knife and plunge it down, straight into the top of its head.

There is no resistance as the blade goes in, and the beast just...stops.

I roll off the beast with an *oomph*, watching as Runa still hasn't let go, shaking her prey back and forth as I try to catch my breath.

Fuck.

Fuck, fuck.

I swallow roughly as I take stock of myself. I'm bleeding in multiple places but nothing life threatening. My clothes are ripped but still in place. I bring a hand up to my heart as I calm myself.

I know what that beast was about to do to me.

I sink deeper into the ground, chest heaving. Too close. That was *too* close.

A pad of paws comes closer, and then Runa is there. She leans down and licks the side of my face, eyes intently on me.

"Good job. You showed that fucker." She growls, snapping her teeth as she looks at the beast. "Are you okay?" I ask, looking at her side and she nuzzles my neck.

I get to my feet with her help and raise my hand, dropping the barrier. I need to go and tell Darius that there was a beast here. That there may be more that have gotten through the barrier.

"Let's go," I say to Runa. She leans down, dropping her

shoulder and I don't even hesitate. I get on her back—blood and all, and then we run.

"*Everyone safe?*" I ask down the link.

"*Yeah Rhea, you okay?*"

"*I'm alive.*"

"*Is it dead?*" Kade asks. "*I tried to come back to help after I got Sam to safety but Hudson wouldn't let me.*"

"*It's dead.*"

"*Are you on your way here?*" Kade asks.

"*I will be soon,*" I tell them, then shut the link down again.

I can hear the sounds of growls and shouting the deeper into the forest we go. The *swoosh* of blades, the calling of males and then the voice I would know anywhere, reaches me next.

"Hold! Do not let them into Eridian!"

Darius.

We head toward him, needing to tell him what happened. His men fight the rogues, and Gods, there are so many of them.

They know we are here, it's the only thing running through my mind.

The rogues are like the sea, waves upon waves coming forward as the Elites battle with them, making sure none get through.

But the forest floor is littered with bodies from both parties.

A dark blur is suddenly next to us, flames licking his back.

"Drax," I whisper, watching as he nuzzles into Runa, his two tails swishing on high alert.

When he smells into her neck and growls, Runa's ears flatten and she moves closer to him. Almost like she is comforting him.

"Rhea!" My head whips to the side, and then I'm jumping down off of Runa and into Darius's arms.

"Fuck, where are you bleeding, where are you hurt!" His hands are frantic on me, his magic pooling at my feet in protection.

"I'm okay, just scratches." I already began healing myself on my way here.

"They are not just scratches!" he fumes, eyes flaring.

"There are beasts here." He pauses, finally stopping his ministrations and looking me in the eye. "The beasts that were in the Drylands." I swallow roughly. "They are here."

And as though summoned by my words, roars are heard and we look up to the tops of the cliffs. Beast after beast look down on us, and then they jump down, landing perfectly at the bottom.

"Fall back!" Darius says, his magic pooling at his feet and then spreading out in the creature's direction. Then he's lifting me onto Drax's back in the next moment. "Go. Get into Eridian,. I'll put a barrier up so you will have enough time to port out of here. I don't have a stone on me. Fuck. Why don't I have a stone on me?"

Because we used all of our resources on getting the injured and my pack back to the cabin.

"You need to come back, we can take them down easier in the forest."

"But they will be closer to Eridian."

"So be it."

"They will not take that from you." His eyes are wild as he says it, so determined. "Nothing," he growls. "Is getting taken from you ever again."

My heart swells with emotion. "We won't let them take it, but they also cannot take you."

We eye each other for a moment, then he looks to the trees. "Fall back into the forest." His men do so on command, turning and sprinting.

Drax turns and then we are moving. Darius runs behind us and Runa stays by his side.

I look back, watching as the beasts and rogures begin their hunt, and at their speed, I know we are not going to make it in time, even with Darius's power wrapping around them from below.

I look at Darius and he knows it too, I can see it in his eyes. Think Rhea, think.

I slice my palm and let my blood drip down. "Va ka reidu, lec fa dienn."

The ground begins to glow a subtle blue, and some of the rogues whimper, affected by my protection, but the beasts are undeterred.

What do we do, what do we do?

We hit the protection barrier, and some are halted at that, but some aren't. Elites get dragged under their paws, screams echoing as they are left to be slaughtered.

Some Elites turn wolf next, turning to defend their Alpha, and then they are locked in battle with them as arrows fly from the side. Leo shoots as fast as he can while Zaide throws knives. Jerrod helps two young males who are injured, and Maverick turns wolf and helps.

And then the worst thing that we could imagine happening right now becomes a reality.

The protection barrier breaks.

Darius uses his power to put his own up, but he can't cast it as wide, and too many are getting in, the cracks form immediately.

Drax snarls as I look at the dying lilk trees, thinking back to the moment before when I created a barrier around the beast.

Then I remember how the barrier came to be.

What if…

"Darius," I say. "I have an idea, I don't know if it will work." The scream of an Elite being ripped apart by a rogue has his whole body tensing. But he's doing what he said, he would walk past everything for me and he is by making sure I'm safe.

"Tell me what to do," he says instantly.

"Cut your hand." He does without hesitation, and I look ahead. Nearly there. "The lilk trees. They became the pillars for the barrier around Eridian. The barrier is made from a sacrifice. From blood." I lean forward on Drax, readying to dismount.

"Please work, please work," I chant.

One.

Two.

I dismount from Drax, and he turns, ready for attack with Runa at his side. Darius is with me in the next second, as we slap our palms on the rotting white bark.

More screams, more snarks and shrieks and— Gods, it's not working.

"It's not working," I whisper, my eyes going to Darius. "Is this it?

"No, stronger, again," Darius demands, his other hand toward the oncoming attack, creating a new barrier every time his breaks to keep them back.

With his eyes on me, I pour my power into the tree, more forcefully this time as my blood paints it.

Come on, come on. Zahariss, please!

It's small at first. So small that I don't even think I feel it.

But the next second, I do.

I gasp at the small pulse of life as it beats between my fingertips. Something new, yet so familiar that I haven't felt in so long.

We don't stop, and I put more of my power into the bark, feeling that pulse getting stronger and stronger as I feel myself depleting. Darius tenses, and I know he must feel it too when his eyes light up in surprise.

"It's there," I tell him, and then I close my eyes.

Please, Zahariss, protect your people. Use our blood and power to put back what was taken.

A heavy pulse happens on my palm, and my eyes spring open. I look to the ground, and I watch as a tiny line of power shoots to the next tree. I follow it, and watch it do the same until I can no longer see it. The line of magic gets brighter, giving off a light purple tint, and then I look to Darius's side, watching as a line appears there.

But it's not from the tree we are connected to, the power has come full circle.

Glancing ahead, some straggling Elites come barreling toward us, Darius's barrier breaks for the final time, while beast and rogure follow.

Vallier, vallier, vallier.

As the men rush past us, Leo, Zaide, Jerrod, Maverick. Injured and young. They all come.

I look down at the magic and it's slow, like waves rising. Just as I close my eyes, Darius reaches for me as the enemy is upon us, cocooning me in his embrace, protecting me, and I wait for the pain, the inevitable.

We are too late. We were too slow.

But all I hear is the whimpers of pain.

I peel my eyes open to find that the rogures and beasts have stopped.

No, not stopped.

They are denied access.

A rogure comes barreling forward as it hits a barrier. Ripples of violet are seen before they disappear again, and the rogure falls to the ground, twitching in pain.

I pant heavily, holding on to Darius while I reach out a hand slowly. The tips of my fingers feel it first, that same feeling of where the barrier once stood. Like it's caressing my soul and I close my eyes, sinking into the feeling.

"We did it," I say in a whisper, looking up and seeing the tree blooming.

Darius breathes heavily against me, clutching me tighter. "*You* did it, little wolf."

He turns us and the Elites are there. Dirty and bloodied, they catch their breath as they nod at us in respect and relief.

Tingles spread through my chest as I look to where Drax and Runa stand, looking at Darius and I.

"*We* did it," I say, looking up at him.

He rubs his nose with mine. "Now we need to kill them all and get them away from your home."

"*Our home*," I say somewhat shyly. He raises a brow and my cheeks heat.

"Ours," he murmurs, nuzzling into my hair.

SIXTY

Darius

Wrapping my power around the beast to immobilize it for a moment, I lunge, blade in hand and aiming for its temple. The iron sinks in, the snarling beast's struggling movements halting before he drops to the floor.

I growl, snarling down at it before looking over at Drax and Runa. They are tearing apart a rogue, arguing over who's kill it is, trying to force each other out the way. I whistle to get Draxton's attention.

"Let her have it, you have had more than your fair share of them over the years." And he has. When others weren't looking, when it was only my closest near, I let Drax out when needed.

He's ferocious, and when his black flames catch on his prey, they consume them until there is nothing left.

Nothing can put them out.

But they don't harm me, or any other who Drax deems worthy.

Drax growls around the rotting flesh at my command, then he huffs and lets go. Runa latches straight on it, dragging it away from Drax. But when he makes a low sound, Runa pauses for a moment, rag-dolling it, but not moving any further away.

Drax must have still wanted her near.

I know the feeling.

I look to Rhea where she lays, a hand on the lilk trees. She wanted to make sure the barrier is at full strength to protect

Eridian while we took care of the enemy.

Her eyes are closed, her lips slightly parted and I can't help but look at my men, glaring to let them know not to look at her.

She looks serene, peaceful, and only I can see that.

As if she can sense my gaze on her, she peels her eyes open and they instantly connect with mine. I feel that pull again, that need to be near, to sink inside of her, to feel her soul.

But I hold off.

There are still some beasts to kill and some rogues to eradicate.

Her cheeks heat when I don't break my stare, a shy smile forming on her lips and I want to bite them, lick them and claim them.

Fuck.

I pull my eyes away, watching as Jerrod brings his axe down, cleaving a rogue in two.

Maybe we don't have many left to kill after all.

Leo and Damian took down the last beast while Drax and Runa go for more rogues. When I hear a noise behind me, I turn to see a rogue tearing into one of my already dead men, fury fills me.

I growl, my magic coating my skin and I go for the rogue.

Sensing the predator behind it, it spins, jaws ready but it's not ready for me.

I punch the side of its face, sending it crashing to the ground and then I'm stabbing it.

It's only when Drax comes over with Runa, who nudges me that I realize the rogue is dead, that I was still stabbing it.

Breathing heavily through my anger, I look to the dead.

We lost seven, maybe more.

Seven males who had families.

Seven letters I need to send out to let them know they are dead.

I hang my head.

With these dead and the ones at the keep...I'm still not enough to protect them.

Four hundred and twenty three men.

That's how many I have lost under my rank in all the years I have been Alpha, that is how many letters I have had to send.

A slender hand comes to my shoulder, and then to the back of my neck, squeezing. I would have never let anyone do such a thing to me, never show anyone this side of vulnerability but just like she cannot hide from me, I cannot hide from her.

I take a full breath, my fist clenching on my knees as I sit back on my heels. "I wasn't quick enough," I tell her. My voice is gruff, angry.

She squeezes. "You did your best."

"Which isn't enough," I snap at her, then instantly regret it and take a calming breath. I reach up and place my hand on top of hers as she begins to take it away from my neck, probably wondering if she made the wrong choice coming over here.

I will not have her second-guessing herself.

Once I have her wrist in my hold, I pull her around and move her until she is straddling me. I place my forehead on hers and just...breathe.

"I didn't mean to snap."

Her breath hits my lips. "I know."

We sit there for a while as I come to terms with losing more men.

"We can take them to the graveyard," Rhea says, her hand caressing the mark on my neck. I feel her power beneath her skin, just like I'm sure she can feel mine.

"You would let Elites be buried there?" I ask, opening my eyes to see hers already on me. "Elites that helped take your home away?"

She's quiet for a moment. "I am ready to move on from what has happened," she whispers, as our wolves come up to us.

Runa lays down, licking her paws as Drax stands over her. After Runa gives him a quick nuzzle, she closes her eyes to rest, letting him protect her.

"There has been too much death, and there are too many regrets. I want to choose how we go forward." She moves her head back to me. "This is me choosing. The Elites are yours, and what's yours is mine." She says it so confidently, so possessively that I squeeze her hips as the beating in my chest becomes stronger.

"And yours is also mine?" I ask.

She nods. "I won't accept anything else."

"I'm not sure it feels like home anymore," Rhea says as she walks through the trees. "It feels like it's been tainted."

I hate that she feels that way, and I clench my teeth.

"I tried to make sure it was back to its usual state. I didn't want you any more upset…" I trail off, uncomfortable.

She looks at me, but I don't meet her eyes for once. "I appreciate you trying."

"It's your home. A home I helped destroy." I resist the urge to growl at myself. "I needed to do something."

A hand reaches my jaw, stroking lightly there, stroking my thumb up and down. "Thank you."

She doesn't need to thank me. I was trying to fix what I helped break.

She drops her hand and she hesitates for a moment.

Slowly, her fingers touch the back of mine. I look down, brows furrowed, then I watch as she slots her much smaller hand in mine.

I pause for a moment, looking at our intertwined hands and then at Rhea. She bites her bottom lip, her cheeks heating again but she doesn't look away from my stare.

I bend and rub my nose with hers, then begin walking again.

I look at her out of the corner of my eye, not making a big deal of this to her as a smile curves her lips.

I've held her hand before, many times now like it is something natural, but I marvel at it every time.

Maybe because it's different now.

Letting her lead the way to the graveyard, we watch the wisps play in the trees as the sun begins to set.

"I'm glad they are back here," Rhea whispers.

I am too.

For her.

Wrapped in a fur cloak, our breath showing in the cold, we crouch over the snow-littered ground and start to climb up a hill.

"It's not far now," she says, sniffling.

"You need to keep warm."

"I will." I eye her. She can't get sick. I'll think of a way to keep her warm on the way back.

Snowflake drops from the sky, floating in front of me and Rhea tilts her head up. She was born on a winter's night, like me, and I have to wonder what she's thinking as I let her have this moment.

"I miss my family," she says, never opening her eyes. I look up too, having difficulty swallowing.

"I do too. They were taken too soon."

"Aren't they all?" I make a sound of agreement.

Yes, they are.

"I think my sister would have loved you," I tell her, and she looks to me then. "And she would have constantly asked you to make her things."

She smiles. "I think I would have liked her too." We continue on our way as she looks down at our joined hands. "Were you born a pup?"

"I wasn't, and you weren't either."

"What does it mean?" she wonders. "Heirs are meant to be born as pups, that is what history states."

"Can we believe what the Highers had put in those scrolls and books? We cannot trust anything anymore."

She shakes her head, deep in thought. "That's true." She's silent for a moment. "My mom passed her Heir powers to me. She had been the Heir of Zahariss for so long, maybe the longest that had ever been. I don't know why she started to pass everything on to me, but it was a gradual thing. Over a full year actually."

I think about that. On how Drax came to me and my power. "I hadn't seen Cazier's Heir at all before I got my powers." My brows furrow in thought. "No one passed anything on to me, I just…was."

"Maybe we aren't born pups at all, maybe that was just something that was said to *protect* Heirs." She looks at me, eyes wide. "Maybe all this time, it wasn't even true."

"That would make the most sense. The Highers would have been looking for pups being born, when in reality, Heirs were here right under their noses."

"But the King said his mate birthed a pup." She tilts her head in thought.

"Maybe they lied too?"

"But why?" she asks.

"I don't know." I shrug.

"My mom was a seer," she begins, her brows scrunching. "Maybe they knew something we didn't." It's not entirely impossible. "And then they had to stay quiet until they couldn't hide it any more, like me."

I hate the look of devastation on her face.

"You were brave to reveal yourself." I let her know that, *feel* like I need her to know that.

"I was a coward, desperate." She frowns, looking down at the ground. "I have many regrets. Especially now knowing that the Highers and my family kept taking children to replace me."

"You can't look at it like that," I say, scanning the area for danger. We may have secured Eridian and the surrounding areas, but I'm more alert than ever after the attack. "These people in Eridian wouldn't have survived if it weren't for you, or Josh and the kid." The last bit comes out on a growl as I mention him. "If you had stayed, you don't know what would have happened if they had experimented on you with you being an Heir. Or..." I can't even say more.

We know they wanted to breed Rhea, for her to birth powerful children, and now we know why.

But the thought of it—

A tendril of Rhea's power wraps itself around my bicep, and I take deep, calming breaths.

"You survived," I say, my tone lower now. I stop and bring her to a halt, turning her to face me. "You survived, little wolf. Through everything that has happened, through the battles of your mind and your soul, the scars on your body, you survived." Her eyes take on a sheen. "And I'm so fucking grateful for that," I say gruffly, clearing my throat but I don't look away from her.

I let her see me.

See all of me.

She releases a breath and reaches up with her free hand, palming my cheek and dragging her fingers softly along my jaw. We stare at each other, and I feel a gentle warmth at my neck. Her eyes go to it, like she can feel it and she smiles, turning to walk again.

"So many 'ifs'," she says, gripping my hand tighter. "For what it's worth," she says quietly, peeking at me out of the corner of her eye. "I'm glad I survived too." I gaze at her, watching as snowflakes float down around her.

Her strength attracts me, her beauty captivates me, but her soul?

That entraps me.

And I let it.

"I guess it is no use to look back on the past. We cannot change it." She nods to herself, as if she has made some sort of decision.

"We cannot," I agree. "But if we have done wrong, the least we can do is make up for it, or try to." I see her look toward me but now I'm the one gazing ahead.

"Maybe we are beginning to, without realizing it," she says softly.

I clear my throat, running my thumb over her knuckles. "Maybe."

SIXTY ONE

Rhea

We walk the familiar path to the graveyard. Darius is silent next to me, taking everything in as we eventually come to a stone wall. It goes around in an odd circle, the back of it stopping just before it goes over the cliffside.

The wall comes to my waist at its full height, haphazardly put together over many days, but we wanted to form some sort of protection around the graveyard. Stones are piled up in mismatched patterns. Some tall, some small, some having three towers in one spot. My heart feels heavy when I gaze upon the graves of the dead. Not one single soul here deserved to have their life shortened.

I take the first step through the opening within the walls, snow crunching underneath my boots as the wind picks up due to the higher elevation. "We have space to the left, I will help create graves soon if you want to start."

I don't wait to hear his answer as I make my way over to the two graves that sit at the very top. The first two that were placed in here.

The sight of the two stone towers piled high has my throat closing, and uncaring that the snow will soak into my pants and cloak, I go to my knees in front of them.

Runa whines inside of me, feeling what I'm feeling.

"Hi mom," I place my hand on the first tower. "Dad." The other on the second.

I close my eyes and try to wrangle my emotions.

After everything that has happened, and what I know now, I want a hug from them more than ever. I want their love and their reassurance that everything will be okay.

I open my eyes when I feel warmth at my side. Darius crouches next to me, looking at the stones. He must realize what they mean because the next words out of his mouth send my heart into a frenzy, the mark on my forearm heating.

He dips his head. "Hello," he says to the graves, and my lips part as I stare at Darius who shifts uncomfortably. "Your daughter is the strongest person I know, and the bravest soul." He clears his throat, then he nods to himself before looking down. "I hurt your daughter, and I'm sorry for that." My eyes well. "I vow to spend the rest of my days making sure she lives in peace, making sure she runs free. And I will make sure to always give her lesia flowers just to see her smile." He looks at me, eyes full of emotion, just like they were on the walk here. "As her Vihnarn, I vow to keep her safe. Thank you for raising such a beautiful daughter."

He opens his hand and places two seeds at the base of their graves. Then he strokes his fingers down my cheek, collecting the tear there as he smiles, before standing and going over to the space for new graves.

I look down at the lesia seeds, stroking over them with a small smile. "He's rugged, arrogant and an asshole," I tell my parents quietly once Darius is out of range. "But...he's mine, just mine. And I'm his." I look at the stones, noticing that moss has started to cover some as I start to clear it off. "I didn't think I would ever have someone just for me, but then he appeared and we are tethered. I don't want to get rid of it anymore, if anything," I say, pulling the sleeve of my top up and touching the middle of my forearm. "I want to strengthen it more now. I want to feel a sliver of what you both felt between you."

I continue picking off the moss and clearing the base of the graves, making sure the seeds Darius put down are in the right place. When I'm satisfied, I place my hand on top of them and with a little power, they grow and bloom.

I smile down at them, taking in their sweet scent.

Darius still carries lesia seeds with him, and I have never been more grateful seeing the flowers at my parents' graves brings me comfort.

Stroking the petals one last time, I go over to Darius and begin to help dig the graves with the shovels we keep here.

"I wanted to meet them," he tells me. "Even if it's like this, I made a vow to them to protect you, to do right by you and kill every fucking thing that threatens you, until I can no more." He shovels dirt into a pile. "I wanted them to know that. I didn't mean to overstep."

"You didn't," I assure him. "It was...sweet."

He makes a rough sound. "It wasn't sweet." He scowls like he ate something bad. "I wanted to be respectful."

I hum, and he scowls harder. I giggle, shaking my head. "Oh how the mighty has fallen," I sing-song, and he stares at me intently.

"Willingly."

I pause at that, a shy smile spreading across my face as we continue digging.

To even be laughing in a graveyard...I would have thought it would be so wrong, but it's not. It's proof of life, proof that these souls may be gone, but they are always with us, and they should hear our laughter. My parents would want to hear my laughter.

Once the graves are finished, I turn at a noise and see that everyone is here. Josh, Taylor, Seb, Hudson and Colten stand on one side, with small, sad smiles on their faces. Kade and Sam are near, Katie and Oscar, and the rest of my pack at the edges of the graveyard too. My eyes move to the left to Belldame, who nods her head. The people from the village in Colhelm next to her, their heads bowed in respect. I look to the Elites next, all of Darius's inner circle as they carry the dead and place them down into their graves, one-by-one.

They are silent as they work, filling in the holes with dirt as I sense the loss coming off of them.

Once they are down, Darius gathers the stones we placed behind him and he begins to start their graves, slowly and methodically, making sure it's right. I bend down and help with the last one, wanting to also show my respect.

This Elite was young, barely out of training and I can see the grief reflected in Darius's eyes as he also puts the last stones on.

The death of others is never easy for the living.

When I think we are done, Darius moves to a spot and brings the bucket of stones with him. When he starts putting them down, beginning two separate towers, I tilt my head in confusion.

"Danny and Josie," he murmurs at my confused look, and my heart skips before beating again. He's doing this for me, to make sure I can say my goodbyes properly.

Clenching my eyes shut from the pain, I nod and crouch next to him, helping him create the towers. Their faces flash through my mind. Their bickering, their joy…their love.

Gods, they loved each other so much. So deeply.

"Thank you for everything you have ever done for me." I begin, once again my throat closing up. I touch Josie's tower. "Thank you for your patience, for teaching me that I can be touched without harm. That I can be hugged without cruelty. That I can…" A choked sound escapes me and Darius's hands come to the nape of my neck, comforting and soothing. "That I can be free," I manage to get out, tears sliding down my face but I don't care.

I loved them.

"How did we get here?" I ask him, sniffling. The life I lived before him seems like an impossibility. Seems like someone else's life, just like the life I had as a girl.

"We got here when I finally opened my eyes." I turn to look at said eyes and he rubs his nose against mine. "Bless them so they are forever running free."

I nod and turn back to the stones, feeling him next to me as my support and my pack at my back, giving me the strength I need to go through with this, a final goodbye but not a forever.

I touch my fingertips to the top of the stones, breathing in the winter air as snowflakes land on the tops of the towers. My lower lip trembles but I breathe deeply, wanting to hold it together for them. For their love.

"Falkvor mah lumn," I say into the wind. It's a blessing from the Gods for the dead. For them to gather and run on the moon together. "Be free in spirit, heart and soul."

Wisps come from the forest behind us, their green-blue glow a gentle warmth amongst the cold. They swirl around the memorials, touching each one gently until they reach Danny and Josie.

They hover over them, swaying gently side to side before gathering together and rising up into a swirl of soft light, disappearing into the night sky. I follow them, snowflakes clinging to my lashes and I close my eyes in relief.

They can rest now.

I look to Darius who is already watching me, and my gaze shows my gratefulness to what he has done. He nods his head, his hand reaching out to stroke my nose before he stands and takes a step back.

My pack comes and fills the space he left behind, their comfort wrapping around me. Josh is on my right and Kade is on my left, the others are at my back and we just breathe in each other. I take Josh and Kade's hand in mine, squeezing gently as we pay our respect to the dead.

We have lost lives since the Elites came to Eridian. Whether from the Highers hands or the rogues, and with that reminder, the determination in me grows even stronger.

To right the wrongs that have been done.

SIXTY TWO

Rhea

I palm the lilk tree, feeling its power thrumming beneath. The relief I feel is indescribable. Eridian is finally a safe haven again, even after the attack on it.

The difference with this barrier and Solvier's though, is that we can be wolf inside of it. I don't know if that is because of Darius and I, or something different altogether.

I look up to the blooming petals and think of Solvier. He would have wise words of what to do next now that we have this. He would be able to guide me, know which path I need to take.

Now I just feel…lost again.

I also feel a sense of foreboding lingering, like anything can change within a moment.

Rogures have come to our home on Charles's command. Word of more hangings have reached us and Charles has given up the façade of caring for his people. Anyone at his gates uninvited are also hanged, and any Elites caught in the lands are punished by death.

The people are more terrified than ever. They are being starved if anyone in their village has attempted to get into the castle for sanctuary, food tax is higher and the Higher's guards are more brutal.

But they are also rallying back, fighting when they can by stealing food that's intended for the castle, running away from guards that are brutal to them. It may be little, but it's a start on losing the control the Highers have over the people.

But there is still so much death.

Starvation, rogure kills, *guard* kills.

I think back to when I was looking down at all those beasts in The Deadlands and shiver. It will be death unbridled if an army of those things roamed the lands.

Darius has told me his men in The Deadlands have started moving rubble to get to the back room to see if what Frederick said was true, but he hasn't received word yet.

"The lands are being lost, and I don't know what to do anymore," I whisper to myself. "What am I supposed to do? How do I right the wrong? How do I help?"

Frustration makes tears spring to my eyes. We are not moving fast enough. I know we aren't. But with the Elite forces split between here, Colhelm and The Deadlands, we don't stand a chance of attacking Charles, but we need to do…something.

A breeze swirls past as a wisp appears in front of me, and I can't help but smile. I raise my hand, ready to play with it like I always do, but it zooms away from me.

My brows furrow. "Do you not want to play with me anymore?" It flies back to me, and then zips away again. I walk towards it, and it moves again.

I pause for a moment.

"Do you want me to follow you?"

The wisp wiggles, and moves further back. I raise my hand and Runa is there, instantly.

She moves toward me, nuzzling into my neck and I reach up and stoke her head. "Go to Darius and bring him. You will both be able to follow my scent." Her wet nose touches my cheek and then she's off.

I follow the wisp through the barrier, feeling the caress on my soul that warms my chest. The wisp doesn't go fast, it makes sure I am within its sight at all times. I pick up the pace, my walk turning into a run and then we are running through the trees.

We go deep into the forest, getting closer to the cliffs on the east side. I think maybe this is a new game we are playing, but when I reach the treeline and step in front of a waterfall, I realize where we are.

Solvier's cave. This was his favorite one behind the waterfall.

Why did this wisp bring me here?

It slows, and I walk toward it, following as we round the pool of water, taking a path up and behind the waterfall.

The rushing of water is all I hear for a few moments as I pass the side of it, my face getting wet. Once inside, the water covering my back, all that greets me is a single glow of the wisp.

"What is it that you wanted me to see?" I follow blindly as it moves further inside.

I haven't been in here much, and even then it was just at the entrance, never wanting to encroach on Solvier's den.

We go through a tunnel or two, my hand on the sides of the walls to guide me when we eventually come out into a larger cave, and I gasp at the space.

It's huge. Stalagmite forms are everywhere, some tunnels leading off here and there, and I look to the lines of light that pierce down from above.

I never knew this was here.

A glow at my face has my attention turning to the wisp, and I continue to follow, careful of my steps on the uneven ground. When it guides me to an edge, I look down in shock.

"What..."

The wisp heads down, and I look carefully for a path. Seeing one to the side, I look behind me, wondering if Darius can even find me and then I shake my head.

That male would be able to find me anywhere.

Walking down the path, I realize it's slowly turning into steps. Lips parting, I watch as the full building comes into view.

The white arches are chipped, dirty and breaking away, and most of the walls are crumbled, but I know what it is instantly.

A place of worship.

"Rhea?!" Speaking of the male.

"Down here!" I call, never once taking my eyes off what's in front of me. Runa is at my side in an instant, and I stroke her back before calling her inside of me.

"Fucking Gods, little wolf," I hear behind me. "Why did you decide to wander off on your own? I know Drax well enough to know that he wanted me to follow Runa, but didn't you stop to realize that seeing her without you made me think something had happened? Do you want me to go mad—"

He stops when he looks up to see what I'm seeing.

"I didn't mean to worry you, Dar. The wisp brought me here and I didn't want to risk losing it." I guide a tendril to his hand and wrap around it. His power instantly coats mine, never taking his eyes off of the structure.

"Wait for me next time." He tilts his head, eyes roaming the building. "Is this...?"

"Yes," I say, reaching for his hand and pulling him toward the building.

We walk over the crumbled walls, and Darius eyes the roof like it's about to cave-in at any second, creating a barrier above our heads for safety.

It looks like there were once tapestries hanging from the walls. All that's left of them now are rotting material, you can't even make out what was on them. Pillars stand tall, thick and strong and I have to wonder how long this has been here.

Entering another room, this must have been a bath before humans invented what we have now. Clever beings they are, but this bath is large and square, murky water now filling it.

"That could fit half of your Elites inside of it," I tell Darius and he grunts.

"Are you saying you want to see my men naked?"

I sigh. "You are more than enough." He nips my ear, but I can tell my answer pleases him.

We round another corner, and both me and Darius halt in

our step.

Flowers cover the whole area, and I wonder if this was maybe a garden room or something with the sheer amount. Water trickles down the sides of what is left of some of the walls, and a sweet scent travels to us.

A white, oval archway rests ahead in the center on a raised platform. It looks almost ethereal as it stands amongst the destroyed room, but that arch isn't touched by the destruction or age of this place of worship. Almost like nothing could if it tried.

Ivy wraps around the arch with flowers blooming amongst it, and I go toward it. Walking up the cracked steps, my foot lands on the floor and it glows a gentle blue.

"Umm, Darius," I say nervously, and he's at my side in an instant.

"What did you do?" he asks.

"Nothing!" He looks to me and then the ground before taking a step.

"Wait!" I say in a panic. But all that occurred was the ground turning black beneath him. My brows furrow. "What does this mean?"

He shakes his head. "I don't know." He looks ahead. "Let's keep going, but stay close."

With his hand on my arm, we take tentative steps toward the middle, the ground a mixture of black and blue.

"It's reacting to us somehow," I say.

"There must be some residue of power beneath us."

We continue until we pause at the arch. It is taller than Darius, and wider than us standing side by side. I look it over in wonder and watch as tendrils of blue and black come up from the ground to slither up the arch. A flower grows and blooms bigger, but the black magic chases it, and it wilts and dies.

"That's not ominous."

Darius looks at me for a moment, then to the dying flowers. "It's a balance," he says, raising a hand and touching the arch.

"We are the balance of the lands and the unknown, and it reacts to it. Put a small amount of power in, just a little and together."

"Like we did with the lilk trees?" He nods. "Okay, I can do that."

Raising my hand on the opposite side to him, I give him a nod, then we are both pushing power into the arch.

The flowers bloom, then die, then bloom and die again, but eventually, we find a balance of having the same amount of power, and the flowers bloom at the top with a single black strand wrapping around the stalk. Living in harmony.

I look to Darius and smile, watching as our power travels to the other flowers covering the area. It spreads out, faster and faster until it's covering the whole room.

"Wow," I whisper, not wanting to disturb the magic flowing here. "It's beautiful—"

A thunderous rumble sounds and the ground begins the tremble.

Darius grabs me instantly, taking us a few steps back and his magic wraps around us at the waist for protection. The arch in front starts to wobble, bits of stone crumbling from it with how forcefully the room is now shaking.

"What's happening?" I ask in shock, huddling closer to Darius. Ahead of us, something comes out of the floor on either side. "Look." I point to it, and Darius moves back more as two statues appear out of the ground.

They are chipped too, huge chunks broken off, but it's so clear as to what they are.

"Darius..." I say nervously.

"It seems we are in a temple of the Gods."

SIXTY THREE

Rhea

The two huge statues of wolves come to a stop, looking down upon us. One dark, one light. They sit proud and strong, ears perked.

There is a feeling in the air, like something out of the lands, like something old and powerful.

"There is magic here," Darius says, looking around for the source.

I nod. "I can feel it, but it doesn't feel threatening."

Darius drops his magic and I look at the two wolf statues. I move forward to the arch between them, and that feeling gets stronger. "Darius, I think it's here."

He moves with me, and we both once again stop in front of the arch. Darius tilts his head, then he reaches out toward it, placing a hand at its center.

A ripple of silver shines, and breath escapes me at the wave of power that rolls over me.

Darius eyes me, probably wondering how to remove me from here if we are in danger, but he decides to bring me close to his side again.

What better way to protect me than to be next to the person who would slay all for me?

Darius calls his power to his hand, the mist coating his fingers as he places his hand further into the arch.

It ripples again.

"There is something on the other side?"

"What?" I ask, looking through the arch to the other side of the room. "There is nothing there."

"It's like a port… I think if we go through here we will be ported somewhere else."

I look at the archway curiously again. "How is that even possible?"

He's deep in thought for a moment, until his gaze turns to me. "I read that long ago, there were portals. You could walk through them and be somewhere else."

"Like a port stone…but stationary?" I ask, and Darius nods.

We both look over the arch and then to each other.

"We need to see where it goes. The wisps led me here for a reason." I point out.

He stares at me intently for a moment, and he nods. "Stay close to me, at all times."

"I will."

With one last 'you better do as you're told' look, we walk through.

Darius is right.

This feels like it does when we port. I feel like I'm being squeezed into nothing, fading away only to be put back together again, to be whole.

We land on hard ground, and Darius instantly takes a defensive stance, but there is no danger here.

Nothing but the ruins in front of us.

"We are in Zakith," I say, recognizing the woods behind us. They run from here all the way to the Aragnis pack home. Though it goes on and on for a long while. "Why would it bring us here?"

"I don't know. We are far away from your old pack, but we need to be vigilant." I nod, my eyes never once leaving the ruins.

I take the steps up to it, and it feels so much different than the one in Eridian.

It feels lifeless, dead.

"Tyeetha," I whisper, remembering what the book said in Darius's library. "It's strange to think they came here a lot, isn't it?"

Darius grunts. "A lot has been lost over time. Everything we have in our history books could all be a lie, including this."

He has a point, but, "I don't think that port arch in Eridian would have taken us here if it didn't mean something. There has to be a reason why."

We walk into what I can only guess could have been a grand room. The pillars on either side are like the other one. Half ruined and destroyed. I feel a sense of sadness as we walk through. As I make out the cracked marble floor before us, I feel this was once a happy place.

Full of warmth and love, instead of feeling so...cold.

"What's wrong?" Darius asks, halting my steps.

My brows furrow. "What?"

He raises a hand and touches my cheek. I lift my own hand, and wetness coats my fingers.

I'm...crying.

"Why are you upset?" he demands, stepping closer and tucking some of my loose hair behind my ear.

"I...I don't know." I swallow over the large lump in my throat. "It just feels so sad here. Like it was once a warm place and now it's not.

"Lifeless," he says and I nod, looking around.

"There were many people in here, once," I begin, as Darius looks at me curiously. "Dancing, blessings, mating ceremonies." I look up and I can see where the ceiling once curved up into a dome, I see where a hole was left in the middle for the moon to shine down. "This was where the Gods visited most, because this is where the people came the most to bless them and receive blessings." I look to Darius sniffling. "This is...home for them."

His eyes bounce between mine. "How do you know that?"

I shrug. "It's a feeling."

He nods, accepting it. He doesn't even try to convince me otherwise, he believes every single word I have just said.

I grab his hand in mine, and we continue to walk through the ruins of what was. It's heartbreaking, really, and I can't help but wonder when the decline of the Gods really started.

We enter through another door to an outdoor space that spans far beyond the temple, but then I spot a familiar platform.

I stop, my heart stops.

My sole focus is on what's in front of me and my whole body starts to shake.

Warm hands hold me, and whispers sound in my ear, but all I can see, all I can hear is my mom's throat being slit.

It's only when Darius picks me up and starts to take me away from here that I finally snap out of it.

"Wait," I croak about, clutching his shoulders tightly as he holds me in his arms.

"Rhea…"

"I know, but we can't leave. Not yet."

I feel his need to take me away from this place, from something that would hurt me so much, but we need to be here.

"We leave whenever you want, no questions." I nod against him, and then breathe in his scent for comfort.

I wriggle and he lets me down. Taking a calming breath, I walk toward the platform, Darius sticks to my side, his hand on the small of my back.

"They defiled this place with what they did," I say into the open space, looking at the trees at the back, the moon high in the sky. "That's why it feels lifeless, that's why I feel so sad."

Darius looks down at the ground, crouching and placing his hand upon it. "The below feels closer." I look down like I can see it, but I know I can't.

We continue toward the center, and I can't help but look at the spot where I think the rogue came out of. "Look." I point, and Darius follows it to the dark patch of grass.

"We need to be careful."

When I'm two steps away from the platform, I swallow before looking down at it. There are lines here that run and connect together, and there are runes and writing that I can't make out.

This just confirms again that this is where my mother was killed.

A chill sweeps through the air and I shiver, pulling my cloak tighter around myself. I look away from the platform when I see red. I don't want to see my mother's blood.

Examining the two pillars, trying to ignore the chains dangling from them, I also see that they have runes on them.

"Why were we brought here?" I wonder, steeling myself before stepping onto the platform.

"Little wolf…"

"I'm okay." I walk to the first pillar, hesitating before running my fingers over the grooves. Feeling compelled to do so. I know why in the next moment.

Without my control, my magic comes to my fingers and enters the stone.

I gasp, pulling my hand back to my chest in surprise as the runes in the pillar begin to glow. I step back, bumping into Darius's chest as he wraps his arms around my waist.

We wait for something to happen, maybe statues appearing like they did in Eridian, but nothing comes.

The pillar still glows, but that's when I realize the other isn't. I move toward it and this time, I'm the one to place my magic there.

It replicates its twin, glowing and pulsing, then a ripple forms between them like a curved wall, but transparent.

"A portal," Darius says. We stand in front of it.

It acts just like the other, the silver ripples moving to an unknown breeze.

"Are we going in?" I grab Darius's hand and hold on tight.

"We have come this far, what is one more unknown place?"

"Here goes nothing."

SIXTY FOUR

Darius

She's smiling again, and I think this one is my favorite.

It's the one where it lights up when she sees something new, when she sees something so beautiful to her that her eyes almost take on a glow.

But when she turns to smile at me, I know I'm wrong. *This* is my favorite.

When she's looking at me like this, it's full of joy and a sense of peace.

This is what I will fight to keep, what I will fight to protect.

This is what I would sacrifice anything for.

"This is…extraordinary," she breathes, turning in a circle and taking everything in, but all I see is her.

There is no danger nearby, almost like the lands would repel it if there were, and that's why I am able to look at her now as she takes in trees taller and thicker than I have ever seen. Able to take in the red and orange blossoms that shouldn't bloom because of winter, of the grass and wildflowers so vibrant and strong where snow should have covered it.

I thought Eridian may be the most life-filled forest there ever was, but this is.

Petals fall as we walk further on the dirt path that could take ten of my Elites walking side by side. The full moon is high up in the sky, stars glittering around it and a gentle breeze flows though. It's not cold, nor warm, it's…magic.

Power.

"This is Vahaliel," Rhea says, holding her hand out and wiggling her fingers like she can feel its magic. She looks at me. "The plane of the Gods."

"How do you know that?" I ask, but it would make the most sense.

She looks ahead and points. "That."

I follow her gaze and see a single tree in the distance that I can only describe as the size of a mountain. No, maybe taller. It's so wide and thick, with long, twining branches expelling from its center. It's full of large blossoms, however, these ones glow.

"Zahariss," Rhea whispers, looking at the tree. "Are you here?"

I can hear the slight desperation in her voice. She wants to know how to make things right within the lands, and what better way to know than to speak to one of its creators.

Apprehension swirls within me as Drax stands alert. I don't know if the Gods are here, I don't even know if they are alive. We could be walking into danger and we don't even know it.

I'm alerted by twigs snapping to my left, and I stand defensively in front of Rhea, power extending out.

A paw comes into sight first, then another, but this is no ordinary wolf.

"Solvier!" Rhea gasps, and then she's running.

The golden-eyed wolf steps forward, lowering his head, he accepts Rhea's hug.

She cries into his fur, her arms wrapped as tightly as she can around his neck as he nuzzles into her.

I loathe her crying, it makes me want to grab what has upset her and take it away. I eye the wolf. I don't think she would appreciate that.

"Hello, Rhea." His voice sounds in my head. *"Dark one."*

My nod is stilted, instantly remembering what he said to me that day in Eridian, but more so, because now I understand it.

"How?...I don't understand," Rhea says, clutching him

tighter.

"This is where I am allowed to be," he says.

"I'm so sorry," Rhea hiccups. "I couldn't protect you, I didn't know what was happening until it was too late, I'm sorry—"

"Hush, now," he says and takes a step back, looking directly into her eyes. *"I knew my fate. I had lived a long time within Eridian without my chosen family, it was time for me to rest with them."*

Just then, another wolf comes out of the forest, and a smaller one follows.

I instantly remember the story Rhea told around the campfire that day, about how his chosen mate was pregnant, but they both died in Eridian when she delivered the babe.

"Oh, Solvier." Rhea sniffles, bowing her head in respect to the other wolves. "Your daughter?" He nods. "She is beautiful." She looks at the other wolf who sits and watches them, clearly nervous.

"You have created a new barrier it seems," he asks, pride in his voice and she nods, smiling when the younger wolf, his daughter, comes up to him, nuzzling his side before going back to her mother. *"You are doing what you must, your path is true."*

"It doesn't feel like it, I feel useless."

He shakes his head and growls low. Rhea's breath hitches, and I'm about to go to her and demand that Solvier tell me what he just did, but then Runa is there, shaking her fur out.

I stand to attention with Drax. He will not hurt her.

"Calm, dark one. I will not hurt her." I relax…a little. *"You think this is useless,"* he says, nudging a wary Runa's side affectionately as she sniffs him. *"You are doing well, you are on the right path."* He looks down to Runa. *"It is so good to see you rather than just feel you."* Her tail wags.

Rhea strokes Runa's head. "But what does that even mean?" Frustration bleeds in her voice. "I am supposed to right the wrong. Make it all better, but how?"

Solvier looks to Rhea and then me, huffing slightly. *"You will know."*

The other female wolf makes a sounds and Solvier looks toward her. *"I must go. Follow the wolves to where you need to go."*

He starts to turn, and the heartbreak in Rhea's voice makes my teeth ache.

"Wait…I—Don't go." Her shoulders shake, and he goes to her, nuzzling her neck as Runa tries to comfort her. "Please."

"I am where I am meant to be," he tells her, licking her face. *"Don't be sad. I am happy to be with my family. You will be okay, my little Heir."*

She nods, a whimper coming from her and she reaches up one last time, rubbing her head on his, and then he's walking away, back to his family.

She watches as they walk back through the trees, Solvier giving her one last look before disappearing from sight.

"Little wolf," I call, opening my arms to her. She doesn't hesitate running into them and I hold her tightly, rubbing her back as I rest my chin on the top of her head. Holding a hand up to Runa, she comes next, nuzzling into me as I stroke behind her ear.

I call Drax and he goes to Rhea's neck, licking there before licking Runa, trying to comfort.

"He has got to make up for his regrets," I tell her. "This is his chance, and now he can be where he truly wants to be."

"You remember the story I told?"

"I remember everything."

She sighs, leaning back into me. "Even in death he found his peace."

"Not many can say that," I tell her, looking to the below like I can see it.

Howls suddenly rent the air and then, from within the trees, a pack of wolves close in on us.

Runa and Drax instantly turn, hackles raised and teeth bared, but these wolves have no body.

"Spirits of wolves," Rhea whispers as we watch the almost transparent wolves. They have a slight, light blue tinge to them to make them visible, and swirls and patterns on them that look ancient, but you can see the trees through them.

They stare at us, their tails wagging high, and then they begin to walk away as one, halting when they notice we aren't following them.

Rhea looks to them for a moment, and then to Runa. The silver wolf moves forward curiously as Drax tenses, readying to protect her. But when the spirit wolves do nothing, Rhea goes to her.

Her feet are off the ground as she climbs on Runa's back, a small smile gracing her lips as she turns toward me.

Her eyes are puffy from crying, but she's always beautiful to me, and even more so on the back of her wolf, absentmindedly stroking Runa.

Drax grunts, and stands next to me. I chuckle because he doesn't let me do this often, but I think the look Runa gave him helped his decision.

"Soft ass," I say to him as I climb on. He growls and I scratch behind his ear. "We can't leave our girls behind now, can we?" He snarls and I smirk. "Thought so." And then we run together with the spirit wolves, heading toward the large tree in the center.

SIXTY FIVE

Rhea

We follow the spirit wolves on Runa and Drax. Darius is alert, as always, but I'm calm. I am calmer than I have ever been. In a place that feels like it is everything right.

I breathe in the sweet scent of the lilk trees, marveling at how tall they are. The ones in Eridian cannot even compare.

Is this where they originated from?

The pack of wolves play and run through the trees along the path, yipping and making excited barks at one another. I can't help but chuckle as one pounced on another unsuspecting one.

"Even here they play," Darius says, patting Drax's neck. The wolf doesn't exactly look happy with having a rider.

I snort.

Draxton's head whips my way, eyes narrowing and I avert my gaze, biting my lip.

"He will shun you, you know," Darius says as Runa makes a scoffing sound.

I shrug. "Maybe, but I doubt it would last long."

Darius tilts his head. "With you, no, it wouldn't."

Exiting out the lilk forest, we halt at the base of the large tree. It's massive. I can't even see the top of it from here, the clouds hiding it. A large petal falls, and it's so big it could fit all of us on it.

I dismount off of Runa, and Darius follows. Giving Runa a nuzzle in thanks, I begin walking toward an opening at the base with Darius at my side. Our wolves at our back.

The spirit wolves seem to stand straighter the closer they get, but it's not in fear...It's in respect.

They look back at us as they reach the dark opening, and then they walk through. I can't see where it leads, but Darius and I don't hesitate to follow.

We pass through a barrier that feels like the one Solvier had in Eridian, and I blink at the sudden light when we pass through it. I grip Darius's arm tightly as I see all the wisps in here. What I thought felt like peace outside, it's nothing like what I feel in here. It's euphoric.

The ground is covered in grass that reaches our ankles, and more lilk trees reside inside with waterfalls flowing out of the bark.

How is that even possible?

I look up and see the tree is completely hollow, winding straight up until I can't see any more.

We walk forward, trailing the wolves through shallow pools of water. Drax and Runa stop briefly to take a drink.

The wolves halt at a wooden balcony at the edge of the water that has no railings, where carved stairs are visible heading down on either side to somewhere below.

The wolves look back at us one last time, waiting until we are near before they *leap*.

I suck in a breath and rush forward, not knowing how deep the drop is, but my eyes widen when I realize they are running on air.

Nothing is helping them, no steps at their feet as they jump and run down into a lower part of the tree.

I can't keep the smile off of my face, but it freezes when I see what is below.

Who is below?

It stands there, it's back to us and seems to be looking down into something dark. It's taller than any other I have ever seen, and I just...know.

"Zahariss," I breathe, hand on my chest to feel my racing

heart as Darius pulls me to his side. "It's really you."

The huge head turns, silver eyes locking on to me and she dips her head.

"Welcome to my home, Heir of mine."

The breath wooshes out of me in a rush, and her presence fills me with so much emotion that I can't decide which one to stick with.

Disbelief, hope, anger, happiness…

She is everything we are in the lands, everything she has instilled in me by making me her Heir, and she is standing there…watching me take it all in.

Suddenly, flashes of two wolves running and playing spring to my mind, they are happy, so in love as they roll around in a meadow…and then pain and devastation comes, and I have to hold on to Darius to stop my knees from buckling.

I gasp, trying to catch my breath as Darius looks at me, with concern in his eyes as I shake my head, unable to say anything.

Zahariss tuts. *"That male."* A buzzing sounds in my ear and then the images are gone, the devastating feeling of heartbreak lifting, and I pant into Darius's chest.

"What the fuck was that?" Darius growls, stroking the back of my head.

"I am sorry on behalf of my Vihnarn, he hasn't got any…etiquette."

"Cazier?" Darius asks, and I blink my eyes open to see her nod.

At least now I know Darius hears her too.

"Come, there is much to discuss," She says, gesturing before her.

Darius's hands land on my cheeks, his jaw ticking. "You okay?" I nod, leaning into his touch as he nudges his nose with mine. "We will leave whenever you want. Just say the word."

"Okay." He grabs my hand and leads me down the stairs to the left.

Runa and Drax move ahead of us, their tails wagging as they rush to Zahariss. Her chuckle echoes in my mind as she greets them, nuzzling their necks.

I can feel the affection she has for them from here, and despite the emotional turmoil I just went through, the sight warms me.

Once we reach the floor, we head to Zahariss and stop a few feet away. She's so tall, my head barely comes up to her ankle.

"I am a God, of course I am large." I blush, hiding half of my face in Darius's arm as she chuckles. *"Now, now, none of that. Let me take a look at you."*

I let go of Darius hesitantly when he gives me an encouraging nod. I stand before her, the wolves now playing with each other off to the side as I watch Zahariss assess me.

"Just like your mother." I pick at my nails to stop the emotions those words cause. *"You who have been through so much pain and heartache, it's no wonder Cazier decided to share his own."* She shakes her head. *"I'll be having words with him shortly."*

"He's here?" Darius asks, looking around.

"In ways." A tinge of sadness nestles in her tone and my brows furrow. *"Now, you have questions I suspect, speak freely, Heir of mine."*

The picking of my fingers worsens, and Darius takes my hand, holding it between both of his as he rubs over them soothingly.

"Why did you leave us?" I ask quietly, as if it is wrong to do so. "The lands are rotting, and you have been nowhere to be seen for years. Do you not care anymore? Did you abandon us?"

Zahariss pauses for a moment, seemingly to think of her answer. *"I have never left the lands, at least not in spirit, just physically,"* she says. *"I know that you already know that. You can feel me all around the lands, in you."* I nod, because I have. *"But physically,"* she says, looking behind her for a moment. *"I had no choice but to leave and stay here. Sit, I will tell you."*

I sit down in the grass, crossing my legs as I look up to Darius. He looks behind him and then back to Zahariss with a question in his eyes.

Zaharis lets loose a soft laugh, *"She is safe here, Heir of Cazier. I assure you."* He tilts his head for a moment and then nods, sitting next to me.

He makes sure his knee is touching mine, and he leans back slightly, his arm coming across my back, palm on the ground.

"It runs deep, doesn't it, Heir of Cazier," Zaharias says, laying down herself and looking between us.

Darius hesitates before nodding. Zahariss nods back and I'm left wondering what it means in their gazes. Before I can ask, she starts to speak.

"To have made the lands, we leave a tiny piece of us in everything. From the water to the mountains, to a tree and a deer. Cazier and I wanted somewhere to reside, to call our home. But of course, over time that became lonely with just the two of us. So we decided to create you."

"The people," I say.

"Correct. With that, we wanted to give the gift of being a wolf, to let people run and feel freedom, to glide on four paws. It didn't work very well at first, we had so many failures. Until we realized one day that the best time to give the people their wolves would be at the age of somewhat maturity."

"Eighteen," Darius says.

Another nod. *"Giving wolves requires some of our power and with that, over the many moon cycles, the people evolved the more or less we gave. Some had power along with their wolves, some came to be witches, as you know them to be. Some went to the other lands and procreated to make something completely new. Some got greedy."*

My heart is in my throat at the sudden tone in her voice.

"In our ignorance, Cazier and I, we didn't see the danger until it was too late. We were happy to share the land with others, to watch life bloom and die, to watch the balance of the cycle repeat again and again, each one bringing something new. The first instance when we thought something was wrong, was the creation of a bloodmate."

"Wait," I sit up straighter. "What?"

"You didn't create that?" Darius asks.

"We did not." Shock vibrates through me, stunning me into silence. *"Cazier and I would never create something so foolish. To be forced to be joined to another against your will, never."*

"But..." I trail off, and she tilts her head at me.

"A Vihnarn is different, we will get to that." I nod, feeling so confused. *"Bloodmates were created by those that enhanced their power. A single touch, a spell here, and suddenly, you find your bloodmate. It was all,"* she scrunches up her nose. *"People made."*

I think back to the story of Solvier, how he was going to run away with his chosen mate when all of a sudden, he found his bloodmate.

My eyes snap up to Zahariss. "They knew of his plans, and they thwarted them."

"Who's plans?" Darius asks as my heart breaks for the golden-eyed wolf.

"Solvier," I reply, and recognition lights his eyes, causing his jaw to tick.

"Continue," he says to Zahariss, and I think she will refuse his command but she doesn't .

"Solvier was meant to mate another to tie two packs together, as was his mate. The moment when that came to be because of a bloodmate, it was only the beginning of more of them. Many more power moves and deception sinking deeper into packs. They grew hungry, they grew greedy. And with that, they caused so much tragedy and pain that it threw the lands out of balance. The king and his mate were the start of the lands downfall after that." I grip my hands between my legs, eager to hear more. *"The King refused the advice of his council to take on more mates, and he was too powerful to be swayed by a bloodmate, as he was Cazier's Heir, though he or anyone else didn't know that at the time."*

The king was Cazier's Heir!? I look at Darius in shock at those words, and he looks just as surprised.

"So the king and his mate, who he loved dearly, bore a child."

"Your Heir," I say, and she bends one of her front paws, seemingly to get more comfortable. "Was she born a pup?

Darius and I weren't."

"She was not, but a lie that was told to protect Heirs. The King's mate also had the gift of sight. Though all she felt was danger, not from who or where it would come from when she was pregnant with her babe. My first," she tells me, and my mind whirls at the lies told for protection. *"She was a brave little thing,"* she continues. *"I was excited to see her grow and try to create some balance in the lands. Cazier and I thought with two Heirs, it would work."*

"But the King and his mate were murdered," Darius fills in. "And the daughter went mad."

"Grief took her. She didn't know how to control the power I gifted to her, she had no balance within herself and in her pain, innocents died."

"And the Highers used that to instill fear of Heirs," I say, my anger rising.

"You know how it feels to have lost those you love, you both do." My hand slips into Darius's as he tenses, but under my touch, he slowly relaxes again. *"So of course, the Highers took the opportunity to capitalize on grief when they formed, and the people, who were lost and scared, held on to the false hope they spewed. With seeing all of this unfold, Cazier and I knew we needed to give more power for our Heirs to be stronger, as we could not intervene any other way."*

My brows furrow. "Why couldn't you have just bitten their heads off?"

She huffs out a laugh, but I'm dead serious. If she had done that, those who were killed would be alive, my family would be alive…

"Do not think like that, Heir of mine." My head snaps up to her, and sadness fills her eyes. *"We may be Gods, but we couldn't interfere like that. There are laws that even we have to abide by, that is why we tried other ways."*

"Heirs," I sigh, understanding.

Another nod. *"If we could create Heirs, they could restore the balance, right the wrongs."*

That phrase again.

"Many have tried and failed," she says sadly, and I can tell she grieves every one of them. *"My Heir, I know you have been through more than most,"* she says, and I tense. *"I couldn't stop what was going to happen to you, though I did try."* Her eyes go behind her again. *"And we were punished for it."*

"Punished?"

"I saw what was going to happen to you many years before they came true. I saw the sheer amount of pain you would endure by the hands of evil. I just couldn't bear the thought of it. I couldn't put another one of my Heirs through that. But for trying to stop it, we have been locked in here. We can send power out only into Heirs, and sometimes, a little more if we really focus hard, but for the most part, we are just here."

"You were a seer, like my mom?" Darius wraps some of his power around my wrist, the cool of it soothing against my skin.

"I was, am. Though I have been cloudy since the day we came here," she says sadly. *"Anyway, the night when Cazier and I tried to go into another soul to end this madness, the laws of the other saw fit to punish us, as it was prohibited."*

"You couldn't overrule?" Darius growls, no doubt thinking about what I had been through.

"Even Gods have a hierarchy," she tells him, eyes softening. *"My punishment was to be banished here, and Cazier's…"* she trails off, sadness coating her like a second skin as she stands and turns. *"He knew how much I loved the lands we created, knew how much joy it brought me. So he tried to fight against them, to help me be free…"*

She pauses and looks down at something, her tail tucking between her legs.

Darius stands, holding a hand out to me and I grasp it as we make our way over to Zahariss.

She looks down into a black hole as we come to a stop next to her, and carefully peer down.

A large, black wolf paces below us, head low and tail high.

Chains clank at his side as spears stick out from his body, blood dripping.

I gasp, hand flying to my mouth. "Cazier," I say, and the wolf's head lifts, violet eyes looking to me, and then to Darius.

"Heir of mine," he rumbles, sitting back on his haunches and looking at Darius. *"I hope you are treating my Vihnarn with respect."*

"Like you treated mine by fucking with her mind?" he growls back, fist clenching and my eyes widen.

"Darius," I hiss. He's a God, does he have a death vow?

"He hurt you, Rhea. I don't give a fuck who he is. I would drop down there and rip his heart out without hesitation."

My eyes widen, a tremble in my hand as I grip his arm in fear of the retaliation of what Cazier will do.

But he just...laughs.

"I chose well," Cazier says. *"You are well now, I see,"* he says as he looks at me and it all comes crashing together.

"I was down there, wasn't I? When I fell into the sea."

"My Vihnarn was very upset, and I don't like her upset. So I brought you to the below and gave you enough power to get back to where you belong." I glance at Darius as he frowns down at Cazier.

"Thank you," I tell Cazier and he nods, his eyes go to Zahariss. They soften when looking at her, and I think back to all he had shown me, all that I had felt.

I realize something at that moment. "He's trapped down there."

Zahariss nods, looking at her mate. *"I was banished here, and Cazier was banished there for trying to stop my punishment. He didn't go willingly, so they had to magically bind him."* The chains, I think to myself, they are stopping him. *"They sealed off the pathway for us to go to one another, so this is all we have been able to do since that day where a mother and her babe died. All we did was for naught, and we became even more helpless and trapped, unable to leave until balance is restored."*

"Do not be too hard on yourself, mate," Cazier says. *"You did all that you could."*

"I didn't do enough," she says back and Cazier growls, and I can tell he's desperate to get to her. To offer her comfort.

How cruel to be able to see but not touch one another.

I look to Darius as he tilts his head, looking down at his God, and I think back to a time when we spoke about how the Gods went mad from not being able to be with each other, and I didn't really get it then...but I think I do now.

Darius looks at me curiously, a question in his eyes but I shake my head and watch as a shimmer flows over Zahariss, and then a female appears in her place.

"You can turn wolf, we can turn human," she tells me, not having to speak in my mind now and I blink in shock.

Even Darius looks shocked as we take a step back.

Her hair is white, her eyes silver and her skin pale as freshly fallen snow. Her dress is as green as the grass below us, and her bare feet wiggle, as if stretching out.

She is beautiful.

"She's mine," I hear Cazier rumble, and I splutter a laugh.

Zahariss looks behind her and shakes her head. She soon sobers though.

"You must fix what we could not," she says, in a more serious tone than I have heard from her.

"I'm trying, we..." I look at Darius. "We are trying. They have beasts roaming the lands, and a Higher more powerful than we even knew."

"He stole from an Heir," she says. "Your mother. He tried to steal her power, and he succeeded a little, but not all."

I nod, thinking as much.

"The beasts?" I asks.

She sighs. "They came from the below. They are the hounds that wrangle up those who deserve to be down there. When that male tried to steal an Heir's power, the power I gave her, Cazier's instincts kicked in and he sent the hounds to bring them to the below for what they did. It should have been a simple thing, but they got corrupted."

"That's why they come out the ground." I look to Darius. "That's why even if they bite you, bite Draxton, you survive." I tell him. "Because you are Cazier's Heir."

"Correct," Cazier says from below. *"My Heir would not be so weak to be harmed by the hounds I command."* He pauses. *"Once commanded."*

"So they have found a way to control the beasts then," Darius confirms.

"And experimented to create something far more deadly," I chime in, thinking of those human-like beasts.

Zahariss's face drops. "I know. We may not be able to do anything in the lands, but we see it all."

"How do we stop them? The lands are rotting as we speak!" The desperation in my voice makes me suck in a breath. "People are dying, the Lands are dying."

Zahariss's face turns hard. "It is not easy for us to see the beautiful thing we had created out of joy and love, only to be tarnished and dying. You think you may be helpless, but it is us who are helpless. But you must send them back. Kill those in the wrong and send them back. Restore balance."

"But how" I say, frustrated. "I'm not strong enough, I can barely control my power now, and Darius can't do everything on his own."

She tilts her head. "You are not on your own. Defy the odds and the lands will fight back. Let the people join you, put a stop to this madness."

"And what if we can't?" I whisper.

"Then all is lost."

A shaky breath releases from me. That isn't an option. I have too much I still want to do.

She looks between Darius and I. "There are people out there that do not want to be under the Highers rule. You just have to look hard enough. More so now than ever."

I peek at Darius. "Many will die," I whisper to him.

"War is death itself, it just has a different name."

My stomach sinks at what is to come, at what we cannot avoid if we are ever to have peace. But we cannot stand back and do nothing, we cannot be silent anymore, we cannot close our eyes and pretend to be blind.

People are dying.

And it is our duty to protect the innocent.

To protect *life*.

I nod, steeling myself and straightening my spine. "Okay. We will do what we must."

"Good," Zahariss says, pride in her voice. "We don't have much time before the magic of this place throws you out. The living cannot be here for long."

"Really?" I ask, watching as Runa and Drax play with the spirit wolves.

"Yes, we are in an in-between of sorts."

"Can we come back?" Darius asks, eyes on the hole behind her. Zahariss's eyes soften.

"I'm not sure. With the Lands in such disarray, I'm surprised you both are even in here, but my power is dwindling to be able to help you with that." She looks down at her hand. "I only have so much left after giving it away to many."

Like she gave it to me, to Mom, and the other Heirs before us.

"Are you dying?" I ask, emotion clogging my throat.

"I don't know," she answers honestly as Cazier growls menacingly and she smiles softly at it. "Having a Vihnarn is a powerful thing, don't you think?" She glances at where Cazier is. "Do you know where it starts?" she asks us.

"No," I say slowly. "I just know what Vihnarn means."

"It starts with the eyes."

As if on cue, Darius and I look at each other, only to be trapped in each other's gaze. He tilts his head, gaze roaming my face before he runs a finger down the bridge of my nose.

"I can believe it," he murmurs. "Those fucking eyes ended me," he sighs, but its full of affection.

I grin.

"A Vihnarn. It is more than a feeling, more than a connection. You are each other's other halves, in mind, body and soul. You are the air you both breathe, the heat of the summer sun, water from rushing waterfalls. It's… Everything. You two are what embodies a Vihnarn down to your souls."

"How can you tell?" Mine and Darius's life has been difficult since our first meeting, how does she know that this is the way it was meant to be?

"It's the way you look at one another, it's hard to not be captured, and hard to look away from. That's when I know, but also, you have seen each other at one's worst, and yet here you stand, united, not afraid of the other, not afraid to go to war *for* one another."

I can't deny her words. At being captured by Darius's eyes or that we have seen our worst.

"When you are Canaric, an Heir, your soul is shown within the other's eyes of your Vihnarn, did you know that?" I shake my head. "It is only shown to the other half of you, no other can see it, even if they are looking, and that is why you are both captivated with the other." I look over at Darius, and he gives me a boyish smirk. Butterflies explode in my stomach and I move instinctively closer to him.

I think back to all the times when I would feel like Darius was looking too closely at me, when I would feel like he was looking at my soul.

Because he was, wasn't he?

Every time I felt that, every look and glance, that was what we were looking at each time.

His arms come around me when I'm before him and he drops his head and rubs his nose with mine.

Zahariss's affectionate chuckle reaches my ears and we both look at her. She nods at us.

"Your path has been hard, for both of you. I'm sure you both questioned our choices at times." We nod. "But we were never wrong in this." Darius moves a hand to the back of my neck, rubbing gently. "We knew as soon as your soul grew, that you were each other's. We knew what pulled you two together, but it is both of you that kept that bond. Do not mistake our input for solidifying. You both chose that." We did? "A Vihnarn is more than a chosen mate, more than a claiming and or life choice. It is soul tied, and both of you have been slowly intertwining since you met, nurturing the bond. I think you both knew that." I did.

I remember thinking about a thread twining with his, connecting us in a way I have never felt. I remember telling Darius I would tear it out and he said he would put it back.

I knew a Vihnarn was more than a simple mate, I have felt it toward Darius, but I never knew it could feel like this.

Be like this.

She stands, brushing off dirt on her dress, her face turning serious. "There is too much darkness in the lands, the balance is wrong. You must put it back," she says again before her eyes move to Darius. "You cannot let it continue." She looks over her shoulder to the hole where Cazier is. "What we are, what you both are, are more than yourselves. When we chose you both, we did not do that on a whim." A huff comes out of her as she looks back towards us. "If you cannot send the rogures back to where they belong, if you cannot rid the darkness, all will be lost."

She walks toward us, her feet seemingly glide over the ground.

When she's in front of me, her hand raises and she cups my cheek. "You are the last, both of you are." Darius and I tense at that, the weight of those words landing. "We have no more to give, nothing to part with." She shakes her head and grabs both of our hands, placing Darius on top of mine and squeezing us together. "We believe in you, both of you. Unite in how you should have always done. Stop hesitating because of the past, over the wrongs you had done to one another, when the situation and circumstances were not in your favor. Do not waste any more time when you do not know how long of that you have left."

Darius drops his head, but Zahariss lifts it with a finger under his chin. A growl slips out without me even knowing, and she lets go, side-eyeing me with a small smile.

"She is yours for more than life." She is talking to Darius, but her eyes are on me. "No matter where you both are, it is for eternity." Her gaze goes to Darius. "She has already let the past go, you have to do so too to move on, to be strong enough for her."

Darius grinds his teeth, but when he looks at me, eyes roaming my face, he seems to settle on some sort of decision.

"Good," Zahariss whispers and steps back. She drops our hands but Darius keeps hold of mine. "I cannot keep you here any longer." She gives us a sad smile. "We will be watching, and waiting, Heirs." Drax and Runa come running to us, and they instantly vanish into our bodies. "Be brave. Even in the face of fear, you can find courage."

I blink, and then we are outside Tyeetha, looking at the ruins.

"We are the last," I whisper to Darius after a long period of silence, both of us left with our thoughts.

"We are." He takes a deep breath. "So let's show them that it was not in vain to choose us, little wolf."

I nod.

Yes. Let's.

SIXTY SIX

Rhea

"Arhh," I shout, throwing the axe and hitting the tree. Sweat runs into my eyes and I wipe them with the back of my hand. The others fare no better.

"Why are you using an axe again?" Seb asks, throwing a knife and watching as it lands perfectly in the center of one of the dummies that we made.

They are about six feet, filled with straw and Seb drew silly faces on all of them. Their eyes look like they're rolling in the back of their head and their mouths gape open, drool spilling down from it.

He said it was his sex face.

We quickly decapitated most of them.

"Anything around you can be a weapon, it's good to use anything you can find," I answer him.

"She's right, you just don't like anything but knives," Taylor chimes in, sparring with Colten, who has Hudson scowling.

I snicker and Hudson's gaze flicks to me for just a moment, before he goes back to watching Colten with such intensity that even my cheeks heat at it.

"Where is the babysitter?" Anna asks. She's practicing off to the side, Zaide volunteering to be *her* dummy as his face grimaces. "Oops, sorry. Too much?" He shakes his head, rolling his shoulders.

"Don't boil him, Anna, Darius wouldn't want that."

She smiles, raising her hand as she pinches her fingers slightly together. "It's just a little."

I shake my head, walking to the tree to grab the axe. "I don't know where Darius is anyway, to be honest."

And I don't. He's been avoiding me, is the only way I can put it.

After going to Vahaliel, I've barely seen him. He just says he is preparing for us to continue with training, making sure Eridian is secure and that we have enough supplies. It's like he doesn't know I'm already doing that, but he insists we do more.

It feels like he's keeping me out of the way and it…hurts, I guess.

A growl from the side has me looking at Kade. He's sparring with Josh, both wolves, and Kade is in full control, which is great to see.

I look further up as Leif and the Alpha wolf sit further back near a tree. They don't come closer, well, the Alpha doesn't, but Leif trots over every now and then.

It must be hard for the both of them to have lost so much.

"How are the new cabins coming along?" Damian asks, now having a knife-throwing competition with Seb.

"Good, The pack from Colhelm excels in carpentry, so it's coming along quicker than expected."

We have had five new cabins constructed in just a few days. It would take us nearly half a moon cycle to do just one.

The plan is to build as many as possible so those that need it can have sanctuary here, and with us having plenty of room in the forest, we can all live here with a decent amount of distance between the little settlements.

Beasts are now hunting the lands, not just Rogues and we need to start evaluating those in need.

At least, that's the plan, along with going back to The Drylands to see if there are any survivors left after the collapse of that place. We are just waiting on news from Darius's Elites after they have cleared a way.

"I'm going to wash up and then go over supplies again," I tell them. They nod and I make my way home.

Yes. Home.

It feels good to say that.

Opening the door, I hear the water through the pipes, thankful it is working properly. I head up the stairs, running my hand up the banister and when I get to the top, Darius comes out of the bathroom, water dripping down his naked torso.

I halt on the last step, my heart beating faster and Darius's eyes instantly darken. After taking a deep breath, he turns and heads to my room.

I blink.

That's it? Where are his arms wrapping around me? Where are his kisses and rumbling sounds as he inhales me?

Part of me wants to go after him, but another part thinks, fuck him, and I go for my shower instead.

The whole time I'm scrubbing myself, I silently snarl at the asshole in my room, cursing him to the below. If that was any other time, he would have dragged me to the nearest surface and had his way with me, but he hasn't touched me in days.

Sulking, yes, I'm sulking, I wrap the towel around me, then realize I didn't bring any clothes in here.

Looks like I am going to have to be near Darius after all.

Padding into the bedroom, ignoring the male within, I rifle through my drawers, looking for anything to put on.

"Are you pouting?" he asks, his deep voice startling me.

I spin, holding the towel to my chest and scowling. "No."

I turn back around as he chuckles, and then I feel his heat at my back.

I try to quiet the intake of breath and the tremble in my body, but he knows what he does to me.

"Yes, you are pouting." He runs his nose up the side of my neck. "Adorable."

I shove him back with a shoulder. "I'm not adorable. Don't you have," I wave my hand around, "I don't know, things to do other than being near me?"

Well I didn't mean to say *that*.

My pout deepens as I internally sigh. Never let a male know how you are hurting, dumbass.

"Are you feeling neglected, little wolf?" I can hear the damn smirk in his voice.

Yes. "No," I say.

He turns me with a hand on my arm. "Come with me." His tone is dead serious now, and my spine straightens. "Nothing is wrong." He reassures me, some of his magic coming out to stroke my arm.

He turns and grabs something off the bed that I hadn't noticed. He hands it to me and as I hold it out, I realize it is another white dress.

This one is a little more sheer though, it's long, to my ankles and has thin straps.

I raise my head in question.

"Get dressed and stay barefoot." He places a piece of my still-wet hair behind my ear "Hair down."

"Why?"

He turns. "We have something to do," he tells me softly. "Get ready."

Looking up at the night sky, thousands of stars twinkle, glittering in the darkness. Darius holds my hand in his, wrapping his power around them as he guides me through the forest.

He's wearing black pants, is shirtless and barefoot, and I'm able to make out the scars on his back, causing my stomach to sink at the reminder of them.

I wear the dress he gave me, self-conscious about being naked but Darius left a cloak for me to wear.

I knew it was because he wanted to make me comfortable,

but I know he also would rip the eyes out of any male seeing me like this.

"Are you taking me somewhere secluded to kill me?" I ask, and he huffs out a laugh.

"No, I would never kill you, Rhea."

"Oh I don't know, you looked very angry when we first met." And he did.

"You had just killed my men and tried to kill me, of course I was angry." He has a point. "But I wouldn't have killed you."

I look at him, but he doesn't meet my gaze. "Because of my sparkling personality?" I ask.

"Because you are you," he says. He does look at me then, and the emotion filling his eyes has my heartbeat playing in my ears.

I duck my head and smile, swinging our hands between us and I'm sure I hear him mutter *adorable* again, but I can't be sure.

When the moon is high in the night sky, I pull my cloak around me tighter as Darius stops. I look around the glade we are surrounded by, smiling at the peeking wisps through the trees ahead.

"Are you going to tell me why we are here now, more training?" I look down at my bare feet. "I'm a bit underdressed for that," I laugh, but Darius doesn't.

"Put your magic to the ground." He nods to the grass tickling our feet.

I swish my foot through the stalks. "Again?" I smile.

"Yes."

I crouch down so fast, nearly ripping Darius's shoulder out of his socket when I forget to let go of his hand. He chuckles, letting go and in my excitement, I don't realize he's moving away from me.

My power is to my palm in the next instant, more controlled, more willing and vibrant, and I smile, closing my eyes and feeling the ground.

"You planted more seeds again, that's why you haven't been around?" He doesn't answer, but that's okay.

I keep focused, feeling them all one-by-one and giving them a bit of magic. I feel them growing, reaching, opening through the ground to bloom under the moonlight.

I still have my eyes closed when Darius says, "that's enough."

I peel my eyes open, grinning at the flowers and picking one, bringing it to my nose and taking in its sweet scent. Finally, I look to where Darius stands in the middle of the lesia flowers. He has made me so many, but somehow, this meadow feels different.

I rise, slowly taking a step but he shakes his head to halt me. I stop, my brows furrowing as I play with the stem in my hand.

He looks up to the moon, his body looking tense for a moment until he eventually takes a deep breath and lets it back out.

"When I first got close to you," he begins, his voice soft. "I thought I saw moonlight in your eyes, I thought I saw my soul." Now I'm the one taking a deep breath at his words. "Who knew this little female—"

"I'm five, seven," I butt in, and he peeks at me, smiling and shaking his head.

"Who knew this female," he says again, giving me a look to not interrupt. "Who is smaller than me, would hold so much power. Who would become more than I could have ever imagined."

His eyes drop to my toes, running up my legs and to the cloak wrapped around me. He gestures for me to drop the cloak, and after a moment's hesitation, I untie it and let it drop to the floor.

He makes a frustrated sound in the back of his throat as he looks at me, taking in my body beneath the sheer dress. When I take another step, he shakes his head again.

"You want to know what I see when I look at you?" he asks, and I swallow roughly.

"You are always looking at me."

"How could I not?" he replies instantly, and my cheeks warm.

"I don't know what you see, Darius," I say quietly.

"I see your heart that's bruised, torn and broken, yet you still give it to those who need it. I see your mind that's been exhausted and full, whirling with memories yet intelligent. Quick and knowledgeable. I see your soul that's stained in death, violence and blood, yet I see the light shine so clearly inside of it. And when I see your eyes... That is my favorite part of you, little wolf. Your eyes light up when you see something new, fill with so much innocence that I just want to wrap you around me and keep you safe. But they can also darken in anger, be brutal when you are protecting those you love, and they burn me alive when they are filled with desire. Desire for me."

"It's only ever been like that with you," I say, chest rising and falling with his words.

"Only you," he agrees, and I know he's also telling me it is the same with him. "But most of all, they still shine like moonlight, like the very first time I got close enough to see it, and they captured me, just like when I first saw you."

"Zahariss said they would," I remind him.

He shakes his head. "You lured me with your presence, and your eyes took me under their spell, but what made me unable to leave your side, unable to escape? It wasn't this bond between us, Rhea, it wasn't the will of the Gods or the moon, or our souls. It was you."

"Your strength, your beauty, your heart, mind and soul. When you look at me, *really* look at me and let me in. Fuck, little wolf." His hands clench at his sides, like he wants to grab me but needing to get the words out. "I see everything that resides in them. My future, my salvation, my forgiveness, my *home*. And with just that look, I would give you anything you ask for, and anything you are too scared to voice aloud." His head hangs back on his shoulders as they rise with another deep breath. "Not being able to see your eyes is like someone taking the moon from the night sky and plunging us into complete darkness, Rhea, and I cannot be without it. That is what I see when I look at you."

"Darius," I choke out, emotions running through me rapidly at his words, at his declaration.

He tilts his head down and smiles. "Come to me, little wolf. Come to me and join our souls, come to me under the moonlight and become my Vihnarn. Just like you were always meant to be."

My heart stops as he holds out his hand to me, at seeing the slight tremble to it as I now realize what this is.

A mating.

I sniffle, clutching the flower tighter in my hand as I watch a number of emotions pass over his face. Determination, adoration, fear and something so much deeper.

Am I ready to be his in the way of the Gods? Do I want to be tied to this male for the rest of my days?

I think back on everything we have been through, and everything that has happened since.

No male will take care of me like him, no other male could even come close. And I don't want them...I want him.

This male that has seen every side of me and is still standing before me. Wanting me.

"Are we still enemies?" I ask softly.

"We could never be that again."

"And you want me? Forever?" I ask.

He nods. I take another step.

"I told you we are effiniar. There is no end for us," he says.

I let out a shaky breath, and then I'm another step closer.

"You will be just for me?"

"Yes."

"Mine?"

"Always," he replies instantly.

"No other?"

"There is no other but you. There never could be." Just like I had always wanted, someone just for me.

I let out a shaky breath, my stomach fluttering with nerves and anticipation.

I take another step.

"Then I will always let you see my eyes, Darius. I will be yours, just like you are mine."

His chest rises and falls deeply as I move closer.

"I will always meet you under the moonlight."

"Under the moonlight," he rasps, hand still out, waiting for me.

I stop just out of reach, needing him to hear my next words, needing him to know how serious I am as I take in a deep breath.

"I forgive you, Darius." His jaw ticks, that hand curling into a fist as he blows out a breath. "And I need you to forgive yourself too."

I look up to the moon and let it wash over my face, while also roaming over my skin. The glamor I wear fades instantly, and I stand there before him, with all my scars on display.

Darius can see them all through my sheer dress, see them all vividly.

"What do you see now?" I ask him, heart pounding in my chest. The last time and *only* time he has ever seen my scars was outside Witches Rest.

When he doesn't say anything, just continues to look over my body, I start to wonder if I did the right thing by showing him, if maybe this was a mistake, but after a few rough swallows, he speaks.

"My everything," he rushes out, chest rising and falling harshly as he closes his eyes briefly, clearing his throat. "I see my everything, Rhea."

I reach for his hand instantly, he grips mine so quickly and pulls me to him, breathing into my neck. He's shaking, holding me impossibly close as I run my hand up his chest and wrap my arms around his neck.

"We will always be, you and I," he mumbles against my skin. "No matter the future, there is no end. Tell me there is no end."

"There is no end," I whisper to him, my eyes filling at the sound of desperation in his tone for my answer.

"My soul is yours, my mind, my strength." He lifts his hand and grabs mine. Locking our fingers together, he places it on his chest. "You have this, my heart. It doesn't beat for another, it hasn't since we met. You own it, control it, it is yours to do what you will with it."

I blow out a shaky breath, grabbing his other hand, I place it over my own heart. "Mine is yours, too," I tell him, laughing softly. "You wouldn't let it be any other way."

"I wouldn't," he murmurs on a smile, rubbing his nose with mine.

I feel my face heat as my markings appear, and Darius's react, pulsing on his neck. A gentle wind comes, and I feel the call before my magic releases from my feet. I look down, seeing it begin to swirl around us gently, like ribbons. Blue and black.

"Our start wasn't a happy one. It wasn't exciting and heart-warming. It was cold and hurtful, unnerving and scary," I tell him, and when I feel him tense, I grip his hand tightly over my heart and look to him. "I'm...I'm not scared anymore, Darius. Not about this connection, not about you, and not about us. Accept my forgiveness, Darius." I stare into his eyes intently, and he doesn't look away. "I forgive you, my former, formidable enemy." He closes his eyes, resting his forehead to mine, rasping my name. "What's done is done. We both bear the scars, physically and mentally, but I don't want to be stuck there. I want to go forward, whatever that may look like. A future that isn't tainted by our past, but one that looks bright with our new beginning." He makes a wounded sound in the back of his throat, and our magic twines tighter around us.

"I told you I will give you anything."

"Then give me this. Hear my words, believe them."

"I do," he says, and now I rub my nose with his.

"Then let's begin, Vihnarn."

His eyes flash at that. "My brave, strong Vihnarn," he rasps against my lips.

"Yours."

"Mine."

I preen at his words, closing my eyes and smiling. "Always you."

"Always mine."

The wind picks up, our powers rising around us as it continues to swirl. We watch it, the moon our ever present witness as they slowly intertwine. The black goes into the blue at first, gentle and soft and the blue doesn't hesitate. I feel it reaching out, guided by something other than us, and they twine like rope connecting, fusing, becoming whole.

And I feel...him.

He's inside of me, that cool power that is always a comfort to me, always reassuring, and I breathe deeply as he purrs from deep within his chest.

"There you are," he breathes, like he's been waiting for this his whole life. Silver flashes in his eyes, and I can see my power within him too.

He will keep it safe, he will be the home in which we were searching for.

"You are my moon, little wolf," he says softly. "I will always chase you to be within your light.

"Then you are my darkness, I will always show you the way."

"You always do," he murmurs, and then he kisses me as our power rises above us and I feel the shift, the connection between us snapping into place.

It's so strong that I gasp into his mouth and he groans, pulling me closer, his hand still in mine, and mine in his. I feel his heart beating strongly, a steady beat as his power fully joins with mine. My whole body tingles from it, thrumming with power.

Darius continues to kiss me like he doesn't need air, like I'm *his* air. He's soft but sure, demanding but relenting. Its connection, soul numbing. It's a kiss from my Vihnarn.

"Under the moonlight," he says roughly as he takes me to the ground.

My dress is off next, and then he's kissing my whole body, scars and all.

"Darius," I stutter, gasping as he licks around my breast and grips it in his hand.

"Shh, little wolf. Let me show you what you do to me. What you mean to me." He licks down my chest, kissing over a deep scar, sending my emotions reeling for a moment, and then it hits me.

"You just spoke to me, like we have a link." I moan, gripping his hair as he moves lower, kissing every inch of me so softly that tears spring to my eyes, even as my pleasure builds.

"You are my Vihnarn, of course we can speak like this."

I feel deep in my mind, but he is there instantly, where he was always supposed to be.

"Home," I say down the link.

"My home," he groans back, eating my pussy and my eyes roll. It's always so good. *"Now I can tell you how good you taste without taking my mouth off of you. I can tell you how hard I am, that I'm leaking all over the ground to be inside of you while taking you higher and higher."*

"Fuck, Darius." My orgasm slams into me suddenly as his fingers enter my pussy at the same time he sucks my clit.

"*Good girl*," he rumbles, and then he's above me, fingers interlink to either side of my head as he thrusts inside of me slowly, eyes never leaving mine. *"Laeliah, my Vihnarn, so fucking beautiful."*

My body rocks gently as he takes me, never once leaving my eyes but my gaze catches his neck, and I inhale sharply. Darius notices my gaze and releases one of my hands, bringing my forearm up to his mouth as he kisses the middle, swirling his tongue around the complete marking there.

"*My Vihnarn,*" he rumbles, and his hips stutter on a moan as my pussy squeezes him at those words.

"*My Vihnarn,*" I echo, and he comes, his face burrowing into my neck, and then I'm floating again, soaring through the night sky as he makes me his under the moonlight over and over.

SIXTY SEVEN

RHEA

"There are around thirty rogues with them," Darius says as we lay on top of a hill, looking down toward the caravan of people traveling toward what we assume, is Wolvorn Castle.

They are with some of my old pack members, as well as some of the Nightshade pack and Highers's guards. They have been slow moving for a while now, and Darius said this was the perfect time to attack, so here we are— just waiting for the command.

My eyes zone in on Patrick at the front, conversing with Higher Berthold. My fists clench in front of me, and without even looking at me, Darius wraps a tendril of magic around them.

"You will have your revenge, little wolf. Calm." I do as he says, taking deep breaths.

Seeing my cousin brings terrible memories to the surface, but most of all, it brings rage.

What he did to me was far more than others, even under Charles's orders. But most of the time he would do it off his own back without being told to do so. He would sneak down to my cage and torment me, assault me and bring his friends.

He is one of the main monsters in my story, and he happily played it.

"I'm not used to having you in my head," I murmur to Darius, trying to distract myself as we wait.

I can hear the grin in his reply. *"I've been waiting to be in yours."*

I look to him then, but his eyes never leave our enemies. *"How long?"*

"Since the moment I met you I have wanted to be inside of you in any way I can." He side-eyes me. *"This is one of them."*

"Possessive"

"Attentive."

"How so?" I laugh. He always has something to say.

"You are my Vihnarn." I shiver at those words, feeling the warmth on my arm that is now forever marked. *"It's my job to take care of you, know your needs."*

"Being able to be inside my head won't tell you that."

"It will, because I can ask you anything no matter the situation or circumstance. I could lose my voice and I would still be able to talk to you."

"You would never lose your voice." He's too strong for that.

"You would though." I glance to him in question. *"When my cock hits that spot inside of you, you can't help but scream my name. Just like last night."*

"Darius!" I hiss.

I hear him laugh. *"Now, you can rest your voice after I'm done with you."*

"You're impossible," I mumble.

"No," he says, finally looking at me. *"I'm your Vihnarn."* I huff, but smile, letting the title fill me with warmth. His magic squeezes over my hand. *"Feel better?"*

I nod. He took my mind off the memories that I knew were beginning to surface at seeing Patrick.

"I know your needs, little wolf, don't doubt that." To the others he says, "Leo, I need you to fire at the back of the group, we need them distracted." Leo nods. "Jerrod, Damian, see that tree line?" He points to the left of the group. "Stay in there, make noise, try and get some rogues to come your way. Take ten men with you. Josh, Taylor." My pack members turn their heads towards him. "Stay near Rhea, watch her back when we start our assault."

"Which will be?" Hudson asks, next to Colten as always.

"As soon as the distraction has worked, my Elites will go forward and attack from their right. We will go in from the side."

"For the Alphas," I say.

"No, for the scum."

I nod.

Darius left some of his men in Eridian, including Zaide and Maverick. I also left Seb and Anna there with Sarah. We still have some wounded that need to heal and she's the greatest help they can have. Kade also stayed behind to protect them if needed, but Seb is keeping a close eye on him.

He's not lashing out as much, but it's too dangerous if it were to happen on a battlefield.

We just cannot risk it.

He understands, but he loathes it. Instead he said he would stay with Sam, who still hasn't spoken a single word to anyone since we got her from The Deadlands, apart from him.

A howl sounds from below, and two rogues start fighting. This is not for play, either. If rogues are even capable of that.

The larger of the two goes for the other's neck, chomping and crushing, snarling that black poison everywhere.

It isn't long before it lays dead on the floor.

Not one person tried to intervene, they just all glanced and carried on walking like it was a normal occurrence.

"Why did it attack?" Taylor asks quietly.

"I don't know, I've never seen one do that."

"They are controlled," Darius murmurs, "Maybe that's causing confusion?"

"You could be right," I mutter, looking over the other rogues.

Darius moves to a crouch, and then he begins to go down the hill, signaling to his men and conversing with them.

I stroke Runa within, not only to calm her since she hasn't stopped snarling, but to calm myself.

We will rid these lands of them one by one for what they did to us, I tell her, and her growl is so terrifying that it causes goosebumps to pepper my skin.

"Ready?" Darius asks, and we all nod.

Yes, I'm ready.

I close my eyes and pray to Zahariss for our safety, and then they open when I hear Leo let loose his first arrow.

It flies through the air, its aim true as it lands at the back, straight into a rogure's hind leg. It turns, snarling and another does the same. But it isn't until a fire arrow comes next that the people notice.

The few in the back turn, eyes wide in alarm as they draw their swords and bellow that there is an attack. I watch as Patrick and Berthold turn, giving their instructions as guards form a defensive position around them for protection.

Cowards.

Jerrod and Damian port out to the trees with some others, and I raise my hand and draw Runa out.

She comes without question, Drax at her side in the next moment as they keep their bodies low.

Darius raises a hand, signaling to his men to get ready. As soon as Patrick and Berthold start moving to the back of their large group, he drops his fisted hand and the Elites move.

Some wolf, some men, they rush down the hill, readying to take anything and anyone out as we are now coming in at the back of them.

They don't notice until the Elites have already begun tearing through the first layer of rogures and guards. Almost all of the men with them turn and see the attack, screams and shouts unleash, warning others that are still dealing with arrows being shot at them.

Some freeze in fear as they notice exactly who their enemy is, and I don't blame them.

The Elites are renowned, well trained and so fucking deadly. Their fear is not uncalled for.

As they are all distracted, Jerrod and Damian come out of the treeline with some men, and then the two sided attack really begins.

Wolves take on Rogures and Elites take on men.

Patrick lands in the middle of the fray with Berthold, who has a barrier around them. They don't attack, they just stay within their protection and bark orders.

"Let's hunt," I say to Runa, and like it is the most natural thing, I climb upon her back and we charge forward, rounding the enemies to come up from the side of them.

Darius is at my side on Drax's back, his hand full of black shards. *"Be ready for anything,"* Darius says through our link.

"I know," I growl, needing to get to Patrick and rip his head off for everything he has ever done to me.

"Good girl," Darius purrs in response to my anger, as I hunker down on Runa's back, running faster.

The Elites fight hard. The sound of metal clashing and the snarls of wolves tearing through the space, equally frightening as we near.

Darius lets loose his shards when we are close enough, and screams follow, arches of blood splattering the air and I have to wonder what caused that.

Then we are there, clashing with the few guards that realize another attack is coming from the side.

One opens his mouth to warn anyone, but Runa pounces, sending him down to the ground and her teeth are around his head in the next moment, tearing it from his body as I lift a blade and injure another, holding onto her fur so I don't fall off.

Darius, however, crouches on the back of Drax, and when Draxton lunges for a rogure, Darius leaps off of him and comes down upon a guard, blade first.

The guard never stood a chance.

Patrick and Berthold shout deeper into the belly of their men, barking more orders.

Darius and I cleave a path to them, taking down rogure and man alike as our wolves protect our back. A punch comes my way, landing just at the edge of my chin and Darius is there, hand around the attacker's throat and squeezing hard.

"You do not touch her!" he roars, and then blood is spurting from his mouth in a rough cough.

He shattered his throat.

A guard tries to take advantage of Darius's distraction and comes at him with a sword, but I'm there.

I block it, moving our blades to the side and then I hit him square in the face, following it up with a strike of my blade across his neck.

I pant, looking down at the male before flicking my gaze to Darius. He's smirking, wiping the back of his hand against his mouth to wipe the blood from there.

"You have a great punch, little wolf."

I eye him. *"It seems you have strong hands, Vihnarn."*

I turn and attack another guard as Darius does the same.

"My hands are capable of much more, as you know."

"Not the time," I growl at him.

"There is always a time. You know what your anger does to me. Now, do not let another touch you."

Black mist forms around my feet and I watch as Darius's magic swirls through the enemy, causing some to buckle and fall to the ground. With that, I spot Patrick up ahead, a rogure at his side, growling at anything and everything nearby.

When I move my gaze from it, it clashes with my cousin's and though his widen for a moment, a smirk forms, eyes full of evil intent.

I'm frozen for a moment, but then I feel Darius's magic still at my feet and no!

I won't be afraid.

I lift my hand and point my blade at him. He laughs, head falling back on his shoulders and it makes me furious.

I gather power in my hand and I release it, causing a ripple of power to push out of me, knocking down a row or two of those who are in my way.

The smirk falls from his lips then, realizing the threat that I pose.

I head toward him, removing anything in my way, then a guard is there, sword in hand as he trembles. Darius throws a shard and it hits him straight in the neck. But as he drops, another rogure sees us, then another and another.

More guards move in front of Patrick, and I spot Berthold now close to his side, hands out as he holds the barrier, but I see it flickering as it weakens.

The others must be on the other side of him.

Darius begins letting loose his attack of shards, Drax and Runa tearing into anything they can grab in their jaws.

"Go for Berthold first, Runa, I will go after Patrick." She growls at that. "You will get your turn. I vow it." She nudges her head with mine and then we both set off.

"I will clear a path," Darius tells me. *"Not a scratch on you Rhea, I'm serious!"*

"I got it."

His power is a blur ahead of me as it goes for anyone in my way, sliding up their body and taking them to the ground. I cut down a man or two, far too easily for my liking, but when two rogures block my way, I realize the men here do not need to be trained or powerful.

They have rogues on their sides.

They both come at me at once, black foam dripping as their jaws open. I throw my blade in the mouth of one and roll to dodge the other. It growls, snarling at my back and I roll again, picking up a dropped sword.

Spinning, sword ready and pointed out, I catch the rogure mid-lunge right in its chest, the weight of it crashing down on me and making my hands shake as I shove it to the side as best as I can.

As it whines and claws at nothing, the other rogure is coming for me, blade handle sticking out of its mouth as Runa jumps on another. I push to my feet, running at it and when it's in range, I twist to the side while also grabbing the handle and pulling.

"That's mine," I growl at it, turning with the momentum and swinging it down on its head.

"We are fucking later," Darius purrs.

"Stop watching me."

"Never."

A shout from ahead has me looking to where Berthold's barrier finally breaks, and I wonder just how powerful he actually is. With Frederick and Mathew, they were able to use their power to attack, but Berthold hasn't done anything with it, and thinking about Higher Aiden when I killed him, he didn't do anything either.

Suddenly, my path is clear and Drax is there, jumping on the Higher as he scrambles for his pocket. Darius growls as he takes down a rogue as I look ahead with Runa, looking for my cousin.

I wipe some blood off my forehead and look within the fight. When I don't see Patrick, I start to panic.

"Where is he?" I ask aloud, pushing forward and now into the other side of the caravan of men.

Josh and Taylor suddenly appear at my side as we head forward, cutting a path as we take on the enemy.

"Their numbers are dwindling," Josh says.

"Colten and Hudson are wolves, some rogues are still breathing so they are taking them down."

I nod but focus, I still don't see Patrick.

"The middle, Rhea, I'll be there soon."

I look to the middle at Darius's words and that's when I see a flash of his face. I rush forward, a growl building up in my chest and when I stab a man in the gut and he falls, I see him fully.

Patrick uses his sword to attack, slashing at the Elites and a wolf while the rogure bites down on an Elite.

"Cousin," I shout, Runa chewing into a rogure at my side.

He turns quickly, a cruel smile on his face. "Lasandrhea," he purrs, "how nice of you to come to me and save me the trouble of finding you."

"You will die today," I tell him, my tone serious.

He tuts. "Is that so?" He holds his arms up. "Do you not see my new pets? They are quite thirsty."

I twirl the blade in my hand. "How are you controlling them?"

"Ah, ah, ah, that's not how this works. But if you come to me quietly, I'll tell you," he whispers like some secret. I say nothing. "Shame," he sighs. "I guess we will do this the hard way!"

He comes for me suddenly, and I lift my sword, blocking the attack. "Show me your power, Lasandrhea, show me what it feels like to be touched by it."

I push back on my sword, and they clang together in a flurry of attacks that he keeps blocking.

"You will die by my hand, not by my power."

"Oh so *noble*," he taunts. "I wonder if you will be so noble when I rip into your cunt!"

He's on the attack now, and out of the corner of my eyes I see rogures coming toward me, toward Runa.

"I'm coming," Darius says, voice frantic.

"You won't touch me, ever again," I say, my voice strong.

I swing my blade, barely missing his stomach and he jumps back, then raises his own blade to try and come down on my head. I block it, swinging my leg out to kick his thigh. It connects and he grunts, wavering for a second and I push him back with the sword.

His eyes flash a hint of fear, and I take advantage of it. Revel in it.

"I'm not a child anymore, I am not *chained* anymore."

"You will be!" he spits, and I push him back again before I

take an opening and swing at him. My fist connects with his cheek, making his head swing to the side. Then I do it again and again, feeling the bone crunch.

I rush for him, next, ready to strangle the life out of him when the rogure that was protecting him all this time, lunges for me.

We tumble, rolling into the dirt and I can hear Darius shouting in my mind, his worry evident in his tone.

My power comes to my hands and I drop my blade in favor of having them both on anywhere I can touch the rogure.

I can't see anything, darkness surrounds me as we are in the fray of the fight, bodies and creatures surrounding me, closing in. Something stabs into my legs, like it's crushing them and I cry out.

I hear the roar from Darius, feel his power coming towards me as I press into the rotting flesh and let it take the brunt of my magic.

"I'm coming!"

"Get Patrick!" I shout down the link to Josh and Darius.

We cannot lose him.

The rogure squeals, its body twitching and shaking, frantically trying to move and get away from the damage I'm causing, but Darius's power is there next, rising from below me and encasing me in its protective hold.

The rogure makes another twitch before it stops moving altogether, its dead weight now at my side.

"Release the barrier, Darius," he does, but I realize it's only because he's at my side, dragging me up and frantically checking me.

"I'm fine," I tell him, readying myself. "We need to...No." My eyes are on Patrick— on the stone he's now holding as Drax and Runa close in on him.

"Until we meet again, cousin." And then he's gone.

Ported out like the fucking coward he is.

SIXTY EIGHT

Darius

I've come to realize that seeing my little wolf upset makes me damn near feral, and since those sad eyes met mine after her cousin ported out, I knew I couldn't sit by and see that look on her face any longer without tearing something apart.

So I will bring him to her. I will give her the revenge she deserves.

"Are you sure he will be here?" Leo asks down the link.

"He would tuck tail and take his ass home, too ashamed to face Charles right now after losing that amount of men and rogues."

And he will. He failed his Lord Higher and is probably taking his time to come up with a good enough excuse as to why so many were killed.

We look down at the Aragnis pack, no, the Kazari pack as Rhea will take back her old home.

She hasn't said that she wants to, but I will make sure I give it back to her so she has the option to decide what she would like to do with it. Knowing my little wolf, she would want it to be another sanctuary for those who need it.

"Does she know you are here?"

"No," I say, *"She thinks I am checking on Elites posted for scouting."*

I didn't lie to my little wolf, I did check in with those men, but I didn't tell her about this detour in case the result brought nothing.

We see movement in the home, three, maybe four figures

inside and I tilt my head.

"Looks like perfect timing."

I smirk. *"Indeed."*

A family massacre it is.

I tilt my head to move forward and Leo holds out a hand. *"After you, Alpha."*

"Shut the fuck up," I growl at him. Rhea isn't the only one who doesn't like the title, though I only loathe it from my closest.

He laughs at my back, uncaring about the blood that's about to be spilled.

He's an alpha himself, his skills are nearly on par with mine, so why is he taunting me now?

"Bloodlust too thick for you?" I ask as we quietly make our way to the back of the home, just like last time."

"A little," he admits after a long pause.

I'll keep my eye on him then.

It's not often Leo can get caught up in the battle, craving for more, but it doesn't mean it cannot happen at any moment.

We just have to keep it under control.

We reach the back entrance, and we instantly hear raised voices inside, a specific male standing out.

"...they just showed up...fucking bitch and her wolf...I can't go and tell him we were defeated, it would look bad and then we...

A woman's voice comes next and I know it's Rhea's aunt. "Just tell him our men let you down, tell him that the Nightshade pack set you up? Or that Berthold betrayed you. Just like Higher Warden has."

"He's dead!" Patrick shouts.

"Exactly."

Me and Leo give each other a quick look and I open the door into the mud room as they try to figure out a way to salvage what had just happened.

There won't be any way, they will be dead.

"Ready?" I ask Leo.

"Always."

When I open the door and enter the kitchen, the family finally realizes they aren't alone anymore.

"Who dares enter my home...oh!" Selene stumbles back, knocking into the kitchen table. "Get...get out!" she screeches, her face paling.

A blade is coming for my throat in the next moment and I easily disarm Richard, another of Rhea's cousins. Another male, who I can't even care to remember his name, brings a blade up, only to have an arrow in his shoulder in the next moment.

I raise a brow at Leo.

He shrugs.

Only he would use a bow indoors.

I shove Richard away from me, eyes on Patrick as he stands at the back, looking between us all, a hand to a bleeding wound on his side.

He must have gotten injured somehow.

"Traitor," he spits at me, eyes wild.

I smirk, showing him my bloodied teeth from battle. "I'm a traitor with what you have all been doing? With what you had done to your own flesh and blood?"

"She is weak," Selene spits, body shaking. "Just like you. I told your father you would not come over to our side, and I was right."

"Yes, you were," I deadpan. "I'm not evil. An asshole, yes, but not evil."

"Leave," the cousin who I can't remember the name of points at the door, just as a creak of a step on the stairs has us looking that way. Sophia, another cousin, walks into the room, eyes hard with a short sword in her hand.

"You are outnumbered," she says, shaking her head, "Leave and we won't report your whereabouts."

Patrick cackles. "Though it will only be so long until Lord Higher has you beneath his paw." He produces a knife from his back pocket and aims it at me. "Though I may take your head first."

I look at Leo. "Do you think Rhea would want this home?" I ask him. "Everyone seems to be here."

He actually looks deep in thought for a moment. "No, I think there are too many bad memories tainting it now."

He's right. And just like a phoenix, she will rise from the ashes anew.

I look at her family. "You're right," I respond, looking around until I see some firewood off to the side. I walk over to it, causally picking them up and placing them on the table as the others back away, still threatening me with weapons.

"What are you doing, get out of my home!" Selene shouts, hands to her chest as she gasps in fright.

"Leo," I nod to the firewood and he grins. Coming over, he gets out a smaller knife and some flint.

Then he begins to stroke the knife over the flint and get some sparks.

"Guards, guards!" Selene cries as the others rush me. I raise a hand and put a barrier around us.

No guards will come, they are with the below now.

When they realize they cannot get through my barrier, they head to the front door, I smirk.

When they open it, they are hit with a black wall.

"There is no leaving this place until I say so...which I won't," I inform them.

"Mother, what does he mean?" Sophia asks, panic in her voice.

"Try the windows," Richard says, but I ignore them all flurrying around, trying to escape when I know they can't. My barrier surrounds all exits to this house.

Patrick stands there, sweat beading his brow and when the fire starts on the table, he trembles.

"The thing is," I tell them, picking up a chair and smashing it on the floor as they start to cough. "I like my little wolf very much, and I need to make her feel better. Understand?"

Patrick shakes his head. "She was mine first!" he gasps, holding onto his throat as the others break out into a coughing fit.

"Ah but you see," I tell him, snapping a leg and throwing it into the fire as it begins to spread. "That's where you are wrong, she was *hers*." I open my barrier a little and go for him. "And you're coming with me."

The others screech as Leo cackles, dragging them close to the fire.

"Where are you?" I ask Rhea as soon as we port back to where we just fought.

"Near a river close by to collect some water. Everything go okay?"

Always such a soft heart.

I breathe deep and feel the connection thrumming through my mind so strongly now that we are closer. I have never felt more complete, more whole since we mated.

Over time, we will be able to connect at a greater distance as we continue to nurture our bond, and with how strong it is already, I don't think it will take long at all.

"Darius?" she calls when I don't answer, and a tremble starts in my fingers. Only she can do this to me.

Render me prey within her hold, yet I would never try to break free from her.

"Did you miss me?"

"You haven't been gone long," she mumbles.

I pause mid-step and tilt my head. *"Is that a no? I can always go longer."*

"No!" She shouts and I smile. *"Gods, why are you so needy?"*

My smile drops. *"I'm not needy."* The Alpha of the Elites does not get needy. *"Come to me, I have something for you."*

She scoffs. *"Sure, not needy at all."*

"I will spank your ass raw if you carry on with that attitude."

She stays silent, and I turn to find Leo watching me. He shakes his head.

"Are you two mind fucking, because usually I'm fine with sex, but even I'm uncomfortable at the thought of that."

I huff out a laugh. "We are not mind fucking." We only did that once.

I see Runa coming toward me, snarling with her head low. I pull the piece of shit to the side, blocking him from her jaws.

"Not yet," I tell her, and she eyes me like she will attack. "Try it, wolf, you will not like the outcome. You will have a turn, okay?" We stare at each other for a moment, and then she relents, bumping her head with mine and I stroke the side of her face. "Good girl. Go to your keeper, go now." She licks me before she heads off.

"Damn she's big, isn't she."

"She is an Heir's wolf," I reply to Leo.

"We have only seen Drax, so to see another is hard to adjust to."

"Why?" I wonder.

He sighs. "It's hard to not feel a little inferior to them."

"I'm afraid to tell you, you are inferior."

"Asshole."

"Now you sound like Rhea."

"Fuck off," he laughs shoving me.

I grow serious. "You may feel inferior in that." I place a hand on his shoulder "But you are just as worthy."

His eyes hold mine for a moment and he nods. "Yeah, I got you, brother. I'll go help the wounded for transport."

I nod and he walks off. A muffled sound comes beside me and I elbow the bastard in the gut, waiting for Rhea as others watch on.

When I see her coming through the trees, a bucket of water in her hand, I nearly snarl when I see no one's been with her. I eye Josh in accusation where he crouches next to an injured male, and as if he can feel it, he turns and eyes me. When I flick my head to Rhea, he looks and then rolls his eyes at me.

I will rip his head—

"Hey," Rhea says, placing the bucket down next to some Elites and then walks over to me.

I shove the piece of shit from behind and he stumbles, falling to the floor. "Just where you belong," I snarl at him. "In the dirt."

Rhea's footsteps falter. "Is that..."

I cross my arms, my chest puffing up a little in pride at the astonishment on her face. I am her Vihnarn, I will provide all things for her.

"I have a gift for you." Her eyes are wide as she looks from me to him.

"How?" she whispers, her hands shaking. I can't tell if it's with anger or nerves— maybe both, but either way, I send out a little strand of my power and wrap it around her wrist in comfort.

She doesn't even blink at it, she just puts her opposite hand over it, and once again, warmth beats within my chest at the unconscious move. At the fact that she just accepts my comfort.

Fuck, what this female does to me...

"How?" she repeats.

"I will always give you what you want and need."

The muffled noises from behind the gag that I put on him, irritates me, causing me to glare down at the fucker. He wiggles, trying to get to his feet but a swift kick to the side has him rolling over, pulling his knees up to his chest in pain.

She walks toward him now, her steps sure as she crouches down near him. I move closer myself, ready in case he lashes out at her.

She looks over him, to his tied hands and the gag, to the bruising on his face.

What? I deserved to get a few hits in. It's taking everything in me not to just kill him, but I know this kill isn't mine to take.

"Will I lose myself if I do this?" she asks in my mind.

I go to stand behind her, placing my hand on top of her head and running my fingers through her hair.

"What makes you think that?"

"All the things I have imagined being able to do to him, all the things he has done to me..." she cuts herself off and looks down. *"There are things in the darkest parts of my mind that scare me."* She finally admits. I bend and place a kiss to the side of her neck.

"You don't need to worry about that," I assure her. *"I am the dark, little wolf, I will always find you within it if you go there."*

She lets out a shaky breath and looks up at me, gratitude shining in her eyes, and a small smile greets her face before she nods.

Trust. That's what that was. She trusts me.

Gods, if anything happened to her, the Lands would feel my wrath until I joined her in Vahaliel. They would know no peace, know no happiness. Just like this fucker won't.

"Be ready," I say, gripping his bound hands and undoing the ties.

She won't want to have this given to her too easy, though it will be. I already rid him of his weapons, all he has now is hands or paws, and Rhea is ready for either.

Draxton growls in excitement as we ready ourselves to watch our girls hunt.

Rhea freezes when the rope comes loose and Patrick kicks out at my leg, which I easily dodge. Then, he crawls backward.

His eyes are wary, looking around at all the Elites still here, looking at Josh who's baring his teeth at him while Hudson holds Colten back with an arm banded around his chest.

When he sees no one is following, he stands and turns, running into the trees, his arms pumping to go as fast as he can.

Rhea watches for a moment or two, and then the change is swift and quick.

The hunt is on.

She gives chase and I follow, also turning wolf. My paws hit the dirt floor, tails high as we keep pace with Rhea, but just a little further back.

I see the brown wolf up ahead that can only be Parick, and he tries to lose Rhea, running around trees, going in and out of them but it is no use. He is but a wolf, not an Heir.

I see the bottom of Rhea's feet pulse a light blue, and then she's off, racing through the trees and gaining on her prey.

"We are not about to be left behind, Drax," I say to him and we pick up the pace.

Watching Rhea hunt her prey ahead does something to me, like the first time I saw her come back with a deer for her pack.

Knowing she had hunted it all on her own, took it down... I growl low, excitement rushing to the surface.

My Vihnarn is strong.

We run until we are parallel to them, just off to the side to give her space, but also close enough if she needs me. The fucker could turn suddenly and try to hurt her, but he will just prolong his suffering if he does.

Rhea reaches him after another boost, and I watch with eagerness as she lands on his back, tackling him to the floor. He thrashes, teeth bared and snapping, his legs scratching for purchase to get her off. Rhea bites the back of his neck, and he growls full of pain.

After everything she has endured, after what I read in the fucking book that I burned, after what she told me, the way she reacts to things, like small, dark spaces...It's taking everything in me to stand back and watch, to not get rid of what hurt her.

He manages to get her off of him, turning and lunging at her and biting her front leg. She yelps and I growl, the flames on my body rising, but Rhea quickly recovers and charges at him again.

She's impressive considering she hasn't been wolf for that long. I suspect even though they hadn't fully connected, Rhea and Runa have connected in other ways over the years, and it shows now with how in sync they are.

They circle each other, and then lunge again, continuing their fight as I stay sentry, watching as his blood coats the floor which has my pulse kicking up.

It makes me want to join her in ripping him to shreds.

When Rhea does a particularly nasty bite to his leg, the wolf once again becomes male with a pained cry, and she follows.

Patrick stands there, bleeding from all sorts of places, sweating and panting. Rhea on the other hand looks cold, hateful. I don't like this look on her face, though it is warranted.

I change, then stride over to them and Patrick notices me, but I lean against a tree as he sneers my way, though fear shines in his eyes.

"Two against one? Who's the coward now?"

I scoff. "I'm simply the observer."

"How fortuitous for me."

"No," I say, "It isn't. I am here to make sure my Vihnarn is well, and I am here if she needs me. Which she won't, she is capable of doing this all on her own."

"But you are here," he sneers, looking over Rhea for any signs of weakness.

He will find none.

"She is mine, where she is, I am."

"Are you going to let him treat you like property," he spits at Rhea. "I knew you were a whore, but spreading them for the Alpha of the Elites?" My whole body locks at his words, remembering that I once said something similar to her. "Vihnarn?" he scoffs. "He doesn't even like you, you know that, right? He just wants power like the Highers do. He probably hates you."

I move toward him, anger flowing over me but Rhea halts me when she lifts up her hand. My jaw tics.

"He treats me like I am the most important thing in the lands," she tells him, and the words settle deep inside of me, soothing all of those little doubts that are telling me that I will fuck all this up. That I'm no good for her. "He is also mine, and he is everything I have ever wanted," she growls, and my body lights up at the possessiveness in her tone. "You treated me like a pet, you abused me! Constantly. He would cut his own hand off before he hurt me again."

He scoffs. "I did what was asked! That is all!"

"And what wasn't!" Rhea shouts at him, her chest heaving. "You would wait until they were gone and come back down with your friends. You would torment me for hours, *use* me for hours. Do not lay there at my fucking feet and lie to my face. I was a child, that doesn't make me too young to not understand what was going on around me, you sick fuck!"

I want to rip his organs out, I want to tear each of his fingers off for ever touching her. Then I want to rip off his cock for ever going near her against her will, ram it down his throat to make him feel what she did. I want him to bleed, bleed and fucking bleed while crying for his life to end...I want to—

"I'm okay Darius." Rhea's voice penetrates my mind and I breathe deeply, closing my eyes briefly and calling the power I didn't realize I had let loose, back.

"Your place was always beneath me, Lasandrhea, don't you remember?" Patrick taunts.

"I will show you my fucking place." Rhea lunges at him.

I circle them as she throws the first punch to his face, bone crunching beneath it as bloodlust coats the air. She doesn't let up, doesn't give him a moment to recover as he tries to block her, grunting in pain as she continues her assault.

"Get off me you stupid bitch!" he shouts.

She doesn't.

"That's it, little wolf, don't let up," I encourage her. I want to hear him scream.

He raises a knee and it connects at her side, I growl, but she doesn't even flinch from the hit—she does, however, manage to pull his arms down and get his face again.

"Good girl," I tell her, as she brings her fist down on his ribs next, hitting him in the same place to break a rib.

She's ruthless in her attack, her face twisted in fury, an angry snarl on her face.

So beautiful.

"Don't let up, keep going," I growl, and her knees join in, smashing them into his sides as he tries to get her off of him, as he wriggles and pushes and tries to attack back, but he has nothing on the *years* of pent up anger inside of her.

Nothing.

"Fuck," I mutter as I circle the other way, getting my own quick kick in. "I love seeing you like this."

She smashes his nose.

"Feisty."

She grabs him by the hair and smashes his head into the ground on a scream.

"Angry."

Her nails scratch his face, breaking the skin as blood pours everywhere.

"So bloodthirsty that I want you wrapped around me, looking like the warrior you are, Vihnarn."

She picks up a rock next, which replaces her fists. Angry little snarls come from her with every blow. Patrick is barely fighting back now, barely moving as he gurgles blood and oh…I look down. He pissed himself.

Pathetic.

Blood splatters Rhea's face and she grimaces. "Don't worry about that, I'll wash it off later."

She pauses and looks to me then, eyes wild and alight with fury. She has Patrick's wrist now in her hand, and I tilt my head to the side as I examine the hold.

"Just a little more pressure and it will snap."

"Just a little?" she whispers, her hair falling down around her.

Gods, she has never been more beautiful.

I nod.

I smirk as a scream follows.

SIXTY NINE

Rhea

My chest heaves as I look down at what's left of my cousin. He's barely recognizable as Runa tears into him, ripping him apart bit by bit, even though he's long since been dead.

He soon lost a lot of blood when his cock was torn from him and shoved down his throat, one of Darius's idea, and I relished in his whimpers of pain as his wide eyes looked at me, begged me to end it.

How the tables turned in his final moments.

I watch on now, somewhat detached. He hurt me, violated me, raped my mouth over and over…and I think I feel…nothing.

That still happened to me, I cannot change it. But one monster is dead, and others are still roaming. Is that why I feel nothing? No relief, no joy. Of course I'm glad he is dead, and I'm still here, alive and left with the scars of what was once done to me.

Hidden or seen.

"Little wolf?"

I know Darius is talking to me, his hands are on my body, trying to get me to relax I think. I hear the worry in his tone, and I can tell he's thinking that maybe he shouldn't have done this for me, brought me one of my monsters, but I'm so grateful to him that he did, even in this state I am in.

He made sure my cousin couldn't escape me, made sure to place him at my feet and let me decide what I wanted to do.

He didn't do it for me, didn't choose for me, he left it to me.

I blink, trying to get myself out of this numbness. I don't know why I can't respond, why I can't move or tear my eyes away from the mutilated, dead body.

It's like I'm not even here.

I just...am.

"Rhea," Darius tries again, running the back of his fingers down the side of my face. "Come back to me." His power goes around my waist, and I feel its coolness sinking into me, feel its reassurance and comfort, feel him.

My darkness.

"Good girl. Keep feeling me." He bends and presses soft kisses to my lips, uncaring of the blood that I'm sure is there. "I'm here." He is.

He's always there, has been since he took me to his keep. He's my soulmate, just mine—all mine, and he wants me more than anything, even knowing what has happened to me.

I cannot let monsters taint it, I refuse to have something else taken away from me because of them.

Darius rubs his nose against mine, something I realize he does a lot, and I think it's how he shows his affection for me, his softer side, as much as Darius can show me.

But it's only ever with me, and that makes me feel...like I'm his everything. Like I know him.

Maybe that side of him is from the boy who has a mother and sister, before they were taken away from him and left him cold.

Maybe I'm his warmth, and everyone needs warmth, so he needs me.

"Vihnarn." That rumbling tone, along with his dominance that washes over me, snaps me out of it and I growl at the audacity of him trying to use that on me, but it's only playful.

I let loose my own dominance, letting him know that doesn't work on me and he smiles, inhaling deeply as I blink up at him.

"There you are," he whispers. "My beautiful, little, wolf."

My eyes go to his chest as he wraps me up in his arms, and my body instantly loses its tension as he runs his fingers through my hair, detangling it the best he can. I relax into him on a sigh, my own arms wrapping around him as I inhale his scent.

His breath hits my ear next. "Talk to me, little wolf."

I don't want to talk, I want to move, I want to run, I want to…His lips are at my neck, nibbling and licking, causing my whole body to shiver.

Darius grabs my hair in a fist and gently pulls my head back. His eyes bounce between mine, a small grin appearing before he nods.

"Run." My brows furrow and he steps back, eyes full of fire and excitement. He licks his lips. "Run, little wolf, let's play and see who's faster." I hesitate for a moment, unsure what to do.

When he steps back with that cocky smirk on his face, he raises his hand and Drax is there, heading straight for Runa, tackling her as they get into their own scuffle over the dead body.

"Just you and me." He bares his teeth. "Now, You either run," he says in a deadly tone, his voice so low and tinged with darkness that it slithers down my spine. "Or I will fuck you next to your cousins corpse."

I wrinkle my nose at that. I don't want to be anywhere near him.

When he takes a step toward me, I freeze, but when I see the determination etched on his face, I turn and run.

His echoing chuckle follows me as I head into the trees, my feet pounding on the ground. I must look a mess, my clothes torn, covered in blood, but the way Darius just looked at me is like he can't see any of that.

"I see you," he murmurs in my mind and I nearly tumble to the ground.

I fling a hand back and place a barrier there, and I don't check to see if it stopped him, I just focus on running ahead, letting my lungs expand as I feel the wind rushing past my face.

I hear him behind me, his steps getting closer, but then they get further, sometimes to the right of me or the left.

He's toying with me.

I press on, placing my magic at my feet for extra speed.

"You know what I'm going to do to you when I catch you?" I don't answer, concentrating on my breathing. *"I'm going to sink myself inside of you, I'm going to make sure you feel every fucking inch of my cock, make you feel what you do to me, what you always do to me."*

A choked breath releases from me, my body heating as I feel my pussy tingle needing to be touched from his words.

"I'm so fucking hard for you right now, my little warrior. Fuck, I love you angry. Get Angry."

"Fuck you!"

His laugh echoes in my mind, and I hear running water up ahead and aim for it.

"Come and play with me, you are the only one who can."

"I will be the only one or I will tear their throats out!" I snarl back. No other will touch him.

His muttered *fuck* is all I hear before I crash into the river, and then he crashes into me.

I gasp, managing to hold my breath before we go under, the ice of the water sinking into our clothes. I'm turned roughly with strong hands, my hair floating around me, and then familiar lips are on mine, hard and demanding.

I groan, trying to push him away but he has a hold on the back of my head, his fingers digging into my skull as he breathes air into my lungs.

He takes us to the surface and I gasp into his mouth. He doesn't seem to care to breathe, doesn't care that water is running down our faces as he walks me back to the bank and hauls me up onto the grass.

He starts peeling off my pants, impatient sounds coming from him, almost like growls, and he gets fed up and just rips them off when he's getting nowhere.

"Darius!" He growls at me, his magic pulling my thighs open and then he's tearing my panties off and entering me.

I arch on a choked gasp, his hand going to my throat, finally removing his mouth from mine as he ruts into me like a wild animal.

"There is only ever you, Rhea," he says on a hard thrust, drawing a moan from me as I claw at his back. "But fuck, it makes me want to make you jealous, makes me want to see how you would react to someone else touching me."

I dig my still booted feet into his lower back, snarling up at him the best I can. "You let anyone touch you and I will kill them before removing your balls. You are mine!" I grab his throat, my power coming to my hand.

His cock twitches inside of me as he squeezes his eyes shut, halting his movements. I pant heavily, rocking my hips, needing him to move. He inhales sharply, eyes flying open as he takes my hand from his throat and slams it beside me, pulling his hips back and then slamming back inside of me.

"What you do to me," he says in my mind, eyes locked on mine. *"This,"* he says, shoving into me impossibly deeper, so much so that my eyes roll. *"Is yours, forever yours, Vihnarn. It has been yours since I locked eyes on you."* I moan as he grabs my other hand and places it next to my head as I move with every thrust.

"Only mine," I whimper, feeling my pussy clench around him. I'm so close.

"Only yours," he groans, snarling down at me and his pace is brutal now, like he's trying to reach every part of me as our skin slaps together. "My moonlight."

Pleasure swirls in my belly, a moan coming from my lips and then his hands are at my hips, rocking me back and forth harshly on his dick as he watches.

"Fuck, Darius." I claw at his chest. It almost feels too much, almost too much.

He growls, dropping his head back on his shoulders as the

cool touch of his magic moves to my stomach, and then lower.

My eyes widen as it skirts across my hips and then over the top of my pussy, caressing the sides and feeling around where his cock is entering me.

"*Ah, Darius,*" I whimper as it begins to roll over my clit, flicking back and forth. "*What—*" I groan at the sensation, and Darius echoes it, dropping his head forward and somehow picking up his pace even more. "*Gods. I can't, it's too much.*" Pressure forms in my lower belly, and I haven't ever felt like this before, I feel like I'm going to combust.

"*You can take it, I know you can.*" I can. I can take anything he gives me. "*Remember our first visit to a river?*" Darius asks. I nod, gasping as his power strokes me faster. "*I wanted to fuck you then, I nearly did, I barely had the restraint to stop…myself…fuck, you're squeezing me so good.*"

"*Close…close..*" I chant, head rocking back and forth as tingles spread all over my body.

"*I know you are, little wolf,*" he grunts out, fingers digging into me. "*You always grip me so tight, and your lips part, those little breathy moans come from you and your breathing stutters. Fuck you are so wet, it's dripping down my balls. Give me all of it, Rhea.. Mark me with your scent.*" I hurtle over the edge, soaring and shaking, gipping his forearms as my legs shake, head tilting back on a silent scream with the intensity of it.

"Such a…good…girl." Darius says on each thrust, then he stills, pressing so close as he leans down, his release filling me. He growls and snarls into my neck, nipping at the skin as I sigh, feeling weightless.

His power lazily strokes around where we are joined, not for anything other than to feel me as Darius places kisses at my neck, nuzzling into me before he bites down.

Hard.

My legs clamp around him, my hands going to the back of his head as he marks me below my ear. I feel his teeth, feel his tongue licking and soothing and it hurts, but not much.

When he's done, he lifts his head and guides my own to his neck. "Mark me, Vihnarn. Show everyone who I belong to." He groans as my pussy contracts at his words, and I lick at his skin, tasting him.

His body trembles as I nuzzle and look for the perfect spot to mark him. When I find it, I bite down. Darius doesn't even flinch, he just pulls me closer and rolls us so I'm on top of him, his hard cock still inside of me as he starts to thrust up in slow glides.

"Only ever you," he says into my ear as we both start to move. I never once let go of him, and he never once removes my teeth.

When my orgasm hits this time, it is gentler as I grind my clit against his taut stomach, but his release seems to go on and on, his groan so loud as he holds me tightly.

I finally let go of him, licking the bite mark and relaxing against him as he rubs my back. I let his scent seep into me, rubbing my face against his cheek, feeling the stubble there and loving it.

"Only you, always," I mumble sleepily.

His barrier comes up and around us, leaving an opening at the top to look up at the night sky.

"Better?" he asks, nuzzling into me, like he can't get enough as his hands trace up my back.

"Better," I sigh.

"That was exactly how I wanted to fuck you the first time we were in a river together in Eridian," he says after some time.

I chuckle and smack his chest. "We can do that any time now."

He's quiet for a moment as I sink deeper into sleep, but I eventually hear him say, "I'm proud of you, little wolf."

Then sleep takes me with a smile on my face.

SEVENTY

Rhea

"What happened here?" I ask, my eyes taking in the terrible scene before me.

We are in a village as close to Fenrikar as we dare, not wanting the Highers or their guards to see us.

Bodies litter the dirt paths, people crying over them as some just sit there, staring into nothing.

I go to an older female as people seem to fuss over her every now and again. She looks tired, bone tired and I crouch before her, raising a hand slowly and holding hers in mine.

"What happened?" I ask as Darius nears, but he begins to help someone who is carrying what looks like another body to where they are all being placed in the center.

We all have our cloaks on, masks covering the bottom half of our face so no one recognizes us. We have no idea how the people will react to our presence, so it is just better all-around for us to keep hiding…for now.

The older woman looks at me, her eyes red from crying. "Death has us all." I shake my head, not understanding.

"Rogues?" I ask quietly.

"Better the rogues than the guards."

Guards?

"What do you mean?" I ask harsher than intended.

We have heard of the Highers guards being more strict, more harsh lately, but why would they fear them over the rogues?

"We had no wheat, this was a lesson."

I pause. "You mean to tell me that you couldn't pay the food tax and this is your punishment?"

"My son," she says, a wrinkled hand going to her mouth as she begins to sob. "My boy, my poor boy." I stand and pull her to me as she sobs into my chest.

I clench my jaw and look at Darius, seeing his own anger rise at what has happened here.

He walks over to his brothers and my pack speaking quietly, and then without words, they all help gather the dead.

"Come with us," I whisper to the older female. "Come with us and we will protect you."

"What can we do against the Highers guards," she says, removing herself from me. "We are but fodder it seems."

I crouch before her again and taking a deep breath, I drop the hood of my cloak, showing her my hair and markings.

"Do not lose hope," I say to her, and her eyes take in the delicate lines on my face.

She looks around and sees Darius nearby, forever imposing with his arms crossed as he makes sure I'm safe, that no one lashes out at me or tries to grab me and take me to the Highers.

You just never know what could happen in the lands anymore.

"Heirs," the old female says. "And Elites."

I nod. "We don't want to be under the Highers rule any longer, but we cannot do it on our own. We also cannot lose any more people. The Lands are dying and we need to fix it, but we need you to fight, too."

She eyes her village, looking between the others who have now stopped to listen to me, to watch us.

"I am but an old female, how can I fight?" she wonders.

"By coming with us and staying alive." I stand and step back, giving her space. "We have a safe haven, Eridian."

"The Deadlands?"

I nod. " It is in the center of it. No rogure can get past the barrier around it, and it is guarded at all times." I look to the dead. "We will help bury your dead, and then we can bring you to Eridian."

"How are you any better than those in power now?" she asks, as a young boy moves toward her, tears streaking down his face.

"Those in power want exactly that. Power. And they know they are losing it over the people of Vrohkaria. We," I say, looking back at Darius who gives a nod encouragingly. "We just want peace."

"How can we believe you," she says on a deep sigh, pulling the young boy closer to her.

I look around at all the village people gathered here, and after tense silence, I remove my cloak.

"Rhea..." Darius's voice is full of weariness.

"It's okay," I reassure him. *"They need to see."*

I lift Darius's t-shirt that I have on beneath off next, leaving me in my bra, which has Darius growling at those looking.

"Ignore my Vihnarn," I chuckle, shaking my head at him.

"What are you doing?" the old female asks.

"Showing you why you can believe me." And then I remove my glamor and show them some of my scars. Gasps ring out, shocked noises and murmurs follow, and Darius moves closer to me, forever the protector as the woman's eyes take in my scarred body.

"Who did that to you?" she asks quietly as the boy clings to her.

"Those in power, who wanted my power," I whisper, holding a hand out and creating a soft ball of light. I float it over to the young boy, and I wait patiently as he reaches out a hand and touches it.

The smile that lights up his face was worth the eyes on my body.

"I want to restore the lands to what they once were," I tell her. "Before power-hungry males decided to slowly destroy it with their greed and laws." Darius picks up my cloak and wraps it around me, pulling me close as he nuzzles the side of my head.

"Why not go and kill the Highers now, rid us of their tyranny?"

"We are not strong enough on our own." I eye the people. "Those who can need to fight, need to help take them down. Charles is more powerful than we know, and he is controlling the rogures that have been plaguing the lands, He is the cause of it all."

A female comes forward, hand to her mouth. "Are you saying that one of those hounds that killed my baby is controlled by the Lord Higher?"

"I am," I say gently, and her knees give out. A male rushes to her side as giant sobs wrack her body, and I swallow over the lump in my throat. "We need to all save ourselves. No one else will do it for us."

"And you are not mad?" a male asks, stepping toward me as Darius lets off a warning growl.

"No," Darius says, pulling me closer. "But if you come any closer to my Vihnarn, I can show you how *mad* I can be."

"Darius," I hiss. "This isn't helping."

He growls. "He doesn't get that close to you."

I'm about to tear him a new asshole when the male actually laughs. "I got it," he says, taking a step back. "Can you keep my family safe?" He nods to the side where a female and a small child stand, covered in dirt and I spot blood at the bottom of her dress.

Gods these children should not be forced to live like this. To see the bloodshed they have.

"We can," Darius tells him.

"That's all I need. Get them to safety and I will fight."

"William," the female gasps, but he shakes his head.

"I will fight."

"Me too," someone else says, walking toward us.

"And me," a female says, eyes hard.

"I will go."

"I can use a sword."

"I'm good with a butcher's knife."

More and more people come toward us, offering to fight for the safety of their family and I grip Darius's arm tight.

But I look to the older female who now stands, heading straight for us.

She stills a foot away, eyes Darius and I, then the Elites and my pack that are still helping move the dead.

"As the elder of this village," she says. I knew she was important here. "Take us to safety and we will fight."

"We will take you to safety either way," Darius lets them know, and I look to him, my hand curling around his in thanks.

"No," the elder says, strong, firm. "I want them dead."

My smile is full of teeth.

"This is where you and your family will stay," I say to Mivera.

She looks around the small, new cabin that was built, a smile on her face. "This is perfect," she tells me, coming over and holding my hand. "Thank you, for everything."

"Don't thank me yet," I say quietly as I walk back out. "War is coming."

"All done?" Josh asks, walking beside me as we make our way to the gathering.

"Yeah," I sigh, leaning into him. "There are so many here now, I thought it would bother me but…"

"But?" he presses.

"It feels right, like it was always meant to be." Like I am actually doing something right.

He curls an arm around my shoulder. "We will get through this. I know it."

"We have to, or all is lost."

We look into the gathering and pause, watching our pack, the Elites and those who have joined us from all over the lands.

It has been a few weeks since that day in the village with the Elder, and since then, we have had many join us to be safe and fight back.

And some we have had to take down, as they have tried to kill us.

Snow covers the ground completely now, as we are all wrapped up in thick cloaks, our breaths showing every time we exhale.

I make sure we all come together once a week as we are all tending to our own duties, or fighting the hounds of the lands. You never know when our last meal will be together, so I make sure we have one to remember by.

"Did the last village get to Colhelm okay?" Josh asks and I nod.

"Damian says it went well." I still don't know where that farmstead is, but I'm in no rush to go back to Colhelm.

"Alpha," Maverick greets me, dipping his head and I sigh.

"It's Rhea, you ass." He smirks and walks to the center, looking into the large pot of stew before he takes a seat.

"If he doesn't remove his arm, he will lose it."

I sigh and nuzzle into Josh, hearing Darius's growl in my head before I move away.

Josh laughs his ass off, and I kick his shin. "Shut up."

"Ow, you little shit." He lunges at me and I squeal, running around the trees. I laugh, listening to his own and when I see a scowling Darius, I head straight for him, launching myself into his lap.

"That's cheating!" Josh points a finger at me as Darius pulls me close, protecting me from his damn tickling hands.

"No, it's smart," I reply, sticking my tongue out at him.

"Fucking cheater." He walks off, grumbling and sitting down next to Sarah. Oh my Gods, is he pouting?

Sarah laughs at the look on his face, trying to hide it behind her hand as Seb and Taylor just outright laugh at him.

"She has a big, bad Heir on her side now," Kade says. "No way can you tickle her."

"I'll get her," Josh grumbles, giving me the stink eye, and I smirk into Darius's neck.

"Not on my watch," Darius growls his way. Darius pulls me closer, inhaling at my neck and releasing a deep growl "Move," he barks at some Elites nearby, and they get up and move away from us without a word at the harsh command.

I roll my eyes.

"Are you ticklish," I ask him, and Leo barks out a rough laugh, like the thought is hilarious.

And I mean, It kind of is.

"No."

My fingers dance to his waist, and I'm suddenly turned, facing outwards on his lap, my arms trapped in his. "Oh my god! You are!"

"I said, no."

I'm so fucking getting him when he least expects it.

"Food's ready." Anna says, stirring the pot as Oscar runs past her legs, diving for a waiting Jerrod who has his arms open.

My mouth drops open as he moves up on the bench, and a timid Katy heads for him, perching on the edge of the seat as she watches her son play with the huge Elite.

"What is happening," I ask Darius through the link.

"I told you he wouldn't hurt them.

"But...but..." What in the Gods happened when I was in my slumber...

The silence is all of a sudden uncomfortable and I realize everyone is looking at me.

"Bless the food, little wolf."

I sit up straighter, having no shame with being on Darius's lap as I look at my pack.

They have small smiles on their faces. Sam sits silently next to Kade, her hand in his, Josh and Sarah huddle close together. Hudson and Colten are shoulder-to-shoulder. Seb sits next to Damian, followed by Anna and Zaide, and then Leo and Taylor. Edward, who is looking far better, sits with a younger boy, who is chatting his ear off and Finn and Sybill are next, then Lacy, Elijah and Nathan with more members and Elites further back.

My eyes sting with unexpected tears. We are all on the same side around this campfire. We are all a united pack.

This is another moment to cherish. We don't know when Charles will attack here again, or if he is just biding his time, but sitting here together like this is important to us all.

I look at the empty seats that have been left, and I realize it's for Danny and Josie.

A breeze flutters past me and I smile. They are here, all around us.

I close my eyes and I bless the food.

"The earth is my witness, of the blood that's been spilt. The moon is my eyes, that food will not wilt. The human is my mind, as I honor this feast. The wolf is my protector, as I safely eat. Zahariss."

"Zahariss," everyone echoes, and they move to grab the food.

Darius picks me up and moves me in his seat as he goes forward, and I sit and wait until everyone has gotten something to eat.

"I have never seen my brother so enamored with anyone," Leo says suddenly, sitting on the bench behind me.

"Why?" I ask, turning to look at him.

"When his family died, he closed his heart off to anything. There was barely anything left for us or the people," he replies quietly.

"That's not true, he has always wanted to protect others."

"Yes, but that was a sense of duty, not heart. Not like now."

Has that always been the case with him?

I know Darius can be...hard. He's an asshole, and I guess

maybe they just see that side of him.

Commanding, arrogant, a leader.

But he's more than that.

So much more.

He's a protector down to the bones of him. A carer, a giver.

I stare at Leo as he stares back. "Thank you," he says suddenly, and I blink.

"For what?"

"For opening up his heart." Then he gets up to join in the line for food.

I sit there deep in my thoughts when I'm picked up and placed back on Darius's lap.

"Eat" there is a large bowl of stew with some homemade bread on the side.

When he dips it in and brings it to my mouth, I wonder how his Elites see him. Doing this in front of them may be considered a weakness.

I subtly look around, but I'm pleasantly surprised to see small smiles on their faces for their Alpha, and that makes me smile too.

I open my mouth and let him feed me, and when he goes to feed himself, I stop him, a hand on his wrist.

I pick off a little bread, dunk it in the stew like he had done for me, then I turn, holding it up to his lips.

"What are you doing, Vihnarn," he asks, but he takes the food from me anyway, chewing thoughtfully.

"Feeding your heart." He pauses mid-chew, eyes bouncing between mine.

"Your presence already does that, it does not need more."

I shake my head, butterflies swirling in my belly as I feed him more bread. "I will give you more, anyway."

SEVENTY ONE

Rhea

I run my hands over my arms, trying to starve off the cold which isn't strictly caused by it being winter, but from the fact that we are walking down the familiar steps toward the place where those beasts are being housed beneath the rubble.

Word was sent to Darius that they have cleared a path to the back rooms, and they are awaiting our arrival to proceed.

"Calm, Rhea."

"I know," I reply through the link. *"I just hope they are there…and that we can help them."*

"You need to prepare for seeing things like we did before…if there even is anything."

I nod and place my hand on his back, my other hand already clutching his as he leads the way.

Josh, Taylor, Leo and Damian are at our backs, Edward at the rear of them as they follow us. We could have ported in, but Darius didn't want to risk doing so and having the place completely collapse on our head.

We reach the room that will take us to the first cluster of cells, and Elites crowd the space, nodding their head to their Alpha as he passes by.

"Rest up," Darius tells them. "We will handle the rest, but prepare to move anyone if they are found."

"Yes, Alpha," they chorus, and Darius leads us through the first cells.

I swallow back the bile threatening to rise once more at what

I will see inside, but a quick glance tells me they are gone.

"We moved and buried them," Darius says. "They deserved rest."

I nod, feeling Josh come to my side in silent support.

"Thank you." My voice is hoarse, unsteady and I clear it, straightening my spine.

No need to be emotional now.

"Is this where they had those beasts?" Edward asks and I nod.

"They gave them the ultrian drug and it made them able to procreate, or something like that."

"Horrific," Edward mutters, and we all agree.

Two Elites guard the doors up ahead to the main room and they open them for us, once again nodding in respect.

We enter the room, the stack of shelving that was once in front of the door, now gone. The stone slab in the middle is half broken, and some cells are crushed on both sides, with large amounts of rubble piled all over.

I look up at the large crack in the ceiling, casting a bright light down upon the center. I let go of Darius's hand and move forward, heading for the grate to see those beasts below, but when I reach one and peer down, none are there. I turn with a questioning look.

"We had them killed," Leo says, climbing over some rubble. "Men went down in small numbers and took them out one at a time."

"All of them?"

"We suspect some escaped, or were transported," Darius says on a growl, anger lighting his eyes.

I nod. That would make sense as there were some that came to Eridian. Speaking of...

"Why do you think Charles hasn't attacked Eridian again?" I wonder aloud as we continue toward the back.

"We don't even know if Charles sent that attack, or if it was random, but we are always on alert."

"I know, it just feels odd."

"Maybe he's toying with us," Josh mutters, nearly slipping over some rocks. "Maybe he's biding his time?"

"Who knows what Charles is thinking," Damain chimes in. "All we know is that we won't be safe forever."

And that's the truth of it.

Once we get to the back rooms, to hopefully find the missing pack members that were on that list, we stop to form a plan of attack.

"What if they transported the people in the back somewhere else, what then?"

Darius looks at Josh and answers him. "Then we will have to find them again. Charles will hold them over us if we don't get them, and then a decision will have to be made, *sacrifices* will have to be made."

The missing people, or the rest of Vrohkaria.

He doesn't say that last part aloud, but it will only be a matter of time before Higher Charles, Higher Aldus, his witches and guards attack us.

Though we have weakened them by killing the other Highers, we don't know if we can defeat them, and we cannot hide forever.

"They will be here," Edward says. "I think if Charles wanted to prioritize what was most important to save, it would have been his creations. There are always more people to steal."

He's right. That would be the easier option for him.

Darius reaches the closed door at his back, and without hesitation, he goes through. I follow, apprehension sending a shiver down my spine as we enter a large room.

With no one here.

My shoulders sag in defeat, helplessness once against weighing me down.

"Let's see what we can find," Darius says as he goes to some scrolls.

Bookshelves filled with scrolls line all the walls, tables with papers scattered on them, along with alchemy sets on others.

Vials of ultrian and dassil flowers are stored in jars, and some are scattered on the floor, broken, as if someone was in a rush.

Drawings of those beasts are on one table, notes and observations written next to them, and I wrinkle my nose as I pick one up and read over it.

"So those beasts are made by having a rogure impregnate a female…." I pick up another paper. "And then they were birthing the beasts it created, then impregnating other females to create even more powerful beasts…"

I throw the papers down on the table, looking away in disgust over the crimes committed in this place.

All of this so they can rule other lands? How can they be so…evil?

These are people's lives they have stolen, children's lives, and then to be thrown in some place like this just to be bred against their will?

I shiver again, and Edward squeezes my shoulder in comfort, but I just shake my head and walk further into the room, Darius's eyes on me as though he can sense the turmoil inside.

Would this still have happened if I just stayed where I was supposed to?

"Do not do that, little wolf," Darius says down the link, and I glance at him, my eyes wet. *"They would have done this either way, only you would have been a part of it."*

I sense the truth to his words, that he really believes that, but these what-ifs can be really hard to swallow.

Bypassing more tables, I see another door leading off into the back, but to the right of me I see a corridor. I start that way.

Walking down, I cast a small ball of power to light the way. I see no end to the corridor, there aren't even doors on either side to lead somewhere else. It isn't until I come to a very large, very long pane of glass that I stop in my tracks. It starts at the ground, and goes halfway up the wall.

Turning, I peer into the glass, my brows furrowed as I try to make out what is on the other side. The glow of my power reflects in it, so I snuff it out and get closer, my forehead touching it.

I see nothing inside, no movement, it's just darkness, complete and utter...wait.

A shadow moved, just there to the right, I'm sure of it.

"What is this," Josh asks, coming to my side.

"There is something in there."

"What?" He looks into the glass. "There isn't anything there, Rhea."

"No, there is." I step back, holding my weight in my left leg and then lifting the other, I call my magic to it and kick the glass.

"Rhea!" Josh shouts in alarm, but I ignore him, continuing to kick at the glass as I hear the others' footsteps approaching. "There could be anything in there! Wait for—"

The glass shatters, raining down shards and I hold out my hand, sending multiple balls of power flying into the room.

Screams reach us, and then we see.

"Gods," I breathe, chest heaving as so many eyes look at us. Small, old, terrified, dirty, skinny, hurt and broken.

"Little wolf!" Darius snarls, hauling me to his chest, but when he follows my line of sight, he tenses, and some of the people within still scream in fright, scrambling back.

"It's okay," Edward tries to calm them, but he's a Higher, and it causes chaos.

People get up and run to the back, some crawl as they are injured, some don't even move, just shiver on the ground in fear and I want to scream at the wrongness of this.

The injustice.

"Calm!" Darius shouts, letting loose his dominance.

"I don't think that will help," I tell him, however, they all freeze in place, which means they are no longer in a panic or harming themselves to get away.

Not like they can go anywhere, only to the back of this...cave.

I squeeze Darius's arm. *"Let me speak to them, you are an Elite and Edward is a Higher, it's scaring them."*

"They could hurt you."

"Darius." He peers down at me and I let his dominance wrap me up in comfort. *"I'm an Alpha, I can take care of myself."*

"You don't need to."

I smile softly at that. *"But I can when I need to."*

After a tense silence, he bends and rubs his nose with mine, stepping back and letting me head toward the opening in the large room.

Darius drops his dominance, and I call more of my power, letting it light up the whole space. I carefully walk forward over the broken glass, palms up, making sure to speak gently to them.

"Hi, I'm Rhea, and I'm Alpha of a place called Eridian." I take another small step toward a woman on the floor. Her legs look broken and she just lays there, eyes on me—but lifeless. "I have been there for over nine years now, and it is a place of sanctuary for wolves and others alike. But more importantly." I bend down next to the woman and place a gentle hand on her arm. Silent tears track down her cheeks as she looks at me, body trembling, but she doesn't utter a word. "Most importantly," I whisper. "It is a place for those who need a safe place to live."

Calling my magic, feeling eyes on me from in front and behind me, I let my power enter the woman.

I hold in my gasp at all the injuries she has sustained, all the pain she must be in, and I don't want to think about the mess of her reproductive organs as I gently coax my power into her slowly, to heal her.

I start with her legs, the tearing in her lower body, stopping the bleeding from the wounds to her chest, moving to her left wrist and to her right fingers. I stitch and pull and press and push my magic through the entirety of her body.

I hear it then, the sharp intake of breath as I close my eyes to focus, the gentle cry as her leg snaps back into place, the increased breathing like she can finally get air into her lungs.

When I have done all I can, I open my eyes, panting softly as sweat beads my brow.

"I will take care of you," I tell the woman as she lifts her hand, slowly moving her fingers like she hasn't done so in such a long time. She then gently, and ever so slowly moves to a sitting position and looks down at her legs, her eyes widen as she moves them, just back and forth a few times.

She will still be in pain and need some serious healing time, but still, she cries.

She cries big, awful sobs and I go to her, wrapping my arms gently around her as my own tears sting my eyes at the pain she is releasing.

The others watch on, eyes wide and wary, but they don't look as fearful anymore.

"Thank you," the female whispers and I pull back, wiping my face as she holds onto my hands tightly.

"Let us help you, let us take you to safety." They look behind me and I hold out a hand. I hear the footsteps, see the fear climbing in their eyes once more. "He will not hurt you. He is the greatest protector I know."

A strong hand curls in mine, and I pull it, urging him to crouch. *"Getting to their level will make them feel better."* I tell him.

He looks at me for a moment, a little uncomfortable, but then he looks at the woman whose eyes are so wide on her drawn face. Darius clears his throat.

"I am Darius Rikoth, Alpha of the Elites and the Higher's enemy." The breath releases from her and the others. "I am also Heir of Cazier, Vihnarn to the Heir of Zahariss, who you will not harm in her attempt to help you.." He looks at me and I blink. They didn't need to know that. "That is our truth. There are only two Highers left, the rest we have killed."

Shocked voices echo throughout the room. "The higher behind you, Higher Warden as you may know him," I say, "he is an ally, not an enemy. He will help you…just as he helped me a long time ago. I vow it."

No one says a word, no one moves or barely breaths.

But the woman I just healed speaks up, then we are porting everyone out of there and into Eridian with sighs of relief.

SEVENTY TWO

Darius

"If we enter here, is there another entrance?"

Edward shakes his head. "No, they blocked it off a long time ago so the servants wouldn't accidentally stumble upon it." He points to the side of the castle where a river seems to run near it. "There are tunnels underground through here."

"But they go to the courtyard," Darius says. "It's to give water to the castle there, access to it whenever they need."

"Yes," he agrees. "But further in, there is a tunnel that leads down into the cellar where Charles stores all the food he has stolen."

And that's what we want— no, what we need.

After going around to villages in the lands, then taking in those who were stolen from packs...our food sources are dangerously low, and this is the only solution.

Steal back what was stolen, or we will all starve.

"That basement has another entrance?" I ask, leaning down to inspect the drawings of Wolvorn Castle.

"Yes, only he, the other Highers and a select few know of that route."

"Then why didn't I?" I ask suspiciously.

I know Edward is Rhea's guardian and he's helped her, but he is also Higher Warden, one of *them*, no matter how many times he tells me he isn't.

I can't trust anything right now.

Not when it comes to Rhea's safety.

"I don't know, Charles once said he will let you know once you take your seat, that way..."

"I would be in on all of his plans and I wouldn't betray him."

"Yes," Edward sighs, a grimace on his face.

"So even after all I had done for him blindly, he still didn't trust me fully."

"Your father went against his words before the end of him. He was too wrapped up in his experiments to see sense. Charles saw that as a betrayal."

I shrug. "My father can rot in the below."

Edward nods. "A lot can."

"So we enter through here and then what?" Leo asks, studying the map just like the rest of us are.

It's Rhea who stays quiet on the other side of the table, her eyes roaming over the castle. She looks tired, a dirt mark on her cheek from cutting down trees and chopping wood earlier. Even the kid told her off for doing too much.

But I can see her need to help the people who are here, her need to make it right.

It is who she is, but it is also a weakness that won't make her think clearly sometimes, and that can jeopardize her safety.

It is why I made sure to include her in this meeting. I could have done this without her knowledge, but the idea of her finding out and going off on her own to try and help would send me over the edge, and her carefully-constructed Eridian would be in ruins if I were to find she was in danger again.

Hand swallowed by water, grasping something solid and then, it disappearing. Water enters my lungs but I need to get to her. I go deeper, lungs burning, legs kicking—

I shake out of those memories and keep my eyes on Rhea, letting my brain take her in to calm the unusual racing of my heart.

The one that belongs to her.

"Little wolf?" I say gently, so as not to startle her.

She picks at her fingers, and I send my power under the table, wrapping around her ankle when she doesn't respond. She jolts, looking at me and she stops at her picking.

"Good girl," I praise down the link, and a pretty, red hue covers her cheeks.

"We need a distraction," she tells the room, brows furrowed.

"Continue," I say, arms folding.

"If we make a disturbance at the front gate, the guards will go there and others can slip by, unnoticed.

"But they are killing anyone who dares defy Charles's orders," Damian says. "Anyone at the gate without invitation is hanged."

"I know." She nods. "But we need to do something to draw their attention, that way some can go through the tunnel unnoticed, or at least, kill those who are guarding it, because there will be guards, won't there?" she asks Edward and he nods.

"But that would mean we will have to split up," Taylor acknowledges, clearly not liking the idea.

"No way," Josh shouts, shaking his head.

"We can't split up," Colton speaks up, body tense, and I notice the way Hudson puts his hand on his back, trying to calm him.

"It's the only way," Rhea tells them. "We need that food."

"We have food in the forest," Leo says, but Rhea is shaking her head.

"There is barely anything left in our own reserves, and we cannot keep killing so much here, there will be nothing left, it goes against everything I stand for. I will not kill more than necessary. But I will not kill off all the animals here."

"This is necessary," Damian fires back.

"Killing the Highers is necessary," Rhea says, "and we need to be alive to do that!"

Leo throws his hands up. "Exactly!"

"We can do both," Zaide says, nodding to the map.

"What do you mean," Jerrod asks, the male sharpening his

axe.

"He means," I start, leaning over the table. "We can split up, cause a diversion, and have people port food out while the rest of us go for the Highers."

Zaide nods.

"Do we have enough people for that, are we even ready for an attack on the castle?"

"You will be," a voice says suddenly, and we turn to see Belldame strolling toward us, witches in tow who are bloodied and bruised.

Rhea gasps rushing over to her. "What happened?!"

I don't even question how the witch got into Eridian through our barrier as I look over the bloodied witches.

"The Highers attacked, our home is overrun by all manner of beasts," she gasps, teetering to the side and Rhea grabs her, holding her steady. "Janelle...She was killed instantly, along with her husband."

The Highers managed to finally enter Witches Rest? Anger rises to the surface and Drax growls within me.

This is bad.

Anna comes bounding over, rushing to her. "Grandmother!" she looks her over, checking for injury as Belldame reassures her. "How did this happen?!" she asks, and I don't see a hint of grief on her face about her sister.

"That is what I would like to know," I say, folding my arms.

"There are far too many, I couldn't hold the barrier," she says, breathing heavily as Anna helps her sit on one of the benches in the gathering, lowering her carefully.

"Many what?" Rhea asks.

"Of beasts and other witches. We were deceived by one of our own. They guided them through the mist and it was already too late by the time we realized. We lost so many..." I look at the witches and children, some lost in what must be horrifying memories.

"Leo, grab supplies and water," I say down the link, and he goes

off with Damian to do so.

If they have managed to get inside Witches Rest...

Belldame starts coughing, the sound deep and I know her lungs are full of liquid. "Grandmother!" Anna says, her hands instantly at her ribs as she closes her eyes and concentrates.

Edward sits beside her, hand on Belldame's shoulder as the old witch gives him a small smile, but suddenly, blood is coming out of her mouth as Anna moves her hands up her sternum.

"Sorry, Grandmother, we need to get it out." The witch nods, still choking and coughing up blood as Edward steadies her.

Rhea watches on, her face pale, but as she turns to me her eyes are full of fury.

I know that look. It is one of a warrior ready for battle, ready to kill those who hurt her family.

I nod.

Ready or not, we are attacking Wolvorn Castle, and many will die from both sides.

I know it.

She knows it.

We all know it.

War does not come without sacrifices, and as I told her before, war is death.

"We will gather everyone over the next week or so to select their role if they are joining the cause," I tell the others and they nod.

"I want...I want them all dead for what they have done to our home," Belldame chokes out.

Rhea nods. "We will kill them all."

"I am going to be fighting, right?" Kade asks as he swings at me and I side-step, dodging his fist and jabbing him in his kidney.

"No," I tell him, and he stops. That's a mistake. I jab at his shoulder, knocking him back and then I go for his legs, taking them out from under him.

He lands with a *thud*, but instead of getting up, he pants heavily on the cold ground, staring up into the breacher that covers us from the heavy snowfall.

"I need to fight," he says.

"No, you need to be here to protect others. That is your job as Alpha of Eridian when Rhea is away."

"That didn't work out so well the last time." It didn't.

"So change it this time. Get up, kid," I growl, pacing back and forth. We have been sparring since that day in the cabin, making sure he gets his frustration out on me, and me alone.

I also won't pass up a chance to hit the kid a time or two, to show him the Alpha he needs to be.

Rhea and her not-brother, but brother, Josh raised him, but they are far too soft on him. They have let him get away with too much for too long.

Well, I won't let him get away with the attitude he has sometimes, and I certainly won't let him get away with hurting Rhea.

Kade doesn't move, so I walk over to him and kick his side.

"Oww," he grumbles, his eyes flashing a moment, but after taking a deep breath, he gets himself under control.

Good, kid.

"Up, we do not have long before Rhea comes looking for either one of us, and you know she hates seeing us like this."

"Practicing?" he says, still laying on the floor and catching his breath.

"We both know it is more than that, kid." He averts his gaze.

What we do is a way to punish himself, let him wallow in self-loathing that I know all too well. But this way I can look out for the kid, for Rhea.

"Does she hate me?" he whispers quietly and I sigh, letting

my head fall back on my shoulders.

I am not the male to talk about this with. Can't he go to the blonde-haired bastard?

When he continues to look at me, I growl to myself. "She doesn't hate *me* kid, so do you really think she would hate you?" he shrugs his shoulders when I look back at him.

I loathe this shit.

I go over and crouch beside him. "The only reason your head is still on your shoulders is because Rhea would be devastated if you were not of these lands." He looks to me then, listening intently. "You hurt her bad, kid, we both have, but that female has the biggest heart of all the lands, and it is our job to make sure we take care of it, okay?"

He nods, moving to a sitting position, eyeing me for a moment.

"Are you two…mating?" he asks awkwardly, and I stare at him.

"She is my Vihnarn," I correct him, my tone serious.

His brows furrow. "But what does she mean to you?"

"She means…" I pause, trying to find the words to describe what she means to me, but the closest thing I can think of is, "everything," I tell him. "She means everything."

He watches me intently, and I see the innocence of a young male peeking through as he thinks about my words.

"Does Mom think it's everything?" he asks quietly, and protectiveness shines in his eyes for Rhea.

Maybe I can like the kid a little for that.

I shrug. Her actions say as much, and when we became one under the moonlight as we were always meant to be, it felt like I meant that much to her. But. "All I can do, kid, is make her happy, safe and give her everything she asks for. She knows I will spend the rest of my days giving that to her."

"And she forgives you? For what you did?"

I look away, then. "She told me she forgives me, and I'm learning to forgive myself, thanks to her. The only reason I am doing that is because she asked it of me."

There is an uncomfortable silence that he eventually breaks. "And what if you can't forgive yourself?"

My eyes swing to his, but he's looking down at his clenched hands.

"We have to try for her, kid. It makes her unhappy, and I won't make her unhappy, we clear?" His head lifts at my tone and he blinks wide eyes at me.

"You love her?"

I rise, holding out my hand to him, which he takes after a moment.

"What I feel for her goes beyond words. Now, let's see how Axis and Drax compare."

He smirks at me for avoiding my answer, and then his wolf is there.

Axis shakes out his fur, and I am glad his control is getting better.

I raise a hand and then Draxton is out, staring down the smaller wolf.

"You may be at a height disadvantage," I tell the kid. "But your opponent, no matter who, always has a weakness. You just have to find it."

Drax gets ready to pounce, and I grab his fur. "No flames." He huffs at me, but the flames on his back die down, and then the wolves collide.

He holds his own as they spar, I will give the kid that, he's getting in his own nips in, though it is clear he is always on the defensive.

But it will keep him alive.

"Where are you?" Rhea's voice sounds in my mind and I smile, leaning back against a tree.

"Missing me again?"

I can't see her roll her eyes, but I know she is. *"Yeah,"* she says, and I still for a moment, not expecting that reply.

I stand straighter, walking away from the wolves and following that pull that will always lead me to her.

"Are you done with checking the perimeter?" I ask, stalking through the trees and making my way to her.

"Yes, no sign of rogues, beasts or anything else."

"Good."

She has been doing this multiple times a day, and once when I watched her go for the fourth time in one day, Josh told me she got like that after an attack years ago also, when some broke through the barrier. He told me to just let her do it for her own peace of mind, so I do.

"So, where are you?" she asks again, and I smirk to myself as I spot her near the lilk trees, palm to it as she closes her eyes.

I lean against a tree, not answering her and just watch the female that has turned me inside out. She's wrapped up in a cloak, hood covering her head and her gentler breaths can be seen with every exhale.

Winter is definitely here, and so too will her heat be soon.

I don't think she knows it, but I have sensed it coming for a little while now.

I have also made sure every male in the vicinity stays well away from her after the gathering. They know their life is in my hands if they so much as go near her with the intent to try to mate with her.

The thought has my magic coming to my feet, and Rhea smiles.

She knows I'm here.

Removing myself from the tree, I walk up behind her and wrap my arms around her waist. She leans back into me, sighing in my embrace as I pull her hood down and nuzzle into her neck, scenting her.

I growl, nipping at her throat as she releases a soft moan.

"Hi," she whispers, her hand coming up to the back of my neck and stroking there. I shiver.

"Found you, little wolf," I murmur the first words that I ever said to her. She releases a small laugh at that, turning in my arms and going on her tiptoes to place a gentle kiss on my lips.

Well, that won't do.

I hold her close to me, my hand going to her jaw to keep her still as she parts her lips for me and lets me in.

I groan at her taste, at the wildness that is always there, and I press her back into the tree, letting her only *feel* what she does to me, my cock straining in my pants, but also what she means to me.

I kiss her like I can't breathe without her, because I can't.

I kiss her like she holds my heart within her, because she does.

And I kiss her like she's everything, because she is.

I break the kiss and Rhea looks up at me, her lips puffy, cheeks slightly red and I run the back of my fingers down them.

"Come," I say, grabbing her hand and leading her.

"Where are we going?"

I smile. "Somewhere we will not be disturbed."

"But don't we need to plan? I know we still need to distribute some weapons, and we are waiting for those in Colhelm—"

I turn, placing a possessive kiss to her lips. "Little wolf?"

"Yeah?" she breathes, looking slightly dazed.

"Hush and let me take care of you."

Her eyes bounce between mine before she says quietly, "okay."

SEVENTY THREE

Rhea

"Will you braid my hair when we eventually leave for Wolvorn?" I ask Darius, as he washes us in my cave.

His fingers freeze briefly before resuming. "I am not very good at it, you know this."

"You're getting better." I tip my head back when he guides me, washing the suds out. "Vallier," I whisper, looking up at him from where I float in the water.

His eyes come to mine, and I see the moment he relents. I smile.

"Sneaky little wolf, you know I cannot resist your eyes." He tries to sound stern, but he fails.

We are silent as he continues to wash my hair, taking more time than needed and I get it, we don't know what will happen tomorrow.

We don't know if we will ever see this cave again…the wisps…or play in a field of lesia flowers.

"If anything were to happen to you…" I voice the thought that has been rolling through my mind since we decided to attack Wolvorn.

We have spent so much time as enemies, I want to spend time as Vihnarns. I want to experience peace with him. I want him to feed me as I feed him, I want to run with our wolves and as wolves. I want a simple life with him by my side.

When I fell off the cliff, I thought that was it, so to be able to be back here, with him and my family, only to then have it ripped away from me again...

Is my fate so cruel?

"Nothing short of your safety could pry me away from you, little wolf," he assures me. "You will lead a distraction while others get the supplies, and then Elites will fight from inside the courtyard. You will make it out of this Rhea, I vow it," he says vehemently, his power coming to wrap beneath me.

I stare up into the opening, watching the few wisps up there as I look to the moon.

"And you?" I whisper, "Will you make it out of this?"

"Where you are, I will be, Rhea." He looks at me, his fingers traveling down my temple as my markings appear. He follows the trail of lines, looking deep in thought as he follows his fingers with his gaze. "The most important thing is for you to be safe through all of this, after this."

"And what about what's important to me," I whisper.

"And what's that?" he murmurs, eyes still fixated on my face.

"You," I reply down the link without hesitation, without holding back and his eyes flash black, causing the breath to stall in my lungs.

He hauls me up into him, my legs instantly going around his waist as he moves us out of the water and then the furs are at my back.

He settles between my legs, his hard cock resting on my stomach but all he does is stare down at me.

It's silent, but his eyes speak loud enough and I swallow at the emotion swimming in them, the emotion he's letting me see and I have never seen so much of it.

It causes a lump to lodge in my throat, it causes me to have my hands dig into his arms so nothing can peel me away from him.

"I never thought," he begins, his voice full of gravel. He clears his throat and tries again, but for some reason, he's unable to get the words out. Instead, he lowers himself so he's hovering above my face, elbows on either side of me as he speaks through our link. *"I never thought I would be blessed enough to have someone in my life after my mother and sister died. I thought about it so deeply that I let it sink into my mind, and then it became so warped that I would never want anyone anyway, because if my family can get ripped away so easily, why would I want anything else to let the same thing happen."* He didn't want to get hurt. Tears sting my eyes at his words. I don't know if he understands why he did that, but he was trying to protect himself. He curls both of his hands into my hair. "Little wolf," he whispers aloud now, eyes bouncing between mine, his voice rough. "I'm glad it's you," he says, rubbing his nose to mine as a tear finally falls.

"I'm glad I tried to kill you that day," I tell him and he grins.

"You were so fierce, little wolf."

"Your little wolf."

"My little wolf."

My throat closes with emotion as I bring my hand up to the marking on his neck. "Always," I vow, my eyes on him, my meaning clear.

We will always be, there is no alternative.

"Effiniar," he murmurs. *Indefinite.*

I push him onto his back and he willingly goes, his eyes curious.

I run my hands over his chest as he grabs my waist, his thumbs rubbing over me. Taking a breath, I lean down, kissing him softly before I leave a trail down his neck. He sucks in a sharp breath when I nip there, and I smile against him as he grunts, his cock hardening further between us. Then I follow a path down his tattoos, paying extra attention to the lesia flower he had done for me and he moans, muscles contracting as his stare burns me alive.

When I move on and get to the trail of hair that leads down, I bite next to it and he growls, his hips lifting and I feel the pre-cum that now coats my skin between my breasts with the position that I'm in.

I look up and his pupils are blown wide, jaw tense and I

smile, rubbing the tattoos on the side of his ribs before I lower further, still trailing kisses. When I get to the base of his cock, he groans, eyes pinned on mine.

I start kissing him, my lips trailing up his hardness, following a vein there, and when I get to the tip I lick the pre-cum there, savoring it and he releases a harsh breath.

"Little wolf." His gruff voice ends on a groan as I take the head in my mouth, swirling my tongue around him slowly, taking my time to taste him. "Fuck."

I look up and see his hands clenching at his sides, the possessiveness and burning desire swirling in his eyes, and I know he's holding himself back.

"There is only you, Vihnarn." His eyes flare at the meaning as he understands. No matter before him, there is only him. The rest do not count.

"Fuck, little wolf." He sounds pained, his brows creasing but I see pride in his eyes, I see adoration for me.

"Touch me," I whisper, before I take the head in my mouth again.

On a groan, Darius raises a hand to me. I expect him to grip my hair tightly, the way I like it, to control my movement as I've given him the okay.

But he does neither.

He leans up on one elbow, his abs rippling with the movement, as he places a hand on top of my head and slides it down my face, stroking my cheek. My eyes flutter shut at the softness of it.

I moan around him, causing him to groan and his muttered curse words spur me on. I'm doing this to him, only me.

Possessiveness takes *me* then, and I get up on my knees and take him deeper, sucking him tighter even as I gag.

"Shit, Rhea you don't have to… *fuck…fuck.*" His cock is nearly in my throat, I feel him there, but I can feel I'm about to gag again so I pull back, making sure my mouth is sealed tightly around him as I breathe through my nose.

I run a hand up his thigh, my short nails scratching there as a heat consumes me, causing more wetness to drip down my thighs. His hand does go to my head then, his fingers tight in my hair and I squirm.

"Keep going," he says in a low tone, his breathing harsh. "Good girl," he praises when I continue. "Take more of me, you can do it, that's it. Your doing so good...*fuck*." I moan around him again at his praise, and his hips thrust up at it, but then he pauses.

My eyes flick up to him, and we stare at each other before I nod. *"I want to taste you , Darius, don't hold back and let me taste you."*

On a groan, his hips pump up into my mouth gently, not going too deep, but his noises of pleasure get louder.

My hands rest on his thighs as I continue to squirm, my pussy pulsing around nothing, needing to be filled and I whine, a cramping in my belly starting and I pause, recognizing it.

Darius inhales and a smile spreads across his face, never once stopping his thrusting as a rumble comes from his chest.

"Your heat is beginning little wolf." I whine again. "This time will be different." He assures me on another pump of his hips. "I'm here from the start, I won't allow you any pain, I will care for you, just like I always should have." Another thrust. "Touch yourself, get ready for me."

I hesitantly lower my hand and skirt around my clit, jolting at the sensation while Darius slowly fucks my mouth.

"Two fingers, Rhea, quickly. Stretch yourself good, I need to be inside you. As much as I want to come down your throat, I need to feel you squeezing me, it will help you. Let me fill you," he groans, his breathing turning heavy.

I whimper, pressing two fingers inside of me and my own hips roll, the sound of my wetness reaching my ears. I'm not even embarrassed that he's watching me do this, it feels too good.

Darius's thrusts speed up, his breathing ragged, and as pleasure builds within me at hearing him, my pussy tightens around my fingers.

Darius pulls me off his cock by my hair, then hauls me on top of him. I cry out at being so close, but I'm crying out even more as he slams me down on his cock.

"Oh Gods." My hands land on his chest as he bounces me up and down, his muscles bulging in his arms as I feel him stretch me. "Darius," I moan, and when he moves a hand to my clit and rubs me in a circular motion. I come instantly.

It hits me so strong and so fast, my nails digging into his flesh as my body shakes almost violently.

"Fuck, fuck, fuck," Darius says on each thrust up into me, his head falling back, his tendons showing in his neck and then I feel the heat of his release inside of me. I rock my hips, my small moans and whimpers echoing around the cave as I can't seem to stop moving.

I want more.

More, more, more.

My stomach cramps, and I prepare myself for the worst of the pain to come, the pain I always get, but it's barely there right now as I move back and forth on Darius.

I realize why. His cock is soothing me.

I whimper as his hands grip my hips softly as he helps me rock back and forth.

"Take what you need from me, little wolf," Darius says, his hands soothing as he calls his power to cool my overheated skin. "I'm here, I won't leave. Use me."

"Darius," I whimper as another cramp comes, and I'm once again afraid of the pain that would follow, but it only hurts a little.

He pulls me down with a hand around my throat, and slowly thrusts up into me, letting me feel all of him. *"He's still hard,"* I think to myself, closing my eyes and feeling myself building again.

"Of course I'm hard," he says back, and I didn't realize I said

that to him in my mind. *"I can smell you. It calls to me, calls to the Alpha in me to make sure your needs are sated."* He glides back and forth inside of me, and every time my pussy squeezes, the fullness he gives me soothes it. *"This time will be different,"* he assures me, now kissing along my neck. *"I will show you how a Vihnarn takes care of you, how only I can take care of you. There will be no fight, just us."*

I groan, falling into him as another cramp hits. His thrusts increase, and my lips go to his neck as I scratch him.

"Be a good girl and bite me." I do, my teeth breaking into his skin and he speeds up his movements, so much so that the slapping of our skin can be heard. A gush of wetness follows and Darius growls, his hands bruising on my hips now as he slams me down on him harder.

My belly swirls and then I'm coming again, calling his name into my bite, my body tingling.

Darius lets out a long groan, his hips losing their rhythm as he once again releases inside of me, growling like the animal he can be.

"Fill me," I say breathlessly as I release him from my teeth. "Fill me up, Vihnarn." My mind begins to turn hazy, my pulse pounding in my ears as my voice becomes slurred. *"Don't stop. Never stop."*

I'm flat on my back, and Darius hovers over me before entering me again, almost violently as his stare looks into my soul.

"Never, I won't ever stop," he snarls down at me, spreading my legs wide as he pounds into my pussy. "You're mine, little wolf, all fucking mine."

"Yours," I whimper, my back arching as I can feel another orgasm right on the edge. Oh Gods, this has never happened so quickly, and I haven't felt one so strong.

"You're about to come again, aren't you." I nod frantically, clawing at the furs beneath me. "Then be a good girl and give it to me." He bends down and takes a nipple in his mouth, sucking and licking and when he bites down, I'm soaring again, getting dizzy from it.

Darius murmurs words to me, tells me how he will always keep me full, that he will feed and fuck me.

I pull him up to my mouth, rolling my hips and I can feel his cum leaking out of me, but I need more.

And when Darius starts to pump his hips again, the haze completely takes over.

Darius is slowly fucking me as I come down from my heat, biting and nibbling at my skin as he rubs his come into my belly.

How did that get there? And why was it wasted?

His chuckles bring my tired eyes to his, and he shakes his head at me. "It was just some that leaked out of you, little wolf. None was wasted."

I hum, feeling the soreness of my body as I wrap my arms around his neck, pulling him down as he comes inside of me once again.

He groans into the kiss that he gives me. It's soft, not full of overwhelming need as we both come down. Sweat drips off of his skin, his power roaming over me to help cool me down and I sigh at the sensation.

He chuckles and breaks the kiss, but I keep my eyes closed as he carries me.

My legs go uselessly around his waist, absolutely boneless but he's so strong that it doesn't matter that I'm dead weight right now.

He lowers us into the pool, sinking down until we are sitting right on the edge. I lean my head on his shoulder tiredly as he splashes water on me. I lift a hand to his chest and feel his strong and steady heartbeat, letting its rhythm relax me further as my aching and tired muscles scream at me.

"I've got you," he whispers into my ear, placing a kiss on my head as he continues to rinse me.

"Thank you," I croak out, and he holds me tighter, wrapping his arms around my waist and burying his face into my neck.

"You do not need to be thankful for what I am supposed to do, little wolf."

I run my hand down his chest and rest it at his hip in the water. "I've never had someone take care of me like that before," I whisper, and I regret it immediately when he tenses. I just ruined it. "I didn't mean…"

"No." He shushes me, playing with the ends of my hair. "I didn't do this last time like I should have. I shouldn't have treated you like I did. I'm sorry."

"No more sorry's," I tell him as sternly as I can as I wrap my hand around his hardening cock. I move over him and sink down, whimpering at being so sore but, I need to be close to him.

"Careful, Rhea, take it easy," he chastises, holding me to keep me still.

"I just need to stay here," I say, cheeks turning red. He pulls my hair back and looks over me, raising a brow.

"Adorable." I start to feel stupid, but then he pulls me closer, settling in more as the small waves of water splash against us. "This is definitely better, why haven't we done this before?" he murmurs, and I can tell he's tired too.

I don't even know how many days it's been, and with the haze slowly lifting from my mind, I can remember the amount of times Darius took me.

Gods he hasn't stopped.

"How long has it been?" I sigh into his skin, feeling so content, feeling so cared for.

His hand rubs at my back as I look at all the marks I have left on him. "Four days."

Four days! It has never lasted that long.

"I didn't realize I was about to have my heat, usually I know."

"Your heat came early last time, and you didn't know then," he reminds me.

"I still don't know why that happened."

"Because your Vihnarn was near." I lift my head at that. "Really?"

He curls a piece of hair around his fingers and he kisses me softly, like he can't help himself. "Yes. I suspect it's also why you didn't know this time either, but I knew it was coming. I am meant to soothe your heat, and make it as comfortable for you as possible, less painful. Maybe that is why you didn't realize." There is a silent question in his eyes at that.

"You soothed everything," I tell him, leaning forward and giving him a gentle kiss, and his body relaxes at that.

Was he worried?

"Good," he says, pulling me back into his neck, his cock twitching inside of me but neither of us do anything about it, just relaxing in the subtle pleasure of it. "Now rest, I got you."

I fully believe he does this time.

SEVENTY FOUR

Rhea

"Hello, um, Rhea?" I pause, the axe held high as I turn and spot Deedrie, the female from The Drylands.

I drop the axe down and wipe my dirty hands on my pants. "Hey, everything okay?"

She swallows roughly and nods. "I just." She shakes her head. "We wanted to thank you?"

"We?" I question, looking at her and then at the tree line behind her. At first, I don't see anyone, but then a female comes through, and then a child. Then more and more come through, walking hesitantly but determined as they come toward Deedrie.

I pick at my fingers, swallowing over the lump in my throat as they all come toward me, small smiles on their faces.

"Breathe, little wolf," Darius says in my mind and I take a breath.

I hear paws behind me, and Runa comes from my back, stepping up beside me. The woman and children eye her warily, but they have seen her walking around Eridian enough to know she won't hurt them.

"Hi," I say to everyone, lifting a hand and stroking Runa's side as she nuzzles my neck in greeting. She has no doubt been off in the forest with Drax as usual.

"We wanted to thank you, for all that you have done for us."

"Oh, there is no need." I wave a hand in the air.

"There is every need," Mivera says, coming through the

crowd toward me. "You saved us all when we thought all was lost."

I shake my head. "I was just there at the right time."

"Do not sell yourself short," Darius murmurs, and my eyes go to the trees, seeing him leaning up against one with Drax at his side.

"You knew of this?"

"I heard them murmuring about thanking you for a while now."

"It is unnecessary," I tell him, eyeing the others.

"What you have done for these people is more than they ever thought they would be able to get. You saved them."

My pack comes through the crowd next, and I clear my throat. "I...I'm just glad you are all okay."

"You made it so, Alpha," Seb says, smiling at me softly.

"I didn't do it on my own," I tell them.

"But without you, we wouldn't have felt safe," Deedrie tells me, then, she gets to her knees and bares her neck.

I watch her in shock, but then Mivera goes to her knees next, and then Seb, and then...they are all on their knees. Even Anna.

"I— What?" I stumble over my words, trying to take deep breaths.

"Thank you, Heir of Zahariss for your protection, and bringing back our hope."

Her words stun me silent, my eyes wide as I look across all the women and children, and my pack.

I spot Josh and Sarah, Taylor, Hudson and Colten. Then I see Katy and Oscar with Jerrod and other members of my pack along with Sybill and Sam. Then I see Leo, Damian, fuck, even Zaide is here, The Elites are here.

My eyes move further back and I spot Kade. My handsome son, pride shining in his eyes as he nods his head at me, and then he also goes to his knees, tilting his head. *"Thank you, mom."*

Oh Gods.

The first tear falls and my eyes go to Darius.

He's still leaning against the tree, a soft, proud smile on his face as he watches me intently. *"You are everything, my Vihnarn. To me, to them. You are the hope that was lost."*

"Darius."

"Accept their loyalty, little wolf."

"And yours?"

"You will always have my loyalty, in this life and the next."

I smile, and then I sob, emotions overwhelming me as I go to Deedrie, my knees joining her on the ground.

"We are hope," I tell her, tell them all as I sniffle and grab her hands in my own. "Without your bravery, hope cannot be there, don't you see?"

She eyes me curiously, as do the others.

"Do not think you are below me. I may be an Heir, I may be an Alpha, but I'm just a female wanting a simple life with those she loves." I smile softly, looking at my pack and then peeking at Darius. "I'm sure you all want that too." They nod, and I stand, holding my hand out. "Let's spend the time we have in whatever peace we can find."

Deedrie laughs, nodding her head as she says, "I want to run." And then she's a wolf. Then another changes, another and another, until all of a sudden, there are dozens of wolves in front of me.

Runa stands at my back, chest puffed out when she lets out a long howl, her head raising and the others joining in, a song of hope and peace as they take off, running past me and Runa and into the trees.

My pack nipping at my fingers as they pass, rubbing up against my legs as they follow after them, the Elites not far behind. Kade is last, his blue eyes on mine as he nuzzles into me before he takes off with Sam on his back, her being too young for her own wolf to have come yet.

I turn and watch them go with Runa, and then she moves away from me but I don't stop staring, hearing them in the distance as they run free for a while.

Is this what the future could be like if I right the wrongs?

Could this be our never-ending peace?

A purring sound comes behind me, and I look over my shoulder to see Runa on her back, legs in the air as Darius rubs her belly.

That fucking traitor.

Drax sits off to the side, giving his keeper the stink eye and I walk over and join him, leaning against the mass of his body as we look down at the begrudging cuteness happening in front of me.

They know we can see them, and they don't even care.

Runa licks Darius's face, and Drax snaps his teeth, a warning growl coming from him, causing Darius to smirk.

"Stop being so possessive Drax." I raise a brow at him.

I walk around Drax and come up behind Darius, and without hesitation, I launch myself at his back, climbing on him. "Hey!" We fall forward on Runa, and Drax comes to us, standing over us as he tries to get to Runa as Runa scrambles to stand. I laugh as Darius rolls us, but I'm soon pushing him off of me as the big oaf weighs far too much.

"Gods," I wheeze, rolling on my belly and breathing deeply. "I thought I was a goner."

"Stop being so dramatic," Darius laughs, hauling me up and placing a kiss to my lips as our wolves play.

"I could have died," I say breathless as he nudges his nose with mine.

"Not in my presence." I smile, and then he's grabbing my hips and placing me on Runa.

He jumps on Drax and they take off, running into the trees toward where we can hear the others howling.

The smile doesn't leave my face as we chase them, and I tilt my head back, releasing my own howl as Darius laughs at me, smiling more than I have ever seen him.

This is what we will be fighting for in the coming days, and I'll be damned if it gets stolen from me before it has even begun.

"Faster, little wolf, let's run until we can't run anymore."

And we do.

That night, when the lands were quiet, Darius took me to a new clearing of lesia flowers and made me see more than stars as he pleasured me over and over again.

Like it was the last time.

Because it might be.

SEVENTY FIVE

Rhea

"We will get through this, child," Belldame says as we stand around the gathering, preparing ourselves to port out to Wolvorn Castle.

Apprehension swirls inside of me, looking over the amount of people from the lands who have chosen to fight with us over staying in Eridian with Kade.

"I hope this plan works."

"I don't think the Highers suspect an attack so soon, especially after their slaughter upon Witches Rest," Belldame says.

I look to her as grief clouds her eyes. She lost so many, and lost her home. I know what that feels like.

"We will help you rebuild," I tell her, grabbing her weathered hand in mine and squeezing.

She nods. "After we kill them all."

"Every single one of them." I agree.

"Us witches have been waiting for this moment for a long time. Now, more than ever." I look over the witches that will come with me to attack the front of the castle walls.

I can tell they are also hurting, but revenge bleeds through their eyes,

An eye for an eye.

Blood for blood.

I turn to her at that, and smile at the hard look in her eyes. "Always so bloodthirsty."

She looks me dead in the eye. "I will boil the blood in their veins until they feel like there is a fire within their belly, and they will be burned from the inside out."

"Make sure it hurts."

Belldame places her palm to my cheek, and I lean into the touch. "Your mother would be so proud of you." I take a deep breath.

"I hope she is."

My eyes glance to Sarah as she helps Josh place blades in the holder on his hips, her eyes shimmering as she mutters soft words to him. Colten and Hudson are off to the side, Hudson's head bowed as he speaks to the younger male, his hands flexing at his sides. Always protective.

My eyes move to Seb next, he stands with Zaide, both flipping a blade in their hands, and I grin at the smile on Seb's face. He's probably taunting him about how he has better knife skills, when really, they are probably the same. Taylor speaks with Jerrod and Damian further ahead, all of their arms folded, and I wonder if they are going over formations, again.

Kade is sitting on a bench, his eyes bruised around the edge and I know he has been sparring with Darius recently. It pains me, but he's having less outbursts that come with confusion, so I'm trying to tell myself that it's helping.

Darius says it is.

Sam perches next to him, her eyes lowered but he looks at her, his eyes shining full of concern. She doesn't speak, she just looks into the fire at the center and I can tell he doesn't like seeing her like this. So sad, so withdrawn.

I can't blame her with the horrors she must have seen in The Drylands, only she hasn't spoken to anyone about it.

I'm not even sure she has told Kade.

She will be staying here with Kade, Sarah, and the rest of our pack, along with the people who chose to stay out of the fight. Not that I blame them. What we are doing is risky, but like Belldame said, they will not suspect an attack so soon.

Even Edward agrees.

Kade strokes a hand over Sam's head, and when she doesn't so much as blink at the contact, Kade's shoulders slump.

"She will be okay," I tell him, and his head whips up to me.

"She hasn't spoken to me since she found out about everyone attacking the castle."

I nod. *"I know, but in time, she will, Carzan, she will."*

He nods, shuffling closer to her to comfort her.

"The kid needs to learn patience."

I huff out a laugh as I reply to Darius. *"Like you?"*

He pauses at that. *"I can be patient."*

"Just not with me," I quip.

"Definitely not with you."

My eyes move to Darius at that. Leo is talking to him, his hands moving as they are obviously deep in conversation, but Darius's eyes are on me.

I nod my head to Leo. *"Don't be rude."*

"I'm not."

"He's talking to you." I laugh.

"And this is more important."

My brows furrow. "*What is?*"

"Looking at you." Damn if my cheeks don't heat at that. "*Adorable.*"

"Shut up."

Runa scratches inside of me, walking forward and I sigh, raising my hand and letting her materialize.

She shakes out her fur, looking back at me and I nod, accepting my damn fate.

"Go on then," I say to her as Belldame chuckles beside me.

She trots over to Darius, who already has his body turned to her, with her tail held high. When she is close enough, her head goes straight to his neck and he raises a hand to hold her there, stroking her neck... I nearly collapse in a puddle.

Yes, my wolf is a traitor for the enemy, well, ex enemy, but I guess I am too as I can't help but smile at them both.

Leo looks to me, to Runa, and then shakes his head. He has

a smile on his face though, and I can tell he's happy for Darius.

All his closest are.

"So, ready to boil blood?" Anna asks suddenly and I startle, just now noticing her. She sighs dramatically. "Don't let a male get the advantage over you, Rhea, I could have attacked you."

I side-eye her. "Don't pretend you didn't come here to get a better look at an Elite yourself."

She glances away. "I don't know what you're talking about.

"Hmm," I say, sharing a grin with Belldame as I see a blade suddenly stop moving out of the corner of my eyes.

"Just don't boil his blood, granddaughter, that's not how we find a mate."

"Can you have mates?" I ask, never hearing that before.

Belldame looks to Anna and then to me. "No, but we can still have a connection that's deep."

"That's enough."

"Is it?" Anna mutters, her eyes flicking to Seb and Zaide before quickly averting them.

"It was for Josie and Danny."

She nods at that. "It was."

"Can you boil their blood much?" I wonder.

Anna turns and smiles at me. I eye her, and when I suddenly feel heat in my legs, an almost bubbling sensation, I look down at that.

"Okay," I mutter. "Point taken, don't do that again." She laughs as Belldame chuckles, but we soon sober up.

"We will live out this day." Anna says, grabbing my hand.

I nod. "We will take nothing less."

Taking a breath, I catch Kade's eyes and nod my head off to the side. With a hesitant look at Sam, he gets up and follows me as I head into the trees.

I can feel Darius's eyes on me, but he doesn't say anything, knowing I need a moment.

We walk through the forest in silence. The snow has stopped falling for now, but the ground is still covered from this morning.

Every step has it crunching under my feet, the cold wrapping around me as I continue until I reach the lilk trees, all still in bloom.

I stop and wait for Kade to catch up as I admire them.

It doesn't take long until he stands beside me, both of us looking up at the trees and feeling the subtle caress of the invisible barrier in front of us.

"It's really been a long time since you first crossed here to get Sarah," he says, and I nod my head.

"It changed everything that day." It was the start of what could be the end.

"I still wonder if it's for the better."

I watch as the branches move, the orange and pink coloring the white of its background, as snow clings to them.

"It has to be for the better," I tell him. "We do not know what will happen today, or the next, or another moon cycle." I turn to him, and he does the same. "We cannot just lay down and roll over anymore." I lift a hand and cup his cheek, smiling at the feeling of the small hairs there. "We have to do better, be better. Nothing will change otherwise."

"There is only us," he says, looking down to the ground.

I pull him to me, my hand going to the back of his head. "It starts with one, Carzan. It just starts with one."

"I won't let anything happen to her," Darius says as he emerges from the trees. I knew he was there for once, the connection thrumming between us.

I give him a thankful glance, and Kade looks at him.

After a moment, he walks towards him, and I tense, wondering how this will go.

I keep out of their way when they spar, and interactions when I have been near have been civil. It still causes worry in the back of my mind, though.

They stare at each other for a moment, the air tense and I pull my cloak around myself, nerves wracking through me.

Kade is the one to eventually breaks that silence.

"She has to come back. Come home." Darius nods, eyeing him. "Vow it to me."

Darius raises a brow at him as Runa can be seen with Drax, plodding around in the background.

"Will you believe it if I do?" Darius asks him.

"I will."

"Then I vow it," he says without hesitation. "She will come back home."

Kade nods, shuffling on his feet but Darius, again, waits him out.

"Take care of my mom," he says, I inhale a breath, closing my eyes and cherishing him calling me that.

When I blink my eyes open, Darius is watching me, seeing the emotions play on my face and his jaw ticks.

Still, he looks back to Kade and says, "she is mine, which means." His hands flex. "You are also mine. So I will protect her, like I will protect you." Kade and I both seem to freeze at that, lost for words. "However, I will kick your ass if I need to."

I huff out a laugh, and Kade follows, shaking his head. "I know. I…I would hope you would. If I need it."

Runa comes out of the forest then, Drax on her tail and she goes to Kade, licking his face and almost purring into him. Drax comes to me, inhaling at my neck and my arms wrap around him, holding him close.

"Arbiel canna," I say.

"Arbiel canna," Kade echoes nuzzling Runa.

We look to Darius, who looks extremely uncomfortable, but still, he says, "arbiel canna."

***

"Eyes sharp, ears alert," Darius says as he lays next to me. "Call me through the link if you need me. I will be there no matter what, Rhea. I will always—"

I cut Darius off by leaning up on my elbow and sealing my lips to his. "I know," I whisper against his lips before laying back down on the ground.

He has told me this many times now, in many different ways and I know he's worried.

We all are.

I snuggle deeper next to him, surrounded by lesia flowers as we look up to the moon. I wanted to be close to him the night before we leave for Wolvorn and Darius always knowing, brought me here, which has become one of my favorite places in all the lands.

"Can we play here when we get back?" I ask him, and he moves so his arm is under my head as a pillow.

"Of course you can play here, little wolf." I smile at that and sigh into him, because well, it's freezing.

Runa runs through the flowers, and we both watch as Drax chases her, playfully nipping at her tail. I chuckle.

"She is so going to beat his ass soon."

"Just the way he likes it." I don't have to look to know he's grinning.

"Are Leif and his dad still in my cave?" I ask, watching our wolves play makes me think of them.

Darius nuzzles into the top of my head as I lean my head on his chest. "Yes. He's fully recovered but I think he knows his son will be safe there."

Thinking about that pack sends a pain through my heart. "It's not fair."

"I know," he says, dragging me so I'm on top of him. Drax and Runa come over after a while and curl themselves around us.

Runa licks Darius's cheek before mine, and then rests her head on his arm, opposite me. Drax comes to her back, laying down and resting his head on her shoulder. Darius calls his magic and twines it around them both and I sigh at the feel of them all.

I yawn. "I don't want to sleep. I don't want to miss anything."

Darius purrs softly and runs a hand through my hair. "You will be back here soon enough."

"Vow it?" I ask him, needing more reassurance. I feel like my future is but within my grasp, and once again, it will somehow get taken away from me.

"I vow it. I won't allow anything to happen to you, Vihnarn. So rest easy," Darius says, and the seriousness in his tone settles me a little.

It makes me believe that maybe, just maybe we have a fighting chance and that we will be back here, playing in the lesia flowers under the moonlight.

Just like we were always meant to be.

I lift my head from Darius, staring into my favorite eyes as he smiles sadly at me, raising a hand to trace along my jaw.

My throat clogs with emotion that this could be the last time we get to be like this.

Darius shakes his head. *"Do not think like that,"* he says in my mind.

"How do you always know?"

"I am your Vihnarn," he replies, like that explains it, and it kind of does.

We are each other's half.

"How can I miss you when you are still right in front of me?" I say aloud, my eyes taking in everything, down to the small scar on his nose.

He breathes deeply, his chest expanding. "Maybe we are missing all the time we spent being enemies, when we could have had this."

"Maybe." My hands come to the side of his neck, running my finger over the mark that calls him my Vihnarn as I watch.

It's a half moon, but at the bottom, it has three lines through it, and at the top, two dots rest above each other, just above the curve of the moon. I have the exact same mark on my forearm, a mirror of its image.

I feel his magic beneath my fingertips, and I sink mine into it, causing Darius to release a purring sound.

"Always," I say, my eyes going back to him.

"Always."

I undo his pants, his hard cock already waiting and he quickly rids me of mine, grabbing my hair and pulling me into his heavy kiss. I place a hand between us, rubbing his cock against me to coat him with my wetness and then I lower myself, moaning into his mouth as he grunts, his hips lifting to chase me as I rise.

"I just want to feel you," I say, never breaking the kiss as we find a rhythm.

Our kiss may be rough and filled with desire, but our movements are slow, cherishing the feeling of one another like this.

"Vihnarn," Darius moans into my mouth and I rock against him. "Fuck, you feel so good."

I whimper, placing my hands on his chest as he watches where we are joined. I look down, seeing his cock shine with me and I release a shuddering breath.

"That's it, take me deeper, good girl." I grind my clit against him, my body trembling and he grits his teeth when I feel him swelling inside of me.

His magic comes to me, the coolness rolling over my clit and I toss my head back.

So close…so close.

"Look at me." The demand has my head falling forward as hands grip my waist, one roaming up my body to pinch my nipple. "You will look at me while you come."

And I do. Never once taking my eyes off the one who is just for me as he fills me, he groans, his grip tightening, and I moan at the look of satisfaction in his eyes as I make him feel that pleasure.

It makes me preen, makes me feel taller.

And when he pulls me down on top of him, catching our breath, we never once break our connections…knowing it could be our last.

SEVENTY SIX

Rhea

The castle looks like a foreboding shadow, standing tall and proud, the Highers's emblems raised on flags, blowing high in the icy wind.

Death feels like it's hanging in the air, and if I breathe in deep enough, I'm sure I can smell the metallic tang that comes with bloodshed.

My pack waits at the back of the large crowd that has gathered, looking at the platform up ahead that must have just been built recently.

It stands just to the right of the castle gates that keep everyone out…and others in.

It didn't take long for us to realize why the crowd had gathered, why melancholy floats through the air like poison.

It's another hanging.

Three women on their tiptoes balance precariously on the stools beneath them, their arms tied behind their backs as they await their fate on the newly-built wooden platform.

It isn't like they can use the battlements on the walls, they are already filled with a sickening number of bodies.

The female's crimes?

Stealing food for a hungry son.

Not paying enough food tax.

Trying to get through the castle gates for safety away from the rogures.

As I hear more and more of these…*crimes* being announced,

I look at the long line of other females waiting their turn to the left of the gate, looking tired and hungry, and I see a pattern here.

They are all females...

We pull our hoods tighter, making sure they are covering us and our masks are firmly in place as we conceal ourselves amongst the people.

The blood witches and some Elites hide within, along with my pack and some villagers who want to help in the fight, waiting for this distraction.

In what could be the last time that we draw breath if we are not careful.

Highers reside beyond the castle walls, well, what's left of them, which are Charles and Aldus. Edward said they are the most powerful among the Highers when I questioned him about why Berthold seemed to be weaker than the others. He said Charles grants power to those that he feels are worthy, whatever that means as Edward didn't seem to know.

Cries begin in the crowd, which soon turns into sobs and shouts as the people watch on helplessly, as they kill more of their kind.

A child screams for her mother somewhere up ahead, and I swear my heart cracks in two.

We cannot allow this.

We cannot let them do this.

My eyes flash to Anna standing next to me, and she nods at whatever she sees in my eyes.

They wanted a distraction? Let's give them one.

"Get ready," I say to Josh down the link.

"Be careful,"

"And you."

I take a breath and remove my hood, letting my hair show. Next, I pull down the mask, allowing my markings to appear as my magic warms in my belly.

Then, I walk through the crowd.

No one notices me at first, they're too busy shouting at the guards, too busy trying to attack them, only to be shoved to the ground and stood on. Repeatedly.

But then, they do.

Gasps sound, of fear and surprise, then the people suddenly start parting for me as I continue my walk to the front gates. To the place where I was whipped.

The place where they killed Josie and Danny.

The place they stole Kade and hurt him.

My pack and others follow behind me, sensing that now is the right time as people watch on. Though they have no idea what is about to happen next.

A guard continues to read off the crimes of the females, trying to justify what they are doing with his chest puffed up and standing tall.

Does it make him feel powerful standing there as he sentences these tied females to death?

Does his little dick stand to attention over the façade that he is more than wolf shit?

I'm near the front now, just close enough to cause some of the guards on the outside to wonder what is going on, and why there is some sort of disturbance.

The guards holding the parchment detailing the female's crimes upon it finally notices me though. I can see the widening of his eyes, the way the paper shakes in his hand and the way his voice trails off.

"Distraction commencing," I tell Darius down the link.

"Be safe, Vihnarn. Hit them quickly, we will join you soon."

"Let them drop!" the guard shouts, and another guard pulls a lever on the platform they are standing on. A breath or two seems to pass through the crowd, through me. And then, the females hang.

I pull out a blade and aim. It slices through the first female's rope, the choking and grunting traumatizing my ears, but she lands with a heavy *thud*.

Two more knives fly through the air, courtesy of Seb, and the others also drop.

The people go crazy, pushing forward to the dropped females while others try to get to the long line of all the others waiting to meet their fateful end, fighting with the guards.

"Control them!" The guard roars, pointing at the others to do something, but we defy the odds and the people push back, fueled by fury, fear, by grief and threat.

My pack helps, pushing the crowd to spread out more, throwing the occasional knife here and there, and I think Anna and others have begun boiling a few guards as I can hear distant screams.

When I reach the edge of the platform, the guards raise the alarm for back up, readying their swords as I smile. Which makes them even more angry.

"I am the Heir of Zahariss," I say loudly. Even though nerves rattle through me, I have to be what I am meant to be.

A balance to the people.

A helping hand.

Hope.

I raise a hand and let Runa out, her growls are menacing. The crowd gasps, rushing to get away from me.

"Let the females go, and you will live."

The guards stare at me as more come to their aid, and then, they laugh.

This is not quiet laughter, this is loud and harsh. My hackles rise.

I take a deep breath. "Last chance."

They laugh harder, and the guard who was announcing the crimes comes to stand at the edge of the platform, looking down at me as more guards come to the battlement's walls above, looking down.

"Now, I'm about to get some hefty coins," the speaker says. "Lord Higher will be delighted with me when I bring him a mad Heir. Don't worry, people of Vrohkaria, we will protect—"

My magic wraps around his neck, squeezing. Choking him. Just like he did to these females.

He grasps at his neck, his mouth opening and closing like a fish, but I simply curl my hand, crushing his windpipe.

When his face turns purple, I frown and step aside, letting him fall off the platform and face-plant the ground.

I shake my hand out. *"Thanks for that little trick, Vihnarn."*

"Which one," he replies on a rumble.

"Choking."

He hums down the link. *"I will use that particular skill the next time I fuck you."* I huff. *"Now, be a good girl and kill them all. I will be there soon."*

I plan on it.

There is a deafening silence as everyone seems to freeze, looking down at the dead guard.

"Die it is," I tell them. "Runa." Her muzzle peels back in a snarl. "Let's hunt and show them just how *mad* an Heir can be."

Runa goes for the guard next to the platform and I go for the one who pulled the lever. The crowd screams, dispersing as guards try to come through them to get to us.

The guards on the battlements shout for archers, but I sense the pulse of magic behind me, knowing the blood witches are about to unleash their power.

The lever-puller draws his sword, his face twisted in anger as we clash, my own blade coming up to meet his.

The crowd screams as they disperse, trying to get away from what is now a battle as the guards shout in alarm. I send magic behind me, and with a push to the male before me, I turn and see more porting in.

"Anna!" I shout, turning and slicing into the speaker's belly.

"Got it." I see her raise two hands toward where the women are captured, and the guards there suddenly tense up, their bodies rigid.

Runa pounces on a guard closing in on me, and I run a hand

over her side in thanks, sending out a pulse of power to knock down two more coming our way up to the platform.

"Go, now," I say to Josh and Taylor when I spot them, and they rush forward to those who were hung, cutting through their bound hands.

Screams sound next, and I look to where Anna and Belldame stand in front of the captured women, the guards screaming as blood pours from their mouths, their eyes bulging as they cry bloody tears.

I jump down and two wolves pass next to me, heading for the guards who just ported in and they lunge, teeth ready as they dig into them. Hudson's wolf is larger than Colten's, and even though he's fighting, he takes a protective stance for Colten, making sure he's safe.

I grab my own blade and move forward to the gates. If we can get the innocents out the way, the witches can blast through it.

Another guard comes at me, swords drawn and I block his first attack, pushing back so he's on the defense and as he trips over a body on the ground, I stab through the side of his neck, not waiting for him to drop before continuing onto the next.

"Rhea!" Taylor shouts, and my head snaps his way, pushing back a guard and wrapping my magic around his legs, once again sending him to the floor.

Blood pours from his mouth, and I look up and find a few blood witches, their faces hidden by cloaks but their hands swirling with power.

Taylor points up to the battlements, and I follow his gaze. Fuck.

"Cover!" I scream while raising my hands up, frantically spreading a barrier out above me as far as I can.

Arrows rain down in the hundreds, some on fire and sweat beads on my brow as they hit the barrier, my legs trembling under the weight of it.

I spot some of the villagers that I rescued as they run toward me, trying to get to cover but it's too late. Arrows pierce their bodies, even the Highers's guards are hit, proving they have no ministration for their own.

Gritting my teeth, I straighten my legs that try to buckle under the weight of the attack, a scream coming from me as I send as much strength as I can to hold them.

Another guard comes for me and *fuck*, if I defend myself the barrier will drop.

"You fucking bitch!" he shouts at me, his sword pulled back to ram me, but he's tackled to the side, Josh stabbing him as he quickly stands again to protect me.

"Thanks," I breathe.

"Concentrate." I nod, holding the barrier as another wave of arrows come.

The fighting never ceases under my protective net, it ripples, dancing just above everyone's head as more blood is spilled.

I whimper as my knees give way, but I keep my arms straight, kneeling in the snow as I growl. Not much longer now, come on come on.

The arrows finally let up, and the barrier drops as I get to my feet, breathing ragged.

"Good job," Josh says, and I nod, swallowing over my dry throat.

"I need to clear a path to the gate," I tell him as we both head into the fray. "I'll call the witches once it is clear—"

"Loose," someone shouts, and my eyes widen, heart stopping.

"Gods," I breathe, as another set of arrows comes. How many do they have ready! "Take cover!" I scream over the fighting. I widen my stance, my hands glowing as I once again cast a barrier while Josh protects me.

As I look up to the battlements, trying to see if there is any way we can cause them to stop their attack, I see Higher Aldus looking down upon us with his witches in tow.

Shit.

"Darius?" I call down the link, needing to see how long he will be, but I soon realize as my heart drops to my stomach, that he's not there.

That the link is shut.

SEVENTY SEVEN

Darius

The need to be with Rhea nearly overwhelms me, nearly makes me port to the front gates to make sure she's safe.

I can't talk to her. I can't get through to her as the link shut down.

The tunnels we are in cancel out that link, even one as powerful as an Heir with the magic running through here.

It makes my skin crawl, makes me feel an urgency that rattles my bones and makes my hackles rise. Drax growls within me.

We are right below Wolvorn Castle, Rhea fighting at the front gates and it doesn't feel right that she is not next to me.

I haven't let her out of my sight since she fell off the cliff and now, here we are, separated again.

We move in another direction, Edward leading the way with the subtle glow of the torch light.

"How long?" I whisper, keeping my senses on high alert.

"Just down this next tunnel, then we will take a right and there's a hidden entrance," Edward says, and Leo and I share a look.

My hand stays on my blade, ready for anything while Drax paces inside of me, trying to break free. He senses the danger, senses Runa is out there fighting while he's in here, but he will have to suffer like me.

Rhea will port out of there if they are overwhelmed. I even told the witch to get her out of there too, and she said she would.

But I don't trust Rhea's sense of judgment.

She would sacrifice anything for those she loves, and with her pack with her...

"Hurry," I say, listening to those behind me.

My brothers are with me, readying themselves to go to the courtyard and sneak up behind those attacking near the front gates, the others— those from various villages, carry port stones on them so that when we get the food storage, they can port back to Eridian and Colhelm with the supplies.

We reach a dead end, and Edward turns to hand me the torch. When I just stare at him, he sighs and passes it to Leo.

"You don't like me very much, do you?" His hands go to the wall as he feels the grooves there.

"I don't."

He presses a stone inward, then the wall moves, opening like a door. He turns and gestures for the torch again. Once in hand, he walks up a set of stairs.

"Good."

"Good?" I question him, and he nods.

"Yes. It means you are protective of Rhea."

"Until my dying breath," I tell him on a growl.

He stops, taking a breath before he turns to look at me. "Then don't die."

My back teeth grind and I nod to the hatch. "Hurry, we are wasting time."

He assesses me, and then turns, unlocking the hatch and pushing upward. It creaks and we all hold our breath, listening for anything on the other side. When nothing can be heard, Edward quickly pushes the wood the rest of the way up and we file in one-by-one, ready and alert.

Torches are scattered around to gently light the space, not enough to be fully lit, but enough to see the vast number of supplies in here.

Barrels and boxes, sacks of grain and oats. Food haphazardly scattered on the floor and I just look at it, wondering how many people would kill to have that spilled food in their bellies.

We move further into the space, keeping quiet as we pass rotting apples and carrots, cabbages and potatoes.

"Fucking bastard," Leo mutters behind me.

"I knew it was bad, but this is..." I trail off.

"No wonder people were starving," Damian growls, kicking a carrot on the floor. "Evil," he mutters to himself as he goes deeper into the room.

I turn to the group that we brought, noticing their wide eyes. "Start grabbing as much as you can in your sacks. Remember, you can place them on the ground to fill more, no matter the weight, others are waiting to help you on the other side." They nod. "Be quiet but quick."

They get to work, walking between the gaps, unfolding their sacks and getting to work on the loose food while dragging already-full barrels together to port.

"Go," Edward says, grabbing a barrel and rolling it to another one. "I can handle this here, go to the gates."

I look at him, really look at him. Rhea trusts him, he's her guardian. It has to mean something because I don't know how much longer I can wait. But Rhea would kill *me* if something went wrong.

"Alpha Darius. I will look after them." The truth in Edwards eyes makes me pause.

I look to my men who watch us. I don't like it, but the need to get to Rhea wins. "Leave if you hear anyone come down here, keep them safe."

He nods. "I vow it, go to Rhea and..."

"And?" I ask, ready to head to the door that will lead me to her.

"And kill them all."

I smile, but it's not a nice one.

It's lethal.

SEVENTY EIGHT

Rhea

Blood splatters the ground, the snow soaking it up as I slash at another guard. Runa snarls beside me, keeping close as more and more port in.

Fuck, we are getting overwhelmed.

"Ahh!" a shout comes, and I spot Anna. A guard is on her, restraining her wrists as he knees her stomach.

"Josh!" I scream down the link. *"Go to Anna."* I see him move out of the corner of my eye.

"Uhh," I grunt as I'm kicked in the ribs, sending me stumbling back. Growling, I curl my hand and form a ball, then, running at whoever just kicked me, I smash my hand to his chest, following him down to the floor as he screams in pain.

"Bastard," I spit with a quick hit to the side of the face. His head crashes to the side and I stand over him, panting as I watch my ball of magic sink into his chest.

I look to the witches, to Belldame as their hands glow with power, chanting up to the battlements to stop the archers from attacking, but also to the Highers witches that have begun to rain down their own attacks as Aldus watches on.

I can also hear their distant chanting, and a shiver rolls down my spine as the sky seems to open up, and then a bolt of lightning comes down. Screams come from that area, and I swallow my fear and bite my arm.

Gathering the blood there and pressing a hand to the ground, a subtle blue spreads out around me, causing any guard near to groan and jolt in pain. But with me only being able to expand its reach so much, that's all the damage I can cause.

"Shit," I say as I look up again. "Take cover!" I raise my hands once more, creating a barrier as best I can, as more arrows are set loose.

We can't go on like this!

My legs wobble on impact, and I can just make out the smiling face of Higher Aldus though the ripples.

I know we don't have a lot of time. There is no way he hasn't informed Charles of what is happening at his gates.

Just as I think it, he smirks, turning to speak to someone and then I notice it.

Snow in some places starts to dip, like small craters forming in on itself. Fuck!

I look up at the archers, at the blood dripping down their mouths as some fall over the walls. I look for Belldame, spotting her further back with a savage grin on her face.

Does she see the ground too? The spots of black?

I back away from one as it appears near me, my heart pounding in my throat. When I see a clawed hand reach out of it, I shake my head.

"No, no, no. *Josh!*" I look around wildly. Only some Elites have noticed it and are trying to get others to move out the way, and some of my pack do the same.

I look at Anna and Josh, Colten and Hudson at their side and fear threatens to overtake me. *"Move, now!"* I scream down the link at him, and without even asking, he grabs Anna and runs to the castle wall, Hudson and Colten following along with some villagers.

More holes appear, and more beasts claw out of them, their snarling mouths and deformed bodies unfurling as they lift themselves out.

Oh Gods.

"Darius!"

I back up, blade out and hand raised, preparing, but we were never ready.

All of a sudden, howl's rent the air, and we all seem to freeze, even the guards that are down here do the same. Rogures follow the beasts out of the ground, and my body starts shaking as I watch black foam drip from their mouths.

We do not have enough numbers for this, or have enough trained warriors.

A beast closest to me sniffs the air, its grunting breaths sound while taking it in and then it crunches its clawed hands spreading out on the snow, as it bends and sniffs the blood there.

Tension fills the air as I see the Elites trying to get members of my pack and villagers to safety, motioning them to port out and some do. I can't even blame them.

But some stay and even though terror rattles through me, pride has me straightening my spine.

When the beast raises his head and lets out his own howl, I'm ready for an attack, then the beast moves and the others follow.

I watch as one beast swipes at a guard and a rogure pounces on another in bloodlust, uncaring who is in their path.

"Port out!" I shout to anyone who can hear me as I move and go for a beast that has its back to me, advancing upon a villager who's trying to stumble away.

I jump on its back, and Runa comes for its front, snapping at its legs as I bring the blade up to stab it. The beast stumbles, and I end up stabbing it in its shoulder as it thrashes, its claws out.

He swipes at Runa and she dodges back as I try to remove the blade from its rotting flesh. I gag at the smell of it, but a flicker of recognition enters my mind.

He smelled of bad blood.

This is what the beast smells like.

Fuck.

Runa continues her attack on its legs, and as the beast tries to stop her, I hold on with an arm around its neck, trying not to fall off. But then I have no choice as pain sears through my back and I'm falling.

I'm thrown left and right on the ground, my head banging on the surface as growls come from behind me.

A rogue has me, ragging me like a doll.

"Rhea!" Josh shouts in a panic but I can't respond as agony licks up my spine.

Calling my magic, I try to aim for it on a gritted scream, feeling the burning in my back, but I miss, and the rogue doesn't let up.

But then it suddenly stops, the snarling growls turning to painful screeches.

Panting into the snow face-first, I get my hands under me, crying out in pain at the wounds on my back and side from its claws. I don't think it bit me, it just managed to grab hold of my cloak and armor as it dragged me around, but its claws definitely sunk in.

I send my power to it, needing to heal so I can get back into the fight. Turning my head to make sure I'm safe to do so, I see Drax on the rogue, tearing into it with furious bites.

Relief fills me, my head pounding as I watch him.

The black-like flames cover his body, then spread onto the rogue and I lean back on my knees with shaky breaths as I wait for my power to heal me.

"It's okay, Drax." I swallow over my dry throat and cough. "He's dead." He stops, coming to me.

I'm not scared of the mist-like flames as I welcome him into my neck. He won't hurt me.

"I'm okay, thank you." I rub in between his eyes and pull back, holding on to him as I stand.

The noise of snarls and cries penetrates my mind, and I want to put my hands over my ears to cover them, wanting to take these people all away from danger.

But we can't.

"Where is your keeper," I say to Drax, and he huffs into my

neck. I try down the link we have, but it feels fuzzy.

"Go help Runa," I tell Drax, and he runs off as Runa takes on another beast.

There are so many of them.

Gods, Darius, please hurry.

Rolling my shoulders, I pick up a blade from the ground, seeing unseeing eyes stare back at me as I look to the battlements. Look at Aldus.

He looks on over the battle, a smirk upon his face as he watches hounds tear apart his people.

Bad blood.

Aldus was the one in Eridian who handed Darius the memory stone. Aldus was the one who taught Edward things, who hurt Kade. Sam said he smelled like bad blood, and if the beasts do…

Then they are connected.

But how?

The Higher's guards are now fighting the rogues, fighting for their lives as those in the battlements or behind the gates come to their aid.

They are left to the slaughter, nothing but fodder for the beasts.

I attack a guard, coming up behind him and ramming my blade through his back. I dodge another sword that comes slicing my way, and I sweep my legs under the male. He cries out in alarm as he hits the ground next to a dead body, but my blade goes through his chest next to quiet him.

I look into the mass of people to find my pack, spotting a few villagers holding their own against two guards. Anna has her hands out next to Belldame's, chanting toward the Higher's witches.

They must be doing okay as no other lightning comes to strike down upon us again.

I see Josh fighting with a rogue to the left, sidestepping an attack and ramming a blade through its temple. When I look further right, Seb just took down a rogure, the hound still twitching at his feet as he looks down at it, his chest heaving. I try to look for Taylor, Hudson and Colten, but I can't see them.

I head Seb's way, cutting a path through and that's when I see a guard come up behind him. Everything slows, but I'm running, pushing and shoving my way through anyone in my way.

"Seb!" I shout for him, but he doesn't hear me over the bloodbath that's happening around him. "Sebastion!" His head turns slowly in my direction. "Watch out!"

I watch in horror as the guard behind him raises his sword, his stance ready to thrust forward and just as I'm pushing another male out the way, lifting my opposite hand to gather my power, Seb fully turns toward me. His brows furrow in concern at the sounds of my voice, and when he spots me, our eyes clashing, the guard thrusts his sword right through his chest.

"No!" The scream tears through my throat as Seb looks down, looking at the sword sticking out of his chest as he wavers on his feet.

His eyes move back up to mine as the guard withdraws his sword, Seb's body jostling with the movement, eyes connecting with mine as villagers tackle the guard to the ground.

"No, no, Seb." I reach him as he falls forward, and I grab him as we collapse to the ground on my knees, cradling him in my arms. "Oh Gods, Seb," I say frantically and I place a hand on his, pushing my power into him. "Vallier, vallier, vallier," I chant.

Please Zahariss, please.

Seb gurgles, blood splattering from his mouth and I turn him gently, tears dripping down my cheeks as I lay him in the snow, both of my hands on his chest now as I pour my power into him.

"Come on, come on." Seb looks up at me, blinking as snowflakes fall and I watch the white beneath us turn red.

I push more power, feeling the tear inside of him, the bleeding, and a sob bursts from my throat.

"No," I whimper, and Seb slowly lifts his hand and places it on mine that's on his chest, coughing up blood as the fight wears on around us. *"Josh!"* I cry down the link.

"I had a good run, Alpha," he croaks, and I cry down at him, my fingers gripping his hand.

"I can fix it, I can, I know I can," I say, trying to repair the damage, but I can't fix this. *"Josh, Darius, please, help me!"*

"I'm coming!" Josh replies frantically.

"It…went through my heart. There is…no use." I shake my head, denying it. "I'm sorry."

"No," I growl down at him, and he tries to give me a smirk. "There is nothing for you to be sorry about, Seb. Just, don't go."

He coughs again, and his eyes dim a little. "Thank you for letting me live out the rest of my days with a…a…family."

"Don't thank me for that, you were always meant to be with us, always meant to teach me how to throw a knife, always making jokes."

He nods, a small smile on his bloodied face. "I get to see her now…you know," he whispers, and he looks up to the sky. "I get…to see my mate. So don't be—" He coughs, nearly choking on his own blood and I lift my hands to put them under his head, to try and help him. "Don't be sad. I…I will see you in another…another…"

"Seb," I whisper, my heart stalling as his head lulls to the side. "Seb," I whimper, shaking him a little, cradling him closer to me.

I stare down at his face, running a hand through his hair as I wait for his reply…But unseeing eyes stare back, and when his essence starts to float up into the air, the finality of his silence, I clutch him to my chest tighter, crying into his hair as his hand falls limply to his side.

"I'm sorry, I'm so sorry." I say as I rock him back and forth.

"We will meet at another time, and you can joke with me all you want." Sniffling, I lay him down gently, while placing a kiss on his forehead and running my hand over his eyes, closing them. "Rest well with your mate."

"Rhea, what?...No." Josh comes to my side, his knees giving way as his bloodied hands go to Seb's chest.

Colten arrives next, Hudson at his side and he grips his shoulders as they shake. Then Taylor is there with Anna, all of us looking down upon our beloved pack member who is no more.

I grasp Seb's hand in mine, bringing it up to my lips to place a kiss there as I close my eyes and let rage consume me.

Let heartbreak eat at me.

Let grief fuel me.

When I hear a rogure coming toward us, I don't even look as I lift my hand and send my power straight for it. I'm not really aware of when I picked up a sword off the ground, and start hacking into a guard like I'm chopping wood.

All I know is that they will all pay.

SEVENTY NINE

Darius

I barge through the door and into the courtyard, hearing the battle ahead of us.

"Rhea?" I shout down the link. It's open now, but she's not answering. *"Rhea?"* I try again.

Guards line the battlements, archers notching their arrows, and witches wait behind the gates, getting ready to either attack those on the outside, or defend.

I sent Elites to watch over Rhea, to help her in any way, but as the battle still rages on, I don't understand why they haven't ported out.

"Attack from the back, get to the gates and open them." I say to my brothers down the link.

They all make affirmative sounds and then, we strike.

They never see us coming from behind, never thought an enemy could be at their back.

But it's more than just an enemy, there is a pissed off Heir who cannot find his Vihnarn.

I grab the first guard I can get to as he turns, gripping his throat and slamming him to the ground. He cries out, causing others to turn at the disturbance, but I'm already bashing his head in with my boot.

Dead.

I bring my blade up and arch it, slashing through another that tries to help his friend, but he falters when he sees who it is.

"Elites!" someone shouts in the gathered crowd, and that sets everyone on high alert.

I catch another guard in the stomach, an arrow whizzing past me as it lands in the eye of another.

"Rhea. Answer me." Still nothing.

Fuck, fuck.

I put my palms to the floor, calling my powers and a rolling, dark mist appears, intertwining with the front line of the guards. They wobble where they stand, eyes rolling into the back of their heads as they try to shake off my power.

But instead they drop, unconscious.

Jerrod is there with his axe, chopping them into pieces as I spot a witch trying to counter my magic, a green-like hue battling with my black.

I pick up a sword, twirl it in my hand and then send it soaring into her hooded face.

Her arms flail, and then she too drops.

A blow to my cheek has my head snapping to the side, blood coating my teeth but I move with the movement, turning and sending my own punch back. I hear the crunch of bone as I connect with the male's face, and he crumples to the floor as I form a shard and send it into his neck.

I grin.

It's feral.

It's mean.

It's fury.

I growl and go into another group of guards as they turn, their eyes widening at my impending assault. I attack first, bringing my blade up and blocking an attack while my magic goes to my back, protecting it like a shield as I dodge and spin, aiming for deadly points of the body to kill those who even dare lift a sword to me.

"Traitor," one spits.

"No," I say, grabbing him by his armor and hauling him to me, my blade shoving into his side. "Heir."

I let my dominance fill the space, scanning the area as some falter under the weight of it. I lift my hand, palm up, then I send five shards outward into the fray, hitting two guards as a knife lands in the other's head.

Zaide is near.

Shouting begins, and I look up, dozens of arrows are pointed our way and I raise my hand, casting a barrier to protect us as they are let loose.

I move under it, still attacking and I hiss when a sword catches my thigh. I spin, punching the guard in the head and he kicks out, trying to weaken me, but I bring a blade down on his thigh and return what he did to me.

He cries out, holding his leg as he hops on the other, I take his foot out from under him. He falls back, cracking his head on the stone floor, bleeding out instantly.

When I feel the arrows no longer hitting my barrier, I release it and look up again.

Aldus smiles down at us, and I grin.

"Come on, Higher Aldus," I say, spreading my arms wide as Drax tears into a male next to me. "Let's settle years of debt. I will fuck with your head like you did mine."

He brings his hands up, purple filling them. "Hello, Heir of Cazier," he says as I hear doors opening at our back, and I know more guards have entered the space. It won't matter, we will kill them all.

Aldus drops his hand and magic slithers down the walls, spreading out when it reaches the stone floor. I eye it curiously, wondering what it will do, but then black patches form.

I growl, twirling my blade in my hand as claws begin to come from the dark. I look up at Aldus, his smirking face infuriating me further.

"I think I shall stay here, Alpha Darius. It is my duty to protect Vrohkaria from mad Heirs." He smiles, hands going behind his back. "The view is also much better on this side…it is more befitting to gaze upon beauty that shall belong to us very soon."

I still, and tilt my head, two tails instantly appearing at my back. "Do not touch her." The ground trembles at my feet, but he just smiles wider.

"You cannot win here, Alpha Darius. And when you are caught, you will be punished accordingly. I think—" he wobbles suddenly, eyes widening before he turns.

I head forward, ready to rip his throat out, when a wave of blue appears on the battlements, followed by an explosion.

Those on the walls stumble, then stone crumbles beneath their feet as they fall to the ground.

Fall to us.

"Attack! Don't let up!" I order on a deadly command.

I spot a black blur, and then Drax is with me. I grip his head in my hands. Checking for injuries before asking, "Where is she?" He looks behind him, toward the gates, and I nod. "Good boy."

Drax instantly enters a battle with a beast, chomping on its legs and dodging its clawed hands. I pick up a discarded sword off the floor and launch it his way. It hits the beast's side, causing enough of a distraction for Drax to leap and his teeth pierce his throat.

I don't watch as he rips it out, instead searching for Aldus. He will not touch my Vihnarn. No one will.

"Rhea! You need to leave. Now." Silence. *"Do you see Rhea near the gates?"* I ask my brothers.

"I haven't seen her," Damian grunts.

"No," Zaide and Jerrod reply.

"I'll help look." Leo answers.

I head for the gates that are under some form of attack, hearing the shouts getting louder as the smell of blood and magic coats the ground. Drax tears into others near my side, coming with me.

A scream comes from ahead, in the middle of the courtyard and my gaze goes to it as one of my Elites drops to the ground, head turned at an unnatural angle.

Aldus casts a barrier, just like the other Highers did, and I watch as he drops it a little to attack, but soon puts it back up like the coward he is.

I go toward him, maneuvering my blade to kill all who get in my way, just like I had been trained for, but this time it is to be rid of them, not protect them.

"Aldus" I shout, and his eyes come to me. "Today, you die."

He scoffs. "Like you could kill me." He looks over me with disgust. "I should have pushed more for your mother to be rid of you when you were in her belly, but your father, the stupid swine, swore he could make you into a Higher. Swore you would lead the next generation."

"He was very wrong,"

"Your mother corrupted you, she was too soft," he tilts his head, smiling. "As she was in other places, according to your father. Just like Lasandrhea will be." Heat prickles up my spine and a blast of power comes from me in a wave. The guards around me all fall to the side as I stalk toward Aldus.

Black spurts up with my footsteps, and my magic coats me like a second skin. I'm furious.

My magic is furious.

And with the little hint of fear creeping into Aldus's eyes, I know what he sees.

An Heir of darkness.

An Heir of the below.

I raise my hand to the right, and in an instant, Drax is within me, standing tall and ready as I come to a halt in front of Aldus, as the battle rages on around me.

"You will not get within the barrier, Alpha Darius, and it is only a matter of time before Lord Higher comes to deal out your punishment, himself."

"All the other Highers are dead, taken out one-by-one. What makes you think you will not be next?"

"They didn't have the power granted to me. It is power

like yours, but closer to the original source as it came from Catherine, and not her swine, which means your power is *weaker*." I ignore him, challenging Drax's own power to my hand. "Why not come back to our side? Has a female really swayed you? I never thought you weak to the wiles of women? Even Maize couldn't sway you."

"Maize is dead," I growl, placing a hand on his barrier and watching as it ripples and sizzles around my palm.

"You Dare!" Beads of sweat form on Aldus's brow, the smirk now none existent. "Why did you kill my protégé?" he asks, anger flashing in his eyes.

"Oh, I didn't." I smirk as he frowns. "My Vihnarn tore her throat out for daring insinuate to touch what is hers."

"Vihnarn!" He shouts, hands forming fists at his side as the ripples expand over his barrier.

"Yes. And I will do the same to you." I press more into the barrier, tiny, black flames appearing slowly. "My mother was kind, and everything that was good and warm. She was everything a son could need or want." I spread my fingers, making a claw shape as the fire rapidly spreads around his protection. "And for her to be killed by the things you all brought to the lands…" I grit my teeth, feeling the cracks in his barrier as I push harder. "For you to have ever touched something else that is good and warm…I will get rid of you all and send you to Cazier, and let him tear you to pieces."

His barrier is engulfed in black flames, and it's like the oxygen is sucked out of the air and everything stills for one moment, then two.

Then his barrier breaks, a look of shock spreads over his face and I see him raising his hands, balls of purple in them but I smirk, letting the change come over me and then my two huge paws are sending him backwards to the floor.

He didn't expect me to turn wolf, didn't expect how quickly I could do it.

He screams in alarm, trying to get his hands up to defend

himself, but it is already too late. I'm already tearing into him.

My claws sink into him and my jaw opens, going around his throat as I rip into him. He screams on a gurgle, and I release him to put my mouth around his head, my teeth piercing into his flesh. His hands hit my sides, causing pain to rattle through me, but I clamp my teeth down, feeling the blood dribble from them as I shake him back and forth.

His body swings left and right, his head still captured between my teeth as I growl, darkness hovering below me like a shadow. I shake him violently, hitting a few guards who try to come at me, but my brothers are there, taking them down.

The pain he pushes into my body becomes worse, and I growl, snarling as I chomp on his head, savagely shaking it, and then I stop.

Aldus is barely breathing now, blood splattering everywhere and I maneuver him to where I want him, placing my front paws on his chest.

Biting a little more to get a better grip with my back teeth, I pull my head back.

It doesn't take much for his head to pop off in my grip, nor does it take much to bite down one last time and let the remains of his head fall from my mouth.

I growl down at his headless body, tearing into his arms next, his chest, his legs and belly. I make sure nothing is left as a haze of fury comes over me.

As I let that feral side come alive, and I don't stop.

I can't stop.

It isn't until something prickles in my mind.

A strand…one that shines so brightly that I pause and look up, distracted from my prey.

The gates of the courtyard are blown open, and the guards and witches who were once there, stumble back from the blast of power following it.

A female stands there, bloody and bruised, a blade in her hand by her side as her other hand is still hanging in the air, magic swirling around it. Her markings are upon her face, looking like the warrior she is as her hair floats around her.

I feel her dominance, feel her power hit me and I inhale sharply.

The change is instant.

Paws turn to hands, and I'm walking towards her, no—running, pushing anyone and anything out of my way with my power as I assess her for injuries.

She looks around the courtyard through barely-seeing eyes that are puffy, red around the edges.

Has she been crying?

"Are you okay? Who the fuck made you cry, Vihnarn?" I ask down the link, as I continue to make my way toward her. Her eyes flick to mine, and they shimmer. It makes me want to rage upon everyone here even more, but I need to get to her, hold her and make sure she is okay. *"Tell me you are okay?"* I demand, picking up the pace. "Rhea!"

She isn't moving to me. It is almost like she can't, like she's frozen in place.

I grab a rogure by the back of its neck and stab it through its head. I shove another guard out the way, punch one to the left and wrap my power around one to the right.

"I'm coming, Vihnarn." Fuck, is she hurt?

I sense a new power entering the space that causes my senses to go on high alert. Even the guards around her turn toward it.

It's powerful.

It's…

A flash comes from behind Rhea where she stands, and she tilts her head, like she can also feel it. I'm running in the next second when it becomes stronger, sending my power out as a form appears behind her.

"Rhea, move!"

I see Josh, Anna and Taylor coming up behind her from the castle walls, I hear my brothers at my back as we all go to Rhea. Drax is out and he heads for her, running as fast as he can.

But a hand lands on her shoulder, and as her eyes widen, she turns to maneuver out of the hold that is on her, a smirk befalls the form's face and then they are both gone.

The rage is instant and I black out.

EIGHTY

Rhea

Gods my head hurts.

I groan, blinking my heavy eyes, trying to keep them open. A taste so vile fills my mouth, and I want to throw the contents of my stomach up, heaving as I try and keep it down.

Breathing heavily through my nose, I try to come around from the heavy feeling that's washing over me. It feels like a cloud in my mind, like I'm floating.

What happened?

Blood, Seb, magic, the gates…

"Darius? Josh?" I mumble down the link, but I can't feel it.

Runa?

Silence.

I'm suddenly aware of my shoulders feeling like they are about to be ripped off, about to be torn from my body and I whimper, trying to move them. It feels more heavy than usual, and the piercing pain at my wrist startles me so much that my eyes spring open to see what is causing it.

My eyes widen, my head shaking back and forth at the chain wrapped around my skin. I look to the other side and it's the same position.

No. Gods, no!

I frantically look around at a familiar space, at the pillars on either side of me that have glowing runes, at the platform below me that gently pulses with power.

I wriggle as I'm suspended above it, kicking my feet and

letting loose a gritted scream as the chains pull tighter.

"Now, now. There is no need for that." I freeze at the voice, fear threatening to swallow me as my eyes go forward to where Charles stands further back.

He has a cloak on him, the hood pulled up but his face is clear to see. His hands are behind his back, his back straight as he watches me.

It all comes back. My fury, my numbness as I killed and slaughtered, sending power into the castle walls, at Darius calling to me, and then Charles…He grabbed me.

"Coward." I snarl at him. He took me away and ran. Charles smiles as I pull at my wrists even though it hurts. I will rip my own hands off rather than be shackled again. "Let me go!" I demand.

I vowed to myself I wouldn't be in this position, that I would never be restricted again.

I feel it then, the terbium within the iron. I call for my magic, I beg it to come in my panic, but it doesn't. It's just quiet, along with Runa.

She shouldn't be as quiet as she is.

"What…What have you done to me?" I hear the fear that creeps into my voice, hating that he can intimidate me, scare me.

His grin is all teeth. He lifts a hand, showing me the vial in his palm.

It's empty.

"Ultrian…it has fascinating effects on males," he says, and the breath lodges in my throat. "It makes them want to breed until they cannot any longer, makes them want to fuck anything within their grasp." Dark patches appear on the ground, following in his wake as he starts walking around the platform. I try to follow him with my eyes, but when he's out of sight at my back, I tense up, watching the craters in the ground with growing fear. "With Heirs, it mutes their power, like the dassil does to normal wolves, dulling down the body to nearly nothing, but still aware." I swallow roughly when I hear the growls. He comes to my right and my eyes track him, my body shaking now. "How do I know that, you may be wondering? You should ask Darius's mother when you eventually see her. It was her mate who helped create it, after all."

Darius's father.

I think I'm going to be sick.

No, I am sick.

I heave, vile liquid coming from me as I hack and cough while Charles watches on with distaste.

"It is time, Lasandrhea. You escaped your fate once, this time shall be different." He clicks his fingers, and braziers that weren't here before light the area, showing piles of bodies.

I gasp, my eyes taking in the amount of piles there are, as he comes to stop in front of me once more.

"What did you do?" I croak out, and he turns, walking over to a pile as those black patches become even darker.

"It seems you have bewitched our Alpha Darius," he says, ignoring my words. "He would have made a fine Higher. Ruthless, fantastic genes, strong, controllable, but he fell into your cunt and never came out, it seems."

My teeth start to chatter as a coldness befalls me.

"He would have never become a Higher, especially after finding out what you have been doing."

"I could have trained him, just like I had been slowly doing over time, waiting for the right moment to strike."

"He woke up and realized it was a nightmare," I snarl, rattling the chains again.

"Shame isn't it?" He sighs like he cares. "These, dear Lasandrhea, are mostly failures," he tells me, pointing to the bodies and swirling a hand. A body is then being dropped into a black hole, the sounds of snarls following it.

"So you killed them?" I croak, devastation washing over. "Because they were not up to your standards?"

He shrugs. "I have no use for them apart from feeding the

hounds."

I watch as he throws another body into another hole.

"How did you control them?"

"Your mother bestowed a curse on the lands when she was passing."

"Killed. She was killed."

"Semantics," he says, and my anger grows. "It was quite a while before I learned that the power she left me." Stolen. "That I can use it to control the hounds of the lands. All I had to do was put a little power into them and they were mine. It was even longer until I realized that we could produce a new species."

A human-like face appears out of the hole closest to him, then claws follow until the beast is dragging himself to stand, looking at Charles.

"When we had rogures breed with females, they produced a hybrid of sorts." He circles the beast. "And with this realization, I wondered if the beasts could then breed with other females and produce something even stronger. The issue was, they wouldn't do as they were told."

"But the ultrian made them."

"Correct." He smiles, all teeth. "You are a clever one, like your mother." I grind my back teeth. "They will create an army, and go across other lands to be under my rule."

"But why? You had Vrohkaria."

"Had? My dear, I still *have* Vrohkaria." The beast turns to me, and my blood runs cold. "Now that I have you within my grasp once again, I can put an end to finding an Heir within others, you are all I need."

"You will never touch me!" I shout, revulsion and panic running through me.

"But I will, and then I will take the children you bare."

He hums, taking his hood down and I'm hit with that smell again. The bad one. I gag, spitting on to the stone below me as he tsks.

"Fitting how you are in the same position as your mother

was."

"Do not talk about my mother," I snarl, trying to call for Runa, anything.

Anyone.

"I intended to take any children she bore and then take her for myself, but she hid her pregnancy from me when you were in her belly. She was cunning that way, with the help of that damn witch. But then I thought, what if I take her power instead, and then take her daughter when she can no longer bear children? She would also be powerful."

"You have killed your own people for your own sick games!" I spit, kicking my legs out again as he comes closer.

His power comes out then, the violet of it striking as it wraps around my throat and squeezes.

"Know your place!" he shouts, malice in his eyes as I cough and splutter, trying to gasp for air as the beast beside him starts growling and snarling. "Look at what you are making him do." He releases me and my head falls forward, taking in much needed air. "Do not anger me. I do not need you awake to breed you."

I am sick again, all over the platform.

The thought of him touching me, him coming anywhere near me like that.

"No," I tell him.

His eyes are wild and filled with excitement as he steps onto the platform and raises himself up to my height. I kick my legs out, a noise much like a wounded animal escaping me as I try to get him away, try to stop him from touching me as he reaches his hands out.

His magic comes out and restrains my ankles, spreading them as his hands land on my hips. A panicked cry comes from me, even as I continue to wriggle and try to get him off me, fuck, I would rather the beast tear into me then him. Not him.

"No!" I scream, my voice cracking as I try to turn this way and that, blood dripping from my wrists as I try and muster the energy, anything to get him away from me.

His fingers dig into my hips, the hold so hard that I know it will bruise my skin. Next, it feels like knives are at his fingertips, and I cry out as I feel blood dripping down from my hips.

"We both know I have no problem seeing you bleed, Lasandrhea. I was the one to command the others, remember. I told them how to hurt you, how to injury you *just* right."

"No," I whimper, squeezing my eyes shut. "Get off me, you cannot have me!"

"Only Alpha Darius can?" he scoffs. "He will soon die. Or shall I make him watch?"

I spit in his face, and I'm choking again.

"Listen here you cunt. My goals are not mere things, they are years in the making. Years! You will bear me powerful children, but not at first, no. You have angered me now. When there is a babe inside of you, I will take its life essence into me, giving me more of the power already coursing through my veins from your mother's." I choke out a noise, but he only squeezes harder. "Only then, when I am satisfied, will you bear my children, and once they are old enough, they will go across other lands on my command and it shall all be mine. But if you bear daughters, they will be given to my pets."

His eyes take on a crazed look, tilting his head back and laughing as more of them crawl out of the ground, joining the other beast who is huffing and chuffing.

"Oh Lasandrhea, I wonder what else is out there…" The delight in his gaze scares me, and my whole body trembles with the lack of air, my lungs burning. "Shall we see what other manner of beings can slide between your thighs and bare other kinds of children?"

He lets me go, my throat on fire as I hack and cough. Tears stream down my face, dripping onto the platform and I can see my blood splattered on it. Sinking into it.

"You were an obedient little thing, once, you shall be again," he murmurs.

"Darius, I need you, please! I'm scared."

A beast walks closer to me from the right, his chuffing sounds terrifying as it sniffs the air.

"Now don't look so frightened, the rutting of those will be much later. Probably when you are close to death."

I watch as one beast goes over to the dead pile of bodies, and when it drops before one, I look away, not wanting to see what it's doing.

I wish I could block out its noises, I wish I could be far away from here.

"Vihnarn, where are you?"

Charles lifts his hand again, and a strand of violet moves around me, coming to wrap around my legs and effectively, loosening the hold they had to keep them open.

I'm relieved instantly, wanting the most vulnerable part of me safe in any way.

No matter how futile the position I am in.

I call for my power again, for Runa.

Still nothing.

"Why are you doing this?" I croak. "I was a child, you have taken countless others and for what? To have other lands in your name?"

He scoffs. "I want *all* the lands in my name and all of its inhabitants. The demons, humans, elves, the fae and the dammed and beyond. Even the damn dragons. They should all bow to me, every single one of them!" he shouts at the end of his rant.

He's completely lost it as he looks at his beasts and urges them toward the pile of bodies, almost cooing at them.

"Go and feast!" he says to them, and I shiver.

"The Gods will never allow this," I whisper to him, my throat sore.

He laughs.

Full on, head tilted back, laughs.

"The Gods?" he cackles. "Oh but they cannot even come out

from their realm, can they?" My breathing stalls. How does he know that? "The entrance to their forevermore home is where you are right now. The veil is thin enough to pass through it if you are welcomed. They can see you, you know," he comes closer again, and a rogure comes out of a hole, snarling, the black foam dripping from his mouth as another and another follow it.

Gods. How many can he possibly have under control?!

"And the Gods can see me, see their new owner."

"You will never control them."

"Never say never, dear. For I *will* be the new God of Vrohkaria, don't you see?" he inhales and sways, the beasts and rogures around him turning their heads toward him.

Charles cracks his neck, rolling it side-to-side as he seems to expand. He grows taller a few inches, his ears lengthening at the tops a little as his chest puffs up.

I feel his dominance hit me, and if I wasn't hanging here, I think my knees would give in.

I try to withstand it, calling my own to keep it at bay but it sneaks past, causing me to almost fold in on myself at the force of it.

The beasts around him whimper and take a few steps back from him.

"Don't you see?" he shouts, arms wide. "I have the Gods's power running through my veins, the power of the below, and you will give me more of it!"

Oh Gods. He's like the half beasts. His ears are the same, and his skin looks a little gray.

Suddenly, cloaked figures port in, hands out and they instantly start a low chant.

Charles comes near the platform, his dark eyes full of greed and malice. He floats up, coming closer to me and I rear back, trying to kick my tired legs out again to no avail.

His finger runs down my cheek, and I turn away, not wanting this monster to touch me.

The ring of his slap echoes in my ears, and I squeeze my eyes shut as he does it again, and again.

"You will not turn away from me." He grabs my jaw painfully, ripping my face to his. "You hid from me all those years, hid what was rightfully mine!" he shouts, getting even closer to my face. "Now you will pay me back tenfold. You will spread your legs and birth as many children as I say you will, and you will let anything between those legs. You will give me the power owed to me and you will give me your wolf."

I blink, struggling against him. "No," I croak, but he just laughs at me.

"Oh, dear. We both know the word *no* is meaningless, don't we."

I'm on a table, laid down, face to the ceiling as I cry, telling them no, not to touch me. Their laughs echo in my ear, Charles's deep voice coming to my side and stroking my hair, telling me that my no really mean yes. That I want this. That it was what I was made for. That I'm just confused, that this was always supposed to happen and everyone goes through this.

It's our rite of passage as a female.

But no.

No, it isn't.

No, no. "No!" I scream at him, leaning forward and biting into his cheek.

"Ahh!" he growls, a hand coming to the back of my head and gripping my hair. "Let go!"

But I don't, I bite down harder, and when his blood reaches the back of my throat, I have to breathe through my nose to not let go of him.

I growl, a horrible sound ripping from me as I dig in deeper as he starts to hit my body.

My ribs, my back, my head.

And still.

I don't let go.

When I feel an almost electrified feeling, pain rattling my

body, I know what it is.

I felt it at Wolvorn castle.

I scream around his cheek as he pulls at my hair, punching the side of my face.

The pain is excruciating, my whole body tensing and when I feel my grip loosen, I bite down harder still, and then I pull back.

The rip of his flesh pierces my brain even as I scream in agony, even as Charles moves back with a shout.

The pain stops in my body when he moves away, and I slump forward, my eyes on Charles as blood drips down from my mouth as I spit the lump of flesh out.

His hand moves to his cheek, that is now missing a chunk as he shouts and curses.

When he looks back at me, I bare my teeth. "You will not touch my wolf."

He curls his lip at me, and electricity fills me again. I scream, legs kicking out wildly as I feel like I'm being torn from the inside out.

Then it's quiet once more as I hang limply, my breathing ragged.

But the reprieve isn't long as Charles starts his attack up again.

"Ahh." I cry, looking into his crazed eyes as blood drips down from his mutilated cheek.

"I can do this for a long time, Lasandrhea. You should have been good."

"Fuck. You." I wheeze, and he intensifies his power as my body shakes, the chains clanging with it.

It goes on and on. He plays with me, toys with me while telling me all the things he's going to do to me.

I slump completely forward, blood dripping from my mouth as he raises a hand and produces a ball of violet.

Of the power he stole from my mother.

That could kill me, but so be it. I would rather die than let him have me.

"You are weak," I say in a weak whisper. "You had to steal power to become something."

"Shut up, you bitch," he growls, and my body lights up once again.

I breathe ragged breaths when it stops. "You will not win. You will die."

"No one can stop my goals," he says vehemently, and I see him patting down his cloak.

"Did you fuck a beast to get some power from the below?" I wonder. Cazier said they came from there.

"Don't be ridiculous."

I laugh, but it turns into a bloody cough. "You look like their bitch."

He sets me alight from within, again. "How dare you—"

The floor begins to tremble, and the pain in my body stops.

It's a slight rumble, the grass vibrating beneath the beasts. Then some little stones bounce on the platform below me.

Charles growls as the rogues and the beasts turn toward something behind them, their hackles raised, and I also look.

I squint through my bleary eyes, at least, nothing at first. Just darkness and the shadows of the woods, until a shape comes into view.

I squint my eyes, my head feeling heavy, exhaustion weighing down on my bones, but I would know that shape anywhere.

I laugh, my lungs causing me pain every time I breathe as Charles growls.

"Oh look," I say breathlessly, my words slurred as I look to Darius as he rides on Drax's back. "You wanted an Heir? Well, now you have two."

EIGHTY ONE

Rhea

"Get him!" Charles shouts to the rogues by his side, and I watch as they pause for a moment, then they do as he says, snarling and running to where Darius comes.

But he is not alone.

Wolves run beside him. The Elites, my pack, and other people of Vrohkaria.

My heart warms despite the circumstances, but fear still licks up my spine at the danger we are all in.

Charles isn't natural.

"Rhea!" The sound of Darius penetrates my mind. I feel our connection, letting it sink into me and I feel like I can breathe again.

You came, I try to say back, but the link is closed off on my end.

"Just hold on, Vihnarn, I'm coming." His voice flutters through my mind and I whimper.

It hurts.

Everything hurts.

I scream as that electrifying feeling rattles my body again, and I can hear a distant, furious roar as my back aches in agony.

Make it stop, make it stop.

"How foolish," I hear Charles say, and I watch through blurry eyes as he spreads his arms wide again.

Bringing them up high, his hands coated in violet, he brings them down in an arch, fingers extended toward the floor. More black holes appear, the ground bubbling as more rogures and beasts appear.

Oh Gods, there are so many of them.

I struggle in the chains that hold me, grunting in frustration and pain that I still can't get free.

I kick my legs from side to side, the metal digging into my wrist, causing more blood to drip down my arms.

Charles turns to me with a cruel smile. "You think you will be free of me?" he asks, once again coming closer to me. "You were *never* free of me in the first place. The marks on your body prove it."

The marks on my body were cherished by Darius. He kissed every one of them, his touch cherishing.

Charles waves a hand, and I feel my glamor disappearing in an instant. Charles's eyes roam over the scars on my body, turning my stomach.

"Fuck you," I croak, and he bares his teeth.

"In good time, but I will do it as I repeat exactly how you got those scars, while the other Heir watches."

I pale at that, instantly remembering the pain, the agony, what he put me through, what he ordered others to put me through.

He lifts a hand and that fire of his is there, and I remember it on the soles of my feet, how I smelled my burning flesh.

It reminds me a little of Draxton's.

I hear the colliding of wolves and beasts before I see it. The screeching howls, the snarling growls, and the shouts and cries of battle all penetrate me.

"Call them back!" I say to Charles as I see half of a body being flung through the air, intestines spilling out of the body as a rogure jumps on a villager. A beast has an Elite in its mouth, his claws on another and I spot Damian jumping on its back.

It's chaos. Carnage. A massacre.

"What will you give me?" Charles smirks, as he calls more and more hounds.

I look to see Darius upon Drax's back, his eyes trained on me, hands covered in black, those two mass-like tails at his back swishing violently.

Darius is closer now, heading toward me but four beasts are directly in his path.

My heart rate kicks up as I watch those human-like beasts train their eyes on him, on something that is mine.

He's not going to make it past them.

"Darius, watch out!"

I watch in horror as the beasts go on the attack. They are going to take him off Drax's back, they are going to hurt him.

My struggle increases, my teeth gnashing together as I try to ignore the pain thrumming through my body.

He's nearly there, a few feet.

I hold my breath when he reaches them, but he doesn't collide with them, he doesn't raise his blade to them.

No.

He moves and crouches upon Drax's back, one hand in the fur at his neck to keep his balance, and when he's close enough to the beasts, Drax leaps for one, his jaws open, but that's not what has me shocked.

When Drax reaches the highest point in his leap, Darius stands to his full height on Drax's back and then, he jumps. His booted foot lands on the head of one beast, as he jumps to the others, smashing its face as I realize his booted feet are also covered in black.

When the beast starts to tumble back, another beast lunges for Darius, but he jumps, and the claws aimed for him end up embedded in his kin. Darius lands on a roll, instantly getting to his feet again and heading our way, trusting Drax to take care of them.

Shards come from him, a rolling, black mist following in his wake, his usual green eyes shrouded in obsidian.

"You think you are on par with me, boy!" Charles snarls, sending more rogures to Darius as he battles through them.

Darius slices the throat of one rogure, and stabs the other before he puts his palm to the floor. One moment, then two, the mist races forward in a rush, like a wave, before it bursts into flames.

Rogures and beasts screech, that black wave of flames looking so much like Drax's, crawling up their skin and burning them alive.

Charles growls as he puts his hand in front of him, sending out a blast of power. Darius spins to dodge the attack, running straight for me once again, as he turns wolf and jumps onto a beast.

He's feral, ripping into the beast and I gasp as claws go into Darius's side, but I don't think he even feels it.

I glance behind him as the battle wages on, the snow-covered ground now a sea of red, and I feel sick to my stomach once again.

I close my eyes and try to feel for my power, for anything that can help, but these fucking chains are blocking everything.

"Ahh!" Charles sends more pain shooting through me and I thrash, shaking my head as I feel like my back is about to snap.

"Let her go." A voice sounds from in front of me, the timbre that of pure darkness, and I peel my eyes open, seeing Darius standing there in human form about twenty feet away, a row of rogures between them as Drax protects his back.

He's covered in blood, chest heaving, eyes hard and furious. Black flames are at his feet, ready and waiting but not burning him at all.

Elites battle in the background, the villages and the people helping, screams tearing through to us as death litters the ground.

Charles growls in front of me and a rogure turns to look at him, sending the power within. That's when I notice that their bone-colored eyes have a slight violet tinge to them...

Is that Charles's magic?

"How sweet," Charles says, and he moves closer to me,

making me tense. "It seems as though you are still bewitched by the Heir's cunt, Alpha Darius," he says to Darius.

My Vihnarn takes a step forward, but freezes when Charles floats up to me, placing a blade at my neck.

Charles laughs, jostling the blade, causing me to hiss at the sting. I feel the blood dripping down.

The ground trembles.

"Now calm down," Charles's slimy voice tells Darius. "It is but a scratch, but it can be much more."

Someone screams behind him, Leo shouting orders, Taylor dragging a villager to safety, Anna fighting with her magic as Zaide slices a rogue nearby.

There is so much slaughtering, and my heart is in my throat for anyone getting hurt.

But Darius?

He doesn't even look back. His sole focus is on me.

"Let her go, now!" Darius brings his hands up, that mist of his violently swirling around them.

"She is mine! She has been mine since she was a child!" Charles roars, and the platform beneath us rattles from the force of it.

"No," Darius says, quiet but deadly. "She has been *mine* since her soul was formed." Then, black rises from below us and he rushes for Charles.

It all happens so fast.

Darius's power snakes up the two pillars, spiraling upward, then it's moving down the chains, focusing on my wrists while another wraps around Charles's arm, yanking it back and effectively taking the blade away from my throat.

I hear a sizzle, and I watch as black flames appear, my wrists burning as he melts the chains wrapped around them, then I drop to the floor with a harsh *thud*.

I cry out, my left side taking the impact as my head bounces off the stone below me. I gasp through panting breaths, my eyes watching as Darius and Charles are colliding.

Charles has his own power around Darius, trying to restrict his arms but Darius fights him off with his black fire, dispelling it. Darius sends shards out, and Charles puts up a barrier to deflect them, and then Darius turns wolf, his big black paws landing on the ground.

I need to help, I need to move, but my legs feel numb.

Runa?

There is a small tingling inside of me, and I focus on it.

"You think you can take her from me? You are a boy! A swine!" Charles throws multiple balls of power at Darius, sending the rogues to him before he turns and wraps a barrier around me, closing me in.

No, not again.

I look around at the barrier, watching it shimmer in and out, knowing it can cause me the same pain he has been inflicting on me for what feels like hours.

Darius claws and bites through rogues, his side now bleeding and my heart is in my throat as he quickly turns back and grabs a blade, hitting it into a rogue's side and slicing it.

"You will die today, Charles," Darius says, his tone dark. "For everything you have done, the crimes you have committed." Darius launches himself at him and connecting his blade with Charles's own as Drax tears into a rogue, flames licking over them.

My vision blurs in and out as they continue to go at each other.

"I have the power of both the Gods within me, and you think *you* can kill me."

Darius grunts, attacking Charles, making him go on the defense as they circle the area, while the others continue their own fight.

And I'm here, useless.

I watch as Leo takes a hit, the beast's claws swiping at him as he stumbles back, Zaide thankfully grabbing his arm and hauling him behind him. I look further and see Anna, hands out, red swirling as rogues seem to be coming for her in slow motion. Josh is there too, stabbing a beast in its thigh as Colten shoves a sword though its neck. A wolf I recognize all too well, Hudson, is in the fray with Jerrod's wolf, snarling and biting. I see them all continuing to fight.

All bruised.

All bleeding.

And I think we are losing.

I look at Darius as he grits his teeth in pain, holding the top of his shoulder for a moment before dropping his hand as he lunges for Charles again.

His armor is ripped there, and the skin bubbles as I catch the remnants of Charles power sizzling into his skin. Darius forms a defensive position, his face full of pain and I think he is causing him the same electrifying pain that he caused me. Charles's laugh seems to confirm it.

He's toying with him.

My eyes slide to Charles as anger settles in my gut, before slowly moving and spreading throughout my body.

Darius groans, his body going taunt for a moment and Charles attacks, striking him with a sword in the side of his stomach. I gasp, my fingers curling into the stone as Darius spins away from him. Charles laughs, watching as blood splatters the floor from his injury and Charles throws more magic at him.

They go back and forth with magic and steel, blow after blow as Darius puts magic at his back to protect against beasts, as Drax continues his own savagery.

"Foolish boy, you could have had it all," Charles spits as he sends magic his way, catching his throat while Darius manages to stab a spike into Charles's shoulder. "Power, females, the people would have bowed at your feet!"

A shadow moves in the corner of my eye, and I glance at it, heart pounding as I see Darius's magic creeping up against the bottom of Charles's barrier, spreading out like cracks, trying to get through.

My eyes slide to Darius.

He's sneakily sent his magic here to try and free me while he's also fighting.

Darius jabs forwards, and Charles places a barrier up to block him before going on the attack again. I notice more dark patches appearing, slower this time, and they are right behind Darius, whose magic seems to have slowed down.

Oh Gods, he's weakening.

I look at his magic on the barrier and swallow roughly.

It's because he's helping me.

Come on, Rhea, move.

"She will never be yours again, Alpha Darius." Charles manages to grab him with magic, binding his arms at his side, squeezing so tight that he drops his blade.

"No!"

"Ahh!" Darius suddenly shouts and my head snaps to him, seeing his body still and rigid. Purple magic circles him in a fast turn, and Darius's own magic tries to swallow it, but it escapes every time.

"Dar!" I whimper as Charles walks toward him. Darius struggles, mindful to send out shards of attack to try and keep Charles at bay, but it's not working, Charles just blocks them with his power, knocking them to the side with shards of his own.

I hear a howl, then I see Drax leaping out of the fray of rogues, coming to his keeper, but the rogues that were slowly appearing out of the ground behind him, arrive.

"Darius, move, you have to move!" I get my arms under me, only for them to give way as I smack my chin off the stone.

"You thought you could best me?" Charles snarls. "I have years on you, boy. I looked after you after your father passed, I taught you how to be a Higher, I praised you to others, and you dare raise a blade to me!" His hand snaps out, and blood seeps from Darius's lips as his head swings to the side.

"Darius!" I shout frantically, eyeing his power next to me. His gaze flicks to mine and I swallow roughly.

He's distracting him, but at what cost?

"Lasandrhea seems worried, shall we go to her?" Charles turns, but Darius's magic comes out and grabs hold of the power binding him. Charles stops. "You think you can get out of my power? You think you could kill me?!" Charles continues as I try to move, to do anything. "I am more than anything you could ever be, Heir of Cazier," he spits, and then his hand is around Darius's throat.

No.

Charles has caused so much pain and suffering. He stole children, stole my childhood and family, controls the rogues and beasts and continues to kill anyone he chooses for his own gains.

He will not take my Vihnarn.

He will not.

Darius's face turns a dark shade of purple and my palms hit the floor, a cry coming from me. I push back and sit on my knees just as a sliver of his magic breaks through, Charles is too distracted with Darius to notice.

He thinks he is unstoppable, that he will be a God, but this is not how it ends.

My face heats and I feel a flicker within me, feel it bubble and expand before it zips around at high speed and I grab hold of it, yanking it to me with so much force that it steals the breath from my lungs.

Zahariss, hear me! Give me the strength I need to break what binds me, to protect the male that's tied to me.

I feel my hair start to float as Darius's power seeps into the space and comes for me.

Let me feel your anger at the injustice that has settled on the lands, let me be the one to release your fury.

I get to my feet, stumbling a little as I stare at the back of Charles in fury, knowing he has the male whom I love in his grasp.

I am the Heir of Zahariss.

I place my hands on the barrier, pain instantly shooting up my arms.

And I will not bend to the whims of a mad man.

My hands glow blue as I send my power into it, watching as cracks appear as Darius's mist circles my wrists.

The pain tries to take me to my knees, but I feel something stronger.

Rage.

"Darius will not be the one to kill you, Lord Higher Charles," I say, my voice not feeling like my own as Charles turns his head to me, his eyes widening for a moment. "I will!"

And then I break his fucking barrier.

EIGHTY TWO

Rhea

This feels like that very first time I felt the power running through me, when I welcomed it home. Only this time, I can control it.

I send a wave of power out, knocking Charles and Darius back as I begin to heal myself. I leap down from the platform, watching as rogues and beasts turn toward us, sensing a new predator in their midst.

I head for Charles as he gets to his feet, a barrier around him as Darius rolls to a stop.

I lift a hand, sending out balls of power to the rogues and beasts, helping Drax on the attack. My power sinks into them when they connect with their skin, dissolving their flesh until my power disintegrates.

The snow falls harder, and the temperature drops lower as I breathe heavily, a puff of white coming from me as I glare at Charles.

"You will pay for that," Charles says, lifting a hand and gathering power.

"Get up, Vihnarn," I say to Darius when he doesn't move.

A wave of blue spreading out beneath me with my every step, the once snow-covered ground now has grass peeking through. I release Runa, knowing she will help Drax as I go to Darius, keeping a wide berth from Charles as he watches me with an evil I feel like I can taste.

Darius growls, getting his knees under him and shaking his

head. He soon stands, looking around wildly until he sees me, instantly coming for me when Charles releases a roar, firing his magic at me.

Darius collides with me, sending us rolling, his power wrapping around us as we dodge Charles's attack.

We get to our feet quickly, Charles advancing on us as more rogues appear. *"Fuck, there are so many of them,"* I say breathlessly.

"The Elites will handle them," Darius says in a rush. I don't know if they can, but I have to trust they will. *"Are you okay?"*

"I'm good."

"Then it's time to hunt, little wolf."

"To the death."

"Only his."

Charles throws his head back and laughs, sporadically sending balls of magic our way. We duck and dodge, putting small barriers in place to protect ourselves as we head toward him.

"Oh, my dear Lasandrhea, shall I let you watch as I give Darius some ultrium? Let you watch him breed anything in sight?"

"That will not happen," Darius growls, throwing a shard his way.

"Won't it?" Charles smiles.

Screams behind us have us halting and turning slightly. My eyes widen in horror as the ground beneath the Elites, my pack and the people seemed to be covered in one huge, dark patch.

Claws and muzzles, pointed, rotted ears and hairy backs slither out from them in the tens…

My eyes swing back to Charles, a cry falling from my lips as I go heavily on the attack, my markings now alight on my face.

"Enough!" I shout, pushing my hand forward and sending another wave of power. It hits Charles's barrier and he's pushed back a little as Darius sends his out to circle around him.

Charles bares his teeth. "If you want to save them, all you have to do is come to me."

I hear another cry, this one full of pain and I try to block it out, try not to think of the swirling dread in my stomach as I can hear the slaughter behind me.

Fuck, fuck, fuck.

"She will not come to you!" Darius sends his power like a tornado around Charles, but in the next moment, it's dispersed.

"They will die, Darius." Charles tells him.

Darius goes on the attack now, hitting Charles's barrier and after a particular hit, it cracks and breaks through his defense, causing Charles to lift his sword to stop his head from being sliced off by Darius.

"Don't you dare, little wolf," Darius says to me as I circle around them, looking for any weaknesses.

"All you have to do is come to me, Lasandrhea, and I will make it all stop."

My mind whirls with what to do.

"Darius, they are dying!"

"You don't get it," he replies harshly.

"Get what?" I ask, my voice shaky.

"Without you, there is no life here. There will be nothing left. I will destroy it all."

"But they will all die."

"So be it. I still choose you."

I let out a heavy breath at that, my hands shaking as I send more attacks toward Charles, making sure no rogues or beasts are sneaking up on us.

I check on Runa and Drax, spot them tearing into the hounds with some Elites at their side. Drax sets it on fire, then moves to the next one.

I look back further and see the devastation, as the people try to fight off their enemies.

But they are losing.

They are *dying*.

I see Josh being knocked to the ground, a rogue upon him as he tries to fight it off. Anna tries to help, Taylor rushing to him. Leo falls next, his bare hands trying to stop a rogure from biting into him, the black poison dripping on him as I see a villager fall, no more than Kade's age as a beast lands on top of another.

They aren't going to make it.

Gods.

"I'll do it!" I shout, and Darius whips his head my way in shock as Charles smirks.

"The fuck you will—" Darius is knocked out of the way from being distracted, flying through the air and I swallow my nerves as he crashes into a tree.

I don't look at him as I head toward Charles, who is grinning from ear to ear.

"Rhea! Don't you dare! Move away from him. Now!" Darius continues to shout in my mind with every step I take toward the monster of my childhood.

"Call them off," I say to Charles, as he rights his clothes. They are dirty, have rips in them but the way he stands, it's not like he has even been in a fight.

"I will, once you put these back on." He lifts a hand, palm to the sky, and a pair of cuffs materialize.

"Rhea!" Darius shouts as he fights off Charles's violet power that is trying to restrain him.

I swallow over the lump in my throat. Those will suppress me, make me helpless once again.

Another cry.

A scream.

A snarl.

A choked breath.

I hear the battle as if it were right next to me.

Hear the people dying.

Feel blood splattering me, my hands covered in the innocent lives that are lost.

I take the last few steps to Charles as Darius screams in my mind. He sends magic my way, trying to wrap me up in it, but it's blocked once again by another barrier. This time it is around me and Charles.

It shrinks as he steps closer to me, and I step back on instinct, feeling the tingle of pain at my back as I'm a breath away from touching his barrier.

My hands shake as he opens the cuffs, his nostrils flaring and eyes full of delight.

"Call them off," I croak again, hating the waver in my voice.

His head dips a little, his dark eyes flickering with purple for but a moment, and then I hear less shouts, less pain.

Less death.

I look toward the beasts and see they have all stopped moving. Some are mid-bite, some have their claws raised, but they are at a complete standstill as the people look at them in confusion.

I breathe out, letting my head fall to my chest in relief as Charles takes hold of one of my wrists, painfully. He runs his thumb over the red marks there, never healed since the last time, and he smiles, pressing down on one until blood seeps beneath his fingers.

I hiss as he sends that fire of his into it, and a *bang* at my back has me jolting, and I can feel Darius there, sending so much power to break the barrier around us, trying to get to me.

Charles laughs, shaking his head as he clasps one cuff around my wrist.

"You were never going to defeat me," he tuts, shaking his head at me like a child. "I am more than both of you, and you will all bow to me when I have punished you for defying me. What a mess I have to clean up," he sighs as his nose wrinkles. "I will say, you saved me the effort of removing the other Highers." He chuckles, yanking on the cuff and pulling me toward him.

His hand goes around my waist, pulling me against his chest and I want to throw up.

Darius goes feral.

The snarls at my back are tinged with so much darkness that I think it will swallow us all.

I take a peek at him, seeing him fully coated in his power, two large tails at his back, eyes wild as he snarls and growls, covering Charles's barrier in complete darkness.

All I can see is the glowing, green eyes.

He's out of control.

"Forgive me," I say to him, but it's like he can't even hear me as he digs his fingers into the barrier.

Charles fills the space with glowing, purple balls as he inhales deeply at my head and pinches my hip. I tremble, revulsion spreading through me as his hand slides up my back to the base of my neck.

He yanks my head back. "I cannot wait to get what has been rightfully mine." His dark eyes bore into mine. "You shall bare my children, and others of course when I allow it." I whimper. "It was so easy to get Mazie to swap out a memory stone to bring you here. So easy to have Alpha Darius see it, think you a traitor and then punish you. The way your back split, the way your blood landed prettily on the floor of my hall." He dips his head. "If Mazie didn't report back to me of her findings in Eridian, I would have never found you, dear girl. How brave of you to try and take on the Elites, my pets." I struggle in his grip and he tuts at me. "That was your downfall, and my fortune. All was so easily manipulated to get you where I wanted you. Within my grasp again." He inhales at my neck and bile rises in my throat. "But first, we need to get that mutt off of you, though. To begin what was always meant to be."

His teeth nip at my neck, just below my ear, and I freeze.

That's Darius's spot.

That's his bite mark.

This is his scent.

No.

It's *our* scent.

When he bites deeper, when he breaks skin...something

inside of me snaps.

"That is not yours to take." I say it quietly, a murmur, really.

Charles pulls his head back, his brows furrowed at my tone.

"What? Speak up!" His grip on my hair tightens painfully, but I look up at him, eyes watering from the harsh grip, but my voice is strong.

"That is not yours. To. Take!" I shove at his chest, causing him to stumble back in surprise, then, I lean back into the barrier. With only one cuff on my wrist in his careless impatience and glee at having me, my power is still there, still useful.

I push my magic into the barrier through my back, merging with Darius's, and the ground shakes. In the next moment, I'm engulfed by Darius as he wraps his arms around me and pulls me through, shattering the barrier completely and into the safety of his embrace.

I waste no time as I lift a hand to Charles, sending a blast of power right into his chest as his eyes widen in shock.

This time, it's not blue.

It's not black.

It's purple.

Taking Darius's magic as if it were my own, it connects within me, building and merging into something more than my own ever was.

This is *our* power.

I walk toward Charles as he stumbles back, but I send another blast out, knocking him down. He tries to put up another barrier, and I even see dark patches following as we walk, calling more rogues, but he is not what we are.

We are Heirs to the Gods, our power was given—not stolen.

Darius's hand comes out at my side, sending more power to Charles and he sweeps him off of his feet, pinning him to the floor, elation fills me.

"Release me!" Charles screams, trying to call his power but every time he does, Darius and I call our own, wrapping it around him and snuffing it out. "You cunt, release me at once!"

Darius breathes heavily into my neck, his tails coming around me and I stroke them in reassurance as Charles continues to scream at us.

He isn't going anywhere.

We come to a stop before Charles, our hands covered in purple as we stare down the male who ruined my life. Ruined Darius's life.

Ruined so many other lives.

Darius growls into my neck, at the wrong scent there and without taking our eyes off of Charles, I tilt my neck and offer it.

Darius's teeth are piercing my skin in the next moment, and I lift a hand to his head, soothing him and pulling him closer, feeling that he needs this right now.

"It's okay," I tell him, and he purrs softly, a rumble coming from his chest as he digs in deeper and I breathe a sigh of relief.

Drax and Runa suddenly come to a stop next to us, growling down at this piece of shit and then I see it in his eyes.

Fear.

I catch my breath as heavy snow falls, the moon high in the sky as Charles continues to struggle.

Darius peels himself from my back and turns me, looking me over for injury. When he finds none, I see the relief in his eyes, along with anger at what I just did but we will deal with that later.

For now...

Darius takes my wrist in his hand, covering it with his power, then in the next moment, the cuff is burning and it drops to the ground.

Warmth rushes through me and I sag in relief.

I don't know how he managed to get it off, but I don't care.

Darius pulls me close, taking my face in his hands and he leans his forehead to mine, a slight tremble to his fingers and I grip his wrists, rubbing my nose with his.

He releases me suddenly, grabbing a sword off the ground

and hands it to me. "Do what you will with him. End it." He tilts my head up toward him, and places a soft kiss to my lips. "End him, Vihnarn."

He steps back and Drax nudges my side. I lift my hand to stroke him before I do the same with Runa, trying to calm her as she growls down at the monster who has plagued our minds.

I look back down at Charles as I move to his side, crouching down. "You took my childhood, as you did with many others, took my parents, as you did with many others." I look down at the sword and turn it this way and that. "You are worse than nothing," I tell him. "You will never accomplish what you have set out to do all these years."

He laughs, eyes crazed. "You think you can end me, girl? Look at you. I can't wait to get you in a cage again, I can't wait to feel you skin-to-skin and test how much you can take—" Darius kicks his side, his feet covered in his power.

Then he does it again and again, taking hold of his hand that he had in my hair and breaking his fingers one by one.

I look to him. "Calm, Vihnarn. He can't hurt me anymore. He cannot hurt anyone." Charles continues to laugh at that, even as he struggles to get free.

I look down at the sword again, and there are so many ways I could hurt him. Torture him even, and I want to.

I can feel it in my bones how much I want to make him suffer. How much I want to constantly cause him pain like he has done to me and so many others.

But as I look down at him, spouting all kinds of ways he will hurt me again, how he will be free, how he is above everyone.

I just want to rid the lands of him.

"I knelt at your feet once, chained and vulnerable. Now you are below me, your life in my hands."

"You think this is the end of me? This is only the beginning!" he spits, wriggling his body from side-to-side.

"You are pathetic. A small male trying to be bigger than he is. You are sick and greedy, Charles. A poison."

"I deserve power! I have given years to these lands, to the people. Why do you get to receive magic as old as the moon, over me!"

"Because I am worthy, and you are not."

He continues spouting all the things he wants to do to me, all things he has done to others as he watches me, but I don't listen to a single word.

Instead, I bring the sword to his throat.

"You will never hurt anyone again." I tell him. "I am the lands, and I will right the wrong. That begins with you."

"You think I'm going to be stuck by your binds?" He struggles more. "I am Lord Higher Charles!" He shouts, "and I am your new God! Release me and lay at my feet—"

He cries out, a cough coming from him as I stab the sword in his stomach. I watch as blood instantly pours from his mouth, watching him struggle in earnest as I pick it up and stab into him again.

He tries to speak, but all that comes out is blood, splattering on my face and I revel in it.

Revel in his end.

I call power to my palm, the color now purple, and then I'm sinking into his chest, my magic carving the way. Pain creases his face, a bloody scream coming from him as his body struggles in the binds as I dig deeper, finding the organ I want as Darius watches on closely.

Gripping it tightly in my palm when I have it, I squeeze and pull.

I hold up Charles's still beating heart in front of him, a smile on my face as he becomes pale, watching my hand flex with every slow beat as blood blooms on his chest.

"May you walk the below forevermore. Cursed to repeat your cycle in nothing but darkness and pain," I tell him as he shivers, his body twitching as his wide eyes stay upon me. "I hope Cazier enjoys playing with you. Lord Higher Charles," I mock, as he takes his last and final breath.

I rise to my feet, sword dangling from my fingertips as I stare at the monster who is no more.

No essence leaves him as I lift my gaze to Darius, his eyes filling with so many emotions as he peers into my soul.

"My little warrior." I smile softly at that, throwing the heart to him and his smirk is deadly as he catches it, squeezing it in his hold before crushing it under his foot.

I pull the sword from his stomach and I start chopping.

Darius watches on, arms folded, ever the protector as I hack, cut, and slice through flesh. When I get to bone and struggle, Darius whistles for Runa to come over, and then her teeth are there, snapping it in half.

When she's done, I wipe the bead of sweat from my brow, and pick up Charles's sword. Twirling it in my hand, I stab it through his chest, and pick up his head, slam it on the hilt.

It's *finally* over.

But when I turn to look at the Elites, my pack and the people who are tending to the wounded, the beasts and hounds that were at a standstill start to twitch, start to growl.

And then, they attack.

EIGHTY THREE

Rhea

I gasp, shock coursing through me as I'm frozen for a moment. We killed Charles, they should go back to where they came from. He controlled them…He…

"Why aren't they going back?" I ask Darius, as we both move in an instant, heading toward them as the others begin shouting in alarm, trying to defend themselves.

"We killed Charles, so the control he had over them must be broken," he replies. "Which means when he commanded them to stop, that no longer matters now."

Gods.

"What do we do?" I lift my hand and send out a wave of power, launching a few rogues to the side as best I can when we reach them, mindful of those I don't want to hurt.

"We get rid of them."

"All of them?" I gasp as I turn and pick up a discarded sword, wrapping two hands around the hilt and stabbing a rogue in the side.

"There are hundreds of them, Darius!" I gasp as more and more come out of the ground.

"Yes," Darius says as he suddenly hauls me to him, a barrier around us. He looks to the rogues, his eyes alert and thoughtful.

"Darius?" I try to free myself, but the frantic look in his eyes stops me.

His eyes bounce between mine before they roam over my

face, his grip almost punishing.

"Be safe," he tells me, his voice gruff.

My brows furrow. "Of course." I nod and go to move, but he hauls me back "Dar—"

He kisses me.

It's brutal and hard, and I gasp into his mouth, his purr sending shivers down my spine. Darius doesn't relent, he just hauls me closer and deepens the kiss, his tongue tangling with mine. Tasting, savoring.

Cherishing.

I whimper, gripping his arm as I feel his power wrap around my waist. When he pulls back, he rubs his nose to mine, squeezing his eyes shut, tightly.

"Darius...?" I question, but he just shakes his head and opens his eyes.

"Stay safe, Vihnarn." He says again, and I nod slowly, unsure what just happened.

"And you," I tell him, and he strokes the backs of his fingers down my face.

"Always you, little wolf."

With one last lingering look, he removes his magic and he rushes into the fray of rogues and beasts, leaving me standing there for a moment.

I reach for our link and feel it there, steady and true, so I shake myself out of my stupor to go to where I last saw Josh.

I stab and kick, push my power to its limits as I fight with the hounds plaguing the land. Runa is at my side, snarling and gnawing her way through as I spot a blonde head just ahead.

I rush for him, climbing on Runa's back in one smooth motion and then I'm there, next to him.

"You okay?" I ask when Josh spots me, and he nods, wiping the blood dripping down the side of his head.

"Yeah, but some need healing, can you do that?" I look at the way the Elites and some of the people have created a wall around what looks like injured people on the ground.

"I can," I tell him, my eyes searching and seeing Darius a ways across from me, battling with ease alongside his brothers.

"I'm going to heal some of the wounded, okay?" I tell Darius. *"Then they can help in the battle?"*

"Good plan, We will try and draw attention away. I'll let my Elites know."

I jump down from Runa, blessing the ground and causing a wave of purple to spread out. Hoping it will help slow some down.

Following Josh, he takes me to the injured and I waste no time. Ignoring the wet ground from the snow as it seeps into me, and the blood staining me, I place my hand on the first person's injury. A nasty gash in his side.

I focus my power there to begin to fix him, stitching my strands in a way to close the wound and begin healing.

"Why aren't they ported out?" I ask Josh, wiping the beads of sweat from my forehead.

I haven't used this much power at all, and it's beginning to take its toll on me.

"They have used them up," Josh says, helping the guy next to me.

"Already?"

He nods solemnly. "We have a lot of injured back at Eridian, but the witches went to help them.

I nod in approval. "That was a smart choice." I wait until the male's side is closed up before I stand. "There, just keep still and wait to heal some more, and then we need to help kill the beasts," I tell him.

"Thank you, Heir of Zahariss." I go to tell him my name is Rhea, but he's already closing his eyes to rest.

I move on to the next one as the battle wages on behind me, and I can tell those defending the injured are beginning to be pushed back.

Shit.

Every now and again, I join them, sending the rogures back

to the below where they belong, only to be called over to help another injured as more beasts appear.

I don't know how long we keep going, but the sun is peaking on the horizon in the distant mountains when I bend over, hands on my knees as I breathe heavily.

My power is waning, and the rogues and beasts don't seem to be stopping.

"Darius," I say down the link. *"We are getting nowhere."*

"They are appearing in the distance too, Zakith will be overrun with them soon."

My blood runs cold.

Charles is dead, we should be celebrating, not fearing for our lives as hounds still plague the lands.

"Why are more appearing, how is it possible?"

"I think they have completely lost all control. The below is out of control.

"Fuck."

He takes a moment to answer. *"We will figure it out, we just have to keep going."*

"How," I croak out, dizziness overcoming me, and Josh having not left my side, makes me sit down as he rubs my back.

"I told you I would keep you safe, and getting rid of these creatures will do that. There is no other option."

"I know."

"So they will be gone from the lands, Vihnarn. I vow it."

The determination in his voice would settle me, but another body just dropped to the floor and I rub my tired eyes.

"When this is over," I say, breathing a lot slower now. *"Take me to the lesia flowers?"* I ask, looking at the blood staining my hands. *"Take me away from the bloodshed and carnage. I want to play in the flowers you gave me, while you watch over me. Like you always have. I want to run and feel the freedom we deserve. I want to watch the moonlight shine down on us and start a simple life."*

Darius doesn't answer straight away, and I look up, like I can see him through the legs of people and creatures.

"Darius?"

He answers in a soft tone, one that makes me blink a few times at it.

"I will make sure you go to the lesia fields, Vihnarn, and you can play there until your heart's content. You will feel the ground beneath your bare feet, because you prefer it that way. You will look up to the moon shining down on you, because you love to bask in its light. Then you will run, and spin, and smile before feeling the petals at your fingertips, because you like to make sure it's real."

I hum down the link, smiling at the image. It truly is my favorite place.

A place he made for me.

Just for me. For Us.

"I can't wait," I tell him as I stand, nodding in thanks to Josh. *"Let's get rid of them quickly, Dar. We are tiring, and I want to sleep with you under the moonlight surrounded by my flowers."*

"As you wish it," he whispers back.

I jump back into it with another sword that I picked up. I don't want to know if its owners are dead as I stab a beast in its leg, waiting for it to turn so Runa can jump on it. It goes down with a tumbling *thud* and Josh and I end it. The battle wages on, rogures die and more people are injured, but we still don't stop. And neither do the creatures.

I stab the hind leg of another beast when it whirls toward me, and I send a ball flying its way in an instant, watching as it sinks into its chest, disintegrating everything in its way. The beast doesn't fall though, and it comes at me with sharp, clawed hands.

I duck and weave its attack, nearly knocking into a villager when I roll and slice it in the back of its ankle.

It wobbles as it spins to follow me, but an Elite is there, stabbing into its side, sending it crashing to the ground.

More and more rogures and beasts come to the surface, quickly overwhelming us and I spin in a circle, slashing and striking, trying to hold them back but it's too much.

We are being overrun.

No.

I scream as a claw rips down my arm, blood dripping on the snow and I turn, stabbing the rogue in the eye and kicking it away from me. Panting heavily, sweat forming at the back of my neck, I hold onto the gash, feeling the heat of my blood.

I feel the hum of my power in my feet, and I look down at it and wonder.

Crouching quickly, I place my palm down, sending out a wave of my power to coat the area around me, but also to call on those who said they would aid us. Hoping it will work.

Kruten, help us.

I send my magic to the dirt beneath the cold snow, thinking of the trolls, thinking about how Kruten said they would aid us.

I hear a scream that soon gets cutoff by growls and snarls, and I swallow roughly.

Fuck!

I get up and attack a rogue, a Higher guard dead at its feet. I launch myself at it, landing on its back and stabbing straight down the center of its head. Quickly clambering off of it, I'm back to back with an Elite, the rogues quickly surrounding us.

"We aren't making it, there are too many!" he says, his breathing uneven. "Quickly, Heir of Zahariss. I'll make a pathway for you to leave."

"I am not leaving you to die."

"It will be an honor to protect you."

"You can shove that honor—" I stab a hound. "Up your ass."

"Alpha Darius will kill us all if something were to happen to you."

"Let me handle my babysitter."

He grunts. "As you wish it."

We fight back-to-back, holding off the beasts trying to attack us as carnage spills across the ground.

"Fuck," the Elite behind me says, and I look over my shoulder, watching as two rogues lunge.

I turn, gripping the back of his armor, ready to pull him out of harm's way when a cloud of dust appears in front of him.

The Elite and I land with a *crash* on the ground, getting to our feet quickly as whimpers are heard in that cloud of dust.

What the...

As it settles, I realize exactly what caused it.

"Hali, we come to aid you!"

"Kruten!" He nods at me, and then he's gripping a rogue's head between his hands and crushing it. I spot more and more trolls in the fray, helping us in this battle as they pop-up in plumes of dust.

They really did come to help.

"Thank you!" I tell him, and he chuffs, picking up a rogue and sending it flying through the air. I spot another troll fighting with a beast, their heights matched and I jump back into the fight.

"We will do what we can, Halis." I nod my head to him as I spot a female troll kicking a rogue in the side, and I instantly recognize her as the mother of the boy I saved.

She looks at me, bowing her head slightly and I smile, throwing myself back into the battle.

"Darius, the trolls are here to help!"

The battle wages on, and I help protect anyone from getting to the wounded while gathering new ones on the way and putting them in the protective circle we have made.

I'm covered in blood and guts, sweat dripping from me but still, we keep at it and we don't give up.

But neither do they.

More and more come. Never ending as we all tire, as more die...

I'm losing hope.

Even with the trolls aid, we are still outnumbered, we are still weakening and tiring, we are still losing.

Why won't they stop? It's like they have been unleashed

upon the lands with no rhyme or reason.

I ready myself for more as a rogure is up next, leaping toward me and I punch it in the side of its head. It skids to the side and that's when I see another rogue coming for me from the right.

Fuck.

Hand out, I send a ball of magic toward it, but I didn't see the third one coming for me head-on.

I step back, lifting the sword and throwing it in the air to hit it. It digs into its chest as it releases a whimpering shriek. It doesn't stall like I thought it would though, instead it continues barreling toward me and it leaps at me, knocking me off my feet with a shocked cry.

We land hard and heavy on the snow, and its teeth are right there, black saliva dripping from its mouth and it's about to snap its jaw shut over the front of my face when it freezes.

I push at it in alarm, scrambling over it as I stand, hand out and ready when I pause.

The rogure is still, like it's frozen in place. White puffs of air still come from its open mouth, so it's still alive but it's…stuck.

This is like when Charles controlled them, but Charles is no more.

I look around in confusion like everyone else, the battle seemingly paused as we wonder what is going on.

"Josh, do you see this?"

"They are frozen over there, too?"

"Yeah?"

I spot a male on the floor beneath a beast, his arm bleeding profusely and I go to him, dragging him up and draping his arm around me.

"I got you."

"Fuck, it hurts." I don't tell him I can see his bone peeking through his armor as I slowly make my way toward where the injured are, subtly using my magic to stem the bleeding.

As we wade through frozen beasts and hounds, dark patches start appearing beneath them and I shout in alarm. "Watch out!"

The others start noticing too, and they all move away from the creatures as best they can with the amount here.

"We need to hurry," I tell the Elite I'm half-dragging. We can't have any more arrive, we won't survive it.

But none do.

A rogure in front of me starts to slowly sink into the ground.

I stare into its bone-colored eyes as I see its breath coming from its open mouth still, see pieces of its gray skin rotting off, but it doesn't move as it slowly sinks.

I look around, watching as others begin to do the same. Even Kruten looks confused.

"They will be gone soon." Darius says, and the breath stalls in my throat.

"To the below?"

"Yes. They won't hurt anyone. Hurt you."

I eye them. *"They won't?"*

"No, little wolf."

I nearly stumble in relief. Oh Gods. We made it.

"They're going back!" I shout to those around me, and their eyes widen, their shoulders slumping in relief.

Kruten lifts his arms and cheers, and the other trolls start stomping their feet.

I haul the injured with the others, keeping an eye on the sinking creatures as Josh rushes for me. He hauls me into a hug and I grip him tightly, breathing in his scent, then Colten, Hudson and Taylor are there, Anna trailing behind them.

We pull each other close, relief spilling from us.

We are alive.

We're alive.

A wet nose touches the back of my neck, and I giggle as Runa pushes her way in, wanting to be a part of it, and the others stroke her too before I call her within me to rest.

"We did it," Josh says, relief in his eyes.

"Thank Gods that's over," Taylor says, and Hudson nods, keeping Colten steady.

"You okay, pup?" He asks, and Colten huffs.

"I'm fine."

We smile at each other, and I'm so ready to go home and bathe for hours, but then grief hits me.

"Seb," I whisper, and their faces fall, eyes instantly to the ground.

"We will make sure he gets home," Anna says, and I nod.

We will take him to the graveyard and bless him to run free. My only hope is that he is with his mate now in Vahaliel. Just like he wanted.

"We need to gather the injured so we can get stones to port them out of here." They nod, their heads held high.

We are bloody, dirty and exhausted, but there are things we still need to do.

"Then we gather the dead and bring them home too. They need to be blessed,"

"Yes, Alpha,"

I scowl. "None of that," I whisper.

They set out to do what I have asked, and I turn, heading to where I last saw Darius.

I need my Vihnarn for a moment.

"I don't know how, but they are still going, Darius. Is it really over now?"

I weave through the mass of creatures that are still sinking into the ground, helping others stand and giving them directions on where to congregate.

"Darius?"

Still no answer. He must be busy, but he's never too busy to answer me.

I spot Maverick as I continue, and he smiles tiredly, nodding his head when he sees me. "Heir of Zahariss."

"It's just Rhea," I tell him, rolling my eyes.

"You are with Alpha Darius, I do not want to lose my head over a title slight." He smiles, teeth bloody.

"Have you seen him? Darius, I mean." I look around, trying

to spot him.

He tilts his head, nodding behind him. "I last saw him heading toward a large pack of rogues that way," he points to the right. "He wanted to make sure they wouldn't come this way as it would have been more than the people here could have handled."

That makes sense.

"Thanks," I tell him, heading toward the direction he told me.

I heal a few people on the way the best I can, knowing I need to be careful with my power. I try to ignore the dead at my feet, trying not to step on them but far too many were lost, and I swallow a few times over the lump in my throat.

Darius will be sending out more letters than I think he ever has.

War is never pretty, but to see it right in front of you is enough to lose the contents of your stomach.

The further I go to Darius, the more the creatures and people dissipate. I still see no sign of him or his brothers, but then I look down and notice his magic.

I pause, crouching and placing my hand on top of it. I feel its coolness seep into me instantly.

I smile and look up, seeing Leo heading toward me through the scattered, frozen creatures.

I rush to him, relief coursing through me with a smile on my face. I like the male now, and I like how protective he is of Darius.

"Hey," I say to him when I reach him, smiling wide with elation. "Do you know where…"

Leo doesn't say anything, but he does look at me.

His mouth turned down, his posture slumped, but it's his eyes that stopped me.

They are sad, dull.

"Leo…?" I ask, daring to place a hand on his arm. Darius would rip it off of him if he saw. "What's wrong?"

"Rhea," he starts, turning his head to look behind him.

My brows furrow and I look in the same direction that he is, and my heart stops.

Just...stops.

Rogures are sinking into the ground, littering the field in the dozens, frozen in various states of attack.

But that isn't what stopped my heart.

Darius does.

He stands in the middle of it all, that black mist of his power swirling around him as he looks up to the coming morning, bathing him in a soft light.

His back is toward us, hands clenching at his side, and there is no sign of Drax with him at all.

But he's slowly sinking into the ground.

I let go of Leo's arm and start to move toward him on shaky legs. They feel numb, like they can barely stand as I start to stumble in his direction, but I don't stop.

"Darius..." I choke out down the link.

He doesn't answer, but his head turns to the side, like he knows I'm here.

Even from this far away, I see his back tense, see his power become more volatile around him.

"Darius!" I try again, and his hands flex.

When he sinks further, I run.

No matter my exhaustion, no matter how I feel like my legs can no longer hold me up.

I run to him.

"Darius!" I scream his name, a cry bubbling up my throat at what I'm seeing.

I dodge rogures, dead men, roaring beasts...I jump over corpses in my bid to go to him and still, he won't turn around, he won't answer me.

"Darius, what are you doing!" I'm so close, so, so close now and I move what little power I have left to my feet to gain speed.

I'm nearly there.

Just a few feet away.

I can grab him and…

I slam into a barrier.

I stare at it in shock, my palms flat against it as I dig my fingers in.

I frantically look around it, looking down to where the dark hole is swallowing Darius.

Taking him.

"Darius, quick, drop the barrier and I'll help you get out of there." I push power into the barrier and I look behind me quickly as Runa whines within me.

His brothers are there, watching me. "Come and help me, quickly," I tell them. They just stand there, faces crumbling. "Why aren't you helping me!" I scream at them, tears rolling down my face as I drop to my knees, clawing at the dirt, trying to dig my way through.

If I can get *under* the barrier, I can help him get out. I can pull him from there.

"Rhea." Darius's voice is a whisper, but I continue to scrape the dirt away. "Little wolf."

A sob bursts from me as I frantically dig at the ground, tearing clumps away and throwing them anywhere I can as I continue.

"Vihnarn."

"No!" I scream, leaning my forehead against the barrier, as I catch my breath, "No," I whimper.

My eyes flutter open, and he's there, directly in front of me now.

His green eyes that I love so much are now full of sadness.

Darius never has sad eyes.

My hands go back to the barrier.

"It will be okay," he tells me, and I shake my head frantically at that.

"No," I whisper. I don't believe it.

I can't.

He raises his palm and places it over mine through the barrier. I feel him there, so close yet out of reach.

He's down to his waist now, and the sound that comes from me is like a dying animal. But that's what I feel like.

I feel like I'm dying.

"I have to keep you safe," he tells me.

"I'm safe where you are."

"They are from the below, Vihnarn," he tells me gently, looking around at the creatures. "They can only be gone if I take them with me."

"Get someone else!"

Zahariss, *please*! Cazier!

He shakes his head. "I would give you anything, but not this. You would never be safe with them roaming the lands, and that would eventually mean you would no longer walk the lands."

"Dar," I whisper, my lips trembling. His eyes tighten and he releases a deep sigh, moving closer toward me, his own fingers flexing on the barrier.

Runa comes to my eyes, watching on with whimpers that rattle around inside of me.

"Remember when you told me you would do anything to protect those you love?" I sob, tears rolling down my cheeks as my fingers curl against his on the barrier. "This is me protecting it, Rhea."

I sag against the barrier, crying, body shaking as I try to breathe. My lungs feel like they are about to give out, and pain travels around my body, my ears ringing.

This isn't fair.

"Vihnarn," he says, his deep voice seemingly trying to reach the bones of me, and the ground begins to shake at my feet.

I look down toward it, seeing black mist rise, getting thicker around his waist until it's touching up against the barrier at the bottom. Like waves splashing against rocks.

"Drop the barrier, Darius." Another head shake. "Darius," I

plead.

"I can't, little wolf."

"What do you mean you can't? You can. Just call your power back and drop it!" My heart begins to race and I push all I have into the barrier, trying to break it.

"The land has always wanted something back." He tilts his head. "To right the wrong."

These words will forever haunt me.

"Not like this." He clenches his jaw and closes his eyes briefly, his features pained as he opens those light green eyes of his, and I see the truth of it all with them. "Darius, please don't go."

"If I don't do this, more will come. They will destroy *everything*."

"It doesn't matter. We can kill them all, just don't leave me, you can't leave me. You said we would go to the lesia field."

"I said *you* would be there, little wolf." That stops me short and I think back. He never said he would be there. "When you walk under the moonlight, remember I will be right there below you, following in your footsteps."

"But you won't be here with me, will you?!" He sinks even deeper and a panicked cry escapes me. "We can find something else to take them back. Why can't Cazier take them back?!"

"He has no control over them now. He is too weak. He told me as much when we were in Tyeetha." And Darius is strong enough being his Heir and full of power. "Rhea," he says, his own voice cracking and pain slices my heart. I shake my head again and again.

He's still sinking, and I start digging into the ground again at the bottom of the barrier, needing to get him out of here, my nails breaking and bleeding.

"Stop, little wolf, you are hurting yourself," he whispers, and I lift my head, his own at the same level now. "It will be okay."

"How could this ever be okay," I cry, a sob ripping from me and I move as close as possible to the barrier, placing my forehead against it and Darius leans in mirroring me. "You can't leave me now." I claw my hands against his barrier, my nails breaking and his face drops. "I can't do this."

"You can." His jaw ticks and he blinks a few times. "I have never chosen you when you needed it, when you deserved it. This is me choosing you now. To keep you safe, to make sure you can still play, and spin, and laugh in those fields of lesia flowers that you love so much."

I shake my head. "I don't want it without you."

"You were okay without me for a long time, you will be okay now." He smiles sadly at me and my heart crumbles.

"Not anymore."

He breathes deeply and stares into my eyes before roaming over my face, cataloging everything he can about me as that mist comes to his shoulders, dragging him down.

"You have my heart, Vihnarn," he murmurs. "Tell me you know that?"

My heart shatters.

Completely shatters.

I nod. "And you have mine," I croak out.

He smiles that boyish smile as he sinks lower, his hand dropping from mine on the barrier, and then…

Darius is gone.

EIGHTY FOUR

Rhea

The trolls are gone now, along with the dead bodies that scattered the floor like grains of sand.

And so are the rogures.

They sank into the ground, along with Darius, back to the below where they came from.

I don't know how long I have been sitting here covered in blood and guts from the battle, but I can't move.

I can't force myself away from the last place I saw him.

Where my heart was last whole.

My pack comes to me. They whisper words of sorrow and reassurance, trying to get me to leave with them but still.

I can't move.

I can't speak.

It's like I'm not in my body anymore.

And I'm not.

Because my heart was taken away from me. It was swallowed up by darkness and I cannot find it.

It's snowing again.

And the ground surrounding me that was once covered in red, is now pure-white once more.

I think I'm cold.

I know my body is shaking.

But again.

I don't move.

Someone places a blanket over me, others place food and

water down.

The Elites come, mourning their loss as I feel furs surrounding me, and I assume they turned wolf to keep me warm.

Wolves like the contact as they all lay around me, but I don't feel a single thing, even as Runa whimpers and whines inside of me.

I look at the darkened ground in front of me.

The snow never covers that bit, like it knows it needs to be seen.

A reminder of who was there before it.

I think it's another day now.

   I blink, and the food is changed along with water skins.

   Wolves no longer circle me, but that's okay.

   I like the silence.

   Silence will let me know if I can hear him.

   If I hear his footsteps.

   I look at the dark patch, my fingers stiff but they twitch.

   I lean forward, a blanket falling off my shoulders and I place my hand atop it.

   Trying to sense him.

   Feel him.

   But my shoulders slump.

   Because I feel nothing at all.

I look over the carving that I found in our cave.

It's wonky, chunks are missing, but the two wolves intertwined, wrapped around each other is another stark reminder of what I lost.

Why Darius made this for me, only to make it hurt every time I look at it, I don't know.

Did he know he would have to take the rogures below? Has he known all along?

I shake my head at the questions I don't have answers to, and I port to just outside of Eridian where the lilk trees are.

Spring is here.

Fresh grass is peaking through the snow and I can't bear to look at it.

At the reminder of his eyes that were always watching me.

I nod at my pack as they check on me, moving away from their touch like it burns.

It sort of does.

It's not the touch I want.

Runa whines within again.

Even she doesn't want to come out.

I port again, and as soon as I land, I take the same path I always do.

I see Leo here with Edward, and I know they will probably want to update me on things, but I bypass them.

I don't care.

Everyone is living their lives, but I'm at a standstill.

I know Edward is rebuilding a council, a member from each pack territory will be on it, and Leo was discussing how the Elites will still continue on with their protection of the lands, after abolishing all previous laws.

One being that you are now allowed to have no pack, and you don't have to declare your whereabouts.

There are great changes happening, and though Edward doesn't want to see himself as the leader of this council, he is, and he is already making the lands a great place.

He is fair and strong. He wants what's best for Vrohkaria and I admire him for that.

I just...don't want anything to do with it.

How could I when the one thing that was mine has been taken from me?

I don't feel like I won anything.

I don't feel like my nightmare has ended.

Because I lost *him*.

I place my hand on the lilk tree, closing my eyes and feeling the undercurrent of Darius's power within here.

It is the only place I can feel him, and today, I spend a little extra time here before I port out once again.

When I walk and get to my spot, I look down at the dark patch and crouch.

Undoing the pouch from my side, I open it and rifle through the seeds.

"We will play in the lesia flowers, Darius, just like you said."

The summer heat bathes me as I walk through the new field of lesia flowers.

They circle out from the dark patch, making sure to fill as much space as possible.

It took many days and nights to do it, but I did.

I walk barefoot through them, Runa at my back. I look down at my bare feet, wondering if he is following them below like he said he would.

But I still can't feel him.

I think he lied.

But Darius has never lied to me.

I head to that dark patch, as always.

Runa lays down, head on her paws and I lay in between her, resting my back on her belly.

And there we stay, again.

Waiting.

The lilk trees are still as beautiful as the first day I saw them.

I place my hand on one, feeling the power thrumming within, his power.

It greets me, and I take a breath.

That's getting harder these days.

Breathing.

There is a tightness in my chest that won't leave me.

Painful thumps of my heart that feel like it would bring me to my knees, and it's his heart.

Is he hurting?

My hand trails over the tips of the lesia flowers.

They look dainty, yet still stand strong.

They will not wilt, they will not die.

I'm not sure I can be like a lesia flower.

Edward says it's normal to feel this way, that my heart is broken. I overheard him speaking to Kade and Josh about me, but I think he knew I was there and wanted me to hear.

But I'm not heartbroken.

My soul is broken.

I blink sluggishly as I reach the dark ground.

There is no such thing as forever.

I still can't look at the grass fully.

I can't look at it and not remember him with the green eyes.

It hurts too much.

So I busy myself with other things.

I visit Belldame at Witches Rest, just to keep her mind at ease and see how far she has come with rebuilding. New homes rest on stilts once again, and they laid to rest their dead, blessing them at Da Bier Dall.

Then I go to see Edward at Fenrikar Castle, briefly. He stays there with the other members of the council, and Vrohkaria is thriving.

And I'm dying.

It feels like the rogues were a bad dream to others now, and I guess it will go down in history texts of just another bad thing that happened, and it will be forgotten that someone sacrificed himself for the peace they now have.

My pack is still in Eridian. They didn't want to move and I didn't force them.

Josh has taken over most of the Alpha duties and Kade has been working on himself the best he can for the time being.

The Elites are now revered and respected more than feared after they continue to protect the people from other creatures, and they are doing great under the watchful eye of Leo.

They come and see me often, at least one of them at one time, but I'm not easy to chase down.

I make sure of it.

I can't see them and not think of him.

I can't see them and not be reminded of how they just stood there, even if they told me they were respecting his wishes and it was hard for them.

They should have helped me.

But they didn't.

The leaves are falling now.

And so am I.

I raise my hand to the moon and watch it shine between my fingers. Wiggling each one, letting its glow peek through as I lay on my back, I think of all the things I left unsaid.

I lost track of how long it has been, lost track since the last time my heart beat.

Can he see me? Can he feel me?

Others think I'm getting better day by day, but they are wrong.

I'm just better at hiding it.

I don't want to see their sad or worried looks, I don't want to deal with the dreaded, 'are you okay' questions.

So I paste a smile on my face, talking as I would normally, I even laugh here and there.

Then as soon as they are out of sight, I sag against the closest surface, my smile dropping as sadness clouds my mind.

Runa rests inside of me after a run with the pack. I heard she even played with Kade for a while so I think she enjoyed it.

I didn't even go, I chopped wood instead.

I let my hand drop to the side. It's late. Everyone is sleeping back at Eridian but I couldn't sleep.

So I came here, again.

I roll over, my hands running through the darkness, trying to feel close to him. My eyes blink heavily and I curl up on my side, hiding within the lesia flowers at my back, hoping I see him in my dreams.

But my dreams are few and far between, all that's left is nightmares of a sinking body and darkness.

EIGHTY FIVE

Rhea

Something washes over me.

A niggling feeling that wakes me.

I stretch, a groan coming from the stiffness in my joints at staying in the same position.

Sighing, I sit up, rubbing a hand down my face and look to the moon. It's still high in the sky, so I know I haven't had much sleep.

That is nothing new.

Not when your dreams are nightmares of shadows.

Covering a yawn with my hand, I stand. I may as well head back to Eridian and start early on the daily jobs. We need more wood, and I can go hunting early. We feed more now as some of the refugees didn't leave, so that will keep me busy for longer.

I nod to myself.

Planning the day helps, it keeps me busy.

Keeps me from feeling the emptiness of a heart that is no longer there.

I feel the port stone in my pocket, but with it still being the middle of the night, I can walk a little. Maybe I can look over the Aragnis pack.

Mivera and her pack lie there now, and she has built more cabins for those passing through who are in need of a place to stay.

She once told me that she was giving just a little back to how

I helped her.

I'm glad she has found a place to stay, and I don't resent her having my old home.

My home is lost to me, so I'm not going to kick her out of hers, even though it is rightly mine after Darius burned my other family members and my old cabin to the ground.

I didn't know that until Leo told me. I just walked away.

It wasn't because I was upset that it had happened.

It was because Darius did that for me and he never told me.

He purged more of my monsters and he didn't want recognition for it. He just made it so because they are the people who hurt me.

I trace my fingers over the lesias as I walk, watching the blue light up under the moon's gaze. The space is filled now, going as far as the eye can see, and I have no more lesia seeds to speak of.

I will have to wait for another traveling merchant to come by, but they are few and far between now. They are saying that there are things going on in the west and it is hard to travel through, and it makes me wonder if it has anything to do with Kruten and his tribe. They headed that way after all.

I sigh, picking a flower and bringing it to my nose, the sweetness of its center calming me for a moment, but suddenly, my senses go on high alert at the feel of power at my back.

I blink, my body tense.

Brows furrowing, I breathe steadily, even as a tremble starts in my fingers.

I turn slowly, sensing something here with me.

I drop the flower, hands now at my sides as I look over the field of blue, trying to pinpoint where it came from.

Runa stirs within me, but there is nothing. Not a single thing there.

I turn, shaking my head at myself. I need sleep, maybe that's why I feel so on edge—

A wave of power rushes out over the field, the flowers

swaying with it and a scent follows.

A scent I know all too well filling my lungs, for the first time in what feels like a lifetime.

My heart beats so hard it feels like it's going to come through my chest as I stop dead in my tracks. My breathing is erratic as I turn, hair flying around my face in my haste as I look at the figure in the distance, look to where he stands above a patch of black.

The figure cracks his neck from side to side rolling his shoulders, and a whimper spills from my lips.

His hands flex next, like he's shaking them out and I stare at the dark head of hair.

I take a step, my legs shaking, eyes blinking, praying they are not deceiving me.

Praying this isn't like that last time where I ran to an illusion, only to fall face-first in my flowers as my heart broke all over again.

The figure turns their head to the side, as if sensing someone here.

Another step.

Their shoulders rise, like they are taking a deep breath, and then, they turn.

I pause, a cry building in my throat as we stare at each other.

And then, I'm running.

That cry spills from my lips, my eyes never leaving his face as he tilts his head and smiles a boyish smile, one that he only ever shares with me.

He doesn't move, no, the asshole waits for me and as soon as I'm close enough, I hear his voice flitter around in my mind as our connection floods open.

"Found you, little wolf."

I crash into him, and he's wrapping me up in his arms, his body shaking as I cry into his neck, holding him close as he breathes me in.

"My Vihnarn," he says, his voice like gravel as I hold him like he will disappear in the next breath, because that's what he did. He left me. "Shh, little wolf. I'm here."

I don't recognize the noises coming from me, like a wounded animal, but he holds me just as close, breathing me in.

"I'm here now."

"Are you?" I choke on my own words and I hear his rough swallow. "Are you real?"

"I am."

I pull back, and my hands go to his face, tracing his jaw, his nose and mouth. I move to his hair next, feeling the strands that are a little longer now, until I rest my fingers over his marking, then move them lower to feel the beating of his heart.

"You're here," I breathe, tears spill down my cheeks. "You're really here."

He stares at me so deeply, so intently as those glass-like flecks appear. "I missed you, Vihnarn." His power comes out, wrapping me up in it and I'm sobbing, shoulders shaking, but he looks at me like I'm the most beautiful thing he has ever seen. "Shh." He holds me tighter as I wrap my legs around him, his own body trembling. "Fuck, I'm here now." Runa whimpers within me, and I feel Drax there, just under his skin in greeting. "I'm sorry it took so long to get back to you." He takes some of my hair, wrapping it around his finger. "It took longer than I ever expected." A haunted look crosses his face, his eyes darkening.

"You left me," I croak out. "Why did it take you so long to come back to me?" I inhale his scent, trying to let it calm me as I grip him, scared he will disappear, scared I'm dreaming.

"I had to make sure it was safe before I came back, to make sure beasts that should stay in the below…stay there."

"And will they? Stay there? Do you have to go back?"

"It is done," he tells me and I sag into him, another tear dropping.

"You are such an asshole for leaving me," I whisper, sniffing and he wipes the tears from my face.

I want to be angry at him for leaving, for making me go through months of agony, barely breathing, but I'm filled with so much relief that he is here.

"I'm yours though," he tells me, his voice gruff, like he can barely contain his *own* emotions.

"Mine," I agree softly, sniffling.

He holds the back of my head, moving my face to his neck and I breathe him in fully for the first time in months as his grip on me is almost painful. He doesn't move, just keeps me close to him until his hand goes to the back of my head, grips my hair and pulls my head back.

Our eyes clash, my eyes full of tears and his full of anguish. I see the pain he has been in, so much like my own and I never want to be apart again, never want him to stop looking at me like I'm his everything.

He leans his forehead to mine, his nose rubbing against me in greeting after a long time, and I clutch his shoulder, my nails digging into him.

"My Vihnarn," he breathes against my lips, and then, he's kissing me, breathing air back into my lungs.

Completing me.

Finally, bringing me home.

EIGHTY SIX

DARIUS

I hold Rhea closer as she rests, watching Runa and Drax play. They haven't stopped rubbing up against each other, always playing, nipping and licking, always touching one another in some way.

It must have been just as hard for her as it was for the female in my arms who I refuse to let go of.

I feel like she will disappear from my arms, much like she feels I will, taking her warmth with her after feeling so cold for so long.

She never once wavered when I was taken to the below, never once left my side where she last saw me.

She didn't move for a long time at first, as I paced back and forth, looking up for any sign of movement, unable to do anything but watch her wither away.

My brothers tried to help her too, but still, she never left me.

So I raged in the dark of the below, growling and snarling like the beasts I was locking up down there, until eventually, I looked up again and she moved.

Slowly at first, like she didn't know how, and I was right there with her.

I followed her, tracing her footsteps from the below, just like I said I would.

They looked like raindrops of light every time she took a step, and I was right beneath her watching through the darkness, reaching up with a hand because I wanted to be closer to her in any way I could.

I couldn't feel her though, couldn't sense her, but she was always that light above who stopped the dark from fully consuming me, who stopped me from going mad in my solitude surrounded by beasts.

Because I was close.

Being away from her, not being able to smell her, touch her, look into those eyes that own my heart, my fucking soul, had been a torture, one I now know that Cazier goes through every passing moment as he's separated from Zahariss.

Cazier guided me in the below, teaching me to craft chains of my power to wrap around the beasts and keep them rooted to the ground in there, if you can call it that. It was darkness and what looked like water because when you stepped upon the ground, ripples formed, but you never got wet.

He told me that was also the place he brought Rhea to, to be able to give her enough power to reach back to me, under Zahariss's orders, and I was thankful for that, but I wasn't thankful how long it would take me to get back to her, if I even could.

Cazier said I may not, that the chance was small, but I would move the lands for my Vihnarn and I managed to get the beasts under control enough that Cazier, even with his dwindled power, took over.

And then with his help, he got me to the surface and back to my Vihnarn, rising up to where she waited for me, surrounded by her favorite flowers just like we are laying in now, her on my chest.

And I will never let go of her again.

We are infinite.

And she is mine, just as I am hers, always.

She mumbles something against me, then lifts her head, looking down at me with sleepy eyes.

She blinks a few times likes she's making sure I'm here, and I smile up at her, running a hand through her hair.

She sighs, her own smile forming as I rub her nose with mine.

"Sleep, Vihnarn," I tell her. I feel the exhaustion pulling me down, but I don't want to take my eyes off of her for one moment.

"I don't want to," she yawns, snuggling closer.

"You can rest now, I won't go anywhere."

She looks at me closely. "You really won't?" Her eyes are full of fear at the thought and I pull her closer, knowing exactly what that feels like.

"I'm not going back down there," I say on a rough swallow. "I made sure the rogures and the beasts of the below stay down there. It just took a lot of my power and time to make sure they wouldn't come back, and therefore, be a risk to you. They are chained as they are meant to be, back under Cazier's control as he watches over them. I belong here with you."

"Always?" she whispers, her eyes imploring me.

"Always." I take a piece of her hair and place it behind her ear. "I vow it."

Her hand comes up and she places it over my heart, rubbing gently back and forth. Her eyes flash with so many emotions, until they settle on one that makes my heart pound beneath her fingertips. I'm sure she can feel it when she digs her nails in, taking a deep breath.

"I love you, Darius Rikoth," she says softly, so softly and filled with so much certainty as I stare at her, watching the light of the moon reflecting in her eyes, in awe that this female can even feel such a thing for me. "Please don't ever leave me again."

I don't know how I earned her love. I don't deserve it, I never did and never would, but I will spend the rest of our lives making sure she feels like she didn't give it away uselessly to me.

Make sure she is safe, satisfied and free.

"You have to know how I feel about you, little wolf." I tell her, trying to find the words to let her know what she means to me.

Love is an emotion I haven't felt with anyone other than my mother and sister, and of course I care for my brothers, but it isn't the same. What I feel for her goes beyond the meaning of love.

"And what do you feel?" she asks, a shy smile on her lips that draws me in, and I can't help but place a hand on the back of her head and bring her to my mouth.

The kiss is slow, but I show her my obsession with her, show her my devotion, affection. My need and craving for her will never end. When I break the kiss, and rub her nose, her eyes lock with mine and I have to wonder if she knows just how much power she has over me. Power that I will freely give her for the rest of our days.

I will be her weapon and I will be her home.

"Love is such a small word for what I feel for you, Vihnarn," I start, and she smiles softly. "But if what I feel for you can be said in such a small word to describe it— then, I love you, little wolf. I love you like the night loves the moonlight."

"Then you are my darkness," she whispers.

"And you are my light."

And I will forever chase it.

EPILOGUE

Rhea

Much Later

The gathering is full of life as we all wait around for dinner to be cooked.

We have four pots now, having expanded our home exponentially in the months since the rogues were defeated, and the Highers killed.

Of course, most of the Elites are here too, talking to their Alpha.

They have been around much more since Darius's return, and who can blame them. Damian cried like a pup and well, I can't mock the guy. I even saw Jerrod wiping a tear as Leo punched him and then hugged him.

The reminder makes me smile because Darius didn't even hit him back, knowing he was hurting and that he put them all in a position that would haunt them.

They spoke for many hours about Darius telling them to not interfere, and to never do it again.

It took a while, but Darius agreed. And then they all sparred, acting like nothing happened before going for a run.

"What are you smiling at, Vihnarn?" Whoops.

I sit back on the bench and shrug. *"You are always watching me."*

"Absolutely. Now, why are you smiling."

"Just remembering how Leo punched you."

He growls.

"Are you two mind-fucking again?" Josh asks, and I look at him, Sarah nestled and heavily pregnant at his side.

"Maybe," I say, just to fuck with him.

He shakes his head, but he's smiling, placing a kiss on Sarah's forehead and rubbing her belly.

"Where's Kade?"

"By the river with Sam," Hudson says as he arrives, a very red-faced Colten in tow and I take a drink to hide my smile, side-eying Josh who buries his face in Sarah's neck to hide his own grin.

"They are ridiculous."

"I know."

I don't know why they try to hide it, but I'm sure they will tell us when they are ready.

I think it has more to do with Colten being hesitant, but for what, I'm not sure.

All I know is that Hudson will take care of him.

"Are you and Sam coming for dinner?" I ask Kade down the link.

"She is playing with the butterflies right now, but I'll ask her."

"Okay, be safe."

"I will, mom."

I smile at that, taking another drink.

Kade is doing better, but is not fully healed from his time with the Highers. His outbursts still happen, and he still spars with Darius, but I think because he's busy focusing on Sam, it helps keep him grounded.

He hasn't left her side since he got back, and Sam still barely speaks. We can only hope time will heal her, but we all know time doesn't always heal all wounds.

And that's okay.

We will be here, regardless, waiting for her to open up and tell us her own story.

A *squawk* has me lifting my head and I sit back, waiting until Illium lands on top of my thighs. "Hello, sweet boy." He squawks, and I scratch him under the chin and take the letter.

"Goodbye, go on over to Darius and I'm sure he will give you a treat."

He does just that and without thinking, Darius goes into his pocket pulling out a dried bit of meat giving it to Illium as he perches on his shoulder.

I huff out a laugh and read through Edwards's letter.

With him now one of the ruling authorities over the people of Vrohkaria, along with the new council which Darius and I are on, balance is now restored to the lands.

We are living as we always should have.

"What is it?" Darius asks, as he comes to sit down next to me.

"Crops are growing well, and they found a new river that opened up so we have another water source. He also invited us to the castle next month as he is having local sellers come to fill the courtyard and celebrate the start of summer."

His brows furrow. "None would have you smiling like you are now."

I grin wider and look down at the letter. "Oh, he also mentions two large wolves have been spotted in Zakith." I look up. "Someone from Mivera's pack reported the sighting, and some are concerned."

Darius grins. "How unusual."

"Very." We share a secret smile.

So maybe we haven't told anyone about Zahariss and Cazier's freedom when the hounds went to the below. We decided to let them be, and if they want others aware of their presence, it will be on their terms.

The Gods walk among us once more, allowed to do so after righting the wrong, and I couldn't be happier for them.

"Dinner is ready!" Katy announces, and everyone rushes over to form a line, waiting their turn, but Jerrod and Oscar get there first, and I don't miss how Katy bats her eyes at him.

Darius and I stay seated, choosing to be the last to get some food as we watch on.

"I never thought I would ever have this," I tell him. Thinking about all of those we lost, and all of those we gained.

I feel his gaze on the side of my face, but I continue watching my pack.

"Have what?" He rumbles, pulling me close to him and feeling our wolves greet each other.

I look at him then, raising a hand and running my fingers down the side of his face.

"Freedom," I say, watching as his eyes bounce between mine. "I never thought I would be free. Not truly. I forget we even have it sometimes."

We were hidden for so long, but now we can all openly walk the lands without fear, without retribution. It will take time to get used to, and I'm slowly learning that I can go anywhere I want now.

He stares at me for a moment, and then he's up and taking my hand, guiding me into the trees.

"Where are we going?" I laugh, nearly tripping over myself in his haste.

He doesn't stop until we hit the lilk trees, and he puts his palm to them as we pass, as do I, feeling our combined power still strong within.

When he stops, he turns to me, raising a hand. Drax is there in an instant, licking the side of my face before going to Darius.

I call Runa and she stretches when she lands, wiggling her tail back and forth as she looks at them.

"What are we doing"? He lifts me suddenly, placing me on top of Runa before he climbs onto Drax's back, the wolf huffing which causes me to giggle.

"We are going for a run."

"Now?" I ask, looking behind me in the direction of the gathering. "Do you not want dinner?"

"This is more important."

"What is?"

"Reminding you of your freedom." And then he's off, racing into the trees and looking back at me over his shoulder with a smirk.

I wait a moment, feeling the weight of his words as they settle deep within me, and then we chase after him with a smile on my face and a heart full of warmth.

Because I *am* free.

We play for hours, exhausting ourselves until eventually we come to rest in my favorite flowers as our wolves wander off to drink in a nearby river.

I look over the flowers, watching them sway in a gentle breeze.

"What are you thinking about?" Darius asks, and his arms come around me, pulling me into his safety.

My hand rests on top of his, watching the horizon.

"I'm thinking that some days I may not remember that I am free now, that I don't need to hide who I am or be scared. And I know it will take time," I tell him, turning in his arms. "But I know you will be there to remind me for the rest of my days."

He smiles down at me, and I smile back.

He bends down, plucking a flower and placing it behind my ear, stroking his fingers down the side of my face, making my stomach flutter.

"I will always be here to remind you, Vihnarn."

It's a promise, a vow, one I will return.

He bends and rubs his nose with mine, then we are barreled over by Runa and Drax, and we all fall in a lump on the floor.

I'm stunned for a moment as is Darius, but then he laughs.

And I fall in love all over again, watching as he wrestles with Runa and she playfully nips at him, knowing he will be waiting to catch me with open arms.

Our beginning was one of pain and torment, but it turned into something so precious, this is another moment that I will keep in my memory as one I will cherish.

Because my love for him will not be fleeting, it will be indefinite, and he will always be mine.

Just for me.

And as he looks at me, that boyish grin appearing, his eyes roaming my face, he knows that I am his.

Always.

Just like it was supposed to be.

THE END

Darius and Rhea lived happily,
obsessively,
possessively,
ever after.

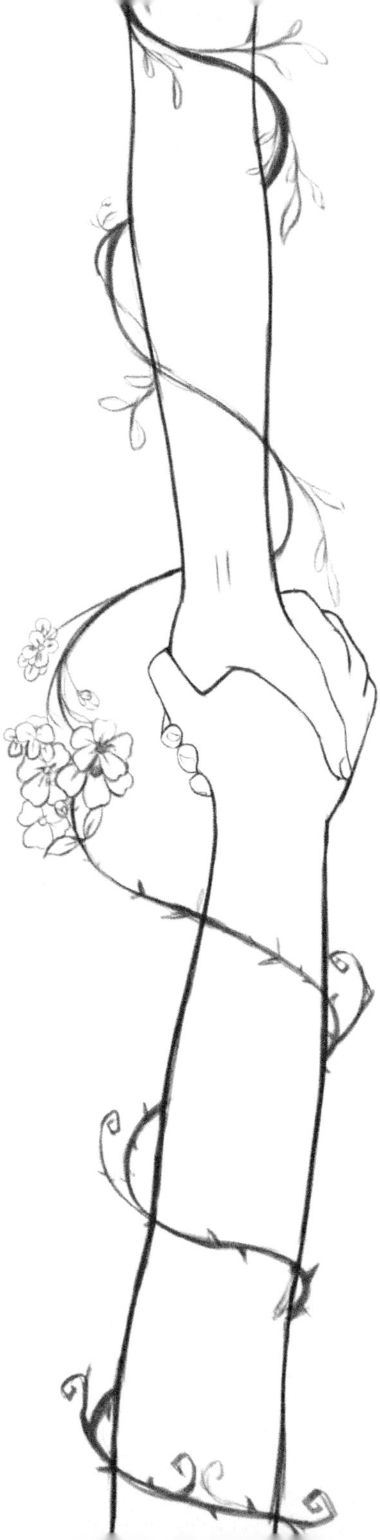

EVER AFTER

DARIUS

"I told you there was no end to us, little wolf, and I meant it. So where do you think you are going without me?" I ask her as she walks away from me.

I would have crawled out of the below if I had to, and she thinks she can leave my sight?

She's my moonlight, always guiding me from the dark.

"Yeah, yeah," Rhea says, rolling her eyes, but the soft smile on her lips gives her fake annoyance away as she looks back at me. "Come on then, Vihnarn, let's go." She carries on walking through her field, the tips of her fingers feeling the petals as always.

Every time she calls me Vihnarn, I can't help the need to be closer to her. Scenting her.

I would crawl into her body and live there if I could.

"Where?" I ask, pulling her close and nuzzling her neck, my hand on her waist as the scent of her flowers encases us. "We can stay here for as long as we want, you know that."

My Vihnarn has been restless lately. Never staying in one place for too long, like she is full of life and it is bursting to escape somehow, but she doesn't know how.

"We are going home," she says, lifting a hand to the back of my head, making a small, happy sound when she plays with the strands of short hair there. "Let's go home and start a new, simple life."

I hold her tighter. at her words, a rough chuckle coming

from me. "There is nothing simple when it comes to us."

She laughs. "Then let's make a new *simple*." She pauses in thought, placing my hand on her belly. "*Our* simple."

I tilt my head in thought, fingers tightening. "Hmm, eventually, only if you vow it."

She turns, lifting up onto her tiptoes, her lips a breath away from mine as she stares into my eyes.

Into my soul.

"I vow it."

I rub her nose with mine. "Then lead the way."

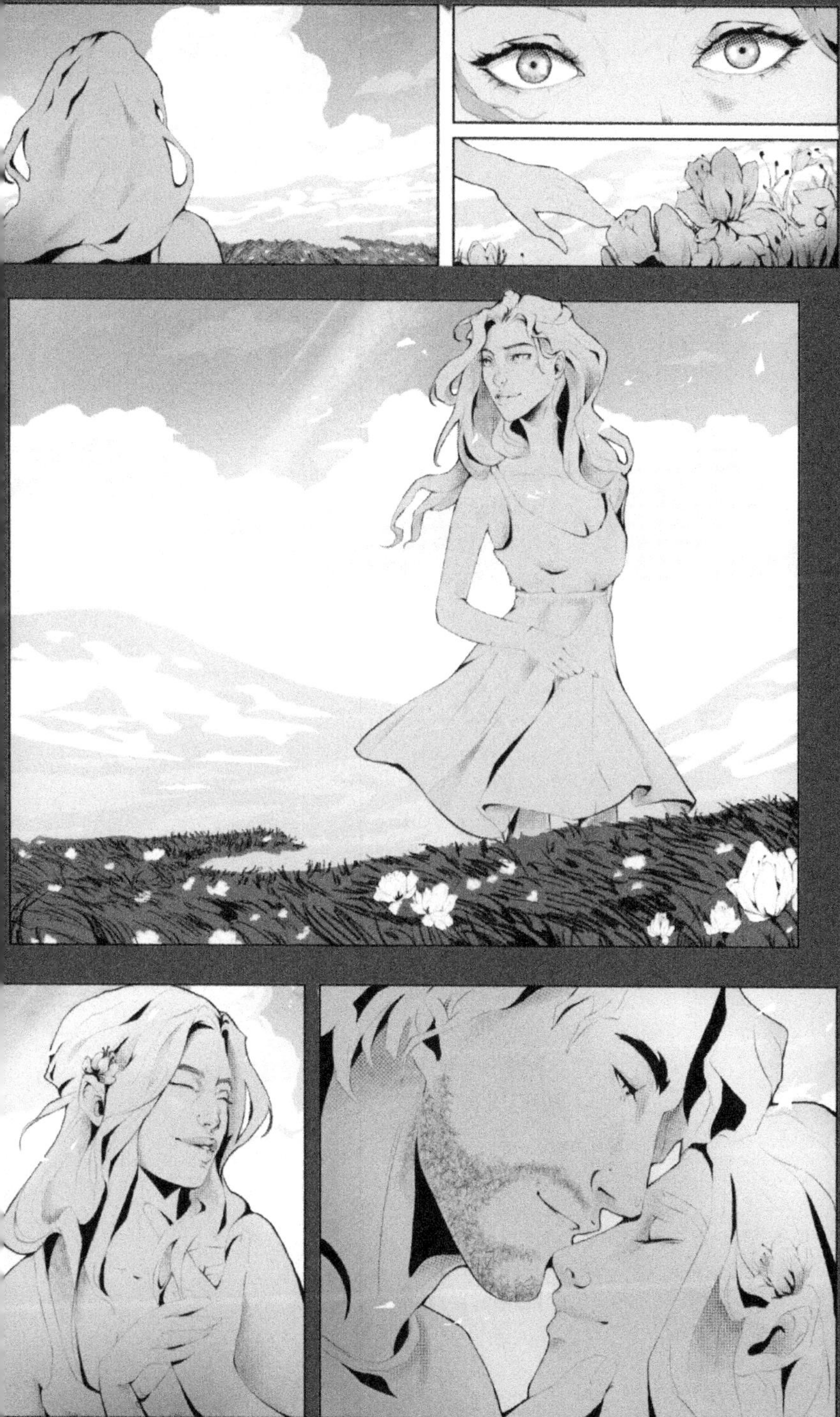

LANGUAGE

Arbiel canna – we bleed wolf
Vallier – please
Milal – female term of endearment
Carzan – male term of endearment
Sion – run
Effiniar – indefinite
Kyt – yes
Dah – I
Ny – my
Zie – you
Zier – your
Lebahn – learn
Brier – fast
Dalie – calm
Eon – down
Uri – for
Ne – me
Laeliah – beautiful
Lumniva – moonlight
Zah - us
Rey - he
Nok - not
Lo - will
Fel - hurt
Hali(s) - Heir(s)

Vihnarn – Someone who is the other half of you.
Your heart
Your soul
Your home

AFTERWARD

My dear reader.

I started writing Rhea and Darius's story in 2020. This was supposed to be an urban fantasy arranged marriage type of thing…

Well, it turned out a little different, didn't it?

I chose to listen to them, to let them guide and show me how they wanted to tell their story.

When I first saw Rhea, she was surrounded by a barrier, chained to the floor and pleading for someone to believe her. Then I followed her gaze and saw Darius standing there, body tense and his eyes hiding how he really felt… and I just knew that it wasn't going to be easy for anyone to love him, even Rhea.

I had doubts that I was even capable of telling such a story where he betrays her so badly, *harms* her so badly, and still have you like him.

I hope I managed to show just how apologetic Darius is in that in his own ways, how much he regrets it and is himself, traumatized from it, and how brave Rhea is for forgiving him.

It has been hard at times, dealing with grief and trauma personally, however, I have seen beautiful things in writing this story that will forever remain close to my heart.

I've seen forests, friendships, waterfalls, relationships, wisps, wolves, magic, Gods, and leisa flowers. So so many beautiful lesia flowers.

Ahh, I'm blabbering, but these characters feel like my family.

It is hard to end a series that is your first love.

I have laughed, cried, hated, giggled, squealed, shouted, raged, gasped, and blushed writing this series, and it will forever remain so close to my soul.

But most of all, I hope I entertained you, I hope I allowed you to escape reality for a little while, I hope I made you feel all the things and by the end, I hope you are satisfied with their ending.

I wanted to thank you all for reading this series. I have learned a lot, and I am always aiming to continue to improve my craft, my storytelling.

This is my baby series, my first ever one, and I cannot believe it's now complete.

Thank you for allowing me to do something I love so much by sharing, liking, reviewing and talking about these books.

You changed my life and breathed passion back into my soul.

Seriously.

Now even though this is the end of Darius and Rhea, we will see them pop up in the future. Some other characters have their stories to tell when they are ready.

But for now, we are going west, past The Deadlands and beyond.

Who's territory is that?

Hmmm, well, there was a little hint in this last book, and I am so excited to dive into these new lands and the creatures that dwell there.

It's about to be a little… hot.

That's all from me, much loves and reading,

and for the last time,

Arbiel canna,

Much loves and reading, Kelly <3

Acknowledgements

My family.
For forgiving my late nights working on this book, and being so proud of all I have accomplished.
And for loving me despite my book buying addiction, and the other book boyfriends in our lives.
To the moon and back, always.

Incognito
Tiddie hugs, always.

My Alpha, Beta reader, proofer.
Mandy, Jessie, Natasha, Veronica, Tori & Katie. You helped make this book, seriously. I appreciate all of you all so so much.

Masochists & Muffins
Always the hype squad anyone could ever want and need.

Reader.
Thank you for seeing it until the end. Without you, this book wouldn't exist.
Here is to the next read in far away lands and beyond.

COME STALK ME

Make sure to join my newsletter and follow me on amazon to always get news of upcoming releases.
Come and join my readers group for updates, teasers, giveaways and more at The Cove
Scan below for all links, or click here including ARC interest forms and signed paperbacks.

Printed in Great Britain
by Amazon